THE
ASTEROID WARS

THE

ASTEROID WARS

The Precipice
The Rock Rats
The Silent War

BEN BOVA

SCIENCE
FICTION

THE

ASTEROID WARS

THE PRECIPICE

CONTENTS

To Irving Levitt, a rare jewel among men
To Barbara, who adorns my life with beauty

ACKNOWLEDGMENTS

Special thanks to Jeff Mitchell, a real rocket scientist; to Chris Fountain, metallurgist and optimist; and to Lee Modesitt, an economist with imagination; true friends all.

The modern tropics and their fringes support more than half the world's population, numbered in the billions. Many already live at the fringe of survival, dependent on food aid transported from the grain belts of more temperate zones. Even a small climatic shift...would physically compress the geographical limits for cereal cropping....I leave it to your imagination what such a pace of climate change would entail for most people.

—Stephen Drury
*Stepping Stones: Evolving
the Earth and Its Life*

...some men have already embarked on a bold new adventure, the conquest of outer space. This is a healthy sign, a clear indication that some of us are still feral men, unwilling to domesticate ourselves by any kind of bondage, even that of the spatial limitations of our planet's surface.

—Carleton S. Coon
The Story of Man (Third Edition)

MEMPHIS

J esus," the pilot kept murmuring. "Jesus, Jesus, Jesus."

The helicopter was racing north, bucking, jolting between the shattered land below and the thick dark gray clouds scudding just above, trying to follow Interstate 55 from the Memphis International Airport to what was left of the devastated city.

You could not see the highway; it was carpeted from horizon to horizon with refugees, bumper to bumper traffic inching along, an unending stream of cars, trucks, vans, buses, people on foot swarming like ants, trudging painfully along the shoulders of the road in the driving, soaking rain, women pushing baby carriages, men and boys hauling carts piled high with whatever they could salvage from their homes. Flood water was lapping along the shoulder embankment, rising, still rising, reaching for the poor miserable people as they fled their homes, their hopes, their world in a desperate attempt to escape the rising waters.

Dan Randolph felt the straps of his safety harness cutting into his shoulders as he stared grimly out the window from his seat behind the two pilots. His head throbbed painfully and the filter plugs in his nostrils were hurting again. He barely noticed the copter's buffeting and jouncing in the choppy wind as he watched the swollen tide of refugees crawling sluggishly along the highway. It's like a war zone, Dan thought. Except that the enemy is Mother Nature. The flooding was bad enough, but the earthquake broke their backs.

Dan put the electronically-boosted binoculars to his eyes once again, searching, scanning the miserable, soaking wet throng below for one face, one individual, the one woman he had come to save. It was impossible. There must be half a million people down there, he thought. More. Finding her will take a miracle.

The chopper bounced and slewed wildly in a sudden gust of wind, banging the binoculars painfully against Dan's brow. He started to yell something to the pilot, then realized that they had run into another blustery squall. Fat, pounding raindrops splattered thickly against the copter's windows, cutting Dan's vision down almost to nothing.

The pilot slid back the transparent sanitary partition that isolated Dan's compartment. Dan suppressed an angry urge to slam it back. What good are sterile barriers if you open them to the outside air?

"We've got to turn back, sir," the pilot yelled over the thrumming thunder of the engines.

"No!" Dan shouted. "Not till we find her!"

Half turning in his seat to face Dan, the pilot jabbed a finger toward his spattered windscreen. "Mr. Randolph, you can fire me when we land, but I ain't going to fly through *that*."

Looking past the flapping windscreen wipers, Dan saw four deadly slim dark funnels writhing across the other side of the swollen Mississippi, dust and debris flying wherever they touched the ground. They looked like coiling, squirming snakes thrashing across the ground, smashing everything they touched: buildings exploded, trees uprooted, autos tossed into the air like dry leaves, homes shattered into splinters, RV parks, housing developments, shopping malls all destroyed at the flick of the twisters' pitiless, mindless malevolence, blasted as completely and ruthlessly as if they had been struck by an enemy missile attack.

The enemy is Mother Nature, Dan repeated silently, numbly, as he stared at the advancing tornadoes. There was nothing he could do about them and he knew it. They couldn't be bought, bribed, flattered, seduced, or threatened into obedience. For the first time since he'd been a child, Daniel Hamilton Randolph felt totally powerless.

As he locked the partition shut again and fumbled in his pockets for his antiseptic spray, the chopper swung away, heading back toward what was left of the international airport. The Tennessee National Guard had thrown a cordon around the grounds; the airport was the Memphis region's last link with the rest of the country. The floods had knocked out electrical power, smashed bridges, covered roads with thick muddy brown water. Most of the city had been submerged for days.

Then came the earthquake. A solid nine on the Richter scale, so powerful that it flattened buildings from Nashville to Little Rock and as far north as St. Louis. New Orleans had already been under water for years as the rising Gulf of Mexico inexorably reclaimed its shoreline from Florida to Texas. The Mississippi was in flood all the way up to Cairo, and still rising.

Now, with communications out, millions homeless in the never-ending rains, aftershocks strong enough to tumble skyscrapers, Dan Randolph searched for the one person who meant something to him, the only woman he had ever loved.

He let the binoculars drop from his fingers and rested his head on the seat back. It was hopeless. Finding Jane out there among all those other people—

The copilot had twisted around in his seat and was tapping on the clear plastic partition.

"What?" Dan yelled.

Instead of trying to outshout the engines' roar through the partition, the copilot pointed to the earpiece of his helmet. Dan understood and picked up the headset they had given him from where he'd dumped it on the floor. He had sprayed it when they'd first handed it to him, but now he doused it again with the antiseptic.

As he clamped it over his head, he heard the metallic, static-streaked voice of a news reporter saying, ". . . definitely identified as Jane Scanwell. The former President was found, by a strange twist of fate, on President's Island, where she was apparently attempting to help a family of refugees escape the rising Mississippi waters. Their boat apparently capsized and was swept downstream, but snagged on treetops on the island.

"Jane Scanwell, the fifty-second President of the United States, died trying to save others from the ravages of flood and earthquake here in what remains of Memphis, Tennessee."

LA GUAIRA

It was raining in Venezuela, too, when Dan Randolph finally got back to his headquarters. Another hurricane was tearing through the Caribbean, lashing Barbados and the Windward Islands, dumping twenty-five centimeters of rain on the island of La Guaira and Caracas, on the mainland, with more to come.

Dan sat behind his big, bare desk, still wearing the rumpled slacks and pullover that he had travelled in from the States. His office smelled musty, mildewed from the incessant rain despite its laboring climate control system. He wasn't wearing the protective nose plugs; the air in his office was routinely filtered and run past intense ultraviolet lamps.

Leaning back into the softly yielding caramel brown leather of his swivel chair, Dan gazed out at the windswept launch complex. The rockets had been towed back into the assembly buildings. In this storm they could not dare to launch even the sturdy, reliable Clipperships. The launch towers were visibly shaking in the gale-force wind, lashed by horizontal sheets of rain; roofs had already peeled off some of the smaller buildings. Beyond the launch towers, the sea was a wild madhouse of frothing whitecapped waves. The wind howled like a beast of prey, rattling even the thick double-paned windows of Randolph's office.

Third storm to hit us and it's not even the Fourth of July yet. Business isn't lousy enough, we've got these double-damned hurricanes to deal with. At this rate I'll be broke by Labor Day.

We're losing, Dan thought. We're in a war and we're losing it. Hell, we've already lost it. What's the sense of pretending otherwise?

The dampness made him ache deep in his bones, an arthritic-like reminder of his age and the dose of radiation sickness he'd contracted years earlier. I ought to get back to Selene, he told himself. A man with a broken-down immune system shouldn't stay on Earth if he doesn't have to.

Yet for hours he simply sat there, staring out at the pounding storm, seeing only the face of Jane Scanwell, remembering the sound of her voice, the touch of her fingers, the soft silkiness of her skin, the scent of her, the way she brightened a room, the way she had filled his life even though they were never really together, not more than a few quick hours now and then before they fell into bitter argument. There was so much separating them. After she had left the White House, they had managed to spend a couple of days together on a tropical atoll. Even that had ended in a quarrel.

But for once they had seen things the same way, had the same goal, fought the same fight on the same side. The greenhouse cliff meant war, a war pitting humankind's global civilization against the blind forces of nature. Jane understood that as well as Dan did. They were going to fight this war together.

And it killed her.

Should I go on? Dan asked himself. What's the use of it? What's the sense of it? He wanted to cry, but the tears would not come.

Dan Randolph had always seemed larger than his actual physical size. He was a solidly-built welterweight, still in trim physical shape, although now, in his sixties, it took grueling hours in the gym to maintain his condition. His once-sandy hair was almost completely gray now; his staff people called him "the Silver Fox" behind his back. He had a fighter's face, with a strong stubborn jaw and a nose that had been flattened years ago by a fist, when he'd been a construction worker in space. Despite all the wealth he'd amassed since those early days, he'd never had his nose fixed. Some said it was a perverse sense of machismo. His light gray eyes, which had often glinted in amusement at the foolishness of men, were bleak and saddened now.

A chime sounded, and the sleek display screen of his computer rose slowly, silently out of the desktop surface.

Dan swiveled his chair to see the screen. His administrative assistant's young, somber face looked out at him. Teresa was a native of Caracas, tall, leggy, cocoa-cream complexion, deep brown almond eyes and thick lustrous midnight dark hair. Years earlier Dan would have tried to bed her and probably succeeded. Now he was simply annoyed at her intrusion into his memories.

"It's almost dinnertime," she said.

"So what?"

"Martin Humphries has been waiting all day to see you. He's the man Zack Freiberg wants you to meet."

Dan grimaced. Zack had been the first one to warn Dan of the impending greenhouse cliff.

"Not today, Teresa," he said. "I don't want to see anybody today."

The young woman hesitated a heartbeat, then asked, softly, almost timidly, "Do you want me to bring you a dinner tray?"

Dan shook his head. "I'm not hungry."

"You have to eat."

He looked at her image on his screen, so intent, so young and concerned and worried that the boss was going off the deep end. And he felt anger rising inside him, unreasoning blind blazing rage.

"No, goddammit to hell and back," he snapped. "*You* have to eat. I can do any goddamned thing I want to, and if you want to keep drawing your paycheck you'd better leave me the hell alone."

Her eyes went wide. Her mouth opened, but she said nothing. Dan snapped his fingers and the screen went blank. Another snap and it folded back into its niche in the desk's gleaming rosewood top.

Leaning back in his chair, Dan closed his eyes. He tried to close his mind against the memories, but that was impossible.

It was all going to be so damned great. Okay, a century or two of global warming would lead to a greenhouse cliff. Not a gradual warmup but a sudden, abrupt change in the world's climate. All that latent heat stored in the oceans would pour into the atmosphere. Ice caps in Greenland and Antarctica melting away. Sea levels shooting up over a decade or two. Big storms and lots of them. Climate shifts turning croplands into deserts.

So what? We'll use the resources of space to solve all those problems. Energy? We'll build solar power satellites, beam energy from space to wherever it's needed. Raw materials? We'll mine the Moon and the asteroids; there's more natural resources in space than the whole Earth can provide. Food production?

Well, that would be a tough one. We all knew that. But with enough energy and enough raw materials we could irrigate the croplands that were being desiccated by the climate shift.

Yeah, sure. And when half the world's major cities got flooded out, what did we do? What could we do? When the electrical power grid got shattered, what did we do? When earthquakes and tsunamis wiped out the heart of Japan's industrial capacity, what did we do? Diddley-squat. When this quake flattened the midwest, what did we do? We tried to help the survivors and Jane got herself killed in the attempt.

The office door banged open and a huge, red-bearded man pushed in, carrying an ornately-carved teak tray laden with steaming dishes. In his massive hands the tray looked like a little child's toy.

"Teresa says you've got to eat," he announced in a high, sweet tenor as he set the tray on Dan's desk.

"I told her I'm not hungry."

"You can't fookin' starve yourself. Eat something."

Dan glanced at the tray. A steaming bowl of soup, a salad, a main course hidden under a stainless steel dome, a carafe of coffee. No wine. Nothing alcoholic.

He pushed the tray toward the red-haired giant. "You eat it, George."

Pulling one of the upholstered chairs up close to the desk, Big George looked his boss in the eye and pushed the tray back toward Randolph.

"Eat," he said. "It's good for ya."

Dan stared back at George Ambrose. He'd known Big George since he'd been a fugitive on the Moon, hiding out from the Selene City authorities with a handful of other free souls who styled themselves the Lunar Underground. Big George was Dan's personal bodyguard now; he wore custom-tailored suits instead of patched coveralls. But he still looked like a barely-tamed frontiersman: big, shaggy, the kind of man who could gleefully pound your head down into your ribcage with no personal malice at all.

"Tell you what," Dan said, feeling a reluctant smile bend his lips a little. "I'll split it with you."

George grinned back at him. "Good thinking, boss."

They ate in silence for several minutes, George gobbling the entire main course, which turned out to be a thick slab of prime rib. Dan took a few spoonfuls of soup and nibbled at the salad.

"Better than the old days, huh?" George said, still chewing prime rib. "Fookin' soyburgers and recycled piss for water."

Dan ignored the younger man's attempt to jolly him. "Has Teresa gone home?" he asked.

"Nope."

Nettled, Dan glanced at his wristwatch. "She's not my nursemaid, double-damn it. I don't want her hovering over me like—"

"That Humphries bloke is still waitin' to see you," George said.

"Now? He's out there now? It's almost nine o'clock, for chrissakes. What's wrong with him? Is he stuck here because of the storm? Doesn't Teresa have the smarts to put him up in one of the guest suites?"

George shook his shaggy head. "He said he'll wait until you're ready to see 'im. He did have an appointment, y'know."

Dan let his breath out in a weary sigh. I just got back from the funeral and they expect me to stick to a schedule made out weeks ago.

"Teresa says he's makin' her nervous."

"Nervous?"

"He's comin' on to her. I can see it meself."

Frowning, Dan muttered, "Teresa can take care of herself."

"The voice of experience?" George grinned.

"He's been hitting on her all the time he's been waiting for me?"

"Want me to shoo 'im off?" George asked.

For a moment Dan relished the image of George hustling his visitor out of the building. But then he realized that the man would simply come back tomorrow. I'll have to get back to business, he told himself. Can't avoid it forever.

"Take the tray out," he said to Big George, "and show this Humphries guy in."

George smacked his lips. "I can bring in dessert and coffee."

"Fine," Dan said, unwilling to argue. "Do that."

Grinning, George scooped up the crumb-littered tray in one hand and started for the door. Dan saw that the desktop was sprinkled with crumbs, too. Annoyed, he brushed them to the carpet.

Teresa appeared at the door. "Mr. Martin Humphries," she announced. She looked tense, Dan thought. Humphries must have really rattled her.

Martin Humphries looked quite young. He was on the small side, a couple of centimeters shorter than Teresa, and he seemed soft, with rounded shoulders and a waistline that was already getting thick, despite the careful drape of his burgundy blazer. He seemed to radiate energy, though, as he strode confidently across the office toward Dan's desk.

Dan got to his feet and extended his hand across the desk.

"Sorry to keep you waiting," he said, making himself smile.

Humphries took Dan's hand in a firm grip. "I understand," he replied. "I'm sorry to intrude on your grief."

His eyes told Dan that the words were nothing more than an expected ritual. Martin Humphries's face was round, almost boyish. But his eyes were diamond-hard, cold and gray as the storm-lashed sea outside the window.

As they sat down, George re-entered the office bearing a tray of pastries and the same carafe of coffee, with a pair of china cups and saucers alongside it. For all his size, Big George walked with the lightfooted step of a dancer—or a cat burglar. Neither Dan nor Humphries said a word as George deftly deposited the tray on the desk and swiftly, silently left the office.

"I hope I haven't kept you from your dinner," Dan said, gesturing to the pastries.

Humphries ignored the tray. "No problem. I enjoyed chatting with your secretary."

"Did you?" Dan said thinly.

"She's quite a piece of work. I'd like to hire her away from you."

"Not a chance," Dan snapped.

With a careless shrug, Humphries said, "That's not important. I came here to talk to you about the current situation."

Dan waved toward the window. "You mean the greenhouse cliff?"

"I mean the way we can help the global economy to recover from the staggering losses it's sustained—and make ourselves a potful of profits while we're doing it."

Dan felt his brows hike up. He reached for one of the delicate little pastries, then decided to pour himself a cup of coffee first. Dan's firm, Astro Manufacturing Inc., was close to bankruptcy and the whole financial community knew it.

"I could use a potful of profits," he said carefully.

Humphries smiled, but Dan saw no warmth in it.

"What do you have in mind?" he asked.

"The Earth is in chaos because of this sudden climate shift," said Humphries.

"The greenhouse cliff, yes," Dan agreed.

"Selene and the other lunar communities are doing rather well, though."

Dan nodded. "On the Moon there's no shortage of energy or raw materials. They've got everything they need. They're pretty much self-sufficient now."

"They could be helping the Earth," said Humphries. "Building solar power satellites. Sending raw materials to Earth. Even manufacturing products that people down here need but can't get because their own factories have been destroyed."

"We've tried to do that," Dan said. "We're trying it now. It's not enough."

Humphries nodded. "That's because you've been limiting yourself to the resources you can obtain from the Moon."

"And the NEAs," Dan added.

"The near-Earth asteroids, yes." Humphries nodded as if he'd expected that response.

"So what are you suggesting?"

Humphries glanced over his shoulder, as if afraid that someone might be eavesdropping. "The Belt," he said, almost in a whisper.

Dan looked at Humphries for a long, silent moment. Then he leaned his head back and laughed, long and loud and bitterly.

SPACE STATION *GALILEO*

They were gaining on her.

Still wearing the spacesuit, Pancho Lane zipped weightlessly through the lab module, startling the Japanese technicians as she propelled herself headlong down its central aisle with a flick of her strong hands against the lab equipment every few meters. Behind her she could hear the men yelling angrily.

If any of those dip-brains have the smarts to suit up and go EVA to head me off, she thought, I'm toast.

It had started out as a game, a challenge. Which of the pilots aboard the station could breathe vacuum the longest? There were six Astro Corporation rocket jockeys waiting for transport back to Selene City: four guys, Pancho herself, and the new girl, Amanda Cunningham.

Pancho had egged them on, of course. That was part of the sting. They'd all been hanging around the galley, literally floating when they didn't anchor themselves down with the footloops fastened to the floor around the table and its single pipestem-slim leg. The conversation had gotten around to vacuum breathing: how long can you hold your breath in space without damaging yourself?

"The record is four minutes," one of the guys had claimed. "Harry Kirschbaum."

"Harry Kirschbaum? Who the hell is he? I never heard of him."

"He died young."

They all had laughed.

Amanda, who had just joined the team fresh from tech school in London, had the face of an angelic schoolgirl with soft curly blonde hair and big innocent blue eyes; but her curvaceous figure had all the men panting.

She said, "I had to readjust my helmet once, during a school exercise in the vacuum tank."

"How long did that take?"

She shrugged, and even Pancho noticed the way it made her coveralls jiggle. "Ten seconds, perhaps. Fifteen."

Pancho didn't like Amanda. She was a little tease who affected an upperclass British accent. One look at her and the men forgot about Pancho, which was a shame because a couple of the guys were really nice.

Pancho was lean and stringy, with the long slim legs of her African heritage. Her skin was no darker than a good tan would produce back in west Texas, but her face was just plain ordinary, with what she considered a lantern jaw and squinty little commonplace brown eyes. She always kept her hair cut so short that the rumor had gone around that she was a lesbian. Not true. But she had a man's strength in her long, muscled arms and legs, and she never let a man beat her in anything—unless she wanted to.

The transfer buggy that was slated to take them all back to Selene was running late. Cracked nozzle on one of the thrusters, and the last thing the flight controllers wanted was a derelict transfer vehicle carrying six rocket jocks; they would be rebuilding the buggy forty-five ways from Sunday while they coasted Moonward.

So the six of them waited in the galley and talked about vacuum breathing. One of the guys claimed he'd sucked vacuum for a full minute.

"That explains your IQ," said his buddy.

"Nobody's made it for a full minute."

"Sixty seconds," the man maintained stubbornly.

"Your lungs would explode."

"I'm telling you, sixty seconds. On the dot."

"No damage?"

He hesitated, suddenly shamefaced.

"Well?"

With an attempt at a careless shrug, he admitted, "Left lung collapsed."

They snickered at him.

"I could prob'ly do it for sixty seconds," Pancho announced.

"You?" The man nearest her guffawed. "Now, Mandy here, she's got the lung capacity for it."

Amanda smiled shyly. But when she inhaled they all noticed it.

Pancho hid her anger at their ape-man attitude. "Ninety seconds," she said flatly.

"Ninety seconds? Impossible!"

"You willin' to bet on that?" Pancho asked.

"Nobody can stand vacuum for ninety seconds. It'd blow your eyeballs out."

Pancho smiled toothily. "How much money are you ready to put against it?"

"How can we collect off you after you're dead?"

"Or brain-damaged."

"She's already brain-damaged if she thinks she can suck vacuum for ninety seconds."

"I'll put my money in an escrow account for the five of you to withdraw in case of my death or incapacitation," Pancho said calmly.

"Yeah, sure."

Pointing to the phone on the wall, next to the sandwich dispenser, she said, "Electronic funds transfer. Takes all of two minutes to set up."

They fell silent.

"How much?" Pancho said, watching their eyes.

"A week's pay," snapped one of the men.

"A month's pay," Pancho said.

"A whole month?"

"Why not? You're so freakin' sure I can't do it, why not bet a month's pay? I'll put five months worth of mine in the escrow account, so you'll each be covered."

"A month's pay."

In the end they had agreed to it. Pancho knew that they figured she'd chicken out after twenty-thirty seconds and they'd have her money without her killing herself.

She figured otherwise.

So she used the galley phone to call her bank in Lubbock. A few taps on the phone's touchtone keypad and she had set up a new account and dumped five months' pay into it. All five of the other jocks watched the phone's tiny screen to make certain Pancho wasn't playing any tricks.

Then each of them in turn called their banks and deposited a month's pay into Pancho's new account. Pancho listened to the singsong beeping of the phone as she laid her plans for the coming challenge.

Pancho suggested they use the airlock down at the far end of the maintenance module. "We don't want some science geek poppin' in on us and gettin' so torqued he punches the safety alarm," she said.

They all agreed easily. So they floated through two lab modules and the shabby-looking habitat module where the long-term researchers were housed and finally made it to the cavernous maintenance unit. There, by the airlock, Pancho chose a spacesuit from the half-dozen standard models lined up against the bulkhead, size large because of her height. She quickly wriggled into it. They even helped her put on the boots and check out the suit's systems.

Pancho pulled the helmet over her head and clicked the neck seal shut.

"Okay," she said, through the helmet's open visor. "Who's gonna time me?"

"I will," said one of the guys, raising his forearm to show an elaborate digital wristwatch.

"You go in the lock," said the man beside him, "pump it down and open the outside hatch."

"And you watch me through the port," Pancho said, tapping the thick round window on the airlock's inner hatch with gloved knuckles.

"Check. When I say go, you open your visor."

"And I'll time you," said the guy with the fancy wristwatch.

Pancho nodded inside the helmet.

Amanda looked concerned. "Are you absolutely certain that you want to go through with this? You could kill yourself, Pancho."

"She can't back out now!"

"Not unless she wants to forfeit five months' pay."

"But seriously," Amanda said. "I'm wiling to call off the bet. After all—"

Pancho reached out and tousled her curly blonde hair. "Don't sweat it, Mandy."

With that, she stepped through the open airlock hatch and slid down her visor. She waved to them as they swung the hatch shut. She heard the pump start to clatter; the sound quickly dwindled as the air was sucked out of the metal-walled chamber. When the telltale light by the inner hatch turned red, Pancho touched the button that slid the outer hatch open.

For a moment she forgot what she was up to as she drank in the overwhelming beauty of the Earth spread out before her dazzled eyes. Brilliantly bright, intensely blue oceans and enormous sweeps of clouds so white it almost hurt to look upon them. It was glorious, an overwhelming panorama that never failed to make her heart beat faster.

You've got work to do, girl, she reminded herself sternly.

Turning to the inner hatch, she could see all five of their faces clustered around the little circular port. None of them had the sense to find a radio, Pancho knew, so she gestured to her sealed helmet visor with a gloved finger. They all nodded vigorously and the guy with the fancy wristwatch held it up where Pancho could see it.

The others backed away from the port while the guy stared hard at his wristwatch. He held up four fingers, then three . . .

Counting down, Pancho understood.

. . . two, one. He jabbed a finger like a make-believe pistol at Pancho, the signal that she was to lift her visor *now*.

Instead, Pancho launched herself out the airlock, into empty space.

LA GUAIRA

Martin Humphries looked irked. "What's so funny about the Asteroid Belt?"

Dan shook his head. "Not funny, really. Just . . . I didn't expect that from you. You've got a reputation for being a hard-headed businessman."

"I'd like to believe that I am," Humphries said.

"Then forget about the Belt," Dan snapped. "Been there, done that. It's too far away, the costs would outweigh the profits by a ton."

"It's been done," Humphries insisted.

"Once," said Dan. "By that nutcase Gunn. And he damned near got himself killed doing it."

"But that one asteroid was worth close to a trillion dollars once he got it into lunar orbit."

"Yeah, and the double-damned GEC took control of it and bankrupted Gunn."

"That won't happen this time."

"Why not? You don't think the GEC would seize any resources we bring to Earth? That's the reason the Global Economic Council was created—to control the whole twirling Earth's international trade."

Humphries smiled coldly. "I can handle the GEC. Trust me on that one."

Dan stared at the younger man for a long, hard moment. Finally he shook his head and replied, "It doesn't matter. I'd even be willing to let the GEC run the show."

"You would?"

"Hell yes. We're in a global emergency now. Somebody has to allocate resources, control prices, see to it that nobody takes advantage of this crisis to line his own pockets."

"I suppose so," Humphries said slowly. "Still, I'm convinced there's a lot of money to be made by mining the Belt."

Nodding, Dan agreed, "There's a lot of resources out there, that's for sure. Heavy metals, organics, resources we can't get from the Moon."

"Resources that the Earth needs, and the GEC would be willing to pay for."

"Mining the asteroids," Dan mused. "That's a major undertaking. A *major* undertaking."

"That's why I'm here. Astro Manufacturing has the resources to do it."

"Astro Manufacturing is just about broke and you know it."

"I wasn't talking about financial resources," Humphries said, waving a hand in the air almost carelessly.

"Oh no?"

"No." Pointing a finger toward the window and the storm-battered launch facility outside, Humphries said, "You've got the technological know-how, the teams of trained personnel, the rockets and infrastructure to get us into space."

"And it's bleeding me white because there's less and less of a market for launch services. Nobody can afford to buy electronics manufactured on the Moon, not when they're being driven from their homes by floods and earthquakes."

Humphries's brows rose questioningly.

"I know, I know," Dan said. "There's the energy market. Sure. But how many solar-power satellites can we park in orbit? The double-damned GEC just put a cap on them. We're building the next-to-last one now. After those two, no more powersats."

Before Humphries could ask why, Dan continued, "The goddamned Greater Asia Power Consortium complained about the powersats undercutting their prices. And the double-damned Europeans sided with them. Serve 'em all right if they freeze their asses off when the Gulf Stream breaks up."

"The Gulf Stream?" Humphries looked startled.

Dan nodded unhappily. "That's one of the projections. The greenhouse warming is already changing ocean currents. When the Gulf Stream breaks up, Europe goes into the deep freeze; England's weather will be the same as Labrador's."

"When? How soon?"

"Twenty years, maybe. Maybe a hundred. Ask five different scientists and you get twelve different answers."

"That's a real opportunity," Humphries said excitedly. "Winterizing all of Europe. Think of it! What an opportunity!"

"Funny," Dan retorted. "I was thinking of it as a disaster."

"You see the glass half empty. To me, it's half full."

Dan had a sudden urge to throw this young opportunist out of his office. Instead, he slumped back in his chair and muttered, "It's like a sick Greek tragedy. Global warming is going to put Europe in the deep-freezer. Talk about ironic."

"We were talking about the energy market," Humphries said, regaining his composure. "What about the lunar helium-three?"

Dan wondered if his visitor was merely trying to pump him. Warily, he answered, "Barely holding its own. There's not that many fusion power plants up and running yet—thanks to the kneejerk anti-nuke idiots. And digging helium-three out of the lunar regolith ain't cheap. Fifty parts per million sounds good to a chemist, maybe, but it doesn't lead to a high profit ratio, let me tell you."

"So you'd need an injection of capital to start mining the asteroids," Humphries said.

"A transfusion," Dan grumbled.

"That can be done."

Dan felt his brows hike up. "Really?"

"I can provide the capital," Humphries said, matter-of-factly.

"We're talking forty, fifty billion, at least."

Humphries waved a hand, as if brushing away an annoyance. "You wouldn't need that much for a demonstration flight."

"Even a one-shot demo flight would cost a couple bill," Dan said.

"Probably."

"Where are you going to get that kind of money? Nobody's willing to talk to me about investing in Astro."

"There are people who'd be willing to invest that kind of money in developing the asteroid market."

For an instant Dan felt a surge of hope. It could work! Open up the Asteroid Belt. Bring those resources to Earth's needy people. Then the cost figures flashed into his mind again, as implacable as Newton's laws of motion.

"You know," he said wearily, "if we could just cover our own costs I'd be willing to try it."

Humphries looked disappointed. "Just cover your own costs?"

"Damned right. People need those resources. If we could get them without driving ourselves into bankruptcy, I'd go to double-damned Pluto if I had to!"

Relaxing visibly, Humphries said, "I know how we can do it and make a healthy profit, besides."

Despite himself, Dan felt intrigued. "How?"

"Fusion rockets."

By the seven cities of Cibola, Dan thought, this guy's a fanatic. Worse: he's an enthusiast.

"Nobody's made a fusion rocket," he said to Humphries. "Fusion power generators are too big and heavy for flight applications. Everybody knows that."

With the grin of a cat that had just finished dining on several canaries, Humphries replied, "Everybody's wrong."

Dan thought it over for all of half a second, then leaned both his hands on his desktop, palms down, and said, "Prove it to me."

Wordlessly, Humphries fished a data chip from his jacket pocket and handed it to Dan.

SPACE STATION *GALILEO*

Leaving her five fellow astronauts gaping dumbfounded at the airlock in the maintenance module, Pancho sailed weightlessly to the metal arm of the robotic cargo-handling crane jutting out from the space station. It was idle at the moment; with no mass of payload to steady it, the long, slim arm flexed noticeably as Pancho grasped it in both hands and swung like an acrobat up to the handgrips that studded the module's outer skin.

Wondering if the others had caught on to her sting, Pancho hand-walked along the module's hull, clambering from one runglike grip to the next. To someone watching from beyond the space station it would have looked as if she were scampering along upside down, but to Pancho it seemed as if the space station was over her head and she was swinging like a kid in a zero-gee jungle gym.

She laughed inside her helmet as she reached the end of the maintenance module and pushed easily across the connector section that linked to the habitation module.

"Hey Pancho, what the hell are you doing out there?"

They had finally gotten to a radio, she realized. But as long as they were puzzled, she was okay.

"I'm taking a walk," she said, a little breathless from all the exertion.

"What about our bet?" one of the men asked.

"I'll be back in a few minutes," she lied. "Just hang tight."

"What are you up to, Pancho?" asked Amanda, her voice tinged with suspicion.

Pancho fell back on her childhood answer. "Nothin'."

The radio went silent. Pancho reached the airlock at the end of the hab module and tapped out the standard code. The outer hatch slid open. She ducked inside, sealed the hatch and didn't bother to wait for the lock to fill with air. She simply pushed open the inner hatch and quickly sealed it again. A safety alarm shrilled automatically, but cut off when the module's air pressure equilibrated again. Yanking off the spacesuit's cumbersome gloves, Pancho slid her visor up as she went to the wallphone by the airlock hatch.

Blessed with perfect pitch and a steel-trap memory, Pancho punched out the numbers for each of the five astronauts' banks in turn, followed by their personal identification codes. Mother always said I should have been a musician, Pancho mused as she transferred almost the total amount of each account into her own bank account. She left exactly one international dollar for each of them, so the bank's computers would not start the complex process of closing down their accounts.

As she finished, the hatch at the other end of the habitation module swung open and her five fellow astronauts began to push through, one at a time.

"What's going on?" demanded the first guy through.

"Nothin'," Pancho said again. Then she dived through the hatch at her end of the long narrow module.

Into the Japanese lab module she swam, flicking her fingers along the equipment racks lining both sides of its central aisle, startling the technicians working there. Laughing to herself, she wondered how long it would take them to figure out that she had looted their bank accounts.

It didn't take very long. By the time Pancho had reached the galley once again, they were roaring after her, the men bellowing with outrage.

"When I get my hands on you, I'm gonna break every bone in your scrawny body!" was one of their gentler threats.

Even Amanda was so furious she lapsed back to her native working-class accent: "We'll 'ang you up by your bloody thumbs, we will!"

As long as I can stay ahead of them, I'm okay, Pancho told herself as she skimmed through the European lab module and into the observatory section, ducking under and around the bulky telescopes and electronics consoles. They were still yelling behind her, but she wondered if all five of them were still chasing. By now there'd been plenty of time for one or more of them to pop into a suit and cut across the top of the tee-shaped station to cut her off.

Sure enough, when she barged into the Russian hab module, two of the guys were standing at the far end in spacesuits, visors up, waiting for her like a pair of armored cops.

Pancho glided to a halt. One of the privacy unit screens slid back and a stubbled, bleary, puffy male face peered out, then quickly popped back in again and slid the screen shut with a muttered string of what sounded like Slavic cursing.

The other three—Amanda and two of the men—came through the hatch behind her. Pancho was well and truly trapped.

"What the fuck are you trying to pull off, Pancho?"

"You cleaned out our bank accounts!"

"We oughtta string you up, damn you!"

She smiled and spread her hands placatingly. "Now fellas, you can't hang a person in microgee. You know that."

"This isn't funny," Amanda snapped, back to her faux-Oxford enunciation.

"I'll make restitution, okay?" Pancho offered.

"You damned well better!"

"And you lost the bet, too, so we each get a month's pay from you."

"No," Pancho said as reasonably as she could. "We never went through on the vacuum breathing, so the bet's off."

"Then we want our money back from your goddamned escrow account!"

"Sure. Fine."

Amanda pointed to the wallphone by the hatch. "You mentioned restitution," she said.

Meekly, Pancho floated to the phone and tapped out her number. "You'll have to give me your account numbers," she said. "So I can put the money back in for you."

"We'll punch in the account numbers ourselves," Amanda said firmly.

"You don't trust me?" Pancho managed to keep a straight face, but just barely.

They all growled at her.

"But it was only a joke," she protested. "I had no intention of keeping your money."

"Not much you didn't," one of the guys snapped. "Good thing Mandy figured out what you were up to."

Pancho nodded in Amanda's direction. "You're the brightest one around, Mandy," she said, as if she believed it.

"Never mind that," Amanda replied tartly. To the men she said, "Now we'll all have to change our ID codes, since she's obviously figured them out."

"I'm going to change my account number," said one of the guys.

"I'm gonna change my *bank*," another said fervently.

Pancho sighed and tried her best to look glum, chastised. Inwardly, she was quivering with silent laughter. What a hoot! And none of these bozos realizes that the half hour or so they've spent chasing me means half an hour's worth of interest from each of their accounts into mine. It's not all that much, but every little bit helps.

She just hoped they wouldn't figure it out while they were all cooped up in the transfer buggy on the way to the Moon.

Well, she thought, if they try to get physical I'll just have to introduce them to Elly.

CHENGDU, SICHUAN PROVINCE

Dan had to shout through his sanitary mask to make himself heard over the din of construction.

"All I'm asking, Zack, is can he do it or can't he?"

He'd known Zack Freiberg for more than twenty years, since Zack had been an earnest young planetary geochemist intent on exploring asteroids and Dan had hired him away from his university post. Freiberg had taken flak from his friends in academia for joining big, bad Dan Randolph, the greedy capitalist founder and head of Astro Manufacturing. But over the years a mutual respect had slowly developed into a trusting friendship. It had been Zack who'd first warned Dan about the looming greenhouse cliff, and what it would do to the Earth's climate.

The greenhouse cliff had arrived, and the Earth's politicians and business leaders had sailed blindly over its edge as the planet plunged into catastrophic warming. Zack was no longer the chubby, apple-cheeked kid Dan had first met. His strawberry hair had gone iron gray, although it was still thick and tightly curled. The past few years had toughened him, made him leaner, harder, boiled away the baby fat in his body. His face had hardened, too, as he watched his equations and graphs turn into massive human suffering.

The two men were standing on the edge of a denuded ridge, looking out across a barren coal-black valley where thousands of Chinese workers toiled unceasingly. By all the gods, Dan thought, they really do look like an army of ants scurrying around. In the middle of the valley four enormously tall smokestacks of a huge electricity-generating plant belched dark gray fumes into the hazy sky. Mountainous piles of coal lay by the railroad track that ran alongside the power plant. Off on the horizon, beyond the farther stripped-bare ridge, the Yangzi River glittered in the hazy morning sunshine like a deadly boa constrictor slowly creeping up on its prey. A sluggish warm breeze smelled of raw coal and diesel fumes. Dan shuddered inwardly, wondering how many billions of microbes were worming their way through his sanitary mask and nose plugs, eager to chew past his weakened immune system and set up homes for themselves inside his body.

"Dan, I really don't have time for this," Freiberg hollered over the roar of a huge truck carrying twenty tons of dirt and rubble down into the valley on wheels that dwarfed both men.

"I just need a few hours of your time," Dan said, feeling his throat going hoarse from his shouting. "Jeez, I came all the way out here to get your opinion on this."

It was a sign of the Chinese government's belated realization that the greenhouse warming would decimate China as well as the rest of the world that they had asked Freiberg to personally direct their massive construction program. At one end of the valley, Chinese engineers and laborers were building a dam to protect the electrical power-generating station from the encroaching Yangzi. At the other end, a crew from Yamagata Industries was constructing a complex pumping station to remove the carbon dioxide emitted by the power station's stacks and store it deep underground, in the played-out seams of the coal bed that provided fuel for the generators.

With an exasperated frown, Freiberg said, "Listen, I know I still get my paycheck from Astro, but that doesn't mean I can jump whenever you blow the whistle."

Dan looked into the other man's light blue eyes and saw pain there, disappointment and outright fear. Zack blames himself for this catastrophe, Dan knew. He discovered the greenhouse cliff and he acts as if it's all his fault. Instead of some fathead king shooting the messenger, the messenger wants to shoot himself.

"Look, Zack," he said, as reasonably as he could manage, "you have to eat a meal now and then, don't you?"

Freiberg nodded warily. He'd been sweet-talked by Dan into doing things he hadn't wanted to do often enough in the past.

"So I brought you lunch," Dan said, waving his arm in the direction of the oversized mobile home he'd arrived in. Its roof glittered with solar panels. "When the noon whistle blows, come in and break some bread with me. That's all I'm asking."

"You want me to look at this proposal over lunch? You think I can make a technical decision about this in an hour or less?"

Dan shrugged disarmingly. "If you can't, you can't. All I'm asking is that you give it a look."

Freiberg gave Dan a look that was far from happy.

Yet five minutes after noon he climbed up through the open door of Dan's big mobile home.

"I might have known," he muttered as he stepped past Big George, standing by the doorway.

The van was luxuriously fitted out. George was Dan's major domo and bodyguard. An attractive young Japanese woman, petite and silent, was stirring steaming vegetables in an electric wok. Dan was sitting in the faux-leather couch that curved around the fold-down dinner table, a suede jacket draped over his shoulders even though the van felt uncomfortably warm to Freiberg. Zack could see the crease across Dan's face that the sanitary mask had left.

"Drink?" Dan asked, without getting to his feet. A half-empty tumbler of something bubbly sat on the table before him.

"What are you having?" Freiberg asked, sliding into the couch where it angled around the table's end. The table was already set for two.

"Ginger beer," said Dan. "George turned me on to it. Non-alcoholic and it's even good for the digestion."

Freiberg shrugged his rounded shoulders. "Okay, I'll have the same."

George quickly pulled a brown bottle from the refrigerator, opened it, and poured Freiberg a glass of ginger beer.

"Goes good with brandy, y'know," he said as he handed the glass to Freiberg.

The scientist accepted the glass wordlessly and George went back to his post by the door, folding his heavy arms over his massive chest like a professional bouncer.

After a sip of his drink, Dan asked, "Might have known what?"

Freiberg waved a hand around the compartment. "That you'd be living in the lap of luxury, even out here."

Dan laughed. "If you've got to go out into the wilderness, you might as well bring a few creature comforts with you."

"Kind of warm in here, though," Freiberg complained mildly.

Dan smiled gauntly at him. "You're accustomed to living in the wild, Zack. I'm not."

"Yeah, guess so." Freiberg glanced at the painting above Dan's head: a little girl standing by a banyan tree. "Is that real?"

"Holoprint," said Dan. "A Vickrey."

"Nice."

"What're you living in, out here?"

"A tent," said Freiberg.

Nodding, Dan said, "That's what I thought."

"It's a pretty good tent, as tents go, but it's nothing like this." His eyes swept the dining area appreciatively. "How many other rooms in here?"

"Just two: office and bedroom. King-sized bed, of course."

"Of course."

"You like it, it's yours."

"The holoprint?"

"The van. The whole shebang. I'll be leaving later this afternoon. If you can find somebody to drive George and me to the airstrip you can keep this for yourself."

Surprised, Freiberg blurted, "Can you afford to give it away? From what I've heard—"

"For you, Zack," Dan interrupted, "my last penny. If it comes to that."

Freiberg made a wry face. "You're trying to bribe me."

"Yep. Why not?"

With a resigned sigh, the scientist said, "All right, let me see this proposal you want me to look at."

"Hey George," Dan called, "bring me the notebook, will you?"

Almost an hour later, Freiberg looked up from the notebook's screen and said, "Well, I'm no rocket engineer, and what I know about fusion reactors you could put into a thimble, but I can't find anything obviously wrong with this."

"Do you think it'll work?" Dan asked earnestly.

"How the hell should I know?" Freiberg snapped irritably. "Why in hell did you come all the way out here to ask my opinion on something you *know* is outside my expertise?"

Dan hesitated for several heartbeats, then answered, "Because I can trust you, Zack. This guy Humphries is too slick for me to believe. All the experts I've contacted claim that this fusion rocket is workable, but how do I know that he hasn't bought them off? He's got something up his sleeve, some hidden agenda, and this fusion rocket idea is just the tip of the iceberg. I think he wants to get his paws on Astro."

"That's a helluva mixture of metaphors," Freiberg said, grinning despite himself.

"Never mind the syntax. I don't trust Humphries. I do trust you."

"Dan, my opinion doesn't mean a damned thing here. You might as well ask George, or your cook."

Hunching forward over the table, Dan said, "You can talk the talk, Zack. You can contact the experts that Humphries has used and sound them out. You can talk to other people, the real specialists in these areas, and see what they think. They'd talk to you, Zack, and you'd understand what they're saying. You can—"

"Dan," Freiberg said icily, "I'm working twenty-six hours a day already."

"I know," Dan said. "I know."

Freiberg had thrown himself totally into the global effort to cut down on the greenhouse gas emissions given off by the world's fossil-fueled power-generating stations, factories, and vehicles.

Faced with disastrous shifts in climate due to the greenhouse warming, the nations of the world were belatedly, begrudgingly, attempting to remedy the cataclysm. Led by the Global Economic Council, manufacturers around the world were desperately trying to convert automobiles and other vehicles to electrical motors. But that meant trebling the global electricity-generating capacity, and fossil-fueled power plants were faster and cheaper to build than nuclear plants. There was still plenty of petroleum available, and the world's resources of coal dwarfed the petroleum reserves. Fission-based power plants were still anathema because of the public's fear of nuclear power. The new fusion generators were costly, complex, and also hindered by stubborn public resistance to anything nuclear.

So more and more fossil-fueled power plants were being built, especially in the rising industrial nations such as China and South Africa. The GEC insisted that new plants sequester their carbon dioxide emissions, capture the dangerous greenhouse gas and pump it safely deep underground.

Zachary Freiberg had devoted his life to the effort to mitigate the greenhouse disaster. He had taken an indefinite leave of absence from his position as chief scientist of Astro Manufacturing and criss-crossed the world, directing massive construction projects. His wife had left him, he had not seen his children in more than a year, his personal life was in tatters, but he was driven to do what he could, what he had to do, to help slow the greenhouse warming.

"So how's it going?" Dan asked him.

Freiberg shook his head. "We're shoveling shit against the tide. There's just no way we can reduce greenhouse emissions enough to make a difference."

"But I thought—"

"We've been working our butts off for . . . how long has it been? Ten years? Not even a dent. When we started, fossil fuel burning pumped six billion tons of carbon dioxide into the air every year. Know how much we're putting out now?"

Dan shook his head.

"Five point three billion tons," Freiberg said, almost angrily.

Dan grunted.

Pointing through the van's window to the massive trucks rumbling by, Freiberg grumbled, "Yamagata's trying to convert their whole fleet of trucks to electricity, but the Chinese are still using diesels. Some people just don't give a damn! The Russians are starting to talk about cultivating what they call the 'virgin lands' in Siberia, where the permafrost is melting. They think they can turn the region into a new grain belt, like the Ukraine."

"So something good might come out of all this," Dan murmured.

"My ass," Freiberg snapped. "The oceans are still warming up, Dan. The clathrates are going to break down if we can't stop the ocean temperature rise. Once they start releasing the methane that's frozen in them . . ."

Dan opened his mouth to reply, but Freiberg kept right on agonizing. "You know how much methane is locked up in the clathrates? Two times ten to the sixteenth tons. Twenty quadrillion tons! Enough to produce a greenhouse that'll melt all the ice in Greenland *and* Antarctica. Every glacier in the world. We'll all drown."

"All the more reason," Dan said, "for pushing out to the Asteroid Belt. We can bring in all the metals and minerals the Earth needs, Zack! We can move the world's industrial operations into space, where they won't screw up the Earth's environment."

Freiberg gave Dan a disbelieving look.

"We can do it!" Dan insisted. "If this fusion rocket can be made to work. That's the key to the whole damned thing: efficient propulsion can bring the cost of asteroid mining down to where it's economically viable."

For a long moment Freiberg said nothing. He merely glared at Dan, half angry, half sullen.

At last he mumbled, "I'll make a few calls for you, Dan. That's all I can do."

"That's all I ask," Dan replied, forcing a smile. Then he added, "Plus a ride to the airstrip for George and me."

"What about your cook?"

With a laugh, Dan said, "She goes with the van, old buddy. She only speaks Japanese, but she's terrific in the kitchen. And the bedroom."

Freiberg flushed deep red. But he did not refuse Dan's gift.

SELENE CITY

The customs inspector looked startled when he saw the plastic cage and the four live mice huddled in it among the loose food pellets.

He set his face into a scowl as he looked up at Pancho. "You can't bring pets into Selene."

The other astronauts had sailed through the incoming inspection without a hitch, leaving Pancho to face the grim-faced inspector alone. They had cruised to the Moon without incident, none of the others realizing that Pancho had milked each of their bank accounts for a half-hour's interest. Pancho figured that even if they eventually discovered her little scam, the amount of money involved was too small to fight over. To her, it wasn't the amount so much as the adroitness of the sting.

"They're not pets," she said coolly to the inspector. "They're food."

"Food?" The man's dark eyebrows hiked halfway to his scalp line.

"Yeah, food. For my bodyguard." Most of the customs inspectors knew her, but this guy was new; Pancho hadn't encountered him before. Not bad-looking, she thought. His dark blue zipsuit complemented his eyes nicely. A little elderly, though. Starting to go gray at the temples. Must be working to raise enough money for a rejuve treatment.

As if he knew he was being maneuvered into giving straight lines, the customs inspector asked, "Your bodyguard eats mice?"

Pancho nodded. "Yes, sir, she does."

The inspector huffed. "And where is this bodyguard?"

Pancho lifted a long leg and planted her softbooted foot on the inspector's table. Tugging up the cuff of her coverall trouser, she revealed what looked like a bright metallic blue ankle bracelet.

While the inspector gaped, Pancho coaxed Elly off her ankle and held her out in front of the man's widening eyes. The snake was about thirty-five centimeters long from nose to tail. It lifted its head and, fixing the inspector with its beady, slitted eyes, it hissed menacingly. The man flinched back nearly half a meter.

"Elly's a genetically-modified krait. She'll never get any bigger'n this. She's very well-behaved and wicked poisonous."

To his credit, the inspector swiftly recovered his composure. Most of it, at least.

"You . . . you can't bring a snake in," he said, his voice quavering only slightly. "That's against the regulations and besides—"

"There's a special exception to the regulations," Pancho said calmly. "You can look it up. Paragraph seventeen-dee, subclause eleven."

With a frown, the inspector punched up the relevant page on his palmcomp. Pancho knew the exception would be there; she had gone all the way up to the Selene health and safety executive board to get it written into the regs. It had cost her a small fortune in time and effort; many dinners with men old enough to be her grandfather. Funny thing was, the only overt sexual pass made at her was from the woman who chaired the executive board.

"Well, I'll be dipped in . . ." The inspector looked up from his hand-held's tiny screen. "How in hell did you get them to rewrite the regs for you?"

Pancho smiled sweetly. "It wasn't easy."

"That little fella is poisonous, you say?"

"Her venom's been engineered to reduce its lethality, but she's still fatal unless you get a shot of antiserum." Pancho pulled a slim vial from her open travelbag and wagged it in front of the inspector's bulging eyes.

He shook his head in wonder as Pancho coaxed the snake back around her ankle. "And he eats mice."

"She," Pancho said as she straightened up again. "When I stay up here for more than a month I have to send Earthside for more mice. Costs a bundle."

"I'll bet."

"The mice never get out of their cage," Pancho added. "Once every other week I put Elly in with them."

The inspector shuddered visibly. He took Pancho's entry forms and passed them in front of the electronic reader. The machine beeped once. Pancho was cleared. The inspector put the transparent mouse cage back into her flight bag and zipped it shut.

"You're okay to enter Selene," he said, almost as if he didn't believe it himself.

"Thank you."

Before she could hoist her bag onto her shoulder, he asked, "Uh . . . what're you doing for dinner tonight?"

Pancho smiled her sweetest. "Gee, I'd love to have dinner with you, but I already have a date."

Dressed in a crisp white pantsuit set off by the flowery scarf she'd tied around her neck, Pancho followed the directions Martin Humphries had videomailed to her.

In Earthside cities, height meant prestige. In hotels and condo towers, the higher the floor, the higher the price. Penthouses were considered the most desirable, and therefore were the most expensive. On the Moon, where human settlements were dug into the ground, prestige increased with depth. The airless lunar surface was dangerous, subject to four-hundred-degree temperature swings between sunlight and shadow, bathed in hard radiation from deep space, peppered with meteoric infall. So in Selene and the other communities on the Moon, the deeper your living quarters, the more desirable it was, and the more expensive.

Martin Humphries must be rotten rich, Pancho thought as she rode the elevator down to Selene's lowest level. According to the biofiles on the nets Humphries was supposed to be one of the wealthiest men in the Earth/Moon system, but that could be public relations puffery, she thought. The tabloids and scandal sites had more on him than the biofiles. They called him "Hump," or "the Humper." He had a reputation as a chaser, married twice and with lots of media stars and glamour gals from the upper crust to boot. When Pancho looked up the pix of his "dates" she saw a succession of tall, languid, gorgeous women with lots of hairdo and skimpy clothes.

Pancho felt completely safe: the Humper wouldn't be interested in a gangly, horse-faced tomboy. Besides, if he tried anything Elly would protect her.

He had called her personally. No flunky; Martin Humphries his own self had phoned Pancho and asked her to come to his home to discuss a business proposition. Maybe he wants to hire me away from Astro, she thought. Astro's been a good-enough outfit, but if Humphries offers more money I'll go to work for him. That's a no-brainer. Go where the money is, every time.

But why did he call me himself, instead of having his personnel office interview me?

There were only a few living units carved into the rock this far underground. Big places, Pancho realized as she glided along the well-lit corridor in the practiced bent-kneed shuffle that you had to use to walk in the Moon's low gravity. The walls of the corridor were carved with elaborate low-relief sculptures, mostly astronomical motifs, but there were some Earthly landscapes in with the stars and comets. She counted about a hundred strides between doors, which meant that the living units on the other sides of the corridor walls were bigger than a whole dorm section on the floors above. The doors were fancy, too: most of them were double, all of them decorated one way or another. Some of them looked like real wood, for crying out loud.

But while all this impressed Pancho, she was totally unprepared for Martin Humphries's home. At the very end of the corridor was a blank metal door, polished steel from the look of it. More like an airlock hatch or a bank vault than the fancy-pants doors she'd passed along the corridor. It slid open with a soft hiss as Pancho approached within arm's length.

Optical recognition system, she thought. Or maybe he's got somebody watching the corridor.

She stepped through the open doorway and immediately felt as if she'd entered another world. She found herself in a wide, high-ceilinged cavern, a big natural cave deep below the lunar surface. Flowers bloomed everywhere, reds and yellows and green foliage spread out on both sides of her. Trees! She gaped at the sight of young alders and maples, slim white-boled birches, delicately fronded frangipani. The only trees she'd seen in Selene were up in the Grand Plaza, and they were just little bitty things compared to these. After the closed-in gray sameness of Selene's warren of corridors and tightly-confined living quarters, the openness, the color, the heady scent of flowers growing in such profusion nearly overwhelmed Pancho. Boulders jutted here and there; the distant walls of the cave and the ceiling high above were rough bare rock. The ceiling was dotted with full-spectrum lamps, she saw. Jeez, it's like being in Oz, Pancho said to herself.

Like Oz, there was a path winding through the shrubbery, littered with flower petals. Pancho liked that much better than yellow bricks.

She realized that there were no birds singing in the trees. No insects buzzed among the flowers. There was no breeze sighing past. This ornate garden was nothing more than a big, elaborate hothouse, Pancho decided. It must cost a freaking fortune.

She glide-walked along the path until a final turn revealed the house set in the middle of the cavern, surrounded by still more trees and carefully-planted beds of roses, irises and peonies. No daisies, Pancho noted. No marigolds. Too ordinary for this layout.

The house was enormous, low but wide, with a slanted roof and walls of lunar stone, smoothed and glazed over. Big sweeping windows. A wide courtyard framed the big double doors of the front entrance, with a fountain gurgling busily in its center. A fountain! Pancho approached the door slowly, reached out her hand to touch its carved surface. Plastic, her fingertips told her, stained to look like wood. For several moments she stood at the door, then turned to look back at the courtyard again, the gardens, the trees, the fountain. What kind of a man would spend so much money for a private palace like this? What kind of a man would have that much money to spend?

"Welcome, Ms. Lane."

The sound of his voice made Pancho flinch. He had opened the door silently while her back had been turned as she surveyed the greenery. She saw a man apparently about her own age, several centimeters shorter than she, a little on the pudgy side. He was wearing an open-necked pale yellow tunic that came down to his hips. His slacks were cinnamon brown, perfectly creased. His feet were shod in fancy tooled leather boots. His skin was doughy white, his hair dark and slicked back.

"I'm here to see Mr. Humphries," she said. "I've been invited."

He laughed lightly. "I'm Martin Humphries. I gave my staff the night off."

"Oh."

Martin Humphries gestured Pancho to come into his house. Knowing Elly was comfortably wrapped around her ankle, Pancho stepped right in.

The house was just as luxurious as the grounds around it, perhaps even more so. Big, spacious rooms filled with the most beautiful furniture Pancho had ever seen. A living room long enough to hold a hockey rink, sofas done in gorgeous fabrics, holowindows showing spectacular Earthside scenery: the Grand Canyon, Mt. Fujiyama, Manhattan's skyline the way it looked before the floods.

The dining room table was big enough to seat twenty, but it was set for just the two of them: Humphries at its head, Pancho at his right hand. Humphries walked her past it, though, and into a book-lined library where the single holowindow showed the star-strewn depths of space.

There was a bar along one side of the library.

"What would you like to drink?" Humphries asked, gently guiding her to one of the plush-cushioned stools.

"Whatever," Pancho shrugged. A good way to judge a man's intentions was to let him select the drinks.

He looked at her for a fleeting, intense moment. Like being x-rayed, Pancho thought. His eyes were gray, she noted, cold gray, like lunar stone.

"I have an excellent champagne," he suggested.

Pancho smiled at him. "Okay, fine."

He pressed a button set into the bar's surface, and a silver tray bearing an opened bottle of champagne in a refrigerated bucket and two tall fluted glasses rose up to serving height with a muted hum of an electrical motor. Humphries pulled the bottle from its bucket and poured two glasses of champagne. Pancho noticed that the ice-cold bottle quickly beaded with condensation. The glasses looked like real crystal, prob'ly made at Selene's glass factory.

The bubbles tickled her nose, but the wine was really good: crisp and cold, with a delicate flavor that Pancho liked. Still, she merely sipped at it as she sat beside Martin Humphries on the softly-cushioned bar stool.

"You must be awful rich to have this place all to yourself," she said.

His lips edged into a thin smile. "It's not mine, really."

"It's not?"

"Legally, this building is a research center. It's owned by the Humphries Trust and operated jointly by a consortium of Earthside universities and the Selene executive board."

Pancho took another sip of champagne while she sorted that out in her mind.

Humphries went on, "I live here whenever I'm at Selene. The research staff uses the other end of the house."

"But they don't live here."

He laughed. "No, they live a few levels up, in . . . um, more ordinary quarters."

"And you get the whole place rent-free."

With a waggle of his free hand, Humphries said, "One of the advantages of wealth."

"The rich get richer."

"Or they lose what they've got."

Nodding, Pancho asked, "So what do they research down here?"

"Lunar ecology," Humphries replied. "They're trying to learn how to build Earthlike ecologies here on the Moon, underground."

"Like the Grand Plaza, up topside."

"Yes. But completely closed-cycle, so you don't have to put in fresh supplies of water."

"That's what all the flowers and trees are about."

"Right. They've been able to make a lovely garden, all right, but it's incredibly expensive. Very labor-intensive, with no birds or insects to pollinate the plants. The idiots running Selene's environmental safety department won't let me bring any up here. As if they could get loose! They're so stupidly narrow-minded they could look through a keyhole with both eyes."

Pancho smiled at him, remembering how hard it had been for her to get the approval to bring Elly and her food into Selene. *I must be smarter than he is,* she thought. *Or maybe Selene's execs just don't like megazillionaires trying to push them around.*

"And those full-spectrum lamps cost a fortune in electricity," Humphries went on.

"Electricity's cheap, though, isn't it?"

Humphries took a long draft of his champagne, then answered, "It's cheap once you've built the solar energy farm up on the surface . . . and the superconducting batteries to store electrical energy during the night. High capital costs, though."

"Yeah, but once you've got the equipment in place the operating costs are pitiful low."

"Except for maintenance."

"Keeping the solar farms clean, up on the surface, you mean. Yeah, I guess that ain't cheap."

"Any work on the surface is damned expensive," he grumbled, bringing his champagne flute to his lips.

"So how rich are you?" she asked abruptly.

Humphries didn't sputter into his champagne, but he did seem to swallow pretty hard.

Pancho added, "I mean, do you *own* any of this or are you just livin' in it?"

He thought a moment before answering. Then, "My grandfather made his fortune in the big dot-com boom around the turn of the century. Gramps was smart enough to get into the market while it was still rising and get out before the bubble burst."

"What's a dot-com?" Pancho asked.

Ignoring her question, Humphries went on, "My father took his degrees in biology and law. He bought into half a dozen biotech firms and built one of the biggest fortunes on Earth."

"What're your degrees in?"

"I have an MBA from Wharton and a JD from Yale."

"So you're a lawyer."

"I've never practiced law."

Pancho felt alarm signals tingling through her. That's not a straight answer, she realized. But then, what do you expect from a lawyer? She recalled the old dictum: How can you tell when a lawyer's lying? Watch his lips.

"What do you practice?" she asked, trying to make it sound nonchalant.

He smiled again, and there was even some warmth in it this time. "Oh . . . making money, mostly. That seems to be what I'm best at."

Glancing around the luxurious library, Pancho replied, "I'd say you're purty good at spendin' it, too."

Humphries laughed aloud. "Yes, I suppose so. I spend a lot of it on women."

As if on cue, a generously-curved redhead in a slinky metallic sheath appeared at the doorway to the dining room, a slim aperitif glass dangling empty from one manicured hand. "Say, Humpy, when is dinner served?" she asked poutily. "I'm starving."

His face went white with anger. "I told you," he said through clenched teeth, "that I have a business meeting to attend to. I'll be with you when I'm finished here."

"But I'm starving," the redhead repeated.

Glancing at Pancho, Humphries said in a low voice, "I'll be with you in a few minutes."

The redhead looked Pancho over from head to toe, grinned, and flounced off.

Visibly trying to contain his fury, Humphries said, "I'm sorry for the interruption."

Pancho shrugged. So I'm not invited for dinner, she realized. Should've known.

"Is that your wife?" she asked coolly.

"No."

"You are married, aren't you?"

"Twice."

"Are you married *now?*"

"Legally, yes. Our lawyers are working out a divorce settlement."

Pancho looked straight into his icy gray eyes. The anger was still there, but he was controlling it now. He seemed deadly calm.

"Okay," she said, "let's finish up this business meeting so y'all can get down to dinner."

Humphries picked up his glass again, drained it, and placed it carefully back on the bar. Looking up at Pancho, he said, "All right. I want to hire you."

"I already have a job," she said.

"As a pilot for Astro Manufacturing, I know. You've been working for them for more than six years."

"So?"

"You won't have to quit Astro. In fact, I want you to stay with them. The task I have in mind for you requires that you keep your position with Astro."

Pancho understood immediately. "You want me to spy on them."

"That's putting it rather crudely," Humphries said, his eyes shifting away from her and then back again. "But, yes, I need a certain amount of industrial espionage done, and you are ideally placed to do it."

Pancho didn't think twice. "How much money are we talkin' about here?"

CUENCA

an Randloph felt a wave of giddiness wash over him as he stood at his hotel window and looked down into the rugged gorge of the Júcar River.

This is stupid, he told himself. You've been in high-rises a lot taller than this. You've been on top of rocket launch towers. You've been to the Grand Canyon, you've done EVA work in orbit, for god's sake, floating hundreds of miles above the Earth without even an umbilical cord to hold onto.

Yet he felt shaky, slightly light-headed, as he stood by the window. It's not the height, he told himself. For a scary moment he thought it was one of the woozy symptoms of radiation sickness again. But then he realized that it was only because this hotel was hanging over the lip of the gorge, six stories down from the edge.

The old city of Cuenca had been built in medieval times along the rim of the deep, vertiginous chasm. From the street, the hotel seemed to be a one-story building, as did all the buildings along the narrow way. Inside, though, it went down and down, narrow stairways and long windows that looked out into the canyon cut by the river so far below.

Turning from the window, Dan went to the bed and unzipped his travel bag. He was here in the heart of Spain to find the answer to the world's overwhelming problem, the key to unlock the wealth of the solar system. Like a knight on a quest, he told himself, with a sardonic shake of his head. Seeking the holy grail.

Like a tired old man who's pushing himself because he doesn't have anything else left in his life, sneered a bitter voice in his head.

The flight in from Madrid had turned his thoughts to old tales of knighthood and chivalrous quests. The Clippership rocket flight from La

Guaira had taken only twenty-five minutes to cross the Atlantic, but there was nothing to see, no portholes in the craft's stout body and the video views flashing across the screen at his seat might as well have been from an astronomy lecture. The flight from Madrid to Cuenca, though, had been in an old-fashioned tiltrotor, chugging and rattling and clattering across a landscape that was old when Hannibal had led armies through it.

Don Quixote rode across those brown hills, Dan had told himself. El Cid battled the Moors here.

He snorted disdainfully as he pulled his shaving kit from the travel bag. Now I'm going to see if we can win the fight against a giant bigger than any windmill that old Don Quixote tackled.

The phone buzzed. Dan snapped his fingers, then realized that the hotel phone wasn't programmed for sound recognition. He leaned across the bed and stabbed at the ON button.

"Mr. Randolph?"

The face Dan saw in the palm-sized phone screen looked almost Mephistopholean: thick black hair that came to a point almost touching his thick black brows; a narrow vee-shaped face with sharp cheekbones and a pointed chin; coal-black eyes that glittered slyly, as if the man knew things that no one else knew. A small black goatee.

"Yes," Dan answered. "And you are . . . ?"

"Lyall Duncan. I've come to take you to the test site," said the caller, in a decidedly Highland accent.

Dan puffed out a breath. They certainly aren't wasting any time. I'm not even unpacked yet.

"Are you ready, sir?" Duncan asked.

Dan tossed his shaving kit back onto the bed. "Ready," he said.

Duncan was short, rail-thin, and terribly earnest about his work. He talked incessantly as they drove in a dusty old Volkswagen van out into the sun-drenched countryside, past scraggly checkerboards of farms and terraced hillsides, climbing constantly toward the distant bare peaks of the Sierras. The land looked parched, poor, yet it had been under cultivation for thousands of years. At least, Dan thought, it's far enough from the sea to be safe from flooding. But it looks as if it's turning into a brown, dusty desert.

". . . tried for many a year to get someone to look at our work, *anyone*," Duncan was saying. "The universities were too busy with their big reactor projects, all of them sucking on one government teat or another. The private companies wouldn't even talk to us, not without some fancy university behind us."

Dan nodded and tried to stay awake. The man's soft Scottish burr was hypnotic as they drove along the winding highway into the hills. There were hardly any other cars on the road, and the hum of the tires on the blacktop was lulling Dan to sleep. Electric motors don't make much noise, he told himself, trying to fight off the jet lag. He remembered that auto makers such as GM and Toyota had tried to install sound systems that would simulate the *vroom* of a powerful gasoline engine, to attract the testosterone crowd. The GEC had nixed that; silent, efficient, clean electrical cars had to be presented as desirable, not as a weak second choice to muscle cars.

". . . none of them wanted to see that a compact, lightweight, *disposable* fusion generator could work as well as the behemoths they were building," Duncan droned on. "No one paid us any attention until we caught the ear of Mr. Martin Humphries."

Dan perked up at the mention of Humphries's name. "How did you reach him? He's pretty high up in the corporate food chain."

Duncan smiled craftily. "Through a woman, how else? He came to Glasgow to give a speech. The anniversary of his father's endowment of the new biology building, or something of that sort. He took a fancy to a certain young lady in our student body. She was a biology major and had quite a body of her own."

With a laugh, Dan said, "So she did the Delilah job for you."

"One of the lads in our project knew her—in the biblical sense. He asked her if she'd help the cause of science."

"And she agreed."

"Willingly. 'Tisn't every day a lass from Birmingham gets to sleep with a billionaire."

"Oh, she was English?"

"Aye. We couldn't ask a Scottish lass to do such a thing."

Both men were still laughing as the car pulled into the test site's parking lot.

It wasn't much of a site, Dan thought as he got out of the car. Just a flat, open area of bare dirt with a couple of tin sheds to one side and a rickety-looking scaffolding beyond them. Rugged hills rose all around, and in the distance the Sierras shimmered ghostlike in the heat haze. The sun felt hot and good on his shoulders. The sky was a perfect blue, virtually cloudless. Dan inhaled a deep breath of clean mountain air; it was cool and sharp with a tang of pines that even got past his nose plugs. Dan thought about taking them out; it would be a relief to do without them. But he didn't remove them.

There were six people in the "office" shed, two of them women, all but one of them young, wearing shabby sweaters and slacks or jeans that hadn't known a crease for years. Dan felt overdressed in his tan slacks and suede sports jacket. One of the women was tall, with long, lank blond hair that fell past her broad shoulders. She looked like a California surfer type to Dan. Or maybe a Swede. The other was clearly Japanese or perhaps Korean: short and chunky, but when she smiled it lit up her whole face.

They all looked eager, excited to have Dan Randolph himself here to see their work, yet Dan caught a whiff of fear among them. Suppose it doesn't work today? Suppose something goes wrong? Suppose Randolph doesn't understand its value, its importance? Dan had felt that undercurrent in research labs all around the world; even on the Moon.

The one older man looked professorial. He wore baggy tweed trousers and a matching vest, unbuttoned. His long face was framed by a trim salt-and-pepper beard. Duncan introduced him as "Dr. Vertientes."

"I am delighted to meet you, sir," Dan said, automatically lapsing into Spanish as he took the man's hand.

Vertientes's brows rose with surprise. "You speak Spanish very well, sir."

"My headquarters is in Venezuela." Dan almost added that he'd once been married to a Venezuelan, but that had been too brief and too painful to bring into the conversation.

"We are a multinational group here," Vertientes said, switching to British English, overlaid with a Castilian accent. "We speak English among ourselves."

"Except when we curse," said the Japanese woman.

Everyone laughed.

Much to Dan's surprise, Duncan was the leader of the little group. The tall, distinguished Vertientes turned out to be the group's plasma physicist. Duncan was the propulsion engineer and the driving force among them.

"You know the principle of nuclear fusion," the Scotsman said as he led the entire group out of the office shack and toward the slightly larger shed that served as their laboratory.

Nodding, Dan said, "Four hydrogen atoms come together to form a helium atom and release energy."

"Nuclei," Duncan corrected. "Not atoms, their nuclei. The plasma is completely ionized."

"Yep. Right."

"Seven-tenths of one percent of the mass of the four original protons is converted into energy. The Sun and all the stars have been running for billions of years on that seven-tenths of one percent."

"As long as they're fusing hydrogen into helium," Dan said. To show that he wasn't entirely unlettered, he added, "Later on they start fusing helium into heavier elements."

Duncan gave him a sidelong glance from beneath his deep black brows, then said, "Aye, but it's only hydrogen fusion that we're interested in."

"Aye," Dan murmured.

The laboratory shed wasn't large, but the equipment in it seemed up-to-date. It looked more like a monitoring station to Dan's practiced eye than a research laboratory. Beyond it was a bigger building that couldn't be seen from the parking lot. The group trooped through the lab with only a perfunctory glance at its equipment, then went on to the other building.

"This is where the dirty work gets done," Duncan said, with his devilish grin.

Dan nodded as he looked around. It was a construction shack, all right. Machine tools and an overhead crane running on heavy steel tracks. The sharp tang of machine oil in the air, bits of wire and metal shavings littering the floor. Yes, they worked in here.

"And out there," Duncan said, pointing to a dust-caked window, "is the result."

It didn't look terribly impressive. Even when they stepped outside and walked up to the scaffolding, all Dan could see was a two-meter-wide metal sphere with a spaghetti factory of hoses and wires leading into it. The metal looked clean and shiny, though.

Dan rapped on it with his knuckles. "Stainless steel?"

Nodding, Duncan said, "For the outside pressure vessel. The containment sphere is a beryllium alloy."

"Beryllium?"

"The alloy is proprietary. We've applied for an international patent, but you know how long that takes."

Dan agreed glumly, then asked, "Is this all there is to it?"

With a fierce grin, Duncan said, "The best things come in the smallest packages."

They went back to the lab and, without a word, the six men and women took their stations along the bank of consoles that lined two walls of the shed. There was an assortment of chairs and stools, no two of them alike, but no one sat down. Dan saw that they were nervous, intense. All except Duncan, who looked calmly confident. He cocked a brow at Dan, like a gambler about to shuffle cards from the bottom of the deck.

"Are you ready to see wee beastie in action?" Duncan asked.

Tired from traveling, Dan pulled a little wheeled typist's chair to the middle of the floor and sat on it. Folding his arms across his chest, he nodded and said, "You may fire when ready, Gridley."

The others looked slightly puzzled, wondering who Gridley might be and what his significance was. Duncan, though, bobbed his head and grinned as though he understood everything.

He turned to Vertientes and said softly, "Start it up, then."

Dan heard a pump begin to chug and saw the readout numbers on Vertientes's console start to climb. The other consoles came to life, display screens flickering on to show multi-colored graphs or digital readouts.

"Pressure approaching optimum," sang out the blonde. "Density on the curve."

"Fuel cells on line."

"Capacitor bank ready."

Duncan stood beside Dan, sweeping all the consoles with his eyes.

"Approaching ignition point," said Vertientes.

Leaning slightly toward Dan, Duncan said, "It's set to ignite automatically, although we have the manual backup ready."

Dan got to his feet and stared out the window at the stainless steel sphere out in the scaffold. There was a crackling air of tension in the lab now; he could feel the hairs on the back of his neck rising.

"Ignition!" Vertientes called.

Dan saw nothing. The metal sphere outside didn't move. There was no roar or cloud of smoke, not even a vibration. He looked at Duncan, then over to the six others, all of them standing rigidly intent at their consoles. Numbers flickered across screens, curves crawled along graphs, but as far as Dan could see or feel nothing was actually happening.

"Shutdown," Vertientes said.

Everyone relaxed, sagged back a bit, let out their breaths.

"Thirty seconds, on the tick," someone said.

"Power output?" Duncan asked.

"Design maximum. It reached fifty megawatts after four seconds and held it there right to cutoff."

Vertientes was beaming. He turned and clutched Duncan by both shoulders. "Perfecto! She is a well-behaved little lady!"

"You mean that's it?" Dan asked, incredulous.

Duncan was grinning too. They all were.

"But nothing happened," Dan insisted.

"Oh no?" said Duncan, grasping Dan's elbow and turning him toward the row of consoles. "Look at that power output graph."

Frowning, Dan remembered a scientist once telling him that all of physics boiled down to reading a bloody gauge.

"But it didn't go anywhere," Dan said weakly.

They all laughed.

"It isn't a rocket," Duncan said. "Not yet. We're only testing the fusion reactor."

"Only!" said the Japanese woman.

"Thirty seconds isn't much of a test," Dan pointed out.

"Nay, thirty seconds is plenty of time," Duncan rebutted.

"The plasma equilibrates in five seconds or less," said Vertientes.

"But to be useful as a rocket," Dan insisted, "the reactor's going to have to run for hours . . . even weeks or months."

"Si, yes, we know," Vertientes said, tapping a finger into the palm of his other hand. "But in thirty seconds we get enough data to calculate the heat transfer and plasma flow parameters. We can extrapolate to hours and weeks and months."

"I don't trust extrapolations," Dan muttered.

The blonde stepped between them. "Well, of *course* we're going to build a full-scale model and run it for months. For sure. But what Doc Vee is saying is we've done enough testing to be confident that it'll work."

Dan looked her over. California, he decided. Maybe Swedish ancestry, but definitely California.

"We intend to mate the reactor with an MHD generator," Vertientes said, earnestly trying to convince Dan. "That way the plasma exhaust from the reactor can provide electrical power as well as thrust."

"Magneto . . ." Dan stumbled over the word.

"Magnetohydrodynamic," Vertientes finished for him.

The blonde added, "The interaction of electrically-conducting ionized gases with magnetic fields."

Dan grinned at her. "Thank you." She's showing off, he thought. She wants me to know that she's a *smart* blonde, despite her surfer chick looks.

Then he caught Duncan watching him with that sly look in his glittering coal-black eyes, and remembered the student from Birmingham who had convinced Humphries to pay attention to their work. He shook his head ever so slightly, to tell Duncan that he wouldn't need to be convinced that way.

Once he would have scooped up a young available woman and enjoyed every minute of their brief fling together. But not now. He grimaced inwardly at the weird curves fate throws. When Jane was alive I chased every woman I saw, trying to forget her. Now that she's dead I don't want anyone else. Not now. Maybe not ever again.

SELENE CITY

Don't you intend ever to return to Earth?"

Martin Humphries leaned back in his exquisitely padded reclining chair and tried to hide the dread he felt as he gazed at his father's image on the wall screen.

"I'm working hard here, Dad," he said.

It takes almost three seconds for radio or light waves to make the round-trip between the Earth and the Moon. Martin Humphries used the time to study his father's sallow, wrinkled, sagging face. Even though the old man had made his fortune in biotech, he still refused rejuvenation treatments as "too new, too risky, too many unknowns." Yet he wore a snow-white toupee to hide his baldness. It made Martin think of George Washington, although George was alleged never to have told a lie and anyone who had ever dealt with W. Wilson Humphries knew that you had to count your fingers after shaking hands with the old scoundrel.

"I need you here," his father admitted grudgingly.

"*You* need *me?*"

"Those bastards from the New Morality are pushing more tax regulations through the Congress. They won't be satisfied until they've bankrupted every corporation in the country."

"All the more reason for me to stay here," Martin replied, "where I can protect my assets."

"But what about *my* assets? What about me? I need your help, Marty. I can't fight these psalm-singing fundamentalists by myself!"

"Oh, come on, Dad. You've got more lawyers than they do."

"They've got the whole damned Congress," his father grumbled. "And the Supreme Court, too."

"Dad, if you'd just come up here you'd be able to get away from all that."

His father's face hardened. "I'm not going to run away!"

"It's time to admit that the ship is sinking, Dad. Time to get out, while you can. Up here on the Moon I'm building a whole new organization. I'm creating Humphries Space Systems. You could be part of it; an important part."

The old man glared at him for much longer than it took his son's words to reach him. At last he growled, "If you stay up there too long your muscles will get so deconditioned you won't be able to come back to Earth."

He hasn't heard a word I've said, Humphries realized. He talks and he never listens.

"Dad, I'm in the middle of a very complicated deal here. I can't leave. Not now." He hesitated, then said, "I might never come back to Earth."

Once he heard that reply, his father's image went from its normal unhappy scowl to a truly angry frown. "I want you here, dammit! This is where you belong and this is where you're going to be. That's final."

"Father," said Martin, feeling all the old fear and frustration swirling inside him like a whirlpool pulling him down, drowning him. "Father, come here, come be with me. Please. Before it's too late."

His father merely glowered at him.

"Give it up, Dad," Humphries pleaded. "Earth is finished. Everything down there is going to crash; can't you understand that?"

The old man sputtered, "Dammit, Marty, if you don't listen to me . . ." He faltered, stopped, not knowing what to say next.

"Why can't you listen to me for a change?" Martin snapped. Without waiting for a response, he said, "I'm trying to build an empire up here, Dad, an empire that's going to stretch all the way out to the Asteroid Belt and beyond. I'm putting the pieces together right now. I'm going to be the wealthiest man in the solar system, richer than you and all your brothers put together. Maybe then you'll treat me with some respect."

Before his father could reply, Humphries sat up in his recliner and pressed the stud set into the armrest to terminate the videophone link. The old man's face disappeared from the wall, revealing a holowindow that showed a realtime view of Jupiter as seen by the twenty-meter telescope at the Farside Observatory.

For a long moment Humphries simply sat there, alone in the office he had set up for himself in the house deep below the lunar surface. Then he took a long slow breath to calm the furies that raged inside him. The old man has no understanding of the real world. He's still living in the past.

He'd rather go down with the ship than admit that I'm right and he's wrong.

Unbidden, the memory of his drowning engulfed him again. Nine years old. His father insisting that the trimaran was in no trouble despite the dark storm winds that heaved the boat so monstrously. The wave that washed him overboard. The frothing water closing over him. Desperately clawing for the surface but sinking, sinking, can't breathe, everything going dark.

Martin Humphries died at the age of nine. After they revived him, he learned that it had been one of the crew who'd dived into the sound to rescue him. Watching the boy sink out of sight, his father had stayed aboard the trimaran and offered a bonus to any crewman who could rescue his son. Form that moment on, Humphries knew that there was no one in the world he could trust; he was alone, with only his inner fears and yearnings to drive him. And only his money to protect him.

Talking with his father always brought those terrible moments back to mind. And the gasping, choking paralysis that clamped his chest like a merciless vise. He reached into the top desk drawer for his inhalator and took a desperate whiff of the cool, soothing drug.

All right, Humphries thought, waiting for his breathing to return to normal, trying to calm himself. He's going to stay down there and try to fight the New Morality until they burn him at the stake. Nothing I say will budge him a millimeter. Very well, then.

I'll stay here in Selene where it's safe and everything's under control. No storms, no rain; a world built to suit me in every detail. From here I can pull the strings just as effectively as if I were down in New York or London. Better, really. There's no reason for me to go Earthside anymore.

Except for the divorce hearing, he remembered. I'm supposed to show up in the judge's chambers for that. But I can do even that from here, get my lawyers to make the excuse that I can't return to Earth, I've been on the Moon too long, it would be dangerous to my health. I can get a dozen doctors to testify to that. No sweat.

Humphries laughed aloud. I won't have to be in the same room with that bitch! Good! Wonderful!

He leaned back again and stared up at the ceiling. It was set to a planetarium display, the sky as it appeared above Selene. Briefly he thought about calling up a porno video, but decided instead to put on the latest informational release from the International Astronautical Authority about the microprobes searching through the asteroids in the Belt.

The IAA's motivation for investigating the asteroids was to locate rocks that might one day hit the Earth. They had good tracks on all the hundreds of asteroids in orbits that brought them close. Now they were sorting through the thousands of rocks out in the Belt big enough to cause serious damage if they were ejected from the Belt and impacted Earth.

The good news was that so far they had not found any asteroid in an orbit that threatened the homeworld—although the asteroids in the Belt were always being jostled by Jupiter and the other planets, perturbing their orbits unpredictably. A constant watch was a vital necessity.

The better news was that, as a byproduct of the impacter watch, the IAA was getting detailed data on the composition of the larger asteroids. Iron, carbon, nickel, phosphorus, nitrogen, gold, silver, platinum, even water was out there in vast abundance. Ripe for picking. Waiting for me to turn them into money, Humphries told himself, smiling happily.

Dan Randolph will send a team out to the Belt on a fusion rocket. The first mission will fail, of course, and then I'll have Randolph where I want him. I'll take control of Astro Corporation and we can put Randolph out to pasture, where he belongs.

Then a thought clouded his satisfaction. It's been damned near six months since I hired Pancho Lane to keep an eye on Randolph. Why haven't I heard from her?

LA GUAIRA

Aren't you nervous?" Amanda Cunningham asked.

Sitting beside her as the Clippership returned to Earth, Pancho shook her head. "Nope. You?"

"A bit."

"Uh-huh."

"I mean . . . meeting the head of the corporation. It's rather exciting, don't you think?"

Pancho and Amanda had been summoned to Astro Manufacturing's corporate headquarters in La Guaira, on an island across the strait from Caracas. Something about a new assignment that Dan Randolph himself would decide.

"Well, meeting the big boss is important, I guess," Pancho said as nonchalantly as she could manage.

They were riding the Clippership down from the aging space station *Nueva Venezuela* to the landing field at La Guaira, riding comfortably in the nearly empty passenger cabin with a sparse handful of paying customers rather than in the cramped cockpit where the crew worked. Amanda reveled in the luxury of spacious seats and entertainment videos; Pancho figured that something important was waiting for them when they landed, something important enough for Astro to undergo the expense of letting them ride deadhead from Selene.

Well, she said to herself, the pilots up in the cockpit are really deadheading, too. Clipperships flew under control from the ground; they didn't need an onboard crew any more than a ballistic missile did. But even after all these years—decades, really—the politicians refused to allow spacecraft that carried passengers to fly fully automated. The pilots had to go along; there had to be a cockpit and full controls for them even though they had absolutely nothing to do.

Don't complain, she said to herself. If the aerospace lines didn't need to hire pilots you wouldn't have gotten a job in the first place. You'd still be sitting in front of a display screen in some cubicle back in Lubbock doing tech support and barely making enough money to keep Sis alive.

Amanda was flicking through the entertainment channels, eyes locked on her little pop-up screen. Pancho eased back in the comfortable passenger's chair and closed her eyes.

Why me? she asked herself. Why has the CEO of Astro Manufacturing called me all the way back from Selene to see him in person? Amanda I can understand. One look at her ID vid and the Big Boss prob'ly started panting like a dog in heat. Still, in the six months since they'd first met, Pancho had acquired a healthy respect for Amanda's piloting skills, boobs notwithstanding. This is her first job and she's already as good as I am . . . well, almost. I'm the best pilot Astro's got, flat out, but what's that got to do with seeing the CEO? Why does he want to see me?

Does Humphries have anything to do with this? He wants me to spy on Astro, which means he prob'ly wants me to spy on Randolph himself. So maybe he's worked things out so's I get to see Randolph face-to-face. Is Humphries pulling strings inside Randolph's own company?

It never occurred to Pancho that Dan Randolph wanted to see her for reasons of his own.

The Clippership rode smoothly through re-entry, with only a few moments of turbulence as it plunged into the Earth's atmosphere like a squat, cone-shaped meteor, plummeting so fast that the very air outside the craft heated to incandescence. We're a falling star, Pancho told herself as she sat tightly buckled into her seat while the ship shuddered and jounced. She could hear the muted howl of the tortured air on the other side of the hull, mere centimeters from her seat. A falling star. Some kid down there's prob'ly making a wish on our trail.

The shaking and banshee wail of re-entry ended swiftly and the flight smoothed out.

"We'll be landing in four minutes," the captain's rich baritone voice announced over the intercom. "Don't be alarmed by all the banging and roaring. It's just the retrorockets and the landing struts deploying."

Pancho smiled. That's what we need the crew for: reassuring announcements.

It felt as if they were falling until the retros fired briefly, pushing Pancho deep into her seat. Another drop, so short she barely had time to feel it before the retros roared out a longer blast. Then everything went silent and still.

"We're on the ground," the captain said, sounding relieved.

Pancho had expected that she and Amanda would be sent directly to Randolph's office for their interview with the CEO, or at least to the personnel department for a briefing on what they should expect. Instead, once they cleared the access tunnel they were met in the terminal by a good-looking young Latino in a business suit who led them out to the garage and a sleek-looking sedan.

"Your luggage is being picked up and will be waiting for you in your quarters at the corporate housing center," he said in impeccable American English, opening the car's rear door for the two women.

As she and Amanda got into the back seat, Pancho saw there was a driver sitting behind the wheel. The young man slid in beside him.

She grinned. "What, no limo?"

The young man half-turned in his seat and said quite seriously, "Mr. Randolph doesn't believe in unnecessary frills. This is comfortable enough, isn't it?"

"Quite," said Amanda.

By the time they got to the test site Amanda had set up a dinner date for herself with their handsome young escort.

The test site was on the shoulder of a green hillside that sloped down into the warm Caribbean. Late afternoon sunshine slanted down from between massive cumulus clouds that were visibly growing, boiling up into towering thunderheads, getting darker and more menacing by the minute. Pancho smelled the salt tang in the air, heard the surf rolling in gently below, felt the warm steady breeze on her face. A tropical paradise, she thought.

Or it would be, if it weren't for all that danged hardware squatting in the middle of the field.

Following their Latino escort, they walked from the car to the small knot of people standing around what looked like a set of man-tall dewar flasks crusted with frost, a small crane, lots of plumbing and tubing, a medium-sized truck carrying what looked like a pair of major-league fuel cells on its bed, a smaller truck loaded with a bank of capacitors, and a corrugated-metal shed off to one side. Several automobiles and semivans were parked on the other side of the shed.

As they got closer, Pancho saw that the people were gathered around a small swept-winged aircraft that was resting on a pair of skids. It was an ancient cruise missile, she saw, an unmanned jet airplane. She knew they'd been outlawed by the disarmament treaties. Only the Peacekeepers

had such weapons, and this one looked too old to be a Peacekeeper missile. The markings on it were faded, the serial number stenciled on its tail
barely legible.

Before she could ask a question, a trim-looking man with silver hair
and a rugged fighter's face stepped out of the crowd around the missile.
He wore a light tan windbreaker zippered to the throat despite the warm
sunshine, a baseball cap perched jauntily on his head, well-faded jeans,
and cowboy boots. Their escort stiffened almost like a soldier coming to
attention.

"Señor Randolph," he said, "may I introduce—"

"You must be Amanda Cunningham," said Dan Randolph, with a
crooked smile. He put his hand out and Amanda took it briefly. "I'm Dan
Randolph."

Then he turned to Pancho. "And you've got to be Priscilla Lane."

"Pancho," she corrected, taking his extended hand. His grip was firm,
friendly. "Priscilla's too fussy, and anybody calls me Pru or Prissy, I'll
belt him."

"Pancho," Randolph said, his smile widening. "I'll remember that."

"What's this all about?" Pancho asked. "Why've you brought us
here?"

Randolph's eyes showed momentary surprise at her bluntness, but
then he shrugged and said, "You're going to see some history being
made . . . if this double-damned jury-rigged kludge works right."

He introduced Amanda and Pancho to Lyall Duncan and the others
gathered around the missile. Almost all of them were male, engineers or
technicians. One of the women was a tall blonde; competition for
Amanda, Pancho thought. Duncan looked like a fierce little gnome, or
maybe a troll, even when he smiled.

Puzzled, intrigued, Pancho allowed Randolph to usher her and
Amanda to the shed. It was packed with instruments and consoles and one
rickety-looking desk with a lopsided chair in front of it.

"You just stay here and watch," he said, with a curious grin. "If it
works, you'll be witnesses. If it blows up, this ought to be far enough
away to keep you from getting hurt."

The dark-haired troll called Duncan chuckled. "Experimental
physics, you know. Always the chance of an explosion."

The crane was on its own caterpillar tractor. A pair of technicians
used it to hoist the missile off the ground and trundle it out almost half a
kilometer. They put the missile gently onto the grassy ground, pointing
into the wind blowing steadily in from the sea.

Consoles were coming to life in the shed. Engineers were speaking to
each other in their clipped jargon. Pancho watched Randolph. The man

seemed outwardly relaxed as he stood with both hands jammed into his windbreaker pockets, watching the missile while the crane waddled back toward them.

Duncan buzzed around the shed like a bee in a flower bed. The tension built up; Pancho could feel it radiating from the backs of the crew standing by the consoles.

"Do you think it's going to rain?" Amanda whispered.

Pancho looked up at the looming thunderheads. "Sooner or later."

At last Duncan said to Randolph, "We're ready to launch."

"Okay," said Randolph. "Do it before it starts pouring."

Duncan said crisply, "Launch!"

Pancho turned her attention to the missile sitting out on the grass. For a moment nothing happened, but then its tail-end spurted flame and it lurched forward. Just as she heard the whining scream of the jet engine, another sound cut in: a deeper, more powerful roar. The missile leaped off the ground, angling sharply toward the cloud-filled sky, trailing a billow of smoke.

Something fell away from the climbing missile. A rocket pack, Pancho realized. They used it to get the bird off the ground.

The plane levelled off a scant hundred meters in the air and circled the field once.

"Nominal flight," one of the engineers called out.

"Fusion drive ready?" Duncan asked.

"Primed and ready."

"Light it."

The missile seemed to falter for a moment, as if it had stalled in midair. Pancho saw the slightly smoky exhaust wink out, heard the jet engine's screech die away. The missile glided for several moments, losing altitude.

Then it seemed to bite into the air, raising its nose and climbing steeply upward as it howled a thin, screeching ethereal wail.

"Programmed flight trajectory," Pancho heard someone call out. "On the money."

The bird flew out to sea until it was a barely visible speck, then turned back and rushed toward them, climbing almost to the base of the thunderheads, its ghostly wail barely audible, streaking past, heading inland. Then it turned again and headed seaward once more. Racetrack course, Pancho realized.

Lightning was flickering in the clouds now.

"Coming up on the two-minute mark," said one of the engineers. "*Mark!* Two minutes."

"Bring her in," Duncan commanded.

"Automatic trajectory," came the answer.

Pancho watched as the missile turned back toward them once again, dropped its flaps, slowed, and gracefully descended for a landing out in the area where it had taken off. The grass was scorched out there from the takeoff rocket's hot exhaust.

Turning slightly, she saw that Randolph was standing just outside the door, eyes riveted to the approaching missile, mouth slightly open, fists clenched.

The missile was still moving fast when it touched the ground, bounced into the air again, wobbled back to the ground, and then plowed nose-first into the dirt, throwing a spray of grass clods and pebbles as it flipped over onto its back and banged down so hard one of the wings tore off. It sounded like a junkyard falling out of the sky.

But the engineers and technicians were all cheering, jumping up and down, pounding each other on the back, yelling and waving like a team that had just scored a gold medal in the Olympics. Randolph yanked off his cap and pegged it out toward the sea.

"Och, what a divot!" Duncan shouted. He raced through the open door to Randolph and launched himself into the older man's arms, wrapping his legs around Randolph's middle. Randolph staggered backward and they fell to the ground together, laughing like maniacs.

Pancho looked at Amanda. She seemed just as puzzled as Pancho felt.

With a shrug, Pancho said, "I guess any landing you can walk away from is a good landing."

Amanda shook her head. "I shouldn't think you'd walk away from that one if you'd been aboard it."

Randolph was disentangling himself from Duncan and getting to his feet. Brushing dirt from his windbreaker, grinning hugely, he walked over to Amanda and Pancho while Duncan scampered toward the shed.

"It works!" Randolph said. "You've just witnessed history, ladies. The first actual flight of a fusion-powered vehicle."

"Fusion?" Pancho gaped at him. "You mean that little bird had a fusion engine on her?"

Amanda said, "But I thought fusion generators were great immense things, like power stations."

Duncan raced back to them, waving a dark bottle in one hand. The rest of the crew gathered around. Pancho wondered why no one went to the poor little aircraft, smashed and crumpled on the grass.

Someone produced paper cups and Duncan began to splash liquor into them. At first Pancho thought it was champagne, but the bottle wasn't the right shape. Scotch, she realized. Scotland's gift to the world.

"Hey," said Randolph, "I need some ice with this."

Duncan actually shuddered. "Ice? With good whisky? You Americans!"
Pancho took a sip of hers, neat. "Wow!" she managed to gasp.

"To the Duncan Drive," Randolph toasted, lifting his paper cup.

"To the stars!" Duncan countered. "We'll ride this engine to Alpha Centauri one day!"

Randolph laughed. "The Asteroid Belt will be far enough, for now."

A couple of the men quaffed their drinks down in one gulp, then trotted out toward the wrecked cruise missile. Others headed for the shed.

"Check the cameras, too," Duncan called after them.

Pancho asked Randolph again, "That little ship has a fusion engine in it?"

Nodding, Randolph replied, "In place of its warhead."

"The engine's that small?"

"It's only a wee test engine," said Duncan. "Just to prove that it can provide controllable thrust."

"Now we can build one big enough to carry a real payload to the Belt," Randolph said.

"Once you raise the money," added Duncan.

With a glance at Amanda, Pancho asked Randolph, "But why did you bring Mandy and me out here? Just to have a couple more witnesses?"

His grin growing even wider, Randolph answered, "Hell no. I wanted you to see this because you two are gong to pilot the first fusion rocket to the Asteroid Belt."

NEW KYOTO

The Yamagata family estate was set on a rugged hillside high above the office towers and apartment blocks of New Kyoto. Built like a medieval Japanese fortress, the solid yet graceful buildings always made Dan think of poetry frozen into shapes of wood and stone. It had suffered extensive damage in the earthquakes, Dan knew, but he could see no sign of it. The repairs had flawlessly matched the original structures.

Much of the inner courtyard was given to an exquisitely maintained sand garden. There were green vistas at every turn, as well: gardens and woods and, off in the distance, a glimpse through tall old trees of Lake Biwa, glittering in the late afternoon sun.

The tiltrotor plane settled down, turbines screeching, in the outer courtyard. Dan pulled off his sanitary mask and unbuckled his safety belt. He was through the hatch before the pilot was able to stop the rotors. Squinting through the dust kicked up by the downwash, Dan saw Nobuhiko Yamagata waiting at the gate to the inner courtyard, wearing a comfortable kimono of deep blue decorated with white herons, the Yamagata family's emblem.

For an instant Dan thought he was seeing Saito Yamagata, Nobuhiko's father, the man who had been Dan's boss in the old days when Randolph had been a construction engineer on the first Japanese solar power satellite. Nobo had been ascetically slim when he was younger, but now his face and body had filled out considerably. He was tall, though, some thirty centimeters taller than his father had been, even several centimeters taller than Dan himself.

The two men bowed simultaneously, then grasped each other's shoulders.

"By damn, Nobo, it's good to see you."

"And you," Nobuhiko replied, smiling broadly. "It's been much too long since you've visited here." His voice was deep, strong, assured.

"You're looking well," Dan said as Yamagata led him past the flowering shrubbery of the inner courtyard, toward the wing of the old stone and wood house where the family lived.

"I'm too fat and I know it," Nobo said, patting his belly. "Too many hours behind a desk, not enough exercise."

Dan made a sympathetic noise.

"I'm thinking of taking a trip to Selene for a nanotherapy session."

"Aw, come on, Nobo," Dan said, "it's not that bad."

"My doctors nag me constantly."

"That's what the double-damned doctors always do. They learn it in medical school. No matter how healthy you are, they always find something to worry you about."

They walked along a winding path of stones set across the middle of the carefully-raked sand garden. Dan noticed the miniature olive tree off in one corner of the garden that he had given Nobo's father many years earlier. It looked green and healthy. Before the greenhouse cliff had struck, even in June the tree would have been covered by a heated transparent plastic dome to protect it from the occasional frost. Now the winters were mild enough to leave the tree in the open all year long.

"What's your father's status?" Dan asked as they removed their shoes at the open door to the main house. Two servants stood silently just inside the door, both women, both in carnelian-red robes.

Nobuhiko grimaced as they walked down the hallway lined with shoji screens.

"The medical researchers have removed the tumor and cleaned father's body of all traces of cancerous cells. They are ready to begin the revival sequence."

"That can be tricky," Dan said.

Ten years earlier, Saito Yamagata had had himself declared clinically dead and then frozen in liquid nitrogen, preserved cryonically to await the day when his cancer could be cured and he would be revived.

"Others have been thawed successfully," Nobo said as they entered a spacious bedroom. It was paneled in teak, with bare floors of bleached pine, and furnished sparely: a western-style bed, a desk in the opposite corner, two comfortable-looking recliner chairs. One wall consisted of sliding shoji screens; Dan figured they covered a closet, built-in drawers, and the lavatory. Dan saw that his one travel bag had already been placed on a folding stand at the foot of the bed.

"Still," he said, "thawing must be pretty dicey."

Yamagata turned to face him, and Dan saw Saito's calm brown eyes, the certainty, the power that a long lineage of wealth and privilege can bring to a man.

"We have followed the research work very thoroughly," Nobo said. He smiled slightly. "We have sponsored much of the work ourselves, of course. It seems that Father could be revived."

"That's great!" Dan blurted. "Sai will be back with us—"

Nobuhiko raised a hand. "Two problems, Dan."

"What?"

"First, there are very strong political forces opposing revival of any cryonically-preserved person."

"Opposing . . . oh, for the love of Peter, Paul, and Peewee Reese. The New Morality strikes again."

"Here in Japan it's an offshoot of the New Dao movement. They call themselves the Flowers of the Sun."

"Flowers of crackpots," Dan grumbled.

"They have a considerable amount of political power. Enough to get nanotechnology banned in Japan, just as your New Morality people got it banned in the States."

"And now they're against reviving corpsicles?"

A reluctant grin cracked Yamagata's solemn expression. "Delicately put, Dan. My father is a corpsicle."

Waving a hand, Dan said, "You know I don't mean any disrespect."

"I know," Nobuhiko admitted. "But the unhappy fact is that these Flowers of the Sun are attempting to pass a law through the Diet that would forbid cryonics altogether and make it a crime to attempt to revive a frozen body."

"Why, for god's sake? On what grounds?"

Nobuhiko shrugged. "They say the resources should be spent in rebuilding our ravaged cities. They say that we don't need rich old people to be brought back among us, what we need are healthy young people who can work hard to rebuild Japan."

"Bullcrap," Dan muttered. Then he brightened. "Hey, I know how you can get around them! Fly your father up to Selene. They'll revive him there. They can even use nanomachines if they have to."

Nobo sat on the bed, his shoulders sagging. "I've thought of that, Dan. I'm tempted to do it, especially before the government bars removal of frozen bodies from the country."

"They can't do that!"

"They will, before the next session of the Diet is over."

"Goddammit to hell and back!" Dan shouted, pounding his fist into his palm. "Has the whole stupid world gone crazy?"

"There's something else," Nobo said, his voice barely above a whisper. "Something worse."

"What on earth could be worse?"

"The people who have been revived. Their minds are gone."

"Gone? What do you mean?"

With a helpless spread of his hands, Nobuhiko repeated, "Gone. The body can be revived, but apparently the freezing process wipes out the brain's memory system. Those we've revived are mentally like newborns. They even have to be toilet trained all over again."

Dan sank into one of the plush recliners. "You mean Sai's mind . . . his personality . . . gone?"

"That's what we fear. Apparently the neural connections in the brain break down when the body is frozen. The mind comes out a virtual *tabula rasa.*"

"Shit," Dan muttered.

"We have our research scientists working on the problem, of course, but there's no point to reviving my father until we know definitely, one way or the other, how his mind has been affected by the freezing."

Dan hunched forward, forearms on his thighs. "Okay. I understand now. But get Sai's body to Selene. Now! Before these religious fanatics make it impossible to move him."

Nobuhiko nodded grimly. "I believe you're right, Dan. I've felt that way myself for some weeks now, but I'm glad that you agree."

"I'm heading up to Selene next week," Dan said. "If you like, I'll take him with me."

"That's very good of you, but this is a family matter. I'll take care of it."

Dan nodded. "Okay. But if you need any help—anything at all, just let me know."

Nobuhiko smiled again, and for the first time there was real warmth in it. "I will, Dan. I certainly will."

"Good."

The younger man rubbed at his eyes, then looked up at Dan again. "Very well, I've told you my problem. Now tell me yours. What brings you here?"

Dan grinned at him. "Oh, nothing much. I just need a couple of billion dollars."

Nobo's face remained completely impassive for a long moment. Then he said, "Is that all?"

"Yep. Two bill should do it."

"And what do I get in return for such an investment?"

With a chuckle, Dan replied, "A bunch of rocks."

LA GUAIRA

Pancho looked up, bleary-eyed, from her desktop screen. Across the room that she and Amanda were sharing, Mandy sat at her desk with virtual reality glasses and earphones covering half her face, peering intently at her own screen.

"I'm goin' for a walk," she said, loudly enough to get through Mandy's earphones.

Amanda nodded without taking off the VR glasses. Pancho squinted at the screen, but it was nothing but a jumble of alphanumerics. Whatever Mandy was studying was displayed on her glasses, not the computer screen.

Their dorm room opened directly onto the patio. Cripes, it's almost sundown, Pancho saw as she stepped outside. The late afternoon was still tropically warm, humid, especially after the air-conditioned cool of their quarters.

Pancho stretched her long arms up toward the cloud-flecked sky, trying to work out the knots in her back. Been settin' at that stupid ol' desk too damned long, she said to herself. Mandy can sit there and study till hell freezes over. She's like a dog-ass computer, just absorbing data like a friggin' machine.

Dan Randolph had put them to studying the fusion drive and working with the engineering team that was converting a lunar transfer buggy into the ship that would carry them out to the Belt. They saw Randolph rarely. The man was jumping all across the world like a flea on a hot griddle, hardly ever in the same place more than one night. When he was in La Guaira he drove the whole team hard, and himself hardest of all.

Peculiar place for a corporate headquarters, Pancho thought as she walked from the housing complex out past the swaying, rustling palm trees, toward the seawall. La Guaira was more suited to being a tourist resort than a major space launching center. Randolph had settled his Astro Manufacturing headquarters here years ago, partly because its location near the equator gave rockets a little extra boost from the Earth's spin, partly because he found the government of Venezuela easier to deal with than the suits in Washington.

Strange, though. Randolph was rumored to have been in love with President Scanwell. There were whispers about their being lovers, off and on, a stormy romance that only ended when the ex-President lost her life in the big Tennessee Valley earthquake.

It all seemed so far away. Pancho followed the winding path toward the seawall, her softboots crunching on the gravel. The Sun was just about touching the horizon, turning the Caribbean reddish gold. Massive clouds were piling up, turning purple and crimson in the underlighting. With the breeze coming off the sea, making the palms bow gracefully, this was as close to a tropical paradise as she could imagine.

But the seawall reminded her of a harsher reality. It was shoulder high, an ugly reinforced concrete barrier against the encroaching waters. It had originally been painted a pastel pink, but the paint had faded in the sun, and the concrete was crumbling here and there where storm tides had pounded against it. The old beaches were all underwater now, except at the very lowest tides. The surf broke out there, long combers tumbling and frothing with a steady, ceaseless growling hiss. And still the sea was rising, a little bit more every year.

"Looks pretty, doesn't it?"

Startled, she turned to see Randolph standing there, looking glumly out to sea. He was wearing a wrinkled white shirt and dark slacks that had gone baggy from long hours of travel.

"Didn't see you coming up the path, boss," said Pancho. "Come to think of it, I didn't even hear you on the gravel."

"I walked on the grass," Randolph said, quite seriously. "Stealth is my middle name."

Pancho laughed.

But Randolph said gloomily, "When Greenland melts down this will all go under."

"The whole island?"

"Every damned bit of it. Maybe some of the gantry towers will stick up above the surface. The hilltops. Not much else."

"Cripes."

"This used to be part of the mainland, you know. When I first brought the company here, that strait cutting us off from the hills didn't exist. The sea level's gone up that much in less than twenty years."

"And it's still goin' up," Pancho said.

Randolph nodded gloomily, then leaned his arms on the shoulder-high seawall and propped his chin on them.

"How's the job going?" he asked.

"We're workin' at it," she replied. "It's a lot to learn, all this fusion stuff."

With a tired nod, he said, "Yeah, but you've got to know every bit of it, Pancho. It anything breaks down out there, you've got to be able to diagnose it and fix it."

"We'll have an engineer on board," she said. "Won't we?"

"Maybe. But whether you do or not, *you've* got to know everything there is to know about the systems."

"Yeah. I guess."

"And you've got to get the new navigational technique down, too," he added.

"Point and shoot, yeah. Kinda weird."

With the thrust and efficiency of the fusion rocket, their spacecraft did not have to travel in an energy-conserving ellipse from Earth orbit to the Belt. Fusion-driven trajectories were almost straight lines: travel times would be days instead of months.

"It's a lot to learn, I know," Randolph said.

She saw the weariness in his eyes, and yet there was something else in them, something more. Hope, she thought. Or maybe just plain mulish stubbornness. He wants to make this fusion ship work. And he's trusting me to drive it. Me and Mandy.

"We could use a weekend off," she said. "Or even a night on the town."

The sun had sunk behind the mainland's mountains. They could see the lights on the mainland beginning to wink on.

"Sorry, kid, no can do," Randolph said. He started walking along the seawall. "I told you when you agreed to take this assignment, you stay here in the complex."

"Security, yeah, I know," Pancho said, following him.

"Your own security, too," Randolph said. "Not just the company's. You're very valuable now. You and Amanda are crucial to this entire operation. I don't want you running any risks."

Pancho thought it over. He's trusting us with this whole operation, right enough. Can't blame him for being careful. Still . . .

She looked across the strait again at the lights of the city.

Then a new thought struck her. Does he know I'm supposed to be snooping on him? Is he keeping us bottled up here so's I can't get in touch with Humphries?

"Can I ask you somethin'?"

Randolph smiled tiredly at her in the fading light. "Sure, go right ahead."

"I've heard rumbles that you were—well, that Astro's got money problems."

Randolph hesitated a moment. Then, "Corporations always have money problems."

"I mean, like, you're purty close to broke."

"Pretty close," he admitted.

"Then why're you sinkin' all this money into the fusion ship?"

The light was dying fast. Pancho could barely see his face. But she heard the determination in his voice.

"Two reasons, kid," he said. "First, if it works, Astro can get first licks at the Belt. Our stock will zoom up, our profits will skyrocket, and the only money problem I'll have is how to spend all the cash flowing in."

Pancho said nothing, waiting for his second reason.

"And also," Randolph went on, "opening up the Belt is crucial for the human race's survival."

"You really think so?"

He stopped walking and turned toward her. "We can't take much more of this climate warming, Pancho. Millions have died already, tens of millions. But the worst is yet to come. If Greenland goes—"

"And Antarctica," she interjected.

"And Antarctica," he agreed. "If they melt down, civilization drowns. Billions will die, not just from the floods but from starvation and disease. We can't support the Earth's population now, for god's sake! There's famine in half the world, and it's getting worse, not better."

"You think the asteroids can help?"

"We need those natural resources. We have to rebuild our industrial base, rebuild our wealth."

"In space."

"Yep. Where we should've been building for the past half-century."

Pancho made a low whistle. "That's a big order, boss."

"You're damned right it is. But if we fail, the human race fails. Only a handful of people will live through this, and they'll be thrown back to a pre-industrial level. Subsistence farming. No electricity. No machinery. No medicines."

"The Middle Ages."

"More like the Stone Age," Randolph grumbled.

"That's why you're hangin' everything on this flight to the Belt."

She couldn't see his face in the deepening darkness, but she sensed him nodding.

"Everything I've got," he said flatly.

Everything he has. The enormity of it suddenly hit Pancho like an avalanche. He's risking everything he has on this flight, his whole company, his whole life. He's willing to gamble everything he's worked for and built up over his lifetime on this one mission. And he's trusting me to fly it for him. Me.

The responsibility felt like the weight of the world on her shoulders.

"Lemme ask you somethin' else," Pancho said, her voice trembling slightly. "Why'd you pick me to make this flight? You've got lots of other pilots with more experience."

Randolph chuckled softly. "More experience, sure. But they've got families to support. Spouses. Kids."

I've got a sister, Pancho thought. But she said nothing.

"Besides," Randolph went on, "none of them have your abilities."

"My abilities?"

"Listen, kid, I went through every scrap of data on every pilot in Astro's employ and quite a few who aren't on the company's payroll. You came out on top. You are the best we've got."

Pancho felt suddenly breathless. Hell, I know I'm good, but am I really *that* good?

"Before you ask for a raise," Randolph said, "I've got to tell you that my personnel people don't agree with me. They think you're a flake."

"Whattaya mean, a flake?" Pancho demanded.

"The rap on you, kid, is that you're not serious. You like to take risks, play games."

"Not with my flyin'."

"Oh no? Like the time you raced Wally Stinson from Selene to the Farside site?"

"Aw, c'mon, I was only havin' some fun," Pancho protested. "Wally let his testosterone do his thinkin' for him."

"And this bet a few months ago about vacuum breathing?"

"That was just a hoot."

He chuckled in the growing darkness, but then said, "You're a gambler, Pancho. That scared the hell out of the personnel gurus."

"I won't gamble with your fusion ship," she said firmly.

Randolph was silent for a few heartbeats, then he said, "I know you won't, Pancho. That's why I picked you to fly her."

"What about Amanda?" she heard herself ask. "She's better'n me, isn't she?"

"She's got more education, she's more cautious. But she's not better than you. Close, but not better. Anyway, if you go, I want you to have another woman pilot with you. Guys get funny ideas after a couple of weeks locked up in an aluminum can."

The plan was to carry an engineer/technician and at least one geologist or planetary astronomer on the flight. The mission was designed to be more than a mere test of the fusion drive; it was supposed to bring back results. It had to.

"I can handle the guys," Pancho said.

"Yep, I'm sure you can. But why bring up the problem?"

"You don't think Mandy'll cause a problem?"

Randolph laughed softly in the darkness. "I see your point. She can raise temperatures when she wants to."

"Even when she doesn't want to."

"I had a long talk with Amanda yesterday. She's going to be prim and proper during the flight. No bedroom eyes. No tight uniforms. She agreed to behave herself."

Pancho was shocked. *The little sneak never said a word to me about talking with the boss.*

"She'll be strictly business. She promised."

"I don't know if she can help herself," Pancho said.

"You think I should take her off the mission?"

Pancho blurted, "No, I think you should take me off it."

"You? Why?"

Don't do it! She raged at herself. *Don't go blabbing it out to him. He'll fire your butt out of here like a hot rocket and then make sure nobody'll ever hire you again. But he trusts me. He's hangin' his whole world on me because he trusts me to get the job done even when his personnel office doesn't.*

"Why should I take you off the mission?" Randolph insisted.

Cursing herself for six kinds of a fool, Pancho said, "Martin Humphries hired me to spy on you."

"He did, huh?" In the starlit darkness, Randolph sounded much less surprised than she thought he would. "When was this?"

"More'n six months ago," Pancho said, barely able to get the words out. "Last time I was up at Selene."

Randolph fell silent and resumed pacing slowly along the seawall. Pancho walked beside him, listening to the sighing of the wind, the grumble of the surf, waiting for him to explode or snarl or say *something*.

At last he started to laugh. Not loud, joyful laughter. Just a low, cynical snickering. "I knew the sonofabitch would try to plant snoops in my drawers, but I never figured he'd recruit you."

"You can fire me if you want to."

"What did he offer you?"

"Money."

"Is that all you're after?"

Pancho hesitated a heartbeat. "I got . . . family to take care of."

"Your sister, yes, I know."

"You know?"

"I told you, I went over every nanobit of data about you. I know about your sister."

"Well . . ." Pancho had to take a breath before she could repeat, "You can fire me, I guess." She was surprised at what an effort it was to say the words.

"Why would I do that?" Randolph sounded genuinely puzzled.

" 'Cause I'm supposed to be spyin' on you."

"That's all right. No need to panic, kid. Go ahead and spy all you want. I knew he'd plant a few spooks into Astro. I'm glad you told me about it. I appreciate your honesty—and loyalty."

"But—"

"No, no it's okay," Randolph said, his tone almost bantering now. "You go ahead and report everything you're doing to him. I'll even make it easier for you. I'll transfer you and Amanda to Selene. That's where the sonofabitch is living, isn't it?"

"I think so, yeah."

"Good," Randolph said. "I ought to go there myself. It's a lot healthier there than here, that's for sure."

"Healthier?"

"Climate controlled. Decontaminated air. I don't need filter plugs stuffed up my nose when I'm there."

Before Pancho could ask why he needed filter plugs at all, Randolph grasped her by the shoulder and turned her gently to look up into the darkening sky. A half-Moon rode among the scudding clouds, the unwinking brilliant beacon light of Selene visible along its terminator between night and day.

"That's where you're going, kid. To Selene."

Pancho wondered if Randolph was truly pleased with her confession, or if he was exiling her to the most remote spot he could find.

SELENE

Pancho had no trouble getting through customs this time. The same inspector went through her bags perfunctorily, not even blinking at the mice in their sealed plastic cage.

But he paid elaborate attention to Amanda. Pancho groused to herself as the inspector carefully went through Amanda's travel bag, alternately grinning at Mandy and reddening as he saw her lacy underclothes.

He'd strip-search her if he could find the slightest excuse, Pancho thought, fuming.

Mandy simply stood on the other side of the table, looking wide-eyed and innocent while she kept up a constant nervous chatter.

"I don't know why they always go through my bag, Pancho. I really don't. You'd think that after all these times we've come to Selene they would simply let me pass through without all this bother."

"He went through my bag, too, Mandy," Pancho replied.

"Yes, but he didn't paw through your underwear."

Grinning with gritted teeth, Pancho said, "Yours are a lot purtier than mine."

The inspector kept his head down as he searched diligently through Amanda's one piece of luggage, but Pancho could see the back of his neck turn beet red.

"All the other passengers have already gone through," Amanda noticed. "We're the last ones."

"The rest of 'em are either up here to start a long-term work contract or they're tourists. We come and go all the time, so we could be smugglers."

"Smugglers?" Amanda looked shocked. "Us? *Me?*"

Pancho reached across the table and tapped the inspector on the shoulder. "Ain't that right? What're you looking for, dope or contraband seeds or maybe illegal bottles of air?"

The inspector mumbled something incomprehensible.

At last he finished and pushed the bag back across the table toward Amanda.

"There you go, Ms. Cunningham. Sorry to have delayed you. I'm just doing my job, miss."

Amanda thanked him politely as she zipped her bag shut and hefted it to her shoulder. Pancho saw that the inspector couldn't help but stare at Mandy's expansive chest. Even in a standard-issue flight suit she looked sexy.

Visibly working up his courage, the inspector said, "Um . . . Ms. Cunningham . . . could I take you out to dinner some time while you're here?" He made a sweaty smile. "To, uh, make up for inconveniencing you and all."

Mandy smiled sweetly at him. "Why, that would be lovely. Call me, won't you?"

"I sure will!"

Pancho seethed as the two of them left the customs station and headed for one of the electric carts that carried new arrivals through the tunnel from the spaceport into the underground city. *He asked me to dinner when I was alone, but with bimbo boobs here he never even saw me. I could've carried the Eiffel Tower up here and he wouldn't have noticed.*

The message light was blinking on their phone by the time they got to the quarters they were sharing. When Pancho had first come to work for Astro Manufacturing, six years earlier, pilots still got private quarters when they worked on the Moon. Not any more. The rumor back at La Guaira was that Randolph was going to rent a dormitory area for the spacecraft pilots and crews.

Why not just fire all of us? Pancho wondered. *If Randolph had any real sense he'd talk the IAA into getting rid of their stupid regulations about keeping human crews aboard the ships.*

Yeah, fine, she answered herself. *Then what do you do? Get a job as a mission controller? Fat chance!*

As soon as they opened the door to their quarters and saw the phone blinking on the nightstand between their two beds, Amanda dropped her bag on the floor; it landed with a gentle lunar thump as Mandy stretched out on the bed and put the handset to her ear.

With a surprised look on her face, Mandy held the phone out to Pancho. "It's for you," she said, as if she didn't really believe it.

Pancho took the handset and saw on the phone's tiny console screen that the caller was Martin Humphries. Rather than activate the speaker, Pancho put the handset to her ear.

"Pancho, is that you?" Humphries's voice said, sounding annoyed. "You're standing outside the camera view."

She stepped between the beds and swiveled the phone console. "It's me," she said, sitting on the bed opposite the one Mandy lay upon.

"I heard that Randolph sent you up here," Humphries said. "But I had to learn it from another source. I haven't heard a peep from you in months."

With a glance at Mandy, who was watching her with intense curiosity, Pancho replied guardedly. "Well, I'm here now."

"Who answered the phone? You're not alone, are you?"

"Nope, I'm here with Mandy Cunningham."

"She's an Astro employee too?"

"That's right."

Mandy was straining to see Humphries's face, but Pancho kept the phone turned away from her.

"Well, I've got to talk to you. I've been paying you for information but so far I've gotten nothing from you but a big, fat silence."

Pancho made a smile. "I'd love to see you, too. I've got a lot to tell you."

Humphries snapped, "All right, get down here right away."

"You want me to come to dinner?" Pancho replied pleasantly.

"Dinner?" Humphries glanced at his wrist. "All right. In two hours."

"Tonight?" Pancho cooed. "That'll be just fine. I'll see you at nineteen hundred. Okay?"

"Seven o'clock," Humphries said. "Sharp."

"I'll be there."

Pancho hung up the phone and said to Amanda, "I'll use the shower first, Mandy. I've got a dinner date."

She left Mandy standing by the bed, staring at her with wide-eyed astonishment.

Martin Humphries clicked his phone off and stretched back in his recliner. Maybe she's smarter than I gave her credit for. She hasn't gotten in touch with me before this because she doesn't want to get caught. Okay, that's reasonable. She's being cautious. She's been surrounded by Randolph's people all the time. There's even somebody in her quarters with her.

Humphries broke into a satisfied grin. Randolph's making his people double up, to save money. He's on the ropes, and he thinks I'm going to save him from bankruptcy.

He laughed aloud. "Me! The savior of Dan Randolph!"

He was still giggling when he put through his call to Nobuhiko Yamagata.

The head of Yamagata Industries was in his Tokyo office, from the looks of it. Humphries could see through the window behind Yamagata several construction cranes and the spidery steelwork of new towers going up. Rebuilding from the last earthquake. They'd better build stronger, he thought grimly. A lot stronger.

"Mr. Yamagata," Humphries said, nodding his head once in imitation of a polite bow. "It's good of you to take the time to talk with me."

He thought about putting Yamagata's image on the wallscreen, but that would make the Japanese look too big. He preferred the smaller desktop screen.

"Mr. Humphries," said Nobo, nearly three seconds later, barely dipping his chin. "It is always a pleasure to converse with you."

Blasted bullshit, Humphries thought. You can't come right out and say what you want with these Japs. You have to make polite fucking conversation for half an hour before you can get down to business.

To his surprise, though, Yamagata said, "Dan Randolph has asked me to invest in a new venture."

"Let me guess," Humphries said. "He wants to build a fusion rocket system."

Again the wait for the microwaves to reach Tokyo and return. "Yes, to go out to the Asteroid Belt and begin developing the resources there."

"And what will your answer be?"

Once Yamagata heard Humphries's question, his normally impassive face showed a tic of annoyance.

"I will be forced to tell him that Yamagata Industries is fully committed to rebuilding the cities that were damaged so heavily by the tsunamis and earthquakes. We have no funds to spare on space developments."

"Good," said Humphries.

Yamagata seemed to freeze into stone. At last he murmured, "It will be as we agreed."

"You'd like to help him, wouldn't you?"

The seconds stretched. At last Yamagata said, "He is an old friend."

"You two were competitors at one time."

"Yamagata Industries no longer has any operations in space," the Japanese said slowly. "All of our energies are devoted to terrestrial developments."

"So I understand."

"But I agree with Dan. The resources from space can be of vital importance to our rebuilding efforts."

"I think so, too."

Yamagata seemed to be searching Humphries's eyes, trying to penetrate to his secret thoughts. "Then why do you insist that I refuse to help him?"

"You misunderstand me," Humphries said, putting on an expression of injured integrity. "I want Randolph to succeed. I intend to fund his fusion rocket venture myself."

"Yes, so I understand," said Yamagata, once Humphries's answer reached him. "What I do not understand is why you pressured me to refuse Dan."

"Could you help him if you wish?"

Yamagata hesitated, but at last replied, "I could put together two billion for him."

"Without hurting your rebuilding projects?"

The hesitation was longer this time. "There would be some . . . repercussions."

"But I can provide the funding and you don't have to take a penny from your existing projects."

Yamagata said nothing for many long moments. Then, "You have put considerable pressure on the banks to make certain that I do not fund Dan Randolph. I want to know why."

"Because I believe the same as you do," Humphries replied, earnestly, "that all of Japan's resources of capital and manpower should be devoted to rebuilding your nation. This fusion rocket venture is very speculative. Suppose it doesn't work? The money will be wasted."

"Yet you are willing to risk your own money."

"I have the money to risk," Humphries said.

After an even longer pause, Yamagata said, "You could invest that two billion in Japan. You could help to house the homeless and feed the hungry. You could assist us to rebuild our cities."

Humphries worked hard to avoid grinning. Now I've got the little bugger, he told himself. To Yamagata he said, "Yes, you're right. Tell you what I'll do: I'll give Randolph one billion only, and invest the other billion in Yamagata Industries. How's that?"

The Japanese industrialist's eyes flickered when he heard Humphries's words. He sucked in a deep, shrill breath.

"Would you be willing to invest your billion in the Renew Nippon Fund?"

"That's essentially a charity, isn't it?"

"It is a nonprofit organization dedicated to helping those who have been displaced by our natural disasters."

This time Humphries hesitated, paused, let Yamagata believe that he was thinking it over before he came to a decision. The damned fool. Thinks he's so fucking smart, keeping me from putting any money into his own corporation. Okay, keep me shut out from your company. I'll get you sooner or later.

With as much of a show of concern as he could muster, Humphries said, "Mr. Yamagata, if you think that's the best way for me to help Japan, then that's what I'll do. One billion for Randolph, and one billion for the Renew Nippon Fund."

Yamagata was actually smiling as they ended their conversation. Once he had switched off the phone, Humphries burst into enormously satisfied laughter.

They're all so dense! So blind! Yamagata wants to rebuild Japan. Randolph wants to save the whole fricking world. Damned fools! None of them understand that the world is done for. Nothing's going to save them. The thing is to build a new civilization off-Earth. Build a new society where it's safe, where only the best people are allowed to live. Build it . . . and rule it.

LONDON

The Executive Board of the Global Economic Council met in a spacious conference room on the top floor of the undistinguished neomodern glass-and-steel office tower that served as the GEC's headquarters. Originally, GEC's offices had been in Amsterdam, but the rising sea level and pounding storms that raged through the North Sea made that city untenable. The Dutch struggled in vain to hold back the IJsselmeer, only to see their city's narrow streets and gabled houses flooded time and again as the canals overflowed and the unrelenting sea took back the land that had been reclaimed by centuries of hard work. The GEC fled to London.

Not that London itself was immune to the rampaging storms and flooding. But the Thames was easier to control than the North Sea. And most of London was still above even the new, rising sea level.

Meetings of the Global Economic Council were usually restricted to the nine regular members and the privileged few who were invited to explain their positions or plead their causes. The news media were barred from the meetings, and there was no gallery for the public to attend.

Still, Vasily Malik dreaded this meeting of the Executive Board. Dan Randolph had demanded a hearing, and Randolph always made trouble.

Vasily Sergeivitch Malik was handsome enough to be a video star. He was tall for a Russian, slightly over one hundred eighty centimeters, broad-shouldered and heavily muscled. About the same age as Dan Randolph, Malik kept his body in good trim through a rigid schedule of daily exercise—and rejuvenation therapies that he kept secret from everyone except his doctors in Moscow. Most people thought he dyed his once-graying hair; no one knew that injections of telomerase had returned youthful vigor to him. Malik enjoyed his secret. His Arctic blue eyes sparkled with good humor.

Until he thought about Dan Randolph. Once they had been deadly enemies in politics, in business, even in romance. The catastrophic greenhouse cliff had forced them into a reluctant alliance. The old enmities were buried; not forgotten, but put aside while they each strove in their own way to save what remained of Earth's civilization.

We still don't think alike, Malik said to himself as he took his chair at the long committee table. He was serving as chairman for this session, so he knew that Randolph's principal fire would be directed at him. It's nothing personal, Malik repeated silently over and over. That was finished long ago. Our differences now are differences of attitude, differences of outlook and expectation.

Still, his stomach knotted at the thought of tangling with Randolph again.

The conference room was comfortable without being ostentatious. The carpeting was neutral gray, although thick and expensive. The sweeping windows that extended along one entire wall were discreetly curtained; a long sideboard of polished mahogany stood there, bearing a variety of drinks from spring water to iced vodka, and trays of finger foods. The table at which the board members sat was also mahogany; each place was set with a built-in computer and electronic stylus. The chairs were high-backed, luxuriously padded and upholstered in matte black leather.

Randolph had insisted, however, that the room be sprayed with disinfectant before the meeting began. Malik had been assured that the spray was necessary, and odorless. Still, his nose wrinkled as he took his chair in the exact middle of the table. Once all nine Board members were comfortably seated at the long table, Malik nodded to the uniformed guard at the door to admit the day's witnesses.

Dan Randolph came through the door and strode straight to the witness table. He looked firm and fit to Malik, dressed in a respectable business suit of dark blue. Randolph's chin was sticking out pugnaciously. He expects a fight, Malik thought.

Behind Randolph came two others. One was a gnomish, dark-haired man, Randolph's technical expert. Malik glanced at the agenda notes on the display screen built into the table before him: Lyall Duncan, an engineer. The other person was a tall blond woman who looked too young to be an expert at anything, except perhaps warming Randolph's bed. A few keystrokes and the display screen identified her as an electronics engineer from California.

Malik caught Randolph's eye as the American took his seat at the witness table. A slight crease across his face showed he had been wearing a sanitary mask. Randolph's usual cocky grin was absent. He looked determined, and deadly serious.

Suppressing a groan, Malik called the meeting to order.

They went through the standard agenda items first, while Randolph sat tensely, watching them like a leopard sizing up a herd of antelope. Finally they came to Randolph's item: *Request for funding new space propulsion system.*

Malik formally introduced Randolph to the other Board members, most of whom already knew Dan. Then, wishing he were elsewhere, Malik asked Dan to explain his proposal.

Randolph looked up at the Board and surveyed the long table from one end to the other. There were no notes before him, no slides or videos. Nothing on the little table except a silver carafe of water and a single crystal tumbler beside it. Slowly, he got to his feet.

"Ever since the greenhouse cliff hit," he began, "and our world's climate began to shift so drastically—no, actually, even *before* the greenhouse cliff came—it's been clear that the people of Earth need the resources that exist off-planet. Energy, raw materials, metals, minerals, all of the resources that Earth needs to rebuild its crippled economy lie in tremendous abundance in interplanetary space."

He paused for a heartbeat, then resumed. "In fact, if we have any hope of stabilizing the global climate and avoiding even worse warming than we've experienced so far, then a significant portion of the Earth's heavy industries must be moved off-planet."

"That's not possible," snapped the representative from North America, a dough-faced white-haired professor in an academic's tweed jacket.

Randolph stared at him bleakly. Once Jane Scanwell had been the North American on the Board.

"It's not economically feasible today," he replied softly. "But if you'll provide the funding, it will be possible within a year."

"One year?"

"Impossible!"

"How can you—"

Malik tapped lightly on the tabletop with his notebook stylus and their voices fell silent.

Randolph smiled tightly at him. "Thank you, Mr. Chairman."

"Please explain your statement," Malik said.

"The key to the economic development of space lies in the costs of acquiring the raw materials in the Asteroid Belt. With the metals and organic minerals from the asteroids, the people of Earth will have access to a pool of natural resources that's far greater than the entire planet Earth can provide."

"The people of the Earth?" questioned the representative from Pan Asia. "Or the corporations that reach the asteroids and begin mining them?"

"The people," Randolph said flatly. "If you provide the funding necessary for this, my corporation will do the work at cost."

"At cost?"

"No fees whatsoever?"

"At cost," Randolph repeated.

"We would certainly want our own accountants examining your cost figures," said the woman representing Black Africa, very seriously.

"Of course," Randolph replied with a wan smile.

"Wait a moment," Malik intervened. "Just what would our money be funding? You haven't told us what you actually propose to do."

Randolph took a deep breath, then said, "We have to develop a fusion rocket system."

Again the Board broke into querulous chatter. Malik had to tap his stylus sharply before they fell silent.

"A *fusion* rocket system?" he asked Randolph.

"We have developed and tested a small flight model of a fusion rocket," Randolph said. Turning slightly in his chair, he went on, "Dr. Duncan can explain it, if you like. We sent detailed notes to each of you when we applied for this hearing; I'm sure your own technical experts have gone over them."

Reluctant nods from the Board.

"I can show you a video of the flight tests we've done, if you wish."

"That won't be necessary," Malik said.

"The key to any and all operations in space is the cost of transportation," Randolph said. "The Clipperships that Masterson Aerospace developed have brought down the costs of going into Earth orbit. They opened up the Earth–Moon system for development."

"And encouraged Selene to thumb its nose at us," grumbled the representative from Latin America.

"Why do we need fusion rockets?" Malik asked, raising his voice enough to cut off any possible digression into the politics of the lunar nation's insistence on remaining independent of the GEC.

"Transportation costs," Randolph answered quickly. "Fusion rockets will cut the trip times and fuel costs for missions to the asteroids down to the point where they can be practical and profitable."

"Profitable for whom?"

"For the entire human race," Randolph snapped, looking slightly irked. "As I've already said, I'm willing to develop the fusion system and operate expeditions to the Asteroid Belt at cost."

"Under GEC management?"

Randolph visibly gritted his teeth. "No. That would be a bureaucratic disaster. But I'll agree to run the show under GEC oversight. You'll have complete access to our books. That's fair enough, I think."

Malik leaned back in his padded chair and allowed the other Board members to grill Randolph. Most of their questions were trivial, or repeated questions already asked and answered. Most of the Board members talked mainly to hear the beloved sound of their own voices, Malik knew.

He had seen the video of Randolph's flight tests. He had reviewed the technical data on the fusion rocket with the best scientists and engineers in the world. The Duncan Drive worked. There was no technical reason to believe that it would not work in a full-scale interplanetary spacecraft. It would cut the travel time to the Asteroid Belt from years to weeks, or less.

We should fund it, Malik thought. We should back Randolph to the hilt. But we won't, of course.

"But what's the fuel for this rocket?" one of the Board members was asking.

Patiently, Randolph replied, "The same as the fuel for the fusion powerplants that generate electricity here on the ground: isotopes of hydrogen and helium."

"Like the helium-three that's mined on the Moon?"

"Right." Randolph nodded.

"That is very expensive fuel," muttered the representative from Greater India. "Very expensive."

"A little goes a long way," Dan said, with a forced smile.

The representative from the League of Islam said irritably, "Selene has raised the price of helium-three twice in the past year. Twice! I have no doubt they are preparing to raise it again."

"We can get the fuel from space itself," Dan said, raising his voice slightly.

"From space itself?"

"How?"

"The solar wind blows through interplanetary space. It's the solar wind that deposits helium-three and hydrogen isotopes on the lunar soil."

"You mean regolith," pointed out the representative from United Europe.

"Regolith, right," Randolph admitted.

"How can you get the fuel from the solar wind?"

"The same way a jet airplane gets air for its engines," Randolph replied. "We'll scoop it in as we go."

Malik saw that the Scottish engineer, sitting off to Randolph's side, squirmed uncomfortably in his chair.

"Scoop it in? Really?"

"Sure," Randolph answered. "We'll use an electromagnetic scoop . . . a big funnel-shaped magnetic field. That way we'll be able to scoop in the fuel we need as we travel."

"How large a scoop will be necessary?"

Randolph made an exaggerated shrug. "That's for the tech people to work out. For the first missions to the Belt we'll carry the fusion fuel in tankage, just like other rockets. But eventually we'll be able to scoop fuel from the solar wind. That'll allow us to carry an even bigger payload, per unit of thrust." Turning slightly in his chair, Randolph asked, "Isn't that right, Lon?"

Duncan, the engineer, looked dubious, but he knew enough to answer, "Right."

With a glance at his wristwatch, Malik tapped his stylus again on the tabletop and said, "Thank you, Mr. Randolph, for a most interesting presentation."

Randolph fixed his gray eyes on Malik. The Russian went on, "The Board will discuss the question and inform you of its decision."

"Time is of the essence," Randolph said.

"We understand that," said Malik. "But we must have a full and thorough discussion of this concept before we can decide whether or not to commit any funding to it."

Reluctantly, Randolph got to his feet. "I see. Well, thanks for hearing me out. You have a tremendous opportunity here . . . and a tremendous responsibility."

"We are well aware of that," Malik said. "Thank you again."

Randolph nodded and headed out of the conference room, followed by the engineer and the blond Californian.

Malik now had to go through the formality of a discussion with the other Board members, but he already knew what the answer would be. He was framing the Board's reply to Randolph even while Dan was leaving the conference room:

Dear Mr. Randolph: While your proposal to develop a fusion rocket system appears to be technically feasible, the Global Economic Council cannot devote such a significant portion of its resources to what is essentially a space-born venture. GEC funding is fully committed for the next five years to programs aimed at alleviating the effects of global climate shift and assisting national efforts at rebuilding and resettling displaced population groups.

SELENE

Dan went by tube train from the GEC Board meeting to the spaceport at old Heathrow. He rode a commercial Clipper-ship to space station *Galileo,* then hitched a ride on a high-thrust Astro transfer buggy to Selene. He was in the offices that Astro Manufacturing rented in Selene by midnight, Greenwich Mean Time, of the day after the GEC meeting.

Duncan and his electronics engineer had gone back to Glasgow, hoping that the GEC Board would find the money to build at least a prototype spacecraft. Dan thought otherwise. He could see it in Malik's eyes: the GEC isn't going to spend diddley-squat on us.

Dan pushed through the empty office suite, ceiling lights flicking on as he entered each area and off as he breezed past, paying scant attention to the unoccupied desks and blank holowindows. He reached the private suite where he bunked down while he was in Selene, peeled off his jacket, tossed his travel bag onto the king-sized bed and stepped into the shower, still dressed in his pullover shirt and micromesh slacks. He kicked off his softboots and banged on the water. It came out at the preset temperature. He popped the plugs out of his nostrils and stripped off the rest of his clothes as the hot, steaming water began to ease the knots of tension in his back and shoulders.

It was an old and very personal indulgence of his: long, hot showers. Back when he'd been a kid working on the early construction projects in orbit and then on the Moon, a hot shower was an incredibly rare luxury. He'd had his nose broken for the second time over the right to a long shower. For years, before Moonbase became the independent nation of Selene, lunar shower stalls were rarer than ten-meter high jumps on

Earth. Even when you did find an incredibly luxurious living unit with a real shower, back in those days the water shut off automatically after two minutes, and there was no way to get it to turn back on again until a full hour had elapsed.

Even now, Dan thought as he let the hot water sluice over him, being on Selene's water board carries more real political clout than being a member of the governing council.

He turned off the water at last and let the built-in jets of hot air dry him. Dan preferred old-fashioned towels, but the air blowers were cheaper.

Naked, he crawled into bed and tried to get some sleep. But his mind kept churning with his hopes, his plans, his frustrations.

Yamagata isn't going to put up any money, he realized. Nobo would have called me by now if he were going to come in with me. He hasn't called because he's reluctant to give me the bad news. Malik and the GEC are a lost cause. I shouldn't even have wasted the time to appear before them, but at least if and when we get this fusion drive going we can say we offered it to the double-damned bureaucrats and they turned us down. So they've got no claim on us whatsoever.

Astro's hanging on by the skin of its teeth, one jump ahead of the bankruptcy courts, and I need to raise a couple of billion to make this fusion system work. Humphries is dangling the money at me, but he'll want a big slice of Astro in return. I need somebody else. Who can I turn to? Who the hell else is there?

Selene, he realized. They don't have the capital, but they've got trained people, equipment, resources. If I can talk them into coming in with me . . .

Then it hit him. Bypass Selene's governing council. Or, at least, end-run them. Douglas Stavenger still outvotes everybody else up here. And Masterson Aerospace is his family's company. If he'll go for this, Masterson will get behind it and Selene's council will fall in step with him.

Doug Stavenger.

He fell asleep thinking about the possibilities. And dreamed of flying past Mars, out to the Asteroid Belt.

"Who's your boyfriend?" Amanda asked.

She and Pancho were exercising in Selene's big gymnasium complex, working up a fine sheen of perspiration on the weight machines. Through the long window on one side of the room Pancho could see two men strapped into the centrifuge, both of them grimacing as the big machine's arms swung round and round, faster and faster. She knew one of the men, a maintenance tech out at the tractor garage, a thoroughly nice guy.

The gym was packed with sweating, grunting, grimacing men and women working the treadmills, stationary bikes, and weight machines. The only faces that didn't look miserable were the kids; they scampered from one machine to another, laughing, sometimes shrieking so loud the adults growled at them.

Every person in Selene, adult or child, citizen or visitor, had to follow a mandatory exercise regimen or be denied transport back to Earth. The low lunar gravity quickly deconditioned muscles to the point where facing Earth's gravity became physically hazardous. Daily exercise was the only remedy, but it was *boring.*

Pancho wore a shapeless T-shirt and faded old shorts to the gym. Amanda dressed as if she were modeling for a fashion photographer: brand-new gym shoes, bright pink fuzzy socks, and a form-fitting leotard that had men tripping over their own feet to gawk at her. Even the women stared openly.

"I don't have a boyfriend," Pancho replied, grunting as she pulled on the weighted hand grips. A favorite gambit of tourists was to have a picture taken while lifting a barbell loaded with enormous weights. What looked superhuman to Earth-trained eyes was merely ordinary in the one-sixth gravity of the Moon.

"You've gone out to dinner twice since we arrived here, and you're going out again tonight, aren't you?" Without waiting for an answer, Amanda added, "I have the impression it's been with the same fellow each night."

Mandy was sitting at the machine next to Pancho, doing pectoral crunches, her arms outstretched with her hands gripping the ends of two metal bars. Then she brought her hands together in front of her, pulling the weighted "wings" and thereby strengthening her chest muscles.

The rich get richer, Pancho thought.

"So?" Amanda insisted. "Who's your fellow?"

"It's strictly business," Pancho said.

"Really? And what business would that be, dear?"

Pancho suppressed a sudden urge to sock Mandy in her smirking face.

"Listen," she said, with some heat, "you go out just about every damned night, don't you? What's the matter with me havin' a date now and then?"

Mandy's expression softened. "Nothing, Pancho, really. I'm only curious, that's all. I think it's fine for you to have an enjoyable social life."

"Yeah, sure. You're just wonderin' who my date could be, 'cause you've got all the other men in Selene sewed up for yourself."

"Pancho, that's not true!"

"Like hell."

"I can't help it if men are attracted to me! I don't do anything to encourage them."

Pancho laughed out loud.

"Really, I don't."

"Mandy, all you have to do is breathe and the men swarm around you like flies on horseshit."

Amanda's cheeks flushed at Pancho's deliberate crudity. But then she smiled knowingly. "Well, it is rather fun to flirt. If men want to take me out to dinner, why not? I just bat my eyes at them and let them tell me how terrific they are."

"And then you bed down with 'em and everybody's happy."

Amanda flared with sudden anger. She started to reply, but stopped before saying a word. For several moments she stared down at her shoe-tops, then at last said in a lower voice, "Is that what you think?"

"It's the truth, ain't it?"

"Really, Pancho, I'm not a slut. I don't sleep with them, you know."

"You don't?"

"Well . . . once in a while. A great while."

Pancho looked at Amanda, really looked at her, and saw a very beautiful, very young woman trying to make her way in a world where a woman's physical appearance still categorized her in men's eyes. Jeez, she thought, Mandy prob'ly has to spend half her life keeping guys' hands off her. So she just smiles at them and jollies 'em along and splits before it gets serious. It's either that or carry a gun, I guess. Or a snake.

"Maybe we could ugly you up," Pancho muttered.

Amanda smiled ruefully. "That's what Mr. Randolph said."

"Huh? Randolph?"

"He told me that if I want to go on the mission with you I'll have to stop making myself so attractive to the men that go with us."

Pancho nodded. "We've gotta find you some big, bulky sweatshirts. Or maybe keep you in a spacesuit the whole damn trip."

The two women laughed together. But after a few moments, Amanda asked again, "So tell me, Pancho, who's your boyfriend?"

Exasperated, Pancho snapped, "You want to meet him? Come on along tonight."

"Really? Do you mean it?"

"Sure, why not?" Pancho said. "I bet he'd like to meet you."

Pancho knew that Humphries would go ballistic over Mandy. Good.

The man had been pressuring her to find out more about what Dan Randolph was up to. Humphries had been getting downright nasty about it.

Humphries had snarled at her when they'd had dinner, Pancho's first night back at Selene. The man had seemed cordial enough when he'd ushered her into that big, formal dining room in the house down at Selene's lowest level. But once he had started asking Pancho what information she had for him, and she had been forced to reply that she had little to report, his mood swiftly changed.

"That's it? That's all you've got to tell me?" Humphries had snarled.

With a helpless shrug, Pancho had answered, "He's had us cooped up in La Guaira, studyin' the fusion system."

"I'm paying you a small fortune and I'm not getting a damned bit of information from you! Nothing! A big, fat zero!"

It was a pretty dinky fortune, Pancho thought. Still, she had tried to placate the man. "But Mr. Humphries, other than the flight tests with that beat-up ol' cruise missile, he hasn't been *doin'* anything."

"He's been flitting all around the fucking world," Humphries had snapped, "from Kyoto to New York to Geneva to London. He's been talking to bankers and development agencies—even to the GEC, and he *hates* the GEC!"

Pancho had tried to be reasonable. "Look, I'm just a rocket jockey. He says he wants me to test-fly the fusion drive once it's built but it might be years before that happens."

"So what does he have you doing in the meantime?" Humphries demanded.

Pancho shrugged. "Nothin' much. He's sent me and Mandy here to Selene. His personal orders. We're supposed to be learnin' about the asteroids out in the Belt. He's got an astronomer from the Farside Observatory tutoring us."

Humphries's expression grew thoughtful. "Maybe he knows you're working for me. Maybe he's just put you on ice for the time being, until he figures out how to get rid of you."

Pancho didn't want Humphries to think about the possibility that she had told Randolph everything.

"Wouldn't it be easier for him just to fire me?" she suggested mildly.

"He's on his way here right now, you know," Humphries muttered.

"He is?" Pancho couldn't hide her surprise.

"You don't even know where he is?"

"I'm not on the mailing list for his personal itinerary," Pancho retorted.

"Now you listen to me, lady. *I* got your name to the top of Astro's personnel list so that Randolph would take you into this fusion rocket program of his. *I'm* the one who's gotten you promoted. I want results! I want to know when Randolph goes to the toilet, I want to know when he inhales and when he exhales."

"Then get yourself another spy," Pancho had said, trying to hold on to her swooping temper. "Whatever he's up to, he hasn't even been on the same continent with me most of the time. I only saw him that once, at the first flight test in Venezuela. You hired the wrong person, Mr. Humphries. You want somebody who can be his mistress, not a pilot."

Humphries had glared at her over the dinner table. "You're probably right," he had muttered. "Still . . . I want you on the job. It might take a while, but sooner or later he's going to use you to test-fly the fusion drive. That's when you'll become valuable to me. I just hired you too soon, that's all."

He made a forced little smile. "My mistake, I guess."

Puffing and sweating at the weight machine, Pancho thought, Yep, it's time for Humphries to meet Mandy. That might solve all my problems.

She laughed to herself. What a setup! Humphries sends Mandy after Randolph and she doesn't know that I've already told Randolph I'm supposed to be spyin' on him for the Humper. And Mandy would go for it, too; she'd love to have Randolph in her bed.

And meantime, she thought, I can be spyin' on Humphries for Randolph! Whatta they call that? I'll be a double agent. Yeah, that's it. A double agent. Terrific.

But what if Humphries drops me altogether once he sees Amanda? That's a possibility. Then you won't be any kind of an agent; you'll be out in the cold.

Okay, so what? she told herself. So you won't be getting the extra money from Humphries, came the answer. So you'll have to maintain Sis on your Astro salary. Yeah, yeah, she argued back. I've been doin' that for years now, I can keep on doin' it.

Wait a minute, she said to herself. Humphries can't fire me. If he tried to, he'd be afraid that I'd tell Randolph everything. The Humper has to keep me on his payroll—or get rid of me altogether.

Pancho got off the weight machine and went to the exercise bike. Pedaling furiously, she thought, The trick is not to get fired by both Humphries *and* Randolph. I don't want to be left out in the cold. And I don't want Humphries to start thinkin' he'd be better off if I happened to get myself killed. No sir!

MASTERSON AEROSPACE CORP.

You can't see them, Mr. Randolph."

Dan was startled by Douglas Stavenger's words.

"I was staring, wasn't I?" he admitted.

Stavenger smiled patiently. "Most people do, when they first meet me. But the nanomachines are all safely inside me. You can't get infected by them."

The two men were sitting in Stavenger's spacious office, which looked more like a comfortable sitting room than a business center. Wide windows made up two of the room's walls. No desk, not even a computer screen in sight; only upholstered chairs and a small sofa off to one side of the room, with a few low tables scattered here and there. Dan had to remind himself that the windows were really transparent, not holoviews. They looked out on Selene's Grand Plaza, the only public greenspace within nearly half a million kilometers.

Douglas Stavenger's office was not buried deep underground. It was on the fifteenth floor of one of the three office towers that also served as supports for the huge dome that covered the Grand Plaza. Masterson Aerospace Corporation's offices took up the entire fifteenth floor of the tower.

Spread out beyond those windows was the six-hundred-meter-long Plaza itself, a grassy expanse with paved footpaths winding through it, flowered shrubbery and even small trees here and there. Dan could see people walking along the paths, stopping at the shopping arcades, playing lunar basketball in the big enclosed cage off by the orchestra shell. Kids were doing fantastically convoluted dives from the thirty-meter platform at one end of the Olympic-sized swimming pool, twisting and somersaulting in dreamlike slow motion before they splashed languidly into the water. A pair of tourists soared past the windows on brilliantly colored plastic wings, flying like birds on their own muscle power in the low lunar gravity.

"It's a pleasant view, isn't it?" Stavenger said.

Dan nodded his agreement. While most people on the Moon instinctively wanted to live as deep underground as possible, Stavenger stayed up here, with nothing between him and the dangers of the surface except the reinforced lunar concrete of the Plaza's dome, and a meter or so of rubble from the regolith that had been strewn over it.

And why not? Dan thought. Stavenger and his family had more or less created the original Moonbase. They had fought a brief little war against the old United Nations to win their independence—and the right to use nanotechnology even though it had been banned on Earth.

Stavenger was filled with nanomachines. Turning his gaze back to him, Dan saw a good-looking young man apparently in his thirties smiling patiently at him. Stavenger wasn't much bigger than Dan, though he appeared more solidly built. Smooth olive complexion, sparkling blue eyes. Yet Douglas Stavenger was at least his own age, Dan knew, well into his sixties. His body was filled with nanomachines, tiny, virus-sized mechanisms that destroyed invading microbes, kept his skin smooth and young, took apart plaque and fatty deposits in his blood vessels atom by atom and flushed them out of his body.

The nanomachines apparently kept him youthful as well. Far better than any of the rejuvenation therapies that Dan had investigated. There was only one drawback to the nanos: Douglas Stavenger was forbidden to return to Earth. Governments, churches, the media, and the mindless masses feared that nanomachines might somehow get loose and cause unstoppable plagues or, worse, might be turned into new genocidal bioweapons.

So Stavenger was an exile who lived on the Moon, able to see the bright beckoning Earth hanging in the dark lunar sky but eternally prohibited from returning to the world of his birth.

He doesn't look upset about it, Dan thought, studying Stavenger's face.

"Whatever they've done for you," he said, "you look very healthy. And happy."

Stavenger laughed softly. "I suppose I'm the healthiest man in the solar system."

"I suppose you are. Too bad the rest of us can't have nanos injected into us."

"You can!" Stavenger blurted. Then he added, "But you wouldn't be able to go back Earthside."

Dan nodded. "We can't even use nanomachines to help rebuild the damage from the flooding and earthquakes. It's outlawed."

Stavenger hunched his shoulders in a slight shrug. "You can't blame them, really. More than ten billion people down there. How many maniacs and would-be dictators among them?"

"Too damned many," Dan mumbled.

"So you'll have to rebuild without nanotechnology, I'm afraid. They won't even allow us to sell them machinery built with nanos; they're frightened that the machinery is somehow infected by them."

"I know," said Dan. Selene built spacecraft of pure diamond out of piles of carbon soot, using nanomachines. But they were allowed no closer to Earth than the space stations in low orbit. Stupid, Dan said to himself. Nothing but ignorant superstition. Yet that was the law, everywhere on Earth.

It also made more jobs for people on Earth, he realized. The spacecraft that Astro used to fly from Earth's surface into orbit were all made basically the same way Henry Ford would have manufactured them; no nanotechnology allowed. Typical politician's thinking, Dan thought: bow to the loudest pressure group, keep outmoded industries alive and turn your back on the new opportunities. Even with the greenhouse warming wiping out half Earth's industrial base, they still think the same old way.

Leaning back in his easy chair, Stavenger said, "I understand you're trying to raise the capital to develop a fusion drive."

Dan smiled crookedly at him. "You're well informed."

"It doesn't take a genius," Stavenger said. "You've had talks with Yamagata and most of the major banks."

"Plus the double-damned GEC."

Stavenger's brows rose slightly. "And now you're talking to me."

"That I am."

"What can I do for you, Mr. Randolph?"

"Dan."

"Dan, okay."

"You can help me save those ten billion people down there on Earth. They need all the help they can get."

Stavenger said nothing. He merely sat there, his face serious, waiting for Dan to go on.

"I want to open up the Asteroid Belt," Dan said. "I want to move as much of Earth's industrial base into orbit as we can, and we need the resources from the Belt to do that."

Stavenger sighed. "It's a pretty dream. I believed in it myself, once. But we found that it costs more than it's worth."

"Selene's sent spacecraft to the NEAs," Dan pointed out.

"Not for many years, Dan. It's just too expensive. We decided a long time ago that we can live on the resources that the Moon provides. We have to. No asteroids."

"But with fusion, it becomes economically feasible to extract resources from the NEAs. And even the Belt."

"Are you certain of that?" Stavenger asked softly.

"Positively," Dan agreed. "Same situation as the Clipperships. Your Clipperships brought down the cost of going into orbit to the point where it became economically feasible to build space stations and solar power satellites and full-scale factories."

"They're not *my* Clipperships, Dan."

"Masterson Corporation is your family's outfit, isn't it?"

Stavenger shifted uneasily in his chair, his smile fading. "Masterson was founded by my family, true enough. I still own a big slice of its stock, but I'm only the Chairman Emeritus. I'm not really involved in the company's operations any longer."

"But they still listen to you."

The smile returned, but it was more guarded now. "Sometimes," Stavenger said.

"So how would Masterson like to come in with me on this fusion system? It'll be a gold mine."

Stavenger hesitated before replying, "I've been told that Humphries Space Systems is backing your fusion program."

"Martin Humphries has offered to, that's true," Dan admitted.

"But you're not satisfied with his offer?"

"I don't know if I can trust him. He comes waltzing into my office and drops this fusion deal in my lap. Why? Why didn't he do it for himself? What's he want me for?"

"Maybe it's Astro Manufacturing that he wants," Stavenger said.

Dan nodded vigorously. "Yep, that's what scares me. The man has a reputation for being a grabber. He's built Humphries Space Systems by swallowing up other companies."

Again Stavenger hesitated. At last he said, "He's on the verge of acquiring a majority of Masterson's stock."

"What?" A jolt of surprise flashed through Dan.

"I'm not supposed to know, really," Stavenger said. "It's all been very hush-hush. Humphries is on the verge of buying out two of our biggest shareholders. If he's successful, he'll have enough clout to load the board of directors with his own people."

"Damn," grumbled Dan. "Double dammit to hell and back."

"I'm afraid you'll have to play with Humphries whether you like it or not. In his court."

Suppressing an urge to get up and pound on the walls, Dan heard himself say, "Maybe not."

"No?"

"There's one other possibility."

"And what might that be?" Stavenger was smiling again, as if he knew precisely where Dan was heading.

"Selene."

"Ahh," said Stavenger, leaning back in his cushioned chair. "I thought so."

"Selene has trained technical personnel and manufacturing facilities. I could bring my fusion people up here and we could build the prototype together."

"Dan," said Stavenger gently, "who would pay Selene's technical personnel? Who would pay for using our facilities?"

"We could share the cost. I can divest a couple of Astro's operations and raise some cash that way. Selene could donate—"

The expression on Stavenger's face stopped him. It reminded Dan of the look that his geometry teacher would give him, back in high school, when he went off on the wrong tangent.

"You know something that I don't," Dan said.

Stavenger laughed gently. "Not really. You know it, too, but you're not thinking of it. You're overlooking the obvious."

Dan blinked, puzzled.

"You are staring at the solution to your problem," Stavenger prompted.

"I'm looking at you and you say that I'm—" The light finally dawned in Dan's mind. "Oh for my sweet old Aunt Sadie! Nanomachines."

Stavenger nodded. "Nanotechnology can build your fusion engine for you, and do it faster and cheaper than the orthodox way."

"Nanotechnology," Dan repeated.

"It would mean your spacecraft could never get any closer to Earth than low orbit."

"So what?" Dan exclaimed. "The double-damned ship is for deep-space operations. It'll never touch down on Earth or any other planetary surface."

"Then you should have no problem," said Stavenger.

"You mean Selene will back us?"

Very carefully, Stavenger replied, "I believe the governing council will allocate personnel and facilities to demonstrate that a prototype fusion engine can be built by using nanotechnology."

Dan grinned widely. "Yep, and once the prototype proves out, Selene will have a major new product line to manufacture: fusion drives."

"And access to the asteroids."

"Damned right! And any comets that come waltzing by, too."

"Selene and Astro Manufacturing will be partners," Stavenger said.

"Partners!" Dan agreed, sticking out his hand. Stavenger gripped it firmly and they shook on the deal.

THE CATACOMBS

It had started as a temporary storage section, just off Selene's small hospital, up by the main airlock and the garage that housed the tractors and other equipment for work on the surface.

Bodies were stored along the blank corridor walls, sealed into protective metal canisters to await transport back to Earth. In earlier days, most of the people who died on the Moon were workers killed in accidents, or visitors who made fatal mistakes while outside on the surface. Hardly anyone died of natural causes until later, when people began settling at Selene to live out their lives.

So the bodies awaiting shipment back Earthside were stored in the corridor between the hospital and the garage, convenient to the tunnel that led to the spaceport.

Eventually, of course, people who had spent their lives on the Moon wanted to be buried there, usually in the farms that provided food and fresh oxygen for the community. But often enough families back Earthside demanded the bodies of their deceased loved ones, despite the deceased's wishes. Some legal wrangles took years to unravel. So the bodies were put into metal dewars filled with liquid nitrogen, frozen solid at cryogenic temperature while the lawyers argued and ran up their fees.

It took several years for Selene's governing council to realize that a new trend had started. Cryonics. People were coming to Selene to be declared legally dead, then frozen into suspended animation in the hope that they could one day be cured of the disease that killed them, thawed, and returned to life once more.

Cryonics had been banned in most of the Earth's nations. The faithful of many religions considered it an affront to God, an attempt to evade the

divinely-mandated limits on human lifespan. While rejuvenation therapies could be done in relative secrecy, having one's body preserved cryonically was difficult to hide. With global warming causing catastrophes
all over the world and many nations barely able to feed their populations,
attempts to forestall death and elongate lifespan were frowned upon, if
not banned altogether.

So those who wanted to avoid death, and had the money to reach the
Moon, came to Selene for their final years, or months, or days. Thus the
catacombs grew, row upon row of gleaming stainless steel dewars, each
filled with liquid nitrogen, each holding a human body that one day might
be revived.

Pancho Lane had brought her sister to Selene, back when the
teenager had been diagnosed with an inoperable brain tumor. Sis was losing her memory, losing control of her body functions, losing her ability to
speak or smile or even to think. Pancho had given Sis the final injection
herself, had watched her younger sister's inert body being slid into the
cold bloodless canister, watched the medical team seal the dewar and
begin the long, intricate freezing process, her tears mingling with the cold
white mist emanating ghostlike from the hoses.

Six years ago, Pancho thought as she walked slowly along the quiet
corridor, looking for her sister's name on the long rows of metal cylinders
resting along the blank stone walls.

She had heard rumors that a few people had actually been revived
from cryonic immersion, thawed back to life. And other rumors, darker,
that claimed those revived had no memories, no minds at all. They
were like blank-brained newborns; they even had to be toilet-trained all
over again.

Doesn't matter, Pancho said to herself as she stopped in front of Sis's
dewar. I'll raise you all over again. I'll teach you to walk and talk and
laugh and sing. I will, Sis. No matter how long it takes. No matter what it
costs. As long as I'm alive, you're not going to die.

She stared at the small metal nameplate on the dewar's endcap.
SUSAN LANE. That's all it said. There was a barcode next to her name,
all Sis's vital information in computer-readable form. Not much to show
for a human lifetime, even if it was only seventeen years.

Her wristwatch buzzed annoyingly. Brushing at the tears in her eyes,
she saw that the watch was telling her she had one hour to get cleaned up
and dressed and down to Humphries's place.

With Amanda.

Mandy wore virginal white, a sleeveless mandarin-collared dress with a
mid-thigh skirt that clung lovingly to her curves. She'd done her hair up

in the latest piled-high fashion: some stylist's idea of neoclassical. Pancho had put on her best pantsuit, pearl gray with electric blue trim, almost the same shade of blue as Elly. Next to Amanda, though, she felt like a walking corpse.

She'd phoned Humphries several times to tell him she was bringing Amanda, and gotten the answering machine each time. It wasn't until she'd been on her way to the catacombs that Humphries had returned her calls, angrily demanding to know who this Amanda Cunningham was and why Pancho wanted to bring her to their meeting.

It was tough holding a reasonable conversation through the wrist-phone, but Pancho finally got across the information that Amanda was going to be her co-pilot on the mission and she'd thought he might be interested in recruiting her to help Pancho's espionage work.

In the wristphone's tiny screen it was almost impossible to judge the expression on Humphries's face, but his tone was clear enough.

"All right," he said grudgingly. "Bring her along if you think she might be able to help us. No sweat."

Pancho smiled sweetly and thanked him and clicked the phone off. No sweat, huh? she thought, laughing inwardly. He'll change his mind once he gets a look at Mandy. He'll sweat plenty.

Pancho spent the time on the electric stairways to Selene's lowest level telling Mandy everything she knew about Humphries. Everything except the fact that he'd hired her to spy on Dan Randolph.

"He's actually a billionaire?" Amanda's big blue eyes went wider than ever when Pancho described Humphries's underground palace.

"Humphries Biotech," Pancho replied. "The Humphries Trust, lord knows what else. You can look him up in the financial nets."

"And you're dating him!"

Frowning slightly at her incredulousness, Pancho replied, "I told you, it's strictly business. He's . . . eh, he's tryin' to hire me away from Astro."

"Really?" A suspicious, supercilious tone dripped from the one word.

Pancho grinned at her. "More or less."

Once they stepped through the airlock-type door and into Humphries's underground garden, Amanda gasped with awe. "It's heavenly!"

"Pretty neat," Pancho agreed.

Humphries was standing at the open door to the house, waiting for them, eying Amanda as they came up the walk.

"Martin Humphries," Pancho said, as close to a formal introduction as she knew, "I would like you to meet—"

"Ms. Amanda Cunningham," Humphries said, all smiles. "I looked up your dossier when I got Pancho's message that you were joining us this evening."

Pancho nodded, impressed. Humphries can tap into Astro's personnel files. He must have Dan's offices honeycombed with snoops.

Humphries took Amanda's extended hand and bent over it, his lips barely touching her satiny white skin. Amanda looked as if she wanted to faint.

"Come in, ladies," Humphries said, tucking Amanda's arm under his own. "Come in and welcome."

To Pancho's surprise, Humphries didn't come on to Amanda. Not obviously, at least. A human butler served aperitifs in the library-cum-bar and Humphries showed off his collection of first editions.

"Pretty rare, some of them," he boasted mildly. "I keep them here because of the climate control system. Back home in Connecticut it would cost a considerable sum to keep the old family home at a constant temperature and humidity. Here in Selene it comes automatically."

"Or we breathe vacuum," Pancho commented. Amanda gave her a knowing look.

The butler showed them to the dining room, where the women sat on either side of Humphries. A pair of squat, flat-topped robots trundled back and forth from the kitchen carrying plates and glasses. Pancho watched intently as the robots' padded claws gripped the chinaware and crystal. They didn't drop a thing, although while clearing the salad plates one of them missed Pancho's dish by a fraction of a millimeter and almost knocked it off the table. Before anyone could react, though, it recovered, grasped the plate firmly and tucked it into its recessed storage section.

"That's a pretty good optical recognition system they've got," Pancho said.

"I don't believe it's optical," Amanda countered. To Humphries she asked, "Is it?"

"Very sharp, Amanda," he said, impressed. "Very sharp. The dishes have monomolecular beacons sprayed on their bottoms. The robots sense the microwave signals."

Pancho lifted up her water tumbler and squinted at its bottom.

"The chip's too small to see with the naked eye," Humphries said.

"What powers 'em?"

"The heat from the food or drink. They have trouble with iced drinks . . . and your salad."

Pancho thought it over for half a second. "Dishes pick up residual heat when we handle them, huh?"

"That's right."

Pancho smiled as the other robot placed a steaming plate of frogs' legs before her. Don't want Humphries to think Mandy's the only smart one here, she told herself.

All through dinner Humphries was charming, solicitous, all smiles. He paid almost as much attention to Pancho as he did to Amanda, up to the point where he encouraged Mandy to tell them about her early life. She began to talk, hesitantly at first, about growing up in London, winning a scholarship to the International Space University.

"It wasn't easy," Amanda said, with almost childlike candor. "All the men seemed to think I was better suited to be a photographer's model than an astronaut."

Humphries made a sympathetic murmur. Pancho nodded, understanding all over again that Mandy's good looks had been as much of a problem for her as an advantage.

"But I made it," she finished happily, "and here we all are."

"Good for you," said Humphries, patting her hand. "I think you've done wonderfully well."

As dessert was being served—fresh fruit from the botanical garden outside with soymilk ice cream—Amanda asked where the lavatory was.

Once she had left the room Pancho leaned closer to Humphries and asked in a lowered voice, "Well, whattaya think?"

He frowned with annoyance. "About what?"

"About Mandy." She almost added, *lunkhead,* but stopped herself just in time.

"She's wonderful," Humphries said, beaming. "Beautiful but brainy, too. You don't see that very often."

Pancho thought, Women don't let you see their brains very often, not if they can get by on their looks.

Aloud, she asked, "So d'you think she'd be any good cozyin' up to Dan Randolph?"

"No!" he snapped.

"No?" Pancho was astonished. "Why not?"

"I don't want her anywhere near Randolph. He'll seduce her in a hot second."

Pancho stared at the man. I thought that was the whole idea, she said to herself. Get Mandy into Randolph's bed. I thought that's what he'd want.

"She's much too fine a woman to be used that way," Humphries added.

Oh, for cryin' out loud, Pancho realized. He's fallen for her! This guy who picks up women like paperclips and dumps 'em when he feels like it, he doesn't just have the hots for Mandy. He's fallen in love with her. Just like that!

SELENE GOVERNING COUNCIL

Dan couldn't help contrasting in his mind this meeting of Selene's governing council with the meeting of the GEC's executive board he'd attended a few weeks earlier in London.

The meeting took place in Selene's theater, with the council sitting at student's desks arranged up on the stage in a semi-circle. Just about every seat on the main floor and the balconies was taken, although the box seats on either side of the stage were all empty. Maybe they've been roped off for some reason, Dan thought. Must be two thousand people out there, he thought as he peeked out at the audience through the curtains screening the stage's wings. Just about every voting citizen in Selene's showed up for this meeting.

As he stood in the wing of the stage, the council members filed past him, taking their seats. For the most part they looked young, vigorous. Six women, five men, none with white hair. A couple of premature baldies among the men; they must be engineers, Dan thought. He knew that membership on the council was a part-time task assigned by lottery; no one was allowed to duck their public service, although they could take time off their regular jobs to attend to their extra duties.

"Nervous?"

Dan turned at the sound of Doug Stavenger's voice.

Smiling, he answered, "When you've had to sit through as many board meetings as I have, you don't get nervous, you just want to get it the hell over with."

Stavenger patted Dan lightly on the shoulder. "This one will be different from all the others, Dan. It's more like an old-fashioned New England town meeting than one of your board of directors' get-togethers."

Dan agreed with a brief nod. Often in his mind he'd spelled it b-o-r-e-d meeting. This one would be different, he felt sure.

It was.

Stavenger served as non-voting chairman of the governing council, a largely honorary position. More pomp than circumstance, Dan thought. The chairman stood at the podium set up at one end of the stage, only a few meters from where Dan stood waiting for his turn to speak. The meeting agenda was displayed on a wallscreen along the back of the stage. Dan was dismayed to see that he was last on a list of nine.

The first five items went fairly quickly. The sixth was a new regulation tightening everyone's water allotment. Several people from the audience shot to their feet to make their opinions heard in no uncertain terms.

One of the council members was chairman of the water board, a chubby, balding, red-faced man wearing the coral-red coveralls of the Tourism Department. The student's desk at which he sat looked uncomfortably small for him.

"There's no way around it," he said, looking flustered. "No matter how efficiently we recycle our water, it's not a hundred percent and it never will be. The more people we allow in, the less water we have to go around."

"Then why don't we shut down tourism," came an angry voice from the floor.

"Tourism's down to a trickle anyway," the water chairman replied. "It's less than five percent of our problem. Immigration is our big difficulty."

"Refugees," someone said in a harsh stage whisper.

"Don't let 'em in!" an angry voice snapped.

"You can't do that!"

"Why the hell not? They made the mess on Earth. Let 'em stew in their own crap."

"Can't we find new sources of water?" a citizen asked.

Stavenger answered from the podium, "Our exploration teams have failed to locate any other than the polar ice fields we've been using all along."

"Bring up a few loads from Earthside," someone suggested.

"Yeah, and they'll gouge us for it."

"But if we need it, what else can we do?"

The audience stirred restlessly. A dozen conversations buzzed through the theater.

The water board chairman raised his voice to be heard over the chatter. "We're negotiating with the GEC for water shipments, but they want to put one of their own people onto the water board in return."

"Hell no!"

"Never!"

"Those bastards have been trying to get control of us since day one!"

The audience roared its angry disapproval.

Stavenger, still standing at the podium, pressed his thumb on a button set into its control panel and a painfully loud hooting whistle rang through the theater, silencing the shouters. Dan covered his ears until the shriek died away.

"We've got to maintain order here," Stavenger said in the numbed silence. "Otherwise we'll never get anywhere."

Reluctantly, they accepted the fact that water allotments would be decreased slightly. Then the water board chairman held out a potential carrot.

"We'll have the new recycling system on-line in a few months," he said, drumming his fingers nervously on his desktop. "If it works as efficiently as the simulations show it should, we can go back to the current water allotments—at least for a year or so."

"And what happens if this recycling system fails?" asked a stern-faced elderly woman.

"It's being thoroughly tested," the water chairman answered defensively.

"This is just a way for the people running the damned hotel to put up their own swimming pool and spa," grumbled a lanky, longhaired citizen. He looked like a physicist to Dan. "Tourism is down so they want to fancy up the hotel to attract more tourists."

Dan wondered about that. Tourism is down because the world's going down the toilet, he thought. Then he admitted, But, yeah, people running tourist facilities will try their damnedest to attract customers, no matter what. What else can they do, except go out of business altogether?

In the end, the council decided to accept the water allotment restrictions until the new recycling system had been in operation for three continuous months. Then they would have a new hearing to decide on whether they could return to the old allotments.

Two more items were swiftly disposed of, then at last Stavenger said, "The final item on our agenda tonight is a proposal by Dan Randolph, head of Astro Manufacturing." He turned slightly and prompted, "Dan?"

There was some scattered applause as Dan stepped up to the podium. Astro employees, Dan thought. Stavenger moved off-stage.

He gripped the edges of the podium and looked over the crowd. He had no notes, no visual aids. For several moments he merely stood there, thinking hard. The audience began to murmur, whisper.

Dan began, "Halley's Comet will be returning to the inner solar system in a few years. Last time it came by, Halley's blew out roughly thirty million tons of water vapor in six months. If I remember the numbers right, the comet lost something like three tons of water per second when it was closest to the Sun."

He waited a heartbeat, then asked, "Do you think you could use that water?"

"Hell yes!" somebody shouted. Dan grinned when he saw that it was Pancho Lane, sitting up in the first row of the balcony.

"Then let's go get it!" Dan said.

He spent the next fifteen minutes outlining the fusion rocket system and assuring them that it had performed flawlessly in all its tests to date.

"A fusion-driven spacecraft can bring in all the water you need, either from hydrate-bearing asteroids or from comets," Dan said. "I need your help to build a full-scale system and flight test it."

One of the women councilors asked, "Are you asking Selene to fund your corporation? Why can't you raise the money from the regular sources?"

Dan made himself smile at her. "This project will cost between one and two billion international dollars, Earthside. None of the banks or other funding sources that I've approached will risk that kind of money. They're all fully committed to rebuilding and mitigation programs. They've got their hands full with the greenhouse warming; they're not interested in space projects."

"Damned flatland idiots," somebody groused.

"I agree," Dan said, grinning. "They're too busy doing what's urgent to even think about what's important."

"Out of all the corporations on Earth," someone called out, "surely you can make a deal or two to raise the capital you need."

Dan decided to cut the discussion short. "Listen. I could probably put together a deal that would raise the money we need, but I thought I'd give you a chance to come in on this. It's the opportunity you've been waiting for."

"Selene doesn't have that kind of money at its disposal," said one of the councilmen.

"No," countered Dan, "but you have the trained people and the facilities to build the fusion rocket with nanomachines."

A hush fell over the theater. Nanotechnology. They all knew it was possible. And yet . . .

"Nanomachines aren't magic wands, Mr. Randolph," said the councilor seated closest to Dan, a lean, pinch-faced young man who looked like a jogging fanatic.

"I understand that," said Dan.

"At one time we thought we could develop nanomachines to produce water for us by taking hydrogen from the incoming solar wind and combining it with oxygen from the regolith. It was technically feasible but in practice a complete failure."

Recognizing the councilman as one who loved the sound of his own voice, Dan said curtly, "If nanomachines can build entire Clipperships they can build fusion drives."

Another woman councilor, with the bright red hair and porcelain-white complexion of the Irish, spoke up. "I've been stuck with the job of treasurer for the council, the thanks I get for being an honest accountant."

Dan laughed, along with most of the audience.

"But it's a sad fact that we don't have the funds to spare on your program, Mr. Randolph, no matter how admirable it may be. The money just isn't in our hands."

"I don't want money," Dan said.

"Then what?"

"I want volunteers. I need people who are willing to devote their time to the greatest challenge of our age: developing the resources of the entire solar system."

"Ah, but that boils down to money, now, doesn't it?"

"No it doesn't," said a deep voice from the middle of the theater. Dan saw a squat, heavily-built black man get to his feet.

"I'm Bernie James. I retired from the nanotech lab last year. I'm only a technician, but I'll work with you on this."

A few rows farther back, a taller man, blond hair cropped short, got to his feet. "Rolf Uhrquest, Space Transportation Department," he said, in a clear tenor voice. "I would be willing to take my accumulated vacation time to work on this fusion project."

Dan smiled at them both. "Thank you."

"And I believe," Uhrquest continued, "that Dr. Cardenas would be interested also." Turning slightly, he called, "Dr. Cardenas, are you here?"

No one answered.

"I will find her," Uhrquest said, very seriously. "It is a shame she is not present today."

Dan looked expectantly out at the audience, but no one else stood up. At last he said, "Thank you," and stepped away from the podium, back into the wings of the stage. Stavenger gave him a quick thumbs-up signal and returned to the podium for the final item on the meeting's agenda: a request from a retired couple to enlarge their living quarters so they could have enough space to start a new business for themselves.

Once the meeting broke up, Stavenger said, "If Kris Cardenas had been anywhere in Selene I would have introduced you to her. Unfortunately, she's in a space station in near-Earth orbit, working on developing nanomachines to bring down the costs of the Mars exploration centers."

"Which station?" Dan asked.

"The one over South America."

Dan grinned at him. "*Nueva Venezuela.* I helped build that sucker. Maybe it's time for me to pay a visit there."

ALPHONSUS

Pancho watched the safety demonstration very carefully. No matter that she had put on a spacesuit and done EVA work dozens of times; she paid patient attention to every word of the demo. This was going to be on the surface of the Moon, and the differences between orbital EVAs and a moonwalk were enough to worry about.

The tourists in the bus didn't seem to give a damn. Hell, Pancho thought, if they're stinky-rich enough to afford a vacation jaunt to the Moon, they must have the attitude that nothing bad'll happen to them, and if it does they'll get their lawyers to sue the hell out of everybody between here and Mars.

They had all suited up in the garage at Selene before getting onto the bus. It was easier that way; the bus was way too tight for fourteen tourists to wriggle and squeeze into their spacesuits. They rode out to the Ranger 9 site in the hard-shell suits, their helmets in their laps.

After all these years, Pancho thought, they still haven't come up with anything better than these hard-shell suits. The science guys keep talking about softsuits and even nanomachine skins, but it's still nothing more'n talk.

Even the teenagers went quiet once they cleared the garage airlock and drove out onto the cracked, pockmarked surface of Alphonsus. A hundred and eight kilometers across, the crater floor went clear over the horizon. The ringwall mountains looked old and weary, slumped smooth from eons of being sandpapered by the constant infall of meteoric dust.

It was the dust that worried Pancho. In orbital space you were floating in vacuum. On the surface of the Moon you had to walk on the powdery regolith, sort of like walking on beach sand. Except that the "sand" billowed up and covered your boots with fine gray dust. Not just your boots, either, Pancho reminded herself. She'd heard tales about lunar dust getting into a suit's joints and even into the life-support backpack. The dust was electrostatically charged from the incoming solar wind, too, and this made the freaking stuff cling like mad. If it got on your visor it could blind you; try to wipe it off with your gloves and you just smeared it worse.

They'd had some trouble finding Pancho a suit that would fit her comfortably; in the end they had to break out a brand new one, sized long. It smelled new, like pristine plastic. When the bus stopped and the guide told the tourists to put on their helmets, Pancho sort of missed the familiar scents of old sweat and machine oil that permeated the working suits she'd worn. Even the air blowing gently across her face tasted new, unused.

The tour guide and the bus driver both checked out each tourist before they let the visitors climb down from the bus's hatch onto the lunar regolith. Pancho's helmet earphones filled with "oohs" and "lookit that!" as, one by one, the tourists stepped onto the ancient ground and kicked up puffs of dust that lingered lazily in the gentle gravity of the Moon.

"Look how bright my footprints are!" someone shouted excitedly.

The guide explained, "That's because the topmost layer of the ground has been darkened by billions of years of exposure to hard radiation from the Sun and deep space. Your bootprints show the true color of the regolith underneath. Give 'em a few million years, though, and the prints will turn dark, too."

For all the years she'd worked in space, Pancho had never been out on a Moonwalk. She found it fascinating, once she cut off the radio frequency that carried the tourists' inane chatter and listened only to the prerecorded talk that guided visitors to the Ranger 9 site.

To outward appearances she was just another tourist from one of the three busloads that were being shepherded along the precisely-marked paths on the immense floor of Alphonsus. But Pancho knew that Martin Humphries was in one of the other buses, and her reason for being here was to report to him, not to sightsee.

She let the cluster of tourists move on ahead of her while she lingered near the parked buses. The canned tourguide explanation was telling her about the rilles that meandered near the site of the old spacecraft crash: sinuous cracks in the crater floor that sometimes vented out thin, ghost-like clouds of ammonia and methane.

"One of the reasons for locating the original Moonbase in Alphonsus's ringwall mountains was the hope of utilizing these volatiles for—"

She saw Humphries shuffling toward her, kicking up clouds of dust as if it didn't matter. It had to be him, she thought, because his spacesuit was different from the ones issued to the tourists. Not different enough to be obvious to the tenderfeet, but Pancho recognized the slightly wider, heavier build of the suit and the tiny servo motors at the joints that helped the wearer move the more massive arms and legs. Extra armor, she thought. He must worry about radiation up here.

Humphries had no name tag plastered to the torso of his suit, and until he was close enough to touch helmets she could not see into his heavily-tinted visor to identify his face. But he walked right up to her, kicking up the dust, until he almost bumped his helmet against hers. She recognized his features through the visor: round and snubby-nosed, like some freckle-faced kid, but with those cold, hard eyes peering at her.

Pancho lifted her left wrist and poised her right hand over the comm keyboard, asking Humphries in pantomime which radio frequency he wanted to use. He held up a gloved hand and she saw that he was holding a coiled wire in it. Slowly, with the deliberate care of a person who was not accustomed to working in a spacesuit, he fitted one end of the wire into the receptacle built into the side of his helmet. He held out the other end. Pancho took it and plugged into her own helmet.

"Okay," she heard Humphries's voice, almost as clearly as if they were in a comfortable room, "now we can talk without anyone tapping into our conversation."

Pancho remembered her childhood, when she and some of the neighborhood kids would create telephone links out of old paper cups and lengths of waxed string. They were using the same principle, linking their helmets with the wire so they could converse without using their suit radios. This'll work, Pancho thought, as long as we don't move too far apart. She judged the wire connecting their helmets to be no more than three meters long.

"You worried about eavesdroppers?" she asked Humphries.

"Not especially, but why take a chance you don't have to?"

That made sense, a little. "Why couldn't we meet down at your place, like usual?"

"Because it's not a good idea for you to be seen going down there so often, that's why," Humphries replied testily. "How long do you think it would be before Dan Randolph finds out you're coming to my residence on a regular basis?"

Teasingly, Pancho said, "So he finds out. He'll just think you're inviting me to dinner."

Humphries grunted. Pancho knew that he had invited Amanda to dinner at his home twice since they'd first met. And he'd stopped asking Pancho to report to him down there. Now they met at prearranged times and places: strolling in the Grand Plaza, watching low-gravity ballet in the theater, doing a tourist moonwalk on the crater floor.

Pancho would have shrugged if she hadn't been encased in the suit. She said to Humphries, "Dan made his pitch to the governing council."

"I know. And they turned him down."

"Well, sort of."

"What do you mean?" he snapped.

"A couple of citizens volunteered to work on Dan's project. He's goin' down to the Venezuela space station to try to get Dr. Cardenas to head up the team."

"Kristine Cardenas?"

"Yup. She's the top expert at nanotech," Pancho said.

"They gave her the Nobel Prize," Humphries muttered, "before nanotechnology was banned on Earth."

"That's the one he's gonna talk to."

For several long moments Humphries simply stood there unmoving, not speaking a word. Pancho thought he looked like a statue, with the spacesuit and all.

At length he said, "He wants to use nanomachines to build the rocket. I hadn't expected that."

"It's cheaper. Prob'ly better, too."

She sensed Humphries nodding inside his helmet. "I should've seen it coming. If he can build the system with nanos, he won't need my financing. The sonofabitch can leave me out in the cold—after I gave him the fusion idea on a silver fucking platter!"

"I don't think he'd do that."

"Wouldn't he?" Humphries was becoming more enraged with every word. "I bring the fusion project to him, I offer to fund the work, but instead he sneaks behind my back to try to raise funding from any other source he can find. And now he's got a way to build the fucking rocket without me altogether! He's trying to cut my balls off!"

"But—"

"Shut up, you stupid bitch! I don't care what you think! That prick bastard Randolph thinks he can screw me out of this! Well, he's got another think coming! I'll break his back! I'll *destroy* the sonofabitch!"

Humphries yanked the wire out of Pancho's helmet, then pulled the other end out of his own. He turned and strode back to the bus that had carried him out to the Ranger 9 site, practically boiling up a dust storm with his angry stomping. If he hadn't been in the heavy spacesuit, Pancho thought, he'd hop two meters off the ground with each step. Prob'ly fall flat on his face.

She watched as he gestured furiously to the bus driver, then clambered aboard the tourist bus. The driver got in after him, closed the hatch, and started off for the garage back at Selene.

Pancho wondered if Humphries would allow the driver to come back out and pick up the other tourists, or would he leave them stranded out here? Well, she thought, they can always squeeze into the other buses.

She decided there was nothing she could do about it, so she might as well enjoy what was left of her outing. As she walked off toward the wreckage of the tiny, primitive Ranger 9, though, she thought that she'd better tell Dan Randolph about this pretty damned quick. Humphries was sore enough to commit murder, it seemed to her.

SPACE STATION *NUEVA VENEZUELA*

It was almost like coming home for Dan. *Nueva Venezuela* had been one of the first big projects for the fledgling Astro Manufacturing Corp., back in the days when Dan had moved his corporate headquarters from Texas to La Guaira and married the daughter of the future president of Venezuela.

The space station had lasted much better than the marriage. Still, the station was old and scuffed-up. As the transfer craft from Selene made its approach, Dan saw that the metal skin of her outer hulls was dulled and pitted from long years of exposure to radiation and mite-sized meteoroids. Here and there bright new sections showed where the maintenance crews were replacing the tired, eroded skin. A facelift, Dan thought, smiling. Well, she's old enough to need it. They're probably using cermet panels instead of the aluminum we started with. Lighter, tougher, maybe even cheaper if you consider the length of time they'll last before they need replacing.

Nueva Venezuela was built of a series of concentric rings. The outermost ring spun at a rate that gave the occupants inside it a feeling of normal Earthly gravity. The two other rings were placed where they would simulate Mars's one-third g and the Moon's one-sixth. The docking port at the station's center was effectively at zero gravity. The tech guys called it microgravity, but Dan always thought of it as zero g.

A great place to make love, Dan remembered. Then he chuckled to himself. Once you get over the heaves. Nearly everybody got nauseous their first few hours in weightlessness.

Dan went through customs swiftly, allowing the inspector to rummage through his one travelbag while he tried to keep himself from making any sudden movements. He could feel his sinuses starting to puff up as the liquids in his body shifted in response to weightlessness. No postnasal drips in zero *g,* Dan told himself. But you sure can get a beaut of a headache while the fluids build up in your sinuses before you adapt.

The main thing was to make as few head motions as possible. Dan had seen people suddenly erupt with projectile vomiting from merely turning their heads or nodding.

The inspector passed him easily enough and Dan gratefully made his way along the tube corridor that led "down" to the lunar-level wheel.

He dumped his bag in the cubbyhole compartment he'd rented for this visit, then prowled along the sloping corridor that ran through the center of the wheel, checking the numbers on each door.

Dr. Kristine Cardenas's name was neatly printed on a piece of tape stuck above her door number. Dan rapped once, and opened the door.

It was a small office, hardly enough room for the desk and the two plain plastic chairs in front of it. A good-looking young woman sat at the desk: shoulder-length sandy hair, cornflower blue eyes, broad swimmer's shoulders. She wore an unadorned jumpsuit of pastel yellow; or maybe it had once been brighter, but had faded after many washings.

"I'm looking for Dr. Cardenas," said Dan. "She's expecting me. I'm Dan Randolph."

The young woman smiled up at him and extended her hand. "I'm Kris Cardenas."

Dan blinked. "You . . . you're much too young to be *the* Dr. Cardenas."

She laughed. Motioning Dan to one of the chairs in front of the desk, she said, "I assure you, Mr. Randolph, that I am indeed *the* Dr. Cardenas."

Dan looked into those bright blue eyes. "You too, huh? Nanomachines."

She pursed her lips, then admitted, "It was a temptation I couldn't resist. Besides, what better way to test what nanotechnology can do than to try it on yourself?"

"Like Pasteur injecting himself with the polio vaccine," Dan said.

She gave him a sidelong look. "Your grasp of the history of science is a bit off, but you've got the basic idea."

Dan leaned back in the plastic chair. It creaked a little but accommodated itself to his weight. "Maybe I ought to try them, too," he said.

"If you don't have any plans to return to Earth," Cardenas replied, with a sudden sharpness in her voice.

Dan changed the subject. "I understand you're working with the Mars exploration program."

She nodded. "Their budget's being slashed to the bone. Beyond the bone, actually. If we can't develop nanos to take over the life-support functions at their bases, they'll have to close up shop and return to Earth."

"But if they use nanomachines they won't be allowed to come back home."

"Only if they use nanomachines in their own bodies," Cardenas said, raising a finger to emphasize her point. "The IAA has graciously decided they can be allowed to use nanotechnology to maintain and repair their equipment."

Dan caught the sarcasm in her tone. "I'll bet the New Morality was thrilled with that decision."

"They don't run the entire show. At least, not yet."

Dan huffed. "Good reason to live off Earth. I've always said, When the going gets tough, the tough get going—"

"—to where the going's easier," Cardenas finished for him. "Yes, I've heard that."

"I don't think I'd be able to live off-Earth forever," Dan said. "I mean . . . well, that's home."

"Not for me," Cardenas snapped. "Not for a half a dozen of the Martian explorers, either. They've accepted nanomachines. They have no intention of returning to Earth."

Surprised, Dan said, "I didn't know that."

"There hasn't been much publicity about it. The New Morality and their ilk have a pretty tight grip on the news media."

Dan studied her face for a long, silent moment. Dr. Cardenas was physically youthful, quite attractive, a Nobel laureate, the leader in her chosen field of study. Yet she seemed so indignant.

"Well, anyway," he said, "I'm grateful that you've taken the time to see me. I know you're busy."

She broke into a pleased smile. "Your message seemed kind of . . ." she fished for a word, " . . . mysterious. It made me wonder why you wanted to see me in person, rather than by phone."

Dan grinned back at her. "I've found that it's always easier to discuss matters face-to-face. Phones, mail, even VR meetings, they can't replace person-to-person contact."

Cardenas's smile turned knowing. "It's more difficult for someone to say 'no' to your face."

"You got me," Dan replied, raising his hands in mock surrender. "I need your help and I didn't want to tell you about it long-distance."

She seemed to relax somewhat. Easing back in her chair, she asked, "So what's so important that you came up here to see me?"

"Down here. I came in from Selene."

"What's your problem? I've been so wrapped up with this Mars work that I haven't been keeping up with current events."

Dan took in a breath, then started, "You know I'm the head of Astro Manufacturing."

Cardenas nodded.

"I've got a small team ready to build a prototype fusion rocket, using nanomachines."

"A fusion rocket?"

"We've tested small models. The system works. Now we need to build a full-scale prototype and test it. We're planning a mission to the Asteroid Belt, and—"

"Spacecraft have gone to the Belt on ordinary rockets. Why do you need a fusion system?"

"Those were unmanned vehicles. This mission will carry a crew of four, maybe six."

"To the Asteroid Belt? Why?"

"To start prospecting for the metals and minerals that the people of Earth need," Dan said.

Cardenas's face turned stony. Coldly, she asked, "What are you trying to accomplish, Mr. Randolph?"

"I'm trying to save the Earth. I know that sounds pompous, but if we don't—"

"I see no reason to save the Earth," Cardenas said flatly.

Dan gaped at her.

"They got themselves into this greenhouse mess. They were warned, but they paid no attention. The politicians, the business leaders, the news media . . . none of them lifted a finger until it was too late."

"That's not entirely true," Dan said softly, remembering his own struggles to get the world's leaders to recognize the looming greenhouse cliff before it struck.

"True enough," Cardenas replied. "And then there's the New Morality and all those other ultraconservative cults. Why do you want to save them?"

"They're people," Dan blurted. "Human beings."

"Let them sink in their own filth," Cardenas said, her words dripping acid. "They've earned whatever they get."

"But . . ." Dan felt completely at sea. "I don't understand . . ."

"They exiled me." She almost snarled the words. "Because I injected nanomachines into my body, they prevented me from returning to Earth. Their fanatics assassinated anyone who spoke in favor of nanotechnology, did you know that?"

Dan shook his head mutely.

"They attacked Moonbase, back before it became Selene. One of their suicide killers blew up Professor Zimmerman in his own lab. And you want me to help them?"

Shocked by her vehemence, Dan mumbled, "But that was years ago . . ."

"I was there, Mr. Randolph. I saw the mangled bodies. And then, when we won and even the old United Nations had to recognize our independence, those hypocritical ignoramuses passed laws exiling anyone who had accepted nanomachines into her body."

"I understand that, but—"

"I had a husband," she went on, blue eyes snapping. "I had two daughters. I have four grandchildren in college that I've never touched! Never held them as babies. Never sat down at the same table with them."

Another woman might have burst into tears, Dan thought. But Cardenas was too furious for that. How the hell can I reach her? he wondered.

She seemed to recover herself. Placing both hands on her desktop, she said more mildly, "I'm sorry for the tirade. But I want you to understand why I'm not particularly interested in helping the people of Earth."

Dan replied, "Then how about helping the people of Selene?"

Her chin went up a notch. "What do you mean?"

"A working fusion drive can make it economical to mine hydrates from the carbonaceous asteroids. Even scoop water vapor from comets."

She thought about that for a moment. Then, "Or even scoop fusion fuels from Jupiter, I imagine."

Dan stared at her. Twelve lords a-leaping, I hadn't even thought of that. Jupiter's atmosphere must be loaded with hydrogen and helium isotopes.

Cardenas smiled slightly. "I presume you could make a considerable fortune from all this."

"I've offered to do it at cost."

Her brows rose. "At cost?"

He hesitated, then admitted, "I want to help the people of Earth. There's ten billion of them, less the millions who've already been killed in the floods and epidemics and famines. They're not all bad guys."

Cardenas looked away from him for a moment, then admitted, "No, I suppose they're not."

"Your grandchildren are down there."

"That's a low blow, Mr. Randolph."

"Dan."

"It's still a low blow, and you know it."

He smiled at her. "I'm not above a rabbit punch or two if it'll get the job done."

She did not smile back. But she said, "I'll spin this Mars work off to a couple of my students. It's mostly routine now, anyway. I'll be back in Selene within the week."

"Thanks. You're doing the right thing," Dan said.

"I'm not as sure of that as you are."

He got up from his chair. "I guess we'll just have to see where it all leads."

"Yes, we will," she agreed.

Dan shook hands with her again and then left her office. Don't linger once you get what you want. Never give the other side the chance to reconsider. He had Cardenas's agreement, no matter that it was reluctant.

Okay, I've got the team I need. Duncan and his crew can stay Earthside. Cardenas will direct the construction job.

Now to confront Humphries.

SELENE

And he's madder'n hell," Pancho finished.

Dan nodded somberly as they rode an electric cart through the tunnel from the spaceport to Selene proper. Pancho had been at the spaceport to meet him on his return flight from *Nueva Venezuela,* looking worried, almost frightened about Humphries.

"I guess I'd be ticked off, too," he said, "if our positions were reversed."

The two of them were alone in the cart. Dan had deliberately waited until the four other passengers of the transfer ship had gone off toward the city. Then he and Pancho had clambered aboard the next cart. The automated vehicles ran like clockwork along the long, straight tunnel.

"What do you want to do?" Pancho asked.

Dan grinned at her. "I'll call him and arrange a meeting."

"At the O.K. Corral?"

"No," he said, laughing. "Nothing so grim. It's time he and I talked about structuring a deal together."

Frowning, Pancho asked, "Do you really need him now? I mean with the nanotech and all? Can't you run this show yourself and keep him out of it?"

"I don't think that would be the smart thing to do," Dan replied. "After all, he did start me off on this fusion business. If I tried to cut him out altogether he'd have a legitimate gripe."

"That's what he expects you to do."

Dan watched the play of shadows over her face as the cart glided silently along the tunnel. Light and shadow, light and shadow, like watching a speeded-up video of the Sun going across the sky.

"I don't play the game the same way he does," he said at last. "And I don't want this project tied up by lawyers for the next ninety-nine years."

Pancho grunted with distaste. "Lawyers."

"Humphries brought the fusion project to me because he wants to get into Astro. I know how he works. He figures that he'll finance the fusion work in exchange for a bloc of Astro's stock. Then he'll finagle some more stock, put a couple of his clones on my board of directors, and sooner or later toss me out of my own company."

"Can he do that?"

"That's the way he operates. He's snatched half-a-dozen corporations that way. Right now he's on the verge of taking over Masterson Aerospace."

"Masterson?" Pancho looked shocked.

Dan said, "Yep. Half the world drowning and the rest cooking from this double-damned greenhouse, and he's using it to snatch and grab. He's a goddamned opportunist. A vampire, sucking the life out of everything he touches."

"So what are you gonna do?"

"Keep his investment in the fusion project to a minimum," Dan said. "And keep the fusion project separate and apart from Astro Corporation."

"Good luck," she said glumly.

Dan grinned at her. "Hey, don't look so worried. I've been through this kind of thing before. This is what the corporate jungle is all about."

"Yeah, maybe, but I think he'll get rough if he doesn't get his way. Real rough."

With a brash shrug, Dan replied, "That's why I keep Big George around."

"Big George? Who's he?"

Dan had made his quick trip to *Nueva Venezuela* without George. He didn't feel the need for a bodyguard once he was off-Earth. In fact, he hadn't seen the Aussie since they'd arrived together in Selene for his meeting with Doug Stavenger.

"I'll have to introduce you to him."

The cart reached the end of the tunnel and stopped automatically. Dan and Pancho got off; he grabbed his travel-bag and they walked to the customs inspection station. Dan saw that the two uniformed inspectors were still checking the quartet of people who had arrived on his flight. On the other side of the area, by the entrance gate, an elderly couple was saying goodbye to a young family with two children, one of them a tot squirming in her mother's arms.

"So whattaya want me to tell Humphries?" Pancho asked. "He'll wanna know how you did with Dr. Cardenas."

"Tell him the truth. Cardenas is joining the team. She'll be here in a few days."

"Should I tell him you want to set up a meeting with him?"

Dan thought it over as they stepped up to the customs desk. "No," he said at last. "I'll call him myself as soon as we get down to our quarters."

Humphries seemed surprised when Dan called him, but he quickly agreed to a meeting the very next morning. He insisted on having the meeting in the Humphries Space System's suite of offices, up in the same tower on the Grand Plaza that housed Doug Stavenger's office.

Dan accepted meekly enough, laughing inwardly at Humphries's gamesmanship. He tried to phone Big George, got only his answering machine, and left a message for George to call him first thing in the morning. Then he undressed, showered, and went to bed.

He dreamed about Jane. They were together on Tetiaroa, completely alone on the tropical atoll beneath a gorgeous star-strewn sky, walking along the lagoon beach while the balmy wind set the palm trees to rustling softly. A slim crescent of a Moon rode past scudding silvery clouds. Jane was wearing a filmy robe, her auburn hair undone and flowing past her shoulders. In the starlight he could see how beautiful she was, how desirable.

But he could not speak a word. Somehow, no matter how hard he tried, no sound would come out of his mouth. This is stupid, Dan raged at himself. How can you tell her you love her if you can't talk?

The clouds thickened, darkened, blotted out the Moon and stars. Beyond Jane's shadowy profile Dan could see the ocean stirring, frothing, an enormous tidal wave rising up higher, higher, a mountain of foaming water rushing down on them. He tried to warn her, tried to shout, but the water crashed down on them both with crushing force. He reached for Jane, to hold her, to save her, but she was wrenched out of his arms.

He woke, sitting up and drenched with sweat. His throat felt raw, as if he'd been screaming for hours. He didn't know where he was. In the darkness of the bedroom all he could see was the green glowing numerals on the digital clock on the night table. He rubbed at his eyes, working hard to remember. Selene. I'm in the company suite in Selene. I'm going to see Humphries first thing in the morning.

And Jane's dead.

"You've been quite a busy fellow," Humphries said, with obviously false joviality.

Instead of meeting in his personal office, he had invited Dan to a small windowless conference room. Not even holoviews on the walls, only a few paintings and photographs of Martin Humphries with celebrities of various stripes. Dan recognized the current President of the United States, a dour-faced elderly man in black clerical garb, and Vasily Malik of the GEC.

Leaning back relaxedly in the comfortable padded chair, Dan said, "I guess I have been on the go quite a bit since we last met."

Sitting across the table from Dan, Humphries clasped his hands together atop its gleaming surface. "To tell you the truth, Dan, I get the feeling you're trying to screw me out of this fusion operation."

Laughing, Dan said, "I wouldn't do that, Marty, even if I could."

Humphries laughed back at him. It seemed more than a little forced to Dan.

"Tell me something," Dan said. "You didn't stumble across Duncan by accident, did you?"

Humphries smiled more genuinely. "Not entirely. When I started Humphries Space Systems I went out and backed more than a dozen small, long-shot research groups. I figured that one of them was bound to come through with something. You ought to see some of the kooks I had to deal with!"

"I can imagine," Dan said, grinning. He'd had his share of earnest zanies trying to convince him of one wild scheme or another over the years.

"I got lucky with Duncan and this fusion rocket," Humphries went on, looking pleased with himself.

"It was more than luck," Dan said. "You were damned smart."

"Maybe," Humphries agreed. "It only takes one swing to hit a home run."

"And it doesn't cost much, either, at the laboratory stage."

Nodding, Humphries said, "If more people backed basic research we'd get ahead a lot faster."

"I should've done it myself," Dan admitted.

"Yes, you should have."

"My mistake."

"Okay then, where do we stand?" Humphries asked.

"Well . . . you financed Duncan's original work."

"Including the flight tests that you saw," Humphries pointed out.

Dan nodded. "I've been trying to put together the financing for building a full-scale spacecraft and sending a team out to the Belt."

"I can finance that. I told you I'd put up the money."

"Yep. But it'd cost me a good chunk of Astro Corporation, wouldn't it?"

"We can negotiate a reasonable price. It won't cost you a cent out of pocket."

"But you'd wind up owning Astro," Dan said flatly.

Something flashed in Humphries's eyes for a moment. But he quickly put on a synthetic smile. "How could I take over Astro Manufacturing, Dan? I know you wouldn't part with more than fifteen-twenty percent of your company."

"More like five or ten percent," Dan said.

"Even worse, for me. I'd be a minority stockholder. I wouldn't even be able to put anybody on the board—except myself, I imagine."

Dan said, "H'mm."

Hunching closer, Humphries said, "I hear you're going the nanotech route."

"You hear right," Dan replied. "Dr. Cardenas is returning to Selene to head up the job."

"I hadn't thought about using nanomachines. Makes sense."

"Brings the cost down."

"Makes my investment smaller," Humphries said, straight-faced.

Tired of the fencing, Dan said, "Look, here's the way I see this. We bring Selene in as a third partner. They provide the facilities and nanotech personnel."

"I thought you were recruiting retirees," Humphries said.

"Some," Dan admitted, "but we'll still need Selene's active help."

"So we've got a third partner," Humphries said sullenly.

"I want to form a separate corporation, separate and apart from Astro. We'll each be one-third owners: you, me, and Selene."

Humphries sat up straighter. "What's the matter, Dan, don't you trust me?"

"Not as far as I can throw the Rock of Gibraltar."

Another man might have laughed grudgingly. Humphries glared at Dan for a moment, his face reddening. But then he got himself under control and shrugged nonchalantly.

"You don't want to let me have any Astro stock, do you?"

"Not if I can help it," Dan said pleasantly.

"But then what are you bringing into this deal? I've got the money, Selene's got the personnel and facilities. What do you offer?"

Dan smiled his widest. "My management skills. After all, I'm the one who came up with the nanotech idea."

"I thought it was Stavenger's idea."

Dan felt his brows hike up. And his respect for Humphries's sources of information. *He didn't get that from Pancho; I didn't tell her. Does he have Stavenger's office bugged? Or infiltrated?*

"Tell you what," said Dan. "Just to show you that I'm not such a suspicious sonofabitch, I'll chip in five percent of Astro's stock. Out of my personal holdings."

"Ten," Humphries immediately shot back.

"Five."

"Come on, Dan. You can't get out of this so cheaply."

Dan looked up at the paneled ceiling, took a deep breath, looked back into Humphries's icy gray eyes.

Finally he said, "Seven."

"Eight."

Dan cocked his head slightly, then murmured, "Deal."

Humphries smiled, genuinely this time, and echoed, "Deal."

Each man extended his hand across the table. As they shook hands, Dan said to himself, Count your fingers after he lets go.

SELENE NANOTECHNOLOGY LABORATORY

Dan was watching intently as Kris Cardenas manipulated the roller dial with one manicured finger, her eyes riveted on the scanning microscope's display screen. The image took shape on the screen, blurred, then came into crisp focus.

The picture was grainy, gray on gray, with a slightly greenish cast. Dan could make out a pair of fuel tanks with piping that led to a spherical chamber. On the other side of the sphere was a narrow straight channel that ended in the flared bell of a rocket nozzle.

"It's the whole assembly!" he blurted.

Cardenas turned toward him with a bright California smile. "Not bad for a month's work, is it?"

Dan grinned back at her. "Kinda small, though, don't you think?"

They were alone in the nanotech lab this late at night. The other workstations were empty, all the cubicles dark, the ceiling lights turned down to their dim nighttime setting. Only in the corner where Dan and Cardenas sat on a pair of swivel stools were the overhead lights at their full brightness. The massive gray tubing of the scanning microscope loomed above them both like a hulking robot. Dan marveled inwardly that the big, bulky machine was capable of revealing individual atoms.

Cardenas said, "Size isn't important right now. It's the pattern that counts."

"Swell," said Dan. "If I want to send a team of bacteria to the Belt, you've got the fusion drive all set for them."

"Don't be obtuse, Dan."

"I was trying to be funny."

Cardenas did not appreciate his humor. Tapping a bright blue-polished fingernail against the microscope's display screen, she said, "We've programmed this set of nanos to understand the pattern of your fusion system: the tankage, the reactor chamber, the MHD channel, and the rocket nozzle."

"Plus all the plumbing."

"And the plumbing, yes. Now that they've learned the pattern, it's just a matter of programming them to build the same thing at full scale."

Dan scratched his chin, then said, "And the full-scale job will be able to handle the necessary pressures and temperatures?"

"Most of it's built of diamond."

That wasn't an answer to his question, Dan realized. Okay, so the virus-sized nanomachines could take individual atoms of carbon from a pile of soot and put them together one by one to build structures with the strength and thermal properties of pure diamond.

"But will that do the job?" he asked Cardenas.

Her lips became a tight line. She was obviously unhappy about something.

"Problem?" Dan asked.

"Not really," Cardenas said, "But . . ."

"But what? I've got to know, Kris. I'm hanging my *cojones* out in the breeze on this."

Raising both hands in a don't-blame-me gesture, she said, "It's Duncan. He refuses to come up here. None of his team will leave Earth."

Dan had known that Duncan, Vertientes, and the rest of the team had opted to remain Earthside and communicate with Cardenas and her nanotech people electronically.

"You talk to him every day, don't you?"

"Sure we do. We even have interactive VR sessions, if you can call them interactive."

Feeling alarmed, Dan asked, "What's wrong?"

"It's that damned three-second lag," Cardenas said. "You can't really be interactive, you can't even have a normal conversation when there's three seconds between your question and their answer every blasted time."

"Is it actually hindering your work?"

She made a face somewhere between a grimace and a pout. "Not hindering, exactly. It's just so damned inconvenient! And time-consuming. Sometimes we have to go over a thing two or three times just to be sure we've heard them right. It soaks up time and makes everybody edgy."

Dan thought it over. "Maybe I can talk them into coming up here."

"I've tried to, god knows. Duncan won't budge. Neither will any of his people. They're terrified of nanomachines."

"No!"

"Yes. Even Professor Vertientes. You'd think he'd know better, at his age."

"They're scared of nanomachines?"

"They won't admit it, of course," said Cardenas. "They say that they might not be allowed to return to Earth if the authorities know that they've been working with nanomachines. I think that's a crock; they're just plain scared."

"Maybe not," Dan said. "Those Earthside bureaucrats get wonky ideas, especially about nanotechnology. I sure haven't told anybody that I'm dealing with nanomachines."

Her brows shot up. "But everybody knows—"

"Everybody knows that *you* and your staff are building a fusion rocket with nanos. As far as the general public is concerned, I don't come near 'em. I'm a bigshot tycoon, I don't get involved in the dirty work. I've never even been in your lab."

Cardenas nodded with newfound understanding. "That's why you sneak in here late at night."

"I don't sneak anywhere," Dan said, with great dignity. "I've never been here. Period."

She laughed. "Of course."

"Kris," he said, more seriously, "I think Duncan and the rest of them have legitimate reasons to be scared of coming up here and working with you. I'm afraid you're going to have to live with that three-second lag. It's their safety net."

Cardenas took a deep breath. "If I have to."

"You've accomplished a helluva lot in just four weeks," Dan pointed out.

"I suppose that's true. It's just . . . it'd be so much easier if we could all work together under the same roof."

Smiling gently, Dan said, "I never promised you a rose garden."

She was about to reply when the door to the corridor banged open, all the way across the mostly-darkened laboratory. Instinctively, Dan started to duck behind the big microscope tube, like a boy hiding from his mother.

Then he recognized the hulking, shaggy, red-bearded figure of Big George Ambrose.

"That you, Dan?" George called as he strode between workstations toward them. "Been lookin' everywhere for you, y'know."

Despite his size, George moved gracefully, light on his feet and perfectly at home in the low lunar gravity.

"I'm not here," Dan growled.

"Right. But if you were, I'd hafta tell you that Pancho Lane's missin'."

"Missing?"

"Not in her quarters," George said as he approached. "Not in any of the Astro offices. Not in the spaceport or the Grand Plaza. Not anyplace I've looked. Blyleven's worried about her."

Frank Blyleven was chief of Astro's security department. Dan glanced at Cardenas, then said to George, "She could be in someone else's quarters, you know."

George looked surprised at the idea. "Pancho? She doesn't have a guy and she doesn't sleep around."

"I wouldn't worry—"

"She didn't show up at the office t'day. She's never missed an hour of work, let alone a whole day."

That worried Dan. "Didn't show up at all?"

"I asked everybody. No Pancho, all day. I been lookin' for her all night. Nowhere in sight."

"Did you ask her roommate?"

"Mandy Cunningham? She was out havin' dinner with Humphries."

"She should be back by now."

George made a leering smirk. "Maybe. Maybe not."

Turning to Cardenas, Dan said, "I'd better look into this. George is right, Pancho's had her nose to the grindstone ever since she came up here."

"So maybe she's taking a little r and r," Cardenas said, unruffled.

"Maybe," Dan admitted. But he didn't think so.

PELICAN BAR

Pancho had spent the entire day being invisible.

The night before, she had gone to the Pelican Bar for a little relaxation after another long, grueling day of study and simulation runs in the Astro office complex.

The incongruously-named Pelican Bar had been started by a homesick Floridian who had come to Selene back in the days when the underground community was still known as Moonbase. Hired to be the base's quartermaster, he had developed a case of hypertension that kept him from returning to Earth until a regime of exercise and medication brought his blood pressure under control.

He took the pills, largely ignored the exercise, and started the bar in his own quarters as a clandestine drinking club for his cronies. Over the years he had grown into a paunchy little barrel of a man, his bald head gleaming under the ceiling fluorescents, a perpetual gap-toothed smile on his fleshy, tattooed face. He often told his patrons that he had found his true calling as a bartender: "A dispenser of cheer and honest advice," as he put it.

The bar was several levels down from the Grand Plaza, the size of two ordinary living suites, carved out of the lunar rock. And quiet. No music, unless someone wanted to sit at the synthesizer that lay dusty and rarely touched in the farthest, most shadowy corner of the room. The only background noise in the place was the buzz of many conversations.

Pelicans were everywhere. A holographic video behind the bar showed them skimming bare centimeters above the placid waters of the Gulf of Mexico against a background of condo towers and beachfront hotels that had long since gone underwater. Photos of pelicans adorned every wall. Statues of pelicans stood at each end of the bar and pelican mobiles hung from the smoothed-rock ceiling. A meter-tall stuffed toy pelican stood by the bartender's computer, dressed in garish, outlandish Florida tourist's garb and peering at the drinkers through square little granny sunglasses.

Pancho liked the Pelican Bar. She much preferred it to the tidy little bistro up in the Grand Plaza where the tourists and executives did their drinking. The Pelican was a sort of home away from home; she came often enough to be considered one of the steady customers, and she usually bought as many rounds as any of the drinkers clustered around the bar.

She exchanged greetings with the other regulars while the owner, working behind the bar as usual, broke away from an intense conversation with a despondent-looking little redhead to waddle down the bar and pour Pancho her favorite, a margarita with real lime from Selene's hydroponic fruit orchard.

Although a set of booths lined the back wall, there were no stools at the bar itself. You did your drinking standing up, and when you could no longer stand your buddies took you home. House rules.

Pancho had wedged herself into the crowd in between a total stranger and a retired engineer she knew only as a fellow Pelican patron whose parents had hung the unlikely name of Isaac Walton around his neck. The word was he had originally come to the Moon to get away from jokes about fishing.

Walton's face always seemed slightly askew; one side of it did not quite match the other. Even his graying hair seemed thicker on one side than the other. Normally a happy drinker, he looked morose as he leaned both elbows on the bar and stared into his tall, frosted drink.

"Hi, Ike," Pancho said brightly. "Why the long face?"

"Anniversary," Walton mumbled.

"So where's your wife?"

He gave Pancho a bleary look. "Not my wedding anniversary."

"Then what?"

Walton stood up a little straighter. He was about Pancho's height, stringy and loose-jointed. "The eighth anniversary of my being awarded the Selene Achievement Prize."

"Achievement Prize?" she asked. "What's that?"

The bartender broke into their conversation. "Hey, Ike, don't you think you've had enough for one night?"

Walton nodded solemnly. "Yup. You're right."

"So why don't you go home to your wife," the bartender suggested. Pancho heard something more than friendliness in his tone, an undercurrent of—jeeps, she thought, he almost sounds like a cop.

"You're right, pal. Absolutely right. I'm going home. Whatta I owe you?"

The bartender waved a meaty hand in the air. "Forget it. Anniversary present."

"Thank you very much." Turning to Pancho, he said, "You wanna walk me home?"

She glanced at the bartender, who still looked unusually grim, then shrugged and said, "Sure, Ike. I'll walk you home."

He wasn't as unsteady on his feet as Pancho had thought he'd be. Once outside the bar Walton seemed more depressed than drunk. Yet he nodded or said hello to everyone they passed.

"What's the Achievement Prize?" Pancho asked as they walked down the corridor.

"Kind of a secret."

"Oh."

"I did the impossible for them, y'see, but I did it too late to be of any use and they don't want anybody to know about it so they gave me the prize as hush money and told me to keep my trap shut."

Confused, Pancho asked, "About what?"

For the first time that evening, Walton broke into a smile. "My cloak of invisibility," he answered.

Little by little Pancho wormed the story out of him. Walton had been working with Professor Zimmerman, the nanotech genius, when the old U.N. had sent Peacekeeper troops to seize Moonbase.

"Stavenger was in a sweat to develop nonlethal weapons so we could defend ourselves against the Peacekeepers when they got here without killing any of them," Walton said, growing steadier and gloomier with each step along the corridor. "Zimmerman promised Stavenger he'd come up with a way to make our guys invisible, but the bastards killed him when they attacked. Suicide bomber got down to his lab and blew the old man to smithereens."

"Himself, too?" Pancho asked.

"I did say 'suicide,' didn't I? Anyway, the so-called war ended pretty quick and we got our independence. That's when we changed the name from Moonbase to Selene."

"I know."

"For a while there I didn't have anything to do. I'd been Zimmerman's assistant and now the old man was gone."

Walton had doggedly kept working on Zimmerman's idea of finding a method for making a person invisible. And eventually he succeeded.

"But who needs to be invisible?" Walton asked. Before Pancho could answer he went on, "Only somebody who's up to no damn good, that's who. Spies. Assassins. Crooks. Thieves."

Selene's governing council decided to mothball Walton's invention. Bury it so that no one would even know it existed.

"So they gave me the big fat prize to keep me quiet. It's a pension, really. I can live in comfort—as long as I stay in Selene and keep my mouth shut."

"Sounds cool to me," Pancho said, trying to cheer him up.

But Walton shook his head. "You don't understand, Pancho. I'm a freaking genius and nobody knows it. I've made a terrific invention and it's useless. I'm not even supposed to mention it to anybody."

Pancho said, "Aren't you taking a chance, talking to me about it?"

He gave her a sidelong glance. "Aw, hell, Pancho, I hadda tell somebody tonight or bust. And I can trust you, can't I? You're not gonna steal it and go out and assassinate anybody, are you?"

" 'Course not," Pancho answered immediately. But she was thinking that it might be a hoot to be invisible now and then.

"Wanna see it?" Walton asked.

"The invisibility dingus?"

"Yeah."

"If it's invisible, how can I see it?"

Walton broke into a cackle of laughter. Clapping Pancho on the back, he said, "That's what I like about you, Pancho ol' pal. You're okay, with a capital oke."

Walton turned down the next cross-corridor and led Pancho up to the level just below the Grand Plaza, where most of Selene's life-support machinery chugged away, purifying the air, recycling the water, rectifying the electrical current coming in from the solar farms. Pumps clattered. The air hummed and crackled. The ceilings of these chambers were rough, unfinished rock. Pancho knew that on their other side was either the manicured lawn of the Grand Plaza or the raw regolith of the Moon's surface itself. And along a corridor not far from where they walked lay the catacombs.

"Isn't the dingus under lock and key?" Pancho asked as Walton led her past a long row of metal lockers.

"They don't even know it exists. They think I destroyed it when they gave me their lousy prize. Destroy it, hell! I'll never destroy it. It's the only one in the whole wide solar system."

"Wow."

He nodded absently. "And it's not a 'dingus,' it's a stealth suit."

"Stealth suit," Pancho echoed.

"Like a wetsuit, covers you from head to toe," he explained in a hushed voice, as if afraid someone would hear him. Pancho strained to listen to him over the background hum and chatter of the machinery.

Pancho followed Walton down the long row of metal lockers. The corridor smelled dusty, unused. The overhead lights were spaced so far apart that there were shadowy pools of darkness every few meters. Walton stopped in front of a locker identified by a serial number. Pancho saw that it had an electronic security lock.

Feeling uneasy, Pancho asked, "Don't they have any guards patrolling up here?"

"Nah. What for? There's cameras at the other end of the corridor, but this old tunnel's like an attic. People store junk up here, personal stuff they don't have room for down in their quarters."

Walton tapped out the security code on the electronic lock and pulled the metal door open. It squealed slightly, as if complaining.

"There it is," he said in a hushed voice.

Hanging inside the locker was a limp bodysuit, deep black.

"Ain't she a beauty?" Walton said as he carefully, lovingly, took the suit from the locker and held it up by its hanger for Pancho to admire.

"Looks almost like a wetsuit," Pancho said, wondering how it could make someone invisible. It glittered darkly in the feeble light from the overhead fluorescents, as if spangled with sequins made of onyx.

"The suit's covered with nanocameras and projectors, only a couple of molecules thick. Drove me nuts getting 'em to work right, lemme tell you. I *earned* that prize money."

"Uh-huh," Pancho said, fingering one of the gloved sleeves. The fabric felt soft, pliable, yet somehow almost gritty, like grains of sand.

"The cameras pick up the scenery around you," Walton was explaining. "The projectors display it. Somebody standing in front of you sees what's behind you. Somebody on your left sees what's on your right. Just like they're looking through you. To all intents and purposes you're invisible."

"It really works?" she asked.

"Computer built into the belt controls it," Walton said. "Batteries are probably flat, but I can charge 'em up easy enough." He pointed to a set of electrical outlets on the smoothed-rock wall of the corridor, opposite the lockers.

"But it really works?" she repeated.

He smiled like a proud father. "Want to try it on?"

Grinning back at him, Pancho said, "Sure!"

While Pancho wriggled into the snug-fitting suit Walton plugged the two palm-sized batteries into the nearby electrical outlet. By the time she had pulled on the gloves and fitted the hood over her head, he was snapping the fully-charged batteries into their slots on the suit's waist.

"Okay," Walton said, looking her over carefully. "Now pull the face mask down and seal it to the hood."

Narrow goggles covered Pancho's eyes. "I must look like a terrorist, Ike," she muttered, the fabric of the mask's lining tickling her lips.

"In a minute you won't look like anything at all," he said. "Unlatch the safety cover on your belt and press the pressure switch."

Pancho popped the tiny plastic cover and touched the switch beneath it. "Okay, now what?" she asked.

"Give it fifteen seconds."

Pancho waited. "So?"

With a lopsided grin, Walton said, "Hold your hand up in front of your face."

Pancho lifted her arm. A pang of shock bolted through her. "I can't see it!"

"Damn right you can't. You're invisible."

"I am?"

"Can you see yourself?"

Pancho couldn't. Arms, legs, booted feet: she could feel them as normally as always but could not see them.

"You got a full-length mirror in your locker?" she asked excitedly.

"Why the hell would I have a full-length mirror in there?"

"I want to see what I look like!"

"Cripes, Pancho, you don't look like anything. You're completely invisible."

Pancho laughed excitedly. She made up her mind at that moment to borrow Ike's stealth suit. Without telling him about it, of course.

HUMPHRIES TRUST RESEARCH CENTER

Covered from head to toes in the stealth suit, Pancho crept slowly, silently along the corridor of Martin Humphries's palatial underground house. She had come down to the mansion with Amanda, although Mandy didn't know it.

For weeks Pancho had been dying to root around in Humphries's mansion. The man was so stinky rich, so ruthlessly powerful and sure of himself, Pancho figured that there must be plenty of dirt under his fingernails. Maybe she could find something that would help Dan. Maybe she could find something that would profit her. Or maybe, she thought, burglarizing Humphries's house would just be a hoot, a refreshing break from the endless hours of study that she and Mandy were grinding through. Besides, it'd be fun to wipe that smug smile off the Humper's face.

So she had borrowed the stealth suit from Walton's locker the very next morning after he'd shown it to her. Pancho had gone to bed that night arguing with herself over whether or not she should ask Ike's permission to use the suit. She had awakened firmly convinced that the less Ike knew the better off each of them would be. So, with a tote bag swinging from her shoulder, she'd gone to the catacombs instead of to work with Mandy, then detoured to the dusty, seldom-used corridor where Walton had stashed the suit. She remembered the singsong of the locker's electronic security code and tapped it out without a flaw.

With a glance at the tiny red eye of the security camera on the ceiling at the far end of the corridor, Pancho quickly bundled the suit into her tote bag. Security people can't watch every screen every minute, she told herself. Besides, even if one of 'em's watchin', I ain't doin' anything to rouse an alarm.

Pancho then went back to her quarters. Amanda was busily at work in the simulations lab; Pancho had the apartment to herself. Immediately she started putting on the stealth suit.

Once she got it on—and saw in the bedroom's full-length mirror that she was truly invisible—she went out to test the suit. It worked wonderfully well. Pancho walked slowly, carefully, through Selene's corridors, threading her way through the pedestrian traffic. Now and then someone would glance her way, as if they'd seen something out of the corner of their eyes. A stray reflection from the overhead lights, Pancho thought, an unavoidable momentary glitter off the array of nanocameras and projectors. But no one really saw her; she drifted through the crowds like an unseen phantom.

She spent the day wandering ghostlike through Selene, gaining confidence in the suit and her ability to use it. The suit fit her snugly, but the boots attached to its leggings were Ike's size, not her own. Pancho had solved that problem by wadding stockings into the boots. They weren't exactly comfortable, but she could walk in them well enough.

For kicks she lifted a soyburger from the counter of the fast-food cafeteria up in the Grand Plaza when no one was working the place except a dumbass robot. She immediately realized, though, that if anyone saw a soyburger floating in midair it would cause a fuss, so she dropped it into the recycler at the end of the counter before anyone noticed her.

By mid-afternoon Pancho returned briefly to her quarters, took off the suit, and dashed out for a quick meal. She was famished. Being invisible makes you hungry, she joked to herself. By the time Amanda returned from her day's work and began dressing for her dinner with Martin Humphries, Pancho was back in the stealth suit, standing quietly in a corner of the bedroom, waiting for Amanda to finish her damned primping and go out.

A cloak of invisibility, Pancho thought as she rode the escalators a few steps ahead of Amanda, down to Selene's bottom layer. What did they call those fancy suits the toreadors wear? A suit of lights, she remembered. Well, I'm wearing a suit of darkness. A cloak of invisibility.

She had to keep her distance from everyone. If somebody jostled into her they'd know she was there, invisible or not. Pancho felt glad that Selene did not allow pets. A dog would probably have sniffed her out easily.

The escalators got less and less crowded as she went down level after level. By the time she was riding down to the last level, she and Amanda were alone on the moving stairs. Once at the bottom, she waited for Amanda, then fell into step behind her. Mandy was heading for a private little dinner with Humphries. Just the two of them, they thought. Pancho smiled to herself. If the Humper tries anything Mandy doesn't like, I'll coldcock him. I'll be her guardian angel. Then she wondered just how far Mandy was willing to go with Humphries—and how far she could tease him without getting herself into real trouble. Well, she shrugged to herself, Mandy's a grownup, she knows what she's doing. Or she ought to.

Mandy looked like a princess in a fairy tale, wearing a short-sleeved frock of baby blue with a knee-length fringed skirt. Modest enough, Pancho thought, although on Mandy nothing could look really modest. Not in the eyes of a man like Humphries, anyway. Pancho couldn't recall seeing the dress before; Mandy must have bought it in one of Selene's shops. Everything cost a fortune there, except for stuff actually made on the Moon. Is Humphries buying her clothes? Pancho wondered. He hadn't given Mandy any jewelry, she was sure of that. Mandy would have showed it off if he had.

Amanda walked purposively down the length of the corridor and into the grotto that housed the Humphries Trust research garden and house. Humphries was at the front door to greet her, all smiles. Pancho slipped in behind her, nearly brushing Humphries's hand as he pulled the door shut. If the Humper felt anything, he didn't show it. Pancho was in the house and he didn't know it.

As Humphries guided Amanda off to the bar, Pancho stood stock-still in the foyer. A man like Humphries would have a state-of-the-art security system in his home, she reasoned. No matter that the house was in Selene; Humphries would insist on topflight security. He might give the human staff the night off for his dates, but he wouldn't turn off his alarm systems. Motion sensors were her big worry. Humphries obviously wouldn't have any working in the residential wing of the house. But the offices would be another thing altogether. She could see the long, spacious living room and the corridor that led to the formal dining room and, beyond it, the library/bar. That was the direction Humphries and Amanda had gone.

On the other side of the foyer was a single closed door. Pancho guessed that it opened onto the suite of offices and laboratories that the ecologists used. Would he have motion sensors set up in there? Probably not, she thought, but if he did . . .

There must be a central control for the security system. Most likely in Humphries's own bedroom or his office. His bedroom? Pancho grinned at the thought. That's one room in the house where he'd have any motion sensors definitely turned off!

Slowly, on tiptoes despite the thick carpeting, Pancho made her way up to the second floor. The master bedroom was easy to find: beautifully-carved double doors at the end of the hallway. She eased the door open. No sirens, no hooting klaxons. Could be silent alarms, she told herself, but if he's dismissed the servants for the night he'll have to come up here his own self, and I can handle that, easy.

The room was sumptuous, and Humphries's bed was enormous, like a tennis court. That bed could handle a whole squad of cheerleaders, she thought. Prob'ly has, Pancho told herself.

Through a half-open door she saw a desktop computer, its screen saver showing some old master's painting of a nude woman. As Pancho cautiously approached the door and eased it all the way open, the screen's image dissolved into another painting of another nude. Huh! she grunted. Some art lover.

Pancho sat at the desk and saw that the computer had a keyboard attached to it. Tentatively, she pecked at the ENTER key. The artwork vanished, and a honey-warm woman's voice said, "Good evening, Mr. Humphries. The time is eight-twelve and I'm ready to go to work anytime you are."

Frowning, Pancho turned the audio down to zero. The screen displayed a menu of options. Hell, he doesn't have any protection on his programs at all. She pictured Humphries at his computer, too impatient to deal with code words and security safeguards. After all, who'd have the balls to break into his home, his own bedroom?

Grinning from ear to ear, Pancho delved into Martin Humphries's computer files.

It turned out that most of the individual file names were indeed coded and incomprehensible to her. So he does have some security built into his programs, she realized. Many of the files required special keywords. One, though, was labelled BED. Curious, Pancho called it up. The screen went blank, except for the words INITIATING HOLOTANK. An eyeblink later the screen announced STARTING HOLOTANK. Then the screen went to a blank gray, except for a bar across its bottom that bore video commands.

Puzzled, Pancho saw a blur of color reflected off the blanked screen. Turning slightly in the desk chair, she saw that what had appeared to be a cylindrical glass *objet d'art* had metamorphosed into a hologram, a full-color three-dimensional moving picture of Humphries naked in bed with some woman.

Son of a bitch, Pancho said to herself. He vids his own sex life. She watched for a few moments. They weren't doing anything that unusual, or thrilling, for that matter, so Pancho touched the fast-forward button on the screen.

It was downright funny watching Humphries and his women in fast-forward. He's a Humper, all right, Pancho thought as she watched a succession of beautiful naked women performing arduously with him. She recognized the redhead from her first visit to the house. I wonder if they know they're being videoed, she asked herself.

After a half-dozen of Humphries's home videos, Pancho got a little bored. She cut the program and returned to the screen's menu of options, but she had new respect for the program labelled VR – PERSONAL. She looked into just one of its files for a few minutes, then angrily clicked it off, revolted.

The nasty S.O.B. uses his bedmates as models for his virtual reality fantasies, she realized. What he can't get them to do in real life he has them doing in his VR wet dreams. Creep!

With a disgusted shake of her head she decided to leave Humphries's sex life alone and started hacking into the other files.

When she glanced at the digital clock in the corner of the screen, Pancho was shocked to realize that nearly two hours had elapsed. It had been a fruitful time, though. The Humphries Trust was now paying the rent on Susan Lane's cryonic storage unit, a big burden off Pancho's shoulders and a picayune pinprick in the Trust's multibillion funds.

Most of the files were incomprehensible to Pancho; some were technobabble and equations, lots of them were stock manipulations and business deals encoded in so much jargon and legalese that it would take a team of lawyers to decipher them. But now they all contained a new subroutine that allowed Pancho to tap into the files from a remote site. Codeword: Hackensack. Which was just what Pancho was preparing to do.

Got to be careful, though, she warned herself. Don't get greedy enough for him to recognize he's being hacked. A man like Humphries'll have you slapped into the slammer so fast it'll break the sound barrier. Or he'll just have somebody pay you a visit and rip out your arms.

Satisfied with her work, Pancho closed down the computer and left Humphries's office, careful to leave the door ajar just the way she'd found it. As she made her way downstairs, she wondered if Mandy and Humphries were still at dinner, after all this time.

They were. Peeking in on the dining room, Pancho saw the remains of some fancy dessert melting in their dishes, and half-empty flutes of champagne sparkling in the subdued light from the crystal chandelier above the table.

Mandy was saying, ". . . it's certainly beautiful, Martin, and I appreciate your thoughtfulness, but I can't accept it. Really, I can't."

Pancho crept closer, staring. Humphries held an open jewelry case in one hand. It contained a stunning sapphire necklace.

"I got it specially for you," he was saying, his voice almost pleading.

"Martin, you're a dear man, but I can't get myself involved in a relationship now. You of all people should understand that."

"But I don't understand," he said. "Why not?"

"I'll be heading off on the mission in a few months. I might never come back."

"All the more reason to grab whatever happiness we can now, while we can."

Amanda looked genuinely distressed. Shaking her head, she said, "I simply can't, Martin. I can't."

In a gentle whisper he said, "I could have you removed from the mission. I could see to it that you stay here, with me."

"No. Please . . ."

"I could," he repeated, stronger. "By god, that's what I'll do."

"But I don't want you to," Amanda said, alarmed.

"You don't have to go through with it," Humphries insisted. "I know it's dangerous. I had no idea that you're afraid of—"

"Afraid!" Mandy snapped. "I'm not afraid! Simply because I understand the risks involved does *not* mean that I'm afraid."

Humphries puffed out an exasperated breath. "Then you're using the mission as an excuse to keep your distance from me, is that it?"

"No!" Amanda said. "That's not it at all. I simply . . ." Her voice trailed off into silence.

"Then what's wrong?" Humphries asked. "What's the problem? Is it me?"

She stared down at the table for a long, miserable, silent moment. Pancho thought she saw tears glistening in Mandy's eyes. The expression on Humphries's face was somewhere between bafflement and anger.

"Martin, please," Amanda said at last. "We've only known each other for a few weeks. You're a very wonderful man in many ways, but I'm not ready for a meaningful relationship. Not now. Not with this mission coming up. Perhaps afterward, when I return, perhaps then."

Humphries pulled in a deep breath. It seemed obvious to Pancho that he was trying to control his temper.

"I'm not a patient man," he said, his voice low. "I'm not accustomed to waiting."

No, Pancho thought. What you're accustomed to is taking your women up to your bedroom and videoing the whole thing for playback. And then VR games.

"Please bear with me, Martin," Amanda whispered, her voice husky with tears. "Please."

If he tries to get rough with Mandy, Pancho told herself, I'll kick his balls into next week. She wished she'd brought Elly, but the stealth suit was too confining for the snake; she'd left Elly back at her quarters.

Humphries snapped the jewelry case shut with a click that sounded like a gunshot.

"All right," he said tightly. "I'll wait. I wish I'd never started this fusion business."

Amanda made a sad smile. "But then we'd never have met, would we?"

He conceded the point with a hopeless shrug, then got up and led Amanda to the front door of the house.

"Will I see you again?" he asked as he opened the door for her.

"It might be best if we don't, Martin. Not until after I return."

He nodded, grim-faced. Then he grasped both her wrists and said, "I love you, Amanda. I really do."

"I know," she said, and kissed him swiftly, lightly, on the cheek.

She hurried down the walk away from him so quickly that Pancho almost didn't make it through the door before Humphries slammed it shut.

LIVING QUARTERS

P ancho had to sprint up the escalators to get back to the quarters she shared with Amanda before Mandy did. Twice she nearly stumbled and fell; it wasn't easy to run up moving stairs when you can't see your own feet.

It was late enough that the corridors were not crowded. Pancho easily dodged around the few people still up and about, leaving a couple of them bewildered as she brushed past them; they felt certain that someone had just rushed by, yet there was no one in sight. She got to their quarters well ahead of Amanda, powered down the stealth suit as soon as she slid the door shut behind her, stripped to her skivvies, and stuffed the suit under her bed. Elly was snoozing comfortably in her plastic cage, actually a box that still smelled faintly of the strawberries it had carried from China to Selene. Pancho had packed it with several centimeters of gritty regolith dirt, stuck in an artificial cactus, and kept a saucer of water in it for Elly's comfort.

She was kneeling beside the plastic box, pouring fresh water into the saucer when Amanda came in.

Pancho looked up at her roommate. Mandy's eyes were red, as if she'd been crying.

"How'd your date go?" she asked, innocently.

Looking troubled, Amanda said, "Oh, Pancho, I think he wants to marry me."

Pancho got to her feet. "He's not the marrying kind."

"He's been married. Twice."

"That's what I mean."

Amanda sat on her bed. "He . . . he's different from any other man I've ever met."

"Yeah. He's got more money."

"No, it isn't that," Amanda replied. "He's . . ." She searched for a word.

"Horny?" Pancho suggested.

Amanda frowned at her. "He's *powerful*. There's something in his eyes . . . he almost frightens me."

Thinking about Humphries's home videos, Pancho nodded.

"I can't see him again. I simply can't."

She sounded to Pancho as if she were trying to convince herself.

"He's so accustomed to getting whatever he wants," Amanda said, more to herself than Pancho. "He doesn't like being turned away, rejected."

"Nobody does, Mandy."

"But he . . ." Again her words faltered. "Pancho, with other men I could smile and flirt and let it go at that. But Martin won't be satisfied with that. He wants what he wants, and if he doesn't get it he can be . . . I just don't know what he'd do, but he frightens me."

"You think he wants to marry you?"

"He said he loves me."

"Aw hell, Mandy, guys have said that to me, too. All they want is to get into your pants."

"I think he really believes that he loves me."

"That's a strange way to put it."

"Pancho, I can't see him again. There's no telling what he might do. I've got to stay away from him."

Pancho thought that Amanda looked scared. And she's got plenty to be scared of, she told herself.

First thing the following morning, Pancho phoned Dan Randolph and asked to meet with him. One of Randolph's assistants, the big beefy-faced guy with the sweet tenor voice, said he'd call her back. In five minutes, he did. Randolph would see her in his office at ten-fifteen.

Astro Corporation's offices were just down the corridor from the living quarters that the company rented. In most corporations, executive country was conspicuously more luxurious than the regular troops' territory. Not so at Astro. There was no discernible difference along the length of the corridor. As she walked along the row of doors, looking for Randolph's name, Pancho decided that she wouldn't tell him about the stealth suit. She'd returned it first thing that morning to Walton's locker. Ike knew nothing of her borrowing the suit; if there was any bad fallout, he couldn't be blamed for anything.

Randolph looked tense when Pancho was ushered into his office by the big Aussie she'd talked to on the phone.

"Hi, boss," she said brightly.

It was a small office, considering it belonged to the head of a major corporation. There was a desk in one corner, but Randolph was standing by the sofa and cushioned chairs arranged around a coffee table on the opposite side of the room. Pancho saw that the walls were decorated with photos of Astro rockets launching from Earth on tongues of fire and billowing smoke. Nothing personal. No pictures of Randolph himself or anyone else. Pancho grinned inwardly when she saw that Randolph's desk was cluttered with papers, despite the computer built into it. The paperless office was still a myth, she realized.

Gesturing to the sofa, he said, "Have a seat. Have you had breakfast?"

Instead of sitting down, Pancho asked, "Is that a trick question? Astro employees are up at the crack of dawn every day, boss, and twice on Sundays."

Randolph laughed. "Coffee? Tea? Anything?"

"Can I use your computer for a minute?" she asked.

He looked puzzled, but said, "Sure, go ahead." Louder, he called, "Computer, guest voice."

Pancho went to the desk and leaned over the upright display screen. She gave her name and the computer came to life. Within a few seconds, she waved Randolph over to look at the screen.

He peered at the display. "What the hell's that?"

"Martin Humphries's personal menu of programs."

"Humphries?" Randolph sank into his desk chair.

"Yep. I hacked into his machine last night. You can tap in anytime you want."

Randolph looked up at Pancho, then back at his screen. "Without his knowing it?"

"Oh, he'll figger it out sooner or later, I guess. But right now he doesn't know it."

"How the hell did you do this?"

Pancho smiled at him. "Magic."

"H'mp," Randolph grunted. "It's a shame you couldn't do this a few days earlier."

"How come?"

"We're partners now."

"You and Humphries? Partners?"

"Humphries, Selene and Astro. We've formed a limited partnership: Starpower, Limited."

"Hot spit! Where can I buy stock?"

"It's not public. Duncan and his people will get a block of shares, but otherwise, it's Humphries, me, and the good citizens of Selene. It should help keep Selene's taxes down, if it works."

Feeling a bit disappointed, Pancho grumbled, "Oh, just the big boys, huh?"

Randolph gave her a sly grin. "I suppose," he said, running a finger across his chin, "that we'll award a few shares here and there, for exceptional performances."

"Like piloting a bird to the Belt and back."

Randolph nodded.

"Okay," Pancho said, with enthusiasm. "Meanwhile, you can poke into Humphries's files anytime you want to."

Randolph cleared the screen with a single, sharp, "Exit." To Pancho, he said, "You're wasting your time jockeying spacecraft. You make a mighty fine spy, kid."

"I'd rather fly than spy," she said.

Randolph looked at her. He's got really neat eyes, she thought. Gray, but not cold. Deep. Flecked with gold. Nice eyes.

"I'm not sure that I want to poke into Humphries's files," he said.

"No?"

"A man named Stimson was the U.S. Secretary of State back a century or more ago," Randolph said. "When he found out that the State Department was routinely intercepting the mail from the foreign embassies in Washington he stopped the practice. He said, 'Gentlemen do not read each other's mail.' Or something like that."

Pancho snorted. "Maybe you're a gentleman, but Humphries sure ain't."

"I think you're half right."

"Which half?"

Instead of answering, Randolph tapped a button on the phone console. The big Australian came through the door from the outer office almost instantly.

"You two know each other?" Randolph asked. Without waiting for a reply from either of them, he said, "George Ambrose, Pancho Lane."

"Pleased," said Big George. Pancho made a quick smile.

"George, who do we have who can download a complete hard drive without letting the hard drive's owner know it?"

Big George glanced at Pancho, then asked, "You want this done as quiet as possible, right?"

"Absolutely right."

"Then I'll do it meself."

"You?"

"Don't look so surprised," George said. "I used to be an engineer, before I hooked up with you."

"You were a fugitive from justice before you hooked up with me," Randolph countered.

"Yeah, yeah, but before that. I came to the Moon to teleoperate tractors up on the surface. My bloody degree's in software architecture, for chrissakes."

"I didn't know that," Randolph said.

"Well now you do. So what needs doing here?"

"I'd like you to work with Pancho here. She'll explain the problem."

George looked at her. "Okay. When do we start?"

"Now," said Randolph. Then, to Pancho, he added, "You can tell George anything you'd tell me."

"Sure," Pancho agreed. But in her mind she added, Maybe.

FACTORY #4

T his is more like it," said Dan.

He heard Kris Cardenas's nervous laughter in his helmet earphones.

There were five of them standing on the factory floor, encased in white spacesuits like a team of astronauts or tourists out for a jaunt on the Moon's surface. Before them, on the broad, spacious floor of the otherwise empty factory, stood a set of spherical fuel tanks, the smaller sphere of a fusion reaction chamber, and the unfinished channel of an MHD generator, all connected by sturdy-looking piping and surrounded by crates of various powdered metals and bins of soot: pure carbon dust. Dan, Cardenas and three of her nanotechnicians stood in a group, encased in their spacesuits, watching the results of the nanomachines' ceaseless work.

It was daylight outside, Dan knew. Through the open sides of the factory he saw the brilliant sunlight glaring harshly against the barren lunar landscape. But inside the factory, with its curved roof cutting off the glow from the Sun and Earth, the components of the fusion system looked dark and dull, like the unpolished diamond that they were.

"We start on the pumps next," Cardenas said, "as soon as the MHD channel is finished. And then the rocket nozzles."

Dan heard an edge in her voice. She did not like being out on the surface. Despite all her years of living on the Moon—or maybe because of them—being outside bothered her.

Selene's factories were built out on the Moon's surface, exposed to the vacuum of space, almost completely automated or run remotely by operators safe in control centers underground.

"You okay, Kris?" he asked.

"I'd feel better downstairs," she answered frankly.

"Okay, then, let's go. I'm sorry I dragged you out here. I just wanted to see for myself how we're doing."

"It's all right," she said, but she turned and started toward the airlock hatch and the tractor that had carried them to the factory.

"I know that the vacuum out here is great for industrial processing," she said, apologizing. "It just scares the bejesus out of me."

"Even buttoned up nice and cozy in a spacesuit?" Dan asked, walking across the factory floor alongside her.

"Maybe it's the suit," she said. "Maybe I'm a closet claustrophobe."

Contamination was something that flatlanders from Earth took for granted. Living on a planet teeming with life, from bacteria to whales, thick with pollution from human and natural sources, and deep within a turbulent atmosphere that transports spores, dust, pollen, smog, moisture and other contaminants everywhere, cleanliness for Earthsiders was a matter of degree. That was why Dan, with his immune system weakened by the radiation doses he'd been exposed to in space, wore filter plugs and sanitary masks when he was on Earth.

In the hard vacuum of the lunar surface, a thousand times better than the vacuum of low Earth orbit, not only was the environment clean of external pollution sources, the contaminants inside most materials could be removed virtually for free. Microscopic gas bubbles trapped inside metals percolated out of the metal's crystal structure and boiled off into the void. Thus Selene's factories were out on the lunar surface, open to the purifying vacuum of the Moon.

"We don't need to go through the carwash again," Dan said, touching the arm of Cardenas's suit. "We can go straight to the tractor."

He walked around the bulky airlock and hopped off the concrete slab that formed the factory floor, dropping in lunar slow-motion three meters to the regolith. His boots puffed up a little cloud of dust that floated lazily up halfway to his knees.

Cardenas came to the lip of the slab, hesitated, then jumped down to where Dan waited for her.

Like all the lunar factories, this one was built on a thick concrete platform to keep the factory floor above the dusty ground. With no winds, there was little danger of contaminants blowing in from the outside. A curving dome of honeycomb lunar aluminum protected the factory from the constant infall of micrometeoroids and the hard radiation from the Sun and deep space.

The most worrisome source of pollution came from the humans who occasionally entered the factories, even though they had to wear spacesuits. Before they were allowed onto the factory floor, Dan and the others had to go through the "carwash," a special airlock equipped with electrostatic scrubbers and special powdered detergents that removed the traces of oil, perspiration and other microscopic contaminants that clung to the spacesuits' outer surfaces.

As the tractor slowly trundled back to Selene's main airlock, Dan thought about what he had just seen. Before his eyes, the MHD channel was growing: slowly, he admitted, but it was visibly getting longer as the virus-sized nanomachines took carbon and other atoms from the supply bins and locked them into place like kids building a tinkertoy city.

"How much longer?" he asked into the microphone built into his helmet.

Cardenas, sitting beside him, understood his question. "Three weeks, if they go as programmed."

"Three weeks?" Dan blurted. "Looks like they're almost finished now."

"They've still got to finish the MHD channel, which is a pretty tricky piece of work. High-current-density electrodes, superconducting magnets and all. Then comes the pumps, which is no bed of roses, and finally the rocket nozzles, which are also complex: buckyball microtubes carrying cryogenic hydrogen running a few centimeters away from a ten-thousand-degree plasma flow. Then there's—"

"Okay, okay," Dan said, throwing up his gloved hands. "Three weeks."

"That's the schedule."

Dan knew the schedule. He had been hoping for better news from Cardenas. Over the past six weeks his lawyers had hammered out the details of the new Starpower, Ltd. partnership. Humphries's lawyers had niggled over every detail, while Selene's legal staff had breezed through the negotiation with little more than a cursory examination of the agreement, thanks largely to Doug Stavenger's prodding.

So now it was all in place. Dan had the funding to make the fusion rocket a reality, and he still had control of Astro Manufacturing. Astro was staggering financially, but Dan calculated that the company could hold together until the profits from the fusion system started rolling in.

Still, he constantly pushed Cardenas to go faster. It was going to be a tight race: Astro had already started construction of its final solar power satellite. When that one's finished, Dan knew, we go sailing over the disaster curve. No new space construction contracts in sight.

"Can't this buggy go any faster?" Cardenas asked, testily.

"Full throttle, ma'am," said the imperturbable technician at the controls.

To take her mind off her fears of being out in the open, Dan asked her, "Did you see this morning's news from Earthside?"

"The food riots in Delhi? Yeah, I saw it."

"They're starving, Kris. If the monsoon fails again this year there's going to be a monster famine, and it'll spread a long way."

"Not much we can do about," Cardenas said.

"Not yet," Dan muttered.

"They got themselves into this mess," she said tightly, "breeding like hamsters."

She's really bitter, Dan thought. I wonder how she'd feel if her husband and kids had decided to stay on the Moon with her. With a sigh, he admitted, She's got plenty to be bitter about.

Big George was waiting for Dan in his private office, sitting on the sofa, a sheaf of printouts scattered across the coffee table.

"What's all this?" Dan asked, sitting in the chair at the end of the coffee table. When George sat on the couch there really wasn't much room for anyone else.

"Stuff I lifted from Humphries's files," George said, his red-bearded face wrinkled with worry. "He's out for your balls, y'know."

"I know."

Tapping a blunt finger on the pile of printouts, George said, "He's buyin' every share of Astro stock he can get his hands on. Quietly. No greenmail, no big fuss, but he's pushin' his brokers to buy at any price."

"Great," Dan grunted. "Maybe the damned stock will go up a little."

George grinned. "That'd be good. Been in free fall long enough."

"You're not thinking of selling, are you?"

With a laugh, George replied, "The amount I've got? Wouldn't make any difference, one way or the other."

Dan was not amused. "If you ever do want to sell, you come to me first, understand? I'll buy at the market price."

"Humphries is buyin' at two points above the fookin' market price."

"Is he?"

"In some cases, where big blocks of stock are involved."

"Son of a bitch," Dan said fervently, pronouncing each word distinctly. "He knows I don't have the cash to buy out the minor stockholders."

"It's not all that bad," George said. "I did a calculation. At the rate he's acquiring Astro shares, it'll take him two years to buy up a majority position."

Dan stared off into space, thinking hard. "Two years. We could be making profits from the Asteroid Belt by then. Should be, if everything goes right."

"And if it doesn't go right?"

Dan shrugged. "Then Humphries will take control of Astro and throw me out on my butt."

"I'll take his head off his fookin' shoulders first," George growled.

"A lovely sentiment, pal, but then we'd have to deal with his lawyers."

George rolled his eyes toward heaven.

GRAND PLAZA

This is getting silly, Pancho thought. Humphries doesn't trust phones or electronic links, too easy to tap, he says. So we have to meet face-to-face, in person, but in places where we won't be noticed together. And he's running out of places.

He had stopped inviting Pancho to his home, down at the bottom level. Worried about somebody seeing her down there where she doesn't belong, he claimed. But Pancho knew he'd stopped inviting her down there once she'd introduced him to Mandy. So his house was now out.

Going outside on tourist jaunts is dumb, she thought. Besides, sooner or later some tourist is gonna recognize the high and mighty Martin Humphries on his bus. And how many times can an Astro employee take an afternoon off to go on a bus ride up on the surface? It's silly.

So now she was strolling along one of the paved paths that meandered through the Grand Plaza. Lots of grass and flowery shrubs and even some trees. Nothing as lush as Humphries had down at his grotto, but the Plaza was pleasant, relaxed, open and green.

For a town that's only got about three thousand permanent residents, Pancho thought, there's an awful lot of people up here sashaying around. The walking paths weren't exactly crowded, but there were plenty of people strolling along. Pancho had no trouble telling the Selene citizens from the rare tourists: the locals shuffled along easily in the low gravity and dressed casually in coveralls or running suits, for the most part; the few tourists she spotted wore splashy tee-shirts and vacation shorts and hopped and stumbled awkwardly, despite their weighted boots. Some of the women had bought expensive frocks in the Plaza shops and were showing them off as they oh-so-carefully stepped along the winding paths.

The Selenites smiled and greeted each other as they passed; the tourists tended to be more guarded and uncertain of themselves. Funny, Pancho thought: anybody with enough money and free time to come up here for a vacation oughtta be more relaxed.

The outdoor theater was jammed, Pancho saw. She remembered a news bulletin about Selene's dance club performing low-gravity ballet. All in all, it seemed a normal weekday evening in the Plaza, nothing out of the ordinary.

All the paths winding through the greenery led to the long windows set into the far end of the Plaza dome. Made of lunar glassteel, they were perfectly transparent yet had the structural strength of the reinforced concrete that made up the rest of the dome's structure. It was still daylight outside, and would be for another two hundred-some hours. A few tourists had stopped to gape out at the cracked, pockmarked floor of Alphonsus.

"It looks so *dead!*" said one of the women.

"And empty," her husband muttered.

"Makes you wonder why anyone ever came up here to live."

Pancho huffed impatiently. You try growing up in Lubbock, or getting flooded out in Houston, see how much better the Moon looks to you.

"Good evening," said Martin Humphries.

Pancho had not seen him approaching; she'd been looking through the windows at the outside, listening to the tourists' comments.

"Howdy," she said.

He was wearing dark slacks with a beige pullover shirt. And sandals, no less. His "ordinary guy" disguise, Pancho thought. She herself was in the same sky-blue coveralls she'd been wearing all day, with an Astro Corporation logo over the left breast pocket and her name stenciled just above it.

Gesturing to a concrete bench at the edge of the path, Humphries said, "Let's sit down. There are no cameras out here to see us together."

They sat. A family strolled by, parents and two little boys, no more than four or five. Lunatics. Selenites. The kids might even have been born here, she thought.

"What have you been up to lately?" Humphries asked casually.

Truthfully, Pancho reported, "We've started the detailed mission planning. Randolph's picked out a couple of target asteroids for us to rendezvous with, and now Mandy and me are workin' out the optimum trajectory, trip times, supply needs, failure modes . . . stuff like that."

"Sounds boring."

"Not when your life hangs on it."

Humphries conceded the point with a nod. "The construction of the propulsion system is proceeding on schedule?"

"You'd know more about that than I would."

"It is," he said.

"That's what I figured. Dan'd go ballistic if there were any holdups there."

"Amanda refuses to see me," he said.

For a moment Pancho was jarred by the sudden change of subject. Recovering quickly, she replied, "Mandy's got enough on her hands. This isn't the time for her to get involved with somebody . . . anybody."

"I want her off the mission."

"You can't do that to her!" Pancho blurted.

"Why not?"

"It'd ruin her career, that's why. Bounced off the first crewed mission to the Belt: how'd that look on her resume?"

"She won't need a resume. I'm going to marry her."

Pancho stared at him. He was serious.

"For how long?" she asked coldly.

Anger flared in Humphries's eyes. "Just because my first two marriages didn't work out, there's no reason to think this one won't."

"Yeah. Maybe."

"Besides," Humphries went on, "if it doesn't work out she'll get a very handsome settlement out of me. She'll never have to work again."

Pancho said nothing. She was thinking, If it doesn't work out he'll use every lawyer he's got to throw Mandy out into the cold without a cent. If it doesn't work out he'll hate her just as much as he hates his first two wives.

"I want you to help convince her to marry me," Humphries said.

Pancho's mind was spinning. You gotta be careful here, she warned herself. Don't get him mad at you.

"Mr. Humphries, that's something I just plain can't do. This isn't a business deal, I can't talk her into doin' something she doesn't want to do. Nobody can. Except maybe you."

"But she won't see me!"

"I know, I know," she said, as sympathetically as she could. "It's just too much pressure for her, what with the mission and all."

"That's why I want her off the mission."

"Don't do that to her. Please."

"My mind's made up."

Pancho sighed unhappily. "Well, you're just gonna have to talk to Dan Randolph about that. He's the boss, not me."

"Then that's what I'll do," Humphries said firmly.

"I wish you wouldn't. Whyn't you let us go out to the Belt. When we get back Mandy'll be able to give you her full attention."

"No." Humphries shook his head. "You might not get back."

"We will."

"You might not. I don't want to take the chance of losing her."

Pancho looked into his eyes. They were still cold, unreadable, like the eyes of a professional card shark she'd known once while she'd been supporting herself through the University of Nevada in Las Vegas by working at one of the casinos. Not the eyes of a lovesick swain. Not the eyes of a man whose heart might break.

"Better talk to Randolph, then," she said.

"I will."

Feeling weary and more than a little afraid of what was going to happen with Mandy, Pancho got to her feet. Humphries stood up, too, and she noticed that he was several centimeters shorter than she'd thought him to be. Glancing down at his sandals, she thought, The sumbitch must have lifts in his regular shoes.

"By the way," Humphries said, his voice hard-edged, "someone's hacked into my private files."

She was genuinely surprised that he'd found out so quickly. It must have shown on her face.

"Randolph is a lot smarter than I thought he was, but it won't do him any good."

"You mean he's the one who hacked you?"

"Who else? One of his people, obviously. I want you to find out who. And how."

"I can't do that!" Pancho blurted.

"Why not?"

"I'll get caught. I'm not a chip freak."

His eyes bored into her for a painfully long moment. "You find out who did it. And how it was done. Or else."

"Or else what?"

With a grim smile, Humphries answered, "I'll think of something."

ASTRO CORPORATION OFFICES

Ⅰf he finds the account I set up for him to pay the rent on my sister's dewar I'm toast," Pancho said as she paced across Dan's office.

Sitting behind his desk, Dan said, "I'll get George to scratch the program. Astro can pay the storage fees for your sister."

Pancho shook her head. "That'll just call attention to what I did."

"Not if we erase the subroutine completely. He'll never know."

"No!" Pancho insisted. "Don't go anywhere near it. It'll tip him off for sure."

Dan could see how agitated she was. "You just want to leave it there? He might stumble across it any minute."

"He knows I did it," Pancho said, crossing the room again in her long-legged strides. "I know he knows. He's just playin' cat-and-mouse with me."

"I don't think so. He's not the type. Humphries is more a sledgehammer-on-the-head kind of guy."

She stopped and turned toward Dan, her face suddenly white, aghast. "Jesus H. Christ . . . he might turn off Sis's life support! He might pull the plug on her!"

Dan knew she was right. "Or threaten to."

"That'd give him enough leverage to get me to do whatever he wants."

"What does he want?"

"He wants Mandy. He wants her scrubbed from the mission so he can talk her into marrying him."

Dan leaned back in his desk chair and stared at the ceiling. He'd had the office swept for bugs only an hour earlier, yet he had the uneasy feeling that Humphries knew everything that he said or did. Pancho's not the only Astro employee he's recruited, Dan reminded himself. My whole double-damned staff must be honeycombed with his snoops. Who can I trust?

He snapped forward in the chair and said into the phone console, "Phone, find George Ambrose. I want him here, now."

In less than a minute Big George came through the doorway from the outer office.

"George, I want this whole suite swept for bugs," Dan commanded.

"Again? We just did it an hour ago."

"I want you to do it this time. Yourself. Nobody else."

Scratching at his shaggy beard, George said, "Gotcha, boss."

It took a maddening half hour. Pancho forced herself to sit on the sofa while George went through the office with a tiny black box in one massive paw.

"Clean in here," he said at last.

"Okay," said Dan. "Close the door and sit down."

"You said you wanted the outer offices done, too," George objected.

"In a minute. Sit."

Obediently, George lowered his bulk into one of the cushioned chairs in front of Dan's desk.

"I've been thinking. Tonight, the three of us are going to move a dewar out of the catacombs," Dan said.

"Sis? Where—"

"I'll figure that out between now and then," Dan said. "Maybe somewhere else on the Moon. Maybe we'll move her to one of the space stations."

"You've gotta have the right equipment to maintain it," George pointed out.

Dan waved a hand in the air. "You need a cryostat to keep the nitrogen liquified. Not much else."

"Life support monitors," Pancho pointed out.

"Self-contained on the dewar flask," said Dan.

"Not the equipment," Pancho corrected. "I mean you need some people to take a look every few days, make sure everything's running okay."

With a shake of his head, Dan said, "That's a frill that you pay extra for. You don't need it. The equipment has safety alarms built in. The only time you need human intervention is when the flask starts to exceed the limits you've set the equipment to keep."

"Well, yeah . . . I guess," Pancho agreed reluctantly.

"Okay, George," Dan said. "Go sweep the rest of the place. We can all meet here for dinner at . . ." he called up his appointment screen with the jab of a finger, ". . . nineteen-thirty."

"Dinner?" Pancho asked.

"Can't do dirty work on an empty stomach," Dan said, grinning mischievously.

"But where are we taking her?" Pancho asked as she disconnected the liquid nitrogen feed line. Despite its heavy insulation, the hose was stiff with a rime of frost. Cold white vapor hissed briefly from its open end, until she twisted the seal shut.

"Shh!" Dan hissed, pointing to the baleful red eye of the security camera hanging some fifty meters down the corridor.

This late at night they were quite alone in the catacombs, but Dan worried about that security camera. There was one at each end of the long row of dewars, and although the area was dimly lit, the cameras fed into Selene's security office where they were monitored twenty-four hours a day. Pancho figured that, like security guards anywhere, the men and women responsible for monitoring the cameras seldom paid them close attention, except when a warning light flashed red or a synthesized voice warned of trouble that some sensor had detected. That's why they had hacked into the sensor controls on Sis's dewar and cut them out of the monitoring loop.

Dan and George were sweating with the effort of jacking up the massive dewar onto a pair of trolleys. Even in the low gravity of the Moon, the big stainless-steel cylinder was heavy.

"Where're we goin'?" Pancho repeated.

"You'll see," Dan grunted.

Pancho plugged the nitrogen hose into the portable cryostat they had taken from one of the Astro labs, several levels below the catacombs.

"Okay, all set," she whispered.

"How're you doing, George?" Dan asked.

The shaggy Australian came around the front end of the dewar. "Ready whenever you are, boss."

Dan glanced once at the distant camera's red eye, then said, "Let's get rolling."

The caster wheels on the trolleys squeaked as the three of them pushed the dewar down the long, shadowy corridor.

"Don't the security cameras have a recording loop?" Pancho asked. "Once they see Sis's dewar is missing, they'll play it back and see us."

"That camera's going to show a nice, quiet night," Dan said, leaning hard against the big dewar as they trundled along. "Cost me a few bucks, but I think I found an honest security guard. She'll erase our images and run a loop from earlier in the evening to cover the erasure. Everything will look peaceful and calm."

"That's an honest guard?" Pancho asked.

"An honest guard," Dan said, panting with the strain of pushing, "is one who stays bought."

"And I'll put an empty dewar in your sister's place," George added, "soon's we get this one settled in." Pancho noticed he was breathing easily, hardly exerting himself.

"But where're we takin' her?" Pancho asked again. "And why're we whisperin' if you got the guard bought?"

"We're whispering because there might be other people in the catacombs," Dan replied, sounding a bit irked. "No sense taking any chances we don't need to take."

"Oh." That made sense. But it still didn't tell her where in the hell they were going.

They passed the end of the catacombs and kept on going along the long, dimly-lit corridor until they stopped at last at what looked like an airlock hatch.

Dan stood up straight and stretched his arms overhead until Pancho heard his vertebrae crack.

"I'm getting too old for this kind of thing," he muttered as he went to the hatch and pecked on its electronic lock. The hatch popped slightly open; Pancho caught a whiff of stale, dusty air that sighed from it.

George pulled the hatch all the way open.

"Okay, down the tunnel we go," said Dan, unclipping a flashlight from the tool loop on the leg of his coveralls.

The tunnel had been started, he explained to Pancho, back in the early days of Moonbase, when Earthbound managers had decided to ram a tunnel through the ringwall mountains to connect the floor of Alphonsus with the broad expanse of Mare Nubium.

"I helped to dig it," Dan said, with pride in his voice. Then he added, "What there is of it, at least."

The lunar rock had turned out to be much tougher than expected; the cost of digging the tunnel, even with plasma torches, had risen too far. So the tunnel was never finished. Instead, a cable-car system had been built over the mountains. It was more expensive to operate than a tunnel would have been but far cheaper to construct.

"I've ridden the cable car up to the top of Mt. Yeager," Pancho said. "The view's terrific."

"Yep," Dan agreed. "They forgot about the tunnel. But it's still here, even though nobody uses it. And so are the access shafts."

The access shafts had been drilled upward to the outside, on the side of the mountain. The first of the access shafts opened into an emergency shelter where there were pressure suits and spare oxygen bottles, in case the cable-car system overhead broke down.

"And here we are," Dan said.

In the scant light from the flashlights that Dan and George played around the tunnel walls, Pancho saw a set of metal rungs leading up to another hatch.

"There's a tempo just above us," he said as George started climbing the ladder. "We'll jack into its electrical power supply to run the dewar's cryostat."

"Won't that show up on the grid monitors?" Pancho asked.

Shaking his head, Dan replied, "Nope. The tempos have their own solar panels and batteries. Completely independent. The panels are even up on poles to keep 'em out of the dust."

Pancho heard the hatch groan open. Looking up, she saw George squeeze his bulk through its narrow diameter.

"How're we gonna get Sis's dewar through that hatch?" she demanded.

"There's a bigger hatch for equipment," Dan said.

As if to prove the point, a far wider hatch squealed open over their heads. Dim auxiliary lighting from the tempo filtered down to them.

Even with the little winch from the tempo, it was a struggle to wrestle the bulky dewar and its equipment up through the hatch. Pancho worried that Sis would be jostled and crumpled in her liquid nitrogen bath. But at last they had Sis hooked up in the temporary shelter. The dewar rested on the floor and all the gauges were in the green.

"You'll have to come back here once a month or so to check up on everything. Maybe once every six or seven months you'll have to top off the nitrogen supply."

A thought struck her. "What about when I'm on the mission?"

"I'll do it," George said without hesitation. "Be glad to."

"How the hell can I thank you guys?"

Dan chuckled softly. "I'm just making certain that my best pilot isn't blackmailed by Humphries into working against me. And George . . ."

The big Aussie looked suddenly embarrassed.

"I used to live in one of the tempos," he said, his tenor voice softer than usual. "Back when I was a fugitive, part of the underground. Back before Dan took me under 'is wing."

Dan said, "This is a sort of homecoming for George."

"Yeah," George said. "Reminds me of the bad old days. Almost brings a fookin' tear to my eye."

Dan laughed and the Aussie laughed with him. Pancho just stood there, feeling enormously grateful to them both.

STARPOWER, LTD.

Dan had offered space in Astro Corporation's office complex for the headquarters of the fledgling Starpower, Ltd. Humphries had countered with an offer of a suite in his own Humphries Space Systems offices. Stavenger suggested a compromise, and Starpower's meager offices opened in the other tower on the Grand Plaza, where Selene's governmental departments were housed.

Yet Stavenger had not been invited to this working meeting. Dan sat on one side of the small conference table, Martin Humphries on the other. The room's windowless walls were bare, the furniture strictly functional.

"I hear you've been having some problems with hackers," Dan said.

For just a flash of a second Martin Humphries looked startled. He quickly regained his composure.

"Whoever told you that?" he asked calmly.

Dan smiled knowingly. "Not much happens around here without the grapevine getting wind of it."

Humphries leaned back in his chair. Dan noticed that it was a personally fitted recliner, unlike the other chairs around the table, which were inexpensive padded plastic.

"The leak's been fixed," Humphries said. "No damage done."

"That's good," said Dan.

"Speaking of the grapevine," Humphries said lightly, "I heard a funny one just this morning."

"Oh?"

"There's a story going around that you and a couple of your employees stole a dewar from the catacombs last night."

"Really?"

"Sounds like something out of an old horror flick."

"Imagine that," Dan said.

"Curious. Why would you do something like that?"

Trying to find a comfortable position on his chair, Dan replied, "Let's not spend the morning chasing rumors. We're here to set our budget requirements."

Humphries nodded. "I'll get one of my people to track it down."

Or one of *my* people, Dan grumbled to himself. But it'll be okay as long as he can't find Pancho's sister. Only she and George and I know where we stashed her.

He said to Humphries, "Okay, you do that. Now about the budget . . ."

They spent the next hour going over every item in the budget that Humphries's staff had prepared for Starpower, Ltd. Dan saw that there were no frills: no allocations for publicity or travel or anything except building the fusion drive, testing it enough to meet the IAA's requirements for human rating, and then flying it with a crew of four to the Asteroid Belt.

"I've been thinking that it makes more sense to up the crew to six," Dan said.

Humphries's brows rose. "Six? Why do we need two extra people?"

"We've got two pilots, a propulsion engineer, and a geologist. Two geologists would be better . . . or a geologist and some other specialist, maybe a geochemist."

"That makes five," Humphries said warily.

"I want to keep an extra slot open. Design the mission for six. As we get closer to the launch, we'll probably find out we need another hand."

Suspicion showed clearly in Humphries's face. "Adding two more people means extra supplies, extra mass."

"We can accommodate it. The fusion system's got plenty of power."

"Extra cost, too."

"A slight increment," Dan said easily. "Down in the noise."

Humphries looked unconvinced, but instead of arguing he asked, "Have you picked a specific asteroid yet?"

Dan tapped at his handheld computer, and the wall screen that covered one entire side of the conference room displayed a chart of the Belt. Thousands of thin ellipsoidal lines representing orbital paths filled the screen.

"It looks like the scrawling that a bunch of kindergarten brats would make," Humphries muttered.

"Sort of," said Dan. "There's a lot of rocks moving around out there."

He tapped at the handheld again and the lines winked out, leaving the screen deep black with tiny pinpoints of lights glittering here and there.

"This is what it really looks like," Dan said. "A whole lot of emptiness with a few pebbles floating around here and there."

"Some of those pebbles are kilometers across," Humphries said.

"Yep," Dan replied. "The biggest one is—"

"Ceres. Discovered by a priest on New Year's Day, 1801."

"You've been doing your homework," Dan said.

Humphries smiled, pleased. "It's a little over a thousand kilometers across."

"If that one ever hit the Earth . . ."

"Goodbye to everything. Like the impact that wiped out the dinosaurs."

"That's just what they need down there," Dan muttered, "an extinction-level impact."

"Let's get back to work," Humphries said crisply. "There's no big rock heading Earth's way."

"None has been found," Dan corrected. "Yet."

"You know," Humphries said, musing, "if we were really smart we'd run a demo flight to Mars and do a little prospecting on those two little moons. They're captured asteroids, after all."

"The IAA has ruled the whole Mars system off-limits for commercial development. That includes Deimos and Phobos."

Hunching closer to the conference table, Humphries said, "But we could just do it as a scientific mission. You know, send a couple geologists to chip off some rock samples, analyze what they're really made of."

"They already have pretty good data on that," Dan pointed out.

"But it could show potential investors that the fusion drive works and there's plenty of natural resources in the asteroids."

Frowning, Dan said, "Even if we could get the IAA to allow us to do it—"

"I can," Humphries said confidently.

"Even so, people have been going to Mars for years now. Decades. Investors won't be impressed by a Mars flight."

"Even if our fusion buggy gets there over a weekend?"

Firmly, Dan said, "We've got to get to the Belt. That's what will impress investors. Show them that the fusion drive changes the economic picture."

"I suppose," Humphries said reluctantly.

"And we've got to lay our hands on a metallic asteroid, one of the nickel-iron type. That's where the heavy metals are, the stuff you can't get from the Moon or even the NEAs."

"Gold," Humphries said, brightening. "Silver and platinum. Do you have any idea of what this is going to do to the precious metals market?"

Dan blinked at him. I'm trying to move the Earth's industrial base into space and he's playing games with the prices for gold. We just don't think the same way; we don't have the same goals or the same values, even.

Grinning slyly, Humphries said, "We could get a lot of capital from people who'd be willing to pay us *not* to bring those metals to Earth."

"Maybe," Dan admitted.

"I know at least three heads of governments who would personally buy into Starpower just to keep us from dumping precious metals onto the market."

"And I'll bet," Dan growled, "that those governments rule nations where the people are poor, starving, and sinking lower every year."

Humphries shrugged. "We're not going to solve all the world's problems, Dan."

"We ought to at least try."

"That's the difference between us," Humphries said, jabbing a finger in Dan's direction. "You want to be a savior. All I want is to make a little money."

Dan looked at him for a long, silent moment. He's right, Dan thought. Once upon a time all I was interested in was making money. And now I don't give a damn. Not anymore. None of it makes any sense to me. Since Jane died—god, I've turned into a do-gooder!

Leaning forward again, toward Dan, his expression suddenly intense, earnest, Humphries said, "Listen to me, Dan. There's nothing wrong with wanting to make money. You can't save the world. Nobody can. The best thing we can do is to feather our own nests and—"

"I've got to try," Dan interrupted. "I can't sit here and just let them drown or starve or sink into another dark age."

"Okay, okay." Humphries raised both hands placatingly. "You go right ahead and beat your head against that wall, if you want to. Maybe the asteroids are the answer. Maybe you'll save the world, one way or the other. In the meantime, we can clean up a tidy little profit doing it."

"Yep."

"If we don't make a profit, Dan, we can't do anybody any good. We've got to make money out of this or go out of business. You know that. We can't do this mission at cost. We've got to show a profit."

"Or at least," Dan countered, "a profit potential."

Humphries considered the idea for a moment, then agreed, "A profit potential. Okay, I'll settle for that. We need to show the financial community—"

"What's left of it."

Humphries actually laughed. "Oh, don't worry about the financial community. Men like my father will always be all right, no matter what happens. Even if the whole world drowns, they'll sit on a mountaintop somewhere, fat and happy, and wait for the waters to go down."

Dan could barely hide his disgust. "Come on, let's get back to work. We've had enough philosophy for one morning."

Humphries agreed with a smile and a nod.

Hours later, after Dan had left the conference room, Humphries went back to his own office and sank into his high-backed swivel chair. As he leaned back and gazed up at the paneled ceiling, the chair adjusted its contours to accommodate his body. Humphries relaxed, smiling broadly. He missed it, he said to himself. The numbers are right there in the budget and Randolph went past them as if they were written in invisible ink.

It was so easy to distract Randolph's attention. Just get him started on his idiotic crusade. He blanks out to everything else. He wants to go to the Belt to save the world. Sounds like Columbus wanting to reach China by sailing in the wrong direction.

Humphries laughed out loud. It's right there in the budget and he paid no attention to it at all. Or maybe he thinks it's just a backup, a redundancy measure. After all, it's not a terribly large sum. Once the nanos have built one fusion system, it only costs peanuts to have them build another one. The real expense is in the design and programming, and that's all amortized on the first model. All the backup costs is the raw materials and the time of a few people to monitor the process. The nanos work for nothing.

He laughed again. Randolph thinks he's so fricking smart, sneaking Pancho's sister out of the catacombs. Afraid I'll terminate her? Or does he want to keep Pancho under his thumb? I won't be able to use her anymore, but so what, who needs her now? I'll be building a second fusion drive and he doesn't even know it!

SPACEPORT ARMSTRONG

Pancho stared across the desolate, blast-scarred expanse of the launch center and wrinkled her nose unhappily. "It sure looks like a kludge."

Standing beside her in the little observation bubble, Dan had to agree. The fusion drive looked like the work of a drunken plumber: bulbous spheres of diamond that sparkled in the harsh unfiltered sunlight drenching the lunar surface, the odd shapes of the MHD channel, the pumps that fed the fuel to the reactor chamber, radiator panels and the multiple rocket nozzles, all connected by a surrealistic maze of pipes and conduits. The entire contraption was mounted on the platform-like deck of an ungainly, spraddle-legged booster that stood squat and silent on the circular launch pad of smoothed lunar concrete.

The observation chamber was nothing more than a bubble of glassteel poking up above the barren floor of Alphonsus's giant ringwall. Barely big enough for two people to stand in, the chamber was connected by a tunnel to the control center of the launch complex.

"We didn't build her for beauty," Dan said. "Besides, she'll look better once we've mated her with the other modules."

Subdued voices crackled from the intercom speaker set into the smoothed wall of the chamber just below the rim of the transparent blister.

"Pan Asia oh-one-niner on final descent," said the pilot of an incoming shuttle.

"We have you on final, oh-one-niner," answered the calm female voice of a flight controller. "Pad four."

"Pad four, copy."

Dan looked up into the star-flecked sky and saw a fleeting glint of light.

"Retrorockets," Pancho muttered.

"On the curve," said the flight controller.

Another quick burst. Dan could make out the shuttle now, a dark angular shape falling slowly out of the sky, slim landing legs extended.

"Down the pipe, oh-one-niner," said the woman controller. She sounded almost bored.

It all seemed to be happening in slow motion. Dan watched the shuttle come down and settle on the pad farthest away from the one on which the fusion rocket was sitting, waiting for clearance to take off. The shuttle pilot announced, "Oh-one-niner is down. All thrusters off."

Pancho let out a puff of pent-up breath.

Surprised, Dan asked, "White knuckles? You?"

She grinned, embarrassed. "I always get torqued up, unless I'm driving the buggy."

Glancing at his wristwatch, Dan said, "Well, we ought to get clearance to launch as soon as they offload the shuttle."

With a nod, Pancho said, "I'd better get suited up."

"Right," said Dan.

The fusion system itself was the last part of their spacecraft to be launched into orbit around the Moon. The propellant tanks and the crew and logistics modules were already circling a hundred kilometers overhead. Pancho would supervise the assembly robots that would link all the pieces together.

Dan went with her along the tunnel and into the locker room where the astronauts donned their spacesuits. Amanda was already there, ready to help check her out. Dan realized it had been a long time since he'd checked out anyone or donned a spacesuit himself. Spaceflight is so routine nowadays that you can come and go from the Earth to the Moon just like you ride a plane or a bus, he thought. But another voice in his head said, You're too old to be working in space. Over the years you've taken as big a radiation dose as you're allowed . . . and then some.

He felt old and pretty useless as he watched Pancho worm into the spacesuit while Amanda hovered beside her, checking the seals and connections. Like Pancho, Amanda was wearing light tan flight coveralls. Dan noticed how nicely she filled them out.

Well, he sighed to himself, at least you're not too old to appreciate a good-looking woman.

But he turned and headed for the tunnel that connected the spaceport to Selene proper, feeling useless, wondering if Humphries was right and he was butting his head against a stone wall.

As he started down the corridor that led to the connector tunnel, he saw Doug Stavenger coming up in the other direction, looking youthful and energetic and purposeful.

Dammitall, he thought, Stavenger's older than I am and he looks like a kid. Maybe I ought to get some nanotherapy.

"Going to watch the launch?" Stavenger asked brightly.

"Think I'll go to the launch center and watch it from there."

"I like to watch from the observation bubble."

"I was just there," Dan said.

"Come on, let's see the real thing instead of watching it on a screen."

Stavenger's enthusiasm was contagious. Dan found himself striding along the narrow tunnel again, out to the bubble.

They ducked through the open hatch and into the cramped chamber. Stavenger climbed the two steps and looked out, grinning. Dan squeezed in beside him, nearly bumping his head on the curving glassteel.

"I used to sneak out here when I was a kid to watch the liftoffs and landings," Stavenger said, grinning. "I still get a kick out of it."

Dan made a polite mumble.

"I mean, we spend almost our whole lives indoors, underground," Stavenger went on. "It's good to see the outside now and then."

"As long as the glass doesn't crack."

"That's what the safety hatches are for."

Dan said, "But you've got to get through them fast, before they shut themselves."

Stavenger laughed. "True enough."

They watched shoulder-to-shoulder in the cramped blister, listening to the flight controllers' crisp voices clicking off the countdown. Stavenger seemed as excited as a child; Dan envied him. A little tractor rolled noiselessly across the crater floor to the launch pad. Pancho's spacesuited figure jumped from it in dreamlike lunar slow-motion, stirring up a lazy puff of gray dust. Then she climbed up the ladder and sealed herself into the booster's one-person crew module.

"This is just an assembly mission, isn't it?" Stavenger asked.

"Right," said Dan. "She not a pilot on this flight, just baby-sitting the robots."

Strangely enough, Dan felt his palms going clammy as the countdown neared its final moments. Relax, he told himself silently. There's nothing to this.

Still, his heart began to thump faster.

". . . three . . . two . . . one . . . ignition," said the automated countdown voice.

The spacecraft leaped off the launch pad in a cloud of smoke and gritty dust that evaporated almost as soon as it formed. One instant the craft was sitting on the concrete, the next it was gone.

"We have liftoff," said one of the human controllers in the time-honored tradition. "All systems in the green."

Pancho's voice came through the speaker. "Copy all systems green. Orbital insertion burn in ten seconds."

It was all quite routine. Still, Dan didn't relax until Pancho announced, "On the money, guys! I'm cruisin' along with the other modules. Time to go to work."

A controller's voice replied, "Rendezvous complete. Initiate assembly procedure."

Dan huffed. "She sounds more like a robot than a human being."

Just then the controller added, "Okay, Pancho. I'll see you at the Pelican tomorrow night."

Stavenger grinned at Dan. "Maybe she drinks lubricating oil."

They walked through the corridor to the tunnel that led back to Selene. As they climbed onto one of the automated carts that plied the kilometer-long tunnel, Stavenger asked, "How soon will you be ready for your flight to the Belt?"

"We've programmed a month of uncrewed flight tests and demo flights for IAA certification. Once we get the nod from the bureaucrats we'll be ready to go."

"Could your craft reach Jupiter?"

Surprised at the question, Dan replied, "In theory. But we won't be carrying enough propellant or supplies for that. Jupiter's almost twice as far as the Belt."

"I know," Stavenger murmured.

"Why do you ask?"

Stavenger hesitated. The cart trundled along the blank-walled tunnel smoothly, almost silently, its electrical motor purring softly. At last Stavenger answered, "Sooner or later we're going to have to go to Jupiter . . . or maybe one of the other gas giants."

Dan saw where he was heading. "Fusion fuels."

"Jupiter's atmosphere is rich in hydrogen and helium isotopes."

"Kris Cardenas mentioned that to me," Dan remembered.

"She and I have been talking about it. Fusion fuels could be a major trade commodity for Selene. And very profitable for Starpower, Ltd."

"Mining asteroids is a lot easier than scooping gases from Jupiter's atmosphere."

"Yes," Stavenger admitted, "but your idea of moving large segments of Earth's industry off the planet is only part of the solution to the greenhouse warming, Dan."

"I know, but it's a big part."

"The other half is to wean them off fossil fuel burning. They've got to stop pumping greenhouse gases into the atmosphere if they're going to have any chance of stopping the global warming."

"And fusion is a way to do that," Dan muttered.

"It's the only way," Stavenger said firmly. "Your solar power satellites can provide only a small fraction of the energy that Earth needs. Fusion can take over the entire load."

"If we can bring in enough helium-three."

"There are other fusion processes that could be even more efficient than burning deuterium with helium-three. But they all depend on isotopes that are vanishingly rare on Earth."

"But plentiful on Jupiter," Dan said.

"That's right."

Dan nodded, thinking, He's right. Fusion could be the answer. If we could replace all the fossil-fueled electricity-generating plants on Earth with fusion plants we could cut down the greenhouse emissions to almost nothing. Fusion power plants could generate the electricity for electric cars. That'd eliminate another big greenhouse source.

He looked at Stavenger with new respect. Here's a man who's exiled from Earth, yet he wants to help them. And he sees farther than I do.

"Okay," he said. "After the flight to the Belt, we make a run out to Jupiter. I'll start the planning process right away."

"Good," said Stavenger. Then he added, "Will this be a Starpower project or will you keep it for Astro Corporation?"

For a moment Dan was dumbstruck. When he found his voice, it was a shocked whisper. "You want to cut out Humphries?"

"He's maneuvering to get a stranglehold on asteroidal resources," Stavenger said, as cold as steel. "I don't think it would be wise to let him control fusion fuels as well."

By all the gods that ever were, Dan thought, this guy is ready to go to war with Humphries.

BOARD MEETING

The filters in his nostrils were giving Dan a headache; they felt as big as shotgun shells. He had come back to Earth reluctantly for this quarterly meeting of his board of directors. Dan always felt he could run Astro Manufacturing just fine if the double-damned board would simply stay out of his way. But they always had to poke their noses into the corporation's operations, complaining about this, asking about that, insisting that he follow every crack-brained suggestion they came up with.

It was all so unnecessary. Dan held a controlling interest of the corporation's outstanding stock; not an absolute majority of the shares, but enough to outvote the other board members if he had to. The board could not throw him out of his seat as corporate president and chief executive officer. All they could do was nibble away, waste his time, drive up his blood pressure.

To top it off, now Martin Humphries had joined the board, smiling, making friends, chatting up the other members as they milled around the sideboard scarfing up drinks and tea sandwiches before sitting in their places at the long conference table. Humphries was out to get an absolute majority, that was as clear to Dan as a gun aimed at his head.

Through the sweeping window that ran the length of the board room Dan could see the surging waters of the Caribbean sparkling in the morning sun. The sea looked calm, yet Dan knew it was inching ever higher, encroaching on the land, patiently, inexorably. Humphries kept his back to the window, deep in intense discussion with a trio of elderly directors.

Dan had flown back to La Guaira specifically for this meeting. He could have stayed in Selene and chaired the meeting electronically, but that three-second lag would have driven him crazy. He appreciated how

Kris Cardenas felt, dealing from the Moon every day with Duncan and his team in Scotland.

Dan stood at one end of the sideboard, beneath the big framed photograph of Astro's first solar-power satellite, glinting in the harsh sunlight of space against the deep black background of infinity. He sipped on his usual aperitif glass of Amontillado, speaking as pleasantly as he could manage with the people closest to him. Fourteen men and women, most of the men either gray or bald, most of the women looking youthful, thanks to rejuvenation treatments. Funny, he thought: the women are taking rejuve therapy but the men are holding back from it. I am myself, he realized. The ultimate machismo stupidity. What's wrong with delaying your physical deterioration? It's not like a face-lift; you actually reverse the aging of your body's cells.

"Dan, could I speak to you for a moment?" asked Harriett O'Banian. She'd been on the board for more than ten years, ever since Dan had bought out her small solar-cell production company.

"Sure, Hattie," he said, walking her slowly to the far corner of the big conference room. "What's on your mind?"

Hattie O'Banian was a trim-looking redhead who had consummated her buyout by Astro Manufacturing with a month-long affair with Dan. It had been fun for them both, and she'd been adult enough to walk away from it once she realized that no matter who shared his bed, Dan Randolph was in love with former President Jane Scanwell.

Glancing over her shoulder to make certain no one was within eavesdropping range, O'Banian half-whispered, "I've been offered a damned good price for my Astro shares. So have half a dozen other board members."

Dan's eyes flicked to Humphries, at the other end of the room, still chatting with the directors gathered around him.

"Who made the offer?" he asked.

"A straw man. Humphries is the real buyer."

"I figured."

"The trouble is, Dan, that's it's a damned good offer. Five points above the market price."

"He's gone up to five, has he?" Dan muttered.

"With the stock in free-fall the way it is, the offer is awfully tempting."

"Yep, I can see that."

She looked up at him and Dan realized that her emerald green eyes, which could be so full of delight and mischief, were dead serious now.

"He can buy up enough stock to outvote you," O'Banian said.

"That's what he's trying to do, all right."

"Dan, unless you're going to pull some rabbit out of your hat at the meeting today, half your board is going to cash out."

Dan tried to grin. It came out more as a grimace. "Thanks for the warning, Hattie. I'll see what kind of rabbits I've got for you."

"Good luck, Dan."

He went to the head of the conference table, tapped the computer stylus against the stainless steel water tumbler there, and called the meeting to order. The directors took their seats; before he sat down, Humphries complained of the glare from the window and asked that the curtains be closed.

The agenda was brief. The treasurer's report was gloomy. Income from the company's final solar-power satellite construction project was tailing off as the project neared completion.

"What about the bonus for finishing the job ahead of schedule?" asked a florid-faced graybeard. Dan thought of him as Santa Claus with hypertension.

"That won't be paid until the sunsat is beaming power to the ground," said the treasurer.

"Still, it's a sizeable amount of money."

"It'll keep us afloat for several months," Dan said, waving the treasurer to silence.

"Then what?"

"Then we have to live off the income from existing operations. We have no new construction projects."

"That's the last of the power satellites?" asked the board member that Dan had privately nicknamed Bug Eyes. His eyes were even wider than usual, as if this was the first time he'd heard the bad news.

Dan clasped his hands as he answered carefully, "Although there are several orbital slots still available to accommodate solar power satellites, the GEC refuses to authorize any new construction."

"It's those damned Chinese," growled one of the older men.

"China is not alone in this," said a plump oriental woman sitting halfway down the table. Dan's name for her was Mama-San. "Many nations prefer to build power stations on their own ground rather than buy electrical power from space."

"Even though the price for that electricity is more than twice as high as our price," Dan pointed out. "And even higher, if you count the costs of sequestering their greenhouse gas emissions."

"Their governments subsidize the greenhouse amelioration," the treasurer pointed out.

"The people still have to pay for it, one way or another."

"What about beaming power from the Moon?"

"You wouldn't need the GEC to allocate any orbital slots for that, by god!" Santa Claus thumped the table with his fist.

"It's a possibility," Dan admitted, "and we've talked about it with the officials of Selene—"

"Selene doesn't own the whole damned Moon! Go off and build solar energy farms in the Ocean of Storms. Cover the whole expanse with solar cells, for god's sake!"

"We've looked into it," Dan said.

"And?"

"The problem is that no matter where the electricity is generated, it's got to be beamed to the ground here on Earth."

"We know that!"

Holding on to his temper, Dan went on, "The Pan-Asia bloc doesn't want to import energy, whether it comes from orbit or the Moon or the Lesser Magellanic Cloud. They won't allow us to build receiving stations on their territory. The Europeans have gone along with them and, between the two blocs, they have the GEC all wrapped up."

"How can we generate electricity from the Lesser Magellanic Cloud?" asked Bug Eyes. "That's quite a long distance away, isn't it?"

Give me strength, Dan prayed silently.

He got them through the various departmental reports at last, fielding what seemed like seventeen thousand questions and suggestions—most of them pointless, several absolutely inane—and went on to new business.

"At least here I have something positive to report," Dan said, smiling genuinely. "Our prototype fusion drive has been assembled in lunar orbit and test-flown successfully."

"You are ready to go to the Asteroid Belt?" asked Mama-San.

"As soon as we get the required crew-rating from the IAA."

From the far end of the table, Humphries spoke up. "We should have IAA approval in two to three weeks, barring any unforeseen setbacks."

"Setbacks?"

"An accident," Humphries said lightly. "Failure of the equipment, that sort of thing."

Or an IAA inspector on the take, Dan added silently. It happened only rarely, but it happened.

"How much is this mission to the asteroids costing us?" asked the sprightly, dapper Swiss gentleman whom Dan had dubbed The Banker.

"The mission is being fully funded by Starpower, Limited," Dan replied.

"Astro owns one-third of Starpower," Humphries pointed out.

"And you own the rest?" The Banker asked.

"No, Humphries Space Systems owns a third, and the other third is owned by Selene."

"How can a city own part of a corporation?"

"All the details are in the reports before you," Dan said, tapping his stylus against the computer screen built into the tabletop.

"Yes, but—"

"I'll explain it after the meeting," Humphries said, full of graciousness. The Banker nodded but still looked unsatisfied.

"The point is," Dan told them, "that once this flight to the Asteroid Belt is accomplished, Astro's stock is going to rise. We'll have taken the first step in opening up a resource base that's enormous—far bigger than all the mining operations on Earth."

"I can see that Starpower's stock will go up," Santa Claus challenged.

"Astro's will, too," Dan said. "Because we have the corner on building the fusion engines."

"Not Humphries Space Systems?" They all turned to Humphries.

He smiled gently, knowingly. "No, this is going to be Astro's product. My corporation is merely supplying the capital, the funding."

Dan thought that Humphries looked like a cat eyeing a helpless canary.

SELENE

o there you have it," Dan said to the IAA inspector. "The system performs as designed."

They were sitting in Starpower, Ltd.'s one and only conference room, a tiny cubicle with an oval table that felt crowded even though only five people were sitting around it. The display screens on all four smartwalls showed data from the test flights of the fusion drive. The first half-dozen flights had been run remotely from the control center underground in Armstrong spaceport. The second string of six flights had been piloted by Pancho and Amanda.

Pointing to the screens, Dan said, "We've demonstrated acceleration, thrust, specific impulse, controllability, shutdown and restart . . . every facet of the full test envelope."

The inspector nodded solemnly. He was a young man with Nordic fair skin and pale eyes, dressed rather somberly in a plain gray pullover shirt and darker slacks. His hair was a thick dirty-blond mop that he wore long, almost down to his shoulders. Despite his conservative outfit, though, he wore several small silver earrings, silver rings on his fingers, a silver bracelet on his right wrist, and a silver chain around his neck. There was a pendant of some sort hanging from the chain but most of it was hidden beneath his shirt.

Pancho and Amanda sat flanking Dan; Humphries was on the other side of the small oval table, next to the inspector. For some long moments there was silence in the conference room. Dan could hear the background hum of the electrical equipment and the soft breath of the air circulation fans.

At last, Dan asked, "Well, what do you think, Mr. Greenleaf?"

"Dr. Greenleaf," the IAA inspector replied. "I have a doctorate in sociology."

Dan felt his brows hike up. Why would the IAA send a sociologist to check out a new spacecraft propulsion system? And why this particular little prig of a sociologist?

Greenleaf steepled his fingers in front of him. "You're surprised that a sociologist is evaluating your test data?"

"Well . . . yes, actually I am," Dan said, feeling decidedly uncomfortable.

"I can assure you, Mr. Randolph—"

"Dan."

"I can assure you, Mr. Randolph, that your data has been examined by the best engineers and physical scientists that the IAA has at its command," Greenleaf said. "We are not taking your application lightly."

"I didn't mean to imply anything like that," Dan said, thinking, This guy is out for blood.

Greenleaf shifted his gaze from Dan to the wall screen before him. "I can see that your device has performed within your design criteria quite reliably."

"Good," said Dan, relieved.

"Except in one respect," Greenleaf went on.

"What? What do you mean?"

"Long-term reliability," said Greenleaf. "The longest flight in your testing program was a mere two weeks, and even then it was at low power."

"I wouldn't call a constant acceleration of one-tenth *g* low power," Dan said, testily. "And the IAA seemed very happy with the data we got from that test flight."

Pancho and Amanda had flown the test rig on a parabolic trajectory that took them around Venus. The ship carried a full panoply of instrumentation for making observations of the planet as it flew by a scant thousand kilometers above Venus's glowing clouds. A team of planetary astronomers had provided the equipment and monitored the flight, all of them from universities that belonged to the IAA, all of them ecstatically happy and grateful for the data that the flight brought back—for free.

"Two weeks is not a sufficient endurance test," Greenleaf said flatly.

Pancho snapped, "It's long enough to get us to the Belt."

"Under full power."

"What else?"

"I cannot authorize a crewed flight to the Asteroid Belt until you have demonstrated that your propulsion system can operate reliably at full power for the time it would take to complete the mission."

Dan felt burning anger rising in his throat. Pancho looked as if she wanted to reach across the table and sock the guy. But then he realized that Amanda was looking not at Greenleaf, but at Humphries, who sat calmly in his chair, his face as expressionless as a professional card shark, his hands in his lap.

"Even your flight past Venus was an infraction of IAA regulations," Greenleaf said, as if justifying himself.

"We filed the flight plan with the IAA," Dan responded hotly.

"But you didn't wait for authorization, did you?"

"It was a test flight, dammit!"

Greenleaf's face flashed red. And Dan finally realized what he was up against. Oh, by all the saints in New Orleans, he said to himself, he's a New Morality bigot. They've infiltrated the IAA.

"I am not going to argue with you," Greenleaf said flatly. "You will be required to fly your device for four weeks at full power before you can receive approval for a crewed mission to the Asteroid Belt."

He pushed his chair back and got to his feet, stumbling in the low lunar gravity despite the weighted boots he wore.

"Four weeks!" Dan blurted. "We can fly to the Belt and back in four weeks under full power."

"Then do so," said Greenleaf, smugly. "But do it under remote control. Without any crew."

He headed for the door, leaving Dan sitting at the table, angry, stunned, and feeling betrayed.

"I'd better go after him," Humphries said, getting up from his chair. "We don't want him angry at us."

"Why the hell not?" Dan grumbled.

Humphries left the conference room. Dan sagged back in his chair. "Flying an uncrewed mission to the Belt doesn't make a dime's worth of sense," he muttered. "It's just an exercise that costs us four weeks' time and almost as much money as a crewed mission."

Pancho said, "Four weeks isn't so bad. Is it?"

"It's four weeks closer to bankruptcy, kid. Four weeks closer to letting that Humper take over my company."

In a very small voice, Amanda said, "It's my fault, actually."

Dan looked at her.

"Martin . . ." she hesitated, then said, "Martin doesn't want me to go on the mission. I'm sure he's had some influence on Dr. Greenleaf's position."

Pancho explained, "He's bonkers about Mandy."

Dan asked, "And how do you feel about him, Amanda?"

"Trapped," she replied immediately. "I feel as though there's nowhere on Earth I can go to get away from him. Or the Moon, for that matter. I feel like a trapped animal."

Dan left the two women and went to his office. As he slipped into his desk chair he commanded the phone to locate his chief counsel, the woman who headed Astro's corporate legal department.

The phone computer system found her on the ski slopes in Nepal. Her image was faint and wavered noticeably. She must be holding her wrist communicator in front of her face, Dan thought. He could see a bit of utterly blue sky behind her. She was in ski togs, polarized sun goggles pushed up on her forehead, and not at all happy about being buzzed by the boss.

"What in the nine billion names of God are you doing in Nepal?" Dan asked, irritated. Then he had to sit, fuming, for the few seconds it took for his message to reach the lawyer and her reply to get back to him.

"Trying to get in some skiing while there's still snow left," she snapped, equally irked.

"Skiing?"

"I do get some vacation time now and then," she said, after the usual pause. "This is the first time I've taken any since lord knows when."

Through gritted teeth, Dan explained the IAA inspector's decision to her.

"You could appeal," she said, once she understood the situation, "but that would take longer than running the uncrewed test flight he wants you to do."

"Couldn't we ask for another hearing, a different inspector?" Dan demanded. "This guy's a New Morality fanatic and they're dead-set against space exploration."

The lawyer's face hardened when she heard Dan's words. "*Mr.* Randolph," she said, "I am a member of the New Morality and I'm not a fanatic. Nor am I against space exploration."

Feeling surrounded by enemies, Dan said, "Okay, okay. So I exaggerated."

She said nothing.

"Can we claim an asteroid with an uncrewed spacecraft?"

"No one can claim ownership of any body in space," her reply came back. It was what Dan had expected. Then she went on, "No planet, moon, comet, asteroid—no celestial body of any kind. That's been international law since the Outer Space Treaty of 1967, and subsequent amendments and protocols."

Trust a lawyer to use two dozen words when one will do, Dan groused to himself.

She went on, "Individuals are allowed to have exclusive use of part or all of a celestial body, for the purpose of establishing a human habitation or extracting natural resources. In that instance, corporations are regarded as individuals."

"So could Astro Corporation claim *use* of an asteroid that an uncrewed spacecraft rendezvouses with?"

Nearly three seconds later she replied, "No. Such a claim can only be made by humans on the scene of the claim itself."

"But the double-dipped spacecraft would be under human control, remotely, from Selene."

Again the lag, and again the answer, "No, Dan. It's not allowed. Otherwise corporations would be able to send miniprobes all over the solar system and claim everything in sight! It would be like the efforts to patent segments of DNA and living organisms, back around the turn of the century."

"So an uncrewed test flight wouldn't do us any good at all," he said.

Once she heard his question, the lawyer answered, "That's a decision that you'll have to make, Dan. I'm just a lawyer; you're the CEO."

"Thanks a lot," Dan muttered.

Martin Humphries had not bothered to chase after the IAA inspector. What was the point? The young bureaucrat had done precisely what Humphries had wanted. Barely able to hide his satisfaction, he rode the moving stairs down to his home deep below the Moon's surface.

It's all working out very neatly, he congratulated himself as he walked along the corridor toward the cavern. Just enough delay to break Randolph's back. Astro's stock is in the toilet, and the other major shareholders will be glad to sell once they hear that the asteroid mission has to be postponed for more testing. By the time they finally get the mission going, I'll own Astro and Dan Randolph will be out on his ass.

And better yet, he thought, once I'm in charge I'll make certain that Amanda stays here on the ground. With me.

LUNAR ORBIT

S he looks better now, doesn't she?" Dan asked as their jumper
coasted toward the fusion-powered spacecraft.

Pancho nodded her agreement. The ship was still utilitarian, not sleek, but now the starkness of the bare engine system by itself was dwarfed by six huge, gleaming spherical propellant tanks. Big white letters stenciled along the cylindrical crew module identified the craft as STARPOWER 1; the logos of Astro Corporation, Humphries Space Systems and Selene adorned one of the propellant tanks.

The jumper was little more than an ordinary lunar transfer buggy with an extra set of tankage and a bigger rocket engine for ascents from the Moon's surface into lunar orbit and descents back to the ground again. Dan and Pancho wore tan Astro coveralls as they rode in the bulbous glassteel crew module, standing with their booted feet anchored in floor loops because seats were not needed for this brief, low-*g* flight. An instrument podium rose at the front of the module, its controls standing unused, since the vessel was being handled by the flight controllers back at Armstrong. Still, Dan felt good that Pancho was a qualified pilot. You never know, he thought.

As they approached the fusion-powered vessel, Pancho whistled at the size of the propellant tanks.

"That's a lot of fuel."

"Tell me about it," Dan said ruefully. "I've had to default on two helium-three contracts with Earthside power utilities to fill those double-damned tanks."

"Default?"

Nodding, Dan said grimly, "Two steps closer to bankruptcy."

Pancho decided to change the subject slightly. "So what've you decided to do about the long-duration test?" Pancho asked.

Dan shook his head. "I've spent the past four days pulling every wire I know."

"And?"

"Nothing so far. Zip. Nobody's going to lift a finger to go against the IAA."

"So you'll have to do the test flight?"

Running a finger across his chin, Dan said reluctantly, "Looks that way."

"Then why are we takin' this ride?"

The shadow of a smile crossed Dan's face. He was thinking of the time, many years earlier, when he had briefly become a privateer, a pirate, hijacking uncrewed spacecraft for their cargoes of ore. It had started as a desperation ploy, the only way a frustrated Dan Randolph could force open the space markets that had been closed by monopolists. He had won his war against monopoly and opened the solar system to free competition among individuals, corporations and governments. But at a price. His smile faded as he remembered the people who had died fighting that brief, unheralded war. He himself had come to within a whisker of being killed.

"So?" Pancho prodded, "Is this a joyride or what?"

Putting his thoughts of the past behind him, Dan replied, "I want to see the crew module for myself. And we're going to meet the planetary geologist that Zack Freiberg's picked out for us."

"The asteroid specialist?"

"Yep. He's aboard the ship now. Came up to Selene yesterday and went straight to the ship. He slept aboard last night."

Pancho huffed. "Eager beaver. College kid, I bet."

"He's got a mint-new degree from Zurich Polytech."

The flight controllers brought the jumper to a smooth rendezvous with *Starpower 1*. While Dan and Pancho stood watching, the little transfer buggy linked its airlock adapter section to the hatch of the bigger vessel. They floated through the womb-like adapter to the fusion ship's airlock hatch.

The airlock opened into the midsection of the crew module. To their left, Dan saw the accordion-fold doors of a half-dozen privacy compartments lining the passageway. Further up were the galley, a wardroom with a table and six small but plush-looking chairs, and—past an open hatch—the bridge. To their right was the lavatory and a closed hatch that led to the equipment and storage bays.

Dan headed left, toward the galley and the bridge.

"Chairs?" Pancho asked, looking puzzled, as they pushed weightlessly past the wardroom, floating a few centimeters above the deck's carpeting.

"You'll be accelerating or decelerating most of the way," Dan pointed out. "You won't be spending much time in zero-g."

She nodded, looking disappointed with herself. "I knew that; it just didn't latch."

Dan understood how she felt. He'd seen the layout of the crew module hundreds of times, viewed three-d mockups and even walked through virtual reality simulations. But being in the real thing was different. He could smell the newness of the metal and fabric; he could reach his hand up and run his fingers along the plastic panels of the overhead. The bridge looked small, but shining and already humming with electrical power.

"Where's our college boy?" Pancho asked, looking around.

"That would be me, I suppose," said a reedy voice from behind them.

Turning, Dan saw a husky-looking young man gripping the edges of the open hatch with both hands. He was a shade shorter than Dan, but broad in the shoulders, with a thick barrel chest. The build of a wrestler. His face was broad, too: a heavy jaw with wide, thin lips and small, deepset eyes. His hair was cropped so close to his skull that Dan couldn't be sure of its true color. He wore a small glittering stone in his left earlobe, diamond or zircon or glass, Dan could not tell.

"I heard you enter. I was in the sensor bay, checking on the equipment," he said in a flat midwestern American accent, pronounced so precisely that he had to have learned it in a foreign school.

"Oh," said Pancho.

"I am Lars Fuchs," he said, extending his hand to Dan. "You must be Mr. Randolph."

"Pleased to meet you, Dr. Fuchs." Fuchs's hand engulfed his own. The young man's grip was strong, firm. "This is Pancho Lane," Dan went on. "She'll be our pilot on the flight."

Fuchs dipped his chin slightly. "Ms. Lane. And, sir, I am not Dr. Fuchs. Not yet."

"That's okay. Zack Freiberg recommends you highly."

"I am very grateful to Doctor Professor Freiberg. He has been very helpful to me."

"And my name is Dan. If you call me Mr. Randolph it'll make me feel like an old man."

"Oh, I wouldn't want to offend you, sir!" Fuchs said, genuinely alarmed.

"Just call me Dan."

"Yes, sir, of course. And you must call me Lars." Turning to Pancho, he added, "Both of you."

"That's a deal, Lars," said Pancho, sticking out her hand.

Fuchs took it gingerly, as if not quite sure what to do. "Pancho is a woman's name in America?"

She laughed. "It's *this* woman's name, Lars old buddy."

Smiling uneasily, Fuchs said, "Pancho," as if testing out the name.

"You handle weightlessness very well," Dan said. "From what Zack told me, this is your first time off-Earth."

Fuchs said. "Thank you, sir . . . Dan. I came up last night so I could adapt myself to microgravity before you arrived here."

Pancho smiled sympathetically. "Spent the night makin' love to the toilet, huh?"

Looking flustered, Fuchs said, "I did retch a few times, yes."

"Ever'body does, Lars," she said. "Nothin' to be ashamed of."

"I am not ashamed," he said, his chin rising a notch.

Dan moved between them. "Have you picked out which cabin you want for yourself? Since you were first aboard you get first pick."

"Hey," Pancho griped, "I've been aboard this buggy before, you know. So has Amanda."

"The privacy compartments are all exactly alike," Fuchs said. "It doesn't matter which one I get."

"I'll take the last one on the left," Dan said, peering down the passageway that ran the length of the module. "It's closest to the lav."

"You?" Pancho looked surprised. "Since when are you comin' on the mission?"

"Since about four days ago," Dan said. "That's when I made up my mind . . . about a lot of things."

PELICAN BAR

S o here's my plan," Dan said, with a grin.

He and Pancho were hunched over one of the postage-stamp-sized tables in the farthest corner of the Pelican bar, away from the buzzing conversations and bursts of laughter from the crowd standing at the bar itself. Their heads were almost touching, leaning together like a pair of conspirators.

Which they were. Inwardly, Dan marveled at how good he felt. Free. Happy, almost. The double-damned bureaucrats have tried to tie me up in knots. Humphries is behind it all, playing along with the IAA and those New Morality bigots. Those uptight psalm-singers don't want us to reach the asteroids. They like the Earth just the way it is: miserable, hungry, desperate for the kind of order and control that the New Morality offers. This greenhouse warming is a blessing for them, the wrath of God smiting the unbelievers. Anything we do to try to help alleviate it, they see as a threat to their power.

Vaguely, Dan recalled from his childhood history lessons something about a group called the Nazis, back in the twentieth century. They came to power because there was an economic depression and people needed jobs and food. If he remembered his history lessons correctly.

So the New Morality has its tentacles into the IAA now, Dan thought. And the GEC too, I'll bet. And Humphries is playing them all like a symphony orchestra, using them to stymie me long enough so he can grab Astro from me.

Well, it's not going to be that easy, partner.

"What's so funny?" Pancho asked, looking puzzled.

"Funny?"

"You say, 'Here's my plan,' and then you start grinnin' like a cat in a canary's cage."

Dan took a sip of his brandy and dry, then said, "Pancho, I've always said that when the going gets tough, the tough get going—to where the going's easier."

"I've heard that one before."

"So I'm going with you."

"You?"

"Yep."

"To the Belt."

"You need a flight engineer. I know the ship's systems as well as anybody."

"Lordy-lord," Pancho muttered.

"I'm still a qualified astronaut. I'm going with you."

"But not until we do the uncrewed test flight," she said, reaching for her beer.

Leaning across the table even closer to her, Dan said in a hoarse whisper, "Screw the test flight. We're going to the Belt. You, Amanda, Fuchs and me."

Pancho nearly choked on her mouthful of beer. She sputtered, coughed, then finally asked, "What're you drinkin', boss?"

Happy as a pirate on the open sea, Dan said, "We'll let 'em think we're doing exactly what they've told us to do, except that the four of us will happen to be aboard the bird when she breaks orbit."

"Just like that?"

"Just like that. We'll calculate a new flight plan once we're underway. Instead of accelerating at one-sixth *g*, as we've planned, we'll goose her up to one-third *g* and cut the flight time by more than half."

Pancho looked unconvinced. "You better bring an astrogator aboard."

"Nope." Pointing a finger at her, Dan said, "You're it, kid. You and Amanda. I'm not bringing anybody into this that we don't absolutely need."

"I'm not so sure about this," Pancho said warily.

"Don't go chicken on me, kid," Dan said. "You two have been studying this point-and-shoot technique for a lot of weeks. If you can't do it, I've been wasting money on you."

"I can do it," Pancho said immediately.

"Okay, then."

"I'd just feel better if you had a real expert on board."

"No experts. Nobody else except the four of us. I don't want anybody tipped off about this. And that includes Humphries."

Pancho waved a hand nonchalantly. "He hasn't said a word to me since we moved Sis."

"I don't think he knows where we stashed her," Dan said, reaching for his drink.

"He knows about ever'thing."

"Not this flight," Dan said firmly. "*Nobody* is going to know about this. Understand me? Don't even tell Amanda or Fuchs. This is just between you and me, kid."

"And the flight controllers," Pancho muttered.

"What?"

"How're you goin' to get the flight controllers to go along with this? You can't just waltz aboard the *Starpower* and light her up without them knowin' it. Hell's bells, Dan, you won't even be able to hop up to the ship if they don't let you have a jumper and give you clearance for takeoff."

Sipping at his brandy-laced ginger beer, Dan admitted, "That's a problem I haven't worked out yet."

"It's a toughie."

"Yep, it is," Dan said, unable to suppress a grin.

Pancho shook her head disapprovingly. "You're *enjoying* this."

"Why not?" Dan replied. "The world's going to hell in a handbasket, the New Morality is taking over the government, Humphries is trying to screw me out of my own company—what could be more fun than hijacking my own spacecraft and riding it out to the Belt?"

"That's weird," Pancho murmured.

Dan saw that his glass was empty. He pressed the button set into the table's edge to summon one of the squat little robots trundling through the crowd.

"Don't worry about the flight controllers," he said casually. "We'll figure out a way around them."

"We?"

"You and me."

"Hey, boss, I'm a pilot, not a woman of intrigue."

"You made a pretty good spy."

"I was lousy at it and we both know it."

"You hacked into Humphries's files."

"And he found out about it in half a minute, just about."

"We'll think of something," Dan said.

Pancho nodded, then realized that she had already thought of something.

"I'll fix the flight controllers," she said.

"Really?" Dan's brows rose. "How?"

"Better that you don't know boss. Just let me do it my way."

Dan looked skeptical, but he shrugged and said nothing.

MISSION CONTROL CENTER

The timing had to be just right.

Nervous despite being invisible, Pancho edged cautiously into the Armstrong spaceport's mission control center. It was nearly two a.m. The center was quiet, only two controllers on duty and both of them were relaxed, one leaning back in his chair while the other poured coffee at the little hotplate off by the door to the lav.

Pancho hadn't told anyone about this caper. She thought it best to borrow the stealth suit and get the job done without bringing anyone else into the picture; not even Dan Randolph. The fewer people who knew about the stealth suit, the better.

No landings or takeoffs were scheduled at this hour; the skeleton crew was in the control center strictly because prudent regulations required that the center always be manned, in case an emergency cropped up.

How could there be an emergency? Pancho asked herself as she slowly tiptoed to the console farthest from those being used by the pair of controllers. Spacecraft don't just zoom in on the spur of the moment; even a max-thrust flight from one of the space stations orbiting Earth takes six hours to reach the Moon. Plenty time to rouse the whole crew of controllers if they were needed. The only possible emergency would be if one of the teams at a remote outpost on the lunar surface ran into a jam. Maybe if an astronomer at the Farside Observatory suddenly developed a case of appendicitis and their radio was out so they sent the poor boob on a ballistic lob to Selene without being able to alert anybody first. That was just about the only emergency Pancho could think of.

Or if an invisible woman sneaked in and jiggered the flight schedule for tomorrow's launches. No, Pancho thought, not tomorrow's. It's already past two in the morning. Today's schedule.

She sat at one of the unattended consoles, as far from the human controllers as possible, and waited for the woman at the coffee urn to return to her post. The overweight guy sitting at his console looked half asleep, feet up on the consoles, eyes closed, a pair of earphones clamped over his head. They weren't the regulation earphones, either. The guy was listening to music; Pancho could see the rhythmic bobbing of his head.

Hope it's a lullaby, she said to herself.

The woman controller took a sip of her coffee and made a sour face. Then she looked straight at Pancho. Inside the stealth suit, Pancho froze. The moment passed. The woman's gaze shifted and she started back toward her console, her steaming coffee mug in one hand. Pancho began to breathe again.

The woman came back to her console, next to the guy, gave him a disapproving frown, then sat down and clapped a regulation earphone and pin-mike set to her head.

Good, thought Pancho. The big chamber was too quiet to suit her. Normally the rows of consoles would be filled with controllers talking to the traffic coming in and out of Selene. There would be plenty of background chatter to hide her pecking at a keyboard. But then there wouldn't be any empty consoles to use; they'd all be occupied during normal working hours.

Pancho tentatively tapped on the keyboard before her, once to silence the voice system, then again to call up the status board. The woman at her console did not hear the faint clicks. Or if she did, she paid no notice. The guy was definitely asleep, Pancho thought, his head lolling on his shoulders now, his bulging belly rising and falling in deep, slow breathing.

Only one craft on the schedule, Pancho saw from the status display. Due to land in five hours. Plenty of time for her to do what she had to and get out before more controllers began filing in for the morning shift.

Slowly, cautiously, with one eye on the bored woman sitting on the other side of the room, Pancho tapped out a set of instructions for the morning's schedule. Then she got up, quietly left the control center, and returned the stealth suit to Ike Walton's locker up in the storage area near the catacombs. She wondered if she'd ever need it again. Maybe I ought to keep it, she thought. But then Ike would discover it was gone, sooner or later, and that would raise a stink. Better to let it stay here and just hope Ike doesn't change the combination on the lock.

Sudden panic hit Pancho. Elly was not in the locker, where she had left her. Pancho had thought that the krait would snooze away in the chilly air of the storage area; she had fed Elly a mouse only a day earlier, and that usually left the snake in a pleasantly drowsy state of digestion. But moving her to Walton's locker must have disturbed Elly's torpor. The snake had slithered through one of the air slits in the bottom of the locker door.

For several frantic minutes Pancho searched for the krait. She found her at last, curled on the floor in front of a heating vent. But when she tried to pick Elly up, the krait reared and hissed at her.

Pancho got down on both knees and frowned at the snake. "Don't you go hissy on me," she said sternly. "I know I disturbed your nap, but that's no reason to get sore."

The snake's tongue flicked in and out, in and out.

"That's right, take a good sniff. It's me, and if you'll just calm yourself down, I'll wrap you around my nice warm ankle and we can get back home. Okay?"

Elly relaxed and sank back into a tight little coil of glittering blue. Pancho slowly extended her hand and when Elly didn't react, she stroked the krait's head gently with one finger.

"Come on, girl," she crooned, "we're gonna take you home where you can sleep nice and comfy."

But not for long, Pancho added silently.

HUMPHRIES TRUST RESEARCH CENTER

Martin Humphries was awakened from a dream about Amanda by the insistent shrill of his personal phone.

It wasn't a sexual dream. Strangely, when he dreamed of Amanda it was never sexual. They were on a yacht this time, sailing across a calm azure sea, standing up by the prow and watching dolphins leaping across the ship's bow wave. He felt nervous on the water, unable to shake the fear of drowning even in this idyllic setting.

Amanda stood by the rail, wearing a lovely pale blue dress, the soft breeze tousling her hair. She gazed at him with sad eyes.

"I'll be leaving soon," she said unhappily.

"You can't leave me," Humphries said to her. "I won't let you leave."

"I don't want to, darling. But they're forcing me to. I must go. I have no choice."

"Who?" Humphries demanded. "Who's forcing you?"

"You know who, dearest," said Amanda. "You know. You're even helping him."

"It's Randolph! He's taking you away from me!"

"Yes," Amanda said, her eyes pleading with him to help her. To save her.

And then the damned phone woke him up.

He sat up in his bed, blazingly angry. "Phone!" he called out. "On the art screen."

A reproduction of a Picasso cubist nude disappeared to reveal the somber face of his security chief.

"Sorry to wake you, sir," the man said, "but you said you wanted to be personally informed of Ms. Cunningham's movements."

With a glance at the digital clock on the nightstand, Humphries demanded, "Where's she going at four in the fricking morning?"

"She's apparently asleep in her room, sir, but—"

"Then what are you bothering me for?" Humphries bellowed.

The security man swallowed visibly. "Sir, her name has just appeared on a flight manifest."

"Flight manifest?"

"Yessir. She and three other people are scheduled to go to the Starpower ship, up in orbit."

"Now? Today?"

"Scheduled for eight this morning, sir."

Four hours from now, Humphries realized. "And this flight manifest just came up on the launch schedule?"

"About an hour ago, sir."

"Why are they going to *Starpower 1*?" Humphries wondered aloud.

"That vessel is scheduled for launch on a test flight at nine o'clock, sir."

"I know that," Humphries snapped. "It's an unmanned long-duration flight."

"Perhaps they're going up for a last-minute checkout, before the ship is launched out of orbit."

"Three other people going with her, you say? Who are they?"

The security chief read off the names. "P. Lane, command pilot; L. Fuchs, mission scientist; and C. N. Barnard, flight surgeon."

"I know Lane," Humphries said. "Who are the other two?"

"Fuchs is a graduate student from Zurich Polytechnical Institute. He just arrived in Selene a few days ago. Barnard is apparently a medic of sorts."

"Apparently?"

Looking uncomfortable, the security chief replied, "He's an Astro employee. We have no background data on Barnard, sir. No ID photo, either. All that we've been able to pull up from Astro's files are his name, his position, and his fingerprints and retinal scan."

"Dan Randolph," Humphries growled. "It's an alias for Randolph!"

"Sir?"

"Check those prints and retinal scan against Dan Randolph's file."

"Yessir."

"And send a couple of men to Amanda Cunningham's quarters. Bring her here, to me."

"Right away, sir."

The wall screen went blank for an instant, then the Picasso image reappeared. Humphries paid no attention. He leaped out of bed, snarling aloud, "That fucking Randolph thinks he's going to zip off to the Belt and take Amanda with him. Like hell he will!"

Dan was already up and dressed in a white flight suit, the kind of coveralls worn by members of Selene's medical staff. "C. N. Barnard" was one of the extra identities he had stored in Astro's personnel files, a hangover from the days when he'd been up to his armpits in international skullduggery. He still had modest bank accounts scattered here and there on Earth under various aliases, just in case he ever needed to disappear for a while.

He grinned to himself as he started for the tunnel that led to the spaceport. I'm going to disappear for a while, all right. Completely out of the Earth–Moon system. Past Mars. Out to the Asteroid Belt. The IAA will go apeshit when they find out we're on board *Starpower 1*. Humphries'll have a fit.

And Astro's stock ought to shoot up when we claim mining rights to a nice, rich asteroid or three. The lawyers may squabble over the details, but a few billion dollars worth of high-grade ores will start a feeding frenzy among the brokers. And the publicity will help, too.

His grin disappeared as he reached the entrance to the tunnel. An electric cart sat waiting to take him to the spaceport, but neither Pancho nor Amanda was in sight. Dammitall to hell and back, Dan fumed. They were supposed to meet me here at five sharp. Women!

"Come on, Mandy," Pancho urged. "Dan's prob'ly waitin' for us already!"

"One more minute," Amanda said, from the lav. "I've just got to—"

Somebody pounded impatiently on the door.

"Oh, hell!" Pancho said.

Amanda came out of the lavatory. "I'm ready, Pancho. Sorry to keep you waiting."

Pancho opened the door. Instead of Dan Randolph, two strangers stood out in the corridor. Both were men, wearing identical dark gray business suits. One with long blond hair and a nice full moustache, the other a taller, darker man with a military crew cut. Both were big-shouldered and stone-faced. They looked like cops to Pancho.

Shit! Pancho thought. They know I hacked into the flight schedule.

But the blond said, "Amanda Cunningham? Come with us, please."

Pancho hiked a thumb over her shoulder. "That's her. And she's not goin' anywhere with you. We're late for work already."

They pushed past Pancho and entered the room. "You'll have to come with us, Ms. Cunningham," the blond said.

"Why? On whose authority?"

"Mr. Humphries wants to see you," the buzz cut said. His partner frowned at him.

Pancho said, "Now wait a minute—"

"Don't interfere," the blond said sharply. "Our orders are to bring Ms. Cunningham to Mr. Humphries's residence. That's what we're going to do."

"Call security, Mandy," Pancho said. "These guys are workin' for Humphries."

Amanda started around the bed to the phone on the night table between their two beds, but the blond moved faster and blocked her way.

"We don't want to get physical," he said to Amanda, "but we've got a job to do and we're going to do it."

"How rough we get depends on you," said the darker man, grinning at Amanda.

She stared at them, wide eyed, somewhere between confusion and terror.

The blond took another step toward Amanda. "Come along now, honey. We don't want to hurt anybody."

Mandy stumbled back, away from him. Pancho saw that both men were focused on her. She swiftly bent down and peeled Elly from her ankle.

"Here, wiseass," Pancho said as she hurled the bright blue snake at the blond.

He turned just fast enough to see the krait sailing in lunar slow motion toward his face. Instinctively he raised his arm to shield himself.

"What the hell!"

Elly bounced off the guy's arm and fell to the floor. She reared up, hissing angrily.

"Jesus Christ, what is it?"

The buzz cut was tugging at something inside his jacket. Pancho chopped at the back of his neck and he sagged to the floor. Elly slithered toward him. The blond seemed frozen with fright, staring at the snake.

Pancho gestured to Amanda, who stepped past the goggle-eyed blond and came to her side.

The guy on the floor pushed himself up on one elbow and saw the snake rearing a bare ten centimeters in front of his face, its beady eyes staring at him.

"Aaaggh," he moaned.

The blond pulled a small pistol from the holster beneath his jacket. Pancho saw that his hand was shaking badly.

"Loud noises annoy her," she said. "Just be quiet and don't move."

The blond glanced at her, then returned his stare to the snake. The buzz cut was sweating as Elly stood before him, her tongue flicking in and out.

"D-do something," he whispered hoarsely.

"Better drop your gun on the bed," said Pancho to the blond. "If you shoot and miss her, she'll bite him for sure."

The blond tossed the gun onto the bed. "Get it out of here," he pleaded.

Pancho started to lean forward, slowly, carefully, bending toward Elly. But the buzz cut's nerve broke. He swung blindly at the snake and tried to scramble to his feet. Elly sank her fangs into the meaty side of his hand.

He screamed and sagged back to the floor, unconscious. Pancho bent over and scooped Elly up, careful to hold her so the krait couldn't twist and bite her.

"He'll be dead in an hour 'less you get the antiserum into him," Pancho said quickly.

The blond stared at his partner helplessly.

"Take him to the hospital!" Pancho shouted.

She headed for her travel bag, still on her bed, next to the blond's discarded gun. Still holding Elly, she rummaged in the bag until she found the vial of antiserum and tossed it to the blond.

"Get him to the hospital! Now! Tell 'em what happened and give 'em this. It's the antiserum."

Then she grabbed her still-open travel bag and headed for the door. Amanda came right behind her, then rushed back in to get her own bag. As they hurried down the corridor together, Pancho glanced back over her shoulder and saw the blond lugging his unconscious partner in the other direction, toward the hospital.

"Good girl, Elly," she said. The krait had wrapped itself contentedly around Pancho's wrist.

When they got to the spaceport tunnel Dan Randolph was pacing angrily.

"Where the hell have you been? We're running late."

"I'll tell you all about it, boss," Pancho said as they climbed aboard the cart.

"It's Martin," Amanda said, her voice low.

"Humphries?" asked Dan.

"He wants Mandy, and I think he knows we're tryin' to get out of here."

"What the hell happened?" Dan demanded.

Pancho told him as the automated cart rode down the tunnel to the spaceport.

• • •

Martin Humphries sat at his desk, staring coldly at the frightened, worried face of the blond security agent. The man was sweating and nervously brushing at his moustache with a fingertip.

"So you let her get away," Humphries said, after the man had explained his failure for the third time.

"My partner was dying!" the blond said, his voice ragged. "That motherfucking snake bit him!"

"And you let Ms. Cunningham get away," Humphries repeated, icily.

"I had to take him to the hospital. He would've died otherwise."

"You didn't phone me, or security, or anyone who might have prevented her leaving."

"I'm phoning you now," the blond said, with some heat. "They're just about making their rendezvous with the *Starpower* ship. You can call the control center and have them abort the mission."

"Can I?"

"There's still time."

Humphries clicked off the connection. Stupid clod, he thought. I send him to do one simple thing and he fucks it up completely.

"Abort the mission," he said aloud. Then he shook his head. I should call the control center and tell them that Dan Randolph is hijacking my vessel and taking the woman I love alone with him. That would be a lovely item for the scandal nets. Everyone would laugh themselves sick at me.

He leaned back in his contoured chair, but its softly yielding padding failed to soothe him. Amanda's running off with Randolph. He's probably been hot for her all the time, just waiting to get her away from me. Well, now they can be together. She prefers him to me. So she can die with him.

His teeth hurt. With some surprise, Humphries realized that he'd clamped his jaw so tight it was making his whole head ache. His neck and shoulders were painfully stiff with tension. His fists were clenched so tightly he could feel his fingernails cutting into his palms.

Amanda's gone off with him. I'll acquire Astro, but I've lost her forever. They'll die together. It's not my fault. I didn't want to kill anybody. They're doing it to themselves. She's killing herself.

He wished he could cry. Instead, he glanced at the list of major Astro stockholders that was displayed on his desktop screen. And he punched his right fist into the screen, exploding it in a shower of sparks and plastic shards.

STARPOWER 1

Fuchs met them at the spaceport, wondering why the four of them were going to the ship a bare hour before it was due to leave orbit and head out to the Belt.

"There's been a change in plans, Lars," Dan told him. "We're going along, too."

The young man's dark brows lifted halfway to his scalp. "The IAA has approved this?"

"That doesn't make any difference," Dan said as Amanda and Pancho clambered into the tractor waiting to take them to the jumper out on the launch pad. "We're going."

Fuchs hesitated, standing in the open airlock hatch of the tractor.

"We're going," Dan repeated. "With you or without you."

A slow smile spread across Fuchs's broad face. "With me," he said, and hopped up into the tractor, clearing its six steps with ease.

Dan grinned and resisted the urge to imitate the younger man's athleticism. Amanda and Pancho had taken the two rear seats, Fuchs the one next to the hatch. Dan sat behind the driver's seat as the driver herself closed the airtight hatch and then checked out the cab's pressurization. She got behind the wheel and slipped on her headset.

She's waiting for authorization from the controller to go out, Dan knew. If they're going to stop us, this'd be the easiest time for them to do it.

But after a few moments' wait, she put the tractor in gear and rolled to the garage's airlock. A few minutes later they were at the jumper, connecting the flexible access tube from the tractor's hatch to the airlock hatch on the jumper's crew module. In their flight coveralls, the four of them stepped carefully along the springy plastic of the narrow tube, hands touching the walls, heads bent slightly to keep from brushing the low ceiling.

Small as it was, the jumper's hab module was better than the claustrophobic tube. It was little more than a few square meters of metal deck enclosed in a glassteel bubble. A control console stood up front on a waist-high pedestal. Pancho went to the control console and pulled on one of the headsets hanging there; Amanda took up her post on Pancho's right.

"Better use the foot loops," Dan said to Fuchs. "We'll be in zero-*g* for a few minutes."

Fuchs nodded. He looked tense, expectant, his thin lips tightly closed.

They can stop us at any time, Dan told himself. But as each second ticked by, he felt better and better.

"Five seconds and counting," Pancho told them. She hadn't bothered to turn on the speaker built into the console.

Just as Dan reached out to clasp one of the handgrips along the curving inner surface of the bubble, the jumper leaped off the ground with a single short, sharp bang of its ascent rocket. Dan's knees flexed, but Fuchs nearly buckled. Dan grabbed his arm to steady him.

"I . . . I'm sorry," Fuchs apologized. "I didn't expect it."

"It's okay," said Dan, impressed by the hard muscle he felt. "This is only your second launch, isn't it?"

Fuchs looked pale. "My second from the Moon's surface. I also rode the shuttle from the Zurich aerospace port."

Dan saw that zero-*g* was making Fuchs queasy. "Are you going to be okay?" he asked. Nothing worse than having the guy next to you upchucking all the way to rendezvous.

With a weak smile, Fuchs pointed to his well-muscled biceps. "I took the precaution of wearing a medicinal patch."

"Good," Dan said.

"And also these." He pulled a thick wad of retch bags from the thigh pocket of his coveralls.

"Smart man," Dan said, hoping that Fuchs wouldn't have to use them.

Under control from the ground, the jumper made rendezvous with *Starpower 1* and docked with the fusion ship's main airlock hatch. Dan felt the slightest of thumps as the jumper's adapter section locked onto the ship's hatch.

"Confirm docking," Pancho said into her pin-mike. "You guys did a good job. I didn't have to touch the controls once."

Whatever the controller said back to her made Pancho laugh. "Yeah, I know; that's why you drag down the big bucks. Okay, we're goin' aboard now."

Turning to Dan, Pancho said, "I'll set her up for automatic separation and return to Selene."

"Right," said Dan, lifting free of his foot restraints and floating to the hatch. As far as the controllers back at Armstrong spaceport were concerned, the four of them were to be aboard *Starpower 1* only for a final checkout before the ship was launched out of orbit. They were expected to return to Selene on the jumper.

"They're gonna be kinda surprised when this li'l buggy lands and nobody's in it," Pancho said with a mischievous grin.

Dan went through the jumper's hatch and into the coffin-sized adapter section. He tapped out the entry code to open the fusion ship's airlock hatch.

"Okay," he said, once the hatch had swung open. "Let's get aboard the Beltline express."

"You first, boss," said Pancho. "You're the owner."

He grunted. "One-third owner. I imagine at least one of the other two is going to be mighty slammed once he figures out what we're doing."

"But he must have figured that out already," Amanda said.

"Right," Pancho agreed. "Why else would he send those goons after Mandy?"

Dan felt his brow furrow. "Then why isn't he raising a howl? Why isn't he trying to stop us?"

Fuchs looked back and forth from Amanda to Pancho to Dan, clearly baffled by their conversation.

"Well, let's get aboard before he does start hollerin'," Poncho said, making a shooing motion toward Dan with both her hands.

Feeling suddenly uneasy, Dan sailed through the hatch and entered *Starpower 1*. He hovered at the airlock's inner hatch as Pancho came through and pushed off straight toward the bridge. Amanda started through the hatch, but stumbled slightly. Fuchs grasped her by the shoulders, steadying her.

"Thank you, Lars," Amanda said.

Dan thought the kid's face turned red for a moment. He let her go and Amanda sailed through both hatches without needing to use her hands or feet. Fuchs, still a newcomer to zero-*g*, gripped the edges of the hatch with both his meaty hands and cannonballed through. He thumped painfully against the far bulkhead. Dan said nothing, suppressing his laughter at the young man's attempted display of athletic prowess.

But as he sealed the hatches Dan's mood darkened. *I warned Amanda about coming on to a guy.* He realized that she was wearing ordinary coveralls, but still—I'll have to play chaperon between her and Fuchs, Dan told himself.

He headed up to the bridge, "swimming" in zero gravity by flicking his fingertips against the passageway bulkheads to propel himself weightlessly forward.

Pancho had strapped herself into the command pilot's chair, busily working both hands across the control board. Through the wide glassteel ports above the board, Dan could see the dead gray curve of the Moon's limb and, beyond it, the beckoning bright crescent of the glowing Earth.

"I just disconnected ground control," she said. "They oughtta start squawkin' about it just about . . . now."

"Put them on the speaker," said Dan.

Amanda glided into the co-pilot's chair and buckled the safety harness. Fuchs came up behind her and slid his feet into the restraint loops on the floor.

"We have a disconnect signal, S–1," came a man's voice from the speaker. He sounded more bored than annoyed.

Pancho looked over her shoulder toward Dan, who placed a finger before his lips. "Run silent, run deep," he whispered.

Cupping her pin-mike with one hand, Pancho said, "I'm ready to separate the jumper."

"Do it," Dan replied.

"Jumper separation sequence initiated," Pancho said into her mike.

"Are you aboard the jumper?" asked the controller. "We can't launch S–1 as long as that disconnect is in effect. We've lost command of the vehicle."

A red light flashed on the control panel, then winked off.

"Jumper separated," Pancho said.

"Repeat, are you aboard that jumper?" the controller asked, his voice rising with irritation.

"Where else would we be?" Pancho asked innocently. And she disconnected the radio link with Selene.

Amanda worked on the launch sequence program, her manicured fingers tapping dexterously on the touchscreen.

"Three minutes to launch," she said calmly.

"Gotcha," said Pancho.

Despite himself, Dan felt his palms go sweaty. Standing there behind the two pilots, ready to ride a man-made star out farther than any sane man had ever gone before, he said to himself, Everything I've got is riding on this bird. If we don't make it, I've got nothing to come back to. Not a double-damned thing.

He looked at Fuchs. The kid was smiling fiercely, like an old-time warrior watching the approach of an enemy army, waiting for the battle to begin, eager to get into it. He's got guts, Dan thought admiringly. We picked the right guy.

"Two minutes," Amanda called out.

"They must be goin' apeshit down there by now," Pancho said, grinning.

"Nothing they can do about it," said Dan. "They can't shoot us down."

"Couldn't they send a Peacekeeper vessel after us?" Fuchs asked.

"Once we light the fusion rocket," Dan answered, "*nothing* in the solar system will be able to catch us."

"Till we come back," said Pancho.

Dan frowned at the back of her head. Then he relaxed. "When we come back, we'll be rich."

"You'll be rich, boss," Pancho said. "The rest of us'll still be employees."

Dan laughed. "You'll be rich, too. I'll see to that. You'll be rich."

"Or dead," Pancho countered.

"One minute," Amanda said. "I really think we should pay attention to the countdown."

"You're right," said Pancho.

Dan watched it all on the displays of the control board. The fusion reactor lit up as programmed. Star-hot plasma began generating energy. Through the MHD channel it roared, where a minor fraction of that heat energy was turned into electrical power. The ship's internal batteries shut off and began recharging. Cryonically-cold liquid hydrogen and helium started pumping through the rocket nozzles' cooling walls. The hot plasma streamed through the nozzles' throats.

"Ignition," Amanda said, using the traditional word even though it was now without physical meaning.

"Thrust building up," Pancho said, Dan watched the curves rising on the thrust displays, but he didn't need to; he could feel weight returning, feel the deck gaining solidity beneath his feet.

"We're off and running," Pancho announced. "Next stop, the Asteroid Belt!"

SPACEPORT ARMSTRONG

lanked by his chief of security and the head of his legal department, Martin Humphries arrived at the spaceport just in time to see *Starpower 1* light up and break orbit.

He stood at the rear of the control center, arms folded across his chest, and watched the telescopic view of the fusion ship displayed on the main wallscreen. It was not a spectacular sight: *Starpower 1*'s four rocket nozzles glowed slightly, and the ship drifted away so slowly that Humphries had to check the numbers running along the right edge of the screen to be certain that it was moving at all.

A smaller screen on the side wall showed a lunar jumper approaching the spaceport.

Four rows of consoles took up most of the control center; only three of the consoles were occupied, but Humphries could sense the consternation and confusion among the controllers.

"Jumper Six, answer!" the controller on the left was practically shouting into his headset mike.

The ponytailed, bearded man sitting in the middle of the trio was whispering heatedly with the woman on his other side. Then he whipped around in his swivel chair and grabbed his own headset from the console.

"Pancho!" he yelled in a rumbling basso voice. "Where the hell are you people? What's going on?"

Humphries knew perfectly well what was going on.

The woman controller looked up and saw Humphries standing there. She must have recognized him. Her face went white and she jabbed the chief controller's shoulder, then pointed in Humphries's direction.

The chief literally jumped out of his chair, sailing high enough almost to clear the console behind his station. But not quite. He banged his shins painfully on the top edge of the console and went sprawling in lunar slow motion into the unoccupied chair behind it, ponytail flying. He was enough of a lunik to reflexively put out his hands and grab the chair's arms to break his fall. But the chair rolled backward into the last row of consoles, and the chief controller crashed ungracefully to the floor with a loud thud and an audible, "Ooof!"

Humphries's security chief instinctively hustled down to the fallen controller and yanked him to his feet while Humphries himself and his lawyer stood impassively watching the idiotic scene.

The security man half-dragged the controller, limping, to Humphries.

"Mr. Humphries," the controller babbled, "we don't know what's going on—"

"Isn't that *Starpower 1* accelerating out of its orbit?" Humphries asked frostily.

"Yessir, it is, but it wasn't scheduled to launch for another half-hour yet and I think Pancho Lane and three other people are *aboard* it and they don't have the authorization for a crewed flight. The IAA is going to—"

"Is there any way to get them back?" Humphries asked, deadly calm.

The chief controller scratched his beard, blinking rapidly.

"Well?"

"Nosir. No way in hell, Mr. Humphries."

"Who else is aboard her?"

"That's just it, we don't know if they're aboard the vessel! They might be on the jumper but they're not answering our calls. Maybe their radio broke down."

"They are aboard *Starpower 1*," Humphries said flatly. "Who else was with Pancho Lane?"

"Um . . ." The chief controller turned to his two assistants, wincing.

The woman called, "Amanda Cunningham, co-pilot; Lars Fuchs, planetary astronomer; and C. N. Barnard, flight surgeon."

"And you allowed them to go aboard my ship?" Humphries asked, his voice sharp as an icepick.

"They had proper authorization," the chief controller said, sweating noticeably. "IAA approval." The other two controllers, still standing at their stations, nodded their agreement.

"Amanda Cunningham was definitely with them?"

All three nodded in unison.

Humphries turned and started out of the control center. The chief controller exhaled a relieved sigh. His coveralls were stained with sweat.

But Humphries stopped at the doorway and turned back toward

him. "I want you to know that the so-called Dr. Barnard is actually Dan Randolph."

All three of the controllers looked stunned.

"You never bothered to check their identifications, did you?"

"We never . . ." The controller's deep voice dwindled into silence under Humphries's furious glare.

"I know you work for Selene, and not for me. But I'm going to do my best to see to it that you three incompetent morons never get within a thousand kilometers of a control center again."

Then he went through the door and headed for the tunnel that led back to Selene proper.

"Shall I start the proceedings for the Astro takeover?" Humphries's lawyer asked him.

He nodded grimly.

With a satisfied smile, the lawyer said, "He won't have any part of the corporation by the time he gets back here."

"He's not coming back," Humphries said darkly. "None of them are."

Sitting in the tiny wardroom behind *Starpower*'s bridge, Dan Randolph felt truly relaxed for the first time in months. The ship was accelerating smoothly. Fuchs looked a lot better now, with the feeling of weight that came from the acceleration. No more floating in zero-*g;* they could sit in chairs without having to strap themselves down.

He marveled at his good mood. The Earth's melting down, your corporation is going broke, you've busted every regulation the IAA ever wrote, Humphries is after your scalp, you're heading out for parts unknown, and you're sitting here with a grin on your face.

He knew why.

I'm free, he told himself. Maybe for only a couple of weeks, but I'm free of all of them, free of all their crap. We're on our own and nobody can bother us.

Until we come back.

Pancho ducked through the hatch and went straight to the juice dispenser.

"How's it going?" Dan asked casually.

"All systems working jus' fine," she said, filling a mug and coming to the table to sit next to Dan.

"Must be okay if you feel good enough to leave the bridge."

"Mandy's up there, keepin' an eye on ever'thing. The bird will actually fly on her own; we don't need to be on the bridge every minute of the day."

"Any incoming calls?" Dan asked.

She shrugged. "Only about six or seven million. Ever'body from Doug Stavenger to the Global News Network wants to talk to you."

"Global News?" Dan's ears perked up.

"Lots of news media. They all want to interview you."

Dan stroked his chin thoughtfully. "Might not be a bad idea. If we're going to do an interview it'll have to be before we get so far away the time lag makes it impossible to have a real-time conversation."

"Better do it quick, then," Pancho said. "Once we goose this bird to one-third *g*, we'll really be sprintin' fast."

Dan nodded his agreement. Pointing to the phone console built into the bulkhead, he asked, "Can you patch me through?"

"Easy."

"Okay . . . lemme talk to La Guaira."

The head of Astro's corporate public relations staff was a sweet-faced brunette who was older—and much tougher—than she looked. Dan asked her if she could arrange a news conference with the world's major news networks.

"It has to be today," he pressed. "We're zipping out so fast that by tomorrow we won't be able to talk back and forth without a four-to-five-minute lag."

"Understood," said the PR woman.

"Can you do it?"

She arched a carefully-drawn brow. "Arrange a major news conference with the man who's hijacked his own superduper spaceship to go out past Mars and start mining the asteroids? Just get off the line, boss, and let me get to work."

Dan laughed and obliged. He was glad that he had decided to keep his public relations team intact, despite the layoffs in other corporate departments. Fire the accountants and the lawyers, he reminded himself. Get rid of the paper shufflers and bean counters. But keep the people who polish your public image. They're the last to go—except for the people who do the *real* work: the engineers and scientists.

Pancho watched him as she sipped at her juice. When Dan ended his call to La Guaira, she asked, "So now what happens?"

"Now we wait while my PR people do their jobs."

"Uh-huh. How long do you think it'll take?"

"We'll know in an hour or so," Dan said. "If it takes longer than that, it's not going to go down."

Pancho nodded. "I could hear it. The lag between you and her's already longer than the usual Earth–Moon delay."

Dan got to his feet and went to the coffee dispenser. He really wanted a pleasant glass of amontillado, but there was no alcohol on the ship.

Remembering the story the two women had told him about the goons Humphries had sent after Amanda, Dan asked, "Whatever happened to your snake?"

"Elly?"

"Is that the snake's name?"

"Yup."

"So what'd you do with her?"

Pancho reached down to her ankle and came up with the glittering blue krait.

Dan flinched back. "You brought that thing aboard?"

Shrugging, Pancho said, "I was gonna leave it with Pistol Pete, he's the guy who owns the Pelican Bar. But with those goons and all, I didn't have the time."

"We've got a poisonous snake on the ship!"

"Relax, boss," Pancho said easily. "I've got four mice in my travel bag. That's enough to keep Elly fat and happy for more'n a month."

Dan stared at the snake. Its beady eyes stared back at him.

He started to shake his head. "I don't want that thing on this ship."

"Elly won't be a problem," Pancho insisted. "I'll keep her in a nice, cool spot. She'll sleep most of the time." Then, with a smirk, she added, "And digest."

"But if something should happen . . ."

Pancho's face went deadly serious. She seemed to Dan to be struggling with herself.

He suggested, "Maybe we could freeze the snake for the duration of the flight. Thaw her out when we get back to Selene."

"She's not poisonous," Pancho blurted.

"What?"

"I don't like to admit it, but Elly's not really poisonous. I just tell people that to keep 'em respectful. You think Selene's safety board would let a poisonous critter into the city?"

"But you said . . ."

Looking almost apologetic, Pancho said, "Aw, you can't believe ever'thing I say, boss. A gal's got to protect herself, doesn't she?"

"But what about that guy she bit?"

"Elly was gengineered. They modified her toxin so she produces a tranquilizer, not a lethal poison."

Dan gave her a hard look. Can I believe anything she says? he wondered.

"The science guys wanted to use Elly to trank animals in the wild that they wanted to study. It never worked."

"And you got the snake for a pet."

"A bodyguard," Pancho corrected.

"What about the antiserum?"

She laughed. "Saline solution. Just a placebo. The guy would've woke up whether they used it or not."

Dan broke into a chuckle, too. "Pancho, you're something of a con artist."

"I suppose," she admitted easily.

Amanda's voice came through on the intercom. "I've got an incoming call from La Guaira."

"I'll take it here," Dan said.

It took several frenzied hours, but Dan's PR director finally set up an interactive news conference with reporters from virtually every major media network on Earth, plus Selene's own news director, Edith Elgin, who happened to be Mrs. Douglas Stavenger when she wasn't on the air.

Dan sat back in the little plastic chair in *Starpower*'s wardroom and smiled into the camera of the phone console set into the bulkhead. His PR director acted as moderator, choosing which reporter was allowed to ask a question, and a backup. Dan found that the time lag from the ship to Earth worked in his favor; it gave him time to think before the next question arrived.

It's always smart to think before you talk, he told himself. Engage brain before putting mouth in gear.

THE INTERVIEW

Cable News: Why did you hijack your own ship?

Dan Randolph: How can you call it a hijacking if it's my own ship? And it's only partially mine, by the way. *Starpower 1* is owned by Starpower, Ltd., which in turn is owned by three organizations: Humphries Space Systems, Astro Manufacturing, and the people of Selene. Far as I know, neither Humphries nor Selene is complaining, so I don't see this as a hijacking.

Cable News: But the International Astronautical Authority says you have no right to be aboard *Starpower 1*.

Dan Randolph: Bureaucratic [DELETED]. There's no reason why a human crew can't ride in this vessel. The IAA is just trying to strangle us in red tape.

BBC: Why do you think the IAA refused to give permission for a human crew to fly in your vessel?

Dan Randolph: I'll be double-dipped in hot chocolate fudge if I know. Ask them.

BBC: Surely you have some opinion on the matter.

Dan Randolph: Paper shufflers tend to be conservative souls. There's always a risk in allowing somebody to do something new, and bureaucrats hate risk-taking. Much safer for them to say no, you need more testing or another round of approvals. Buck the responsibility upstairs and don't stick your own neck out. If the IAA had been running America's expansion westward back in the nineteenth century, they'd still be trying to decide whether to build Chicago or St. Louis.

Nippon News Agency: What do you hope to achieve by this flight?

Dan Randolph: Ah, a substantive question for a change. We intend to stake out a claim to one or more asteroids. Our goal is to open up the vast resources of the Asteroid Belt for the human race.

Nippon News Agency: Have you determined which asteroids you will investigate?

Dan Randolph: Yes, but I'm not at liberty to reveal which they are. I don't want anyone or anything to cloud our claim.

Several questioners simultaneously: What do you mean by that? What are you afraid of? Who would make a rival claim?

Dan Randolph: Whoa! Hey, one at a time. Basically, I fear that if I announce that we're aiming for a certain asteroid, the IAA will find a reason to declare it off-limits to development, just as they've declared the Near-Earth Asteroids and the moons of Mars closed to development.

Network Iberia: But the NEAs have been closed to development because there is the chance that their orbits could be perturbed and they would crash into the Earth, isn't that so?

Dan Randolph: That's the IAA's excuse for keeping the NEAs off-limits, right. Bureaucrats can always find a good excuse to prevent progress.

Network Iberia: Are you saying, then, that the IAA has other motives in this? A hidden agenda?

Dan Randolph: If they do, their agenda isn't hidden terribly well. They've denied the resources of the NEAs to the needy people of Earth. If they could, they'd deny the resources of the Belt, as well. Why? Ask them, not me.

Lunar News: You seem to be implying that the IAA is working against the best interests of Earth.

Dan Randolph: I'm not implying it, I'm saying it loud and clear: The IAA is working against the best interests of Earth.

Lunar News: If that's the case, who do you think they are working for?

Dan Randolph: The status quo, of course. That's what bureaucrats always support. Their goal is to keep tomorrow exactly like today, or yesterday, even—no matter how lousy today or yesterday may have been.

Pan Asia Information: You cast yourself in the position of helping the needy people of Earth. Yet isn't your true goal to make billions in profits for your corporation?

Dan Randolph: My true goal is to open up the resources of the Asteroid Belt. We are running this mission on a shoestring; we don't intend to make a profit from this flight.

Pan Asia Information: But you hope to make profits from future missions, don't you?

Dan Randolph: Certainly! But more important than that, we'll have shown that the people of Earth can tap the enormous treasures of resources waiting for us in the Belt. We'll be glad to see other companies coming out to the Belt to find and develop those resources.

Columbia Broadcasting: You'd be glad to see competitors going to the Belt, but only after you yourself have claimed the best asteroids.

Dan Randolph: That's real flatland thinking. There are millions of asteroids in the Belt. Hundreds of millions, if you count the boulder-sized ones. We could claim a thousand of them and that wouldn't even begin to put a dent into the total number available.

Columbia Broadcasting: You say "claim" an asteroid. But isn't it illegal to claim any object in space?

Dan Randolph: It's been illegal since 1967 to claim sovereignty over any body in space. But since the founding of Selene, it has been perfectly legal to claim *use* of the natural resources of a celestial body.

Euronews: Weren't you accused of piracy at one time? Didn't you hijack shipments of ore on their way from the Moon to factories in Earth orbit?

Dan Randolph: That was a long time ago, and all those legal issues have been resolved.

Euronews: But aren't you doing the same thing now? Stealing a ship and going out to claim resources that rightfully belong to the entire human race?

Dan Randolph: Look, pal, I *own* this ship, one-third of it, at least. And those resources out in the Belt won't do the entire human race one diddley-squat [DELETED] iota's worth of good if somebody doesn't go out there and start developing them.

Anzac Supernet: Is it true that *Starpower 1* runs on fusion rockets?

Dan Randolph: Yes. For more about the Duncan Drive you should talk to Lyle Duncan, who headed the team that built this propulsion system. He's at the university in Glasgow.

Anzac Supernet: Are you really going to be able to reach the Asteroid Belt in two weeks?

Dan Randolph: If we accelerate at one-sixth *g* halfway and then decelerate to our destination, yes, two weeks.

Global News: Do you think this stunt will help the price of Astro Manufacturing stock?

Dan Randolph [grinning]: You must be a stockholder. Yes, if we're successful I think Astro's price should climb considerably. But that's just my guess. I'm in enough trouble with the IAA; I wouldn't want the GEC's regulators on my back, too.

Global News: How many people are on the ship with you? Could you introduce them?

•   •   •

Leaning back in his reclining chair as he watched the interview, Martin Humphries felt whipsawed by emotions. Try as he might to remain calm, he seethed inwardly with cold fury at Dan Randolph and Amanda Cunningham.

Yet when Amanda appeared on the wallscreen, sitting at the ship's control panel alongside Pancho Lane, looking properly businesslike in her flight coveralls and her hair pinned up, his anger melted in the light from her eyes.

How could you? He silently asked Amanda. I offered you everything and you turned your back on me. How could you?

After hardly a minute of seeing her on-screen he abruptly snapped the broadcast off. The wallscreen went blank.

It's over and done with, he told himself as he called up his appointments calendar on his desk screen. Put it behind you. Grimly he searched for the date of the next quarterly meeting of Astro Manufacturing's board of directors. He marked the date in red. Randolph will be dead by then. I'll be able to pick his bones and snap up Astro for a song. They'll all be dead by then. Her too.

Furious at the way his hands trembled, Humphries called up his most reliable dating service and began scrolling through the videos of the women who were available and ready to please him.

None of them were as desirable as Amanda, he realized. But he began making his choices anyway.

OUTWARD BOUND

An adenoidal woman lamented lost love as country music twanged softly in the bridge of *Starpower 1*.

"That was some performance you put on," said Pancho.

She was sitting in the command-pilot's seat at the instrument panel. Dan was in the right-hand seat, beside her, separated by a bank of control knobs and rocker switches. He saw that half the touchscreens on the panel had been personalized by Pancho: they showed data against backgrounds of the Grand Canyon, sleek acrobatic aircraft, even muscular male models smiling reclining on sunny beaches.

"The interview?" Dan laughed softly. "I could've predicted three-quarters of the questions they asked. Maybe more."

He stared out at the view through the wide glassteel port that ran the length of the instrument panel and wrapped around its sides. To his left, behind Pancho, was the Sun, its brilliance toned down by the port's heavy tinting but still bright enough to dominate the sky. It made Pancho look as if she had a halo ringing her close-cropped hair. The zodiacal light stretched out from the Sun's middle clear across the width of the port; dust motes scattered the sunlight, leftovers from the solar system's early days of creation. Beyond was darkness, the deep black infinity of space. Only a few of the brightest stars shone through the port's tinting.

"You really think the stock price'll go up?" Pancho asked, her eyes shifting back and forth among the displays on the panel.

"Already has, a couple of points," Dan said. "That's one of the reasons I did the interview."

She nodded. "From what I heard afterward, the IAA wants to slap your butt in jail the instant you get back into their jurisdiction."

"Wouldn't be the first time I've been in jail," Dan muttered.

"Yeah, but that wouldn't do the stock any good, would it?"

"Pancho, you talk like a worried stockholder."

"I'm a stockholder."

"Are you worried?"

"What, me worry?" she joked. "I got no time for worryin'. But I would like to know exactly where we're heading."

"Would you?"

"Come on, boss, you can razzle-dazzle the reporters but I know you got an asteroid all picked out. Maybe a couple of 'em."

"I want to get to three of them."

"Three?"

"Yep. One of each type: stony, metallic, and carbonaceous."

"How deep into the Belt will we hafta go?"

'We'd better bring Fuchs into this; he's the expert."

In a few minutes the four of them were seated around the table in the ship's wardroom: Amanda and Fuchs on one side, Pancho and Dan on the other. A computer-generated chart of the Asteroid Belt was displayed on the bulkhead screen, a ragged sprinkling of colored dots between thin yellow circles representing the orbits of Mars and Jupiter.

"So you can see that the metallic asteroids," Fuchs was saying, in an almost pedantic drone, "lie mostly in the outer areas of the Belt. This is a region that hasn't been explored as well as the inner zones."

"Which is why we haven't picked a specific metallic rock as yet," said Dan.

"What're we talkin' here?" Pancho asked. "Three AUs? Four?"

"Four astronomical units," Amanda replied, "give or take a fraction."

"And you want to head out there and scout around?" Pancho clearly looked incredulous.

"We have enough fuel for some maneuvering," Dan said.

Pulling her palmcomp from her coverall pocket, Pancho said, "Some maneuvering. But at that distance, not a helluva lot."

"I need a nice chunk of nickel-iron," Dan said. "Doesn't have to be big: a few hundred meters will do just fine."

Fuchs broke into a smile. It made his heavy-featured, normally dour face light up. "I think I understand. A nickel-iron piece a few hundred meters across would contain enough iron ore to feed the world's steel industry for a year or more."

Dan jabbed a forefinger in his direction. "You've got it, Lars. That's what I want to show them, back home."

Amanda spoke up. "Didn't someone bring a nickel-iron asteroid into the Earth–Moon vicinity?"

"Gunn did it," Fuchs answered. "He even named the asteroid Pittsburgh, after the steel-producing center in the United States."

"Yeah, and the double-damned GEC tossed Gunn off the rock and damned near ruined him," Dan recalled sourly.

"You simply can't have people bringing potentially dangerous objects into the Earth–Moon region," Amanda said. "Suppose this Pittsburgh thing somehow was perturbed into an orbit that would impact Earth? It could have been devastating."

Dan scowled at her. "It's been more than four centuries since Newton figured out the laws of motion and gravity. We can calculate orbits with some precision. Pittsburgh wasn't going to endanger anything. It was just the double-damned GEC's way of maintaining control."

Pancho looked up from her palmcomp. "We've got fuel enough to maneuver for three days, out at the four AU range."

"Good enough," Dan said. "We'll be scanning all the way out there. Maybe we'll get lucky and find a nickel-iron baby right away."

Fuchs shook his head gloomily. "There is vast emptiness out there." Pointing to the wallscreen display, he went on, "We think of the Belt as crowded with asteroids, but really they are nothing but infinitesimal bits of matter floating in an enormous sea of emptiness. If that chart was drawn to true scale, the asteroids would be too small to see, except in a microscope."

"A few needles in a tremendous haystack," Amanda added.

Dan shrugged carelessly. "That's why we have radar and telescopes and all the other sensors."

Pancho brought the conversation back to practicality. "Okay, so we have to go huntin' to find a metallic rock. What about the others you want, boss?"

"Lars has already picked them out."

Tapping on his own palmcomp, lying on the table before him, Fuchs highlighted two particular asteroids on the wall display. Bright red circles flashed around them. With another touch of his stylus on the palmcomp's tiny keyboard, the trajectory of *Starpower 1* appeared on the display, with the ship's current position outlined by a flashing yellow circle.

"The closer object is 26–238, an S–type asteroid."

"Stony," Amanda said.

"Yes," Fuchs agreed, smiling at her. "Stony asteroids are rich in silicates and light metals such as magnesium, calcium and aluminum."

Dan stared at the display. The dot showing *Starpower 1*'s position was noticeably moving. *Christ, we're going like a bat out of hell.* He had known the facts and figures of the fusion-driven ship's performance, but now, seeing the reality of it on the chart, it began to hit him viscerally.

"Our second objective," Fuchs was going on, "will be 32–114, a C–type, chondritic object. Chondritic asteroids contain carbon and hydrates—"

"Water," said Pancho, getting up from the narrow table and heading for the food freezer.

"Yes, water, but not in the liquid form."

"The water molecules are linked chemically to the other molecules in the rock," Amanda said. "You have to apply heat or some other form of energy to get the water out."

"But it's water," Dan said, watching Pancho as she pulled a foil-wrapped prepackaged meal from the freezer. "Selene needs water. So does anybody working in space."

" 'You will do your work on water,' " Amanda murmured. " 'An' you'll lick the bloomin' boots of 'im that's got it.' "

"What's that?" Dan asked, puzzled.

She looked almost embarrassed. "Oh . . . Kipling. Rudyard Kipling."

" 'Gunga Din,' " Fuchs added quickly. "A very fine poem."

"By a white European male chauvinist," Pancho quipped as she slid her meal into the microwave oven.

"How can you be hungry?" Amanda asked. "You had a full meal only a few hours ago."

Pancho grinned at her. "I don't have to watch my figure. I burn off the calories just like that." She snapper her fingers.

"But those prepackaged meals," Amanda said. "They're so . . . prepackaged."

"I like 'em," said Pancho.

"Anyway," Dan said, raising his voice slightly to cut off any disagreements, "those are the two rocks we're going after. We'll take some samples to solidify our claim and then head for the outer region of the Belt and find ourselves a metallic body."

"I've been wondering," Amanda said slowly, "about the legal status of any claims we make. If the IAA considers this flight to be illegal . . . I mean, if we're deemed to be outlaws—"

"They could disallow our claims to the asteroids," Dan finished for her. "I've thought about that."

"And?"

A single, sharp, clear *ping* sounded from the open hatch to the bridge. Pancho sprinted from the microwave oven and ducked through the hatch.

She came back into the wardroom a moment later, her face taut. "Solar flare."

Amanda got to her feet and pushed past Pancho, into the bridge. Fuchs looked concerned, almost alarmed.

Dan said, "I'll check out the electron guns."

"Might not hit us," Pancho said. "The plasma cloud's still too far away to know if it'll reach us or not."

"I'll check out the electron guns anyway," Dan said, getting up from his chair. "I've taken enough radiation to last me a lifetime. I don't need any more."

EARTHVIEW RESTAURANT

The instant Martin Humphries saw Kris Cardenas, he realized that she was suffering pangs of guilt. Big time. The scientist looked as if she hadn't slept well recently; dark circles ringed her eyes, and her face looked bleak.

He rose from his chair as the maitre d' escorted her to the table and smiled as the dark-clad man held Cardenas's chair for her while she sat down. Cardenas was not smiling.

Gesturing with an outstretched arm, Humphries said, "The finest restaurant within four hundred million kilometers."

It was an old joke in Selene. The Earthview was the only true restaurant on the Moon. The other two eateries were cafeterias. Ten years earlier, the Yamagata Corporation had opened a top-grade tourist hotel at Selene, complete with a five-star restaurant. But Yamagata was forced to shut down their restaurant as the greenhouse warming throttled the tourist trade down to a trickle. Now they sent their few guests to the Earthview.

At least Cardenas had dressed properly, Humphries saw. She wore a sleeveless forest-green sheath decorated tastefully with accents of gold jewelry. But she looked as if she were ready to attend a funeral, not an elegant dinner.

Without preamble, she leaned across the table so intently she almost touched heads with Humphries. "You've got to warn them," she whispered urgently.

"There's plenty of time for that," he said easily. "Relax and enjoy your meal."

In truth, the Earthview was a fine restaurant by any standard. The staff were mostly young, except for the stiffly formal maitre d', who added an air of grave dignity to the establishment. Carved out of the lunar rock four levels below the surface, the restaurant lived up to its name by having broad, sweeping windowwalls that displayed the view from the lunar surface. It was almost like looking through windows at the barren, gauntly beautiful floor of the great ringwalled plain of Alphonsus. The Earth was always in the dark sky, hanging there like a splendid glowing blue and white ornament, ever changing yet always present.

There were no robots in sight at the Earthview restaurant, although the menus and wine list appeared on display screens built into the table-tops. Instead of tablecloths, each place setting rested on a small mat of glittering lunar honeycomb metal, as thin and flexible as silk.

Humphries ordered wine from their waiter. As soon as the young man walked away from their table, Cardenas hunched forward again and whispered, "Now! Tell them now! The sooner they know the safer they'll be."

He gave her a hard look. Apparently the nanobugs in her bloodstream can't deal with the effects of too little sleep, he thought. Or maybe she has nightmares. She's on a royal guilt trip, that's certain.

"We agreed, Dr. Cardenas," he said softly, "that we would warn them just as they approached the outer fringes of the Belt. That won't happen for another day and a half."

"I want you to warn them now," she insisted. "I don't care what we agreed on."

With the barest shake of his head, Humphries said, "I'm afraid I can't do that. We must stick to our plan."

"I was insane ever to agree to this," Cardenas hissed.

"But you did agree," Humphries pointed out. "In the long run, you'll be glad that you did."

It had been so easy to turn her. Humphries considered that his one major talent was finding the weak spot in other people's personalities, and then playing on their weaknesses to get what he wanted. It worked with Dan Randolph and his ridiculous crusade to save the Earth. It worked with Dr. Cardenas and her burning anger against the Earth and the people who had separated her from her husband and family.

The wine came. Humphries tasted it and sent it back. There was nothing really wrong with it, but Humphries simply felt like asserting himself. Subtly. Cardenas probably doesn't understand what's going on, not at the conscious level, he thought. But down in her guts she's got to know that I'm the one in charge here. I make the decisions. I mete out the rewards and the punishments.

She sat in stony silence while the embarrassed waiter took away the wine and swiftly returned with another bottle. Humphries sipped at it. Not as good as the first one, really, but he had established his point.

"This is fine," he murmured. "You may pour."

They ordered dinner. Cardenas barely picked at hers as, course by course, the dishes came and were taken away again. Humphries ate heartily. He was almost enjoying Cardenas's discomfort.

At last, after the waiter had left their desserts and walked away from the table, Cardenas said, "Well, if you won't tell them, I will."

"That's not what we agreed on," Humphries said tightly.

"To hell with what we agreed on! I don't know why I let you talk me into it."

"You let me talk you into it because I can get you back to Earth, back to your ex-husband and your children and grandchildren."

"He's remarried," she said bitterly. "There's no point in messing up his life any more than I have already."

Humphries almost smiled. She's really riding the guilt train, he said to himself.

Aloud, he coaxed, "But your grandchildren. You do want to see them, don't you? If you prefer, I could arrange to have them come up here, you know."

"I've asked them to come up, just for a visit. Begged them," Cardenas said. "They won't do it. They're terrified that they'll be refused re-entry back to Earth. That they'll be exiled here, just as I am."

Smoothly, Humphries said, "I can arrange a visit for them. Outside normal channels. I can guarantee that they'll be allowed to return to their homes."

He saw new hope kindled in her eyes. "You could?"

"No sweat."

She sat in silence while her dessert slowly melted. Humphries spooned his up, watching her, waiting.

"But don't you understand how dangerous it is?" she blurted at last. "They're going out past Mars, for god's sake. There's no one out there to help them."

"Randolph's no fool," he said sharply. "When the ship's systems start to fail he'll turn around and come back here. In a big hurry."

"I don't know . . ."

"And his pilot's an expert. She won't do anything foolish."

Cardenas either wasn't listening to him or not hearing. "Once those nanos kick in," she said, "there's no stopping them. They'll take the radiation shield apart, atom by atom, and then—"

"They won't have the time," Humphries insisted. "You forget how fast *Starpower* goes. They'll zip back here in a few days."

"Still . . ." Cardenas looked utterly unconvinced.

Trying to sound unconcerned, Humphries said, "Look, I know this is a dirty trick to play on Randolph. But that's the business world. I want his mission to fail so I can buy out his company on the cheap. I don't want to kill him! I'm not a murderer."

Not yet, he added silently. But I'm going to be. And I'm going to have to silence this woman before her guilt trip makes her warn Randolph.

Unbidden, the thought of Amanda came to him. It only hardened his resolve. *He's* making me kill her. Randolph deserves to die. He's forced me to kill Amanda.

As he looked across the table at Kris Cardenas, so troubled, her eyes focused on god-knows-what, Humphries nodded to himself. If I leave her alone she'll warn Randolph. She'll ruin everything. I can't let her do that.

SOLAR STORM

The Apollo missions to the Moon in the mid-twentieth century were timed to avoid periods when the Sun was likely to erupt with a flare that would drench the solar system with killing levels of hard radiation.

Later, spacecraft shuttling between the Earth and the Moon simply scurried for shelter when a solar storm struck. They either returned to the protection that the Earth's magnetic field provides against the storm's lashing hail of protons and electrons, or they landed on the Moon and their crews sought shelter underground.

The earliest spacecraft to carry humans beyond the Earth–Moon system had no such options available to them, for their transit times to Mars were so long that they would inevitably encounter a solar storm while weeks or months away from a safe haven. Thus they were outfitted with storm shelters, special compartments in which the crew could be protected from the intense radiation spewed out by a solar flare. The first explorers sent to Mars spent days on end cooped up in their spacecraft's cramped "storm cellar," until the high-energy particles of the storm's plasma cloud finally passed them by.

Starpower 1 had no storm cellar. The entire crew module was protected in the same manner that a storm shelter would have been. The module was lined with thin wires of an exotic yttrium-based compound that formed a superconducting magnet which generated a permanent magnetic field around the crew module, a miniature version of the Earth's magnetic field. Yet the superconductor could not produce a magnetic field strong enough to deflect the solar storm's most dangerous killers, the high-energy protons.

When faced with a vast cloud of deadly subatomic particles blasted out by a solar flare, the ship was charged to a high positive electrostatic potential by a pair of electron guns. The energetic protons in the cloud were repelled by the ship's positive charge. The magnetic field was strong enough to deflect the cloud's lighter, less energetic electrons—and thus keep the negatively-charged electrons from ruining the ship's positive charge.

Safely cocooned inside the protective magnetic field, the crew of *Starpower 1* watched the swift approach of the storm's plasma cloud.

"Be here in another six hours," Pancho announced, pulling off her headset as she swiveled the command pilot's chair to face Dan.

He frowned at the news. "That's for certain?"

"Certain as they can be. Early-warning spacecraft in Mercury co-orbit have plotted out the cloud. Unless there's a great big kink in the interplanetary field, it's gonna roll right over us."

Nodding, Dan said, "The electron guns are ready to go."

"Better start 'em up," she said. "No sense waitin' till the last minute."

"Right." Dan stepped through the hatch, into the empty wardroom, and headed aft, where the electron guns were housed. Pancho could control them from the bridge, but Dan wanted to be there in case any problems cropped up.

"And send Amanda up here, will you?" Pancho called to him. "I gotta take a break."

"Right," Dan shouted back, over his shoulder.

Where is Amanda? He asked himself. The wardroom was empty. The doors to the privacy compartments along the passageway were closed. And where is Fuchs? he wondered, starting to feel nettled.

He found them both in the sensor bay, where Fuchs was explaining something about the x-ray projector.

"It would be more helpful if we could use a small nuclear device," the planetary astronomer was saying, totally serious. "That would be the most convenient way of generating x-rays and gamma rays all at the same time. But of course, nuclear devices are banned."

"Of course," Amanda said, looking just as intent as Fuchs.

"Pancho needs you on the bridge, Mandy." Dan said.

She looked startled for a flash of a second, then said, "Right."

As she hurried toward the bridge, Dan asked Fuchs, "What in the name of the nine gods of Sumatra do you want a nuke for?"

"I don't!" Fuchs said. "They're illegal, and justly so."

"But you just said—"

"I was explaining to Amanda about x-ray spectroscopy. How we use x-rays to make an asteroid fluoresce and reveal its chemical composition. The x-rays from this solar flare would have been very helpful to us if we were only close enough to the Belt."

"But a nuke?"

Fuchs spread his hands. "Merely an example of how to produce x-rays and gamma rays on demand. An example only. I have no intention of bringing nuclear explosives into space."

"I don't know," Dan said, scratching his chin. "You might be onto something. Maybe we could talk the IAA into letting us use nukes as sources for spectroscopic studies."

Fuchs looked aghast. Dan laughed and slapped him on the shoulder. Fuchs saw the joke and grinned weakly back.

Dan's mood darkened as he edged down the narrow walkway in the aft end of the module. He did not like the thought of being exposed to hard radiation. He had taken a lifetime's worth of radiation back in his earlier days, working in space. Much more of a dose would kill him, he knew. It wouldn't be an easy way to go, either.

As he lifted the covers protecting the electron guns' innards and checked them for the eleventh time since they'd launched out of lunar orbit, Dan thought, Maybe Stavenger's right. Get a jolt of nanomachines, let them clean up the damage the radiation's done, rebuild me from the inside. So I won't be able to go back to Earth. So what? What's down there that I'd miss so much?

He knew the answer even as he asked the question. Sea breezes. Blue skies and soft sunsets. Birds flying. Flowers. Huge ugly brutal cities teeming with life. Vineyards! Dan suddenly realized that no one had yet tried to grow wine grapes off-Earth. Maybe that's what I'll do when I retire: settle down and watch my vineyards grow.

The intercom speaker set into the narrow walkway's overhead carried Pancho's voice. "Dan, you ready for me to light up the guns?"

The electron guns were just as good as they'd been all the other times he'd inspected them. Closing the cover on the one on his right, Dan answered, "You may fire when ready, Gridley."

Pancho retorted, "I don't know who this Gridley guy is, but I can't rev up the guns till you close both their covers and seal 'em right and proper."

"Aye, aye, skipper," Dan said.

By the time he made it back to the bridge, Pancho was nowhere in sight. Amanda sat alone in the right-hand seat, and the bridge was rocking to the beat of high-intensity pop music. As soon as she saw Dan come through the hatch, Amanda snapped the music off.

"Pancho's in the loo," she said as Dan slid into the command-pilot's seat.

"How's the storm?"

"Precisely on track." Amanda tapped at one of her touchscreens; it displayed a simplified map of the inner solar system, the orbits of Earth and Mars shown as thin lines of blue and red, respectively; the position of *Starpower 1* was a blinking bright yellow dot. A lopsided gray miasma was almost touching the dot.

Dan's mouth went dry. "I hate these things," he mumbled.

"It missed the Earth completely. Mars, as well."

"But it's going to swamp us."

"Actually," Amanda said, "we'll merely be brushed by it. A few hours, that's all."

"That's good."

"Our own velocity is helping a lot, you know. An ordinary spacecraft, coasting along the way they do, would be in the cloud for days on end."

Dan had no desire to be in the cloud for even ten minutes. He changed the subject, as much to get away from the fear building up inside him as any other reason. "How friendly are you and Fuchs?"

Amanda's brows shot up. "Lars? He's very earnest—about his work. Nothing more."

"That's all there is to it?"

"Yes."

Dan thought it over. Two healthy young people locked in this sardine can for a couple of weeks. Of course, there's Pancho and me to chaperon them. Dan grinned to himself. Damn, it's like being a teenager's father.

Pancho returned to the bridge. "Hey boss, get outta my chair."

"Yes'm," said Dan.

The plasma cloud hit them less than an hour later. There was no buffeting, no clanging of alarms, nothing to tell them that they were being engulfed in the cloud of killing radiation except the rising curves of fire-engine red on the radiation monitoring screens.

Pancho did not consider the storm so dangerous that someone had to be on the bridge at all times. She came into the wardroom and joined the others for dinner. Dan ate mechanically, not really tasting his food, not really hearing the conversation. Double-damned radiation, he kept thinking. I hate this. Despite two steaming mugs of coffee, he felt cold inside.

But the others seemed completely unfazed by the storm. After the meal Dan said good-night to them all and went to his compartment. He dreamed of floating helplessly in space, slowly freezing as the Sun glowered at him.

NANOTECHNOLOGY
LABORATORY

L ong past midnight, Kris Cardenas sat alone in her office in Selene's nanotechnology lab. The rest of the lab was empty, darkened to its nighttime lighting level.

She had agreed to have dinner with Martin Humphries because she wanted to get the man to warn Dan Randolph about the nanomachines that she had planted in his vessel, virus-sized disassemblers that once were known as "gobblers."

They were the reason that nanotechnology was banned on Earth—and under careful supervision at Selene.

Quis custodiet ipsos custodes? she asked herself. Who will watch the watchmen? Some Roman asked that question more than two thousand years ago, Cardenas knew.

All nanotech work was under very strict control in Selene. No one was allowed to work with gobblers: they had killed people. They had even been used to commit murder. If they ever got loose they could destroy all Selene. The medical work had to be supervised down to the nanometer because the therapeutic nanobugs that took apart plaque in a person's arteries or destroyed tumors atom by atom were forms of gobblers, nothing less. If they ever got loose, if their programming was ever-so-subtly altered . . .

That was why Kris Cardenas's primary duty as head of all nanotech work at Selene was to protect against such a catastrophe. She watched over every aspect of the work done in the nanotech lab.

But who will watch the watchmen? She had produced a microscopic batch of gobblers for Humphries, specifically tailored to damage *Starpower 1* enough so Dan would have to turn the ship around and limp back to Selene. Humphries had promised that he would obtain permission for her to visit Earth again, to see her daughters and her grandchildren.

Now he was offering to bring them up here. Even better. But the price! Dan Randolph and the other people on that ship could get killed.

Is that what Humphries really wants? She asked herself. If I warned Dan now he'd have to return to Selene. Flat and simple. But Humphries wants to wait another day or so, let Dan get to the inner fringes of the Belt and then tell him that his ship's going to fail.

Or maybe he won't warn Dan at all!

Cardenas sat up straight in her desk chair. That's it, she told herself. He wants to kill Dan and the rest of the crew. She knew it with the certainty of revealed truth.

What can I do about it?

Warn Dan, she answered her own question. Warn him *now.*

But how? She wondered. I can't just pick up a phone and put a call through to him. They're out past the orbit of Mars by now.

I've got to get to someone in the Astro office. Someone who can put me through to Dan. Maybe that big Australian bodyguard of his. What's his name? George something.

Martin Humphries could not sleep, despite the exertions he'd been through with the raven-haired woman lying beside him. Nominally an environmentalist on the consulting staff of Humphries Trust, the young woman's favored environment seemed to be a bedroom with plenty of furniture to play on, as far as Humphries could determine.

She was sleeping peacefully. He was wide awake.

Dr. Cardenas. Humphries was worried about her. Even the lure of seeing her grandchildren wasn't going to outweigh her overdeveloped sense of honor, he thought. She wants to warn Randolph; she's probably figured out that I want the sonofabitch dead.

He sat up in the bed and glanced at the woman sleeping beside him. Slowly, carefully, he pulled the silk sheet down from her shoulders. Even with no lights in the room except the green glow from the digital clock, he could see that her body was smooth, flawless, perfectly proportioned. Too bad she's heading back to Earth in a few days.

Cardenas, he reminded himself sternly.

She's going to try to warn Randolph, he felt certain. Maybe that's a good thing. If Randolph turns back now, Amanda will come back with him. With *him.* She won't be coming back to me. She doesn't want me, that's why she ran off with him. If Cardenas warns them, they'll come back here together to gloat at me.

He squeezed his eyes shut and tried to drive out the mental images of Randolph and Amanda together. *I've got to think this through carefully. Logically.*

For Cardenas to warn Randolph she'll have to get somebody here in Selene to set up the message for her. She'll probably go to Astro; that's where Randolph's people are. And if she asks them to let her put through a call to Randolph they'll ask her why. Sooner or later she'll tell them why: Martin Humphries has bugged the Starpower ship with nanomachines. And then they'll know all about it.

Conclusion: For my own protection, I've got to stop her from talking to anyone at Astro. I've got to stop her from even trying to warn Randolph. I've got to stop her. Period.

When Dan awoke from his troubled sleep the solar storm had passed. Pancho was in the wardroom when he shambled in, bleary-eyed.

"Top o' the mornin', boss," she said cheerily, hefting a mug of steaming coffee.

"How's the weather out there?" Dan asked, heading for the juice dispenser.

"Clear and calm, except for a few rocks we should be passin' by this afternoon."

That made Dan smile. "We're at the Belt."

"Will be, by sixteen hundred hours. Right on *shedyule,* as Mandy would say."

"Good. Great. Where's Fuchs? We've got to make some course adjustments."

Ten minutes later the four of them were seated around the table in the wardroom.

"I want to get a metallic nugget first," Dan said.

Fuchs lifted his heavy shoulders slightly. "The metallic bodies are more heavily concentrated towards the outer area of the Belt."

"So we go to the outer edge of the Belt," Dan replied, "and search for a lump of iron. We can pick up the stony and carbonaceous rocks on the way back."

"We'll have to go more than four astronomical units, then," Amanda pointed out. "No one's gone that far before."

Dan said, "We've got the supplies for it. And the fuel. Everything's running all right, isn't it?"

"No major problems," said Pancho.

His brows rising, Dan asked, "What are the minor problems?"

She grinned at him. "The coffee's pretty awful. A couple of li'l maintenance chores to do. You know, a cranky pump, one of the fuel cells is discharging when it shouldn't. Nigglin' stuff. Mandy and I are takin' care of it."

Amanda nodded. Dan looked from her back to Pancho. Neither woman seemed worried. Well, he thought, if the pilots aren't worried, no reason for me to sweat.

"The sensor suite is in perfect working order," Fuchs volunteered. "I'm already recording data."

"We'll have to do the turnaround maneuver soon," said Amanda.

Gesturing vaguely toward infinity, Dan asked Fuchs, "Have you picked a destination point out there?"

"A general area only," he replied. "The outer Belt has not been mapped well enough to pick a precise asteroid. Most of them are not even numbered yet."

"Have you given Pancho the coordinates?"

Fuchs's face colored slightly. "I gave them to Amanda."

"I've put the data into the nav computer," Amanda said quickly, looking at Pancho.

Pancho nodded. "Okay. I'll go check it out."

"Onward and upward," said Dan, rising from his chair. "We'll be breaking distance records, if nothing else."

"Four AUs," Pancho muttered, getting to her feet also.

She headed for the bridge. Dan followed her, leaving Amanda and Fuchs still sitting at the table.

Pancho slid into the pilot's chair and tapped on her main touchscreen, the one showing the hunk on the beach. Standing behind her, Dan saw the navigation computer program come up over the muscles and teeth.

But Pancho was looking at one of the smaller screens, where an amber light was blinking slowly.

"What's that?" Dan asked.

"Dunno," said Pancho, working the screen with her fingers. "Running a diagnostic . . . h'mmph."

"What?"

Without turning her head from the display screens, Pancho muttered, "Says there's a hot spot on one of the superconducting wires outside."

A jolt of alarm surged through Dan. "The superconductor? Our storm shield?"

She glanced up at him. "Don't get frazzled, boss. Happens all the time. Might be a pinhole leak in the coolant line. Maybe a micrometeor dinged us."

"But if the coolant goes—"

"The rate of loss ain't much," Pancho said calmly. "We're due for turnaround in six hours. I can angle the ship then so's that side's in the shade. If the hot spot doesn't go away then, Mandy and me will go EVA and fix the leak."

Dan nodded and tried to feel reassured.

STAVENGER THEATER

Kris Cardenas marveled at the crowd's willingness to leave their comfortable homes and jam themselves cheek-by-jowl into the cramped rows of narrow seats of the outdoor theater. A considerable throng of people was flowing into the theater. It was built in the Grand Plaza, "outdoors." Exactly one thousand seats were set in a shallow arc around the graceful fluted shell that backed the stage.

Even with three-dimensional interactive video and virtual reality programs that were nearly indistinguishable from actuality, people still went to live performances. Maybe it's because we're mammals, Cardenas thought. We crave the warmth of other mammals. We're born to it and we're stuck with it. Lizards have a better deal.

There was one particular mammal Cardenas wanted to see: George Ambrose. That morning she had phoned the Astro corporate office trying to find him, only to reach his video mail. Late in the afternoon he returned her call. When she said she had to talk to him in person as soon as possible, and preferably in a public place, George had scratched at his thick red beard for a moment and then suggested the theater.

"I've got a date comin' with me," he said cheerfully, "but we can get together in the intermission and chat for a bit. Okay?"

Cardenas had quickly agreed. Only as an afterthought did she ask what the theater was playing.

George sighed heavily. "Some fookin' Greek tragedy. This date of mine, she's a nut for th' classics."

Usually the theater was sold out, no matter what the production might be. In the days before the greenhouse cliff, when tourism was building up nicely, Selene's management invited world-class symphony orchestras, dance troupes, drama companies to come to the Moon. Now, most of the performances were done by local amateur talent.

Medea, performed by Selene's very own Alphonsus Players. Cardenas would have shuddered if it had mattered to her at all. Still, the theater was fully booked. Only Cardenas's status as one of Selene's leading citizens wheedled a ticket out of the system, and she had to go all the way up to Doug Stavenger for that. He smilingly admitted that he wasn't going to use his.

She barely looked at the stage during the first half of the performance. Sitting on the aisle in the fourth row, Cardenas spent most of her time scanning the crowd for a glimpse of George Ambrose's shaggy red hair.

When the first half ended, she trudged with the slow-moving throng along the central aisle as they chatted about the play and the performances. Cardenas felt surprised to see so many gray and white heads among the theater-goers. *Selene is aging,* she thought. *And very few of our people are taking nanobugs or other therapies to stop it.* Finally she saw Big George, like a fiery beacon bobbing head and shoulders above the others.

Once past the last row of seats, most of the crowd scattered to the concession stands spread among the plaza's flowering shrubbery. A maintenance robot trundled slowly along the periphery of the crowd, patrolling for litter.

George was at the jam-packed bar. Cardenas hung back, waiting for him to get his drink and work his way out of the crowd. When he did, he had a plastic stein of beer decorated with Selene's logo in one hand and a skinny, hollow-eyed redhead on his other arm. She was pretty, in a gaunt, needy way, Cardenas thought. Nice legs. The drink in her hand was much smaller than Ambrose's.

Big George spotted Cardenas and, leaving his date standing by a flowering hibiscus bush, walked toward her.

"Dr. Cardenas," he said, with a polite dip of his head. "What can I do for you?"

"I've got to get a message to Dan Randolph," she said. "As quickly as possible."

"No worries. Pop over t' the office tomorrow morning. Or tonight, after th' show, if you like."

"Is there some way I could talk to Dan without coming to your offices? I think I'm being watched."

George looked more puzzled than alarmed. "You could phone me, I suppose, and I'll patch you through to the radio link." He took a pull from his stein.

"Can we do it tonight?"

"Sure. Right now, if you like. I wouldn't mind an excuse to leave this show. Pretty fookin' dull, don'tcha think?"

"Not now," she answered. "That would attract attention. After the show. I'll drop in at friend's place and call your office from there."

For the first time, George showed concern. "You're really scared, are you?"

"I think Dan's life is in danger."

"You mean someone's out to kill 'im?"

"Humphries."

George's face hardened. "You certain of that?"

"I'm . . . pretty sure."

"Sure enough to want to warn Dan. From a safe place, where the phone won't be bugged."

"Exactly."

George took a big breath. "All right. Instead of all this pussyfootin' around, you come with me after the show's finished and I'll put you in an Astro guest suite. That way I can protect you."

Cardenas shook her head. "That's kind of you, but I don't think I'm in danger."

"Then why th' cloak and dagger stuff?"

"I don't want Humphries to know that I'm warning Dan. If he knew, then maybe I would be in trouble."

George thought that over for a few moments, a huge red-maned mountain of a man towering over her, scratching his head perplexedly.

"All right," he said at last. "Back to Plan A, then. I'll go to the office after this fookin' show and you call me there. Okay?"

"Yes. Fine. Thank you."

"Sure you don't want some protection?"

She considered his offer for several heartbeats, then said, "Thanks, but I won't need it. And I've got my work to consider. I can't run the lab from an Astro guest suite."

"Okay," said George. "But if you change your mind, just holler."

Martin Humphries was reclining in his favorite chair, watching a home video of his own performance, when the phone buzzed. Irked, he glanced at the console and saw that it was his emergency line. He snapped his fingers, and the wallscreen lit up to show the woman he'd sent to follow Cardenas. She was a nondescript clerk from Astro Corporation's communications department who needed extra money to bring her younger sister up from the ravaged ruins of Moldavia.

"Well?" Humphries demanded.

"She talked with George Ambrose and then went back to the show."

"You have video?"

"Yes, of course."

"Well let me see it," he snapped.

The woman's face was replaced by a slightly jittery video of Cardenas talking earnestly with Randolph's body-guard, that big Australian.

"They went back to the show together?"

The woman's face reappeared on the screen. "No, separately. He had another woman with him."

Glancing at the digital clock on his desk, Humphries asked, "When does the show end?"

"I don't know."

Stupid cow, he fumed silently. Aloud, he commanded, "Stay with her. I'm going to send a couple of men to pick her up. Keep your phone on and they'll home in on the signal. That way, even if they don't get there before the show's over they can find you—and her."

"It is not allowed to keep the phone on during the performance," the woman replied.

"I don't care what's allowed and what isn't! Keep your phone on and stay with Dr. Cardenas or I'll have you shipped back to Moldavia!"

Her eyes widened with sudden fear. "Yes, sir," she said. Sullenly.

"How's the leak?" Dan asked.

He'd been fidgeting around in the wardroom for hours, trying not to pop into the bridge and bother the pilots. But a leak in the superconductor's coolant scared Dan. Without the superconductor they could be fried by the next solar storm.

So when Amanda left the bridge, Dan asked about the leak.

She looked surprised at his question. "Leak?"

"In the coolant line."

"Oh, that. It's nothing much. Pancho will go EVA after turnaround and patch it."

"Just Pancho?" Dan asked. "By herself?"

"It's only a tiny leak," Amanda said lightly. "Pancho decided it won't need both of us out there."

Dan nodded and got up from his chair. "Think I'll go aft and see what Fuchs is doing." If I just sit here I'll turn myself into a nervous wreck, he added silently.

Fuchs was back in the sensor bay, humming tunelessly to himself as he bent over a worktable strewn with parts from an infrared scanner.

"Did it break down?" Dan asked.

Fuchs looked up at him, a pleased smile on his broad face. "No, no," he said. "I decided to upgrade its sensitivity so we could get better data at long range."

"We're going to turn around soon. You'll have to get all these loose parts stowed away safely or they'll slide off the table."

"Oh, I should be finished by then."

"Really?"

With a glance that was part surprise at having his word questioned, and part pride in his abilities, Fuchs said, "Of course."

He bent over his work again, stubby thick fingers handling the delicate parts with the precision of a well-trained mechanic. Dan watched him for a while, then quietly left the man to himself. As he started back to his privacy cubicle, he saw Amanda heading along the narrow passage toward him.

"Going to help Pancho suit up?" he asked. "I can—"

"Oh, there's plenty of time for that," Amanda said brightly. "I thought I'd pop in on Lars for a few minutes and help him get prepared for turnaround."

Dan felt his brows inch upward. "Something going on between you two?" he asked.

She looked genuinely surprised. "Lars is a complete gentleman," Amanda said with great dignity. "And even though you may not believe it, I know how to behave like a lady."

She brushed past Dan, chin high, radiating disdain.

Dan grinned at her retreating back. Something's going on, all right, even if Fuchs doesn't know it yet.

TURNAROUND

O n my mark," Pancho's voice came through the intercom, "turnaround in thirty minutes. *Mark.*"

Dan sat up in his bunk. He had just drifted to sleep, it seemed, after staring at the compartment's overhead for what had felt like hours.

We're well inside the Belt, he thought. The ship's working fine. We're heading for the outer reaches to scout around for a good, solid M–type body.

And there's a leak in the coolant that keeps the superconductor cooled down enough to maintain the magnetic field around us that protects us from the hard radiation of solar storms. Sounds like the house that Jack built, he said to himself, trying to shake the feeling of foreboding that plagued him.

He grabbed a fresh pair of coveralls and marched to the lav. I need a shower and a shave, he thought. And you need to get that leak fixed, a voice in his head reminded.

He wished it didn't bother him so much. Pancho wasn't worried about it; neither was Amanda.

Damned good-looking woman, Amanda, he thought. Even in loose-fitting coveralls she's dynamite. Better make it a cold shower.

The only tricky part of the turnaround maneuver was that they had to shut down the main thrusters. Not the fusion reactor itself; the procedure was to kill the ship's thrust during turnaround, and use the reactor's exhaust gases to turn the ship by venting a fraction of the exhaust through maneuvering jets set into the sides of the propulsion module.

Dan headed up to the bridge after his shower. Both pilots were in their places. No music was playing.

"All systems ready for turnaround," Amanda murmured.

"Check, all systems go," Pancho replied.

Standing behind their chairs, Dan asked, "Where's Fuchs?"

"Prob'ly still in the sensor bay," Pancho said, "playin' with his toys."

Amanda frowned slightly as she touched the comm screen. "Turnaround in five minutes," she announced.

Glancing over her shoulder, Pancho said, "Boss, you oughtta find a chair."

He scowled at her. "I've been in micro-g before, kid." Before you were born, he almost added.

He could see Pancho grinning in her reflection on the port in front of her. "Okay, you're the boss. Footloops on the deck and handgrips on the overhead."

"Aye-aye, skipper," Dan said, grinning back at her.

"Thrust cutoff in two minutes," Amanda called out.

"Two minutes. Check."

When the main thrusters cut off, Dan felt completely at ease. The feeling of gravity dwindled away to nothing, and he floated off the deck slightly. Grabbing one of the handgrips, he hung there and watched the pilots working their touchscreens.

"How's Fuchs doin' back there?" Pancho asked.

Amanda tapped the central screen and it showed Fuchs strapped into the fold-up chair in the sensor bay, looking a little pasty-faced but otherwise okay.

"Maneuver thrust in two minutes," Amanda said.

"Check," Pancho replied.

Dan worked his feet into the loops on the deck without letting go of the overhead handgrips. The maneuvering jets fired and he felt as if somebody suddenly shoved him from one side. He remembered from childhood his first ride in a people-mover at some airport: he'd been standing facing the doors, and when the train lurched into movement he'd nearly toppled over sideways. Only the grownups crowded around him had prevented him from falling.

"Phew," Pancho said, "this bird turns like a supertanker: slow and ugly."

"You're not flying a little flitter now," Dan said.

"Turn rate is on the curve," Amanda pointed out, tracing the curve on the touchscreen with a manicured fingertip. Her screen's background showed the white cliffs of Dover.

"Uh-huh," said Pancho. "Still feels like we're pushin' freight."

Amanda said, "We are: all that deuterium and helium-three."

The fuel weighs a lot, Dan realized. Funny. You think of hydrogen and helium as being light, almost weightless. But we've got tons of the stuff in our tanks. Dozens of tons.

There was nothing much to see through the port. No panoply of stars swinging past. No asteroids in sight. Nothing but emptiness.

"Where's the Sun?" Dan heard himself ask.

Pancho chuckled. "It's there, boss. Hasn't gone away. We're just angled up too much to see it through the windshield, that's all."

As if in confirmation, a stream of light glowed through the port.

"Sunrise in the swamp," Pancho called out.

Dan felt another sideways surge of thrust, pushing from the opposite direction.

"Turnaround maneuver complete," said Amanda.

"Flow to main thrusters," Pancho said, working the touchscreens.

"Main thrusters, confirmed."

Weight returned to the bridge. Dan settled back onto the deck.

Amanda smiled happily. "On course and on velocity vector."

"Hot spit!" Pancho exclaimed. "Now let's see how that leak is doin'."

Kris Cardenas almost made it back to her own apartment before two young men in dark business suits caught up with her.

"Dr. Cardenas?"

She turned. The man who had called her name was taller than his partner, slim and lithe, sallow complexion, his dark hair cropped into a buzz cut. The other was huskier, blond, pink-cheeked.

"Come with us, please," said the dark one.

"Where? Why? Who are you?"

"Mr. Humphries wants to see you."

"Now? At this hour? It's—"

"Please," said the blond, slipping a dead-black pistol from inside his jacket.

"It fires tranquilizing darts," said the dark one. "But you wake up with a bitching headache. Don't make us use it on you."

Cardenas looked up and down the corridor. The only other person in sight was a mousy little woman who immediately turned away and started walking in the opposite direction.

"Now," said the blond, pointing his pistol at her.

With a resigned droop of her shoulders, Cardenas nodded her surrender. The blond put his gun away and they started along the corridor toward the escalators.

"At least this one doesn't have a snake," the blond whispered hoarsely to his partner.

The other man did not laugh.

EVA

P ancho felt an old excitement bubbling up inside her as she wormed her arms through the spacesuit's sleeves. After more than five days of being cooped up in the ship, she was going outside. It was like being a kid in school when the recess bell rang.

Standing by the inner airlock hatch where the spacesuits were stored, she popped her head up through her suit torso's neck ring, grinning happily to herself. This is gonna be fun, she thought.

Dan looked uptight, though, as he held her helmet in his arms and watched her pull on the gloves and seal them to the suit's cuffs.

"Jealous?" she teased.

"Worried," he replied. "I don't like the idea of you going out alone."

"Piece of cake, boss," Pancho said.

"I ought to go with you. Or Amanda, maybe."

With a shake of her head, Pancho countered, "Mandy's gotta stay at the controls. Shouldn't have both pilots out at the same time, if you can help it."

"Then I'll suit up—"

"Whoa! I've seen your medical record, boss. No outside work for you."

"The safety regs say EVAs should be performed by two astronauts—"

"Whenever possible," Pancho finished for him. "And since when did you start quotin' IAA regulations?"

"Safety is important," Dan said.

Inside the spacesuit, with its hard-shell torso and servomotor-amplified gloves, Pancho felt like some superhero out of a kids' video confronting a mere mortal.

"I'll be fine," she said as she took the helmet from Dan's hands. "Nothin' to worry about."

"But if you run into trouble . . ."

"Tell you what, boss. You suit up and hang out here at the airlock. If I run into trouble you can come on out and save my butt. How's that?"

He brightened. "Okay. Good idea."

They called Amanda down from the bridge as Dan struggled into the lower half of his suit and tugged on the boots. By the time he was completely suited up, backpack and all, except for the helmet, Pancho was feeling antsy.

"Okay," she said as she pulled the bubble-helmet over her head and sealed it to the neck ring. "I'm ready to go outside."

Amanda hurried back to the bridge while Dan stood there grinning lopsidedly at her, his head sticking out of the hard suit like some kid posing for a photograph from behind a cardboard cutout of an astronaut.

Pancho opened the inner hatch of the airlock and stepped through. The airlock was roomier than most, big enough to take two spacesuited people at a time. Through her helmet she heard the pump start to clatter, and saw the telltale on the control panel switch from green to amber. The sound dwindled to nothing more than a slight vibration she felt through her boots as the air was pumped out of the chamber. The light flicked to red.

"Ready to open outer hatch," she said, unconsciously lapsing into the clipped argot of flight controllers and pilots.

Amanda's voice came through the tiny speaker set into her neck ring, "Open outer hatch."

The hatch slid up and Pancho stared out at an infinite black emptiness. The helmet's glassteel was heavily tinted, but within a few seconds her eyes adjusted and she could see dozens of stars, then hundreds, thousands of them staring solemnly at her, spangling the heavens with their glory. Off to her left the bright haze of the zodiacal light stretched like a thin arm across the sky.

She turned her back to the zodiacal light's glow and attached her safety tether to one of the rungs just outside the hatch.

"Goin' out," she said.

"Proceed," Amanda replied.

"Gimme the location of the leak," Pancho said as she clambered out and made her way up the handgrips set into the crew module's side.

"On your screen."

She peered at the tiny video screen strapped to her left wrist. It showed a schematic of the module's superconducting network of wires, with a pulsating red circle where the leak was.

"Got it."

Although she knew the ship was under acceleration and not in zero-g, Pancho still felt surprised that she actually had to climb along the hand-grips, like climbing up a ladder, toward the spot marked on the schematic. Deep in her guts she had expected to float along weightlessly.

"Okay, I'm there," she said at last.

"Tether yourself," Dan's voice commanded sternly.

Pancho was still tethered to the rung next to the airlock hatch. Grinning at Dan's fretfulness, she unreeled the auxiliary tether from her equipment belt and clipped it to the closest grip.

"I'm all tucked in, Daddy," she quipped.

Now to find the leak, she thought. She bent close and played her helmet lamp on the module's skin. The curving metal was threaded with thin wires running along the module's long axis. There was no obvious sign of damage: no charred spot where a micrometeor might have hit, no mini-geyser of escaping nitrogen gas.

It can't be more than a pinhole leak, Pancho told herself.

"Am I at the right spot?" she asked.

No answer for a few moments. Then Amanda replied, "Put your beacon on the wire you're looking at, please."

The radio beacon was strapped to Pancho's right wrist. She laid her right forearm on the wire.

"How's that?"

"You're at the proper spot."

"Can't see any damage."

"Replace that section and bring it in for inspection, then."

She nodded inside her helmet. "Will do."

But she felt silly, cutting out what looked to be a perfectly good length of wire. Something's wonky here, Pancho thought. This ain't what we think it is, I bet.

Behind his unkempt beard, Big George was frowning with worry as he sat at one of the consoles in the spaceport's control center. This little cluster of desks was occupied by Astro employees, monitoring *Starpower 1*'s flight. They sat apart from the regular Selene controllers, who handled the traffic to and from Earth.

George wanted to send his message to Dan in complete privacy. The best the Astro controllers could do was to hand him a handset and tell him to keep his voice down.

Wishing they had worked out a code before Dan had impetuously sailed off, George pulled the pin-mike to his lips and said hurriedly, "Dan, it's George. Dr. Cardenas has disappeared. She told me last night she was worried that Humphries wants to kill you. When I called her this morning she wasn't in her office or in her quarters. I can't find her anywhere. I haven't told Selene security about it yet. What do you want me to do?"

He pulled off the headset and nudged the controller who had given it to him. The man had been studiously keeping his back to George.

He swiveled his chair to face the Aussie. "Finished so soon?"

"How long will it take to get an answer?"

The controller tapped at his keyboard and squinted at the display on his console's central screen. "Seventeen minutes and forty-two seconds for your message to reach them. Same amount of time for their answer to get back here, plus a couple additional seconds. They're moving pretty damned fast."

"Thirty-five minutes," George said.

"Got to allow some time for them to hear what you've got to say and decide what to say back to you. Probably an hour, at least."

"I'll wait."

Martin Humphries unconsciously licked at the thin sheen of perspiration beading his upper lip. He hated talking with his crotchety sour-faced father, especially when he had to ask the old man for advice.

"You kidnapped her?" W. Wilson Humphries's wrinkled face looked absolutely astonished. "A Nobel Prize scientist? You kidnapped her?"

"I've brought her here, to my home," Humphries said, holding himself rigidly erect in his chair, exerting every gram of willpower he possessed to keep from squirming. "I couldn't let her warn Randolph."

The conversation between father and son was being carried by a tight laser beam, directly from Humphries Space System's communication center on the top of Alphonsus crater's ringwall mountains to the roof of the senior Humphries's estate in Connecticut. No one could eavesdrop unless they tapped into the laser beam itself, and if someone did, the drop in the beam's output at the receiver would be detectable.

"Killing Randolph isn't bad enough," grumbled the old man. "Now you're going to have to kill her, too."

"I haven't killed anybody," Humphries said tightly. "If Randolph has any brains at all he'll turn back."

It took nearly three seconds for his father's reply to reach him. "Sloppy work. If you want to remove him, you should have done it right."

Humphries's temper flared. "I'm not a homicidal maniac! Randolph is business, and anyway, if he dies it will look like an accident. His ship fails out there in the Belt and he and his crew are killed. Nobody will know what happened and nobody will be able to investigate, not for months, maybe years."

He tried to calm himself as he waited for his father's response.

"Gaining Astro Manufacturing is worth the risk," the old man agreed. "Especially since no one can connect you with the . . . uh, accident."

"She can."

Humphries knew what his father was going to say.

"Then you'll have to get rid of her."

"But that doesn't mean I have to kill her. I don't want to do that. She's a valuable asset. We can use her."

It wasn't a spur-of-the-moment decision, Humphries told himself. Dr. Cardenas and her knowledge of nanotechnology had been part of his long-range plan all along. It's just that this crisis has forced me to move faster than I'd originally planned to, he told himself.

"Use her?" his father snapped. "How?"

Waving a hand in the air, Humphries said vaguely, "Nanotechnology. She's the top expert. Without her it would've taken years to build that fusion rocket."

His father cackled. "You don't have the guts to take her out."

"Don't be an idiot, Dad! She's much more valuable to me alive than dead."

"You want her to be part of your team, then," his father replied.

"Yes, of course. But she's having this goddamned attack of integrity. She's got cold feet about Randolph, and if I don't stop her, she'll tell everyone about the sabotage, even though she's a party to it."

The old man chuckled when he heard his son's complaint. "An attack of integrity, eh? Well, there are ways to get around that."

"How?"

It was maddening to have to wait nearly three seconds for his father's response.

"Make her an offer that she can't accept."

"What?"

Again the interminable wait. Then, "Offer her something that she really wants, but can't agree to. Make her an offer that really tempts her, but she'll have to reject. Then you've shown yourself to be reasonable, and she's being the difficult one. Then she'll be more willing to agree to your next offer."

Humphries was impressed. "That's . . . Machiavellian."

When his father answered, his seamed, sagging face was strangely contorted, as if he were suppressing a guffaw. "Yes, it is, isn't it? And it works."

Humphries could only sit there and admire the old bastard.

More thoughtfully, his father asked, "What's her weak point? What does Cardenas want that she can't get unless you give it to her?"

"Her grandchildren. They'll be our hostages. Oh, I'll do it in a nice, elegant manner. But I'll let her know that either she works for me or her grandchildren suffer. She'll do what I want."

"You really want to be emperor of the world, don't you, Martin?"

Humphries blanched. "*Your* world? God forbid. Earth is a shambles and it isn't going to get any better. You can have it. You're welcome to it. If I make myself emperor, it'll be up here: Selene, the Moon, the asteroids. That's where the power is. That's where the future lies. I'll be emperor of these worlds, all right. Gladly!"

For long moments his father said nothing. At last the old man muttered, "God help us all."

STARPOWER 1

L ars Fuchs was scowling as he peered at the display screen.
"Well?" Dan prompted.

The two men stood in the cramped sensor bay, where
Fuchs had rigged a makeshift laboratory by yanking one of
the ship's mass spectrometers from its mounting and putting
it on the repair bench where he was using it to examine the
sample of dull gray wire that Pancho had brought in. A thin sky-blue
coolant tube lay alongside the wire. Dan knew the wire had originally run
through the tube, like an arm in a sleeve.

"There is no leak in the coolant line," Fuchs said. "I drove pressurized nitrogen through it and it didn't leak."

Dan felt puzzled. "Then what's causing the hot spot?"

Pointing to the tangle of curves displayed on the screen, Fuchs said,
"The composition of the wire seems to match the specifications quite
closely: yttrium, barium, copper, oxygen—all the elements are in their
proper proportions."

"That doesn't tell us diddley-squat," Dan groused.

Fuchs's frown deepened as he studied the display. "The copper level
seems slightly low."

"Low?"

"That might be a manufacturing defect. Perhaps that's the reason for
the problem."

"But there's no leak?"

Fuchs rubbed his broad, square chin. "None that I can detect with this
equipment. Really, we don't have the proper equipment for diagnosing
this. We would need a much more powerful microscope and—"

"Dan, we're receiving a call for you," Amanda's voice came through the speaker in the sensor bay's overhead. "It's from George Ambrose, marked urgent and confidential."

"I'd better get back up to the bridge," Dan said. "Do the best you can, Lars, with what you've got."

Fuchs nodded unhappily. How can a man accomplish anything without the proper tools? he asked himself. With a heavy sigh, he turned back to the display screen while Randolph ducked through the hatch and headed forward.

What other sensors can I take from the set we have to examine this bit of wire? Everything we have here has been designed to measure gross chemical composition of asteroids, not fine details of a snippet of superconducting wire.

With nothing better that he could think of, Fuchs fired up the mass spectrometer again and took another sampling of the wire's composition. When the curves took shape on the display screen his eyes went wide with surprised disbelief.

George held one meaty hand over the earphone clamped to the side of his head, listening intently to Dan Randolph's tense, urgent voice. There was no video transmission; Dan had sent audio only.

". . . you go with Blyleven to Stavenger himself and tell him what's happened. Stavenger can bypass a lot of red tape and get Selene's security people to turn the place upside down. You can't hide much in a closed community like Selene. A really thorough search will find Dr. Cardenas . . . or her body."

George nodded unconsciously as he listened. Once, ten years earlier, he had lived as a fugitive on the fringes of Selene, an outcast among other outcasts who called themselves the Lunar Underground. But they had survived principally on the sufferance of Selene's "straight" community. They could exist on the fringes because nobody cared about them, as long as they didn't make nuisances of themselves.

George agreed with Dan, up to a point. If Selene's security cops wanted to find a person, there wasn't much chance of hiding. But a dead body could be toted outside, concealed in a tractor, and dumped in the barren wilderness of the Moon's airless surface.

"Okay, Dan," he half-whispered into the pin-mike at his lips. "I'll get to Stavenger and we'll find Dr. Cardenas, unless she's already dead."

Frank Blyleven was head of Astro corporate security. A round, florid-faced, jovial-looking man with thinning straw-colored hair that he wore down to his collar, Blyleven seemed to have a grandfatherly smile etched permanently on his face. It unnerved George to see the security director smiling as he explained about Dr. Cardenas's disappearance.

"This is way out of our league," he said, without the slightest change in expression. "I mean, I only have half-a-dozen people in my group. We chase down industrial espionage and petty theft, for the lord's sweet sake, not kidnappings."

George knew how well Astro's security team chased down petty theft. The Lunar Underground lived on small "borrowings" from corporate storerooms.

"Dan said we should go to Stavenger," said George.

Nodding cheerfully, Blyleven turned to his desktop phone and asked for Douglas Stavenger.

When George and Blyleven were ushered into Stavenger's office, up in the Grand Plaza, a fourth man was sitting in front of Stavenger's broad, glistening desk. Stavenger introduced him as Ulrick Maas, director of security for Selene. Maas looked like a real cop to George: muscular build, dark, suspicious eyes, scalp shaved bald.

"You realize that this may be nothing to get alarmed about," Stavenger said once all four men were seated. "But Kris Cardenas isn't the kind of woman who suddenly goes into hiding, so I think we ought to try to find her."

"She's in Humphries's place, down at the bottom level," George said flatly.

Stavenger leaned back in his desk chair. Maas stared at George through narrowed eyes; Blyleven looked as if he were thinking about much more pleasant things. Through the office windows George could see the broad expanse of the Grand Plaza. A couple of kids were flying above the greenspace like a pair of birds, flapping their brightly-colored rented plastic wings.

Grimacing, Stavenger asked, "You're certain of that?"

"It's Humphries she was scared of," George replied. "Where else would he stash her?"

"That area down there is the property of the Humphries Trust," Maas pointed out. "Selene doesn't have legal authority to go in and search it."

"Not even if her life's on the line?" George asked.

Stavenger said to Maas, "Rick, I think you'll have to initiate a search."

"Of Humphries's place?" George asked.

"Of all of Selene proper," Stavenger said. "Humphries's place is a different matter." He turned to the phone and asked it to connect him with Martin Humphries.

• • •

"Dr. Cardenas?" Martin Humphries said to Stavenger's image on his patio wallscreen. "You mean the scientist?"

"Yes," said Stavenger, looking strained. "She's missing."

Humphries got up from the chaise longue on which he'd been reclining while he reviewed his father's holdings in Libya.

"I don't understand," he said to Stavenger's image, trying to look puzzled. "Why are you telling me about this?"

"The security office has initiated a search for her throughout Selene. I'd appreciate it if you allowed them to search your premises, as well."

"My home?"

"It's just a formality, Mr. Humphries," Stavenger said, with an obviously false smile. "You know security types: they want to dot every eye and cross every tee."

"Yes, I suppose they do," Humphries replied, smiling back. "I suppose someone could hide out in the gardens, couldn't they?"

"Or inside the house. It's rather large."

"H'mm, yes, I suppose it is—by Selene standards." He took a breath, then said reluctantly, "Very well, let them send a team down here. I have no objections."

"Thank you, sir."

"You're welcome," said Humphries. He snapped his fingers to shut down the connection. Then he went into the house, walking swiftly to his office.

He snapped his fingers as he entered the office. The phone screen lit up. "Get Blyleven down here on the double. I've got a job for him."

MARE NUBIUM

The tractor plodded slowly along the bleak, empty expanse of *Mare Nubium,* heading away from the ringwall mountains that marked Alphonsus and the site of Selene.

Kris Cardenas fought to keep the terror from overcoming her. She could feel it, trembling deep inside her, crawling up into her throat, making her heart race so hard she could hear its pulse thundering in her ears.

"Where are you taking me?" she asked, her voice muffled by the helmet of the spacesuit they had put her into.

No response from the driver. Of course, Cardenas thought. They've disabled my suit's radio. A neat, high-tech way of gagging me.

The two goons who had picked her up the night before had brought her down to Humphries's extravagant place in Selene's lowest level. Martin Humphries had not deigned to meet her, but she knew whose place it was. The servants had been very polite, offering her food and drink and showing her to a comfortable guest suite where she'd spent the night. The door to the corridor had been locked, of course. She was a prisoner and she knew it, no matter how sumptuous her cell.

Strangely, she slept well. But thinking over the situation the next morning, after a maid had brought a breakfast tray into her sitting room, Cardenas reasoned that Humphries was going to murder her. He'll have to, she thought. He can't let me go and let me tell everyone that he's killed Dan Randolph.

With my help, she added silently. I'm an accomplice to murder. A blind, stupid, stubborn fool who didn't see what she didn't want to see. Not until it was too late.

And now I'm going to be murdered, too. Why else would they be taking me all the way out into the godforsaken wilderness?

The thought of being killed frightened her, intellectually, in the front lobe of her brain. But being outside on the surface of the Moon, out in the deadly vacuum with all the radiation sleeting in from deep space, out here where humans were never meant to be—that terrified her deep in her guts. This tired little tractor had no pressurized cabin, no crew module; you had to be in a spacesuit to survive for a minute out here.

This is a dead world, she thought as she looked through her helmet visor. The gray ground was absolutely dead, except for the cleated trails of other tractors that had come this way. No wind or weather would disturb those prints; they would remain in place until the Moon crumbled. Behind them, a lazy rooster tail of dust floated in the soft lunar gravity.

And beyond that, nothing but the gently undulating plain of barren rock, pockmarked with craters, some the size of finger-pokes, some big enough to swallow the tractor. Rocks strewn everywhere, like the playroom toys of careless children.

The horizon was too close. It made Cardenas feel even jumpier. It felt wrong, dangerous. In the airless vacuum there was no haze, no softening with distance. That abrupt horizon slashed across her field of view like the edge of a cliff.

She saw that the ringwall mountains of Alphonsus were almost below the horizon behind them.

"Where are we going?" she asked again, knowing it was useless.

Beside her, Frank Blyleven was no longer smiling. He sweated inside his spacesuit as he drove the tractor. When he'd made his deal with Martin Humphries, it had been for nothing more serious than allowing Humphries to tap into Astro Corporation's communications net. A good chunk of money for practically no risk. Now he was ferrying a kidnapped woman, a Nobel scientist, for the lord's sweet sake! Humphries was going to have to pay extra for this.

Blyleven had to admit, though, that Humphries had smarts. Stavenger wants to search for Dr. Cardenas? Okay. Who better to spirit her out of Selene for a while than the head of Astro's security department? Nobody asked any questions when he showed up at the garage already suited up, with another spacesuited person alongside him.

"Got to inspect the communications antennas out on Nubium," he told the guard checking out the tractors. "We'll be out about six hours."

Sure enough, three hours into his aimless wandering across the desolate *mare*, he got a radio signal from Humphries's people. "Okay, bring her back."

Smiling again, he leaned his helmet against Cardenas's so she could hear him through sound conduction.

"We're going back now," he said. "They'll have a team to meet you. You behave yourself when we get to the garage."

Kris Cardenas felt a huge surge of gratitude well up inside her. We're going back. We'll be safe once we're back inside.

Then she realized that she was still Humphries's prisoner, and she wasn't really safe at all.

Dan felt simmering anger as he watched George's report on the wall-screen of the ship's wardroom.

"I was in on th' search of Humphries's place. It's big enough to hide a dozen people. We din't find Dr. Cardenas or any trace of her," George ended morosely.

"She must still be alive, then," Dan said. Then he blew out an impatient huff of breath as he realized that George wouldn't hear his words for another twenty minutes or so.

Pancho was sitting beside him in the wardroom, looking more puzzled than worried as George's image faded from the wallscreen.

"If they haven't found her body," Dan said to her, "it means she's probably still alive."

"Or they've stashed the corpse outside," Pancho suggested.

Dan nodded glumly.

"Why would Humphries want to kill Dr. Cardenas?" Pancho asked.

"Because she found out something that she wanted to tell me; something that Humphries doesn't want me to know."

"What?"

"How should I know?" Dan snapped.

Pancho grinned lamely. "Yeah, I guess that was a pretty dumb question."

Dan rubbed his chin, muttering, "Humphries knew the security people were coming to search his place so he just moved her somewhere else until the search was over. I'll bet a ton of diamonds she's back inside his house now. He'll want to keep her close."

"Prob'ly," Pancho agreed.

"I wish there was a way we could get somebody into Humphries's place without him knowing it," Dan mused.

Pancho sat up straighter. "There is," she said, with a sly smile.

George counted it as a sign of Doug Stavenger's respect for Dr. Cardenas that he agreed to a private meeting.

"Invisible?" Stavenger looked shocked. "A cloak of invisibility?"

"I know it sounds nutty," George said, "but Dan told me that—"

"It's not nutty," Stavenger murmured, steepling his fingers before his face. "I'm stunned, though, that Ike Walton told anyone about it."

"You mean it's real? A cloak of invisibility?"

Stavenger eyed the big Aussie from behind his desk. "It's real, all right. But I doubt that it comes in your size. We're going to have to put the loose-lipped Mr. Walton back to work."

The worst part about this, Dan fumed silently, is being so far apart that we can't talk in real time.

He had paced the length of the crew module several times, from the bridge where Pancho and Amanda chatted amiably while monitoring the ship's highly automated systems to the sensor bay at the far end of the passageway, where Fuchs was bent over the sample of superconducting wire.

George's last message had an almost fairy-tale quality to it. "Stavenger's got the guy who made the cloak enlarging it to fit me. He's over in th' nanotech lab now, doin' it. He says I'll be able to sneak into Humphries's place sometime tomorrow morning, if he doesn't run into any snags."

Rumpelstiltskin, Dan thought as he prowled along the passageway. No, he was the guy who spun straw into gold. Who had the cloak of invisibility?

Pancho, he answered himself. Of all the sneaky con artists in the solar system, she's the one who comes up with a cloak of invisibility. Well, chance favors the prepared mind, they say. Pancho was smart enough and fast enough to use what chance offered her.

He found himself at the sensor bay again. There wasn't room for a chair. Fuchs was standing, staring at the same display screen he'd been staring at the last time Dan had looked in at him.

"Anything interesting?" Dan asked him.

Fuchs stirred as if being awakened from a dream. But from the worried expression on his face, Dan thought it might have been a nightmare.

"What is it, Lars?"

"I've found what created the hot spot in this section of wire," Fuchs said, his voice grave, solemn.

"Good!" said Dan.

"Not good," Fuchs countered, shaking his head.

"What is it?"

Pointing to the curves traced across the display screen, Fuchs said, "The amount of copper in the wire is diminishing."

"Huh?"

"The wire is superconducting only if its composition remains constant."

"And it stays cooled down to liquid nitrogen temperature," Dan added.

"Yes, of course. But this length of wire . . . its copper content is diminishing."

"Diminishing? What do you mean?"

"Look at the curves!" Fuchs said, with some heat. Rapping his knuckles on the display screen he said, "In the past two hours the copper content has gone down six percent."

Dan felt baffled. "How could—"

"As the copper content dwindles, the wire goes from a superconducting state to a normal state. It begins to heat up. The hot spot boils off some of the nitrogen coolant. The hot spot grows. It was only microscopic at first, but it eventually became large enough for the monitoring sensors to detect it."

Dan stared at him.

"There is only one agency that I can think of that could selectively remove copper atoms from the wire."

"Nanomachines?" Dan squeaked.

Fuchs nodded solemnly. "This length of wire was seeded with nanomachines that remove copper atoms and release them into the liquid nitrogen coolant. Even now they are removing copper atoms and letting them flow into the air of this compartment."

"Jesus H. Christ on a bicycle," Dan said, his insides suddenly hollow. "That's why Humphries grabbed Cardenas. She's the nanotech expert."

"We are infected," Fuchs said.

"But you caught it in time," Dan countered. "It's only this one length of wire that's infected."

"I hope so," Fuchs said. "Otherwise, we're all dead."

HUMPHRIES TRUST RESEARCH CENTER

George stood to one side of the walkway leading into Humphries's house. It had been eerie, riding down the escalators wearing the enlarged stealth suit that Ike Walton had cobbled together for him. George couldn't see his own feet. At one point, he nearly tripped and tumbled down a flight of escalator stairs.

Walton had looked like a naughty little kid caught peeking at dirty pictures when Stavenger had confronted him in his office and ordered him to enlarge the stealth suit to fit George.

Red-faced, Walton had stammered that he'd need help from the nanolab technicians, and that would ruin the secrecy that had shrouded the stealth suit since he'd first invented it.

"That can't be helped," Stavenger had replied tightly. "Secrecy's already been breached."

In the end, Stavenger himself went with Walton and George to the nanolab and asked the chief technician to clear out the lab and work with Walton by herself. In total secrecy. Once she understood that Dr. Cardenas's life might be at stake, she quickly agreed.

"I'd heard rumors about a stealth suit, off and on," she marveled, once Walton explained what was needed.

"Don't add to them," Stavenger pleaded.

Walton had the programs for the nanomachines buried in his personal files. Within hours, he and the chief technician were watching a spread of darkly-glittering stealth cloth growing on a lab table. George stood slightly behind them, eyes goggling as the invisible virus-sized machines busily turned bins of metal shavings into his new suit.

Now he stood at the entrance to Humphries's house at high noon, trying to figure out a way to get through the front door without being detected. The huge cavern was in its daylight mode, long strips of full-spectrum lamps shining brightly. Wondering if the people inside the house came out for lunch, George edged closer to the door.

It swung open, surprising him, and a pair of Humphries's research scientists came out, deep in earnest conversation. George knew they were scientists from their costumes: the guy wore a shapeless open-necked shirt and faded jeans; he had a long ponytail down his back as well. The woman was in a light sweater and loose, comfortable slacks. They were talking about the life cycle of some Latin-named species.

George slipped behind them as the door started to close and held it halfway open with one extended arm. The two scientists went on their way, chattering intently. George pushed the door open a little more and peered inside. Two hefty men in blue security uniforms stood inside, looking bored. George slipped through the door and then let it swing shut. The two guards never noticed. They were talking about last night's football tournament, videoed live from Barcelona.

An older man in a dark suit came out of a doorway halfway down the hall. He had the frozen-faced expression of a trained butler. George tiptoed past the guards, peeking into each open doorway as he went. He could hear voices from his left, and found a doorway that opened onto a long corridor, with plenty of people shuttling from one office to another along its length. That must be where the research staff works, he thought. Don't they break for lunch?

It was difficult to pick up odors from inside the suit's face mask, but George caught the unmistakable scent of steaks on the griddle, something he hadn't smelled since he'd been on Earth. Steaks! he thought. Humphries doesn't mind spendin' his fookin' money on hauling steaks up here.

The hallway ended in a busy, stainless-steel kitchen big enough to keep a good-sized restaurant going. The staff eats in, George realized. At least they do for lunch. Cooks and assistants were scurrying back and forth, pots were boiling steam, and an industrial-sized grill was sizzling with thick steaks. George counted eleven of them. A banker's dozen, he said to himself.

One of the dark-uniformed maids was putting together a much more modest meal on a large teak tray: a crisp salad, a small sandwich, a slice of melon and a pot of tea. A woman's lunch, George thought.

He followed the maid as she carried the tray past him, down the hallway, and up the stairs to the second floor. One of the doors along the upstairs hall was guarded by a bored-looking young man in a gray business suit. He saw the maid approaching and opened the bedroom door.

"Lunch is here, Dr. Cardenas," he said.

George stopped as the maid went through the bedroom door and came out again less than a minute later, the tray empty at her side. She closed the door. George heard the lock click. The guard gave her a smile and she smiled back, but neither of them said anything as she headed back for the stairs.

George leaned against the wall a half-dozen meters from the lethargic guard, who sat on a wooden chair and pulled a palmcomp from inside his jacket. From the beeps and peeps, George figured the guy was playing a game to pass the time.

Okay, George said, folding his arms across his chest. Cardenas is in there. She's still alive. Now how do I get her out—alive?

He spent the better part of an hour prowling along the upstairs hall, checking out the stairway, studying the lone guard. Humphries apparently insisted on a dress code for his servants: the guards wore suits, the maid and the kitchen help wore uniforms. The scientists stayed on the other side of the house. They'd be no problem, George decided.

The maid returned with the empty tray, went into Cardenas's room, and came out with the lunch dishes. George thought Cardenas might be on a hunger strike; she had hardly eaten anything.

Shortly afterward, Humphries himself came up the hall. He was dressed casually: a white velour pullover and navy blue well-creased slacks. The guard snapped to his feet and stuffed his still-beeping palmcomp into his side pocket. Humphries frowned at him and motioned impatiently for him to open the door.

The door's kept locked, George realized, as Humphries stepped into the room. He waited until the door was almost shut, then tiptoed to it and pushed it slowly open. The guard paid no attention, engrossed once more in his video game. George let the door swing halfway open, then deftly slipped into the room.

Humphries noticed it. Frowning, he marched to the door and snapped at the guard. "Can't you close a goddamned door properly?" Then he slammed it shut.

Suppressing a chuckle, George edged into a corner of the room. Dr. Cardenas was standing tensely by the only window. It was a super room, George thought: big pieces of furniture made from real wood. Hauling it up to Selene must have cost more than the whole kitchen staff's salaries for ten years.

"How do you feel today?" Humphries asked Cardenas, crossing the oriental carpet toward her.

"I want to go home," she said flatly, as if it were a request that they both knew would be ignored.

Sure enough, Humphries acted as if he hadn't heard her. "I'm sorry that we had to take you outside. I understand that you don't like that."

"I want to go home," Cardenas repeated, stronger. "You can't keep me locked up here forever."

"I have a proposition to offer you. If you agree to it, you could go back to Earth and be with your grandchildren."

She closed her eyes wearily. "I simply want to go back to my quarters here at Selene. Let me go. Now."

Humphries sighed dramatically and sat on the upholstered chair near the window. "I'm afraid that's impossible, at this precise moment. Surely you can understand why."

"I won't say a word to anyone," Cardenas replied, walking uncertainly toward the sofa that faced his chair. "I simply want to return to my normal life."

"Without warning Randolph?"

"It's too late to warn Dan by now," she said. "You know that."

Humphries spread his hands. "Really, the best option for you is to return to Earth. You'll be in very comfortable quarters and I'll personally guarantee that your daughters and grandchildren will be brought to you."

"The way I was brought here?"

"You haven't been harmed, have you? You've been treated with great care."

"I'm still a prisoner."

It seemed to George that Humphries was working hard to control his temper. "But if you'll only do what I ask," he said, tightly, "you can return to Earth and be with your family. What more could you ask for?"

"I don't *want* to go to Earth!" Cardenas burst. "I won't be a part of your scheme!"

"You haven't even heard what my . . . scheme, as you put it, is."

"I don't care. I don't want to hear it."

"But it will stop the greenhouse warming. It will save the Earth."

"Nothing can save the Earth and you know it."

He hung his head for a moment, as if trying to find the right words. At last he looked up at her again. "You can save the Earth, Dr. Cardenas. That's the real reason why I brought you here. I need you to run the operation. I need the absolute best person there is. That person is you. No one else could make it work."

"Whatever it is, I won't do it," Cardenas said flatly.

"Not even to save the Earth?"

She gave him a withering look. "What makes you think I want to save the Earth?"

"Not even to save your grandchildren?" He said it with a smile.

Cardenas gasped when she realized what he meant. "You're threatening my family?"

He put on an innocent air. "Did I make a threat?"

"You're despicable!"

Humphries slowly got to his feet, like a man weary of dealing with an obstinate child. "Dr. Cardenas," he said slowly, "your options are few. Please hear me out."

"I won't say a word to anyone."

"I'm not talking about that now."

She started to reply, then thought better of it.

"At least listen to what I have to say."

She stared at him.

"Think of your grandchildren back there on Earth," Humphries coaxed. "Their future is in your hands."

Still without saying a word, Cardenas slowly sat on the sofa, facing Humphries.

"That's better," he said smiling. "We're both reasonable people. I'm sure we can work this out."

George walked softly toward them, listening intently.

STARPOWER 1

Sitting in her command chair on the bridge, Pancho asked, "How do we know the bugs ain't chewin' away at us now?"

Dan had never before seen Pancho look morose. Her long, lantern-jawed face was deadly serious now; her usual cocky grin had vanished.

"They were eating copper," Dan replied. "We got rid of the wire sample. The bugs went out the hatch with it."

"You hope."

"Fervently," said Dan.

"Well, the ship's wiring doesn't use any copper," Pancho said hopefully.

"It's all fiber optic. I know."

"There's plenty of copper here and there, though," Pancho went on. "Maybe only trace amounts, but if we got nanobugs eatin' copper, they could knock out half the microprocessors on board."

"That's great," Dan groused.

"The MHD channel!" she blurted. "It's got a superconducting magnet wrapped around it!"

"Holy Christ!"

"If that goes, the magnet'll dump all its energy—"

"It'll explode?"

"Like a frickin' bomb," Pancho said.

"Great. Just perfect," Dan muttered. "And there's not a double-damned thing we can do about it, is there?"

She shook her head. "Just hope it hasn't been infected."

Dan felt shaky inside. He had to swallow before he could speak. "Not much we can do if it has been."

"Could be worse," Pancho said, with false jollity. "If we had bugs that ate carbon, they'd be chewin' on us."

Dan saw no humor in that. "Where's Amanda?" he asked, pointing to the empty co-pilot's chair. "Shouldn't she be on duty up here?"

"She's back with Lars."

"In the sensor bay?"

"Yup. He's tryin' to jury-rig the electron microscope to get nanometer resolution."

"So he can see nanobugs?"

"If there're any to be seen, right."

"Those two seem to spend a lot of time together," Dan grumbled.

"Come to think of it, that's true."

Dan said nothing. He didn't like the idea of Amanda and Fuchs playing around together, but he had no evidence that they were. Fuchs seemed like a pretty stiff straight arrow. But you never know, Dan said to himself. Amanda certainly seems to enjoy being with him.

Pancho jabbed a finger toward one of the touchscreen displays. "Well, at least the magnetic shield's holdin' up okay. We're safe from radiation storms . . . for th' time being."

For the time being, Dan echoed silently.

"And the MHD channel?"

She tapped at a screen. "Normal as pie."

"The bugs haven't infected it, then."

"Maybe not."

"I think I'll go back to the sensor bay," Dan muttered. "See how those two are getting along."

"Gonna be their chaperon?" Pancho teased.

"Am I that obvious?"

"You sure are, boss. A real worrywart."

"Do you think they need a chaperon?"

"Prob'ly not. Mandy can take care of herself. Lars isn't like Humphries."

Nodding his agreement with Pancho's assessment of the situation, Dan said, "So I'll see how he's doing with the electron microscope."

"Good excuse," Pancho said, laughing.

Wishing he could forget his fears of the nanobugs, Dan left the bridge, poured himself a mug of coffee in the wardroom, and then headed along the passageway to the sensor bay. He could see them through the open hatch to the cramped little compartment, standing amid the humming instruments and flickering display screens, deep in earnest conversation.

My god, they look like Beauty and the Beast, Dan thought. Even in rumpled tan coveralls, with her shining blonde hair pinned up in a sensible, no-nonsense fashion, Amanda looked gorgeous. Her big blue eyes were totally focused on Fuchs. In his usual dead-black pullover and slacks, his barrel-chested thickset body made him look like a feral animal out of some wildlife vid: a boar or a black bear. But he wasn't growling or snarling at Amanda. Far from it.

"How's it going?" Dan asked as he stepped through the open hatch.

They looked startled, as if they hadn't seen him approaching.

Pointing to the gray tube of the miniaturized electron microscope, Dan forced a grin and asked, "Find any nanobugs?"

Fuchs turned away from Dan, toward the microscope. "No, it's hopeless. This machine will never resolve nanometer objects."

Dan wasn't surprised. "It wasn't designed to."

"I had thought perhaps I could boost its power," Fuchs went on, "but that was an idle hope."

"We've been reviewing the long-range sensor data," Amanda said, her cheeks slightly red. "Looking for a suitable asteroid, you know."

"And?"

Fuchs broke into a happy grin. It was so unusual that Dan was taken aback.

"We have an embarrassment of riches," he said, tapping at one of the touchscreens. "There are more than a dozen metal-rich bodies within a day's flight of us, or less."

Amanda said, "We've been trying to decide which one we should aim for."

Dan smiled at her. "That's easy. Go for the biggest one."

George held his breath as he edged closer to the corner of the big bedroom where Humphries and Dr. Cardenas sat. They both looked tense, although he seemed strung high with anticipation, while fear and anger glowered clearly on Cardenas's face.

George knew that they couldn't see him, yet he felt anxious, almost frightened to be this close to them, invisible or not. Don't sneeze, he warned himself. Don't fookin' breathe.

"All right," Cardenas said tightly. "I'm listening."

Leaning slightly toward the sofa on which Cardenas sat, Humphries clasped his hands together and began, "Suppose I set you up in your own laboratory in some remote location on Earth. My father has holdings in Libya, for example. We could bring your grandchildren there, to be with you."

"And what would I be expected to do at this remote laboratory?" Cardenas asked. Her voice was without inflection, like an automaton's, her face a frozen mask.

"Nanomachines could be made to take carbon dioxide out of the atmosphere, can't they? Break the molecules down into carbon and oxygen atoms. The carbon could be buried, the oxygen released back into the air or sold as an industrial gas, whatever. That could stop the greenhouse warming in a year or two!"

Cardenas's expression did not change. "Nanotechnology is banned, you know that. No matter how you want to use it, you can't make nanomachines anywhere on Earth. You'd have the GEC, the world government, every religious nut on Earth going crazy if you even hinted that you're thinking of using nanotechnology."

Humphries smiled patiently. "We won't tell them, for god's sake. We just start doing it. In secret. Out in the Sahara or the middle of the ocean or Antarctica, anywhere. In a year or maybe even less, they'll start noticing the carbon dioxide levels going down. We can take out the other greenhouse gases, as well. They'll see that the greenhouse warming is lessening. *Then* we'll have them all by the balls! They'll have to accept what we're doing. They'll have no choice."

"And what happens if these nanomachines don't work exactly right? What happens if they start taking other carbon compounds apart? Like *you*, for instance. You're made of carbon atoms, aren't you?"

"That won't happen."

"I know it won't happen," she said. "Because I won't do it. It's an absurd scheme."

"What's absurd about it?" Humphries demanded.

A slight, sardonic smile cracked Cardenas's facade. "You don't have any idea of how enormous Earth's atmosphere is. Do you know how many tons of carbon dioxide you'd have to remove? Billions! Tens of billions, at least! You'd have to cover Africa with nanomachines to remove that much carbon dioxide!"

"I'm sure that's an exaggeration," Humphries muttered, scowling.

Cardenas shot to her feet, startling George. "All right, you'd merely have to cover the Sahara desert. It's still beyond belief!"

"But—"

"And you'd never be able to keep it secret. Not a program of that scale."

"But it could be done, couldn't it?"

"It could be started," she admitted. "Until some fanatic drops a nuke on us. Or laces our drinking water with plague bacillus."

"I can protect you against terrorists," Humphries said.

Cardenas paced to the window, obviously thinking furiously. Turning back to Humphries, she said, "Using nanomachines on that scale is an invitation to disaster. Some fruitcake could steal a handful and reprogram them to take apart . . . plastics, for example. Or petroleum. Or use them as assassination weapons. You're talking about gobblers, for Christ's sake!"

"I know that," Humphries said coldly.

Cardenas shook her head. "It won't work. Aside from the sheer physical scale of the project, the authorities on Earth would never grant approval for using nanomachines. Never! And I can't say that I'd blame them."

Humphries slowly got to his feet. "You refuse to even try?"

"It's a hopeless task."

He sighed theatrically. "Well, I've tried to be reasonable. I thought we might be able to work something out."

"Let me go," Cardenas said, with a pleading note in her voice.

"I thought it would be a way for you to be with your grandchildren, as you want to be."

"Just let me go."

He gave her a sad look. "You know I can't do that. It's too great a risk for me."

"You can't keep me here forever!"

With a small shrug, Humphries asked, "What do you propose as a way out of this impasse?"

She stared at him, open-mouthed.

"I mean, you can see my problem. I know you can. How can I let you go when there's every chance that you'll tell people that I'm responsible for Dan Randolph's death?"

"But I'm responsible, too."

"Yes, I know. But you'd confess to it, wouldn't you?"

"I . . ." she hesitated, then said in a low, defeated voice, "I suppose I would, sooner or later."

"There you are," Humphries said softly. "The problem remains."

"You're going to have to kill me."

"I don't want to do that. I'm not a cold-blooded murderer. In fact, I'd like to see you reunited with your grandchildren, if it's at all possible. There must be some way we can work together, some way we can find around this problem."

"I don't see any," Cardenas whispered.

"Well, think it over," Humphries said, heading for the door. "I'm sure you can come up with a solution, if you just put your mind to it."

He smiled as he opened the door and left. George saw the guard standing out in the hallway before Humphries closed the door and its lock clicked shut.

As he strode down the hallway, Humphries mused to himself, It *could* work! If we could spread enough nanomachines I could break the greenhouse warming in a couple of years. They'd be on their knees with gratitude.

He decided to put a small team of experts together to study the possibilities dispassionately. Cardenas isn't the only nanotechnology guru in Selene, he assured himself.

BREAKOUT

K ris Cardenas stared at the locked door for several silent moments after Humphries left, then she suddenly broke into racking sobs. Face buried in her hands, body bent, she stumbled to the bed and threw herself onto it, crying inconsolably.

George stood uncertainly in the far corner of the bedroom, wondering what he should do. She's already hysterical, he said to himself. If I go and tap her on the shoulder and say, "Hi! I'm an invisible man!" she'll probably freak out altogether.

So he waited, fidgeting unhappily, until Cardenas stopped crying. It didn't take long. She sat up on the bed, took a deep breath, then got to her feet and went to the lavatory. When she came out again, it was obvious to George that she had washed her face and put on some makeup. But her eyes were still red, puffy.

Well, you can't stand here like a fookin' idiot forever, George told himself. Do something!

Before he could decide what to do, Cardenas walked to the window and pressed her fingers against the glass. Then she turned and seemed to survey the room. With a slight nod, she walked to the bare little desk and picked up its wooden, cushioned chair. It seemed heavy for her, but she carried it, tottering slightly, to the window.

She wants to crash the window and jump out of here, George realized. She'll just end up hurting herself.

He touched her arm lightly and whispered, "Excuse me."

Cardenas flinched and let the chair thump to the carpeting. She blinked, stared, saw nothing.

"Excuse me, Dr. Cardenas," George whispered.

She spun around in a complete circle, eyes wide.

"Who said that?"

George cleared his throat and replied, a little louder, "It's me, George Ambrose. I'm—"

"Where the hell are you?"

George felt slightly embarrassed. "I'm invisible."

"I'm going crazy," Cardenas muttered. She sank down onto the chair, right there in the middle of the room.

"No you're not," George said, still keeping his voice low. "I'm here to get you out of this place."

"This is a trick."

"Is this room bugged? Do they have any cameras in here?"

"I . . . don't think so . . ."

"Look," George said, then immediately realized it was a foolish term to use. "I'm gonna take off me hood so you can see me face. Don't get scared now."

Cardenas looked more suspicious than frightened. George yanked the hood off his head and pulled off his face mask. It felt good to feel cool air on his skin.

She jumped out of the chair. "Christ almighty!"

"No, it's just me," he said, with a slight grin. "George Ambrose. I work for Dan Randolph, y'know."

Comprehension lit her eyes. "Walton's stealth suit! He didn't destroy it, after all."

"You know about it."

"Me, and four other people."

"There's a few more now," George said.

"How in the world did you ever—"

"No time for that now. We've got to get you out of here."

"How?"

George scratched at his beard. "Good question."

"You didn't bring along a suit for me, did you?" Cardenas said.

"Should have, shouldn't I? We just didn't think of it. We weren't certain where you were."

"So what do we do?"

George thought it over for a few moments. "They keep you in this room all the time?"

Cardenas nodded.

"Door's locked, isn't it?"

"Yes. And there's a guard outside . . . at least, every time they've brought a meal in to me there's been a guard out in the hall. I imagine he's armed."

George's face lit up. "When do they bring you meals? When's the next one coming?"

Several hours later there was a single rap on the door, and then Cardenas heard the lock click. She glanced swiftly about the room but could no longer see George.

The door opened and the same silent, sour-faced woman in dark uniform came in, carrying a dinner tray. Cardenas could see a wiry young man standing on the other side of the doorway. The woman deposited the tray wordlessly on the coffee table in front of the sofa and then departed, still silent and dour. The guard closed the door and locked it again.

Cardenas sat on the sofa. For the first time in days she had an appetite. She felt George's bulk settling on the cushions beside her.

"Smells good," George said.

She took the lid off a platter of fish fillets and vegetables.

"Looks good, too," George added.

"You're hungry," she said.

"Haven't eaten since breakfast."

"Help yourself."

George didn't wait to be coaxed. He lifted off his face mask again and dug in. Cardenas watched as fork and knife moved seemingly by themselves and chunks of dinner rose to his face, which seemed to be floating in midair. She found that if she looked hard enough, directly at him, she could see a faint flickering glitter, almost subliminal. Reflection of the ceiling lights scattered by the chips, she thought. But you have to know he's there to see it, and even then it's almost below the perception level.

"Don't you want any?" George asked.

"No, you go ahead."

"Eat the veggies, at least."

"I'll take the salad."

The meal was finished in a few minutes. George put his mask on again and completely disappeared.

"D'you tell 'em you're finished or do they send the maid back for the tray automatically?"

"I tell the guard. He sends for the maid."

"Okay. Tell the guard you're finished and ask him to take the tray."

"He'll send for the maid."

"Tell 'im you don't want to wait for her. Make some excuse."

Cardenas nodded, got up from the sofa, and went to the door. She could sense George's body warmth as he padded along beside her.

She banged on the door with the flat of her hand. "I'm finished. Could you please take the tray?"

"I'll call the kitchen," came the guard's muffled voice.

"I can't wait! I've got to get to the toilet right away! I'm sick to my stomach. Please take the tray."

A moment's hesitation, then they heard the lock click. The door swung open and the guard stepped in, looking concerned.

"What's the matter? Something in the—"

The punch sounded like a melon hitting the pavement from a considerable height. The guard's head snapped back and his eyes rolled up. He crumpled to the floor. Cardenas saw his arms yanked up into the air and his body dragged into the room.

"Come on, now," George whispered to her.

They stepped out into the hallway. The door shut, seemingly by itself, and locked. She felt his hand engulf half her upper arm as George let her down the hallway to the stairs. The house seemed quiet at this hour, although a glance out the windows showed that the cavern outside was still lit in daytime mode.

The downstairs hall was empty, but Cardenas could hear the sounds of conversation floating through from somewhere. Neither of the voices sounded like Humphries's to her. They got to the foyer just inside the front door. Two young men in gray suits looked surprised to see her approaching them.

Frowning, the taller of the two said, "Dr. Cardenas, what are—"

George's punch spun him completely around. The other guard stared, frozen with surprise, until he was lifted off his feet by a blow to the midsection. Cardenas heard a bone-snapping *crunch!* and the guard fell limply to the tiled floor.

The front door jerked open and George hissed, "Come on, then!"

Cardenas ran out of the house, up the path that wound through the garden, and through the hatch that opened into Selene's bottommost corridor. She could hear George panting and puffing alongside her. Once they were through the hatch, George's hand on her arm brought her to a stop.

"I don't think anybody's followin' us," he said.

"How long do you think it will take for them to realize I'm gone?" she asked.

She sensed him shrugging. "Not fookin' long."

"What now, then?"

"Lemme get outta this suit," George muttered. "Hot enough inside here to cook a fella."

His face appeared, then his entire shaggy head. Within a minute he stood before her, sweating and grinning, a big red-haired mountain of a man in rumpled, stained olive-green coveralls.

"That's better," George said, taking a deep breath. "Could hardly breathe inside that suit."

As they started walking swiftly along the corridor toward the escalator, Cardenas asked, "Where can I go? Where will I be safe? Humphries will turn Selene upside-down looking for me."

"We could go to Stavenger and ask him to take care of you."

She shook her head. "Don't put Doug in the middle of this. Besides, Humphries probably has his own people planted in Selene's staff."

"H'mm, yeah, maybe," George said as they reached the escalator. "Inside Astro, too, for that matter."

Suddenly frightened at the possibilities, Cardenas blurted, "Where can I go?"

George smiled. "I got the perfect hideout for ya. Long as you don't mind sharin' it with a corpsicle, that is."

BONANZA

I t's a beauty," Dan breathed, staring at the image on the control panel's radar screen.

"Purty ugly-lookin' beauty," Pancho countered.

The radar image showed an elongated irregular lump of an asteroid, one end rounded and pitted, the other dented by what looked like the imprint of a giant mailed fist.

"It looks rather like a potato," said Amanda, "don't you think?"

"An iron potato," Dan said.

Fuchs came through the hatch, and suddenly the bridge felt crowded to Dan. Lars isn't tall, he said to himself, but he fills up a room.

"That is it?" Fuchs asked, his eyes riveted to the screen.

"That's it," Pancho said, over her shoulder. She tapped at the keyboard on her left and a set of alphanumerics sprang up on the small screen above it. "Fourteenth asteroid discovered this year."

Amanda said, "Then its official name will be 41–014 Fuchs."

"How's it feel to have your name on an asteroid, Lars?" Pancho asked.

"Very fine," Fuchs said.

"You're the first person to have his name attached to a newly-discovered asteroid in *years*," Amanda said. She seemed almost aglow, to Dan.

"Most of the new rocks have been found by the impact searchers," Pancho said. "Those li'l bitty probes don't get their names into the record."

"Asteroid 41–014 Fuchs," Amanda breathed.

He smiled and shrugged—squirmed, almost, as if embarrassed by her enthusiasm.

"The official name's one thing," Dan said. "I'm calling her Bonanza."

"Her?" Fuchs asked.

"Asteroids are feminine?" Pancho challenged.

Dan held his ground. "Hey, we speak of Mother Earth, don't we? And they call Venus our sister planet, don't they?"

"What about Mars?" Pancho retorted.

"Or Jupiter," said Amanda.

Pointing to the lump imaged on the radar screen, Dan insisted, "Bonanza's going to make us all rich. And very happy. She and her sisters are going to save the world. She's a female."

"Sure she's female," Pancho said laconically. "You want to dig into her, don't you?"

Fuchs sputtered and Amanda said, "Pancho, really!"

Dan put on an innocent air. "What a dirty mind you have, Pancho. I admire that in a woman."

Within three hours they were close enough to Bonanza to see it for themselves: a dark, deformed shape glinting sullenly in the wan light of the distant Sun. The asteroid blotted out the stars as it tumbled slowly end over end in the cold empty silence of space.

"... eighteen hundred and forty-four meters along its long axis," Amanda was reading out the radar measurements. "Seven hundred and sixty-two meters at its maximum width."

"Nearly two kilometers long," Dan mused. He hadn't left the bridge all during their approach to the metallic asteroid.

"Killing residual thrust," Pancho said, her attention focused on the control displays.

"Throttling down to zero," Amanda confirmed.

The asteroid slid out of view as the pilots established a parking orbit around it. Dan felt what little weight remained dwindle away to nothing. He floated up off the deck, stopped himself with a hand against the overhead.

He felt Fuchs come through the hatch behind him.

"Lars, we're going to be in zero *g* for a while," Dan said.

"I know. I think I'm getting accustomed to it."

"Good. Just don't make any sudden head movements and you'll be fine."

"Yes. Thank—*mein gott!* There it is!"

The dark lopsided bulk of Bonanza rose in front of the bridge windows like some pitted, pockmarked monster, huge, overawing, menacing. Despite himself, Dan felt a wave of unease surge through him. It's like confronting an ogre, he thought, a giant beast from a fairy tale.

"Look at those striations!" Fuchs said, his voice vibrant with excitement. "This must have been broken off from a much larger body, perhaps a planetesimal from the early age of the solar system! We've got to get outside and take samples, drill cores!"

Dan broke into laughter. Fuchs turned toward him, looking confused. Even Pancho glanced over her shoulder.

"What so funny, boss?"

"Nothing," Dan said, trying to sober himself. "Nothing." Inwardly, though, he marveled that the same sight that brought back to him memories of childhood dread stirred Fuchs into a frenzy of scientific curiosity.

"Come on," Fuchs said, ducking past the hatch. "We've got to suit up and go outside."

Dan nodded his agreement and followed the scientist. He's forgotten about zero-*g*, Dan realized. He's not worried about upchucking now, he's got too much work that he wants to do.

Amanda remained on the bridge as Pancho followed Dan down to the airlock.

"You're not thinkin' of goin' EVA, are you?" she asked Dan.

"I've been a qualified astronaut since before you were born, Pancho."

"You've been redlined. You can't go outside."

"And rain makes applesauce."

"I mean it, Dan," Pancho said, quite seriously. "Your immune system can't take another radiation dose."

"Fuchs can't go out there by himself," he countered.

"That's my job. I'll go with him."

"Nope. You stay here. I'll babysit him."

"I'm the captain of this craft," Pancho said firmly. "I can order you to stay inside."

He gave her a crooked grin. "And I'm the owner. I can fire you."

"Not till we get back to Selene."

Dan huffed out an impatient sigh. "Come on, Pancho, stop the chickenshit."

"Your medical records say—"

"Dammitall to hell and back, I don't care what the medical records say! I'm going out! I want to *see* this sucker! Touch her with my own hands."

"No gloves?"

They had reached the airlock, where the spacesuits hung in racks like suits of armor on display. Fuchs was sitting on the bench that ran in front of the racks, already into the lower half of his suit, sealing the boots to the cuffs of his leggings. Dan reached for the suit that bore his name stenciled on its chest.

"I thought you were scared of the radiation," Pancho said.

"I'll be okay inside the suit," Dan said. "The weather's calm out there; no radiation storm."

Fuchs looked up at them, said nothing.

"The regulations say—"

"The regulations say you're not supposed to bring pets aboard," Dan said, grinning again as he pulled the lower half of his suit from its rack and sat down beside Fuchs. "But I've got to look into my shoes every morning to make sure your damned snake isn't curled up inside one of them."

"Snake?" Fuchs yelped, looking alarmed.

Pancho planted her fists on her hips and glared down at Dan for a long moment. Then she visibly relaxed.

"Okay, boss," she said at last. "I guess I can't blame you. But I'm gonna monitor your vitals back on the bridge. If I say come in, you come in. Right then. No arguments. Agreed?"

"Agreed," Dan replied instantly. A voice in his head was laughing mockingly. Are you satisfied? the voice asked. You've shown her that you're not a sick old man. Big deal. How are you going to feel when the cold clamps down on you and your bones start hurting again?

Doesn't matter, Dan answered himself. I'm not going to stay cooped up in here like a cripple. To hell with it; I don't really give a damn. If I've got to die, I'd rather wear out than rust out. What difference does it make?

"Clear for EVA." Amanda's voice came through the speaker in Dan's helmet.

He was in the airlock, sealed in his suit, feeling like a robot in a metal womb.

"Opening outer hatch," he said, pressing a gloved finger on the red light of the control panel.

"Copy, outer hatch."

The hatch slid open and Dan felt his pulse start to quicken. How long has it been since I've been outside? he asked himself. That sardonic voice in his head answered, Not since you got the radiation overdose, jiggering commsats in the Van Allen Belt.

Ten years, Dan realized. That's a long time to be away from all this.

He pushed himself through the hatch and floated in emptiness. The universe hung all around him: stars solemn and unwinking, staring at him even through the heavy tinting of his fishbowl helmet. Turning slowly, he saw the Sun, strangely small and pale, with its arms of faint zodiacal light outstretched on either side of it.

Freedom. He knew he was confined inside the spacesuit and he couldn't survive for a minute without it. Yet hanging there weightlessly in the silent emptiness of infinity, Dan felt free of all the world, alone with the cosmos, in tune with the ethereal music of the spheres. Glorious freedom. Radiation be damned; he felt he could soar out into the universe forever and leave the petty lusts and hates of humankind far behind. It wouldn't be a bad way to die.

Then the asteroid slid into his view. Massive, ponderous, an enormous pitted dark looming reality hanging over him like an ominous cloud, a mountain floating free in space. *Starpower 1* looked pitifully small and helpless alongside the two-kilometer-long asteroid; like a minnow next to a whale. Dan suddenly understood how Jonah must have felt.

You can't scare me, he said to the asteroid. You're two kilometers of high-grade iron ore, pal. You're going to look beautiful to a lot of people on Earth. Money in the bank, that's what you are. Jobs and hope for millions of people. Bonanza: that's your name and that's just what you are.

"Ready for EVA." Fuchs's voice broke into Dan's silent monologue.

"Clear for EVA. Lars," he heard Amanda reply.

Dan squeezed the right handgrip on his maneuvering controls with the lightest of touches. The cold gas jet on the backpack squirted noiselessly and he turned enough to be looking back at the ship. *Starpower 1* glinted nicely in the starlight. She still looked brand-new, shining, not a pit or a scratch on her. The airlock hatch slid open and a spacesuited figure stood framed in it.

"Exiting the airlock," Fuchs said, his voice trembling slightly.

"Come on, Lars," Dan called. "Isn't she a beauty?"

Fuchs jetted toward him. Dan saw that his suit was bristling with hammers and drills and all sorts of equipment.

"It's enormous!" He sounded awestruck.

"She's just an average-sized chunk of metal," Dan said. "And as soon as you chip a piece off her, we can claim her."

Fuchs showed no hesitation at all, although he seemed a bit clumsy working the controls of his maneuvering thrusters. For a moment Dan thought he was going to ram into the asteroid, but at the last instant Fuchs fired a braking blast and hovered a scant few meters above its pitted, pebbly surface.

Dan jetted toward him, and with a bare touch of the handgrip controls lowered himself to the surface of the asteroid. He felt his boots make contact and then recoil slightly. Not much gravity, he thought, as he puffed down again and finally stood on the surface of Bonanza. Clouds of dust rose where his boots made contact with the surface; they just hung there, barely moving in the minuscule gravity.

It took Fuchs three tries to get firmly onto the surface; he kept coming down too hard and bouncing off. In the end, Dan had to reach out and yank him down.

"Don't try to walk," he told Fuchs. "The gravity's so light you'll float up and away."

"Then how—"

"Slide your boots along." Dan demonstrated a couple of steps, shuffling up even more dust. "Like you're dancing."

"I don't dance very well," Fuchs said.

"This isn't the smoothest dance floor in the solar system, either."

The asteroid's surface was rough and uneven, covered with a powdery coating of dust, much like the surface of the Moon. Dan thought it was more like standing on the deck of a boat, though, than on solid ground. There wasn't really a horizon; the rock just *ended*. Pinhole craters peppered the surface, pebbles and fist-sized rocks littered it, and out along its far end, Dan could see a more sizeable crater, a big depression with a raised rim all around it.

"How much iron do you think we've got here?" Dan asked.

"We'll have a good measure of its mass by the time we return to the ship," Fuchs said. "With the ship orbiting the asteroid we have a classic two-body system. It's simple Newtonian physics."

Dan thought to himself, He's a scientist, all right. Ask him a simple question and you get a dissertation. Without the answer to your question.

"Lars," he said patiently, "can't you give me some idea of this lump's mass?"

Fuchs spread his hands. In the spacesuit, he looked like a bubble-topped fireplug with arms.

"A back-of-the-envelope guesstimate?" Dan coaxed.

"Oh . . . considering its dimensions . . . nickel-iron asteroids are typically no more than ten percent nickel . . . it must be somewhere in the neighborhood of seven or eight billion tons of iron and eighty million tons or so of nickel."

Dan's eyes went wide. "That's five or six times the world's steel production in its best year! Before the floods and all!"

"There are impurities, of course," Fuchs warned. "Platinum, gold and silver, other heavy metals."

"Impurities, right," Dan agreed, cackling. His mind was spinning. One asteroid is enough to supply the world's steel industry for years and years! And there are thousands of these chunks out here! It's all true!

Everything I hoped for, all those wild promises I made—they're all going to come true!

Fuchs seemed oblivious to it all. "I want to look at those striations," he said, turning toward the far end of the asteroid. His effort made him rise off the surface and Dan had to yank him down again.

"Take a sample here, first," Dan said. "Then we can claim it."

The light was so dim that Dan could see Fuchs's head outlined inside his bubble helmet. He nodded and slowly, very slowly, got down into a kneeling position. Then he pulled a rock hammer from his equipment belt and chipped off a bit of the asteroid. The effort raised more dust and lifted him off the surface again, but this time he clawed at the ground with one gloved hand and pulled himself back down.

"Anchor yourself, Lars," Dan said. "Hammer a piton in and tether it to your belt."

"Yes, of course," Fuchs answered, fumbling with the equipment clipped to his waist.

Dan said, "Record this, Amanda, and mark the time. Starpower Limited has begun taking samples of asteroid 41–014 Fuchs. Under the terms of the International Astronautical Authority protocol of 2021, Starpower Limited. claims exclusive use of the resources of this asteroid."

"I've got it," Amanda's voice replied. "Your statement is being beamed to IAA headquarters on Earth."

"Good," Dan said, satisfied. He recalled from his school days the story of the Spanish explorer Balboa first sighting the Pacific Ocean. From what he remembered of the tale, Balboa waded out into the surf and claimed the whole bloody ocean and all the lands bordering on it for Spain. They thought big in those days, Dan said to himself. No pissant IAA to worry about.

Fuchs got the knack of shuffling along the surface of the asteroid, and started chipping out samples and making stereo videos. Dan worried about the dust they were kicking up. It could get into the joints of our suits, he thought. Damned stuff just hangs there; must take a year for it to settle back again.

He saw a bulge off to his right, like a small knoll or a rounded hill. That must be the tail end of this rock, Dan told himself. Looking back at Fuchs, he saw that the scientist had finally anchored himself to the ground and was busily chipping away, raising lingering clouds of dust.

"I'm going to go up to that ridge," he told Fuchs, pointing, "and see what's on the other side."

"Very well," said Fuchs, still bent over his sampling.

Dan shuffled carefully along, worrying about the dust. On the Moon, dust raised from the ground was electrostatically charged; it clung stubbornly to the suits and helmet visors. Probably the same thing here.

He started up the slight rise. Something didn't feel right. Suddenly his boots slid out from under him and he tumbled, in dreamlike slow motion, face forward. His fall was so gentle that he could put out his hands and stop himself, but he bounced off the dusty ground and found himself floating *up* the rise like a hot-air balloon gliding up the side of a mountain.

Dan's old astronaut training took over his reflexes. In his mind he saw clearly what was happening. The gravity on this double-damned rock is so low that I'm floating off it! He saw the bulbous end of the asteroid sliding slowly beneath him and, beyond it, the star-strewn infinity of space.

Twisting his body so that he pointed himself back toward the asteroid's bulk, Dan squirted his maneuvering jets and lurched back to the asteroid. Gently, tenderly, he touched down again on its surface. Fuchs was still tapping away with his sampling hammer, rising off the ground with every blow, his anchored tether pulling him back again for another crack.

Dan was breathing hard, but otherwise no worse the wear for his little excursion. With even greater care than before he shuffled back to stand beside Fuchs and help bag the samples he'd chipped out.

At last Pancho said sternly, "Time to come in, guys."

"Just one more sample," Fuchs replied.

"*Now,*" Pancho commanded.

"Aye-aye, cap'n," said Dan. He rapped his gloved knuckles on Fuchs's helmet. "Come on, Lars. You've done enough for one day. This rock isn't going to go away; you can come back another time."

Amanda was at the airlock to help them take off their backpacks and dust-spattered spacesuits. Dan caught a strange, pungent smell once he removed his helmet. Not like the sharp firecracker odor of the lunar dust; this was something new, different.

Before he had time to puzzle out the dust's odor, Pancho came down to the airlock area, looking so somber that Dan asked her what was the matter.

While Fuchs chattered happily with Amanda, Pancho said, "Bad news, boss. Another section of the superconductor is heating up. If it goes critical it could blow out the whole magnetic shield."

Dan felt his jaw drop open. Without the shield they'd be cooked by the next solar radiation storm.

"We've gotta get back to Selene pronto," Pancho said. "Before another flare breaks out."

"What're our chances?" Dan asked, his throat dry.

She waggled a hand. "Fifty-fifty . . . if we're lucky."

TEMPO 9

We won't have to go outside, will we?" Cardenas asked nervously.

She was following George through the maze of pumps and generators up on the topmost level of Selene. Color-coded pipes and electrical conduits lined the ceiling; Cardenas wondered how anyone could keep track of which was which. The air hummed with the subdued sounds of electrical equipment and hydraulic machinery. On the other side of the ceiling, she knew, was the grassy expanse of the Grand Plaza—or the bare dusty regolith of the Moon's airless surface.

"Outside?" George echoed. "Naw, there's a shaft connectin' the tempo to the tunnel . . . if I can find th' fookin' tunn—ah, there it is!"

He pulled a small hatch open and stepped over its coaming, then reached a hand back to help Cardenas. The tunnel was dark, lit only by the hand-torch George carried. Cardenas expected to see the evil red eyes of rats in the darkness, or hear the slithering of roaches. Nothing. Selene is clean of vermin, she thought. Even the farmlands have to be pollinated artificially because there aren't any insects here.

Not yet, she thought. Sooner or later, though. Once we start allowing larger numbers of people up here, they'll bring their filth and their pests with them.

"Here we are," George said.

In the circle of light cast by his torch, she saw the metal rungs of a ladder leading up along the wall of the tunnel.

"How much farther does the tunnel go?" she asked in a whisper, even though she knew there was no one else there.

"Another klick or so," George answered. "Yamagata people wanted to drill all the way through the ringwall and out to *Mare Nubium*. Got too expensive. The cable car over the top was cheaper."

He scampered up the ladder, light and lithe despite his size. Cardenas started to follow him.

"Wait a bit," George called down to her. "Got to get this hatch unstuck."

She heard metal groan. Then George said, "Okay, up with you, now."

The ladder ended in an enclosed area about the size of her apartment unit down inside Selene. It was a cylindrical shape, like a spacecraft module.

"We're on the surface?" Cardenas asked, trying to keep her voice from shaking.

"Buried under a meter of dirt from the regolith," George said happily. "Safe as in church."

"But we're outside."

"On the slope of the ringwall. Just below the cable-line. The original idea was, if there's an emergency with the cable-trolley, people could stay in here till help arrives."

She looked around the shelter warily. A pair of double-decker bunks stood at the far end, the hatch of an airlock at the other. Inbetween was a small galley with a freezer, microwave oven, and sink; some other equipment she didn't recognize; two padded chairs; a desk with a computer atop it and a smaller chair in front of it . . .

And a big metal cylinder sitting in the middle of the floor, crowding the already-cramped quarters. One end of the cylinder was attached to a large pair of tanks and a miniaturized cryostat.

"Is that a dewar?" Cardenas asked.

George nodded. "Had to hide the woman inside it from Humphries."

"She's dead?"

"Preserved cryonically," George said. "There's hopes of reviving her."

"She won't be much company."

" 'Fraid not. But I'll pop back here every few days, see that you're okay."

Stepping toward the desk, trying to hide her anxiety, Cardenas asked, "How long will I have to stay here?"

"Dunno. I'll have a chat with Dan, see what we should do."

"Call Doug Stavenger," she said. "He'll protect me."

"I thought you didn't want to put him in the middle of this scrape."

She wrapped her arms around herself, trembling with cold fear. "That's before I knew you were going to put me out here."

"Hey, this isn't so bad," George said, trying to sound reassuring. "I useta live in tempos like this for months at a time."

"You did?"

"Yup. Me and my mates. This is like home-sweet-home to me."

She looked around the place again. It seemed smaller than her first view of it. Closing in on her. Nothing between her and the deadly vacuum outside except the thin metal of the shelter's cylinder and a heaping of dirt over it. And a corpse in the middle of the floor, taking up most of the room.

"Call Stavenger," she pleaded. "I don't want to stay here any longer than I have to."

"Sure," said George. "Lemme talk to Dan first."

"Make it quick."

"The magnetic shield is going to blow up?" Dan asked, for the thirtieth time.

Pancho sat across the table from him in *Starpower 1*'s wardroom. Amanda was on the bridge as the ship raced at top acceleration back toward Selene. Fuchs was in the sensor bay, assaying the samples he'd chipped from Bonanza.

"You know how superconductors work," Pancho said, grimly. "They have to stay cooled down below their critical temperature. If they go above that temperature all the energy in the coil gets dumped into the hot spot."

"It'll explode," Dan muttered.

"Like a bomb. Lots of energy in the superconductor, boss. It's a dangerous situation."

"There's more than one hot spot?"

"Four of 'em so far. Wouldn't be surprised if more of 'em crop up. Whoever bugged this ship didn't want us to get back home."

Dan drummed his fingers on the table top. "I can't believe Kris Cardenas would do this to me."

"It's Humphries, pure and simple," said Pancho. "He could kill you with a smile, any day."

"But he'd need Kris to do this."

"Look," Pancho said, hunching forward in her chair. "Doesn't matter who spit in whose eye. We got troubles and we've gotta figger out how to save our necks before that magnetic coil goes up like a bomb."

Dan had never seen her look so earnest. "Okay, right. What do you recommend?"

"We shut down the magnetic field."

"Shut it down? But then we'd have no radiation shield."

"Don't need it unless there's a flare, and we can prob'ly get back to Selene before the Sun burps another one out."

"Probably," Dan growled.

"That's the chance we take. I like those odds better'n letting the coil's hot spots build up to an explosion that'd rupture the ship's skin."

"Yeah, you're right," Dan said, reluctantly.

"Okay, then." Pancho got up from the table. "I'm gonna shut it down now."

"Wait a minute," said Dan, reaching for her wrist. "What about the MHD channel?"

Pancho shrugged. "No problems so far. Prob'ly hasn't been bugged."

"If it goes, we're dead, right?"

"Well . . ." She drew the word out. "We *could* dump the coil's energy in a controlled shutdown. That wouldn't affect the thrusters."

"But we'd lose our electrical power."

"We could run on the fuel cells and batteries—for a while."

"Long enough?"

Pancho laughed and headed for the hatch. "Long as they last, boss," she said over her shoulder.

"Murphy's Law," Dan growled after her.

If anything can go wrong, it will: that was Murphy's Law. Now I can add Randolph's corollary to it, he thought: If you turn off your radiation shield, you're certain to be hit by a solar flare.

MESSAGES

George shooed everyone out of the mission control center, except for the chief who insisted hotly that the center must have at least one human controller on duty at all times.

If he'd been a man, George would have simply picked him up and heaved him through the door out into the corridor. Instead, the chief on this shift was a rail-thin, pasty-faced, lank-haired woman with the personality of an Arkansas mule. She would not leave the center.

Restraining the urge to lift her off her feet and carry her out to the corridor, George pleaded, "I've got to send a private message to Dan Randolph. I can't have anybody listenin' in on it."

"And why not?" she demanded, hands on hips, narrow nostrils flaring angrily.

"None of your fookin' business," George snarled. "That's why not."

For long moments they glared at each other, George towering over her, but the woman totally unfazed by him.

"It's Dan's own orders," George said at last, stretching the truth a little. "This is ultra-sensitive stuff."

The woman seemed to think that over for a second, then said more reasonably, "You take the console over there, on the end. I'll set you up with a private channel. Nobody else in here but you and me, and I won't eavesdrop. Okay?"

George started to say no, but realized that this was the best he could accomplish, short of physical mayhem.

Before he could agree, though, Frank Blyleven pushed through the double doors, his normally smiling face wrinkled into a puzzled frown.

"What's going on here?" the security chief demanded, walking up the aisle between the consoles. "I got a report that you're throwing controllers out of the center."

Heaving an impatient sigh, George explained all over again that he had to get a message through to Dan. "In private," he said. "Nobody listenin' in."

Blyleven crossed his arms over his chest and tried to look authoritative. It didn't work. To George he looked like a red-faced shopping mall Santa in mufti.

"Very well," he said. "Send your message. I'll sit by the corridor door and make certain nobody disturbs you."

Surprised, George thanked him and headed for the console that the chief controller had indicated. Blyleven went to the last row of consoles and sat down at the one closest to the door. Surreptitiously, he tapped the keyboard a few times. When George finished his message and erased it from the comm system's memory core, Blyleven had a copy that he could pawn to Humphries.

Dan felt nervous as he watched Pancho and Amanda shut down the radiation shield. Dumping all that electromagnetic energy didn't bother him; it was the idea that now they had no protection against another solar storm except the thin hull of the ship itself.

". . . shutdown complete," Pancho announced. "Magnetic field zeroed out."

"Zero field," Amanda confirmed.

"Naked to mine enemies," Dan murmured.

"How's that, boss?" Pancho asked, looking up over her shoulder toward him.

"I feel naked," Dan said.

"Don't worry. Sun looks calm enough for the time being. Even if it shoots out a flare, we can always get into our suits and go for a swim in one of the fuel tanks."

"That wouldn't be very helpful," Amanda pointed out, not realizing that Pancho was joking. "The high-energy protons would set off all sorts of secondary particles from the fuel's atoms."

Pancho frowned at her. Amanda looked from her to Dan and then back to her control panel.

"I think I'll go back and see how Lars is doing," she said, getting up from her chair.

"Have fun," Pancho said.

Dan watched her step through the hatch, then slid into her vacated chair.

"Don't look so glum, boss. We're battin' along at one-third g with no sweat. Be back in lunar orbit in less'n four days."

"I had wanted to stop to sample those other two rocks," Dan said.

"Can't take the chance. Better to—hold on. Incoming message from Selene. George Ambrose."

"I'll take it here," said Dan. "By the way, have you told mission control that we've shut down the shield?"

"Not yet, but they'll see it on the telemetering. It's recorded automatically."

Dan nodded as George's bushy red-maned face appeared on the screen. Quickly, in a worried whisper, George explained how he'd located Cardenas and spirited her off to the temporary shelter.

"She wants t'see Stavenger," George concluded. "I told her I'd talk to you first. She'll be perfectly okay in the tempo for a coupla weeks, if we need to keep her stashed there. So . . . what d'you want me to do, Dan?"

George's image on the screen froze. Dan could see that he must have been at the mission control center when he'd sent the message. Good. He must've cleared out the place to make sure nobody could eavesdrop.

Now I've got to send him a reply that just about anybody can listen to, Dan thought. This is going to be like an old-time mafioso speaking into a tapped telephone.

"George, I think she's right. Do as she asks . . . as carefully as you can. She's important to us; there's a lot she and I have to talk about when I get back. We've got some problems here on the ship and we're heading back home. If all goes well, we should be back in lunar orbit in less than four days. I'll keep you informed, and you let me know how things are going there."

Dan reviewed his own message, decided there was nothing he needed to add to it, then touched the SEND button on the comm panel.

He started to get up from the co-pilot's seat when the comm unit pinged.

" 'Nother message comin' in," Pancho said needlessly.

A young man's face appeared on the screen. He looked annoyed. "General notice to all spacecraft and surface vehicles. A class-four solar flare has been observed by the early-warning sensors in Mercury orbit. Preliminary calculations of the interplanetary field indicate the resulting radiation storm has a ninety percent chance of reaching the Earth–Moon system within the next twelve hours. All spacecraft in cislunar space are advised to return to the nearest safe docking facility. All activities on the lunar surface will be suspended in six hours. Anyone on the surface is advised to seek shelter within six hours."

Dan sagged back into the chair.

Pancho tried to smile. "You called it, boss: Murphy's Law."

STORM SHELTER

Four worried people clustered around the table in *Starpower 1*'s wardroom. The wallscreen showed a chart of the solar system, with the radiation cloud that the solar flare had belched out appearing as a shapeless gray blob twisted by the interplanetary magnetic field. It was approaching Earth and the Moon rapidly. Deep in the Asteroid Belt a single pulsating yellow dot showed where their ship was.

Dan said to the computer, "Show the projections for the next two days."

The cloud grew and thinned, but surged out past the orbit of Mars and then engulfed the inner Belt and overran the blinking dot that marked *Starpower 1*'s position.

Pancho made a sound halfway between a sigh and a snort. "No way around it. We're gonna get hosed."

Amanda looked up from her palmcomp. "If we could pump all our remaining fuel into one tank, it could serve as a shelter . . . of sorts."

"I thought the secondaries would get us," Dan muttered.

"They'd be high," Amanda admitted, "but if we could pressurize the fuel it might absorb most of the secondary particles before they reached us."

"If we're plumb in the middle of the tank," Pancho said.

"Yes. Inside our suits, of course."

"Can the suits handle the temperature? We're talking about liquid hydrogen and helium; damned close to absolute zero."

"The suits are insulated well enough," Pancho said. Then she added, "But nobody's ever tried a dunk in liquid hydrogen with 'em."

"And we'd have to be dunked for god knows how many hours," Dan muttered.

Fuchs had not said a word. His head was bent over his own palmcomp.

"How much protection would the fuel give us?" Dan asked glumly.

Amanda hesitated, looked down at her handheld screen, then said, "We'd all need hospitalization. We'd have to set the flight controls to put us into lunar orbit on automatic."

"We'd all be that sick?" Pancho asked.

Amanda nodded solemnly.

And I'd be dead, Dan thought. I can't take another radiation dose like that. It would kill me.

Aloud, he tried to sound reasonably hopeful. "Well, it's better than sitting here with our thumbs jammed. Pancho, start transferring the fuel."

"How high can we pressurize one of the tanks?" Amanda wondered.

"I'll check the specs," said Pancho. "Come on, we've got to—"

"Wait," Fuchs said, looking up at them. "There is a better way."

Dan looked hard at him. Fuchs's eyes were set so deep that it was difficult to see any expression in them. Certainly he was not smiling. His thin slash of a mouth looked tight, hard.

"Computer," Fuchs called, "display position of asteroid 32–114."

A yellow dot began blinking near the inner edge of the Belt.

"That's where we must go," Fuchs said flatly.

"It's half a day off our course home," Pancho objected.

"Why there, Lars?" Amanda asked.

"We can use it for a storm shelter."

Dan shook his head. "Once the cloud runs over us, the radiation is isotropic. It comes from all directions. You can't hide behind a rock from it."

"Not behind the rock," Fuchs said, with growing excitement. "Inside it!"

"Inside the asteroid?"

"Yes! We burrow into it. The body of the asteroid will shield us from the radiation!"

"That would be great," Dan said, "if we had some deep drilling equipment aboard and a few days to dig. We don't have either."

"We don't need them!"

"The hell we don't," Dan shot back. "You think we're going to tunnel into that rock with your little core sampler?"

"No, no, no," Fuchs said. "You don't understand. That rock is a chondritic asteroid!"

"So what?" Pancho snapped.

"It's porous! It isn't a rock, not like Bonanza. It's an aggregate of chondrites—little stones, held together by gravity."

"How do you know that?" Dan demanded. "We haven't gotten close enough to—"

"Look at the data!" Fuchs urged, waving a thick-fingered hand at the wallscreen.

"What data?" The screen still showed the chart with the radiation cloud.

Fuchs pointed his palmcomp at the screen like a pistol and the wall display suddenly showed a long table of alphanumerics.

"Look at the data for its density," Fuchs said urgently. He jumped up from his chair and bounded to the screen. "Look! Its density isn't much more than that of water! It *can't* be a solid object! Not with such a density. It's porous! An aggregation of stones! Like a . . ." he searched for a word, ". . . like a pile of rubble . . . a beanbag chair!"

Dan stared at the numbers, then looked back at Fuchs. The man was clearly excited now.

"You're sure of this?" he asked.

"The numbers don't lie," Fuchs said. "They can't."

Pancho gave out a soft whistle. "Shore wish we had somethin' more'n numbers to go on."

"But we do!" Fuchs said. "Mathilde in the Main Belt, and Eugenia— several C–class bodies among the Near-Earth Asteroids—they are all aggregates, not solid at all. Microprobes have examined them, even gone inside them!"

"Porous," Dan muttered.

"Yes!"

"We can dig into them without drilling equipment?"

"They are probably highly-tunneled by nature."

Dan stroked his chin, trying to think, trying to decide. If he's right, it'd be better than dunking ourselves in a pool of liquid hydrogen for hours on end. If Fuchs is right. If we can burrow into the asteroid and use it for a storm shelter. If he's wrong, we're all dead.

Pancho spoke up. "I say we go for the asteroid, boss."

Dan looked into her steady light brown eyes. Is she saying this because she knows I won't make it otherwise? Is she willing to take the chance with her own life because it's the only chance we've got to save mine?

"I agree," Amanda said. "The asteroid is the better choice."

He turned back to Fuchs. "Lars, are you absolutely certain of all this?"

"Absolutely," Fuchs replied, without an instant's hesitation.

"Okay," Dan said, feeling uneasy about it. "Change course for—which one is it?"

"Asteroid 32–114," Fuchs and Amanda answered in unison.

"Point and shoot," Dan said.

Dan tried to sleep while *Starpower 1* raced to the chondritic asteroid, but his dreams were troubled with faces and visions from the past and a vague, looming sense of dread. He awoke feeling more tired than when he'd crawled into his bunk.

He felt stiff and sore, as if every muscle in his body were strained. Tension, he told himself. But that sardonic voice in his mind retorted, Age. You're getting to be an old man.

He nodded to his image in the lav mirror. If I live through this I'm going to start rejuve therapy.

Then he realized what he'd said: *if* I live through this.

He put on a fresh set of coveralls and grabbed a mug of coffee on his way to the bridge. Amanda was in the command chair, with Fuchs sitting at her right.

"Pancho's sleeping," Amanda said before Dan could ask. "We'll be making rendezvous with 114 in . . ." she glanced at one of the screens, ". . . seventy-three minutes. I'll wake her in half an hour."

"Can we see the rock yet?" Dan asked, peering into the black emptiness beyond the windows.

"Telescopic view," said Amanda, touching a viewscreen.

A lumpy, roundish shape appeared on the screen. To Dan it looked like a partially-deflated beach ball, dark gray, almost black.

"We're getting excellent data on it," Fuchs said. "Mass and density are confirmed."

"It's porous, as you thought?"

"Yes, it has to be."

"It's certainly no beauty," Amanda said.

"I don't know about that," replied Dan. "It looks pretty good to me. In fact, I think I'll call it Haven."

"Haven," she echoed.

Dan nodded. "Our haven from the storm." Silently he added, If those numbers for its density mean what Fuchs says they do.

SELENE

The worst part of being alone in the temporary shelter was the waiting. There was nothing to do in the tempo except pace its length—an even dozen strides for Kris Cardenas—or watch the commercial video broadcasts that the shelter's antenna pulled in from the relay satellites.

Maddening. And there was the high-tech sarcophagus in the middle of the floor with the frozen woman inside its gleaming stainless steel cylinder. Not much company.

When the hatch in the floor suddenly squeaked open, Cardenas jumped with surprise so hard she nearly banged her head on the shelter's curving roof. For an instant she didn't care who was coming through the hatch; even an assassin would be a welcome relief from the boredom of the past night and day.

But she puffed out a big sigh of relief when she saw George Ambrose's brick-red mane rising through the open hatch. George climbed through and grinned at her.

"Dan says I should take you to Stavenger."

Cardenas nodded. "Yes. Fine."

Doug Stavenger was not happy to see her. He sat behind his desk and eyed her with raw disappointment showing in his expression. Cardenas sat in the cushioned chair before the desk like an accused criminal being interrogated. George stood by the office door, beefy arms folded across his chest.

"You seeded Randolph's ship with gobblers?" he said, his voice hollow with shocked disbelief.

"Specifically tailored to take apart copper compounds," Cardenas admitted, feeling shaky inside. "Nothing more."

"Isn't that enough?"

"It was meant to cripple the ship's radiation shield," she said defensively. "Once they found out about it they'd abort their mission and return here."

"But they didn't find out about it until they were deep in the Belt," Stavenger said.

George added, "And now they're sailing into a fookin' radiation storm without a shield."

"This could become a murder," Stavenger said. "Four murders."

Cardenas bit her lip and nodded.

"And Humphries was behind this scheme," Stavenger said. It was a statement, not a question.

"He wanted Randolph's mission to fail."

"Why?"

"Ask him."

"He's a major investor in the project. Why would he want it to fail?"

"Ask him," she repeated.

"I intend to," said Stavenger. "He's already on his way here."

As if on cue, Stavenger's phone chimed. "Mr. Humphries here to see you," said the phone's synthesized voice.

"Send him in," Stavenger said, touching the stud on the rim of his desk that opened the door.

George stood aside, clearly glowering through his beard as Humphries walked in. Humphries looked at Cardenas, half turned in her chair, then at Stavenger. With a slight shrug he took the other chair in front of the desk.

"What's this all about?" he asked casually as he sat down. "What's going on?"

"It's about attempted murder," Stavenger said.

"Murder?"

"Four people are caught in a solar storm out in the Belt without a working radiation shield."

"Dan Randolph, you mean." Humphries almost smiled. "That's just like him, barging ahead like a bull in a china shop."

Stavenger bristled. "You didn't get Dr. Cardenas here to seed Randolph's ship with gobblers?"

"Gobblers?"

"Nanomachines. Disassemblers."

Humphries glanced at Cardenas, then said to Stavenger, "I asked Dr. Cardenas if there was any way that Randolph's ship could be . . . er, disabled slightly. Just enough to get him to turn back and abort his flight to the Belt."

Cardenas started to reply, but Stavenger said heatedly, "If they die—if any one of them dies—I'll have you arraigned for premeditated murder."

Humphries actually smiled at Stavenger. "That's so far-fetched it's ludicrous."

"Is it?"

"I had Randolph's ship sabotaged so he would abort his flight and come back to Selene. I admit to that. Any sane man would have turned around and headed for home as soon as he found the sabotage. But not Randolph! He pushed on anyway, knowing that his radiation shield was damaged. That's his decision, not mine. If there's a crime in this, it's Randolph committing suicide and taking his crew with him."

Stavenger barely held on to his composure. His fists clenched, he asked through gritted teeth, "And just why did you want to sabotage his ship?"

"So the stock in Astro Corporation would drop, why else? It was a business decision."

"Business."

"Yes, business. I want Astro; the lower its stock, the easier for me to buy it up. Dr. Cardenas here wanted her grandchildren. I offered to get her together with them in exchange for a pinch of nanomachines."

"Gobblers," Stavenger said.

"They weren't programmed to harm anyone," Cardenas protested. "They were specifically set to attack the copper compound of the superconductor, nothing more."

"My father was killed by gobblers," Stavenger said, his voice as cold and sharp as an icepick. "Murdered."

"That's ancient history," Humphries scoffed. "Please don't bring your family baggage into this."

Visibly restraining himself, Stavenger stared at Humphries for a long, silent moment. Electricity crackled through the office. George decided that if Stavenger came around the desk and started beating up on Humphries, he would keep the door closed and prevent anyone from coming to the bastard's aid.

At last Stavenger seemed to win his inner struggle. He took a shuddering breath, then said in a low, seething voice, "I'm turning this matter over to Selene's legal department. Neither of you will be allowed to leave Selene until their investigation is finished."

"You're going to put us on trial?" Cardenas asked.

"If it were up to me," Stavenger said, "I'd put the two of you into leaky spacesuits and drive you out into the middle of *Mare Nubium* and leave you there."

Humphries laughed. "I'm glad you're not a judge. And, by the way, Selene has no capital punishment, does it?"

"Not yet," Stavenger growled. "But if we get a few more people like you here, we'll probably change our laws on that point."

Humphries got to his feet. "You can threaten all you like, but I don't think your courts will take this as personally as you are."

With that, he strode to the door. George stepped aside and let him open it for himself. He noticed that there was a thin sheen of perspiration on Humphries's upper lip as he left the office.

The instant the door closed again, Cardenas broke into sobs. Half doubled over in her chair, she buried her face in her hands.

Stavenger's icy composure melted. "Kris . . . how could you do it? How could you let him . . ." He stopped and shook his head.

Without looking up at him, Cardenas said in a tear-choked voice, "I was angry, Doug. Angrier than you can know. Angrier than I myself knew."

"Angry? At Randolph?"

"No. At *them*. The crazies who let this greenhouse cliff ruin the world. The fanatics who've exiled us, who won't let me come to Earth to see my children, my grandchildren. And they won't come here, not even for a visit. I wanted to punish them, get even with them."

"By killing Randolph?"

"Dan's trying to help them," she said, looking up at him at last, her face streaked with tears. "I don't *want* them helped! They made this mess. They shut me out of their lives. Let them stew in their own juices! They deserve whatever they get."

Stavenger shook his head, bewildered. He handed Cardenas a tissue and she dabbed at her reddened eyes.

"I'm going to recommend that you be placed under house arrest, Kris. You'll be able to go anywhere in Selene except the nanotech lab."

She nodded wordlessly.

"And Humphries?" George asked, still standing by the door.

"Same thing, I suppose. But he's right, the smug slimebag. We don't have capital punishment; we don't even have a jail here in Selene."

"House arrest for him would be a lark," George said.

Stavenger looked disgusted. But then his chin came up and his eyes brightened. "Unless we take it out on his wallet."

"Huh?"

With a slow smile spreading across his youthful face, Stavenger said, "If he's found guilty of murder, or even attempted murder, maybe the court can divest him of his share of Starpower and keep him from taking over Astro Corporation."

George huffed. "I'd rather punch his ribs in."

"So would I," Stavenger admitted. "But I think he'd *rather* have his ribs punched in than to have to give up Astro and Starpower."

HAVEN

T here it is," Pancho sang out. "How's that for navigation?"

Dan crouched slightly behind the command chair and peered through the window. The asteroid was visible to their naked eyes now against the distant glow of the Sun's zodiacal light, a dumbbell-shaped dark mass tumbling slowly end over end.

Fuchs stood beside Dan, his hands on the back of Amanda's chair.

"It's two bodies in contact," he said. "Like Castallia and several others."

"Looks like a peanut," said Dan.

"A peanut made of rock," Pancho said.

"No, no," Fuchs corrected, "a peanut made up of thousands of little stones, chondrules, that are barely holding together in their very weak mutual gravitational attraction."

"Uh-huh."

"Look, you can see craters on the surface."

Dan strained his eyes. How in hell can he see craters on that black slug in this dim lighting?

"They have no rims," Fuchs went on, talking fast in his excitement. "Smaller objects have collided with the asteroid but they don't make impact craters as they would on a solid body. They simply burrow into the loose rubble."

"Same as we're gonna do," Pancho said.

"Our storm cellar," Amanda added, glancing up at Fuchs.

It's our storm cellar only if he's right, Dan added silently. If that chunk out there really is a beanbag and we can dig into it until the storm's over.

Aloud, he asked, "How long before the radiation starts to build up?"

"Four hours, plus a few minutes," Pancho said. "Plenty of time."

You hope, Dan said to himself.

She established *Starpower 1* in a close orbit around the tumbling asteroid, and then the four of them floated weightlessly down to the airlock, where Dan and Fuchs had already assembled six emergency tanks of air. As they wriggled into their spacesuits Fuchs begged to go out the airlock first, but Dan overruled him.

"Pancho goes first, Lars. You're still a tenderfoot out there."

Through his fishbowl helmet, Fuchs's broad face frowned in puzzlement. "But my feet are fine," he said. "Why are you worried about my feet?"

Dan and Pancho both laughed, but Amanda shot an annoyed glance at Dan and said, "It's an American expression, Lars. From their western frontier, long ago."

"Yep," Dan conceded. "I learned it from Wild Bill Hickok."

Getting serious, Pancho said, "We can go together, Lars and me—whenever you guys are ready to stop horsin' around."

"Aye-aye cap'n," said Dan, touching his helmet with a gloved hand in a sloppy salute.

Pancho and Fuchs went through the airlock and, once it cycled, Dan and Amanda. While he stood in the cramped metal chamber, listening to the air-pump's clatter dwindling to silence, he heard Fuchs's excited voice through his helmet speaker:

"It's like a sandpile!"

Dan offered a swift thanks to whatever gods there be. Maybe we'll all live through this, after all.

With Amanda, he went through the airlock and then jetted the hundred meters or so separating the ship from the asteroid. It sure looks solid, Dan thought, staring at the black, slowly tumbling mass as he approached it. And yes, there were craters here and there with no rims to them; just holes, as if some giant had poked his fingers into the asteroid.

Then he saw Fuchs's helmet and shoulders; the rest of him was in some sort of a pit. He's digging like a kid in a sandbox, Dan saw.

As he got closer, Dan saw that the surface of the asteroid looked hazy, blurred. Is he stirring up that much dust? Dan asked himself. No, it's not just where Fuchs is digging. It's everywhere. The whole surface of the asteroid is blurry. What the hell is causing that?

"Are my eyes going bad or is the surface blurred?" he said into his helmet microphone.

"Dust," came Fuchs's immediate reply. "Particles from the solar wind give the dust an electrostatic charge. It makes the dust levitate."

"That doesn't happen on the Moon," Dan objected.

'The Moon is a very large body," said Fuchs. "This asteroid's gravity is too weak to hold the dust on the surface."

Just then Dan touched down on Haven. It was like stepping on talcum powder. His boots sank into the dark dust almost up to his ankles even though he came down with a feather light touch. Cripes, he thought, it's like one of those black sand beaches in Tahiti.

Dan turned and saw Pancho, long and lean even in her spacesuit, gliding across the asteroid's dusty surface toward him.

"Bring out the air tanks, Mandy," Pancho said.

Amanda soared weightlessly to *Starpower 1*'s airlock, then emerged again towing a string of six tall gray cylinders behind her. In her gleaming white spacesuit she looked like a robot nurse followed by a half-dozen unfinished pods.

"Better start diggin', boss," Pancho said.

Dan nodded, then realized that she might not be able to see the gesture. There wasn't all that much light out here, and they had decided to keep their helmet lamps off to save their suit batteries.

"We go with the buddy system," Dan said as he unlimbered the makeshift shovel he had carried with him. "You and me, Pancho. Amanda, you stay with Lars."

"Yes, of course," Amanda replied.

It wasn't quite like digging at the beach. More like working on a giant, black hunk of Swiss cheese, Dan thought. There were holes in the surface, tunnels that had apparently been drilled by stray chunks of rock hitting the asteroid. There was no bedrock, just a loose rubble of black rounded grains, the largest of them about the size of a small pebble. It's a wonder they hold together, Dan thought.

"Here's a ready-made tunnel for two," Pancho called to him. He saw her slowly disappearing into one of the tunnels.

It was wide enough for the two of them, just barely.

"How far down does it go?" Dan asked as he gingerly slid over the lip of the crater, careful not to catch his backpack.

"Dunno," Pancho answered. "Deep enough to ride out the storm. Better start fillin' in the hole."

He nodded inside his helmet and took a tighter grip on his improvised shovel: it had been a panel covering an electronics console. They had to cover themselves with at least a meter of dirt to protect against the oncoming radiation.

As he dug away at the sides of the sloping tunnel, Dan expected the gritty dirt to slide down into their hole. That's what would have happened on Earth, or even on the Moon. But Haven's gravity was so slight that the tunnel walls would not cave in no matter how furiously he dug into them.

In short order he and Pancho, working side by side, had buried themselves as deep as their waists. Not enough, Dan knew. Nowhere near enough, not yet.

"How're we doing . . . on time?" he asked Pancho, panting from the exertion of digging.

She straightened up. "Lemme see," she said, tapping at the keyboard on her left forearm. Dan could see a multi-colored display light up on her bubble helmet.

"Radiation level's not up much over ambient yet," she said.

"How soon?" Dan asked impatiently.

The lights on her helmet's inner face flickered, changed. "Hour and a half, maybe a little less."

Dan went back to digging, blinking sweat out of his eyes, wishing he could wipe his face or just scratch his nose. But that was impossible inside the suit. Should have worn a sweat band, he told himself. Always did when I went outside. Been so long since I've done any EVA work I forgot it. Hindsight's always perfect.

"Y'know we're gonna need at least a meter of this dirt over us," Pancho said, digging alongside him.

"Yep."

"And then dig our way out, after the cloud passes."

"Yep," Dan repeated. It was the most he could say without stopping work. His muscles ached from the unaccustomed exertion.

It seemed like hours later when he heard Pancho's voice in his helmet speaker. "How're you guys doin', Mandy?"

"We're fine. We found a lovely cave and we have it almost completely filled in."

"Once you're all covered over it's gonna degrade our radio link," Pancho said.

"Yes, I'm sure it will."

"Got your air tanks in there with you?"

"Yes, of course."

Dan saw that their air tanks were still lying out on the surface, more than arm's reach away.

"Okay, keep your radio open. If we get completely cut off, you stay in the hole for fourteen hours. Got that?"

"Fourteen hours, check."

"Time count starts now."

"Fourteen hours from now," Amanda confirmed.

"Have a nice day."

"We'll see you in fourteen hours," Fuchs said.

"Right," said Dan, silently adding, Dead or alive.

To Pancho, he said, "I'd better drag the air tanks in here." Before she could object he pushed himself out of the hole and soared up above the dark, uneven ground. Dan glanced around but could not find the shelter that Amanda and Fuchs had dug for themselves. They did a good job, he thought as he tapped his jet thruster controls to push himself back to the surface.

The cylinders weighed next to nothing, but still he was careful with them as he slid them down into the pit. They still have mass, and inertia, Dan knew. I could break open Pancho's helmet or spring her suit's joints if I let one of these things bang into her.

By the time he wormed himself back into the pit beside her, Dan was bathed in cold sweat and puffing hard.

"You're not used to real work, are you, boss?" Pancho teased.

Dan shook his head inside his helmet. "Soon as we get back to Selene I'm going in for rejuvenation therapy."

"Me too."

"You? At your age?"

"Sooner's better'n later, they claim."

Dan humphed. "Better late than never."

"Radiation level's starting to climb," Pancho said, starting to paw at the sides of their pit again. "We better get ourselves buried or neither one of us'll get any younger."

"Or older," Dan muttered.

Buried alive. This is like something out of an Edgar Allan Poe story, Dan said to himself. He knew Pancho was mere centimeters from him; so were the air tanks. But he could see nothing. They were buried under nearly a full meter of loose rubble, curled fetally, nothing to see or hear or do except wait.

". . . are you doing?" He heard Amanda's voice, scratchy and weak, through his helmet's speaker.

"We're okay," Pancho said. "I've been thinkin' we oughtta organize a square dance."

Dan suppressed a groan. That's just we need, he thought, redneck humor. Then, surprisingly, he laughed. He hadn't heard the term "redneck" since he'd been in Texas, long ages ago. There are no rednecks off-Earth, Dan realized. You don't get sunburned out here. Cooked, maybe. Fried by radiation. But not tanned, not unless you sit under the sunlamps in the gym at Selene.

He wiggled his right hand through the loose rubble encasing him and felt for the keyboard on his left forearm. By touch he called up the ship's sensor display. They had programmed the suits to show the displays on the inner surfaces of their bubble helmets. Nothing but streaks of colored hash. Either the pile of dirt atop them or the radiation storm was interfering with their link to the ship. Probably a combination of both, he thought.

"What's the time?" Dan asked.

At least he could talk with Pancho. Even if the radio link broke down completely, they were close enough to scrunch through the dirt and touch helmets so that they could talk through sound conduction.

"More'n thirteen hours to go, boss."

"You mean we've been down here for less than an hour?"

"Forty-nine minutes, to be exact."

"Shit," Dan said, with feeling.

"Take a nap. Best way to spend the time."

Dan nodded inside his helmet. "Nothing else to do."

He heard Pancho giggle softly.

"What's funny?"

"Mandy and Lars. I bet they're tryin' to figger out how to get the two of them into one suit."

Dan laughed, too. "Maybe you and I ought to try that."

"Boss!" Pancho cried in mock shock. "That's sexual harassment!"

"Nothing else to do," he repeated. "I can't even jerk off inside this double-damned suit."

"I can," Pancho teased.

"Now *that's* sexual harassment," Dan grumbled.

"Nope. Just better design."

Dan licked his lips. He felt thirsty, chilled, yet he was sweating. His stomach was queasy.

"How do you feel, Pancho?"

"Bored. Tired. Too jumpy to sleep. How 'bout you?"

"The same, I guess. Every part of me aches."

"How's your blood pressure?"

"How in hell would I know?"

"You hear your pulse in your ears?"

"No."

"Then you're okay, I guess."

"Thank you, Dr. Pancho."

"Go to sleep, boss. That's what I'm gonna try to do."

"I thought you said you were too jumpy."

"Yeah, but I'm gonna give it a try. Close my eyes and think pleasant thoughts."

"Good luck."

"You try it, too."

"Sure."

Dan closed his eyes, but his thoughts were far from pleasant. Opening them again, he fumbled with his wrist keyboard until he got the suit's radiation sensor displayed on his helmet. The graph was distorted by the curve of his helmet, and blurry. He tried to focus his eyes on it. *Looks okay,* he said to himself. *Curve's going up, but the slope is low and it's a far distance from the red zone.*

Try to sleep. He was certainly tired enough for it. *Relax! Think about what you're going to do when you get back to Selene. I'd like to personally punch out Humphries's lights.* Dan pictured Humphries's surprise when he broke his nose with a good straight right.

Somewhere in his mind an old adage sounded: *Revenge is a dish best taken cold.*

Punching in Humphries's face would be fun, but what would really hurt the bastard? He's tried to kill me. He may succeed yet; we're not out of this. If I die he'll move in and take over Astro. How can I prevent him from doing that? How can I stop him, even from the grave?

Dan chuckled bitterly to himself. *I'm already in my grave,* he realized. *I'm already buried.*

NANOTECHNOLOGY
LABORATORY

Charley Engles looked worried, upset. He nervously brushed his sandy hair back away from his forehead as he said, "Kris, I'm not supposed to let you in here."

It was well past midnight. Cardenas was surprised that anyone was still working in the lab complex. Selene's security people hadn't bothered to change the entry code on the main door; she had just tapped it out and the door had obligingly slid open. But Engles had been working in his cubicle, and as soon as he saw Cardenas striding determinedly past the empty work stations toward her own office, he popped out of his cubbyhole and stopped her.

"We got notified by security," he said, looking shamefaced. "You're not allowed in here until further notice."

"I know, Charley," she said. "I just want to clear out my desk."

Charles Engles was a young grad student from New York whose parents had sent him to Selene after he'd been crippled in a car crash. Even knowing that he could never return to them once he'd taken nanotherapy, his parents wanted their son's legs repaired so he could walk again.

"The cameras . . ." Engles pointed to the tiny unwinking red lights in the corners of the ceiling. "Security will send somebody here once they see you."

"It's all right," she said, trying to mask her inner tension. "I'll only be here a few minutes. You can go back to your work."

Instead, he walked with her as she headed for her office.

"What's this all about, Kris? Why do they want to lock you out of your own lab?"

"It's a long story and I'd rather not go into it right now, Charley. Please, I just need a few minutes in my office."

He looked unhappy, almost wounded. "If there's anything I can do to help . . ."

Cardenas smiled and felt tears welling in her eyes. "That's very kind of you, Charley. Thanks."

"I mean, I wouldn't be able to walk if it weren't for you."

She nodded and added silently, And now that you can walk you'll never be allowed to return to Earth.

"Well . . ." he shifted uneasily from one foot to the other. "If there's anything you need, anything at all, just let me know."

"Thanks, Charley. I'll do that."

He stood there for another awkward moment while Cardenas wondered how long it would take Security to send someone to apprehend her. Finally he headed reluctantly back to his own cubicle. She walked slowly toward her office.

Once Charley stepped into his cubicle, though, Cardenas swiftly turned down a side passageway toward the rear of the laboratory complex. She passed a sign that proclaimed in red letters AUTHORIZED PERSONNEL ONLY BEYOND THIS POINT. This was the area where newly developed nanomachines were tested. The passageway here was lined with sealed, airtight chambers, rather than the cubicles out front. The door to each chamber was locked. The passageway itself was lined with ultraviolet lamps along its ceiling. Each nanomachine type was designed to stop functioning when exposed to high-intensity ultraviolet light: a safety precaution.

Cardenas passed three doors, stopped at the fourth. She tapped out its entry code and the steel door opened inward a crack. She slipped into the darkened chamber and leaned her weight against the heavy door, closing it. With a long, shuddering sigh, she reset the entry code from the panel on the wall, effectively locking the door to anyone who might try to get in. They'll have to break the door down, she told herself, and that will take them some time.

By the time they get the door open I'll be dead.

Dan dreamed of Earth: a confused, troubled dream. He was sailing a racing yacht, running before the wind neck-and-neck with many other boats. Warm tropical sunlight beat down on his shoulders and back as he gripped the tiller with one hand while the boat's computer adjusted the sails for every change in the breeze.

The boat knifed through the water, but suddenly it was a car that Dan was driving at breakneck speed through murderously heavy traffic. Dan didn't know where he was; some city freeway, a dozen lanes clogged with cars and buses and enormous semi rigs chuffing smoke and fumes into the dirty gray, sullen sky. Something was wrong with the car's air conditioning; it was getting uncomfortably hot in the driver's seat. Dan started to open his window but realized that the windows had to stay shut. There's no air to breath out there, he said to himself, knowing it was ridiculous because he wasn't in space, he was on Earth and he was suffocating, choking, coughing.

He woke up coughing with Pancho's voice blaring in his ears, "Recharge your backpack, boss! You're runnin' low on air."

Blackness. He couldn't see a thing. For a moment he felt panic surging through him, then it fell into place. Buried in the asteroid. Time to refill his backpack's air tank. In the dark. By touch.

"Lemme help you," Pancho said.

Dan sensed her beside him. The gravelly dirt shifted, crunched. Something bumped into his side.

"Oops. 'Scuse me."

Dan pushed one hand through the gritty stuff, remembering where he'd put the cylinders.

"I've got the hose," he said.

"Okay, good. That's what I was lookin' for."

"Groping for, you mean."

"Whatever. Hand it to me now."

Dan felt her hand pushing against his side. "I can do it," he said.

"Better let me," said Pancho. "You're tired and fatigue makes you sloppy, causes mistakes."

"I'm all right."

'Sure. But just lemme do it, huh? Tired astronauts don't live long."

"And rain makes applesauce," he mumbled, pushing the end of the hose into her waiting hand.

"Don't open it up yet," Pancho warned. "Don't want grit or dust contaminating the air."

"I know," he groused.

It seemed to take hours. Dan tried to keep from coughing but the air in his suit seemed awfully thick; his chest was hurting. He pictured old pantomime comedy routines as he and Pancho haltingly fumbled with the air hose, working blindly, and refilled each other's suit tanks. They filled Dan's backpack first, and within a minute he could take a deep breath again without it catching in his throat.

Once they filled Pancho's backpack he heard her inhale deeply. "Best canned air in the solar system," she announced happily.

"What time is it? How long do we have to go?"

"Lemme see . . . seven and a half hours."

"That's how long we've been down here?"

"Nope, that's how long we still have to go," Pancho answered.

"Another seven and a half hours?"

Pancho laughed. "You sound like a kid in the back seat of a car."

He huffed, then broke into a chastened grin. "I guess I was whining, wasn't I?"

"A little."

A new thought struck Dan. "After the time's up, how do we tell if the radiation's really gone down enough for us to get back to the ship?"

"Been thinkin' about that. I'll worm my extensible antenna wire up to the top of this rubble heap and see if we can link with the ship. Then it'll be purty simple to read the ship's sensors."

"Suppose the ship's comm system's been knocked out by the radiation."

"Not likely."

"But what if?"

Pancho sighed. "Then I'll just hafta stick my head out and see what my suit sensors read."

"Like an old cowboy video," Dan said. "Stick your head out and see if anybody shoots at you."

"Hey, boss, you really did learn a lot from Wild Bill Hickok, didn't ya?"

This late at night there was only one man on duty monitoring Selene's security-camera network. He was a portly, balding former London bobby who had spent his life's savings to bring himself and his wife to the Moon and live in comfortable, low-gravity retirement. He'd found retirement so boring, however, that he pleaded with Selene's personnel department to allow him to work, at least part-time.

The uniform they gave him wasn't much; just a set of glorified coveralls with an insignia patch on the left shoulder and his name badge clipped over its breast pocket. But at least he could spend three nights each week sitting alone and content, watching the videos his wife always complained about while still feeling that he was doing something worthwhile. He half-dozed, leaning back in his padded swivel chair, as the twenty display screens arranged in a semicircle around his desk flashed views from Selene's hundreds of security cameras. Actually, only nineteen of the screens showed the cameras' scenes; the screen directly in front of the desk was showing the football match from Vancouver, live. But with the sound well-muted, of course.

The computer did all the real work. The toffs in the main office programmed the computer with a long list of things that would be considered questionable or downright illegal. If the computer detected any such activity it sounded an alarm and indicated where and what was going on.

With the score still tied and only four minutes left in the final period, the blasted computer buzzed.

The guard frowned with annoyance. His central screen winked out for an instant, then displayed a ceiling-eye-view of a woman walking through one of the labs. UNAUTHORIZED PERSON blinked in red across the bottom of the screen.

It took a few minutes to coax the information out of the computer, but finally the guard phoned the security chief, waking him of course, with the news that Dr. Kris Cardenas had entered the nanotechnology laboratory. The chief grumbled and cast a bleary eye at the guard, but at least had the good grace to say, "Thanks. I'll send somebody down there."

Then he hung up and the guard went back to watching the football game. It was going into overtime.

HAVEN

Try as he might, Dan could not get back to sleep. Pancho had attempted to call Amanda and Fuchs, but there was no response from them.

"Must be a lotta sizzle outside," she said.

Dan thought she sounded worried. Not her usual sassy self. Or maybe she's just tired. Or bored.

How can anybody be bored with this storm only a meter over our heads? Dan asked himself. Some storm. No thunder and lightning. No noise at all, unless you count the crackle and hiss when you try to use the radio.

Quiet. Deadly quiet.

Dan found the water nipple in his suit's collar and took a sip. Flat and warm. Like recycled piss.

More than seven hours to go. I'll go bonkers by then: stark, raving nutty.

Then he tasted blood in his mouth.

It was like an electric shock. His entire body flinched. Everything else disappeared from his mind.

Bleeding gums, he thought, trying to fight down the terror rising in him. One of the prime symptoms of radiation sickness.

Or maybe you accidentally bit your tongue, he told himself.

Yeah, sure, answered that sardonic voice in his head. You've had a bout of radiation sickness before, you know the drill. Only this time there's no place to go to, nothing to do except sit here in this grave and let the radiation do its job on you.

"Pancho," he croaked, surprised at how dry his throat was.

"Right here, boss."

"Can you turn on your suit's recorder?"

"Yeah, I think so . . ."

Dan sensed her fumbling in the dirt. This must be the way moles live, he thought, depending on touch instead of sight. His stomach was fluttering, nauseous. Christ, don't let me toss my cookies inside the double-damned helmet, he begged silently.

Pancho said, "Testing, one, two, three." A moment later he heard the words repeated.

"Okay, the recorder's workin'."

"Good," said Dan. "Get this down." He cleared his throat. It felt raw, raspy. Then, in as normal a voice as he could produce, he pronounced:

"I am Dan Randolph, CEO of Astro Manufacturing Corporation. This is my last will and testament. The recording equipment will automatically mark this statement with the date and time."

"That's right," Pancho said.

"Don't interrupt, kid. Where was I? Oh, right, last will and testament. I hereby bequeath all my stock in Astro Corporation to my friend and loyal employee, Priscilla Lane, together—"

Pancho was so shocked she didn't even bristle at the use of her proper name. "To me? Are you loco?"

"Don't interrupt!" Dan snapped. "All my Astro stock to Priscilla Lane, together with all my personal belongings and possessions." He had to stop and take a few breaths. Then, "And I nominate Priscilla Lane to take my place on the board of directors of Astro Corporation."

He thought about it for a few moments, then nodded, satisfied. "Okay, that's it. You can turn off the recorder now."

"What'd you do that for? How come you—"

"I'm not going to make it, kid," Dan said tiredly. "The radiation's getting to me. I want you to take my place on the board of directors and fight that sumbitch Humphries with every gram of strength you've got."

"Me? I'm just a hick engineer . . . a rocket jock, for cryin' out loud."

"You're my heir, Pancho. Like a daughter. I don't have any family to leave anything to, and besides, you know Astro as well as anyone does."

"Not the board of directors."

Dan laughed weakly. "You'll roll right over them, kid. The board needs some fresh, young blood. You'll have to fight Humphries, of course. He'll want to be made chairman once I'm gone."

In a quieter voice, Pancho asked, "You're talkin' like you're at death's door."

"I think I am. My gums are bleeding. I feel woozy. My ears are ringing. I just hope I don't get the shits."

"The storm's almost over," she said.

"So am I."

"Once we get back into the ship we can zip back to Selene in a couple of days. Maybe faster! I can goose her up to maybe half a *g*."

"And how will you brake her? Impact? Dive right into Alphonsus?"

Pancho fell silent for several moments. Dan was glad she couldn't see him. The way his insides felt, his hands would probably be shaking like a palsied old man's if they weren't buried in the asteroid's rubble.

"They can cure radiation sickness back at Selene," Pancho said at last. "Use nanomachines."

"If I make it back to Selene."

"Only about seven hours to go," she said. "Radiation's levelin' off."

"Not as deep as a well," Dan quoted, "or as wide as a church door, but it's enough. It'll do."

"You goin' delirious?"

"No, that's just Shakespeare. *Romeo and Juliet.*"

"Oh. Yeah, right."

"I'm going to take a nap, kid. I feel pretty tired."

"Good idea, I guess."

"Wake me when it's over."

Kris Cardenas was surprised at how her hands trembled as she worked. Programming nanomachines to disassemble carbon-based molecules was a snap, a no-brainer. Just a slight modification to the procedure they used every day to build diamond mechanisms out of bins of soot.

It wasn't the difficulty of the work. As she sat at the lab bench, peering intently at the desktop screen that displayed what the atomic force microscope was showing, she thought about the consequences.

Gobblers. I'm deliberately creating a batch of gobblers. If they get loose . . .

Calm down! she scolded herself. Go through this logically, step by step.

Okay, they'll break in and find me dead. Lying on the floor. I'll leave a note on the computer screen. Put it in big red letters, so they can't miss it. I'm only making a microsample of gobblers and I'm disabling their assembly capabilities. They can't reproduce. They'll be contained inside my body.

But what if they get outside your body? They'll be taking you apart from the inside. What's to stop them from getting out?

Nothing, she told herself. So I'll turn on the UV overheads before I swallow the bugs. That will destroy them once they get outside my body.

A knock on the door startled her.

"Dr. Cardenas? We know you're in there. Open up, please."

She wiped the display from the AFM and began hurriedly typing her suicide note.

"Warning. I have ingested a microgram of nanomachine disassemblers. They are programmed to take apart carbon-based molecules. Do not allow them to go beyond the confines of this laboratory. Disinfect the lab with high-intensity ultraviolet light before moving my body or touching anything in this room. Notify—"

Someone banged on the door, hard. "Kris! It's Doug Stavenger. You don't have to do this. Come on out."

She scanned the red block letters on the display screen and erased the final word; no need to notify Doug, he's already here.

"Kris, it's not your fault." Stavenger's voice was muffled by the heavy steel door, but she heard the urgency in it well enough. "Come out and talk this over with me."

She got off the spindly-legged stool and went to the sampling site at the end of the bench. A gleaming cup of lunar aluminum sat there, half full of water that contained the nanomachines that were going to kill her.

"Kris," Stavenger called, "you've spent your life developing nanotechnology. Don't throw it all away. Don't give them another reason to say nanomachines are killers."

She picked up the cup and held it in both hands, thinking, I can't live with this guilt. I've committed murder. I've killed four people.

Stavenger was shouting through the locked door, "That's what they'll say. You know that. They'll say that nanomachines killed the foremost researcher in the field. They'll use it to show how dangerous nanomachines are, how right they've been all along to ban them."

She looked from the cup to the closed, locked door. It was Humphries's idea, but I did it. Willingly. He pulled my strings and I danced like a blind, obedient little puppet.

"Don't throw your life away, Kris," Stavenger pleaded. "You'll be destroying everything you've worked for. You'll be giving them the excuse they need to come back here and force us to obey their laws."

Humphries, she thought. Once I'm dead he'll be able to blame the whole thing on me. His lawyers will talk his way out of it. He'll walk away from this. From four murders. Five, counting me.

Cardenas carried the cup back to the sampling site and sealed its aluminum top to its rim. Once the top clicked into place she placed the cup in the disposal oven and closed its door. The inner walls of the oven fluoresced as its ultraviolet lamps bathed the cup.

Why should I die for Martin Humphries? she asked herself. Someone's got to stand up to him. Someone's got to tell the truth about this. No matter what it costs, I've got to face him, face all of them.

"Come on, Kris. Open the door."

They're watching me through the security camera, Cardenas knew. She went back to the computer and erased her message. One of the staff people can destroy the gobblers tomorrow, she told herself. They're safe enough in the oven for now.

Slowly she walked to the door, then stopped at the keypad on the wall next to it.

"Doug?" she called.

"I'm right here, Kris. Open the door, please."

"This is silly," she said, feeling stupid, "but I don't remember the sequence I used to reset the lock."

A mumble of voices on the other side of the door. Then Stavenger, sounding relieved, replied, "Okay, Kris. Security's bringing an analyzer down anyway. We'll have it open in a few minutes."

"Doug?" she said again.

"Yes."

"Thanks."

"*Da nada,*" he answered.

By the time they got the door unlocked, Cardenas was surprised at how calm she felt. She had looked death in the face and discovered that she was strong enough to go on living.

The passageway outside was crammed with men and women in security coveralls, half-a-dozen of her own nanotech people, several medics in white, and Doug Stavenger.

"Are you all right?" Stavenger asked worriedly.

Cardenas felt herself smile a little. "I am now," she said.

DEATH

C'mon, boss, wake up!"

Pancho's voice, muffled, distant. Dan's eyes were gummy, bleary; it took an effort to open them. He tried to wipe them but his hands were still buried in the loose rubble of the asteroid.

"Dan! Wake up!"

He heard the urgency in her voice.

"Yeah. Okay . . ." His stomach heaved.

"Radiation level's down almost to normal," Pancho said. "You okay?"

"Sure," he lied. He felt too weak to move, too tired to care.

"Time to get outta here." She was scrabbling, clawing through the gravelly dirt. Dan wanted to help her but he could barely move his arms. All he wanted to do was sleep. Then his guts suddenly lurched and a wave of nausea swept over him.

"We're up, in the open." Amanda's voice came through his helmet speaker.

"I'm gonna need some help here," Pancho replied. "Dan's in a bad way."

Dan was concentrating on not vomiting. Get me to a toilet, he begged silently. I don't want to let loose inside the suit. Even in the depth of his misery, though, somewhere in the back of his mind he laughed bitterly at himself. It all boils down to this, he thought. Everything you've done in your life doesn't amount to a teaspoon of applesauce. All that's really important is not upchucking or losing control of your bowels.

He sensed somebody digging frantically above him, and then strong arms lifting him, dragging him free of the rubble-filled tunnel. Fuchs. He overdid it, and the two of them went tumbling completely off the asteroid, spiraling crazily in space. Dan saw *Starpower 1* slide past his field of view and then an unstoppable surge of bile rose into his throat and he vomited, spattering his stomach's contents noisomely all over his fishbowl helmet. The stench was overpowering. He groaned and retched again.

"Hang in there, boss," Pancho said. "I gotcha."

Dan thought he heard someone else retching, too. Nothing like the sound of vomiting to make you upchuck, too. I could get the whole Vienna Boys Choir tossing their cookies this way.

He wavered in and out of consciousness, thinking, That's the way they get you. They make you so miserable that you'll be glad to die. He squeezed his eyes shut and tried not to breathe. He desperately wanted to wipe his face but inside the suit and helmet it was impossible.

"Okay, the lock's cycling," he heard Pancho say.

"Bring him inside." Amanda's voice.

"Take him to his own bunk."

"Yes. Careful now."

He didn't dare open his eyes. At one point he heard Pancho say, "You get him out of his suit. I gotta see how much damage the storm did to the ship's systems."

After a while he felt something cool and soothing wiping his face. Opening his eyes at last, Dan saw a blurred image of Amanda bending over him, with Fuchs beside her. They book looked worried, grim.

"How do you feel?" Amanda asked.

"Lousy," he croaked.

Fuchs said, "We are under way. Pancho is accelerating to one-third *g*."

"The ship's okay?"

"Some of the sensors were damaged by the radiation," Fuchs said. "And the communications equipment, too. But the fusion power plant is functioning properly."

"The nanobugs didn't get to the MHD generator's superconductor?" Dan asked. It took most of his strength to get the words out.

"No, they seem perfectly in order," Fuchs answered. Then he added, "Thank god."

We're on our way home, Dan thought. He closed his eyes. On our way home.

"Until you get him here where we can give him proper medical treatment," Selene's chief radiation therapist was saying, "there's nothing you can do for him beyond the chelation pills and antioxidants you're already giving him."

Pancho watched the medic's unhappy image as she sat disconsolately in the command pilot's chair. It had taken more than an hour to contact Selene. *Starpower 1*'s high-gain antenna had been knocked out by radiation damage and she'd had to use the backup laser comm system. Otherwise the ship was running okay, some radiation damage here and there; nothing vital. The nanobugs hadn't gotten to the superconducting coil of the MHD generator, thank whatever gods there be.

But Dan was in a bad way, and the sad-assed medics at Selene couldn't do any more for him than a bunch of witch doctors. Bring him in as fast as you can. Well, sure! That's what I'm doin'. But will it be fast enough?

And Elly was dead. Just before they had abandoned the ship she had left the snake in her box and put the box in the refrigerator, knowing the cold would put Elly into a torpor, hoping that the fridge would provide enough shielding to save the krait. I should've carried her inside my suit, Pancho berated herself. Even if she bit me, I should've brought her with me. The radiation had killed the krait, along with the one remaining mouse.

Her thoughts returned to Dan. He's got it bad. We all took a dose, we'll all need medical attention once we get back to Selene. The chelation pills are helping, but Dan might not make it. He looks half-dead already.

Amanda came into the bridge and slipped into the right-hand seat.

"How is he?" Pancho asked.

"We cleaned him up and he's sleeping now." She made a strange face. "His hair is coming out. In clumps."

Pancho fought down the urge to go back to Dan's compartment. Nothing you can do there, she told herself.

She asked Amanda, "How's Lars?"

"He seems to be fine."

"Did he take the pills?"

"Yes, of course. He's working on the high-gain antenna."

'That circuitry's supposed t'be hardened against radiation," Pancho said angrily. "We oughtta sue the manufacturer when we get back."

"Oh, Pancho, it was exposed to such a high level of radiation. That was an intense storm."

She nodded, but said, "Yeah, but still that comm gear has gotta work right."

"You need a rest," Amanda said.

"We all do."

"I'll take the conn. Go back and catch some sleep."

"Maybe you're right."

"Do it, Pancho."

She looked at Amanda for a brief moment, then made up her mind and slowly got to her feet, surprised at how stiff she felt. "If I'm not back in two hours, wake me up."

Amanda nodded.

"I mean it, Mandy. Two hours."

"Yes. I will."

Satisfied, Pancho made her way back through the wardroom. She hesitated at the door to her privacy compartment, then went a further few steps to Dan's door.

She slid it open a crack. Dan was still sleeping, lying on the bunk, his body sheened with perspiration, the shorts and tee-shirt they had put on him stained by his sweat. His scalp was dotted with bald spots where tufts of hair had come out. God, he's in a bad way, she said to herself.

He opened his eyes and focused on her.

"Hi, kid," he breathed.

"How're you feelin', boss?"

"Not good."

"Anything I can bring you? I could fix some broth or somethin'."

"I'd just chuck it all over myself," he said.

"We'll be in Selene in another day and a half. Just rest yourself and we'll get the medics—"

"Did you send my last will and testament to them?" Dan asked.

Pancho shook her head. "Havin' troubles with the main antenna. Lars is workin' on it."

"How's the laser?"

"The backup? It's okay. We're usin' it to—"

"Send my will," Dan said.

"We don't hafta do that. You're gonna be fine."

"Send it," he insisted. He tried to raise himself on one elbow and failed. "Send it," he whispered.

"You sure you wanta leave everything to me?"

"Will you fight Humphries?"

She nodded solemnly. "Yep. That's a promise, boss."

"Good." He smiled weakly. "Send it. Now."

With a reluctant sigh, Pancho said, "Okay, if that's what you want."

"That's what I want," he whispered. "And put in our claim to Haven, too."

She nearly smiled. That's more like Dan Randolph, she thought.

"One more day," said Fuchs.

He and Amanda sat side by side in the wardroom. Fuchs was picking halfheartedly at a breakfast of prepackaged eggs and soymeat. Amanda hardly looked at her cereal and fruit.

"One more day," she repeated glumly.

"You're not happy."

"Humphries is in Selene. It will start all over again once we get back."

"Not if you're married to me," Fuchs blurted.

She stared at him. He looked totally serious, almost solemn. But then his thin lips curved slowly into a hopeful smile.

Before she could think of anything to say, Fuchs went on, "I love you, Amanda. I'm not proposing to you merely to protect you from Humphries. I love you, and more than anything in the universe I want you to be my wife."

"But Lars, we've only known each other a few weeks. Not even that long."

"How long does it take?" he asked. "I've fallen hopelessly in love with you. It happened in an instant."

She felt stunned. This steady, capable, thoughtful, intelligent man was looking at her expectantly, his whole life shining in his pale blue eyes. He loves me? Amanda wondered. We haven't even kissed and he believes he loves me? Do I love him?

Fuchs licked his lips nervously and asked, "I know I'm only a graduate student and my financial prospects aren't very wonderful, but could you—I mean to say, do you think . . ."

He seemed to run out of words. He simply sat there, gazing at her as if afraid to say anything more.

She thought swiftly, never taking her eyes from his. He's strong. He's steady. He's wanted to come on to me, I've felt that often enough. Yet he didn't. He never even touched me, never said a word until now. He's honorable.

It seemed like an eternity before she heard herself whisper, "Yes, Lars. I'll be happy to marry you."

You can learn to love him, Amanda told herself. You know you can trust him, you know he's gentle and sweet. He'll protect you from Humphries.

Fuchs leaned toward her and slid a strong arm around her waist. Amanda closed her eyes and they kissed, softly, tenderly at first. But she felt him clutch her to him, felt real strength and passion in the lingering kiss. She wound her arms around his neck.

After several minutes they separated slightly. Amanda felt breathless.

Fuchs was beaming like a thousand lasers. "We've got to tell Pancho!" he exclaimed, jumping to his feet. "And Dan!"

Laughing, he took Amanda's arm as she rose to her feet. He let her duck through the hatch to the bridge, then followed right behind her.

"Pancho, Lars has asked me to marry him!"

Pancho turned halfway around in her command chair and grinned at them. "'Bout time," she said. "I was wonderin' when you two would figger it out."

"We've got to tell Dan!"

Pancho nodded, scanned the instrument panel and saw that the ship's systems were performing adequately, then got up and started back with them.

"We oughtta perform the ceremony right here, get you legally hitched before we get back to Selene," she said.

"Oh! Could you?"

"Is the captain of a spacecraft legally empowered to perform marriages?" Fuchs asked.

"Oughtta be," Pancho said, shrugging.

They reached Dan's compartment and softly slid the accordion door back. Dan was lying on his back, his eyes closed, a sweaty sheet covering the lower half of his body.

"He's sleeping," Amanda said.

Dan's eyes popped open. "How can a sick man sleep with all the racket you're making?" he said, barely above a whisper.

Amanda's hands flew to her face. Fuchs started to apologize.

Dan waved a feeble hand to silence him. "If you can establish a comm link, you can get somebody on Earth to perform the ceremony."

"Hey, that's right," Pancho said.

Licking his dry, cracked lips, Dan asked, "You want the Pope in Rome? I've got some connections." Looking at Amanda, he added, "How about the Archbishop of Canterbury?"

"One of the ministers in Selene will do," Amanda said softly.

"I get it," Dan said. "You're in a hurry."

Fuchs turned red.

"I want to give the bride away," Dan said.

"Sure. Fine," said Pancho. "I'll set up the comm link." She headed back toward the bridge.

It took longer to make the arrangements than to perform the ceremony, even with a twelve-minute lag between the ship and Selene. Amanda and Fuchs stood by Dan's bunk with Pancho behind them. They had no flowers, no wedding attire except the coveralls they'd been wearing. The minister appeared on the wall screen opposite Dan's bunk. He was the pastor of Selene's interfaith chapel, a Lutheran: an ascetically thin young German with hair so blond it looked nearly white. Amanda could see that he was in his office, not the chapel itself. That didn't matter, she told herself. He conducted the brief rite in English and with great dignity, despite the time lag between them.

"Do each of you take the other for your lawful spouse?" the young minister asked.

"I do," said Fuchs immediately.

"I do," Amanda said.

They stood there feeling foolish and fidgety for the six minutes it took their response to reach the minister and the six additional minutes it took his words to reach them.

At last he said, "Then I pronounce you husband and wife. Congratulations. You may kiss the bride."

Amanda turned to Fuchs and they embraced. Pancho thanked the minister and cut the electronic link. The wall screen went dark.

They turned to Dan, lying in his bunk.

"He's fallen asleep," Amanda whispered. But she stared at Dan's sweat-stained tee-shirt. His chest didn't seem to be moving.

Fuchs leaned over the bunk and pressed two fingers against Dan's carotid artery.

"I don't feel a pulse," he said.

Pancho grabbed Dan's wrist. "No pulse," she agreed.

"He's dead?" Amanda asked, feeling tears welling up in her eyes.

Fuchs nodded solemnly.

LIFE

Pancho's heart was thumping, and not merely from the heavier gravity of Earth. The quarterly meeting of Astro Corporation's board of directors was about to begin. Would they follow Dan's wishes and vote her onto the board? And what if they do? What do I know about directing a big corporation? she asked herself.

Not much, she admitted. But if Dan thought I could do it, then I gotta at least give it my best shot.

She stared at the other directors as they milled around the sideboard of the luxurious meeting room, pouring drinks for themselves and picking out delicate little sandwiches and stuff. They all looked old, and dignified, and wicked rich. Most of the women wore dresses, by jeeps, or suits with skirts. Expensive clothes. Lots of jewelry, too. Pancho felt shabby in her best pantsuit and no adornments except for a bracelet and pendant earrings of lunar aluminum.

They were ignoring her. They clumped together in twos and threes, talking to each other in low voices, not whispers exactly, but little buzzing heads-together conversations. Nobody even looked her way, yet Pancho got the feeling that were all talking about her.

Not even the plump oriental woman in the bright red dress spoke to her. She must know what it's like to be an outsider, Pancho thought. But she's keeping her distance, just like all the others.

Martin Humphries strode into the board room, decked out in a sky-blue business suit. Pancho clenched her fists. If he's in mourning for Dan he sure ain't showing it, she thought. None of them are.

Humphries nodded here and there, saying hello and making small talk as he made his way past the sideboard toward Pancho. He glanced once out the long window above the sideboard and seemed almost to wince at the view of the sea out there. Then he turned and came toward Pancho. Stopping a meter or so in front of her, Humphries looked Pancho up and down, the expression on his face pretty close to a sneer.

"Do you honestly think we're going to allow a roughneck grease monkey to have a seat on this board?"

Suppressing an urge to punch him out, Pancho said tightly, "We'll see purty soon, won't we?"

"We certainly will."

He was wearing his lifts, Pancho saw; still, Humphries was several centimeters shorter than she.

"What puzzles me," she said looking down into his ice-gray eyes, "is how they can allow a convicted murderer t' stay on the board."

"I wasn't convicted of murder!" Humphries snapped, keeping his voice low.

Pancho made a small shrug. "They found you guilty of causin' Dan Randolph's death, didn't they?"

"I pleaded guilty to involuntary manslaughter. That was the deal my lawyers set up for me."

"Selene's court was way too easy on you. I would've hanged you. And not by the neck, either."

"They made me divest my holdings in Starpower!" he snarled. "Made me turn over my one-third to them!"

"And Astro," Pancho corrected. "You can still make money off Dan's dead body outta the profits Astro's gonna be pullin' in."

"And they exiled me! Threw me out of Selene. Forbade me from returning for twenty years." He glanced over his shoulder at the view of the sea through the long sweeping window like a man looking back at something chasing him.

"You got off light," said Pancho. "Dr. Cardenas got a life sentence. She'll never be allowed to work in her own nanolab again."

"She was just as responsible for his death as I was. And so are you, for that matter."

"Me?"

"You were the captain of the vessel. You could have turned back once you realized the radiation shield was failing."

"Thanks to you."

Humphries smirked at her. "If Randolph had brought a proper medical man aboard, if he hadn't taken the ship before the IAA approved the flight—"

"That's right," Pancho growled, "blame the victim for the crime."

"You didn't even freeze him once he died. You didn't even try to."

"Wouldn't have done any good," Pancho said. "We couldn't've got his core temperature down quick enough."

They had thought about it, she and Mandy and Fuchs. They had even considered putting Dan's body into a spacesuit and dunking him into one of the fuel tanks. But a quick calculation showed the cryogenic fuel would be used up by the time they reached the Moon and Dan's body would thaw before they could transfer him to a proper dewar.

Humphries smiled slyly. "Or maybe you *wanted* him dead, so you could inherit from him?"

Pancho had her right fist cocked before she realized it. Humphries threw his hands up and scuttled several steps back from her. Everything stopped. The board room went absolutely quiet. All faces turned toward them.

With a deep, deliberate breath, Pancho put her hand down. Humphries straightened up, looking sheepish. The other directors turned back to their own conversations, trying to pretend that nothing had happened.

Scowling angrily, Humphries walked away from her. Pancho saw that most of the directors moved out of his way as he approached the sideboard. As if they didn't want to be close enough to touch him or even have him breathe on them.

"I think we'd better start the meeting," said a petite red-haired woman in a forest-green skirted suit.

The directors went to the long polished table in the middle of the room and began to take their chairs. Pancho watched uncertainly for a moment, then saw that two chairs were unoccupied: one at the head of the table and another at its foot. Remembering her childhood bible classes, she took the lowest chair. The redhead sat to the right of the empty chair at the table's head; Humphries sat opposite her, his back to the window.

Everyone looked around, as if wondering what to do next. The redhead slowly got to her feet.

"For those of you who don't know me," she said, looking down the table toward Pancho, "my name is Harriet O'Banian. As vice-chair for the board, I guess I'll have to run this meeting until a new chairperson is elected."

They all nodded. Pancho saw that a small display screen was built into the gleaming surface of the table in front of each place. It showed an abbreviated agenda.

"I'm going to dispense with the usual formalities," O'Banian said, "and proceed directly to—"

"May I interrupt?" Humphries asked, holding up his hand like a schoolboy.

O'Banian murmured, "Of course."

Rising to his feet, Humphries said earnestly, "I wasn't able to attend the emergency meeting of the board that was called when news of Dan Randolph's unfortunate death was revealed."

Unfortunate? Pancho snarled inwardly.

"You all know that his death was partially my own fault. I played too rough, and I've seen the consequences. Please believe me, I never wanted to have Dan die."

The hell you didn't, Pancho said to herself. Looking along the table, though, she was shocked at the sympathetic expressions on many of the directors' faces.

"My real crime," Humphries went on, "was wanting to run Astro Corporation. And I let that ambition override my common sense. I saw Dan driving this fine organization into bankruptcy, and I knew that I could do better."

He stopped, hung his head for a moment. Pancho thought, The sumbitch should've been an actor.

"I'm truly sorry that Dan is dead. I feel a great weight of responsibility for it, even though that is not what I intended. I'll pay the price for my mistake for the rest of my life."

Pancho could barely keep herself from throwing something at him. But the other directors seemed calm, accepting.

Humphries wasn't through. "I know we can pull Astro through its current crisis. Despite Dan's unfortunate death, the mission to the Asteroid Belt was actually a success. Starpower Limited now has rights to two asteroids that are worth several trillion international dollars on today's commodities markets. And Astro, of course, owns one third of Starpower."

"One half," Pancho snapped.

Humphries stared at her for a long, speechless moment. "One half," he admitted at last. "That's right. Astro now owns half of Starpower."

"And Selene owns the other half," said Pancho.

Humphries bristled. Pancho grinned at him, thinking, I hope you choke on the money you'll be makin'.

Hattie O'Banian broke the tension-filled silence. "Thank you, Mr. Humphries. At this time, before we go on to the regular agenda, I would like to welcome Ms. Priscilla Lane to the board."

Pancho watched Humphries raise an eyebrow. Immediately, the oriental woman, sitting across the table from him, said, "Ms. Lane hasn't yet been elected to the board."

"I'm sure we can do that by acclamation," O'Banian said. "After all, Dan specifically—"

"It's customary to vote on a new member," said a florid-faced man with a full gray beard sitting a few chairs down from Humphries. "After all, a position on the board isn't hereditary," the florid man grumbled. He reminded Pancho of Santa Claus, except that he was nowhere near being jolly. "You can't inherit board membership just because a dying man willed it to you."

Pancho understood the implication. *Cripes, they think I was sleepin' with Dan and that's why he named me to the board.*

O'Banian looked displeased. "Very well, then. In that case, I believe we should allow Ms. Lane to say a few words about herself."

All faces turned toward Pancho. Thinking furiously, she got slowly to her feet.

In her mind she heard Dan telling her, *My personnel people think you're a flake, Pancho. The rap on you is that you're not serious.* She knew that each member of the board had seen her personnel file. *Okay, Pancho,* she said to herself, *time to grow up and start bein' serious. You're in the big leagues now. You gotta show them your best.*

She took a deep breath, then started, "I was just as surprised as any of you when Dan Randolph said he wanted me to take his place on this board. I'm an engineer and pilot, not a banker or a lawyer. But Dan said the board needed some fresh blood, and he picked me. So here I am."

Surveying the men and women watching her, Pancho went on, "I think I know why Dan wanted me here—and it wasn't for my good looks, either."

A few chuckles. O'Banian smiled broadly.

"With all due respect to you, I think this board could use somebody who has some practical experience in Astro's activities. Dan sure did, but I don't think any of you have been involved in the company's actual operations. I've been flyin' Astro spacecraft for nearly seven years now. I've been out to the Belt and back. That's where our best chance of makin' real profits lies: out in the Belt. I know what it takes to get the job done. I think I can help this board to make the right decisions as we start to tap the resources of all those asteroids. Thank you."

She sat down. No one applauded. Humphries gave her a hard stare, then swept his eyes along the table, trying to fathom the opinions of the other directors.

"Oh, one more thing," Pancho said, without getting up from her chair. "If you do elect me to the board, I intend to vote for Ms. O'Banian as the new chairman."

Now Humphries scowled openly.

O'Banian said, "Very well. Let's vote, shall we? All in favor of Ms. Lane, raise your hands."

Two hours later, as the meeting broke up, Humphries accosted Pancho.

"Well, now you're a board member," he said "By the margin of two votes."

"And Ms. O'Banian is the chairman of the board."

Humphries scoffed, "Do you think that's going to stop me from taking control of Astro?"

"It won't stop you from tryin', I know that."

"I'll get Astro," he said firmly. "And Starpower, too, eventually."

"Maybe," said Pancho. "And maybe not."

He laughed at her.

"Lissen, Humpy," Pancho growled. "I don't give a shit how your lawyers wiggled you out of it, you killed Dan Randolph. I'm gonna make sure that he haunts you for the rest of your natural days."

"I don't believe in ghosts," said Humphries.

Now Pancho laughed. "You will, Humpy. You surely will."

THE ROCK RATS

To Charles M. Brown and the *Locus* team

Yet each man kills the thing he loves,
  By each let this be heard,
Some do it with a bitter look.
    Some with a flattering word.
  The coward does it with a kiss,
    The brave man with a sword!

Some kill their love when they are young,
  And some when they are old;
Some strangle with the hands of Lust,
    Some with the hands of Gold:
The kindest use a knife, because
    The dead so soon grow cold.

—Oscar Wilde
The Ballad of Reading Gaol

PROLOGUE: SELENE

Amanda clutched at her husband's arm when Martin Humphries strode into the wedding reception, unannounced and uninvited.

The Pelican Bar went totally silent. The crowd that had been noisily congratulating Amanda and Lars Fuchs with lewd jokes and lunar "rocket juice" froze as if somebody had doused the place with liquid nitrogen. Fuchs patted his wife's hand gently, protectively, as he scowled up at Humphries. Even Pancho Lane, never at a loss for a quip, simply stood by the bar, one hand holding her drink, the other balling into a fist.

The Pelican wasn't Humphries's kind of place. It was the workers' bar, the one joint in Selene's underground warren of tunnels and cubicles where the people who lived and worked on the Moon could come for relaxation and the company of their fellow Lunatics. Suits like Humphries did their drinking in the fancy lounge up in the Grand Plaza, with the rest of the executives and the tourists.

Humphries seemed oblivious to their enmity, totally at ease in this sea of hostile stares, even though he looked terribly out of place, a smallish manicured man wearing an impeccably tailored imperial blue business suit in the midst of the younger, boisterous miners and tractor operators in their shabby, faded coveralls and their earrings of asteroidal stones. Even the women looked stronger, more muscular than Humphries.

But if Humphries's round, pink-cheeked face seemed soft and bland, his eyes were something else altogether. Gray and pitiless, like chips of flint, the same color as the rock walls and low ceiling of the underground bar itself.

He walked straight through the silent, sullen crowd to the table where Amanda and Fuchs sat.

"I know I wasn't invited to your party," he said in a calm, strong voice. "I hope you'll forgive me for crashing. I won't stay but a minute."

"What do you want?" Fuchs asked, scowling, not moving from his chair beside his bride. He was a broad, dark-haired bear of a man, thick in the torso, with short arms and legs heavily muscled. The tiny stud in his left ear was a diamond that he had bought during his student days in Switzerland.

With a rueful smile, Humphries said, "I want your wife, but she's chosen you instead."

Fuchs slowly got up from his chair, big thick-fingered hands clenching into fists. Every eye in the pub was on him, every breath held.

Amanda glanced from Fuchs to Humphries and back again. She looked close to panic. She was a strikingly beautiful woman, with a wide-eyed innocent face and lusciously curved figure that made men fantasize and women stare with unalloyed envy. Even in a plain white jumpsuit she looked utterly stunning.

"Lars," Amanda whispered. "Please."

Humphries raised both hands, palms out. "Perhaps I phrased myself poorly. I didn't come here for a fight."

"Then why did you come?" Fuchs asked in a low growl.

"To give you a wedding present," Humphries replied, smiling again. "To show that there's no hard feelings . . . so to speak."

"A present?" Amanda asked.

"If you'll accept it from me," said Humphries.

"What is it?" Fuchs asked.

"*Starpower 1.*"

Amanda's china blue eyes went so wide that white showed all around them. "The ship?"

"It's yours, if you'll have it. I'll even pay for the refurbishment necessary to make it spaceworthy again."

The crowd stirred, sighed, began muttering. Fuchs looked down at Amanda, saw that she was awed by Humphries's offer.

Humphries said, "You can use it to return to the Belt and start mining asteroids. There's plenty of rocks out there for you to claim and develop."

Despite himself, Fuchs was impressed. "That's . . . very generous of you, sir."

Humphries put on his smile again. With a careless wave of his hand, he said, "You newlyweds need some source of income. Go out and claim a couple of rocks, bring back their ores, and you'll be fixed for life."

"Very generous," Fuchs muttered.

Humphries put out his hand. Fuchs hesitated a moment, then gripped it in his heavy paw; engulfed it, actually. "Thank you, Mr. Humphries," he said, pumping Humphries's arm vigorously. "Thank you so much."

Amanda said nothing.

Humphries disengaged himself and, without another word, walked out of the bar. The crowd stirred at last and broke into dozens of conversations. Several people crowded around Fuchs and Amanda, congratulating them, offering to work on their craft. The Pelican's proprietor declared drinks on the house and there was a general rush toward the bar.

Pancho Lane, though, sidled through the crowd and out the door into the tunnel, where Humphries was walking alone toward the power stairs that led down to his mansion at Selene's lowest level. In a few long-legged lunar strides she caught up to him.

"I thought they threw you out of Selene," she said.

Humphries had to look up at her. Pancho was lean and lanky, her skin a light mocha, not much darker than a white woman would get in the burning sunshine of her native west Texas. She kept her hair cropped close, a tight dark skullcap of ringlets.

He made a sour face. "My lawyers are working on an appeal. They can't exile me without due process."

"And that could take years, huh?"

"At the very least."

Pancho would gladly have stuffed him into a rocket and fired him off to Pluto. Humphries had sabotaged *Starpower 1* on its first—and, so far, only—mission to the Belt. Dan Randolph had died because of him. It took an effort of will for her to control her temper.

As calmly as she could manage, Pancho said, "You were pretty damn generous back there."

"A gesture to true love," he replied, without slowing his pace.

"Yeah. Sure." Pancho easily matched his stride.

"What else?"

"For one thing, that spacecraft ain't yours to give away. It belongs to—"

"Belonged," Humphries snapped. "Past tense. We wrote it off the books."

"Wrote it off? When? How in hell can you *do* that?"

Humphries actually laughed. "You see, Ms. Director? There are a few tricks to being on the board that a greasemonkey like you doesn't know about."

"I guess," Pancho admitted. "But I'll learn 'em."

"Of course you will."

Pancho was newly elected to the board of directors of Astro Manufacturing, over Humphries's stern opposition. It had been Dan Randolph's dying wish.

"So we've written off *Starpower 1* after just one flight?"

"It's already obsolescent," said Humphries. "The ship proved the fusion drive technology. Now we can build better spacecraft, specifically designed for asteroid mining."

"And you get to play Santy Claus for Amanda and Lars."

Humphries shrugged.

The two of them walked along the nearly-empty tunnel until they came to the power stairs leading downward.

Pancho grabbed Humphries by the shoulder, stopping him at the top of the moving stairs. "I know what you're up to," she said.

"Do you?"

"You figger Lars'll go battin' out to the Belt and leave Mandy here in Selene."

"I suppose that's a possibility," Humphries said, shaking free of her grip.

"Then you can move in on her."

Humphries started to reply, then hesitated. His face grew serious. At last he said, "Pancho, has it ever occurred to you that I really love Amanda? I do, you know."

Pancho knew Humphries's reputation as a womanizer. She had seen plenty of evidence of it.

"You might tell yourself that you love her, Humpy, but that's just because she's the only woman between here and Lubbock that won't flop inta bed with you."

He smiled coldly. "Does that mean that you would?"

"In your dreams!"

Humphries laughed and started down the stairs. For a few moments Pancho watched him dwindling away, then she turned and headed back toward the Pelican Bar.

As Humphries rode down to Selene's bottommost level, he thought, Fuchs is an academic, the kind who's never had two pennies in his hands at the same time. Let him go out to the Belt. Let him see how much money he can make, and all the things that money can buy. And while he's doing it, I'll be here at Amanda's side.

By the time he reached his palatial home, Humphries was almost happy.

DATA BANK:
THE ASTEROID BELT

Millions of chunks of rock and metal float silently, end-lessly, through the deep emptiness of interplanetary space. The largest of them, Ceres, is barely a thousand kilometers wide. Most of them are much smaller, rang-ing from irregular chunks a few kilometers long down to the size of pebbles. They contain more metals and min-erals, more natural resources, than the entire Earth can provide.

They are the bonanza, the El Dorado, the Comstock Lode, the gold and silver and iron and everything-else mines of the twenty-first century. There are hundreds of millions of *billions* of tons of high grade ores in the asteroids. They hold enough real wealth to make each man, woman, and child of the entire human race into a millionaire. And then some.

The first asteroid was discovered shortly after midnight on January 1, 1801, by a Sicilian monk who happened to be an astronomer. While oth-ers were celebrating the new century, Giuseppi Piazzi was naming the tiny point of light he saw in his telescope *Ceres* after the pagan goddess of Sicily. Perhaps an unusual attitude for a pious monk, but Piazzi was a Sicilian, after all.

By the advent of the twenty-first century, more than fifteen thousand asteroids had been discovered by earthbound astronomers. As the human race began to expand its habitat to the Moon and to explore Mars, mil-lions more were found.

Technically, they are *planetoids,* little planets, chunks of rock and metal floating in the dark void of space, leftovers from the creation of the Sun and planets some four and a half billion years ago. Piazzi correctly referred to them as planetoids, but in 1802 William Herschel (who had earlier discovered the giant planet Uranus) called them *asteroids,* because in the telescope their pinpoints of light looked like stars rather than the disks of planets. Piazzi was correct, but Herschel was far more famous and influential. We call them asteroids to this day.

Several hundred of the asteroids are in orbits that near the Earth, but most of them by far circle around the Sun in a broad swath in deep space between the orbits of Mars and giant Jupiter. This *Asteroid Belt* is centered more than six hundred million kilometers from Earth, four times farther from the Sun than our homeworld.

Although this region is called the Asteroid *Belt*, the asteroids are not strewn so thickly that they represent a hazard to space navigation. Far from it. The so-called Belt is a region of vast emptiness, dark and lonely and very far from human civilization.

Until the invention of the Duncan fusion drive the Asteroid Belt was too far from the Earth/Moon system to be of economic value. Once fusion propulsion became practical, however, the Belt became the region where prospectors and miners could make fortunes for themselves, or die in the effort.

Many of them died. More than a few were killed.

THREE YEARS LATER

CHAPTER 1

I said it would be simple," Lars Fuchs repeated. "I did *not* say it would be easy."

George Ambrose—Big George to everyone who knew him—scratched absently at his thick red beard as he gazed thoughtfully out through the window of *Starpower 1*'s bridge toward the immense looming dark bulk of the asteroid Ceres.

"I di'n't come out here to get involved in daft schemes, Lars," he said. His voice was surprisingly high and sweet for such a shaggy mastodon of a man.

For a long moment the only sound in the compartment was the eternal hum of electrical equipment. Then Fuchs pushed between the two pilots' seats to drift toward Big George. Stopping himself with a touch of his hand against the metal overhead, he said in an urgent whisper, "We can do it. Given time and resources."

"It's fookin' insane," George muttered. But he kept staring out at the asteroid's rock-strewn, pockmarked surface.

They made an odd pair: the big, bulky Aussie with his shaggy brick-red mane and beard, hovering weightlessly beside the dark, intense, thickset Fuchs. Three years in the Belt had changed Fuchs somewhat: he was still burly, barrel-chested, but he had let his chestnut brown hair grow almost to his collar, and the earring he wore was now a polished chip of asteroidal copper. A slim bracelet of copper circled his left wrist. Yet in their individual ways, both men looked powerful, determined, even dangerous.

"Living inside Ceres is bad for our health," Fuchs said.

George countered, "Plenty of radiation protection from the rock."

"It's the microgravity," Fuchs said earnestly. "It's not good for us, physically."

"I like it."

"But the bones become so brittle. Dr. Cardenas says the rate of fractures is rising steeply. You've seen that yourself, haven't you?"

"Maybe," George half-admitted. Then he grinned. "But th' sex is fookin' fantastic!"

Fuchs scowled at the bigger man. "Be serious, George."

Without taking his eyes off Ceres's battered face, George said, "Okay, you're right. I know it. But buildin' a bloody O'Neill habitat?"

"It doesn't have to be that big, not like the L–5 habitats around Earth. Just big enough to house the few hundred people here in Ceres. At first."

George shook his shaggy head. "You know how big a job you're talkin' about? Just the life support equipment alone would cost a mint. And then some."

"No, no. That's the beauty of my scheme," Fuchs said, with a nervous laugh. "We simply purchase spacecraft and put them together. They become the habitat. And they already have all the life support equipment and radiation shielding built into them. We won't need their propulsion units at all, so the price will be much lower than you think."

"Then you want to spin the whole fookin' kludge to an Earth-normal g?"

"Lunar normal," Fuchs answered. "One-sixth g is good enough. Dr. Cardenas agrees."

George scratched at his thick, unkempt beard. "I dunno, Lars. We've been livin' inside the rock okay. Why go to all this trouble and expense?"

"Because we have to!" Fuchs insisted. "Living in microgravity is dangerous to our health. We *must* build a better habitat for ourselves."

George looked unconvinced, but he muttered, "Lunar g, you say?"

"One-sixth normal Earth gravity. No more than that."

"How much will it cost?"

Fuchs blinked once. "We can buy the stripped-down spacecraft from Astro Corporation. Pancho is offering a very good price."

"How much?"

"The preliminary figures work out . . ." Fuchs hesitated, took a breath, then said, "We can do it if all the prospectors and miners put in ten percent of their income."

George grunted. "A tithe, huh?"

"Ten percent isn't much."

"A lot of us rock rats don't make any income at all, some years."

"I know," said Fuchs. "I factored that into the cost estimate. Of course, we'll have to pay off the spacecraft over twenty- or thirty-year leases. Like a mortgage on a house, Earthside."

"So you want everybody here in Ceres to take on a twenty-year debt?"

"We can pay it off sooner, perhaps. A few really big strikes could pay for the entire project all by themselves."

"Yeah. Sure."

With burning intensity, Fuchs asked, "Will you do it? If you agree, most of the other prospectors will, too."

"Whyn't you get one of the corporations t' do it?" George asked. "Astro or Humphries . . ." He stopped when he saw the look on Fuchs's face.

"Not Humphries," Fuchs growled. "Never him or his company. Never."

"Okay. Astro, then."

Fuchs's scowl shifted into a troubled frown. "I've spoken to Pancho about it. The Astro board would not vote for it. They will sell stripped-down spacecraft to us, but they won't commit to building the habitat. They don't see a profit from it."

George grunted. "Lot they care if we snap our bones."

"But you care," Fuchs said eagerly. "It's *our* problem, George; we have to solve it. And we can, if you'll help."

Running a beefy hand through his thick mop of red hair, Big George said, "You're gonna need a techie team to do the integration job. There's more to puttin' this habitat of yours together than just connectin' Tinkertoys, y'know. You'll need a flock of geek boys."

"That's already in the cost estimate," Fuchs replied.

George huffed a mighty sigh, then said, "All right, Lars, I'm in. I guess it would be pretty good to have a base out here in the Belt with some decent gravity to it."

Fuchs smiled. "You can always have sex aboard your own ship."

George grinned back at him. "Believe it, mate. Believe it."

Fuchs went with George to the ship's main airlock and helped the bigger man get back into his hard-shell spacesuit.

"They're testin' lightweight suits back at Selene, y'know," he said as he slid into the rigid torso and worked his arms through the stiff sleeves. "Flexible. Easy to put on."

"And the radiation protection?" Fuchs asked.

"Magnetic field surrounds the suit. They claim it's better'n this stuff." He rapped his knuckles against the torso's cermet carapace.

Fuchs gave a little snort of disdain. "They'll need years of testing before I'd buy one."

As he wormed his hands into the gloves, George said, "Me too."

Handing the bigger man his fishbowl helmet, Fuchs said, "Thanks for agreeing, George. It means a lot to me."

George nodded solemnly. "I know. You two want to have kids."

Fuchs's cheeks reddened. "It's not that!"

"Isn't it?"

"Well, not alone, no." Fuchs looked away from George for a moment, then slowly admitted, "I worry about Amanda, yes. I never thought she would want to stay out here with me. I never thought I myself would be out here this long."

"There's a lot of money to be made here in the Belt. A *lot* of money."

"Yes, yes indeed. But I worry about her. I want her to be in a safer place, with enough gravity to keep her from deconditioning."

"And enough radiation shielding to start a family," George said, grinning. Then he pulled on his helmet before Fuchs could think of a reply.

CHAPTER 2

Once George had cycled through *Starpower 1*'s airlock and jetted back to his own *Waltzing Matilda*, Fuchs went down the ship's narrow central passageway to the compartment where his wife was working.

She looked up from the wallscreen as Fuchs slid the compartment door open. He saw that she was watching a fashion show beamed from somewhere on Earth: slim, slinky models in brightly colored gowns of outrageous designs. Fuchs frowned slightly: half the people of Earth displaced by floods and earthquakes, starvation rampant almost everywhere, and still the rich played their games.

Amanda blanked the wallscreen as she asked, "Has George left already?"

"Yes. And he agreed to it!"

Her smile was minimal. "He did? It didn't take you terribly long to convince him, did it?"

She still spoke with a trace of the Oxford accent she had learned years earlier in London. She was wearing an oversized faded sweatshirt and cutoff work pants. Her golden blonde hair was pinned up off her neck and slightly disheveled. She wore not a trace of makeup. Still, she was much more beautiful than any of the emaciated mannequins of the fashion show. Fuchs pulled her to him and kissed her warmly.

"In two years, maybe less, we'll have a decent base in orbit around Ceres with lunar-level gravity."

Amanda gazed into her husband's eyes, seeking something. "Kris Cardenas will be happy to hear it," she said.

"Yes, Dr. Cardenas will be very pleased," Fuchs agreed. "We should tell her as soon as we arrive."

"Of course."

"But you're not even dressed yet!"

"It won't take me a minute," Amanda said. "It's not like we're going to a royal reception." Then she added, "Or even to a party in Selene."

Fuchs realized that Amanda wasn't as happy as he'd thought she would be. "What's the matter? Is something wrong?"

"No," she said, too quickly. "Not really."

"Amanda, my darling, I know that when you say 'not really' you really mean 'really.' "

She broke into a genuine smile. "You know me too well."

"No, not too well. Just well enough." He kissed her again, lightly this time. "Now, what's wrong? Tell me, please."

Leaning her cheek on his shoulder, Amanda said very softly, "I thought we'd be home by now, Lars."

"Home?"

"Earth. Or even Selene. I never dreamt we'd stay in the Belt for three years."

Suddenly Fuchs saw the worn, scuffed metal walls of this tiny coop of a cubicle, the narrow confines of the ship's passageway and the other cramped compartments; smelled the stale air with its acrid tinge of ozone; felt the background vibrations that rattled through the ship every moment; consciously noticed the clatter of pumps and wheezing of the air fans. And he heard his own voice ask inanely:

"You're not happy here?"

"Lars, I'm happy being with you. Wherever you are. You know that. But—"

"But you would rather be back on Earth. Or at Selene."

"It's better than living on a ship all the time."

"*He's* still at Selene."

She pulled slightly away, looked straight into his deep-set eyes. "You mean Martin?"

"Humphries," said Fuchs. "Who else?"

"He's got nothing to do with it."

"Doesn't he?"

Now she looked truly alarmed. "Lars, you don't think that Martin Humphries means anything to me?"

He felt his blood turning to ice. One look at Amanda's innocent blue eyes and full-bosomed figure and any man would be wild to have her.

Coldly, calmly, he said, "I know that Martin Humphries wants you. I think that you married me to escape from him. I think—"

"Lars, that's not true!"

"Isn't it?"

"I love you! For god's sake, don't you know that? Don't you understand it?"

The ice thawed. He realized that he held in his arms the most gorgeous woman he had ever seen. That she had come to this desolate emptiness on the frontier of human habitation to be with him, to help him, to love him.

"I'm sorry," he muttered, feeling ashamed. "It's just that . . . I love you so much . . ."

"And I love you, Lars. I truly do."

"I know."

"Do you?"

He shook his head ruefully. "Sometimes I wonder why you put up with me."

She smiled and traced a fingertip across his stubborn, stubbled jaw. "Why not? You put up with me, don't you?"

With a sigh, he admitted, "I thought we'd be back on Earth by now. I thought we'd be rich."

"We are. Aren't we?"

"On paper, perhaps. We're better off than most of the other prospectors. At least we own this ship . . ."

His voice faltered. They both knew why. They owned *Starpower* because Martin Humphries had given it to them as a gift.

"But the bills do mount up," Amanda said swiftly, trying to change the subject. "I was going over the accounts earlier. We can't seem to stay ahead of the expenses."

Fuchs made a sound somewhere between a grunt and a snort. "If you count how much we owe, we certainly are multi-millionaires."

It was a classic problem, they both knew. A prospector might find an asteroid worth hundreds of billions on paper, but the costs of mining the ores, transporting them back to the Earth/Moon region, refining them—the costs of food and fuel and air to breathe—were so high that the prospectors were almost always on the ragged edge of bankruptcy. Still they pushed on, always seeking that lode of wealth that would allow them to retire at last and live in luxury. Yet no matter how much wealth they actually found, hardly any of it stayed in their hands for long.

And I want to take ten percent of that from them, Fuchs said to himself. But it will be worth it! They'll thank me for it, once it's done.

"It's not like we're spendthrifts," Amanda murmured. "We don't throw the money away on frivolities."

"I should never have brought you out here," Fuchs said. "It was a mistake."

"No!" she contradicted. "I want to be with you, Lars. Wherever you are."

"This is no place for a woman such as you. You should be living comfortably, happily—"

She silenced him with a single slim finger across his thin lips. "I'm perfectly comfortable and happy here."

"But you'd be happier on Earth. Or Selene."

She hesitated a fraction of a second before replying, "Wouldn't you?"

"Yes," he admitted. "Of course. But I'm not going back until I can give you all the things you deserve."

"Oh, Lars, you're all that I really want."

He gazed at her for a long moment, then said, "Yes, perhaps. But I want more. Much more."

Amanda said nothing.

Brightening, Fuchs said, "But as long as we're out here, at least I can make a decent home for you in Ceres orbit!"

She smiled for her husband.

CHAPTER 3

Build a habitat big enough to house everyone living at Ceres?" asked Martin Humphries, incredulous.

"That's what the rumble is," said his aide, a winsome brunet with long-lashed almond eyes, full pouty lips, and a razor-sharp mind. Even though her image on his bedroom wallscreen showed only her head and shoulders and some background of her office, the sight of her set Humphries's mind wandering.

Humphries leaned back in his wide, luxurious bed and tried to concentrate on business. He had started the morning with a vigorous tussle with a big-breasted computer analyst who nominally worked in Humphries Space Systems' transportation department. She had spent the night in Humphries's bed, yet even in the midst of their most passionate exertions he found himself closing his eyes and fantasizing about Amanda.

His bedmate was in the shower now, and all thoughts about her or Amanda were pushed aside as Humphries talked business with his aide, whose office was several levels up in Selene's underground network of corridors.

"It sounds ridiculous," Humphries said. "How reliable is this information?"

The aide let a wintry smile cross her tempting lips. "Quite reliable, sir. The prospectors are all talking about it, back and forth, from one ship to another. They're chattering all across the Belt about it."

"It still sounds ridiculous," Humphries grumbled.

"Beg to differ, sir," said the aide. Her words were deferential, but the expression on her face looked almost smug. "It makes a certain amount of sense."

"Does it?"

"If they could build a habitat and spin it to produce an artificial gravity that approaches the grav field here on the Moon, it would be much healthier for the people living out there for months or years on end. Better for their bones and organs than sustained microgravity."

"H'mmph."

"In addition, sir, the habitat would have the same level of radiation shielding that the latest spacecraft have. Or even better, perhaps."

"But the prospectors still have to go out into the Belt and claim the asteroids."

"They are required by law to be present at an asteroid in order for their claim to be legal," the aide agreed. "But from then on they can work the rock remotely."

"Remotely? The distances are too big for remote operations. It takes hours for signals to cross the Belt."

"From Ceres, sir," the aide said stiffly, "roughly five thousand ore-bearing rocks are within one light-minute. That's close enough for remote operations, don't you think?"

Humphries didn't want to give her the satisfaction of admitting she was right. Instead he replied, "Well, we'd better be getting our own people out there claiming those asteroids before the rock rats snap them all up."

"I'll get on that right away," said the aide, with enough of a smile curving her tempting lips to show that she had already thought of it. "And mining teams, too."

"Mining operations aren't as urgent as claiming the stupid rocks."

"Understood," she said. Then she added, "The board meeting is this morning at ten. You asked me to remind you."

He nodded. "Yes, I know." Without another word he tapped the keypad on the nightstand and her wallscreen image winked off.

Slumping deeper into the pillows, he heard the woman who'd spent the night in his bed singing in the shower. Off-key. Well, he said to himself, music isn't her best talent.

Fuchs. The thought of Lars Fuchs pushed all other notions out of his mind. He's out there with Amanda. I never realized she'd stay out in that wilderness with him. She doesn't belong there, living in a crummy ship like some gypsy, some penniless drifter wandering out there in the empty wastes. She should be *here*, with me. This is where she belongs.

I made a mistake with him. I underestimated him. He's no fool. He's not just prospecting and mining. He's building an empire out there. With Pancho Lane's help.

The young woman appeared at the bathroom door, naked, her skin dewy and flawless. She posed enticingly and smiled for Humphries.

"Do we have time for one more? Are you up to it?" Her smile turned just a tad impudent.

Despite himself, Humphries felt stirred. But he said gruffly, "Not now. I've got work to do."

And he thought, This twat could get possessive. I'd better transfer her to some job back on Earth.

Martin Humphries drummed his fingers impatiently on his desk, waiting for the lame-brained techs to make all the connections so the board meeting could get underway.

After all these years, he fumed to himself, you'd think that setting up a simple virtual reality meeting with a half-dozen idiots who refuse to leave Earth would be an easy matter. He hated waiting. He loathed being dependent on anyone or anything.

Humphries refused to leave Selene. His home was on the Moon, he told himself, not Earth. Everything he wanted was here in the underground city, and what wasn't here could be shipped to Selene upon his order. He had fought Selene's legal system to a standstill to prevent them from exiling him back to Earth.

Earth was crippled, dying. The greenhouse flooding had wiped out most coastal cities and turned hundreds of millions of people into homeless, starving wanderers. Farmlands withered in droughts while tropical diseases found fresh territories in what used to be temperate climates. Electrical power grids everywhere faltered and sputtered lamely. A new wave of terrorism unleashed man-made plagues while crumbling nations armed their missiles and threatened nuclear war.

It's only a matter of time, Humphries knew. Despite all the efforts by the so-called world government, despite the New Morality's fundamentalism and relentless grip on the political reins of power, despite the suspension of individual freedoms all across the globe, it's only a matter of time until they start nuking each other into extinction.

Safer here on the Moon. Better to be away from all that death and destruction. What was it Dan Randolph used to say? When the going gets tough, the tough get going—to where the going is easier.

Humphries nodded to himself as he sat in his high-backed chair. He was alone in his sumptuous office, a mere twenty meters from his bedroom. Most of Humphries Space Systems' board members also lived in Selene now, yet hardly any of them were allowed into the house. They stayed in their own homes, or came to the HSS offices up in the Grand Plaza tower.

Damned waste of time, Humphries grumbled to himself. The board's just a rubber stamp, anyway. The only member who ever gave me any trouble was Dad, and he's gone now. Probably trying to tell St. Peter how to run heaven. Or more likely arguing with Satan in hell.

"We're ready now, sir," said his aide's silky voice in the stereo earplugs Humphries wore.

"Then do it."

"Are your goggles in place, sir?"

"I've been wearing my *contacts* for damned near fifteen minutes!"

"Of course."

The young woman said nothing else. An instant later, the long conference table that existed only in Humphries's computer chips sprang into existence before his eyes, each seat filled by a board member. Most of them looked slightly startled, but after a few seconds of turning in their chairs to see if everyone was there, they began chatting easily enough with one another. The half-dozen who were still on Earth were at a disadvantage, because it took nearly three seconds for signals to make the round-trip from Moon to Earth and back again. Humphries had no intention of holding up the proceedings for them; the six old farts had little power on the board, no need to worry about them. Of course, they each had a lot to say. Humphries wished he could silence them. Permanently.

He was in a foul mood by the time the meeting ended, cranky and tired. The meeting had accomplished nothing except very routine decisions that could have been made by a troop of baboons. Humphries called for his aide over the intercom phone. By the time he had gone to the lavatory, slipped his VR contacts out of his eyes, washed his face and combed his hair, she was standing in his office doorway, wearing a cool powder blue pantsuit accented with asteroidal sapphires.

Her name was Diane Verwoerd, born of a Dutch father and Indonesian mother, a teenaged fashion model in Amsterdam when her dark, sultry looks first attracted Humphries's notice. She was a little on the skinny side, he thought, but he paid her way through law school anyway and watched her climb his corporate ladder without ever once succumbing to his attempted seductions. He liked her all the more for her independence; he could trust her, rely on her judgment, which was more than he could say about the women who did flop into his bed.

Besides, he thought, sooner or later she'll give in. Even though she knows that'll be the end of her job in my office, she'll crawl into bed with me one of these nights. I just haven't found the right motivation for her yet. It's not money or status, I know that much about her. Maybe power. If it's power she's after, she could be dangerous. He grinned inwardly. Playing with nitroglycerine can be fun, sometimes.

Keeping those thoughts to himself, Humphries said without preamble as he stepped back to his desk, "We need to get rid of the rock rats."

If the statement surprised her, Verwoerd showed no hint of it. "Why should we?" she countered.

"Simple economics. There's so many of them out there claiming asteroids that they're keeping the price of metals and minerals too low. Supply and demand. They're overdoing the supply."

"Commodities prices are low, except for food products," Verwoerd agreed.

"And sinking," Humphries pointed out. "But if we controlled the supply of raw materials—"

"Which means controlling the rock rats."

"Right."

"We could stop selling them supplies," Verwoerd suggested.

Humphries waved a hand in the air. "They'd just buy their goods from Astro. I don't want that."

She nodded.

"No, I think our first step should be to establish a base of operations on Ceres."

"On Ceres?"

"Ostensibly, it will be a depot for the supplies we sell to the rock rats," Humphries said, sliding into his commodious high-backed chair. If he desired, the chair would massage his body or send waves of soothing warmth through him. At this moment, Humphries wanted neither.

Verwoerd gave the appearance of thinking over his statement for several moments. "And actually?"

"It'll be a cover for putting our own people out there; a base for knocking the rock rats out of the Belt."

Verwoerd smiled coldly. "Once we open the base, we cut our prices for the supplies we sell the prospectors and miners."

"Cut our prices? Why?"

"To get them buying from HSS and not Astro. Tie them to us."

Nodding, Humphries said, "We could give them more favorable terms for leasing spacecraft, too."

Now she took one of the upholstered chairs in front of his desk. Crossing her long legs absently, she said, "Better yet, lower the interest rates on purchase loans."

"No, no. I don't want them to own the vessels. I want them to lease the spacecraft from us. I want them tied to Humphries Space Systems."

"Under contract to HSS?"

Humphries leaned back in his chair and clasped his hands behind his head. "Right. I want those rock rats working for me."

"At prices that you set," she said.

"We allow the prices for raw ores to keep going down," Humphries mused. "We *encourage* the independents to bring in so much ore that the prices are forced constantly downward. That will drive them out of the field, sooner or later."

"Leaving only the people who are under contract to HSS," Verwoerd agreed.

"That way, we gain control of the costs of exploration and mining," he said, "and on the other end we also control the prices for the refined metals and other resources that we sell to Selene and Earth."

"But individual rock rats could sell to companies on Earth on their own, independently," she pointed out.

"So what?" Humphries snapped. "They'll just be undercutting each other until they drive themselves out of business. They'll be cutting their own throats."

"Supply and demand," Verwoerd murmured.

"Yes. But when we get the rock rats working exclusively for us, we'll control the supply. No matter what the demand, we'll be able to control prices. And profits."

"A little on the devious side." She smiled, though.

"It worked for Rockefeller."

"Until the anti-trust laws were passed."

"There aren't any anti-trust laws in the Belt," Humphries said. "No laws at all, come to think of it."

Verwoerd hesitated, thinking, then said, "It will take some time to drive out all the independents. And there's still Astro to consider."

"I'll handle Astro when the time comes."

"Then you'll have complete control of the Belt."

"Which means that in the long run it won't cost us anything to set up a base on Ceres." It was a statement, not a question.

"That's not exactly how the accounting department will see it."

He laughed. "Then why don't we do it? Establish a base on Ceres and bring those rock rats under our control."

She gave him a long, careful look, a look that said, *I know there's more to this than you're telling me. You've got a hidden agenda, and I'm pretty sure I know what it is.*

But aloud all she said was, "We can use this base on Ceres to central-ize all the maintenance work, as well."

He nodded an acknowledgement to her. "Good idea."

"Offer the lowest possible terms on the maintenance contracts."

"Get the rock rats to come to HSS for maintenance," he agreed.

"Make them dependent on you."

He laughed again. "Gillette's dictum."

She looked puzzled.

"Give 'em the razor," he explained. "Sell 'em the blades."

DOSSIER:
OSCAR JIMINEZ

T he illegitimate son of an illegitimate son, Oscar Jiminez was picked up by the police in one of their periodic sweeps through the barrios of Manila when he was seven years old. He was small for his age, but already an expert at begging, picking pockets, and worming his way past electronic security systems that would have stopped someone bigger or less agile.

The usual police tactic was to beat everyone mercilessly with their old-fashioned batons, rape the girls and the better-looking boys, then drive their prisoners far out into the countryside and leave them to fend for themselves. Until they got caught again. Oscar was lucky. Too small and scrawny to attract even the most perverse of the policemen, he was tossed from a moving police van into a roadside ditch, bleeding and covered with welts.

The lucky part was that they had thrown him out near the entrance to the regional headquarters of the New Morality. The Philippines were still heavily Catholic, but Mother Church had grudgingly allowed the mostly Protestant reformers to operate in the island nation with only a minimum of interference. After all, the conservative bishops who ran the Philippine Church and the conservatives who ran the New Morality saw eye to eye on many issues, including birth control and strict obedience to moral authority. Moreover, the New Morality brought money from America into the Philippines. Some of it even trickled down enough to help the poor.

So Oscar Jiminez became a ward of the New Morality. Under their stern tutelage his life of crime ended. He was sent to a New Morality *school, where he learned that unrelenting psychological conditioning methods could be far worse than a police beating. Especially the conditioning sessions that used electric shock.*

Oscar swiftly became a model student.

CHAPTER 4

Kris Cardenas still looked little more than thirty. Even in a gritty, shabby one-room habitat carved out of one of Ceres's countless natural crevices, she radiated the blonde, sapphire-blue-eyed, athletic-shouldered look of a California surfer.

That was because her body was filled with therapeutic nanomachines, virus-sized contrivances that pulled apart molecules of fat and cholesterol in her bloodstream, repaired damaged cells, kept her skin smooth and her muscles taut, acted as a purposeful immune system to protect her body from invading microbes. Nanotechnology was forbidden on Earth; Dr. Kristine Cardenas, Nobel laureate and former director of Selene's nanotechnology laboratory, was an exile on Ceres.

For an exile who had chosen to live on the ragged frontier of human settlement, she looked happy and cheerful as she greeted Amanda and Lars Fuchs.

"How are you two doing?" she asked as she ushered them into her quarters. The twisting tunnel outside her door was a natural lava tube, barely smoothed by human tools. The air out there was slightly hazy with fine dust; every time someone moved in Ceres they disturbed the rock dust, and the asteroid's gravity was so slight that the dust hung in the air constantly.

Amanda and Fuchs shuffled their feet across Cardenas's bare rock floor and made their way to the room's sofa—actually a pair of reclining seats scavenged from a spacecraft that had limped to Ceres and never made it out again. The seats still had safety harnesses dangling limply from them. Fuchs coughed slightly as he sat down.

"I'll turn up the air fans," Cardenas said, gliding to the control panel set into the room's far wall. "Settle the dust, make it easier to breathe."

Amanda heard a fan whine from somewhere behind the walls. Despite being dressed in a long-sleeved, high-buttoned jumpsuit, she felt chilled. The bare rock always felt cold to her touch. At least it was dry. And Cardenas had tried to brighten up the underground chamber with holowindows that showed views of wooded hillsides and flower gardens on Earth. She had even scented the air slightly with something that reminded Amanda of her childhood baths in real tubs with scads of hot water and fragrant soap.

Cardenas pulled an old laboratory stool from her desk and perched on it before her visitors, locking her legs around its high rungs. "So, how are you?" she asked again.

Fuchs cocked an eye at her. "That's what we come to you to find out."

"Oh, your physical." Cardenas laughed. "That's tomorrow, at the clinic. How are you getting along? What's the news?"

With a glance at Amanda, Fuchs answered, "I think we'll be able to go ahead with the habitat project."

"Really? Has Pancho agreed—"

"Not with Astro's help," he said. "We're going to do it ourselves."

Cardenas's eyes narrowed slightly. Then she said, "Is that the wisest course of action, Lars?"

"We really don't have that much of a choice. Pancho would help us if she could, but Humphries will hamstring her as soon as she brings it up to the Astro board of directors. He doesn't want us to improve our living conditions here."

"He's going to establish a depot here," Amanda said. "Humphries Space Systems will, that is."

"So you and the other rock rats are going to pursue this habitat program on your own?"

"Yes," said Fuchs, quite firmly.

Cardenas said nothing. She clasped her knees and rocked back slightly on the stool, looking thoughtful.

"We can do it," Fuchs insisted.

"You'll need a team of specialists," Cardenas said. "This isn't something that you and your fellow prospectors can cobble together."

"Yes. I understand that."

Amanda said slowly, "Lars, I've been thinking. While you're working on this habitat project you'll have to stay here at Ceres, won't you?"

He nodded. "I've already given some thought to leasing *Starpower* to someone else and living here in the rock for the duration of the project."

"And how will you earn an income?" Cardenas interjected.

He spread his hands. Before he could reply, though, Amanda said, "I think I know."

Fuchs looked at his wife, clearly puzzled.

"We can become suppliers for the other prospectors," Amanda said. "We can open our own warehouse."

Cardenas nodded.

"We can deal through Astro," Amanda went on, brightening with each word. "We'll obtain our supplies from Pancho and sell them to the prospectors. We can sell supplies to the miners, too."

"Most of the mining teams work for Humphries," Fuchs replied darkly. "Or Astro."

"But they still need supplies," Amanda insisted. "Even if they get their equipment from the corporations, they'll still need personal items: soap, entertainment videos, clothing . . ."

Fuchs's face was set in a grimace. "I don't think you would want to handle the kinds of entertainment videos these prospectors buy."

Undaunted, Amanda said, "Lars, we could compete against Humphries Space Systems while you're directing the habitat construction."

"Compete against Humphries." Fuchs rolled the idea on his tongue, testing it. Then he broke into a rare grin. It made his broad, normally dour face light up. "Compete against Humphries," he repeated. "Yes. Yes, we can do that."

Amanda saw the irony in it, although the others didn't. The daughter of a small shopkeeper in Birmingham, she had grown up hating her middle-class background and the lower-class workers her father sold to. The boys were rowdy and lewd, at best, and they could just as easily become danger-ously violent. The girls were viciously catty. Amanda discovered early that being stunningly beautiful was both an asset and a liability. She was noticed wherever she went; all she had to do was smile and breathe. The trick was, once noticed, to make people see beyond her physical presence, to recog-nize the highly intelligent person inside that tempting flesh.

While still a teenager she learned how to use her good looks to get boys to do what she wanted, while using her sharp intellect to keep one jump ahead of them. She escaped her father's home and fled to London, took lessons to learn to speak with a polished accent, and—to her com-plete astonishment—found that she had the brains and skill to be a first-rate astronaut. She was hired by Astro Manufacturing Corporation to fly missions between Earth and the Moon. With her breathless looks and seeming naïveté, almost everyone assumed she had slept her way to the top of her profession. Yet the truth was just the opposite; Amanda had to work hard to fend off the men—and women—who wanted to bed her.

It was at Selene that she had met Martin Humphries. He had been her gravest danger: he wanted Amanda and he had the power to take what he wanted. Amanda had married Lars Fuchs in part to get away from Humphries, and Lars knew it.

Now, here out on the fringe of humankind's expansion through the solar system, she was about to become a shopkeeper herself. How father would howl at that, she thought. The father's revenge: the child becomes just like the parent, in the end.

"Humphries won't like competition," Cardenas pointed out.

"Good!" exclaimed Fuchs.

Shaken out of her reverie, Amanda said, "Competition will be good for the prospectors, though. And the miners, too. It will lower the prices they have to pay for everything."

"I agree," said Cardenas. "But Humphries won't like it. Not one little bit."

Fuchs laughed aloud. "Good," he repeated.

TWO YEARS LATER

CHAPTER 5

As soon as he stepped out onto the surface of Ceres, Fuchs realized that this was the first time he'd been in a spacesuit in months. The suit still smelled new; he'd only used it once or twice. *Mein gott*, he said to himself, I've become a bourgeois. The suit didn't fit all that well, either; the arms and legs were a trifle too long to be comfortable.

His first venture into space had been aboard *Starpower 1*'s ill-fated maiden voyage, five years earlier. He'd been a graduate student then, heading for a doctorate in planetary geochemistry. He never returned to school. Instead, he married Amanda and became a rock rat, a prospector seeking his fortune among the asteroids of the Belt. For nearly two years now, he had abandoned even that to run a supply depot on Ceres and supervise the habitat project.

Helvetia Ltd. was the name Fuchs had given his fledgling business, incorporating it under the regulations of the International Astronautical Authority. He was Helvetia's president, Amanda its treasurer, and Pancho Lane a vice president who never interfered in the company's operations; she seldom even bothered to visit its headquarters on Ceres. Helvetia bought most of its supplies from Astro Corporation and sold them to the rock rats at the lowest markup Amanda would allow. Humphries Space Systems ran a competing operation, and Fuchs gleefully kept his prices as low as possible, forcing Humphries to cut his own prices or be driven off Ceres altogether. The competition was getting to the cutthroat level; it was a race to see who would drive whom out of business.

The rock rats obviously preferred dealing with Fuchs to dealing with HSS. To his pleasant surprise, Helvetia Ltd. prospered, even though Fuchs considered himself a mediocre businessman. He was too quick to extend credit on nothing more than a rock rat's earnest promise to repay once he'd struck it rich. He preferred a handshake to the small print of a contract. Amanda constantly questioned his judgment, but enough of those vague promises came through to make Helvetia profitable. We're getting rich, Fuchs realized happily as his bank account at Selene fattened. Despite all of Humphries's tricks, we are getting rather wealthy.

Now, gazing around the bleak battered surface of Ceres, he realized all over again how lonely and desolate this place was. How far from civilization. The sky was filled with stars, such a teeming profusion of them that the old familiar constellations were lost in their abundance. There was no friendly old Moon or blue glowing Earth hanging nearby; even the Sun looked small and weak, dwarfed by distance. A strange, alien sky: stark and pitiless. Ceres's surface was broodingly dark, cold, pitted by thousands of craterlets, rough and uneven, boulders and smaller rocks scattered around everywhere. The horizon was so close it looked as if he were standing on a tiny platform rather than a solid body. For a giddy instant Fuchs felt that if he didn't hang on, he'd fall *up*, off this worldlet, into the wild wilderness of stars.

Almost distraught, he caught sight of the unfinished habitat rising above the naked horizon, glittering even in the weak sunlight. It steadied him. It might be a ramshackle collection of old, used, and stripped-down spacecraft, but it was the handiwork of human beings out here in this vast, dark emptiness.

A gleam of light flashed briefly. He knew it was the little shuttlecraft bringing Pancho and Ripley back to the asteroid's surface. Fuchs waited by the squat structure of the airlock that led down into the living sections below ground.

The shuttle disappeared past the horizon, but in a few minutes it came up over the other side, close enough to see its insect-thin legs and the bulbous canopy of its crew module. Pancho had insisted on flying the bird herself, flexing her old astronaut muscles. Now she brought it in to a smooth landing on the scoured ground about a hundred meters from the airlock.

As the two spacesuited figures climbed down from the shuttle, Fuchs easily recognized Pancho Lane's long, stringy figure even in her helmet and suit. This was the first time in nearly a year that Pancho had come to Ceres, doubling up on her roles of Astro board member and Helvetia vice president.

Tapping on the communications keyboard on his left wrist, Fuchs heard her talking with Ripley, the engineer in charge of the construction project.

". . . what you really need is a new set of welding lasers," she was saying, "instead of those clunkers you're workin' with."

Rather than trying to walk in the low-gravity shuffle that was necessary on Ceres, Fuchs took the jetpack control box into his gloved hand and barely squeezed it, feather-light. As usual, he overdid the thrust and sailed over the heads of Pancho and the engineer, nearly ramming into the shuttlecraft. His boots kicked up a cloud of dark dust as he touched down on the surface.

"Lord, Lars, when're you gonna learn how to fly one of those rigs?" Pancho teased.

Inside his helmet Fuchs grinned with embarrassment. "I'm out of practice," he admitted, sliding his feet across the surface toward them, raising still more dust. The ground felt gritty, pebbly, even through his thick-soled boots.

"You were never *in* practice, buddy."

He changed the subject by asking the engineer, "So, Mr. Ripley, will your crew be able to assemble the latest additions on schedule?"

"Believe it or not," Ripley replied archly, "they will."

Niles Ripley was an American of Nigerian heritage, an engineer with degrees from Lehigh and Penn, an amateur jazz trumpet player who had acquired the nickname "Ripper" from his headlong improvisations. The sobriquet sometimes caused problems for the mild-mannered engineer, especially in bars with belligerent drunks. The Ripper generally smiled and talked his way out of confrontations. He had no intention of letting some musclebound oaf damage his horn-playing lip.

"Your schedule will be met," Ripley went on. Then he added, "Despite its lack of flexibility."

Fuchs jabbed back, "Then your crew will earn its bonus, despite their complaints about the schedule."

Pancho interrupted their banter. "I've been tellin' ol' Ripper here that you'd get this job done a lot faster with a better set of welding lasers."

"We can't afford them," Fuchs said. "We are on very tight budget restraints."

"Astro could lease you the lasers. Real easy terms."

Fuchs made an audible sigh. "I wish you had thought of that two years ago, when we started this operation."

"Two years ago the best lasers we had were big and inefficient. Our lab boys just came up with these new babies: small enough to haul around on a minitractor. Very fuel efficient. They've even got a handheld version. Lower power, of course, but good enough for some jobs."

"We're doing well enough with what we have, Pancho."

"Well, okay. Don't say I didn't make you the offer." He heard the resigned, slightly disappointed tone in her voice.

Pointing a gloved hand toward the habitat, which was nearly at the far horizon, Fuchs said, "We've done quite well so far, don't you think?"

For a long moment she said nothing as the three of them watched the habitat glide down the sky. It looked like an unfinished pinwheel, several spacecraft joined end to end and connected by long buckyball tethers to a similar collection of united spacecraft, the entire assembly slowly rotating as it moved toward the horizon.

"Tell you the truth, Lars old buddy," said Pancho, "it kinda reminds me of a used-car lot back in Lubbock."

"Used-car lot?" Fuchs sputtered.

"Or maybe a flyin' junkyard."

"Junkyard?"

Then he heard Ripley laughing. "Don't let her kid you, Lars. She was pretty impressed, going through the units we've assembled."

Pancho said, "Well, yeah, the insides are pretty good. But it surely ain't a thing of beauty from the outside."

"It will be," Fuchs muttered. "You wait and see."

Ripley changed the subject. "Tell me more about these handheld lasers. How powerful are they?"

"It'll cut through a sheet of steel three centimeters thick," Pancho said.

"How long does it take?" asked Ripley.

"Couple nanoseconds. It's pulsed. Doesn't melt the steel, it shock-blasts it."

They chatted on while the habitat sank out of sight and the distant, pale Sun climbed higher in the dark, star-choked sky. Fuchs noticed the zodiacal light, like two long arms outstretched from the Sun's middle. Reflections from dust motes, he knew: microscopic asteroids floating out there, leftovers from the creation of the planets.

As they started toward the airlock, Pancho turned to Fuchs. "Might's well talk a little business."

She raised her left arm and tapped the key on her cuff that switched to a secondary suit-radio frequency. Ripley was cut out of their conversation now.

Fuchs hit the same key on his control unit. "Yes, business by all means."

"You asked us to reduce the prices for circuit boards again," Pancho said. "We're already close to the bone, Lars."

"Humphries is trying to undersell you."

"Astro can't sell at a loss. The directors won't stand for it."

Fuchs felt his lips curl into a sardonic smile. "Humphries is on your board of directors still?"

"Yup. He's promised not to lower HSS's prices any further."

"He's lying. They're offering circuit boards, chips, even repair services at lower and lower prices. He's trying to drive me out of the market."

"And once he does he'll run up the prices as high as he pleases," she said.

"Naturally. He'll have a monopoly then."

They had reached the airlock hatch. It was big enough for two space-suited people, but not three, so they sent Ripley through first.

Pancho watched the engineer close the hatch, then said, "Lars, what Humphries really wants is to take over Astro. He's been after that since the git-go."

"Then he'll have a monopoly on all space operations, everywhere in the Belt . . . everywhere in the whole solar system," Fuchs said, feeling anger rising within him.

"That's what he's after."

"We've got to prevent that! Whatever it takes, we must stop him."

"I can't sell you goods at below cost, buddy. The board's made that clear."

Fuchs nodded wearily. "Then we'll have to think of something else."

"Like what?"

He tried to shrug his shoulders, but inside the spacesuit it was impossible. "I wish I knew," he admitted.

CHAPTER 6

I'm becoming dependant on this woman, Humphries thought, watching Diane Verwoerd as they rode down the moving stairs toward his mansion, in Selene's bottommost level.

She was coolly reading out the daily list of action items from her handheld palmcomp, ticking them off one by one, asking him to okay the staff assignments she had already made to handle each item.

Humphries rarely left his house. Instead, he had made it into a haven of luxury and security. Half the house was living quarters, the other side given over to the scientists and technicians who maintained and studied the gardens that surrounded the mansion. It had been a brilliant idea, Humphries thought, to talk Selene's governing board into letting him create a three-hundred-hectare garden down in the deepest grotto in Selene. Officially, the house was the Humphries Trust Research Center that ran the ongoing ecological experiment: Can a balanced ecology be maintained on the Moon with minimal human intervention, given adequate light and water? Humphries didn't care in the slightest what the answer was, so long as he could live in comfort in the midst of the flourishing garden, deep below the radiation and other dangers of the Moon's surface.

He relished the knowledge that he had fooled them all, even Douglas Stavenger, Selene's founder and youthful éminence grise. He had even talked them into rescinding their foolish decision to exile him from Selene after his part in Dan Randolph's death had become known. But he hadn't fooled the tall, exotic, silky Diane Verwoerd, he knew. She saw right through him.

He had invited her to lunch at the new bistro just opened in the Grand Plaza. She had turned down his earlier offers of dinner, but a "working lunch" outside the house was something she could not easily refuse. So he had taken her to lunch. And she had worked right through the salad and soy cutlets, barely taking a sip of the wine he ordered, refusing dessert altogether.

And now, as they rode on the powered stairs back to his office/home, she held her palmcomp before her and rattled off problems facing the company and her solutions for them.

She's become almost indispensable to me, he realized. Maybe that's her game, to become so important to me businesswise that I'll stop thinking of her as a hotbody. She must know that I don't keep a woman around for long once I've had her in bed.

He grinned inwardly. You're playing a tricky game, Ms. Verwoerd. And, so far, you've played it just about perfectly.

So far.

Humphries refused to admit defeat, although it was obvious that this luncheon idea had been no victory. He listened to her long recitation with only half his attention, thinking, I'll get you sooner or later, Diane. I can wait.

But not much longer, another voice in his head spoke up. No woman is worth waiting for this long.

Wrong, he answered silently. Amanda is.

As they neared the bottom of the last flight of moving stairs, she said something that abruptly caught his full attention.

"And Pancho Lane flew all the way out to Ceres last week. She's on her way back now."

"To Ceres?" Humphries snapped. "What's she doing out there?"

"Talking to her business associates, Mr. and Mrs. Fuchs," Verwoerd replied calmly. "About undercutting our prices, I imagine."

"Undercutting me?"

"What else? If they can drive HSS out of Ceres they'll have the whole Belt for themselves. You're not the only one who wants to control the rock rats."

"Helvetia Ltd.," Humphries muttered. "Silly name for a company."

"It's really a front for Astro, you know."

He looked around the smooth walls of the escalator well without replying. At this deep level beneath Selene, no one else was riding down. There was no sound except the muted hum of the electric motor powering the stairs.

"Pancho's using Fuchs and his company to make it much tougher for you to take control of Astro. The more business she does through Helvetia, the more the Astro board sees her as a real hero. They might even elect Pancho chairman when O'Banian steps down."

"Drive me out of the Belt," Humphries growled.

"That's what we're trying to do to them, isn't it?"

He nodded.

"We'd better do it, then, before they do it to us," said Diane Verwoerd. Humphries nodded again, knowing she was right.

"What we need, then," she said slowly, "is a plan of action. A program aimed at crushing Helvetia once and for all."

He looked at her, really looked at her for the first time since they'd finished lunch. She's thought this whole thing through, he realized. She's leading me around by the nose, by god. Humphries saw it in her almond eyes. She has this all figured out. She knows exactly where she wants to lead me.

"So what do you suggest?" he asked, really curious about where she was heading.

"I suggest a two-pronged strategy."

"A two-pronged strategy?" he asked dryly.

"It's an old technique," Verwoerd said, smiling slyly. "The carrot and the stick."

Despite his efforts to remain noncommittal, Humphries smiled. "Tell me about it," he said as they reached the bottom of the stairs and stepped off.

Once he got back to his office, Humphries cleared his calendar and leaned back in his chair, thinking, worrying, planning. All thoughts of Diane left his conscious mind; he pictured Amanda out there with Fuchs. Amanda wouldn't try to hurt me, he told himself. But *he* would. He knows I love her and he'd do *anything* to damage me. He's already taken Amanda away from me. Now he wants to drive me out of the Belt and stop me from taking Astro. The sonofabitch wants to ruin me!

Diane is right. We've got to move, and move fast. Carrot and stick.

Abruptly, he sat up straight and ordered the phone to summon his chief of security. The man rapped softly at his office door a few moments later.

"Come in, Grigor," said Humphries.

The security chief was a new hire: a lean, silent man with dark hair and darker eyes. He wore an ordinary business suit of pale gray, the nondescript costume of a man who preferred to remain in the background, unnoticed, while he noticed everything. He remained standing despite the two comfortable chairs in front of Humphries's desk.

Tilting his own chair back slightly to look up at him, Humphries said, "Grigor, I want the benefit of your thinking on a problem I have."

Grigor shifted slightly on his feet. He had just been recruited from an

Earth-based corporation that was floundering financially because most of its assets had been destroyed in the greenhouse flooding. He was on probation with Humphries, and he knew it.

"Those rock rats out in the Belt are getting a bigger and bigger share of their supplies from Helvetia Ltd. instead of from Humphries Space Systems," Humphries said, watching the man closely, curious about how he would respond.

Grigor said nothing. His face betrayed no emotion. He listened.

"I want Humphries Space Systems to have exclusive control of the rock rats' supplies."

Grigor just stood there, unmoving, his eyes revealing nothing.

"Exclusive control," Humphries repeated. "Do you understand?"

Grigor's chin dipped in the slightest of nods.

"What do you think must be done?" Humphries asked.

"To gain exclusive control," said Grigor, in a throaty, guttural voice that sounded strained, painful, "you must eliminate your competitor."

"Yes, but how?"

"There are many ways. One of them is to use violence. I presume that is why you have asked my opinion."

Raising one hand, Humphries said sharply, "I don't mind violence, but this needs to be done with great discretion. I don't want anyone to suspect that Humphries Space Systems has anything to do with it."

Grigor thought in silence for a few heartbeats. "Then the action must be taken against individual prospectors, rather than Helvetia itself. Eliminate their customers and the company will shrivel and die."

Humphries nodded. "Yes," he said. "Exactly."

"It will take some time."

"How much time?"

"A few months," Grigor said. "Perhaps a year."

"I want it done faster than that. Sooner than a year."

Grigor closed his eyes briefly, then said, "Then we must be prepared to escalate the violence. First the individual prospectors, then personnel and facilities on Ceres itself."

"Facilities?"

"Your competitor is constructing an orbital habitat there, is he not?"

Humphries fought to suppress a satisfied grin. Grigor's already been studying the situation, he realized. Good.

When his employer failed to reply, Grigor continued, "Stopping the habitat project will help to discredit the man who started it. If nothing else, it will show that he is powerless to protect his own people."

"It's got to look accidental," Humphries insisted. "No hint of responsibility laid at my doorstep."

"Not to worry," said Grigor.

"I never worry," Humphries snapped. "I get even."

As Grigor left his office, silent as a wraith, Humphries thought, Carrot and stick. Diane will offer the carrot. Grigor's people will provide the stick.

ONE MONTH LATER

THE LADY OF THE LAKE

Ooh, Randy," gushed Cindy, "you're so *big*."

"And hard," added Mindy.

Randall McPherson lay back in the small mountain of pillows while the naked twins stroked his bare skin. Some guys liked sex in microgravity, but Randy had spun up his ship to almost a full terrestrial g for his encounter with the twins. His partner, Dan Fogerty, complained about the fuel cost of spinning up the ship, but Randy had ignored his bleating. Fogerty was known to all the miners as Fatso Fogerty, he had allowed himself to blubber up so shamelessly, living in microgravity most of the time. McPherson spent hours of his spare time in their ship's exercise centrifuge, or had the whole ship spun up to keep his muscles in condition. Fogerty was lucky to have a levelheaded man such as McPherson to team with him, in McPherson's opinion.

The twins were actually back at Ceres, of course, but the virtual reality system was working pretty well. Hardly a noticeable lag between a request by Randy and a smiling, slinky, caressing response from Cindy and Mindy.

So Randy was more than a little irked when Fogerty's voice broke into his three-way fantasy.

"There's a bloomin' ship approaching us!"

"What?" McPherson snapped, sitting up so abruptly that the VR images of the twins were still wriggling sensuously on the pillows even though he was no longer lying between them.

"A ship," Fatso repeated. "They're askin' to dock with us."

McPherson muttered a string of heartfelt profanities while the twins lay motionless, staring blankly.

"Sorry, ladies," he said, pushing himself up off the pillows, feeling half embarrassed, half infuriated. He lifted the VR goggles off and saw the real world: a dreary little compartment on a scruffy clunker of a ship that badly needed a refit and overhaul after fourteen months of batting around the Belt.

Awkwardly peeling off his VR sensor suit and pulling on his coveralls as he made his way up to the bridge, McPherson bellowed, "Fatso, if this is one of your goddam jokes I'm gonna wring your neck till I hear chimes!"

He ducked through the hatch and into the cramped, overheated bridge. Fogerty overflowed the pilot's seat, one hand clenching half a meat pie; most of the rest of it was spattered over his chins and his coveralls front. He was globulously lumpy, stretching the faded orange fabric of his coveralls so much that McPherson was reminded of an overripe pumpkin. He smelled overripe, too, and the additional spicy aroma from the meat pie made McPherson's stomach churn. Reckon I don't smell much better, McPherson told himself, trying to keep an even temper.

Fogerty half-turned in the creaking chair and jabbed a thick finger excitedly toward the main display screen. McPherson saw the two-kilometer-long chunk of rock they had just claimed, dark and lumpy, and a silvery spacecraft that looked too sleek and new to be a prospector's ship.

"A mining team?" Fogerty half-suggested.

"Out here already?" McPherson snapped. "We just sent in our claim. We haven't contacted any miners."

"Well, there they are," said Fogerty.

"That's not a miner's ship."

Fogerty shrugged. "Shall I give 'em permission to come aboard?"

McPherson had to squeeze past his partner's bulk to get into the right-hand seat. "Who in blazes are they? And what are they doing here? With the whole Belt to poke into, why are they sticking their noses into our claim?"

Fogerty grinned at his partner. "We could ask 'em."

Grumbling, McPherson flicked on the communications channel. "This is *The Lady of the Lake*. Identify yourselves, please."

The screen swirled with color momentarily, then a darkly bearded man's face took form. He looked vaguely oriental to McPherson: high cheekbones, hooded eyes.

"This is *Shanidar*. We have a boxful of videodisks that we've viewed so often we can lip-synch the dialogue. Do you have any to trade?"

"What've you got?" Fogerty asked eagerly. "How recent are they?"

"Private stuff, mostly. *Muy piquante*, if you know what I mean. You can't get them through the normal channels. They were brand-new when we left Selene, six months ago."

Before McPherson could reply, Fogerty broke into a dimpled, many-chinned smile. "We can swap you one-for-one, but our stuff is older."

"That's okay," said the bearded man. "It'll be new to us."

"What're you doing out here?" McPherson demanded. "We claimed this rock, you know."

"We're not prospecting any more," came the reply. "We've hit our jackpot and made a deal with Humphries Space Systems to process the ores. Got our money in the bank. We just thought we'd unload these videodisks before we head back home."

"Sure," said Fatso. "Why not?"

McPherson felt uneasy. But he saw the eager look on his partner's fleshy face. After fourteen months in the Belt they had barely cleared the payments on their ship. They needed another week, at least, to negotiate a mining contract with one of the corporations. McPherson had no intention of accepting the first offer they received. And the prices for ores just kept going down; they'd be lucky if they netted enough to live on for six months before they had to go out again.

"Okay," he said reluctantly. "Come on over and dock at our main airlock."

Fogerty nodded happily, like a little kid anticipating Christmas.

CHAPTER 7

Amanda thought again about how housekeeping on Ceres—inside Ceres, actually—was different from living on a ship. Not that their living quarters were that much more spacious: the single room that she and Lars shared was a slightly enlarged natural cave in the asteroid, its walls, floor, and ceiling smoothed and squared off. It wasn't much bigger than the cubic volume they had aboard *Starpower*. And there was the dust, always the dust. In Ceres's minuscule gravity, every time you moved, every time you took a step, you stirred up the everlasting dust. It was invisibly fine inside the living quarters, thanks to the air blowers. Once they moved up to the orbiting habitat, the dust would be a thing of the past, thank god.

In the meantime, though, it was a constant aggravation. You couldn't keep anything really clean: even dishes stored in closed cupboards had to be scoured under air jets before you could eat off them. The dust made you sneeze; half the time Amanda and most of the other residents wore filter masks. She worried that her face would bear permanent crease marks from the masks.

But living in Ceres offered something that shipboard life could not duplicate. Company. Society. Other people who could visit you or you could drop in on. Strolls through the corridors where you could see neighbors and say hello and stop for a chat. The corridors were narrow and twisting, it was true; natural lava tubes through the rock that had been smoothed off enough for people to shuffle through in a low-gravity parody of walking. Their walls and ceilings were still curved and unfinished raw stone; it was more like walking through a tunnel than a real corridor.

And there was the dust, of course. Always the dust. It was worse in the tunnels, so bad that everyone wore face masks when they went for a stroll.

Lately, though, people's attitudes had changed noticeably. There was an aura of expectation in the air, almost like the slowly building excitement that the year-end holiday season had brought when she'd been a child on Earth. The habitat was growing visibly, week by week. Everyone could see it swinging through the sky on their wallscreens. We're going to live up there, everyone was saying to themselves. We're going to move to a new, clean home.

When Lars had first told Amanda about the orbiting habitat, she'd been worried about the radiation. One advantage of living inside a big rock was that it shielded you from the harsh radiation sleeting in from the Sun and deep space. But Lars had shown her how the habitat would use the same magnetic radiation shielding that spacecraft used, only stronger, better. She studied the numbers herself and became convinced that the habitat would be just as safe as living underground—as long as the magnetic shielding worked.

Lars was up on the unfinished habitat again with Niles Ripley. He and the Ripper were working on a recalcitrant water recycler that refused to operate as programmed. Meanwhile, she was running the office, routing prospectors' requests for supplies and equipment to the proper inventory system, and checking to make certain that the material actually was loaded aboard a ship and sent to the people who had requested it.

Then there was the billing procedure. Miners were usually no problem: most of them were on corporate payrolls, so whatever they owed could be deducted automatically from their paychecks. Prospectors, though, were something else. The independents had no paychecks to deduct from. They were still searching for an asteroid to mine, waiting to find a jackpot. Yet they needed air to breathe and food to eat just as much as did miners working a claim. At Lars's insistence, Amanda ran a tab for most of them, waiting for the moment when they struck it rich.

Strange, Amanda thought, how the system works. The prospectors go out dreaming of making a fortune. Once they find a likely asteroid they have to make a deal to mine its ores. That's when they realize that they'll be lucky if they can break even. The prices for metals and minerals roller coasted up and down—mostly down—depending on the latest strikes; the commodities markets Earthside were hotbeds of frantic speculation, despite the sternest efforts of the Global Economic Council to keep things under control.

Yet there were just enough really big finds to keep the stars in the prospectors' eyes. They kept doggedly searching for the one asteroid that would allow them to retire in wealth and ease.

The real way to make a fortune, Amanda had learned, was to be a supplier to the prospectors and miners who seemed to be rushing out to the Belt in steadily increasing numbers. They did the searching and the finding, the mining and refining. But the people here on Ceres were the ones who were getting rich. Lars had already amassed a small fortune with Helvetia Ltd. Humphries's people were piling up bigger and bigger sums in their bank accounts, too. Even the twins, with their virtual reality bordello, were millionaires several times over.

The real profits, though, went to the corporations. Astro and Humphries Space Systems made most of the money; only a small percentage of it stays with people like Lars and me, Amanda knew.

Amanda rubbed at the aching back of her neck. It had become stiff from staring at the wallscreen for so many hours on end. With a tired sigh, she decided to call it a day. Lars would be coming in soon. Time to scrub up and put on a clean set of coveralls for dinner and maybe take a walk to the Pub afterward. Before shutting down for the day, though, Amanda flicked through the list of incoming messages awaiting her attention. Routine. Nothing that needed immediate attention.

Then she noticed that one of the messages had come in not from the ships plying the Belt, but from Selene. From the headquarters of Humphries Space Systems.

Her first instinct was to ignore it. Or perhaps delete it altogether. Then she saw that it was addressed to Lars, not her. It was not marked personal, and did not bear Martin Humphries's signature. No harm in reading it, Amanda thought. It won't be a two-way conversation, face-to-face. She glanced at her mirror by the bed, across the narrow room. I'm certainly not dressed to impress anyone, she thought. But even if it is from Martin, it was recorded and sent hours ago. Whoever sent it won't see me.

She didn't bother to take off her filter mask as she called up the message from HSS.

The wallscreen flickered momentarily, then showed an attractive dark-haired woman with the kind of sculpted high cheekbones that Amanda had always envied. The ID line beneath her image read DIANE VERWOERD, SPECIAL ASSISTANT TO THE CEO HUMPHRIES SPACE SYSTEMS.

"Mr. Fuchs," said Verwoerd's image, "I have been authorized by the management of Humphries Space Systems to engage in negotiations for buying out Helvetia Limited. The buyout would include your supply depot, inventory, and all the services that Helvetia performs. I'm sure you'll find our terms very attractive. Please call me at your earliest convenience. Thank you."

The screen blanked to the HSS logo against a neutral gray background. Amanda stared at it, seeing the woman's image, hearing her words. Buy us out! We could go back to Earth! We could live well and Lars could even go back to graduate school and get his doctorate!

She was so excited that she paid no attention to the message from the supply ship that was supposed to make rendezvous with *The Lady of the Lake*.

CHAPTER 8

Don't you see, Lars?" Amanda said eagerly. "We could go home! To Earth! You could go back to your studies and get your doctorate."

Fuchs was sitting on the edge of their bed, his thin slash of a mouth turned down grimly, Amanda beside him. Together they had watched Diane Verwoerd's full message offering him ten million international dollars for his supply service and its facilities on Ceres.

"It's a bribe," he growled.

"It's the opportunity of a lifetime, darling. Ten million international dollars! Think of it! Ten million, free and clear, just like that!" She snapped her fingers. "For nothing more than signing your name."

"And getting out of Ceres."

"And returning to Earth. We could go to London, or Geneva, if you prefer."

"It's a bribe," he repeated stubbornly.

Amanda took both his big, callused hands in hers. "Lars, darling, we can go back to Earth and live comfortably wherever you choose. We can begin a new life together."

He said nothing, simply stared at the blanked wallscreen as if he were looking down the muzzle of a gun.

"Lars, we could have children."

That stirred him. He turned his head to look into her eyes.

"I want to have a baby, Lars. Your baby. We can't do that here, you know that."

He nodded bleakly. "The gravity . . ." he muttered.

"If we lived on Earth, we could lead normal lives. We could raise a family."

"The frozen zygotes are waiting for us at Selene," he said.

She slid her arms around his neck. "We won't need them, Lars. Not if we live on Earth like normal people."

He started to pull her to him, but then something crossed his face. His expression changed; he looked almost as if he were in pain.

"They want us to leave Ceres."

"And you want to *stay*?" Amanda had meant it to be joking; light-hearted. But it sounded bitter, almost like nagging, even to her.

"The prospectors. The miners," he said, almost whispering. "All the others rock rats out here . . . our friends, our neighbors."

"What of them?"

"We'd have to leave them."

"We'll make new friends. They'll understand."

He pulled away from her and got to his feet. "But we'll be leaving them to *him*, to Humphries."

"What of it?"

"Once we're out of his way, once he's bought us out, he'll be the only source for supplies in the entire Belt. No one else would dare to compete against him."

"Astro might. Pancho—"

"He's on Astro's board of directors. Sooner or later he'll take control of Astro, too. He'll control everything! And everybody."

Amanda had known all along that her husband would stick on this point. She had tried to keep it out of her mind, but there it was, in the open, standing between them.

"Lars," she said slowly, picking her words with care, "whatever feelings Martin may have once had for me are long gone, I'm certain. There is no need to view this as a competition between you and he."

He walked away from her, paced the little room in six strides and then turned back toward her, a barrel-chested bear of a man dressed in faded dark gray coveralls, his broad heavy-featured face glowering with distrust.

"But it *is* a competition, Amanda. Between Humphries Space Systems and Helvetia Limited. Between him and Astro, actually. We're caught in the middle of it, whether we like it or not."

"But we can get out of it," she said. "You can take me back to Earth and we'll be rid of Humphries and Astro and the rock rats for good."

He strode to the bed and dropped to his knees before her. "I want to take you back home, dearest. I know how much you want to be away from here, how brave you've been to stay here with me—"

"I love you, Lars," she said, reaching out to tousle his dark hair. "I want to be with you wherever you are."

He sighed heavily. "Then we must remain here. At least for a little while longer."

"But why . . . ?"

"Because of them. The rock rats. Our neighbors and friends here on Ceres. We can't leave them to Humphries."

Amanda felt her eyes misting over. "We can't let this opportunity pass us by, Lars. Please, *please* accept their offer."

He started to shake his head stubbornly, but then he noticed the tears in her eyes. He got to his feet and sat heavily beside her again on the edge of the bed.

"Amanda, dearest, I can't turn my back on all the people here. They trust me. They need me."

"I need you, too, Lars," Amanda said. "We've been out here for five years. I haven't complained once, have I?"

"No, you haven't," he admitted. "You've been very wonderful."

"I'm asking you now, Lars. I'm begging you. Please accept this offer and take me back home."

He stared into her glistening eyes for long, silent moments. She could see that he was thinking, searching for some way to do what she wanted without feeling that he had betrayed the other rock rats in the Belt.

At last he said, "Let me talk to Pancho."

"Pancho? Why?"

"To see if Astro will make a similar offer."

"And if they won't?"

With obvious, painful reluctance, Fuchs said, "Then we'll accept Humphries's offer."

"You will?"

He nodded, smiling sadly. "Yes, I'll take his money and leave the Belt and bring you home to Earth."

DOSSIER:
JOYCE TAKAMINE

The name on her birth certificate read Yoshiko Takamine, but once she started at public school everyone called her Joyce. Her parents didn't mind; they were fourth-generation Americans, with only a vague feeling of nostalgia for the family's roots in Japan. The first time one of her schoolmates called her a "Jap," Joyce thought she meant "Jewish American Princess."

Father moved them to the hills above Sausalito, but when the greenhouse floods wiped out most of the electrical power generation plants in the Bay area, they were plunged into darkness along with everyone else. Those were desperate times, with half the county thrown out of their jobs. No electricity, no work. Joyce's class held their senior prom by candlelight, and there was talk of bringing in drilling companies to bore wells deep enough to tap the natural gas that lay kilometers belowground.

All the kids had to find some kind of job to help support the family. Joyce did what her great-grandmother had done more than a century earlier: migrant stoop labor in the farms down in the rich valleys of California. The floods hadn't reached that far inland, although prolonged drought was searing the orchards and vineyards mercilessly. It was hard, bitter work, picking fruits and vegetables beneath the hot sun while grim-faced men armed with shotguns kept on patrol against wandering bands of starving looters. They expected casual sex from the workers. Joyce quickly learned that it was better to please them than to go hungry.

When Joyce returned home that winter, she was shocked to see how much her parents had aged. An epidemic of dengue fever had swept the coast and even reached into the hills where they lived. Her mother sobbed *softly at night; her father stared into the hot cloudless sky, racked with bouts of coughing that left him gasping for breath. When he looked at his daughter he seemed ashamed, as if all this devastation, all this ruination of the family's plans, was his fault alone.*

"I wanted you to become an engineer," he told Joyce. "I wanted you to rise beyond my station in life."

"I will, Dad," she told him, with the careless assurance of youth. And when she turned her eyes to the sky, she thought about the wild frontier out along the Asteroid Belt.

CHAPTER 9

"He's put in a call to Pancho Lane," said Diane Verwoerd.

She and Humphries were strolling through the courtyard outside his mansion. Humphries claimed he enjoyed taking a walk in the "outdoors"—or as near to outdoors as you could get on the Moon. Humphries's home was in the middle of a huge grotto down at the deepest level of Selene's network of underground corridors and habitation spaces. The big, high-ceilinged cavern was filled with flowered shrubbery, profusions of reds and yellows and delicate lilacs blooming from one rough-hewn rock wall to the other. Taller trees rose among the profusion of flowers: alders and sturdy maples and lushly flowering white and pink gardenias. No breeze swayed those trees; no birds sang in the greenery; no insects buzzed. It was a huge, elaborate hothouse, maintained by human hands. Hanging from the raw rock ceiling were strips of full-spectrum lamps to imitate sunlight.

Verwoerd could see the enormous garden beyond the ornate fountain that splashed noisily in the courtyard. The house itself was massive, only two stories high, but wide, almost sprawling. Built of smoothed lunar stone, its roof slanted down to big sweeping windows.

Compared to the gray underground drabness of the rest of Selene, this garden and home were like a paradise in the midst of a cold, forbidding desert. Verwoerd's own quarters, several levels up from this grotto, were among the best in Selene, but they seemed cramped and colorless compared to this.

Humphries claimed he enjoyed walking in the open air. The only other open space in Selene was the Grand Plaza, under the big dome up on the surface, and *anyone* could take a stroll up there. Here he had his privacy, and all the heady color that human ingenuity and hard work could provide on the Moon. Verwoerd thought he enjoyed the idea that all this was his more than any aesthetic or health benefits he could gain from walking among the roses and peonies.

But any pleasure he might have enjoyed from this stroll was wiped away by her announcement.

"He's called Pancho?" Humphries snapped, immediately nettled. "What for?"

"She scrambled his message and her reply, so we don't know the exact words as yet. I have a cryptologist working on it."

"Only one message?"

With a small nod, Verwoerd answered, "His incoming to her, and hers outgoing to him immediately after."

"H'mm."

"I can guess what the subject was."

"So can I," Humphries said sourly. "He wants to see if she'll better our offer."

"Yes."

"He's playing her against me."

"It would seem so."

"And if she outbids me, then Astro gets full control of his Helvetia Limited." He pronounced the name sneeringly.

Verwoerd frowned slightly. "He's already using Astro as his supplier. What does Pancho have to gain by buying him out?"

"She keeps us from buying him out. It's a preventive strike, that's what it is."

"So we increase our bid?"

"No," Humphries snapped. "But we increase our pressure."

Seyyed Qurrah laughed with delight as he gazed through the thick quartz observation port at his prize, his jewel, his reward for more than two years of scorn and struggle and near starvation. He feasted his eyes as the irregular chunk of rock slid across his view, grayish brown where the sunlight struck it, pitted and covered here and there with boulders the size of houses.

"Allah is great," he said aloud, thanking the one God for his mercy and kindness.

Turning to the sensor displays in his cabin's control panel, he saw that this lump of stone bore abundant hydrates, water locked chemically to the silicates of the rock. Water! In the desert that was the Moon, water fetched a higher price than gold. It was even more valuable at Ceres, although with only a few hundred people living at the big asteroid, the demand for precious water was not as high as that of Selene's many thousands.

Qurrah thought of the contempt and ridicule that they had heaped upon him back home when he'd announced that he intended to leave Earth and seek his fortune in the new bounty of the Asteroid Belt. "Sinbad the Sailor" was the kindest thing he'd been called. "Seyyed the Idiot" was what most of them said. Even when he had reached Ceres and leased a ship with the last bit of credit his dead father had left him, even there the other prospectors and miners called him "Towel Head" and worse. Well, now the shoe was on the other foot. He'd show them!

Then he pictured how happy Fatima would be when he returned to Algiers, wealthy and happy at last. He would be able to shower her with diamonds and rich gowns of silk with gold threading. Perhaps even acquire a second wife. He was so pleased that he decided to take a full meal from his meager foodstocks, instead of his usual handful of boiled couscous.

But first he would register his claim with the International Astronautical Authority. That was important. No, before that, he must make his prayer to Allah. That was more important.

He realized he was nearly babbling out loud. Taking a deep breath to calm himself, Qurrah decided, prayer first, then register with the IAA, then celebrate with a whole meal.

He kept his ship spinning all the time, counterbalancing his habitation unit with the power generator and other equipment at the end of the kilometer-long tether. Not for him the long months in microgee, with his muscles going flabby and his bones decalcifying so that he would have to spend even longer months in lunar orbit rebuilding his body cells. No! Qurrah lived in almost a full earthly gravity.

So he had no trouble unfurling his prayer rug once he had taken it from its storage cabinet. He was spreading the rug on the one uncluttered area of his compartment when his communications receiver chimed.

A message? He was startled at the thought. Who would be calling me out here, in this wilderness? Only Fatima and the IAA knows where I am—and the people back at Ceres, of course, but why would they call a lonely prospector?

Fatima! he thought. Something has happened to her. Something terrible.

His voice trembled as he answered, "This is the *Star of the East*. Who is calling, please?"

A bearded man's face appeared on his main screen. He looked almost Asian to Qurrah, or perhaps Hispanic.

"This is *Shanidar*. You are trespassing on territory that belongs to Humphries Space Systems, Incorporated."

"This rock?" Qurrah was instantly incensed. "No sir! There is no registered claim for this asteroid. I was just about to send in my own claim when you hailed me."

"You haven't registered a claim for it?"

"I am going to, right now!"

The bearded man shook his head, very slightly, just a small movement from side to side.

"No you're not," he said.

They were the last words Qurrah ever heard. The laser blast from *Shanidar* blew a fist-sized hole through the thin hull of his ship. Qurrah's death scream quickly screeched to silence as the air rushed out and his lungs collapsed in massive hemorrhages of blood.

THE PUB

George Ambrose cradled his stone mug of beer in both his big paws. They call it beer, he grumbled inwardly. Haven't seen a decent beer since I came out here. Fookin' concoction these rock rats call beer tastes more like platypus piss than anything else. The real stuff was available, but the price was so high for anything imported that George gritted his teeth and sipped the local brew.

As joints went, the Pub wasn't so bad. Reminded George of the Pelican Bar, back at Selene, except for the twins in their spray-paint bikinis. They worked behind the bar, under the protective eye of the owner/barkeep. More'n two hundred and sixty million kilometers away, the old Pelican was. Nearly a week's flight, even in the best of the fusion ships.

He looked over the crowd. The Pub was a natural cave in Ceres's porous, rocky crust. The floor had been smoothed down but nobody'd ever bothered to finish the walls or ceiling. Be a shame to leave this behind when we move to the habitat, George thought. He'd grown fond of the joint.

Everything in the Pub was either scavenged or made from asteroidal materials. George was sitting on an old packing crate, reinforced by nickel-iron rods and topped with a stiff plastic cushion cadged from some ship's stores. The table on which he was leaning his beefy arms was carved rock, as was his mug. Some of the crowd were drinking from frosted aluminum steins, but George preferred the stone. The pride and joy of the the Pub was its bar, made of real wood, ferried in here by the daft old poppy who owned the joint. Maybe he isn't so daft, George mused. He's makin' more money than I am, that's for sure. More money than any of these rock rats.

Men and women were jammed four deep at the bar and sitting at all the tables spotted across the place like stalagmites rising from the stone floor, four or five men to every sheila. A dozen or more stood along the back wall, drinks in their hands. A pair of women and another bloke were sitting at the same table as George, but he hardly knew them and they were chatting up each other, leaving him alone with his beer.

A strange crowd, he thought. Prospectors and miners ought to be rough, hard-handed men, outback types like in the old videos. These blokes were college boys, computer nerds, family men and women with enough education and smarts to operate spacecraft and highly automated mining machinery. Not one of 'em ever used a pick or shovel, George knew. Hell's bells, I never did meself. Lately, though, a different sort had been drifting in: snotty-looking yobbos who kept pretty much to themselves. They didn't seem to have any real jobs, although they claimed they worked for HSS. They just hung around, as if they were waiting for something.

Off in the far corner of the cave a couple of blokes were unpacking musical instruments and connecting their amplifiers. Niles Ripley walked in, loose-jointed and smiling at his friends—just about everybody—with his trumpet case in one hand. George pushed himself to his feet and shambled to the bar for a refill of his platypus brew. Several people said hello to him, and he made a bit of chat until Cindy slid the filled mug back to him. Or was it Mindy? George could never tell the twins apart. Then he went back to his table. Nobody had swiped his seat. That's the kind of place the Pub was.

As the music began, low and sweet, George found himself thinking about his life. Never dreamed I'd be out here in the Belt, digging ores out of fookin' asteroids. Hard work, but better than prospecting, poking around the Belt for months on end, looking for a really rich asteroid that the corporations haven't already claimed, hoping to make the big strike so you can go home and live in luxury. Life takes weird turns.

The Ripper, who had been playing along with the other musicians, finally stood up and tore into a solo that rocked the cave. His trumpet echoed off the stone walls, bringing everyone to their feet, swaying and clapping in time to his soaring notes. When he finished they roared with delight and insisted on more.

The evening flew by. George forgot about the ship that he owed money on, forgot about getting up early tomorrow morning to finish the repair job on *Matilda*'s main manipulator arm so he could get the hell out of Ceres and finish the mining job he'd signed up for before the contract deadline ran out and he had to pay a penalty to Astro Corporation. He just sat there with the rest of the crowd, grooving on the music, rushing to the bar along with everyone else when the band took a break, drinking all night long yet getting high on the music, not the beer.

It was well past midnight when the band broke up, after several encores, and started to pack their instruments and equipment. People began to file out of the Pub, tired and happy. The twins had disappeared, as usual. Nobody laid a hand on them, except in virtual reality. George plowed through the crowd and made his way to the Ripper.

"Lemme buy you a beer, mate?"

Ripley clicked his trumpet case shut, then looked up.

Smiling, he said, "Maybe a cola, if you can afford it."

"Sure thing, Rip. No worries."

A few determined regulars still stood at bar, apparently with no intention of leaving. George saw four of the new guys there, too, grouped together, bent over their drinks and talking to one another in low, serious tones. They all wore coveralls with the HSS logo over their name tags.

"Another beer for me and a cola for the Ripper, here," George called to the barkeep.

"A cola?" sneered one of the yobbos. The others laughed.

Ripley smiled down the bar at them. "Can't have any alcohol after midnight. I'm working on the habitat in the morning."

"Sure," came the reply.

George scowled at them. They were so new to Ceres they didn't realize that an imported cola cost half the earth. He turned back toward Ripley. "Helluva show you put on tonight."

"They seemed to like it."

"Ever think of playin' professionally? You're too good to be sittin' out on this rock."

Ripley shook his head. "Naw. I play the trumpet for fun. If I got serious about it, it'd become work."

"You hurt my ears with that damned noise," said another of the yobbos.

"Yeah," said one of his mates. "Why the hell d'you hafta play so damned loud?"

Before George could say anything, Ripley replied, "Gee, I'm sorry about that. Maybe next time I'll use a mute."

The complainer walked down the bar toward Ripley. "Next time my ass. What're you going to do about the frickin' headache you've given me?"

He was a tall, rangy sort, athletically built; short blond hair, with a funny little tail in the back, like an old-time matador. He was young, George saw, but old enough to have better manners.

The Ripper's smile started to look a little forced. Very gently, he replied, "I guess I could treat you to a couple of aspirins."

"Fuck you and your aspirins." The guy threw his drink into the Ripper's face.

Ripley looked shocked, totally at a loss. He blinked in confusion as beer dripped from his nose, his ears.

George stepped between them. "That wasn't very smart," he said.

"I'm not talking to you, Red. It's this wiseass noisemaker I'm talking to."

"He's my friend," said George. "I think you owe him an apology."

"And I think you ought to pull your shaggy ass out of this before you get hurt," said the yobbo, as his three companions came up to stand with him.

George smiled pleasantly. This was getting interesting, he thought. To the beer-thrower, he said, "Mr. Ripley, here, isn't the sort to get involved in a barroom brawl. He might hurt his lip, y'see, and then everyone here would be upset with the people who made that happen."

The guy looked around. The Pub was almost empty now. The few remaining regulars had backed away from the bar, drinks in their hands. A handful of others who had been leaving now stood at the doorway, watching. The barkeep had faded back to the other end of the bar, the expression on his face somewhere between nervous and curious.

"I don't give a fuck who gets upset with who. And that includes you, big ass."

George grabbed the guy by the front of his shirt and lifted him, one hand, off the floor to deposit him with a thump on the bar. He looked very surprised. His three friends stood stock-still.

Ripley touched George's other arm. "Come on, pal. Let's not have a fight."

George looked from the yobbo sitting on the bar to his three standing partners, then broke into a shaggy grin.

"Yeah," he said to the Ripper. "No sense breakin' the furniture. Or any heads."

He turned and started for the door. As he knew they would, all four of them leaped at him. And none of them knew beans about fighting in low gravity.

George swung around and caught the first one with a backhand swat that sent him sprawling. The next two tried to pin his arms but George threw them off. The original troublemaker came at him with a high-pitched yowl and a karate kick aimed at his face. George caught his foot in mid-kick and swung him around like a kid's toy, lifted him totally off his feet, and then tossed him flying in a howling slow-motion spin over the bar. He crashed into the decorative glassware on the shelves along the back wall.

"Goddammit, George, that costs money!" the barkeep yelled.

But George was busy with the three recovered yobbos. They rushed him all at once, but it was like trying to bring down a statue. George staggered back a step, grunting, then smashed one to the floor with a single sledgehammer blow between his shoulderblades. He peeled the other two off and held them up off the floor by the scruffs of their necks, shook them the way a terrier shakes a rat, then banged their heads together with a sound like a melon hitting the pavement after a long drop.

He looked around. Two men were unconscious at his feet, a third moaning facedown on the floor. The barkeep was bending over the yobbo on the floor behind the bar amid the shattered glassware, shouting, "Well, somebody's got to pay for this damage!"

"Are you all right, George?" Ripley asked.

George saw that the Ripper had a packing-crate-chair in his hands. He laughed. "What're you gonna do with that, post 'em back to Earth?"

Ripley broke into a relieved laugh, and the two men left the Pub. Half a minute later the Ripper ran back in and retrieved his trumpet. The bartender was on the phone, calling Kris Cardenas, the only qualified medical help on Ceres. He held a credit chip from one of the yobbos in his hand.

CHAPTER 10

Even after five years on Astro Corporation's board of directors, Pancho Lane still thought of herself as a neophyte. You got a lot to learn, girl, she told herself almost daily.

Yet she had formed a few working habits, a small set of rules for herself. She spent as little time in Astro's corporate offices as possible. Whether at La Guaira on Earth or in Selene, Pancho chose to be among the engineers and astronauts rather than closeting herself with the suits. She had come up through the ranks, a former astronaut herself, and she had no intention of reading reports and studying graphs when she could be out among the workers, getting her hands dirty; she preferred the smell of machine oil and honest sweat to the quiet tensions and power jockeying of the corporate offices.

One of her self-imposed rules was to make decisions as soon as she had the necessary information, and then to act on her decisions quickly. Another was to deliver bad news herself, instead of detailing some flunky to handle the chore.

Still, she hesitated to put in the call to Lars Fuchs. It won't make him happy, she knew. Instead, she called his wife. Pancho and Amanda had worked together five years earlier; they had copiloted *Starpower 1*'s maiden mission to the Belt. They had watched helplessly as Dan Randolph died of radiation poisoning—murdered by remote control, by Martin Humphries.

And now the Humper was offering to buy out Lars and Mandy, get them off Ceres, establish his own Humphries Space Systems as the sole supplier for the rock rats out there. Pancho had tried to fight Humphries, tried to keep Astro in the competition through Fuchs's little company. But she had been thoroughly outmaneuvered by Humphries, and she knew it.

Angry more at herself than anyone else, she marched herself to her office in La Guaira and made the call to Amanda. She paid no attention to the lovely tropical scenery outside her office window; the green, cloud-topped mountains and gently surging sea held no attraction for her. Planting her booted feet on her desktop, wishing there was some way to help Mandy and Lars, she commanded her phone to send a message to Amanda Cunningham Fuchs, on Ceres.

"Mandy," she began unceremoniously, "I'fraid I got bad news for you and Lars. Astro won't top Humphries's buyout offer. The board wouldn't vote to buy you out. Humphries has a nice little clique on the board and they voted the whole proposition down the toilet. Sorry, kid. Look me up when you get back to Selene, or wherever you're goin'. Maybe we can spend some time together without worryin' about business. See ya."

Pancho was startled when she realized she'd been sitting at her desk for nearly half an hour without instructing the phone to transmit her message.

Finally she said, "Aw shit, send it."

The headquarters of the International Astronautical Authority were still in Zurich, officially, but its main working offices were in St. Petersburg.

The global warming that had melted most of the glaciers in Switzerland and turned the snowpacks of the Alpine peaks into disastrous, murderous floods had forced the move. The administrators and lawyers who had been transferred to Russia complained, with some resentment, that they had been pushed off the greenhouse cliff.

To their surprise, St. Petersburg was a beautiful, cosmopolitan city, not at all the dour gray urban blight they had expected. The greenhouse warming had been kind to St. Petersburg: winters were nowhere near as long and bitter as they had once been. Snow did not start to fall until well into December and it was usually gone by April. Russian engineers had doggedly built a series of weirs and breakwaters across the Gulf of Finland and the Neva River to hold back the rising seas.

Even though the late winter sunlight had to struggle through a slate-gray layer of clouds, Erek Zar could see from his office window that most of the snow had already melted from the rooftops. It promised to be a good day, and a good weekend. Zar leaned back in his desk chair, clasped his hands behind his head, looked out across the rooftops toward the shimmering harbor, and thought that, with luck, he could get away by lunchtime and spend the weekend with his family in Kraków.

He was not happy, therefore, when Francesco Tomasselli stepped through his office door with a troubled expression on his swarthy face. Strange, Zar said to himself: Italians are supposed to be sunny and cheerful people. Tomasselli always looked like the crack of doom. He was as lean as a strand of spaghetti, the nervous sort. Zar felt like Shakespeare's Julius Caesar: *Let me have men about me that are fat; sleek-headed men, and such as sleep o' nights.*

"What's the matter, Franco?" Zar asked, hoping it wasn't serious enough to interfere with his travel plans.

Tomasselli plopped into the upholstered chair in front of the desk and sighed heavily. "Another prospecting ship is missing."

Zar sighed too. He spoke to his desktop screen and the computer swiftly showed the latest report from the Belt: a spacecraft named *Star of the East* had disappeared; its tracking beacon had winked off, all telemetry from the craft had ceased.

"That's the third one this month," Tomasselli said, his lean face furrowed with worry.

Spreading his hands placatingly, Zar said, "They're out on the edge of nowhere, sailing alone through the Belt. Once a ship gets into trouble there's no one near enough to help. What do you expect?"

Tomasselli shook his head. "When a spacecraft gets into trouble, as you put it, it shows up on the telemetry. They send out distress calls. They ask for help, or advice."

Zar shrugged.

"We've had ships fail and crews die, god knows," Tomasselli went on, the faint ring of vowels at the end of most of his words. "But these three are different. No calls for help, no telemetry showing failures or malfunctions. They just disappear—*poof!*"

Zar thought a moment, then asked, "Had they claimed any asteroids?"

"One of them had: *Lady of the Lake*. Two weeks after the ship disappeared and the claim was officially invalidated, the asteroid was claimed by a vessel owned by Humphries Space Systems: the *Shanidar*."

"Nothing irregular there."

"Two weeks? It's as if the Humphries ship was waiting for *Lady of the Lake* to disappear so they could claim the asteroid."

"You're getting melodramatic, Franco," said Zar. "You're accusing them of piracy."

"It should be investigated."

"Investigated? How? By whom? Do you expect us to send search teams through the Asteroid Belt? There aren't enough spacecraft in the solar system for that!"

Tomasselli did not reply, but his dark eyes looked brooding, accusing.

Zar frowned at his colleague. "Very well, Franco. I'll tell you what I'll do. I'll talk to the Humphries people and see what they have to say about it."

"They'll deny everything, of course."

"There's nothing to deny! There's no shred of evidence that they've done anything wrong!"

Tomasselli muttered, "I am going to examine all the claims made by HSS ships over the past month."

"What for?"

"To see if there are any in the regions where those two other missing ships disappeared."

Zar wanted to scream at the man. He's nothing but a suspicious-minded young Italian, Zar thought, seeing nefarious plots and skullduggery wherever he looks. But he took a deep breath to calm himself and said in an even, measured tone:

"That's fine, Franco. You check the claims. I'll speak to the HSS people. Monday. I'll do it first thing Monday morning, after I come back from the weekend."

CHAPTER 11

There was no meeting hall in Ceres, no single place designated for public assemblies. That was mainly because there had never been a need for one; Ceres's ragtag collection of miners and prospectors, repair people and technicians, merchants and clerks had never come together in a public assembly until now. The closest thing to a government on Ceres was a pair of IAA flight controllers who monitored the takeoffs and landings of the ships that were constantly arriving for supplies and maintenance, then departing into the dark emptiness of the Belt.

So when Fuchs called for a public meeting, it took some doing for him to convince the other rock rats that a gathering was necessary and beneficial. As it was, hardly forty men and women out of the several hundred in the asteroid showed up at the Pub, which Fuchs had commandeered for his meeting. A few dozen others attended electronically, from their ships in transit through the Belt. Big George was among those latter; he had left Ceres in his *Waltzing Matilda* several days before Fuchs's meeting convened.

It was a good-natured crowd that came together in the Pub at 1700 hours that afternoon. Like most spacecraft and off-Earth facilities, Ceres kept Universal Time. The Pub's owner/barkeep had allowed his place to be used for the meeting upon Fuchs's promise that it would take no longer than an hour. The "six o'clock swill" could proceed as usual.

"I'm no public speaker," Fuchs said, standing atop the bar so everyone in the milling, chattering crowd could see him. Three big flatscreens had been wheeled into the back of the room; they showed nearly a score of individuals attending the meeting remotely. Many of the prospectors refused to do even that, claiming that they didn't want anyone to know where they were, outside of the usual IAA trackers, whom they tolerated only because of the IAA's tradition of confidentiality and non-interference in spacecraft operations, except for safety conditions.

"I'm no public speaker," Fuchs repeated, louder.

"Then what're you doing up there?" came an irreverent voice from the crowd. Everyone laughed.

Grinning back at the heckler, Fuchs rejoined, "It's a dirty job . . ."

". . . but somebody's got to do it," the whole crowd finished with him.

Fuchs laughed, a little sheepishly, and looked at Amanda, standing off by the wall toward his right. She smiled encouragement at him. The twins stood beside her, fully clothed in glittering metallic outfits. Even in plain coveralls Amanda still looked far more beautiful than they, in Fuchs's eyes.

"Seriously," he said, once the crowd settled down, "it's time we talked about something that most of us find distasteful—"

"What'samatter Lars, the toilets backing up again?"

"The recycler breaking down?"

"No," he said. "Worse than that. It's time to start thinking about forming some kind of a government here."

"Aw, shit!" somebody yowled.

"I don't like the idea of rules and regulations any more than you do," Fuchs said quickly. "But this community is growing and we don't have any laws or law enforcement."

"We don't need 'em," a woman shouted.

"We've been getting along okay without any."

Fuchs shook his head. "There have been two brawls right here in the Pub in the past month. Someone deliberately damaged Yuri Kubasov's ship last week. Deliberate sabotage."

"That's a private matter," came a voice from the back of the chamber. "Yuri was chasing the wrong woman."

A few people snickered knowingly.

"Then there was the break-in in my warehouse," Fuchs added. "That was no minor affair; we lost more than a hundred thousand dollars worth of inventory."

"Come on, Lars," a woman challenged. "Everybody knows that you're competing against HSS. So they're playing a little rough; that's your problem, not ours."

"Yeah, if you and Humphries are battling it out, why try to drag us into your fight?"

Glancing again toward Amanda, Fuchs answered, "It's not my fight. It's yours."

"The hell it is!" said one of the men, heatedly. "This is between you and Humphries. It's personal and it's got nothing to do with us."

"That's not true, as you'll soon find out."

"What's that supposed to mean?"

Reluctantly, surprised at how hard it was to bring out the words, he told them, "It means that Amanda and I will be leaving Ceres shortly. We'll be returning to Earth."

"Leaving?"

Feeling real pain, Fuchs went on, "Humphries has made an offer that's much too generous for us to us to ignore. HSS will be taking over Helvetia's warehouse and all its services."

For several heartbeats there was absolute silence through the Pub.

Then, from one of the flatscreens, Big George said, "That means HSS will be our only supplier."

"They'll have a monopoly here!" someone else wailed.

With a grave nod, Fuchs said, "That's why it's important for you to form some kind of government, some group that can represent you, maybe get Astro to set up another facility—"

"FIRE," said the synthesized computer voice from the speakers by the Pub's entryway. "FIRE IN SECTION FOUR-CEE."

"That's my warehouse!" Fuchs blurted.

The crowd bolted through the entryway and out into the tunnel. Fuchs jumped down from the bar, grabbed Amanda by the hand, and raced along behind the others.

Each section of the underground settlement was connected to the others by the tunnels. Airtight hatches stood in the tunnels every hundred meters or so, programmed to seal themselves shut in case of a drop in air pressure or other deviation from normal conditions. By the time Fuchs reached the entrance to his warehouse, still grasping Amanda's hand, the hatch that sealed off the cave had long been shut tight. He pushed through the crowd from the Pub, coughing violently at the dust they had raised, and touched the hatch's metal surface. It felt hot.

"The warehouse cameras are out," said one of the technicians. "Must be a pretty intense fire."

Fuchs nodded, scowling. "Nothing to do but wait until it consumes all the air in there and kills itself off."

"Was anyone inside?" Amanda asked.

"I don't believe so," Fuchs said. "Not any of our people; they were all at the meeting."

"So we wait," said the technician. He fumbled in his coverall pocket, then pulled out a breathing mask and slipped it on.

Several people in the crowd murmured condolences. Most of the others drifted off, buzzing with low-voiced conversations. Here and there someone coughed or spluttered from the dust.

"He did this," Fuchs muttered.

"Who?" asked Amanda.

"Humphries. One of his people."

"No! What would he—"

"To convince us to leave Ceres. The money offer he made was a ruse. We haven't told him of our decision to accept it, so now he uses force."

"Lars, I can't believe that he'd do that."

"I can."

Amanda looked at the few people remaining in the tunnel and said to her husband, "There's nothing we can do here. We should go home; we can come back later, when the fire's burned itself out."

"No," Fuchs said. "I'll wait here."

"But you don't have a breathing mask and—"

"You go. I'll wait here."

Amanda tried to smile, failed. "I'll wait with you."

"There's no need . . ."

"I'd rather be with you," Amanda said, taking his big-knuckled hand in both of hers.

Standing there with nothing to do except wait, coughing in the gritty dust, Fuchs felt a seething anger rising within him, a burning hatred for the man who could order such a thing and his henchmen who actually did it.

The swine, he said to himself. The filthy, sneaking, murderous swine. A fire! In a sealed community like this. If the safety hatches didn't work they could have killed us all! The fire could consume all our air and asphyxiate every one of us!

Murderers, he told himself. I'm dealing with men who would commit murder to get what they want. I'm taking Humphries's money and running away from this place like a lackey being paid off by the lord of the manor.

"Lars, what wrong?" Amanda asked.

"Nothing."

She looked truly worried. "But you were trembling. You looked—I've never seen such an expression on your face before."

He tried to control the rage boiling inside him, tried to hide it, keep it bottled up where no one could see it, not even his wife.

"Come on," he said gruffly. "You were right. There's nothing we can do here until we can open the hatch and see how much damage has been done."

When they got back to their apartment, he picked at the dinner Amanda set before him. He could not sleep. The next morning, when he and a pair of technicians went back to the warehouse, the airtight hatch was fused shut. They had to use one of Astro's mining lasers to cut it open and then wait several minutes for the big, gutted chamber to fill with breathable air.

The warehouse was a blackened shambles. The technicians, both of them young men new to Ceres, stared at the wreckage with round eyes.

"Jeez," muttered the one on Fuchs's right as they played their hand lights around the still-hot ruins.

Fuchs couldn't recognize the place. The shelving had collapsed, metal supports melted by the heat of the blaze. Tons of equipment were reduced to molten lumps of slag.

"What could've caused such a hot fire?" wondered the kid on Fuchs's left.

"Not what," Fuchs muttered. "Who."

CHAPTER 12

I t's a good thing that it takes so long for communications to go back and forth, Amanda thought. Otherwise Lars would be screaming at the woman by now.

She had watched her husband, his face grimed from the ashes of the warehouse and his mood even darker, as he placed his call to their insurance carrier to inform them of the fire. Then he had called Diane Verwoerd, at Humphries Space Systems' offices in Selene.

Even though messages moved at the speed of light, it took more than an hour for Ms. Verwoerd to respond. With the distance between them, there could be no real conversation between Ceres and the Moon. Communications were more like video mail that true two-way links.

"Mr. Fuchs," Verwoerd began her message, "I appreciate your calling me to inform us about the fire in your warehouse. I certainly hope that no one was injured."

Fuchs started to reply automatically, and only stopped himself when Verwoerd coolly went on, "We will need to know the extent of the damage before opening our negotiations on acquiring Helvetia Limited. As I understand it, a major part of your company's assets consisted of the inventory in your warehouse. I understand that this inventory was insured, but I'm certain that your insurance won't cover much more than half the value of the damaged property. Please inform me as soon as you can. In the meantime, I will contact your insurance carrier. Thank you." Her image winked out, replaced by the stylized logo of Humphries Space Systems.

Fuchs's face looked like a thundercloud, dark and ominous. He sat at the computer desk of their one-room apartment, staring silently at the wallscreen. Amanda, sitting on the bed, didn't know what she could say to make him feel better.

"We won't be getting ten million," he muttered, turning to her. "Not half that, I imagine."

"It's all right, Lars. Three or four million is enough for us to—"

"To run away with our tails between our legs," he snapped.

Amanda heard herself answer, "What else can we do?"

Fuchs's head drooped defeatedly. "I don't know. I don't know. We're wiped out. The warehouse is completely gutted. Whoever set the fire did a thorough job."

Warily, she asked, "Do you still think it was deliberately set?"

"Of course!" her husband shouted angrily. "He never intended to pay us ten million! That was a lure, a ruse. He's kicking us off Ceres, out of the Belt entirely."

"But why would he make the offer . . . ?" Amanda felt confused.

Almost sneering with contempt, Fuchs said, "To put us in the proper frame of mind. To get us accustomed to the idea of leaving the Belt. Now he's waiting for us to come crawling to him and beg for as much of the ten million as he's willing to give us."

"We won't do that," Amanda said. "We won't crawl and we won't beg."

"No," he agreed. "But we will leave. We have no choice."

"We still have the ship."

His heavy brows rose. "*Starpower*? You'd be willing to go prospecting again?"

Amanda knew that she really didn't want to take up the life of a rock rat again. But she nodded solemnly, "Yes. Why not?"

Fuchs stared at her, a tangle of emotions burning in his deep-set eyes.

Niles Ripley was dead tired as he shuffled slowly across the desolate dark ground, heading for the airlock. A four-hour shift of working on the habitat was like a week of hard labor anywhere else, he felt. And riding the shuttlecraft back down to the surface of Ceres was always nerve-racking; the ground controller ran the little hopper remotely from underground, but Ripley twitched nervously without a human pilot aboard. The shuttle had touched down without mishap, though, landing a few meters from a Humphries craft being loaded for a supply run to one of the miners' ships hanging in orbit.

It'll be good to get to the Pub and sip a brew or two, Ripley said to himself. By god, I'll even spring for the imported stuff tonight.

The construction work was going well. Slower than Fuchs had expected, but Ripley was satisfied with the progress that the crew was making. Looking up through his fishbowl helmet, he could see the habitat glinting in the sunlight as it spun slowly, like a big pinwheel.

Okay, he thought, so maybe it does look like a clunky kludge. Bunch of spacecraft tacked together in a circle, no two of 'em exactly the same. But by god the kludge was pretty near finished; soon people could go up and live in that habitat and feel just about the same gravity as on the Moon.

Got to get the radiation shielding working first, he reminded himself. Sixteen different sets of superconducting magnets and more to come. Getting them to work together is gonna be a bitch and a half.

The work was so damned tedious. Flatlanders back on Earth thought that working in microgee was fun. And easy. You just float around like a kid in a swimming pool. Yeah. Right. The reality was that you had to consciously plan every move you made; inside the spacesuit you had to exert real strength just to hold your arms out straight or take a few steps. Sure, you could hop around like a jackrabbit on steroids if you wanted to. Hell, I could jump right off Ceres and go sailing around like Superman if I had a mind to—and I if didn't worry about breaking every bone in my legs when I landed. Working in microgee is *tough*, especially in these damned suits.

Well, I'm finished for today, he said to himself as he watched the habitat slowly disappear beyond the sharp, rugged horizon. Ceres is so small, he thought. Just a glorified hunk of rock hanging in the middle of nothing. Ripley shook his head inside his bubble helmet, amazed all over again that he was working 'way out here, in this no-place of a place. He started back toward the airlock again, kicking up lingering clouds of gritty dust with each careful, sliding step. Looking down awkwardly from inside the helmet, he saw that the suit was grimy with dark gray dust all the way up the leggings, as usual. The arms and gloves were crummed up, too. It'll take a good half-hour to vacuum all this crud off the suit, he told himself.

The airlock was set into a dome of local stone, its thick metal hatch the only sign of human presence on Ceres's surface, outside of the two spindly-looking shuttlecraft sitting out there. Ripley was almost at the hatch when it swung open and three spacesuited figures stepped out slowly, warily, as if testing each step they made in this insubstantial gravity. Each of their spacesuits showed a HSS logo on the left breast, just above their name tags. Ripley wondered if they might be the guys Big George had shellacked in the Pub. They had all been Humphries employees, he recalled.

They were carrying bulky packing crates, probably filled with equipment. In Ceres's low gravity, a man could carry loads that required a small truck elsewhere. All of them had tools of various sorts clipped to belts around their waists.

"Where you goin', guys?" Ripley asked good-naturedly over the common suit-to-suit radio frequency.

"Loading up the shuttle," came the answer in his earphones.

"Same old thing every day," another of them complained. "More crap for the mining ships up in orbit."

They got close enough to read Ripley's name stenciled on the hard shell of his suit. Ripley realized that they were so new to Ceres they hadn't gotten their own individual suits yet. They had apparently picked the suits they were wearing from HSS's storage; their names were lettered on adhesive strips pasted onto the torsos.

"Buchanan, Santorini, and Giap," Ripley read aloud. "Hi. I'm Niles Ripley."

"We know who you are," Buchanan said sourly.

"The horn player," said Santorini.

Ripley put on his peacemaking smile, even though he figured they couldn't see it in the dim lighting.

"Hey, I'm sorry about that brawl couple nights ago," he said placatingly. "My friend got carried away, I guess."

All three of them put their crates down on the pebbled, dusty ground. Buchanan said, "I hear they call you the Ripper."

"Sometimes," Ripley said guardedly.

"Where's your trumpet?"

With a little laugh, Ripley said, "Back in my quarters. I don't carry it with me everywhere I go."

"Too bad. I'd really like to jam it up your ass."

Ripley kept smiling. "Aw, come on now. There's no reason to—"

"That big ape of yours put Carl in the infirmary with three crushed vertebrae!"

"Hey, I didn't start the fight. And I'm not looking for one now." Ripley started to walk past them, toward the still-open airlock hatch.

They stopped him. They grabbed his arms. For a ridiculous instant Ripley almost felt like giggling. You can't fight in spacesuits, for chrissakes! It's like boxers wearing suits of armor.

"Hey, come on, now," Ripley said, trying to pull his arms free.

Buchanan kicked his feet out from under him and Ripley fell over backward, slowly, softly, in the dreamy slow motion of microgee. It seemed to take ten minutes as he toppled over; numberless hordes of stars slid past his field of view, silently, solemnly. Then at last he hit the ground, his head banging painfully inside the helmet, a thick cloud of dust enveloping him.

"Okay, Ripper," Buchanan said. "Rip this!"

He kicked Ripley in the side of his spacesuit. The others laughed and started kicking, too. Ripley bounced around inside the suit, unable to get up, unable to defend himself. It didn't hurt that much, at first, but each kick got worse and he worried that they might tear his air line loose. He tasted blood in his mouth.

When they finally stopped kicking him, every part of Ripley's body throbbed with pain. They were still standing over him. Buchanan stared down at him for a long, silent moment. Then he unhooked a tool from the belt at his waist.

"You know what this is?" he asked, holding it up in his gloved hand. It was a short, squat, smooth greenish rod with a helical glass flashlamp coiled around its length and a pistol grip beneath. A heavy black cord ran from the heel of the grip to a battery pack clipped to Buchanan's belt.

Before Ripley could say anything Buchanan explained.

"This is a Mark IV gigawatt-pulse neodymium laser. Puts out picosecond pulses. We use it to punch neat little holes in metal. What kind of a hole do you think it'll punch through you?"

"Hey, Trace," said Santorini. "Take it easy."

Ripley tried to move, to crawl away. His legs wouldn't carry him. He could see the laser's guide beam walking up the front of his spacesuit, *feel* it come through his transparent helmet, inch over his face, past his eyes, onto his forehead.

"Trace, don't!"

But Buchanan slowly lowered himself to one knee and bent over Ripley, peering into his eyes. This close, their helmets almost touching, Ripley could see a sort of wild glee in the man's eyes, a manic joy. He moved one arm, tried to push his tormentor away; all he accomplished was to pull the name tag off Buchanan's suit.

"They didn't say to kill him," Santorini insisted.

Buchanan laughed. "So long, noisemaker," he said.

Ripley died instantly. The picosecond laser pulse pulped most of his brain into jelly.

CHAPTER 13

Lars Fuchs was sitting at his desk talking to the prospector to whom he'd leased *Starpower*. The woman flatly refused to give up the ship until the term of her lease expired, four months in the future.

"I've been snookered out of two good rocks by HSS people," she said, her anger showing clearly in her image on Fuchs's wallscreen. "I'm going out to the far side of the Belt and get me a good-sized metallic 'roid. Anybody comes near me, I'll zap 'em with the cutting laser!"

Fuchs stared at her face. She couldn't be much more than thirty, a former graduate student like himself. Yet she looked far harder, more determined, than any graduate student he remembered. Not a trace of makeup; her hair shaved down to a dark fuzz; her cheek bones and jawline gaunt, hungry.

"I can arrange for you to transfer to another ship that's available for lease," Fuchs said reasonably.

The prospector shook her head. "No deal. I'm working my way around the far side. By this time tomorrow it'll take half an hour for messages to catch up with me. Sayonara, Lars."

The screen went blank. Fuchs leaned back in his creaking desk chair, his thoughts churning slowly. There is no way I can force her to bring *Starpower* back. She's on her way out and she won't be back for at least four months. When she returns she'll either have claim to a rich metallic asteroid or she'll be so dead broke she won't even be able to pay me the final installment on the lease.

No matter which way he looked at it, he could find no answer to his problem. If we're going back to Earth it will have to be as passengers on someone else's ship.

Amanda came through the door from the tunnel at the same moment that the phone chimed. Fuchs automatically said, "Answer," to the phone, but then he saw the awful expression on his wife's face.

"What is it?" he asked, rising from his chair. "What's wrong?"

"Ripley," she said in a voice that sounded frightened. "They found him by the airlock, outside. He's dead."

"Dead?" Fuchs felt shocked. "How? What happened?"

"That's what I want to talk to you about," said Kris Cardenas, from the wallscreen.

Fuchs and Amanda both turned to her image.

Cardenas looked grim. "They brought Ripley's body to me, here in the infirmary."

"What happened to him?" Fuchs asked again.

Cardenas shook her head warily. "Nothing wrong with his suit. He didn't die of asphyxiation or decompression. The suit's scuffed up a lot, but there was no system failure."

"Then what?" Amanda asked.

She frowned with uncertainty. "I'm going to do a multi-spectral scan and try to find out. The reason I called you was to find out if he has any next-of-kin here on Ceres."

"No, no one closer than New Jersey, in the United States," said Fuchs. "I'll transfer his personnel file to you."

"He was working on the habitat?" Cardenas asked, even though she knew the answer.

"Yes," said Fuchs absently. "Now the project will have to stop until we find someone to replace him."

Amanda said, "We're coming to the infirmary, Kris. We'll be there in five minutes."

Cardenas said, "Hang on. Give me an hour or so to do this scan. I'll know more about it by then."

Amanda and Fuchs both nodded their agreement.

Despite her youthful appearance, Kris Cardenas looked grave, almost angry as she ushered Amanda and Fuchs into her tiny infirmary. It was the only medical facility on Ceres, the only medical facility between the Belt and the exploration bases on Mars. Cardenas could handle accident cases, if they weren't too severe, and the usual run of infections and strains. Anything worse was sent to Selene, while Cardenas herself remained among the rock rats.

She was twice an exile. Because her body was teeming with nanoma-chines, no government on Earth would allow her to land on its territory. This had cost her her husband and children; like most of Earth's inhabi-tants, they were terrified by the threat of runaway nanotechnology caus-ing pandemic plagues or devouring cities like unstoppable army ants chewing everything into a gray goo.

Her anger at Earth and its unreasoning fears led her to cause Dan Randolph's death. It was inadvertent, true enough, but Selene banned her from her own nanotech laboratory as a punishment for her actions and a precaution against future use of nanomachines for personal motives. So she left Selene, exiled herself among the rock rats, used her knowledge of human physiology to establish the infirmary on Ceres.

"Have you found what killed Ripley?" Amanda asked her as she and Fuchs took the chairs in front of Cardenas's desk.

"I wouldn't have caught it, normally," Cardenas said tightly. "I'm not a pathologist. It damned near slipped right past me."

The office was small, crowded with the three of them in it. Cardenas tapped a keypad on her desktop and the wall opposite the doorway turned into a false-color display of Niles Ripley's body.

"There was nothing obviously wrong," she began. "No visible trauma, although there were a few small bruises on his chest and back."

"What caused them?" Fuchs asked.

"Maybe when he fell down, inside his suit."

Fuchs scowled at her. "I've fallen down in a spacesuit. That doesn't cause bruising."

Cardenas nodded. "I know. I thought maybe he died of a cardiac infarction, a heart attack. That's when I went for the scan," she explained. "But the coronary arteries look clean and there's no visible damage to the heart itself."

Fuchs squinted at the image. A human body, he thought. One instant it's alive, the next it's dead. What happened to you, Ripley?

Amanda echoed his thoughts. "So what happened to him?"

Cardenas's expression grew even tighter. "The next thing I looked for was a stroke. That's still the number one killer, even back on Earth."

"And?"

"Look at his brain."

Fuchs peered at the wallscreen, but he didn't know what was normal in these false-color images and what was not. He could make out the white outline of the skull and, within it, the pinkish mass of the man's brain. Tangles of what he took to be blood vessels wrapped around the brain and into it, like a mass of tiny snakes writhing inside the skull.

"Do you see it?" Cardenas asked, her voice as sharp as a bayonet.

"No, I don't see . . . wait a minute!" Fuchs noticed that while most of the brain was a light pink color, there was an area of deeper hue, almost a burnt orange, that ran straight through the brain mass, from front to back.

"That orange color?" he said, not certain of himself.

"That orange color," Cardenas repeated, hard as ice.

"What is it?" Amanda asked.

"It's what killed him," said Cardenas. "Ruptured neurons and glial cells from the front of his skull to the back. It did as much damage as a bullet would, but it didn't break the skin."

"A micrometeor?" Fuchs blurted, knowing it was stupid even as his mouth said it.

Amanda objected, "But his suit wasn't ruptured."

"Whatever it was," said Cardenas, "it went through the transparent plastic of his helmet, through his skin without damaging it, through the cranial bone, and pulped his brain cells."

"*Mein gott,*" Fuchs muttered.

"I have two more bits of evidence," Cardenas said, sounding more and more like a police investigator.

The wallscreen image changed to show Ripley's dead face. Fuchs felt Amanda shudder beside him and reached out to hold her hand. Ripley's eyes were open, his mouth agape, his milk-chocolate skin somehow paler than Fuchs remembered it. This is the face of death, he said silently. He almost shuddered himself.

Cardenas tapped her keyboard again and the image zoomed in on the area just above the bridge of Ripley's nose.

"See that faint discoloration?" Cardenas asked.

Fuchs saw nothing unusual, but Amanda said, "Yes, just a tiny little circle. It looks . . . almost as if it had been charred a little."

Cardenas nodded grimly. "One more piece of the puzzle." She reached into her desk drawer.

Fuchs saw her pull out a thin strip of tape, not even ten centimeters long.

"This was stuck on Ripley's right glove when he was found," Cardenas said, handing the tape to Fuchs.

He stared at it. Hand-lettered on the tape in indelible ink was BUCHANAN.

Coldly, mercilesslly, Cardenas said, "Buchanan is a mechanic for Humphries Space Systems. He has access to tools such as hand lasers."

"A hand laser?" Fuchs asked. "You think a hand laser killed Ripley?"

Cardenas said, "I got one from the HSS warehouse and tried it on my soysteak dinner. One picosecond blast ruptures the cells pretty much the way Ripley's brain cells were destroyed."

"Do you mean that this man Buchanan deliberately murdered Ripley?" Amanda asked, her voice faint with shock.

"That's exactly what I mean," said Cardenas, as hard and implacable as death itself.

CHAPTER 14

By the time he and Amanda got back to their own quarters, Fuchs was blazing with rage. He went straight to the closet by the minikitchen and started rummaging furiously through it.

"Lars, what are you going to do?"

"Murderers!" Fuchs snarled, pawing through the tools and gadgets stored on the closet shelves. "That's what he's brought here. Hired killers!"

"But what are you going to do?"

He pulled out a cordless screwdriver, hefted it in one hand. "It's not much, but it will have to do. It's heavy enough to make a reasonable club."

Amanda reached for him, but he brushed her away.

"Where are you going?" she asked, breathless with fear.

"To find this man Buchanan."

"Alone? By yourself?"

"Who else is there? How much time do we have before this Buchanan takes off in one of Humphries's ships and leaves Ceres altogether?"

"You can't go after him!" Amanda pleaded. "Let the law handle this!"

Storming to the door, he roared, "The law? What law? We don't even have a village council. There is no law here!"

"Lars, if he's really a hired killer, he'll kill you!"

He stopped at the door, tucked the screwdriver into the waistband of his slacks. "I'm not a complete fool, Amanda. I won't let him kill me, or anyone else."

"But how can you . . ."

He grabbed the door, slid it open, and marched out into the tunnel, leaving her standing there. Billows of dust followed his footsteps.

The Pub was crowded when Fuchs got there. He had to push his way to the bar.

The barkeep recognized him, but barely smiled. "Hello, Lars. Gonna call another town meeting?"

"Do you know a man named Buchanan?" Fuchs asked, without preamble.

The barkeep nodded warily.

"Do you know where I can find him?"

The man's eyes shifted slightly, then came back to lock onto Fuchs's. "What do you want him for?"

"I need to talk to him," said Fuchs, struggling to keep his voice even, calm.

"He's a badass, Lars."

"I'm not here to start a fight," Fuchs said. He even felt it was true.

"Well, that's Buchanan right down there at the end of the bar."

"Thank you."

Fuchs accepted a frosted aluminum goblet of beer, then wormed his way through the crowd until he was next to Buchanan. The man was with two friends, talking to a trio of miniskirted young women, their drinks on the bar in front of them. Buchanan was tall, with wide sloping shoulders, and young enough to have a flat midsection. His blond hair was cut short, except for a tiny imitation matador's twist at the back of his head. His face was lean, unlined, relaxed.

"You are Mr. Buchanan?" Fuchs asked, putting his aluminum goblet on the bar.

Buchanan turned to him, looked Fuchs over and saw a stocky older rock rat in a shapeless gray velour pullover and wrinkled slacks with the build of a weasel and a sour expression on his broad, heavy-featured face. The guy had a tool of some sort tucked in his waistband.

"I'm Buchanan," he said. "Who the fuck are you?"

Fuchs replied, "I am a friend of the late Niles Ripley."

He said it quietly, flatly, but it was as if he had shouted the words through a power megaphone. Everything in the Pub stopped. Conversation, laughter, even motion seemed to freeze in place.

Buchanan leaned his right elbow on the bar as he faced Fuchs. "Ripley won't be blowing his horn around these parts anymore," he said, grinning. One of the men behind him snickered nervously.

Fuchs said, "Your name tag was found in his dead hand."

"Oh, so that's where it got to. I was wondering where I'd lost it."

"You killed him."

Buchanan reached slowly behind him and pulled a hand laser from the pouch strapped to his waist. He laid it down carefully on the bar, next to his drink. Its power cord trailed back to his belt; its business end pointed at Fuchs.

"If I did kill him, what're you going to do about it?"

Fuchs took a breath. The lava-hot rage he had felt only a few minutes earlier had turned to ice now. He felt cold, glacially calm, but not one nanobit less enraged than he had been before.

He replied softly, "I thought you and I could go back to Selene and let the authorities there investigate the murder."

Buchanan's jaw dropped open. He gawked at Fuchs, standing like a stubborn little bull in front of him. Then he lifted his head and brayed with laughter. His two friends laughed, also.

No one else did.

Fuchs slapped Buchanan's laughing face, hard. Shocked, Buchanan touched his bleeding lip, then reached for the laser on the bar. Fuchs was prepared for that. He clamped Buchanan's hand to the bar with a viselike grip and pulled the screwdriver from his waistband with his right hand.

The laser cracked once. Fuchs's aluminum goblet went spinning, leaking beer through a tiny hole, while Fuchs thumbed the screwdriver on and jammed it into Buchanan's chest. Blood geysered and Buchanan looked terribly surprised, then slumped to the floor, gurgling briefly before he went silent forever.

Splashed with Buchanan's blood, still holding the buzzing screwdriver in his right hand, Fuchs picked up the hand laser. Buchanan's fall had wrenched the power cord out of the base of its grip.

He glanced down at the dead body, then looked at Buchanan's two friends. Their eyes were wide, their mouths agape. Unconsciously, they both backed away from Fuchs.

Without another word, Fuchs turned around and strode out of the silent Pub.

THREE WEEKS LATER

CHAPTER 15

They held a trial of sorts. Under Fuchs's own prodding, the people of Ceres picked a judge by sorting through the computerized personnel files and coming up with a woman who worked for Humphries Space Systems as a contracts lawyer. A jury was selected by lot; no one picked was allowed to refuse the duty. For the defense, Fuchs represented himself. No less than the owner and barkeep of the Pub volunteered to prosecute the case.

The trial, held in the Pub itself, took all of forty-five minutes. Practically everyone in Ceres jammed into the rock-walled chamber. Chairs and two tables had been moved up to the bar to accommodate the accused and the counselors. The judge sat on a high laboratory stool behind the bar. Everyone else stood.

Six different witnesses told substantially the same story: Fuchs had asked Buchanan to go to Selene with him for a formal investigation of Ripley's murder. Buchanan reached for the laser. Fuchs stabbed him with the power tool. Even Buchanan's two companions admitted that that was the way it had happened.

Fuchs's punctured beer goblet was presented as evidence that Buchanan had indeed fired his laser with intent to kill.

The only question arose when the prosecutor asked Fuchs why he had come into the Pub armed with the tool that eventually killed Buchanan.

Fuchs admitted openly, "I knew that he was a dangerous man. I knew that he had murdered Niles Ripley—"

The judge, sitting on a high stool behind the bar, snapped, "That's inadmissible. This trial is about you, Mr. Fuchs, not about Ripley's death."

With only the slightest of frowns, Fuchs said, "I was afraid he would be dangerous. I had been told that he had come to the Pub before and started a fight. And that he had several friends with him."

"So you armed yourself with a lethal weapon?" asked the prosecutor.

"I thought it might be useful as a club, if it came to a fight. I had no intention of using it to stab him."

"Yet that's exactly what you did."

"Yes. When he tried to shoot me I suppose I reacted without thinking of the consequences. I defended myself."

"Very thoroughly," the judge grumbled.

The verdict was never in doubt. Fuchs was acquitted, the killing called justifiable self-defense. Then the prosecutor displaced the judge behind the bar and proclaimed that there would be a round of drinks on the house for everybody.

Amanda was delighted with the outcome, but Fuchs was morose for the next several days.

"This isn't the end of it," he told her one night as they lay in bed together.

"Lars darling," said Amanda, "you mustn't let this get you down so. You acted in self-defense."

"I really would have gone with him to Selene," Fuchs said. "But I knew he would never do that. Never."

"It's not your fault that you had to kill him. It was self-defense. Everyone knows that. You mustn't feel bad about it."

"But I don't!" He turned to face her. In the darkened room, lit only by the glow of the digital clock numerals in one corner of the wallscreen, he could barely make out the puzzled expression on her lovely face.

"I don't feel bad about killing that vermin," Fuchs said, in a low, firm voice. "I knew I would have to. I knew he would never listen to reason."

Amanda looked surprised, almost fearful. "But Lars—"

"No one would do a thing about it. I knew I was the only one who would bring him to justice."

"You knew? All along you knew?"

"I *wanted* to kill him," Fuchs said, his voice almost trembling with fervor. "He deserved to die. I wanted to kill the arrogant fool."

"Lars . . . I've never seen you this way."

"What's worrying me," he said, "is Humphries's reaction to all this. The negotiations for buying out Helvetia are obviously finished. Buchanan was part of his attempt to force us out of the Belt. What is he going to try next?"

Amanda was silent for a long while. Fuchs watched her adorable face, so troubled, so filled with care for him. He almost smiled. The face that launched a thousand spaceships, he thought. Well, at least several hundred.

Yet she was thinking that her husband had turned into an avenging fury. Perhaps only for an hour or so, but Lars had gone out to the Pub deliberately to kill a man. And it didn't worry him, didn't frighten him at all.

It terrified her.

What can I do? Amanda asked herself. How can I stop him from becoming a brute? He doesn't deserve this; it isn't fair to force him to become a monster. She racked her brain, but she could see only one way back to sanity.

At last she said, "Lars, why don't you speak directly to Martin?"

He grunted with surprise. "Directly? To him?"

"Face-to-face."

"Over this distance that's not possible, really."

"Then we'll go to Selene."

His expression hardened. "I don't want you that near to him."

"Martin won't hurt me," she said. Tracing a hand across his broad chest, she went on, "And you're the man I love. You have nothing to fear from Martin or any other man in the universe, on that score."

"I don't want you at Selene," he whispered firmly.

"We can't go to Earth unless we go through weeks and weeks of reconditioning."

"The centrifuge," he muttered.

Amanda said, "I'll stay here, Lars, if that's what you want. You go to Selene and talk this out with Martin."

"No," he said immediately. "I won't leave you here."

"But . . . ?"

"You come to Selene with me. I'll talk to Humphries, assuming he'll agree to talk to me."

Amanda smiled and kissed his cheek. "We can put an end to this before it becomes an out-and-out war."

Pulling her to him, Fuchs said gently, "I hope so. I truly hope so."

She sighed. That's more like it, she thought. That's more like the man I love.

But he was thinking, It's Amanda that Humphries wants, nothing less. And the only way he'll get Amanda is over my dead body.

"She's coming here?" Martin Humphries asked, hardly daring to believe what his aide had just told him. "Here, to Selene?"

Diane Verwoerd allowed a tiny frown of displeasure to crease her forehead. "With her husband," she said.

Humphries got up from his high-backed chair and practically pranced around his desk. Despite his aide's sour look he felt like a little kid anticipating Christmas.

"But she's coming to Selene," he insisted. "Amanda is coming to Selene."

"Fuchs wants to talk to you face-to-face," Verwoerd said, folding her arms across her chest. "I doubt that he'll let his wife get within a kilometer of you."

"That's what *he* thinks," Humphries countered. He turned to the electronic window on the wall behind his desk and tapped at his wristwatch several times. The stereo image on the wide screen flicked through several changes. Humphries stopped it at an Alpine scene of a quaint village with steeply-pitched roofs and a slim church steeple against a background of snow-covered peaks.

That's ancient history, Verwoerd thought. There hasn't been that much snow in the Alps since the great avalanches.

Turning back to her, Humphries said, "Fuchs is coming here to surrender. He'll try to wheedle as much of the ten million we offered him as he can get. But he's bringing Amanda because he knows—maybe in his unconscious mind, maybe not consciously—but he knows that what I really want is Amanda."

"I think we should look at this a little more realistically," Verwoerd said, stepping slowly toward the desk.

Humphries eyed her for a moment. "You think I'm being unrealistic?"

"I think that Fuchs is coming here to negotiate your buyout of his company. I very much doubt that his wife will be part of the deal."

He laughed. "Maybe you don't think so. Maybe he doesn't think so. But I do. That's what's important. And I bet that Amanda does, too."

Verwoerd had to deliberately keep herself from shaking her head in disagreement. He's insane about this woman. Absolutely gonzo over her. Then she smiled inwardly. How can I use this? How can I turn his craziness to my advantage?

DOSSIER:
OSCAR JIMINEZ

When he finished the New Morality high school, at the age of seventeen, Oscar was sent to far-off Bangladesh for his two years of public service. It was compulsory; the New Morality demanded two years of service as partial repayment for the investment they had made in a youth's education and social reformation.

Oscar worked hard in what was left of Bangladesh. The rising sea levels and the terrifying storms that accompanied each summer's monsoon inundated the low-lying lands. Thousands were swept away in the floods of the Ganges. Oscar saw that many of the poor, miserable wretches actually prayed to the river itself for mercy. In vain. The swollen river drowned the heathens without pity. Oscar realized that just as many of the faithful were drowned, also.

Luck touched him again, once he finished his two years of public service. The New Morality administrator in Dacca, an American from Kansas, urged Oscar to consider accepting a job in space, far away from Earth.

Oscar knew better than to argue with authority, but he was so surprised at the idea that he blurted, "But I'm not an astronaut."

The administrator smiled a kindly smile. "There are all kinds of jobs up there that need to be filled. You are fully qualified for many of them."

"I am?" Oscar's qualifications, as far as he knew, were mainly lifting and toting, handling simple invoices, and following orders.

With a nod, the administrator said, "Yes. And, of course, there is God's work to be done out there among the godless humanists and frontier ruffians."

Who could refuse to do God's work? Thus Oscar Jiminez went to Ceres and was hired by Helvetia, Ltd., to work in their warehouse.

CHAPTER 16

Selene's Hotel Luna had gone through several changes of management since it was originally built by the Yamagata Corporation.

In those early days, just after the lunar community had won its short, sharp war against the old United Nations and affirmed its independence, tourism looked like a good way to bring money into the newly-proclaimed Selene. Masterson Aerospace's lunar-built Clipperships were bringing the price of transportation from Earth down to the point where the moderately well-heeled tourist—the type who took "adventure vacations" to Antarctica, the Amazonian rain forest, or other uncomfortable exotic locales—could afford the grandest adventure vacation of them all: a trip to the Moon.

Sadly, the opening of the hotel coincided almost exactly with the first ominous portents of the greenhouse cliff. After nearly half a century of scientific debate and political wrangling, the accumulated greenhouse gases in Earth's atmosphere and oceans started an abrupt transition in the global climate. Disastrous floods inundated most coastal cities in swift succession. Earthquakes devastated Japan and the American midwest. Glaciers and ice packs began melting down, raising sea levels worldwide. The delicate web of electrical power transmission grids collapsed over much of the world, throwing hundreds of millions into the cold and darkness of pre-industrial society. More than a billion people lost their homes, their way of living, everything that they had worked for. Hundreds of millions died.

Tourism trickled down to nothing except the extremely wealthy, who lived on their financial mountaintops in ease and comfort despite the woes of their brethren.

Hotel Luna became virtually a ghost facility, but it was never shut down. Grimly, hopefully, foolishly, one owner after another tried to make at least a modest success of it.

To a discerning visitor, the lavish, sprawling lobby of the hotel would appear slightly seedy: the carpeting was noticeably threadbare in spots, the oriental tables and easy chairs were scuffed here and there, the ornate artificial floral displays drooped enough to show that they needed to be replaced.

But to Lars Fuchs's staring eyes, Hotel Luna's lobby seemed incredibly posh and polished. He and Amanda were riding down the powered stairway from the hotel entrance up in the Grand Plaza. Glistening sheets of real, actual water slid down tilted slabs of granite quarried from the lunar highlands. The water was recycled, of course, but to have a display of water! What elegance!

"Look," Fuchs exclaimed, pointing to the pools into which the waterfalls splashed. "Fish! Live fish!"

Beside him, Amanda smiled and nodded. She had been brought to the hotel on dates several times, years ago. She remembered the Earthview Restaurant, with its hologram windows. Martin Humphries had taken her there. The fish in those pools were on the restaurant's menu. Amanda noticed that there were far fewer of them now than there had been back then.

As they reached the lobby level and stepped off the escalator, Fuchs recognized the music wafting softly from the ceiling speakers: a Haydn quartet. Charming. Yet he felt distinctly out of place in his plain dark gray coveralls, like a scruffy student sneaking into a grand palace. But with Amanda on his arm, it didn't matter. She wore a sleeveless white pantsuit; even zippered up to the throat it could not hide her exquisitely-curved body.

Fuchs didn't pay any attention to the fact that the spacious lobby was practically empty. It was quiet, soothing, an elegant change from the constant buzz of air fans and faint clatter of distant pumps that was part of the everyday background of Ceres.

As they reached the registration desk, Fuchs remembered all over again that Martin Humphries was footing their hotel bill. Humphries had insisted on it. Fuchs wanted to argue about it as they rode a Humphries fusion ship from Ceres to Selene, but Amanda talked him out of it.

"Let him pay for the hotel, Lars," she had advised, with a knowing smile. "I'm sure he'll take it out of the price he pays you for Helvetia."

Grudgingly, Fuchs let her talk him into accepting Humphries's generosity. Now, at the hotel desk, it rankled him all over again.

When it had originally opened as the Yamagata Hotel, there had been uniformed bellmen and women to tote luggage and bring room service orders. Those days were long gone. The registration clerk seemed alone behind his counter of polished black basalt, but he tapped a keyboard and a self-propelled trolley hummed out of its hidden niche and rolled up to Fuchs and Amanda. They put their two travel bags onto it and the trolley obediently followed them into the elevator that led down to the level of their suite.

Fuchs's eyes went even wider once they entered the suite.

"Luxury," he said, a reluctant smile brightening his normally dour face. "This is real luxury."

Even Amanda seemed impressed. "I've never been in one of the hotel's rooms before."

Suddenly Fuchs's smile dissolved into a suspicious scowl. "He might have the rooms bugged, you know."

"Who? Martin?"

Fuchs nodded gravely, as if afraid to speak.

"Why would he bug the rooms?"

"To learn what we plan to say to him, what our position will be in the negotiation, what our bottom figure will be." There was more, but he hesitated to tell her. Pancho had hinted that Humphries videotaped his own sexual encounters in the bedroom of his palatial home. Would the man have cameras hidden in *this* bedroom?

Abruptly, he strode to the phone console sitting on an end table and called for the registration desk.

"Sir?" asked the clerk's image on the wallscreen. A moment earlier it had been a Vickrey painting of nuns and butterflies.

"This suite is unacceptable," Fuchs said, while Amanda stared at him. "Is there another one available?"

The clerk grinned lazily. "Why, yessir, we have several suites unoccupied at the moment. You may have your pick."

Fuchs nodded. Humphries can't have them all bugged, he thought.

"I'm glad you decided to meet me in person," Martin Humphries said, smiling from behind his wide desk. "I think we can settle our business much more comfortably this way."

He leaned back, tilting the desk chair so far that Fuchs thought the man was going to plant his feet on the desktop. Humphries seemed completely at ease in his own office in the mansion he had built for himself deep below the lunar surface. Fuchs sat tensely in the plush armchair in front of the desk, feeling uneasy, wary, stiffly uncomfortable in the gray business suit that Amanda had bought for him at an outrageous price in the hotel's posh store. He had left Amanda in the hotel; he did not want her in the same room as Humphries. She had acquiesced to his demand, and told her husband that she would go shopping in the Grand Plaza while he had his meeting.

Humphries waited for Fuchs to say something. When he just sat there in silence, Humphries said, "I trust you had a good night's sleep."

Suddenly Fuchs thought of hidden cameras again. He cleared his throat and said, "Yes, thank you."

"The hotel is comfortable? Everything all right?"

"The hotel is fine."

The third person in the room was Diane Verwoerd, sitting in the other chair in front of the desk. She had angled it so that she faced Fuchs more than Humphries. Like her boss, she wore a business suit. But while Humphries's dark burgundy suit was threaded with intricate filigrees of silver thread, Verwoerd's pale ivory outfit was of more ordinary material. Its slit skirt, however, revealed a good deal of her long slim legs.

Silence stretched again. Fuchs looked at the holowindow behind Humphries's desk. It showed the lush garden outside the house, bright flowers and graceful trees. Beautiful, he thought, but artificial. Contrived. An ostentatious display of wealth and the power to flaunt one man's will. How many starving, homeless people on Earth could Humphries help if he wanted to, instead of creating this make-believe Eden for himself here on the Moon?

At last Verwoerd said crisply, all business, "We're here to negotiate the final terms of your sale of Helvetia Limited to Humphries Space Systems."

"No, we are not," said Fuchs.

Humphries sat up straighter in his chair. "We're not?"

"Not yet," Fuchs said to him. "First we must deal with several murders."

Humphries glanced at Verwoerd; for just that instant he seemed furious. But he regained his composure almost immediately.

"And just what do you mean by that?" she asked calmly.

Fuchs said, "At least three prospectors' ships have disappeared over the past few weeks. Humphries Space Systems somehow acquired the claims to the asteroids that those prospectors were near to."

"Mr. Fuchs," said Verwoerd, with a deprecating little smile, "you're turning a coincidence into a conspiracy. Humphries Space Systems has dozens of ships scouting through the Belt."

"Yes, and it's damned expensive, too," Humphries added.

"Then there is the out-and-out murder of Niles Ripley on Ceres by a Humphries employee," Fuchs went on doggedly.

Humphries snapped, "From what I hear, you took care of that yourself. Vigilante justice, wasn't it?"

"I stood trial. It was declared justifiable self-defense."

"Trial," Humphries sniffed. "By your fellow rock rats."

"Your employee murdered Niles Ripley!"

"Not by my orders," Humphries replied, with some heat. "Just because some hothead on my payroll gets himself into a brawl, that's not my doing."

"But it was to your benefit," Fuchs snapped.

Coolly, Verwoerd asked, "How do you come to that conclusion, Mr. Fuchs?"

"Ripley was the key man in our habitat construction program. With him gone, the work is stopped."

"So?"

"So once you acquire Helvetia, the only organization capable of finishing the project will be HSS."

"And how does that benefit me?" Humphries demanded. "Finishing your silly-assed habitat doesn't put one penny into my pocket."

"Not directly, perhaps," said Fuchs. "But making Ceres safer and more livable will bring more people out to the Belt. With your company in control of their supplies, their food, the air they breathe, even, how can you fail to profit?"

"You're accusing me—"

Verwoerd interrupted the budding argument. "Gentlemen, we're here to negotiate the sale of Helvetia, not to discuss the future of the Asteroid Belt."

Humphries glared at her again, but took in a breath and said grudgingly, "Right."

Before Fuchs could say anything, Verwoerd added, "What's done is done, and there's no way of changing the past. If an HSS employee committed murder, you made him pay the full price for it."

Fuchs searched for something to say.

"Now we should get down to business," said Verwoerd, "and settle on a price for Helvetia."

Humphries immediately jumped in with, "My original offer was based on your total assets, which have gone down almost to nothing since the fire in your warehouse."

"Which was deliberately set," Fuchs said.

"Deliberately set?"

"It was no accident. It was arson."

"You have proof of that?"

"We have no forensics experts on Ceres. No criminal investigators."

"So you have no proof."

"Mr. Fuchs," Verwoerd said, "we are prepared to offer you three million international dollars for the remaining assets of Helvetia Limited, which—frankly—amounts to the good will you've generated among the miners and prospectors, and not much more."

Fuchs stared at her for a long, silent moment. So sure of herself, he thought. So cool and unruffled and, yes, even beautiful, in a cold, distant way. She's like a sculpture made of ice.

"Well?" Humphries asked. "Frankly, three million is pretty much of a gift. Your company's not worth half that much, in real terms."

"Three hundred million," Fuchs murmured.

"What? What did you say?"

"You could make your offer three hundred million. Or three billion. It doesn't matter. I'm not going to sell to you."

"That's stupid!" Humphries blurted.

"I won't sell to you at any price. Never! I'm going back to Ceres and starting all over again."

"You're crazy!"

"Am I? Perhaps so. But I would rather be crazy than give in to you."

"You're just going to get yourself killed," Humphries said.

"Is that a threat?"

Again Humphries looked at Verwoerd, then turned back to Fuchs. He smiled thinly. "I don't make threats, Fuchs. I make promises."

Fuchs got to his feet. "Then let me make a promise in return. If you want to fight, I can fight. If you want a war, I'll give you a war. And you won't like the way I fight, I promise you that. I've studied military history; it was required in school. I know how to fight."

Humphries leaned back in his desk chair and laughed.

"Go ahead and laugh," Fuchs said, pointing a stubby finger at him. "But consider: you have a great deal more to lose than I do."

"You're a dead man, Fuchs," Humphries snapped.

Fuchs nodded agreement. "One of us is."

With that, he turned and strode out of Humphries's office.

For several moments, Humphries and Verwoerd sat there staring at the doorway Fuchs had gone through.

"At least he didn't slam the door," Humphries said with a smirk.

"You've made him angry enough to fight," Verwoerd said, with a troubled frown. "You've backed him into a corner and now he feels he has nothing to lose by fighting."

Humphries guffawed. "Him? That little weasel? It's laughable. He knows how to fight! He's studied military history!"

"Maybe he has," she said.

"So what?" Humphries replied testily. "He's from Switzerland, for god's sake! Hardly a martial nation. What's he going to do, smother me in Swiss cheese? Or maybe yodel me to death."

"I wouldn't take it so lightly," said Verwoerd, still looking at the empty doorway.

CHAPTER 17

Piracy?" Hector Wilcox's eyebrows rose almost to his silver-gray hairline.

Erek Zar looked uncomfortable, unhappy, as the two men strolled along the lane through the park just outside the IAA office building. Spring was in the air, the trees were beginning to bud, the local St. Petersburg populace was thronging the park, glad to see the sun. Women were sunbathing on the grass, their long dark coats thrown open to reveal their lumpy, thick bodies clad only in skimpy bikinis. It's enough to make a man take a vow of celibacy, Wilcox thought, eying them distastefully.

Zar was normally a placid, cheerful, good-natured paper shuffler whose most urgent demands were for an extra day off here and there so he could nip off to his family in Poland for a long weekend. But now the man's ruddy, round face was dead serious, flushed with emotion.

"That's what he's charging," Zar said. "Piracy."

Wilcox refused to have his postprandial constitutional destroyed by an underling suddenly gone bonkers.

"Who is this person?"

"His name is Lars Fuchs. Tomasselli brought the matter to me. Fuchs is accusing Humphries Space Systems of piracy, out in the Asteroid Belt."

"But that's ridiculous!"

"I agree," Zar said swiftly. "But Tomasselli's taken it seriously and opened an official file on it."

"Tomasselli," said Wilcox, as if the word smelled bad. "That excitable Italian. He saw a conspiracy when Yamagata made that takeover offer to Astro Corporation."

"The takeover was never consummated," Zar pointed out, "mainly because Tomasselli got the GEC to go on record as opposing it."

"And now he's taking accusations of *piracy* seriously? Against Humphries Space Systems?"

Nodding unhappily, Zar said, "He claims there's some evidence to substantiate the accusation, but as far as I can see it's all circumstantial."

"What on earth does he expect me to do about it?" Wilcox grumbled mildly. He was not the kind of man who lost his self-control. Not ever. You didn't get as far up on the intricate chain of command of the International Astronautical Authority as he had by recklessly blowing off steam.

"It's an open file now," Zar said, apologetically.

"Yes. Well, I suppose I'll have to look it over." Wilcox sighed. "But, really, *piracy*? In the Asteroid Belt? Even if it's true, what can we do about it? We don't even have an administrator on Ceres, for goodness' sake. There isn't an IAA presence anywhere in the Belt."

"We have two flight controllers at Ceres."

"Bah!" Wilcox shook his head. "What do they call themselves out there? Rock rats? They pride themselves on their independence. They resisted the one attempt we made to establish a full-fledged office on Ceres. So now they're crying to us about piracy, are they?"

"It's only one person making the accusation: this man Fuchs."

"A maniac, no doubt," said Wilcox.

"Or a sore loser," Zar agreed.

WALTZING MATILDA

Big George's stomach rumbled in complaint.

He straightened up—no easy task in the spacesuit—and looked around. *Waltzing Matilda* hung in the star-strewn sky over his head like a big dumbbell, its habitat and logistics modules on opposite ends of a kilometer-long buckyball tether, slowly rotating around the propulsion module at the hub.

Been too many hours since you've had a feed, eh? he said to his stomach. Well, it's gonna be a few hours more before we get any tucker, and even then it'll be mighty lean.

The asteroid on which George stood was a dirty little chunk of rock, a dark carbonaceous 'roid, rich in hydrates and organic minerals. Worth a bloody fortune back at Selene. But it didn't look like much: just a bleak lump of dirt, pitted all over like it had the pox, rocks and pebbles and outright boulders scattered across it. Not enough gravity to hold down a feather. Ugly chunk of rock, that's all you are, George said silently to the asteroid. And you're gonna get uglier before we're finished with ya.

Millions of kilometers from anyplace, George realized, alone in this cold and dark except for the Turk sittin' inside *Matilda* monitoring the controls, squattin' on this ugly chunk of rock, sweatin' like a teen on his first date inside this suit and me stomach growlin' 'cause we're low on rations.

And yet he felt happy. Free as a bloomin' bird. He had to make a conscious effort not to sing out loud. That'd startle the Turk, he knew. The kid's not used to any of this.

Shaking his head inside the fishbowl helmet, George returned to his work. He was setting up the cutting laser, connecting its power pack and control module, carefully cleaning its copper mirrors of clinging dust and making certain they were precisely placed in their mounts, no wobbles. It was all hard physical work, even though none of the equipment weighed anything in the asteroid's minuscule gravity. But just raising your arms in the stiff, ungainly suit, bending your body or turning, took a conscious effort of will and more muscular exertion than any flatlander could ever appreciate. Finally George had everything set, the laser's aiming mirrors pointing to the precise spot where he wanted to start cutting, the power pack's superconducting coil charged and ready.

George was going to slice out chunks of the asteroid that *Matilda* could carry back to Selene. The prospector who'd claimed the rock wouldn't make a penny from it until George started shipping the ores, and George was far behind schedule because the wonky laser kept malfunctioning time and again. No ores, no money: that was the way the corporations worked. And no food, George knew. It was a race now to see if he could get a decent shipment of ores off toward Selene before *Matilda*'s food locker went empty.

As he worked, a memory from his childhood school days back in Adelaide returned unbidden to his mind; a poem by some Yank who'd been in on the Yukon gold rush nearly two centuries ago:

> *Were you ever out in the Great Alone, when the moon was awful clear,*
> *And the icy mountains hemmed you in with a silence you most could hear;*
> *With only the howl of a timber wolf, and you camped there in the cold,*
> *A half-dead thing in a stark, dead world, clean mad for the muck called gold;*
> *While high overhead, green, yellow and red, the North Lights swept in bars?—*
> *Then you've a hunch what the music meant . . . hunger and night and the stars.*

George nodded solemnly as he checked out the laser's focus. Hunger and night and the stars, all right. We've got plenty of that. And a stark, dead world, too, aren't you? he said to the impassive asteroid. Come to think of it, you've prob'ly got some gold tucked away inside you, huh? Strange kinda situation when water's worth more'n gold. Price of gold's dropped down to its value as an industrial metal. Jewelers must be going bonkers back Earthside.

"George?" the Turk's voice in his helmet speaker startled him.

"Huh? What'sit?"

The kid's name was Nodon. "Something is moving out at the edge of our radar's resolution range."

"Moving?" George immediately thought that maybe this asteroid had a smaller companion, a moonlet. But at the extreme range of their search radar? Not bloody likely.

"It has a considerable velocity. It is approaching very fast."

That was the longest utterance the kid had made through the whole flight. He sounded worried.

"It can't be on a collision course," George said.

"No, but it is heading our way. Fast."

George tried to shrug inside the spacesuit, failed. "Well, keep an eye on it. Might be another ship."

"I think it is."

"Any message from 'im?"

"No. Nothing."

"All right," said George, puzzled. "Say hullo to him and ask his identification. I'm gonna start workin' the ores here."

"Yes, sir." The kid was very respectful.

Wondering what—or who—was out there, George thumbed the activator switch and the laser began to slash deeply into the asteroid's rocky body. In the airless dark there was no sound; George couldn't even feel a vibration from the big ungainly machine. The dead rock began to sizzle noiselessly along a pencil-slim line. The cutting laser emitted in the infrared, but even the guide beam of the auxiliary laser was invisible until the cutting raised enough dust to reflect its thin red pointing finger.

Be a lot easier if we could get nanomachines to do this, George thought. I've got to twist Kris Cardenas's arm when we get back to Ceres, make her see how much we need her help. Little buggers could separate the different elements in a rock, atom by atom. All we'd hafta do is scoop up the piles and load 'em on the ship.

Instead, George worked like a common laborer, prying up thick, house-sized slabs of asteroidal rock as the laser's hot beam cut them loose, clamping them together with buckyball tethers, and ferrying them to *Matilda*'s bulky propulsion module, which was fitted with attachment points for the cargo. By the time he had carried three such loads, using the jetpack of his suit to move the big slabs, feeling a little like Superman manhandling the massive yet weightless tonnages of ores, he was soaked with perspiration.

"Feels like a bloody swamp in this suit," he complained aloud as he started back toward the asteroid. "Smells like one, too."

"It is a ship," said Nodon.

"You're sure?"

"I can see its image on the display screen."

"Give 'em another hail, then. See who they are." George didn't like the idea of another ship in the vicinity. *It can't be coincidence,* he told himself.

He landed deftly on the asteroid about fifty meters from where the laser was still slicing up the rock. *Why would a ship be heading toward us? Who are they?*

Dorik Harbin sat at the controls of *Shanidar,* his dark bearded face impassive, his darker eyes riveted on the CCD display from the ship's optical sensors. He could see the flashes of laser-heated rock spurting up from the asteroid and the glints of light they cast on the *Waltzing Matilda,* parked in orbit around the asteroid. The information from Grigor had been accurate, as usual. There was the ship, precisely where Grigor had said it would be.

Death was no stranger to Dorik Harbin. Orphaned from birth, he was barely as tall as the assault rifle the village elders gave him when Harbin had dutifully marched with the other preteens to the village down the road, where the evil people lived. They had killed his father before Harbin had been born and raped his pregnant mother repeatedly. The other boys sometimes sniggered that Dorik was conceived by one of the rapists, not the father that the rapists had hacked to death.

He and his ragamuffin battalion had marched down to that evil village and shot everyone there: all of them, men, women, children, babies. Harbin even shot the village dogs in a fury of vengeance. Then, under the pitiless eyes of the hard-faced elders, they had set fire to each and every house in that village. Dousing the bodies with petrol where they lay, they burned the dead, too. Some of them were only wounded, pretending to be dead to escape the vengeance they had reaped, until the flames ignited their clothing.

Harbin still heard their screams in his sleep.

When the blue-helmeted Peacekeeper troops had come into the region to pacify the ethnic fighting, Harbin had run away from his village and joined the national defense force. After many months of living in the hills and hiding from the Peacekeepers' observation planes and satellites, he came to the bitter conclusion that the so-called national defense force was nothing more than a band of renegades, stealing from their own people, looting villages and raping their women.

He ran away again, this time to a refugee camp, where well-clad strangers distributed food while men from nearby villages sold the refugees hashish and heroin. Eventually Harbin joined those blue-helmeted soldiers; they were looking for recruits and offered steady pay for minimal discomfort. They trained him well, but more importantly they fed him and paid him and tried to instill some sense of discipline and honor in him. Time and again his temper tripped him; he was in the brig so often that his sergeant called him "jailbird."

The sergeant tried to tame Harbin's wild ferocity, tried to make a reliable soldier out of him. Harbin took their food and money and tried to understand their strange concepts of when it was proper to kill someone and when it was not. What he learned after a few years of service in the miserable, pathetic, deprived regions of Asia and Africa was that it was the same everywhere: kill or be killed.

He was picked for a hurry-up training course and sent with a handful of other Peacekeeper troops to the Moon, to enforce the law on the renegade colonists of Moonbase. They even allowed the specially-selected troopers dosages of designer drugs which, they claimed, would enhance their adaptation to low gravity. Harbin knew it was nothing more than a bribe, to keep the "volunteers" satisfied.

Trying to fight the tenacious defenders of Moonbase from inside a spacesuit was a revelation to Harbin. The Peacekeepers failed, even though the lunar colonists took great pains to avoid killing any of them. They returned to Earth, not merely defeated but humiliated. His next engagement, in the food riots in Delhi, finished him as a Peacekeeper. He saved his squad from being overrun by screaming hordes of rioters, but killed so many of the "unarmed" civilians that the International Peacekeeping Force cashiered him.

Orphaned again, Harbin took up with mercenary organizations that worked under contract to major multinational corporations. Always eager to better himself, he learned to operate spacecraft. And he quickly saw how fragile spacecraft were. A decent laser shot could disable a vessel in an eyeblink; you could kill its crew from a thousand kilometers away before they realized they were under attack.

Eventually he was summoned to the offices of Humphries Space Systems, the first time he had returned to the Moon since the Peacekeepers had been driven off. Their chief of security was a Russian named Grigor. He told Harbin he had a difficult but extremely rewarding assignment for a man of courage and determination.

Harbin asked only, "Who do I have to kill?"

Grigor told him that he was to drive the independent prospectors and miners out of the Belt. Those working under contract to HSS or Astro were to be left untouched. It was the independents who were to be "discouraged." Harbin grimaced at the word. Men like Grigor and the others back at Selene could use delicate words, but what they meant was anything but refined. Kill the independents. Kill enough of them so that the rest either quit the Belt or signed up with HSS or Astro Corporation.

So this one had to die, like the others.

"This is *Waltzing Matilda*," he heard his comm speaker announce. The face on his display screen was a young male Asian, head shaved, eyes big and nervous. His cheeks seemed to be tattooed. "Please identify yourself."

Harbin chose not to. There was no need. The less he spoke with those he must kill, the less he knew about them, the better. It was a game, he told himself, like the computer games he had played during his training sessions with the Peacekeepers. Destroy the target and win points. In this game he played now, the points were international dollars. Wealth could buy almost anything: a fine home in a safe city, good wines, willing women, drugs that drove away the memories of the past.

"We are working this asteroid," the young man said, his shaky voice a little higher-pitched than before. "The claim has already been registered with the International Astronautical Authority."

Harbin took in a deep breath. The temptation to reply was powerful. It doesn't matter what you have claimed or what you are doing, he answered silently. The moving finger has written your name in the book of death, nor all thy piety nor wit shall lure it back to cancel half a line; nor all thy tears wash out a word of it.

By the time he'd made his eighth ore-ferrying trip, George felt dead tired. And starving.

He turned off the laser and said into his helmet microphone, "I'm comin' in."

The Turk replied only, "Copy that."

"I'm sloshin' inside this suit," George said. "The power pack needs rechargin', too."

"Understood," said Nodon.

George unhooked the power pack and toted it in his arms back to *Matilda*'s airlock. It was twice his size, and even though it weighed virtually nothing he was careful handling it; a mass that big could squash a man no matter what the ambient gravity. The law of inertia had not been repealed.

"What's our visitor doin'?" he asked as he sealed the lock's outer hatch and started pumping air into it.

"Still approaching on the same course."

"Any word from 'im?"

"Nothing."

That worried George. By the time he had wormed his way out of the ripe-smelling suit and plugged the big power pack into the ship's recharging unit, though, his first priority was food.

He half-floated up the passageway to the galley.

"Spin 'er up a bit, Nodon," he hollered to the bridge. "Gimme some weight while I chow down."

"One-sixth g?" the Turk's voice came back down the passageway.

"Good enough."

A comfortable feeling of weight returned as George pulled a meager prepackaged snack from the freezer. Should've loaded more food, he thought. Didn't expect to be out here this long.

Then he heard a scream from the bridge. The air-pressure alarm started hooting and the emergency hatches slammed shut as the ship's lights went out, plunging George into total darkness.

CHAPTER 18

Amanda was aghast. "You refused to sell at any price?"

Fuchs nodded grimly. Some of the blazing fury he had felt during his meeting with Humphries had burned off, but still the smoldering heat of anger burned deep in his guts. Only one thing was certain: he was going to fight. On the way from Humphries's office to their hotel suite Fuchs had made up his mind once and for all. He was going to wipe the smug smile from Humphries's face, no matter what it cost.

Amanda was in the sitting room of their suite when Fuchs barged through the door, angry and impatient. He saw the expectant look on her face and realized she'd been waiting for him all the while; she'd never gone shopping or done anything other than wait for his return.

"I couldn't do it," Fuchs said, so low that he wasn't sure she'd heard him. He cleared his throat, repeated, "I couldn't sell to him. Not at any price."

Amanda sank into one of the small sofas scattered about the room. "Lars . . . what do you expect to do now?"

"I don't know," he told her. That wasn't quite true, but he wasn't sure of how much he could tell her. He sat in the chair next to Amanda and took her hands in his. "I told him I was going back to Ceres and start over."

"Start over? How?"

He tried to smile for her, to hide his true thoughts. "We still have *Starpower*. We can go back to prospecting, I suppose."

"Live aboard the ship again," she murmured.

"I know it's a step backward." He hesitated, then found the courage to say, "You don't have to come with me. You can stay on Ceres. Or . . . or wherever you would prefer to live."

"You'd go without me?" She looked hurt.

Fuchs knew that if he told her his real plans, his true goal, Amanda would be terrified. She would try to talk him out of it. Or worse, once she realized that he was unshakable, she would insist on staying with him every step of the way.

So he temporized. "Amanda, dearest . . . it wouldn't be fair for me to ask you to live that way again. I've made a mess of things, it's up to me to—"

"Lars, he'll kill you!"

She was truly frightened, he saw.

"If you go back to the Belt by yourself," Amanda said urgently, "he'll have someone track you down and murder you."

Fuchs remembered Humphries's words: *You're a dead man, Fuchs.*

"I can take care of myself," he said grimly.

Amanda thought, I've got to go with him. Martin won't strike at Lars if there's a possibility of hurting me.

Aloud, she said to her husband, gently, soothingly, "I know you can take care of yourself, darling, but who's going to take care of me?" And she reached up to stroke his cheek.

"You'd go with me?"

"Of course."

"You *want* to go with me?" He was filled with joyful wonder at the idea.

"I want to be with you, Lars," Amanda said softly, "wherever you go."

To herself, though, she said, It's me that Martin wants. I'm the cause of all this. I'm the reason my husband is in such danger.

And Fuchs was saying to himself, She wants to be away from Humphries. She's afraid of him. She's afraid that if I'm not near enough to protect her, he'll steal her away from me.

And the embers of his anger burst into flaming rage again.

WALTZING MATILDA

The emergency lights came on, dim but better than utter darkness. George groped through the shadows along the narrow passageway from the galley to the closed hatch of the bridge. He tapped the code on the bulkhead keypad and the hatch popped open slightly.

At least there's proper air pressure in the bridge, George thought as he pushed the hatch all the way open. Hatch wouldn't have opened otherwise.

Nodon was sitting in the command pilot's chair, eyes wide with shock or fright, hands racing along the console keyboard. The regular lights came back on, but they seemed weaker than usual.

"What th' fook happened, mate?" George asked, sliding into the copilot's chair.

"I got an electric shock," said Nodon. "A spark jumped from the panel and the lights went out."

George could see the kid was checking out all the ship's systems. The control panel's displays flickered almost too quickly for the eye to register as Nodon raced through one system diagnostic after another.

The kid's good, George thought. I made the right decision when I hired him.

Nodon was a skinny youngster who'd claimed to be twenty-five, but George figured the kid was barely out of his teens. No real experience, outside of working on computers back on Ceres, but he had an intensity, a bright eager desire to succeed, that made George pick him as his crewman for this mining job. George called him "Turk" but Nodon was actually a Mongol, with the decorative spiral tattoos on both his cheeks to prove it. He claimed he'd been born on the Moon, of miners who'd fled

Earth when the Gobi Desert engulfed the grasslands of their ancestral homeland. He was all bone and sinew, skin the color of old parchment, head shaved bald, big expressive deep brown eyes. He'd look damned handsome if it weren't for those bloody scars, George thought. He was trying to grow a moustache; so far it was nothing more than a few wisps that made his upper lip look dirty.

Sitting tensely in the command chair, flicking through diagnostics almost faster than George could follow, Nodon wore only a comfortable sleeveless mesh shirt over a pair of ragged shorts.

"The power generator is off-line," he said. "That's why the lights went out."

"We're on batteries now?" George asked.

"Yes, and—"

The alarms hooted again and George felt his ears pop. The airtight hatch slammed shut once more.

"Jeezus God!" George shouted. "The bugger's shootin' at us!"

Dorik Harbin scowled at his display screens. His first shot should have taken out the ship's habitat module, but they'd increased their spin just a split second before he'd fired. He'd hit *something*, he was certain of that, but it wasn't a fatal hit.

It had taken a few minutes for the big laser to recharge; this had given Harbin enough time to choose his target carefully. He had the full schematics of *Waltzing Matilda* on one of the screens, courtesy of Humphries Space Systems. Their intelligence data was well-nigh perfect. Harbin knew where to find the ships he went after, and what each ship's layout was.

Not much of a challenge to a soldier, he thought. But then, what soldier wants challenges? When you put your life on the line, the easier the job the better. For just the flicker of a moment he thought about the fact that he was shooting at unarmed civilians. Perhaps there was a woman aboard that ship, although the HSS intelligence data didn't indicate that. What of it? he told himself. That's the target and you're being paid to destroy it. It's a lot easier than killing people face to face, the way you had to in Delhi.

That had been a mess, a fiasco. One battalion of mercenary troops trying to protect a food warehouse against a whole city. That idiot commander! Stupid Frenchman. Harbin still saw the maddened faces of the ragged, half-starved Indians, bare hands against automatic rifles and machine guns. Still, they nearly swarmed us down. Only when he was foolish enough to let one of the women get close enough to knife him did his blood-rage surge and save him. He shot her point-blank and led a howling murderous charge that sent the mob running. He stopped firing into their backs only when his automatic rifle finally jammed from overheating.

He pushed the nightmare images out of his mind and concentrated on the job at hand. By the time he was ready to fire again, *Matilda*'s spin had moved the hab module enough so that it was partially shielded by the big slabs of ores the miners had hung on their central propulsion module. But their main comm antenna was in his sights. He squeezed off a shot. The laser's capacitors cracked loudly and he saw a flash of light glance off the rim of the antenna. A hit.

Now to get the auxiliary antennas, he said to himself. I'll have to move in closer.

"Shooting at us?" Nodon's voice went high with sudden fright.

"Fookin' bastard," George growled. "Get into your suit. Quick!"

Nodon bolted from his chair and went to the hatch. He tapped out the keyboard code swiftly and the hatch swung open all the way.

"The air pressure is falling," he called over his shoulder as George followed him down the passageway toward the airlock.

George was thinking, If we had the bloody laser on board we could give the bastard a taste of his own medicine. But the laser was sitting on the asteroid and its power pack was recharging; at least, it had been until the generator had been hit.

As they scrambled into their suits, George said, "We'd better power down the ship. Save the batteries."

Nodon was already pulling his bubble helmet over his head. "I'll go to the bridge and do it," he said, his voice muffled by the helmet.

"Turn off everything!" George yelled after his retreating back. "Let 'em think we're dead!"

He added silently, It won't be far from wrong, either.

Nodon returned from the bridge as George was closing the neck seal of his helmet. Leaning toward the kid so their helmets touched, he said, "Don't even use the suit radio. Play dead."

The kid looked worried, but he forced a sickly grin as he nodded back to George.

They got to the airlock and went out together. George grasped Nodon's suited arm and, without using his jetpack, pushed off toward the big slabs of ores attached to *Matilda*'s fusion engine. Get into the shadow of those chunks, he thought. Huddle up close to 'em and maybe this fookin' killer won't see us.

Perspective is tricky in microgravity. Once George and his young crewman got to the nearest of the slabs, it seemed as if they were lying on a huge hard bed, side by side, looking up at the slowly-revolving shape of their habitation module as it swung on its long tether.

The other ship glided into George's view. It was small, little more than a hab unit set atop a fusion engine and a set of bulbous propellant tanks. It looked almost like a cluster of mismatched grapes. Then he recognized the bulky shape of a high-power laser hanging just below the hab module. This ship was meant to be a destroyer, nothing else.

The guide beam from the ship's auxiliary laser played over *Matilda*'s habitation module. George watched as the smaller ship maneuvered leisurely, the evil red spot of the guide beam sliding away from the hab unit. For a moment it was lost in the depth of space, but then George's heart clutched in his chest. The red spot was moving across the slab to which he and Nodon were clinging.

He knows we're here! George thought, sweat breaking out on his face. He's gonna slice us!

But the red spot slid across the slab more than ten meters below their boots. It stopped on the bell-shaped nozzle of their fusion engine, then walked slowly up to the throat of the nozzle. A light flashed there. George blinked against the sudden, unexpected glare.

Nodon bumped his helmet against George's. "The engine!" he whimpered.

Another flash. This time George saw shards of metal fly off the rocket nozzle, glinting briefly in the pale sunlight as they spun out of sight, into the endless darkness.

Again the laser fired. This time it hit the piping that fed cryogenic hydrogen into the nozzle's cooling capillaries. Fookin' bastard knows his business, George thought grimly. He's disabled the engine with three bloody shots.

The attacking ship maneuvered leisurely, drifting out of George's sight, beyond the edge of the slab on which he and Nodon hid. For moments that seemed like hours, the two men lay there unmoving. What are we gonna do? George wondered. How can we get home without the main engine?

In the darkness, George felt Nodon's helmet touch his again. "Do you think he's gone?" the young man asked.

Before George could answer, he caught another glint in the corner of his eye. Pushing slightly away from the slab, he saw that their attacker was punching holes in their propellant tanks. Thin cold jets of cryogenic hydrogen and helium-three hissed noiselessly into the vacuum, brief whitish wisps of gas that dissipated into the emptiness of space in an eyeblink.

"We're movin'," George muttered, even though Nodon could not hear him. Like a child's balloon when he lets the air out of it, the gases escaping from the punctured tanks were pushing *Matilda* slowly away from the asteroid.

"We're gonna get a fookin' tour of the solar system," George said aloud. "Shame we'll be too dead to enjoy the sights."

CHAPTER 19

I'm surprised he hasn't had us thrown out of this hotel already," Fuchs said morosely.

Pancho Lane tried to smile encouragingly. Lars and Amanda both looked so down, so—*bewildered* was the word for it, Pancho decided. Overrun by events and their own emotions.

"Hey, don't worry about the hotel," she said, trying to sound cheerful. "Astro'll pay for it if Humphries reneges."

Fuchs was still in the light gray business suit he'd worn for his meeting with Humphries. Amanda was wearing a pale turquoise knee-length frock, modest enough, but she still made Pancho feel gawky and shapeless, as usual. Mandy didn't mean to, but whenever Pancho was near her she felt like a beanpole standing beside a vid star.

"We're going back to Ceres," Amanda said. "Back to prospecting."

The two of them were sitting glumly on the sofa set beneath a hologram of Valles Marineris on Mars: the grandest Grand Canyon in the solar system.

"What about Helvetia, Ltd.?" Pancho asked. "You're not gonna let Humphries muscle you out of business, are you?"

Fuchs grunted. "What business? Our inventory went up in flames."

"Yeah, but the insurance oughtta cover enough of it to get you started again."

Fuchs shook his head wearily.

"You got a lot of good will out there on Ceres," Pancho urged. "Shouldn't oughtta let that go to waste."

Amanda's brows rose hopefully.

"Don't want to let Humphries get a monopoly, do you, Lars ol' buddy?"

"I'd prefer to strangle him," Fuchs growled.

Pancho leaned back in her chair, stretched her long lean legs. "Tell you what: Astro'll advance you the credit to restock your warehouse, up to the limit that the insurance will pay you."

Fuchs looked at her. "You can do this?"

"I'm learnin' how to play the board of directors. I got a clutch of 'em on my side. They don't want Humphries to monopolize the Belt any more'n you do."

Amanda asked, "Is your group strong enough to let you do what you just offered to do?"

Nodding, Pancho replied, "Take my word for it."

Turning to her husband, Amanda said hopefully, "Lars, we could start Helvetia all over again."

"With a smaller inventory," he grumbled. "The insurance won't cover everything we lost."

"But it's a start," Amanda said, smiling genuinely.

Fuchs did not smile back. He looked away from his wife. Pancho thought there was something going on inside his head that he didn't want Mandy to see.

"I'm going back to prospecting," he said, his eyes focused on the far wall of the sitting room.

"But—"

"I'll take *Starpower* back as soon as the current lease on her is finished."

"But what about Helvetia?" Amanda asked.

He turned toward her once more. "You'll have to run Helvetia. You can stay on Ceres while I take the ship out."

Pancho studied them. There was something going on between them, some hidden agenda someplace, that she couldn't fathom.

"Lars," said Amanda, in a very soft voice, "are you certain that this is what you want to do?"

"It's what I must do, darling." His voice sounded implacable.

Pancho invited them both to dinner at the Earthview Restaurant, off the hotel's lobby.

"Strictly a social evening," she told them. "No talk about Humphries or Ceres or any kind of business at all. Okay?"

They agreed, halfheartedly.

So naturally they talked about business through the entire meal. Pancho's business.

The standing joke about the Earthview was that it was the finest restaurant within four hundred thousand kilometers. Which was perfectly true: the two other eateries in Selene, up in the Grand Plaza, were mere bistros. Two levels beneath the lunar surface, the Earthview featured sweeping windowalls that displayed holographic views from the Moon's surface. It was almost like looking through real windows at the gaunt, cracked floor of the giant crater Alphonsus and its worn, slumped ringwall mountains. But the Earth was always in that dark sky, hanging like a splendid glowing jewel of sparkling blue and glowing white, ever changing yet always present.

The Earthview prided itself on having a human staff, no robots in sight. Pancho always felt that a truly top-rate restaurant should use tablecloths, but the Earthview used glittering placemats made of lunar honeycomb metal, thin and supple as silk.

None of them had changed clothes for dinner. Fuchs was still wearing his gray suit, Amanda her turquoise knee-length dress. Pancho, who favored coveralls and softboots, had started the day in a business outfit of chocolate-brown slacks, pale yellow sweater, and light tan suede vest. Amanda had loaned her a light auburn Irish lace stole to "dress up your outfit."

Once their handsome young waiter had brought their drinks and taken their dinner order, an awkward silence fell over their table. They had agreed not to talk business. What other topic of conversation was there?

Pancho sipped at her margarita and watched the waiter's retreating back. Nice buns, she thought. Wonder if he's married?

"So what have you been doing lately, Pancho?" Amanda finally said, more to break the silence than any other reason.

"Me? I'm followin' up on something Dan Randolph talked about years ago: scoopin' fusion fuels from Jupiter."

Fuchs's ears perked up. "Fusion fuels?"

"Yeah. You know, helium-three, tritium, other isotopes. Jupiter's atmosphere is full of 'em."

"That's a steep gravity well," said Amanda.

"Tell me about it," Pancho said. "You know I've been approached by some nuts who want to go skimmin' Jupiter's atmosphere as a *stunt*? They even brought a network producer with 'em."

"Insanity," Fuchs muttered.

"Yeah, sure." Pancho pronounced the word *shore*. "But then there's a gaggle of scientists who wanta set up a research station in orbit around Jupiter. Study the moons and all."

"But the radiation," Amanda said.

"Tight orbit, underneath the Jovian Van Allen belts. Might be doable."

"Astro would fund this?"

"Hell no!" Pancho blurted. "Universities gotta come up with the funding. We'll build the sucker."

"And use it as a platform for mining Jupiter's atmosphere," Amanda added.

Pancho smiled at her. Sometimes I forget how smart she is, Pancho thought. I let her sweet face and nice boobs fool me.

Then she looked at Fuchs. He sat with his drink untouched before him, his eyes staring off into some private universe. Whatever he's thinking about, Pancho realized, he's a zillion kilometers from here.

WALTZING MATILDA

Once they got back inside the ship, it took George and Nodon hours to patch the holes punched through the hull by the attacker's laser and check out all the systems. They were both dead tired by the time they were able to take off their spacesuits and clump wearily, fearfully to the bridge.

George took the command chair, Nodon slipped into the chair at his right.

"You run a diagnostic on the power generator," said George. "I'll check the nav computer and see where th' fook we're headin'."

They worked in silence for another twenty minutes.

At last Nodon said, "I can repair the generator. He knocked out one set of electrodes. We have spares."

George nodded. "Okay, then. If you can get the generator back on line we won't hafta worry about electrical power for the life support systems."

Nodding, Nodon said, "That is good news."

"Right. Now here's the bad news. We're up shit's creek without a paddle."

Nodon said nothing. He held his bony face impassive, but George saw that even his shaved pate was sheened with perspiration. It sure isn't the temperature in here, George told himself. In fact, the bridge felt decidedly chilly.

With a heavy sigh, George said, "He knocked enough holes in the propellant tanks to send us jettin' deeper into the Belt."

"And the main engine is beyond repair."

"Prob'ly."

"Then we will die."

"Looks that way, mate. Unless we can get some help."

"The comm system is down. He must have lasered the antennas."

George nodded. "So that's what the soddin' bastard was doing."

"He was very thorough."

Sitting there, staring at the control panel with half its telltale lights glowering red, George tried to think.

"We're okay on life support," he mused aloud.

"Once the generator is running again," Nodon corrected. "Otherwise the batteries will run out in . . ." He glanced at the displays ". . . eleven hours."

"Better fix the generator, then. That's our first priority."

Nodon started to get up from his seat. He hesitated, asked, "And our second priority?"

"Figurin' out if we can nudge ourselves into a trajectory that'll bring us close to Ceres before we starve to death."

CHAPTER 20

Amanda would have preferred to stay in Selene for just a few days more, but Fuchs insisted that they start back for Ceres as soon as possible. He learned from Pancho that an Astro ship was due to depart for Ceres the next day, carrying a load of equipment that Helvetia had ordered before the warehouse fire.

"We'll go back on that ship," Fuchs told his wife.

"But it's a freighter. It won't have passenger accommodations," Amanda protested.

"We'll go back on that ship," he repeated.

Wondering why her husband was so insistent on returning as quickly as possible, Amanda reluctantly packed her travel bag while Fuchs called Pancho to beg a ride.

The next morning they rode the automated little tractor through the tunnel that led out to Armstrong Spaceport and climbed aboard the spindly-legged shuttlecraft that would lift them to the *Harper*. The ship was in lunar orbit, but rotating at a one-sixth g spin. Fuchs felt grateful that he would not have to endure weightlessness for more than the few minutes of the shuttlecraft's flight.

"Newest ship in the solar system," said her captain as he welcomed them aboard. He was young, trim, good-looking, and stared openly at Amanda's ample figure. Fuchs, standing beside her, grasped his wife's arm possessively.

"I'm afraid, though, that she's not built for passenger service," the captain said as he led them down the habitat module's central passageway. "All I can offer you is this cabin."

He slid an accordion-pleated door back. The cabin was barely large enough for two people to stand in.

"It's kind of small," the captain said, apologetically. But he was smiling at Amanda.

"It will do," said Fuchs. "The trip is only six days."

He stepped into the compartment, leading Amanda.

The captain, still out in the passageway, said, "We break orbit in thirty minutes."

"Good," said Fuchs. And he slid the door shut.

Amanda giggled at him. "Lars, you were positively rude to him!"

With a sardonic grin back at her, he said, "I thought his eyes would fall out of his head, he was staring at you so hard."

"Oh, Lars, he wasn't. Was he?"

"He most certainly was."

Amanda's expression became sly. "What do you think he had on his mind?"

His grin turned wolfish. "I'll show you."

Even though they took place in the tropical beauty of La Guaira, on the Caribbean coast of Venezuela, the quarterly meetings of Astro Manufacturing Corporation's board of directors had turned into little less than armed confrontations. Martin Humphries had built a clique around himself and was working hard to take control of the board. Opposing him was Pancho Lane, who had learned in her five years on the board how to bring together a voting bloc of her own.

As chairman of the board, Harriett O'Banian tried her best to steer clear of both groups. Her job, as she saw it, was to make Astro as profitable as possible. Much of what Humphries wanted to do was indeed profitable, even though Pancho opposed virtually anything Humphries or one of his people proposed.

But now Pancho was proposing something that might become an entirely new product line for Astro, and Humphries seemed dead set against it.

"Scoop gases from the atmosphere of Jupiter?" Humphries was scoffing. "Can you think of anything—any idea at all—that carries more risk?"

"Yeah," Pancho snapped. "Lettin' somebody else get a corner on the fusion fuels market."

Red-haired Hattie O'Banian was no stranger to outbursts of temper. But not while she chaired the board. She rapped on the long conference table with her knuckles. "We *will* have order here," she said firmly. "Mr. Humphries has the floor."

Pancho slumped back in her chair and nodded unhappily. She was seated almost exactly across the table from Humphries. O'Banian had to exert some self-control to keep from smiling at her. Pancho had come a long way since her first awkward days on the board. Underneath her west Texas drawl and aw-shucks demeanor, she had a sharp intelligence, quick wit, and the ability to focus on an issue with the intensity of a laser beam. With Hattie's help, Pancho had learned how to dress the part of a board member: today she wore a trousered business suit of dusky rose, touched off with accents of jewelry. Still, Hattie thought, her lanky, long-legged tomboy image came through. She looked as if she wanted to reach across the table and sock Humphries between the eyes.

For his part, Humphries seemed perfectly at ease in a casual cardigan suit of deep blue and a pale lemon turtleneck shirt. He wears clothes well, Hattie thought, and hides his thoughts even better.

"Martin," said O'Banian. "Do you have anything else to add?"

"I certainly do," Humphries said, with a crafty little smile. He turned his gaze to Pancho for a moment, then looked back at O'Banian. "I am opposed to fly-by-night schemes that promise a jackpot at the end of the rainbow but are in reality fraught with technical risks. And human dangers. Sending a ship to Jupiter in a crazy attempt to scoop hydrogen and helium isotopes from that planet's atmosphere is utter madness, pure and simple."

Half a dozen board members nodded agreement. O'Banian noticed that a couple of them were not usually on Humphries' side in these quarrels.

"Ms. Lane? Do you have anything more to say in support of your proposal?"

Pancho sat up ramrod straight and looked squarely at Humphries. "I sure do. I've presented the facts, the engineering analysis, the cost estimates and the profit probabilities. The numbers show that scooping fusion fuels is within the capabilities of existing technology. Nothing new needs to be invented."

"A ship that dives into Jupiter's atmosphere to collect its gases?" blurted one of the older men down the table. He was paunchy, bald, red-faced.

Pancho forced a smile at him. "A ship that's being teleoperated from Jupiter orbit. It's well within existing capabilities."

"There's no base in the Jupiter system for a remote operating team; we'd have to set it up it ourselves."

"That's true," Pancho said evenly. "I didn't say it was existing state-of-the-art hardware. But it is within existing capabilities. We just have to build it and test it."

"At what cost?" asked the gray-haired woman sitting two chairs down from Pancho.

"You have all the cost figures in my presentation," Pancho said. Then, turning to O'Banian, she asked, "Can I finish my say without bein' interrupted, please?"

O'Banian nodded. Raising her voice slightly, she said, "Let's give Pancho the same courtesy we gave Martin, everyone."

Pancho said, "Thanks, y'all. Earth needs energy sources that won't put greenhouse gases into the atmosphere. Fusion is the answer, and fusion based on helium-three is the most efficient fusion system that's been built so far. There's trillions of dollars *per year* waitin' for the company that can supply fusion fuels for Earth. And don't forget that Selene, the Mars bases, Ceres, and lots of other facilities off Earth will buy fusion fuels, too. Not to mention the market for spacecraft propulsion."

"Selene sells us deuterium-three," said the red-faced bald man. "They scoop it up out of the ground."

Pancho countered, "There's not enough deuterium on the Moon to satisfy the potential market demand."

"But going all the way out to Jupiter . . . that will make the price too damned high, won't it?"

"Not once we get the facilities runnin'. It'll be a long-haul cargo run, a pipeline operation. We won't hafta undercut Selene's price; we'll just offer a million times more fusion fuels than Selene can dig up."

The man mumbled to himself, unconvinced.

Pancho looked back to O'Banian, but before the chairwoman could say anything, she went on, "One more thing. If we don't do this, Humphries Space Systems will."

Humphries shot up from his chair and pointed an accusing finger at Pancho. "That's a deliberate insult!"

"That's the truth and you know it!" Pancho fired back.

The board room erupted with angry voices.

O'Banian banged on the table, hard. "Quiet! All of you."

"Do I still have the floor?" Pancho asked, once the commotion calmed down. Humphries was glaring at her from across the table.

O'Banian threw an irritated look at Pancho. "As long as you refrain from personal attacks on other board members," she answered stiffly.

"Okay," said Pancho. "But it seems to me like we got a problem here. *Mr.* Humphries here is in a position to block new ideas and then take 'em back to his own corporation and run with 'em."

"You're accusing me of unethical behavior!" Humphries barked.

"Damn right," said Pancho.

"Wait! Quiet!" O'Banian demanded. "I will not have this meeting break down into a personal quarrel."

The oldest member of the board, a frail-looking gentleman who hardly ever said a word, spoke up. "It seems to me," he said in a whispery voice, "that we do indeed have a conflict of interest here."

"That's nonsense," Humphries snapped.

"I'm afraid that the point has to be considered," O'Banian said. She tried to make it as mild and noncommittal as possible, but she was not going to let this point pass without a full discussion. She deliberately kept her eyes away from Pancho, afraid that her gratitude would show.

The discussion wrangled on for nearly two hours. Each board member demanded to have his or her say, whether or not the same sentiment had already been expressed by someone else. O'Banian sat patiently through it all, watching their egos on parade, trying to figure out how she could bring this to a vote. Throw Humphries off the board? Gladly. But there weren't enough votes for that. The best she could hope for was to pull his fangs.

Humphries was no fool. He too listened to the board members' repetitious ramblings, clearly impatient, obviously calculating his odds. By the time it was his turn to speak in his own defense, he had come to a decision.

Rising to his feet, he said slowly, calmly, "I'm not going to dignify the accusation that Ms. Lane made by trying to defend myself against it. I think the facts speak for themselves—"

"They sure do," Pancho muttered, loud enough for everyone to hear.

Humphries kept his temper, barely. "Therefore," he continued, "I will withdraw my opposition to this Jupiter concept."

O'Banian realized she had been holding her breath. She let it out with a gush, surprised at how displeased she felt. She had hoped that Humphries would do the gentlemanly thing and resign from the board.

"But let me tell you this," Humphries added, with an upraised finger. "When the costs mount up and the whole idea collapses around our heads, don't say I didn't warn you."

O'Banian took another breath, then said, "Thank you, Martin, on behalf of the entire board."

But Humphries's clique on the board still opposed the Jupiter project. The best they would agree to was to allow Pancho to seek a partner that would share at least one quarter of the project's costs. Failing that, the board would not allow the program to be started.

"A partner?" Pancho groused. O'Banian threw her a sharp warning look. If Pancho complained openly that no one would join Astro in such a partnership, it merely proved Humphries's point that the idea was impractically far-fetched.

"I think you might open up a dialogue with some of the major utilities corporations," O'Banian suggested. "After all, they have the most to gain from an assured supply of fusion fuels."

"Yeah," Pancho mumbled. "Right."

As the meeting broke up and the board members made their way out of the conference room, muttering and chattering to one another, Humphries came up to O'Banian.

"Are you satisfied?" he asked, in a low, confidential voice.

"I'm sorry it had to come to this, Martin," she replied.

"Yes, I can see how sorry you are." He glanced across the room, to where Pancho was talking to the old red-faced man as they filed out of the room. "Clever work, using Pancho as your stalking horse."

O'Banian was genuinely shocked. "Me? Using . . . ?"

"It's all right," Humphries said, smiling thinly. "I expect sneak attacks now and then. It's all part of the game."

"But, Martin, I had no idea—"

"No, of course you didn't. Well, go ahead with this Jupiter nonsense, if you can find some idiot foolish enough to go along with you. Once it flops I'll be able to use it to get you off the board. And that damned grease monkey, too."

WALTZING MATILDA

W hat spooks me," George was saying, "is how the fookin' bastard knew where our antennas were."

He and Nodon were taking off their spacesuits, dog-tired after a five-hour EVA. They had patched the laser-punched holes in the propellant tanks, but most of the hydrogen and helium had already leaked away. Their communication antennas, even the backups, were slagged and useless.

"He must have had complete specs on this ship," Nodon said, as he lifted off the torso of his hard-shell suit and placed it carefully on its rack. "Every detail."

"Every fookin' detail," George agreed. He sat on the tiny bench in front of the suit racks, filling it so completely that Nodon sat on the deck to start removing his boots. George felt too weary even to bend over and pull his boots off.

Piece by piece they finished unsuiting at last, then made their way to the galley. George mused aloud, "Y'know, somebody must've given him the specs for this ship."

"Yes," Nodon agreed, trailing along behind him. The passageway was too narrow for them to proceed side by side.

"But who? This is a piece of private property, its specs aren't public knowledge. You can't look 'em up in a fookin' net site."

Nodon scratched his lean, bristly chin, then suggested, "Could he have access to the manufacturer's records?"

"Or to the maintenance files at Ceres, maybe," George muttered.

"Yes, that is possible."

"Either way," said George, with growing conviction, "it has to be somebody in Humphries Space Systems. Their people do the maintenance on it."

"Not Astro?"

"Naw. HSS offered me a bargain price if I signed up for the maintenance contract."

"Then it must be someone in HSS," Nodon agreed.

"But why? Why did the bastard attack us?"

"To invalidate the claim to the asteroid, certainly."

George shook his head irritatedly. "There's millions of rocks in the Belt. And Humphries is the richest shrewdie in the fookin' solar system. What's he need a lousy asteroid claim for?"

"Perhaps not him," Nodon said. "Perhaps someone in his corporation."

"Yeah." George nodded. "Maybe."

With a resigned shrug, Nodon said, "It is all academic, anyway."

"Whatcha mean, mate?"

Tapping a lean finger against the small wallscreen that displayed the galley's contents, Nodon pointed out, "We have enough food for only another twenty-two days. Perhaps as much as forty days, if we cut our daily ration to starvation level."

George grunted at him. "No sense starvin' ourselves. We're gonna die anyway."

CHAPTER 21

Through the week-long trip on the *Harper*, Amanda sensed a strangeness in her husband, something odd, different, something she couldn't put her finger on. He seemed—not distant, exactly—certainly not distant: Lars spent almost the entire journey in bed with her, making love with a fierce intensity she had never known before.

And yet, even in the midst of their passion there was something withdrawn about him; something that he was hiding from her. She had always been able to read his thoughts before: one look at the set of his jaw and she knew. He had never held anything back from her. But now his face was impassive, his expression guarded. His deepset blue eyes showed her nothing.

It frightened Amanda to realize that Lars was keeping a secret from her. Perhaps more than one.

Once they arrived back at their quarters on Ceres and began unpacking their travel bags, Amanda decided to confront the issue directly.

"Lars, what's the matter?"

He was stuffing a handful of socks and underwear into his bureau drawer. "The matter?" he asked, without looking up at her. "What do you mean?"

"Something's on your mind and you're not sharing it with me."

Straightening up, he came back toward her at the bed. "I'm thinking of everything that we have to do. The insurance, restocking the warehouse, getting *Starpower* back."

Amanda sat on the bed, next to her opened bag. "Yes, of course. And what else?"

His eyes shifted away from her. "What else? Isn't that enough?"

"There's something more, Lars. Something that's been bothering you since we left Selene."

He looked down at her, then turned his attention to his travel bag again, started rummaging through it, muttering about his shaving kit.

Amanda put her hand atop his, stopping him. "Lars, please tell me."

He straightened up. "There are some things you shouldn't know, dear."

"What?" She felt shocked. "What things?"

He almost smiled. "If I told you, then you would know."

"It's about Martin, isn't it? You've been this way ever since your meeting with him."

Fuchs took a deep breath. She could see his chest expand and then deflate again. He pushed his bag aside and sat next to her on the bed.

"All through our trip back here," he said, his voice heavy, low, "I've been trying to think of a way that we can stop him from gaining complete control of the Belt."

"So that's it."

He nodded, but she could see that there was still more. His eyes looked troubled, uncertain.

"He wants that. He wants complete control of everyone and everything out here. He wants absolute power."

Amanda blurted, "What of it? Lars, we don't have to fight against him. We can't! You're only one man. You can't stop him."

"Someone has to do it."

"But not you! Not us! We can cash in the insurance money and go back to Earth and forget about all this."

With a slow shake of his head, Fuchs said, "Perhaps you can forget about it. I can't."

"You mean you won't."

"I can't."

"Lars, you're obsessed with a foolish macho delusion. This isn't a battle between you and Martin. There's nothing to fight about! I love you. After all these years, don't you know that? Don't you believe it?"

"It's gone beyond that," Fuchs said grimly.

"Beyond . . . ?"

"He's killed people. Friends of ours. Ripley. The men and women aboard the ships that have disappeared. He's a murderer."

"But what can you do about it?"

"I can fight."

"Fight?" Amanda felt truly frightened now. "How? With what?"

He held up his thick-fingered hands and slowly clenched them into fists. "With my bare hands, if I have to."

"Lars, that's crazy! Insane!"

He snapped, "Don't you think I know it? Don't you think it horrifies me down to the bottom of my soul? I'm a civilized man. I'm not a Neanderthal."

"Then why . . . ?"

"Because I *must*. Because there's an anger in me, a fury that won't let go of me. I *hate* him! I hate his smug certainty. I hate the idea that he can push a button and men are murdered millions of kilometers away while he sits in his elegant mansion and dines on pheasant. And fantasizes about you!"

Amanda's heart sank. I'm the cause of all this, she realized all over again. I've turned this sweet, loving man into a raging monster.

"I'd like to smash his face in," Fuchs growled. "Kill him just as he's killed so many others."

"The way you killed that man in the Pub," she heard herself say.

He looked as if she had slapped him in the face.

Shocked at her own words, Amanda said, "Oh, Lars, I didn't mean—"

"You're right," he snapped. "Absolutely right. If I could kill Humphries like that, I'd do it. In a hot second."

She reached up and stroked his cheek as gently, soothingly as she could. "Lars, darling, please—all you're going to accomplish is getting yourself killed."

He pushed her hand away. "Don't you think I'm already marked for murder? He told me he would have me killed. *You're a dead man, Fuchs.* Those were his exact words."

Amanda closed her eyes. There was nothing she could do. She knew that her husband was going to fight, and there was nothing she could do to stop him. She knew he would get himself killed. Worse, she saw that he was turning into a killer himself. He was becoming a stranger, a man she didn't know, didn't recognize. That frightened her.

"And to what do I owe the pleasure of your visit?" asked Carlos Vertientes.

He's a handsome devil, Pancho thought. Aristocratic Castilian features. Good cheekbones. Neat little salt-and-pepper beard. He really looks like a professor oughtta, not like the slobs and creeps back in Texas.

She was strolling along the *Ramblas* in Barcelona with the head of the university's plasma dynamics department, the tall, distinguished physicist who had helped Lyall Duncan build the fusion propulsion system that now powered most of the spacecraft operating beyond the Moon's orbit. Vertientes looked truly elegant in a dove-gray three-piece suit. Pancho was wearing the olive green coveralls she had traveled in.

Barcelona was still a vibrant city, despite the rising sea level and greenhouse warming and displacement of so many millions of refugees. The *Ramblas* was still the crowded, bustling, noisy boulevard where everyone went for a stroll, a sampling of tapas and good Rioja wine, a chance to see and be seen. Pancho liked it far better than sitting in an office, even though the crowd was so thick that at times they had to elbow their way past clusters of people who were walking too slowly. Pancho preferred the chatting, strolling crowd to an office that might be bugged.

"Your university's a shareholder in Astro Corporation," Pancho said, in answer to his question.

Vertientes's finely-arched brows rose slightly. "We are part of a global consortium of universities that invests in many major corporations."

He was slightly taller than Pancho, and slim as a Toledo blade. She felt good walking alongside him. With a nod, she replied, "Yup. That's what I found out when I started lookin' up Astro's stockholders."

He smiled dazzlingly. "Have you come to Barcelona to sell more stock?"

"No, no," Pancho said, laughing with him. "But I do have a proposition for you—and your consortium."

"And what might that be?" he asked, taking her arm to steer her past a knot of Asian tourists posing for a street photographer.

"How'd you like to set up a research station in orbit around Jupiter? Astro would foot three-quarters of the cost, maybe more if we can jiggle the books a little."

Vertientes's brows rose even higher. "A research station at Jupiter? You mean a manned station?"

"Crewed," Pancho corrected.

He stopped and let the crowd flow around them. "You are suggesting that the consortium could establish a manned—and womanned—station in Jupiter orbit at one-quarter of the actual cost?"

"Maybe less," Pancho said.

He pursed his lips. Then, "Let's find a cantina where we can sit down and discuss this."

"Suits me," said Pancho, with a happy grin.

WALTZING MATILDA

George looked sourly at the screen's display.

"Four hundred and eighty-three days?" he asked. He was sitting in the command pilot's chair, on the bridge; Nodon sat beside him.

Nodon seemed apologetic. "That is what the navigation program shows. We are on a long elliptical trajectory that will swing back to the vicinity of Ceres in four hundred and eighty-three days."

"How close to Ceres?"

Nodon tapped at the keyboard. "Seventy thousand kilometers, plus or minus three thousand."

George scratched at his beard. "Close enough to contact 'em with our suit radios, just about."

"Perhaps," said Nodon. "If we were still alive by then."

"We'd be pretty skinny."

"We would be dead."

"So," George asked, "what alternatives do we have?"

Nodon said, "I have gone through all the possibilities. We have enough propellant remaining for only a short burst, nowhere nearly long enough to cut our transit time back to Ceres to anything useful."

"But the thruster's bunged up, useless."

"Perhaps we could repair it."

"Besides, if we use the propellant for thrust we won't have anything left for the power generator. No power for life support. Lights out."

"No," Nodon corrected. "I have reserved enough of the remaining propellant to keep the power generator running. We are okay there. We won't run short of electrical power."

"That's something," George huffed. "When our corpses arrive back in Ceres space the fookin' ship'll be well lit."

"Perhaps we can repair the rocket thruster," Nodon repeated.

George scratched at his beard again. It itched as if some uninvited guests had made their home in it. "I'm too fookin' tired to go out again and look at the thruster. Gotta get some shut-eye first."

Nodding his agreement, Nodon added, "And a meal."

Surveying the depleted list on the galley inventory screen, George muttered, "Such as it is."

CHAPTER 22

Amanda looked up from her screen and smiled as Fuchs entered their one-room apartment. He did not smile back at her. He had spent the morning inspecting the ruins of Helvetia's warehouse. The fire had turned the rock-walled chamber into an oven, melting what it did not burn outright. Before it consumed all the oxygen in the cave and died out, it reduced all of Fuchs's stock, all that he had worked for, all that he had planned and hoped for, to nothing but ashes and twisted stumps of melted metal. If the airtight hatches hadn't held, the fire would easily have spread down the tunnels and killed everyone in Ceres.

Fuchs trembled with rage at the thought. The murdering vermin didn't worry about that. They didn't care. So everyone in Ceres dies, what is that to Humphries? What does it matter to him, so long as he gets his way and removes the thorn in his side?

I am that thorn, Fuchs told himself. I am only a little inconvenience, a minor nuisance in his grandiose plans for conquest.

Thinking of the blackened, ruined warehouse, Fuchs said to himself, This thorn in your side will go deeper into your flesh, Humphries. I will infect you, I will inflame you until you feel the same kind of pain that you've inflicted on so many others. I swear it!

Yet by the time he trod back to his home, coughing in the dust stirred up by his strides, he felt more weary than angry, wondering how he had come to travel down this path, why this weight of vengeance had fallen onto his shoulders. It's not vengeance, he snarled inwardly. It's justice. Someone has to stand for justice; Humphries can't be allowed to take everything he wants without being accountable to anyone.

Then he slid back the door to his quarters and saw Amanda's beautiful, radiant smile. And the anger surged back in full fury. Humphries wants her, too, Fuchs reminded himself. The only way he'll get Amanda is over my dead body.

Amanda got up from her desk and came to him. He took her in his arms, but instead of kissing him, she rubbed her fingers against his cheek.

"You have a smudge on your face," she said, still smiling. "Like a little boy who's been out playing in the streets."

"Soot from the warehouse," he said bleakly.

She pecked him on the lips, then said, "I have some good news."

"Yes?"

"The insurance money was deposited in Helvetia's account this morning. We can get started again without borrowing from Pancho."

"How much?"

Amanda's smile faded a fraction. "Just a tad less than half of what we applied for. About forty-eight percent of our actual loss."

"Forty-eight percent," he muttered, heading for the lav.

"It's more hard cash than we had when we started Helvetia, darling."

He knew she was trying to cheer him. "Yes, that's true, isn't it?" he said as he washed his face. His hands were grimy with soot, too, he saw.

He let the dryer blow over his face, noisy and rattling, remembering the luxury of having actual cloth towels at the hotel in Selene. We could do that here, Fuchs told himself. Vacuum clean them on the surface just as they do at Selene. It would save us electrical power, if we could keep the dust from up on the surface out of the laundry.

"Any word from *Starpower*?" he asked as he stepped back into the main room.

"She's on the way in," Amanda said. "She'll be here when the lease is up, at the end of the month."

"Good."

Amanda's expression turned grave. "Lars, do you think it's a good idea for you to take *Starpower* out? Can't you hire a crew and stay here?"

"Crews cost money," he said. "And we'd have to share whatever we find with the crew. I can handle the ship by myself."

"But you'll be alone. . . ."

He knew what she meant. Ships had disappeared out in the Belt. And he was marked for murder by Humphries.

"I'll be all right," he said. "They won't know where I'm going."

Amanda shook her head. "Lars, all they have to do is tap into the IAA's net and they'll see your tracking beacon. They'll know exactly where you are."

He almost smiled. "Not if the tracking beacon is coming from a drone that I release a day or so after I've left Ceres."

She looked totally surprised. "But that would be a violation of IAA regulations!"

"Yes, it would. It would also make my life much safer."

The work of cleaning up the charred mess of his warehouse took several days. It was hard to find men or women to do the menial labor; they demanded the same level of pay they could get working someone's computer systems or crewing one of the prospecting ships. So Fuchs hired all four of the teenagers on Ceres. They were eager to have something to do outside of their school hours, happy to be away from their lesson screens, happier still to be earning spendable money. Still, Fuchs did most of the labor himself, since the kids could only work a couple of hours each day.

After several days, though, the four youngsters failed to show up for work. Fuchs phoned each of them and got a variety of lame excuses.

"My parents don't want me working."

"I got too much studying to do."

Only one of them hinted at the truth. "My father got an e-message that said he could lose his job if he let me work for you."

Fuchs didn't have to ask who the father worked for. He knew: Humphries Space Systems.

So he labored alone in the warehouse cave, finally clearing out the last of the charred debris. Then he started putting together new shelving out of discarded scraps of metal from the maintenance bays.

One evening, as he scuffed wearily along the dusty tunnel after a long day of putting up his new shelving, Fuchs was accosted by two men wearing HSS coveralls.

"You're Lars Fuchs, aren't you?" said the taller of the pair. He was young, not much more than a teenager himself: his dirty-blond hair was cropped close to his skull, and his coverall sleeves were rolled up past his elbows. Fuchs saw tattoos on both his forearms.

"I am," Fuchs answered, without slowing down.

They fell in step with him, one on either side. The shorter of the two was still a couple of centimeters taller than Fuchs, with the chunky build of a weightlifter. His hair was long and dark, his face swarthy.

"I've got a piece of friendly advice for you," said the taller one. "Take your insurance money and leave Ceres."

Still shuffling along the tunnel, Fuchs said, "You seem to know something about my business."

"Just get out of here, before there's trouble," the other one said. His accent sounded Latino.

Fuchs stopped and looked them up and down. "Trouble?" he asked. "The only trouble that happens here will be trouble that you start."

The taller one shrugged. "Doesn't matter who starts it. What matters is, who's still standing when it's over."

"Thank you," said Fuchs. "Your words will be useful evidence."

"Evidence?" They both looked startled.

"Do you think I'm a fool?" Fuchs said sharply. "I know what you're up to. I'm wearing a transmitter that is sending every word you say to IAA headquarters in Geneva. If anything happens to me, you two have already been voiceprinted."

With that, Fuchs turned on his heel and strode away from the two toughs, leaving them dumbfounded and uncertain. Fuchs walked carefully, deliberately, stirring up as little dust as possible. He didn't want them to think he was running away from them; he also didn't want them to see how his legs were shaking. Above all, he didn't want them to figure out that his transmitter was a total bluff, invented on the spot to allow him to get away from them.

By the time he got home, he was still trembling, but now it was with anger. Amanda flashed a welcoming smile at him from the computer desk. Fuchs could see from the wallscreen that she was ordering inventory to stock the warehouse. Most of the machinery and electronic gear she ordered came from Astro Corporation. Now, he saw, she was dealing with foodstuffs and clothing, which came from other companies. He went to wash up as she stared wistfully at the latest Earthside fashions.

By the time he came back into the room, she was finished with the computer. She slid her arms around his neck and kissed him warmly.

"What would you like for dinner?" she asked. "I just ordered a shipment of seafood from Selene and I'm famished."

"Anything will do," he temporized as he disengaged from her and sat at the computer desk.

Amanda went to the freezer as she asked, "Will you be ready by the time the supplies start arriving?"

Working the computer, his eyes on the wallscreen display, Fuchs barely nodded. "I'll be ready," he muttered.

Amanda saw that he was studying the specifications for handheld lasers.

Frowning slightly, she said, "That looks like the laser that that Buchanan fellow killed Ripley with."

"It is," Fuchs said. "And he tried to kill me with it, too."

"I've already ordered six of them, with an option for another half-dozen when they're sold."

"I'm thinking of ordering one for myself," said Fuchs.

"For *Starpower*?"

He looked up at her. His face was grim. "For myself," he said. "As a sidearm."

CHAPTER 23

Starpower swung lazily in the dark star-choked sky above Ceres. Strange, Fuchs noted as he climbed aboard the shuttle-craft, that the sky still seems so black despite all those stars. Other suns, he thought, billions of them blazing out their light for eons. Yet here on the rubble-heap surface of Ceres the world seemed dark, shadowy with menace.

Shaking his head inside the fishbowl helmet, Fuchs clambered up the ladder and ducked through the shuttlecraft's hatch. No sense taking off the suit until I'm inside *Starpower*, he told himself. The shuttle flight would take mere minutes to lift him from the asteroid's surface to his waiting ship.

The shuttle's hab module was a bubble of glassteel. Two other prospectors were already aboard, waiting to be transferred to their space-craft. Fuchs said a perfunctory hello to them through his suit radio.

"Hey, Lars," one of them asked, "what are you gonna do about the habitat?"

"Yeah," chimed in the other one. "We put up good money to build it. When's it going to be finished so we can move in?"

Fuchs could see their faces through their helmets. They weren't being accusative or even impatient. They looked more curious than anything else.

He forced a weak smile for them. "I haven't had a chance to recruit a new project engineer, someone to replace Ripley."

"Oh. Yeah. Too bad about the Ripper."

"You did a good thing, Lars. That sonofabitch murdered the Ripper in cold blood."

Fuchs nodded his acknowledgment of their praise. The voice of the IAA controller told them the shuttlecraft would lift off in ten seconds. The computer counted off the time. The three spacesuited men stood in the hab module; there were no seats, nothing except a tee-shaped podium that held the ship's controls, which weren't needed for this simple flight, and foot loops in the deck to hold them down in microgravity.

Liftoff was little more than a gentle nudge, but the craft leaped away from Ceres's pitted, rock-strewn surface fast enough to make Fuchs's stomach lurch. Before he could swallow down the bile in his throat, they were in zero-g. Fuchs had never enjoyed weightlessness, but he put up with it as the IAA controller remotely steered the shuttle to the orbiting ship of the other two men before swinging almost completely around the asteroid to catch up with *Starpower*.

Fuchs thought about hiring a replacement for Ripley. The funding for the habitat was adequate, barely. He had put the task on Amanda's list of action items. She'll have to do it, Fuchs said to himself. She'll have to use her judgment; I'll be busy doing other things.

Other things. He cringed inwardly when he thought of the angry words he had flung at Humphries: *I've studied military history. . . . I know how to fight.* How pathetic! So what are you going to do, go out and shoot up Humphries spacecraft? Kill his employees? What will that accomplish, except getting you arrested eventually, or killed? You think too much, Lars Fuchs. You are quick to anger, but then your conscience frustrates you.

He had thought long and hard about searching out HSS vessels and destroying them. Hurt Humphries the way he's hurt me. But he knew he couldn't do it.

After all his bold words, all his blazing fury, the best he could think of was to find an asteroid, put in a claim for it, and then wait for Humphries's hired killers to come after him. Then he'd have the evidence he needed to make the IAA take official action against Humphries.

If he lived through the ordeal.

Once the shuttle made rendezvous with *Starpower* and docked at the spacecraft's main airlock, Fuchs entered his ship and began squirming out of the spacesuit, grateful for the feeling of gravity that the ship's spin imparted. The bold avenger, he sneered at himself. Going out to offer yourself as a sacrificial victim in an effort to bring Humphries down. A lamb trying to trap a tiger.

As he entered the bridge, still grumbling to himself, the yellow MES-SAGE WAITING signal was blinking on the communications screen.

Amanda, he knew. Sure enough, the instant he called up the comm message, her lovely face filled the screen.

But she looked troubled, distraught.

"Lars, it's George Ambrose. His ship's gone missing. All communications abruptly shut off several days ago. The IAA isn't even getting telemetry. They're afraid he's dead."

"George?" Fuchs gaped at his wife's image. "They've killed George?"

"It looks that way," said Amanda.

Amanda stared at her husband's face on the wallscreen in their quarters. Grim as death, he looked.

"They killed George," he repeated.

She wanted to say, No, it must have been an accident. But the words would not leave her lips.

"*He* had George killed," Fuchs muttered. "Murdered."

"There's nothing we can do about it," Amanda heard herself say. It sounded more like a plea than a statement, even to her own ears.

"Isn't there?" he growled.

"Lars, please . . . don't do anything . . . dangerous," she begged.

He slowly shook his head. "Just being alive is dangerous," he said.

Dorik Harbin studied the navigation screen as he sat alone on the bridge of *Shanidar*. The blinking orange cursor that showed his ship's position was exactly on the thin blue curve representing his programmed approach to the supply vessel.

Harbin had been cruising through the Belt for more than two months, totally alone except for the narcotics and virtual reality chips that provided his only entertainment. A good combination, he thought. The drugs enhanced the electronic illusion, allowed him to fall asleep without dreaming of the faces of the dead, without hearing their screams.

His ship ran in silence; no tracking beacon or telemetry signals betrayed his presence in space. His orders had been to find certain prospectors and miners and eliminate them. This he had done with considerable efficiency. Now, his supplies low, he was making rendezvous with a Humphries supply vessel. He would get new orders, he knew, while *Shanidar* was being restocked with food and propellant.

I'll have them flush my water tanks, too, and refill them, Harbin thought idly as he approached the vessel. After a couple of months recycled water begins to taste suspiciously like piss.

He linked with the supply vessel and stayed only long enough for the replenishment to be completed. He never left his own ship, except for one brief visit to the private cabin of the supply vessel's captain. She handed him a sealed packet that Harbin immediately tucked into the breast pocket of his jumpsuit.

"Must you leave so soon?" the captain asked. She was in her thirties, Harbin judged, not really pretty but attractive in a feline, self-assured way. "We have all sorts of, um . . . amenities aboard my ship."

Harbin shook his head. "No thank you."

"The newest recreational drugs."

"I must get back to my ship," he said curtly.

"Not even a meal? Our cook—"

Harbin turned and reached for the cabin's door latch.

"There's nothing to be afraid of," the captain said, smiling knowingly.

Harbin looked at her sharply. "Afraid? Of you?" He barked out a single, dismissive laugh. Then he left her cabin and went immediately back to his own ship.

Only after he had broken away from the supply vessel and was heading deeper into the Belt did he open the packet and remove the chip it contained. As he expected, it contained a list of ships to be attacked, together with their planned courses and complete details of their construction. Another death list, Harbin thought as he studied the images passing across his screen.

Abruptly, the specification charts ended and Grigor's lean melancholy face appeared on the screen.

"This has been added at the last moment," Grigor said, his dour image replaced by the blueprints of a ship. "The ship's name is *Starpower*. We do not have a course for it yet, but that data will be sent to you via tight-beam laser as soon as it becomes available."

Harbin's eyes narrowed. That means I'll have to get to the preplanned position to receive the laser beam and loiter there until they send the information. He did not like the idea of waiting.

"This is top priority," Grigor's voice droned over the image of *Starpower*'s construction details. "This must be done before you go after any other ships."

Harbin wished he could talk back to Grigor, ask questions, demand more information.

Grigor's face appeared on the screen again. "Destroy this one ship and you might not need to deal with any of the others. Eliminate *Starpower* and you might be able to return to Earth for good."

WALTZING MATILDA

I have good news," Nodon said as George pushed through the hatch into the bridge. "While you were EVA I wired the backup laser into the comm system."

George squeezed into the right-hand seat. "The backup laser?"

"From our supply stocks. Back in the storage section."

"And it works?"

Nodon beamed happily. "Yes. The laser can carry our communications signals. We can call for help now."

Breaking into a guarded smile, George asked, "We'll hafta point it at Ceres, then."

"The pointing is the problem," Nodon said, his happiness diminishing. "At the distance we are from Ceres, the beam disperses only a dozen kilometers or so."

"So we hafta point it straight onto the optical receivers, then."

"If we can."

"And the fookin' 'roid rotates in about nine hours or so, right?"

"I believe so," Nodon said. "I can look it up."

"So that means we'd hafta hit their optical receivers bung on at just the right time when they're pointin' toward us."

"Yes," said Nodon.

"Like playin' a fookin' game o' darts over a distance of thousands of kilometers."

"Hundreds of thousands."

"Fat chance."

Nodon bowed his head. For a moment George thought he might be praying. But then he looked up again and asked, "What of the engine? Can you repair the thruster?"

George grunted. "Oh, sure. Yeah."

"You can?"

"If I had a repair shop available and a half-dozen welders, pipefitters and other crew."

"Oh."

Heaving a weary sigh, George said, "We'll hafta depend on the laser, pal. The fookin' engine's a lost cause."

CHAPTER 24

Lars Fuchs didn't spend more than five minutes deciding what he was going to do. He called up the flight history data on *Waltzing Matilda*. Sure enough, Big George and his crewman had been working a fair-sized carbonaceous asteroid, according to the data they had telemetered back to the IAA. They had started mining it, then all communications from their ship had abruptly cut off. Efforts by the IAA controllers on Ceres to contact them had proved fruitless.

Evidence, Fuchs thought as he studied the flight data on his main comm screen. If I can locate *Waltzing Matilda* and find evidence that the ship was attacked, deliberately destroyed, then I can get the authorities Earthside to step in and do a thorough investigation of all these missing ships.

Sitting alone on the bridge of *Starpower*, he tapped the coordinates of the asteroid George had been working into his navigation computer. But his hand hovered over the key that would engage the program.

Do I want the IAA to know where I'm going? He asked himself. The answer was a clear *no*. Whoever is destroying the prospectors' and miners' ships must have exact information about their courses and positions. They can use the telemetry data that each ship sends out automatically to track the ships down.

I must run silently, Fuchs concluded. Not even Amanda will know where I am. The thought of the risk bothered him; the reason for sending out the telemetry signal was so the IAA would know where each ship was. But what good is that? Fuchs asked himself. When a ship gets in trouble, no one comes out to help. The Belt is too enormous. If I run into a problem I'm on my own. All the telemetry data will do is tell the IAA where I was when I died.

It took the better part of a day for Fuchs to take out *Starpower*'s telemetry transmitter and install it into the little emergency vehicle. Each ship carried at least one escape pod; six people could live in one for a month or more. An example of so-called safety regulations that looked important to the IAA and were in fact useless, ridiculous. An escape pod makes sense for spacecraft working the Earth/Moon region. A rescue ship can reach them in a few days, often in a matter of mere hours. But out here in the Belt, forget about rescue. The distances were too large and the possible rescue ships too few. The prospectors knew they were on their own as soon as they left Ceres.

Fuchs grinned to himself as he thought about all the other uses the emergency vehicles had been put to: extra storage capacity; extra crew quarters; micrograv love nest, when detached from the spinning ship so the pod could be weightless.

But you, he said silently as he installed the telemetry transmitter into *Starpower*'s escape pod, you will be a decoy. They will think you are me, while I head silently for George's asteroid.

Once he returned to the bridge and sat in the command chair, he thought of Amanda. Should I tell her what I'm about to do? He wanted to, but feared that his message would be overheard by Humphries's people. It's obvious that they have infiltrated the IAA, Fuchs thought. Perhaps the flight controllers on Ceres are secretly taking money from him.

If something happens to the escape pod, Amanda will think I've been killed. How can I warn her, let her know what I'm doing?

Then he felt an icy hand grip his heart. What would Amanda do if she thought I was dead? Would she mourn me? Try to avenge me? Or would she run to Humphries? That's what *he* wants. That's why he wants me dead. Will Amanda give in to him if she thinks I'm out of the way?

He hated himself for even thinking such a thought. But he could not escape it. His face twisted into an angry frown, teeth clenched so hard it made his jaws ache, he banged out the keyboard commands that ejected the pod into a long, parabolic trajectory that would send it across the Belt. It took an effort of will, but he did not send a message back to his wife.

I'm alone now, Fuchs thought as he directed *Starpower* toward the asteroid where Big George had last been heard from.

Diane Verwoerd was reading her favorite Bible passage: the story of the crooked steward who cheated his boss and made himself a nice feather bed for his retirement.

Whenever she had qualms about what she was doing, she called up Luke 16:1–13. It reassured her. Very few people understood the real message of the story, she thought as she read the ancient words on the wallscreen of her apartment.

The steward was eventually fired when his boss found out about his cheating. But the key to the tale was that the steward's thefts from his master's accounts were not so huge that the master wanted vengeance. He just fired the guy. And all through the years that the steward had been working for this master, he had put away enough loot so he could live comfortably in retirement. A sort of golden parachute that the boss didn't know about.

Verwoerd leaned back languidly in her recliner. It adjusted its shape to the curves of her body and massaged her gently, soothingly. It had originally belonged to Martin Humphries, but she had shown him an advertisement for a newer model, which he had immediately bought and then instructed her to get rid of this one. So she removed it from his office and installed it in her own quarters.

With a voice command she ordered the computer to show her personal investment account. The numbers instantly filled the wallscreen. Not bad for a girl from the slums of Amsterdam, she congratulated herself. Over the years you've avoided the usual pitfalls of prostitution and drug dependency and even steered clear of becoming some rich fart's mistress. So far, so good.

She spoke to the computer again, and the list of asteroids that she personally owned the claims for appeared on the screen. Only a half dozen of the little rocks, but they were producing ores nicely and building up profits steeply. Taxes would take a sizeable chunk of the money, but Verwoerd reminded herself that no government can tax money that you don't have. Pay the taxes and be glad you owe them, she told herself.

Of course, Martin thought that HSS owned the claims to those asteroids. But with so many others in his clutches, a mere half-dozen was down below his radar horizon. Besides, whenever he wanted to check on anything, he always asked his trusted assistant to do it. So he'll never find out about this little pilfering until after I've left his employment.

She cleared the list from the screen, and the verses from Luke came up again.

I'll be able to retire very comfortably in a couple of years, Verwoerd told herself. It will all work out fine, as long as I don't get too greedy— and as long as I keep Martin at arm's length. The moment I give in to him, my days as an HSS employee are numbered.

She looked at her reflection in the mirror across the room and smiled to herself. Maybe I'll give him a little fling, once I'm ready to retire. Once he fires me, I'll get severance pay. Or at least a nice little going-away present from Martin. He's like that.

Turning from her own image back to the words from the Bible, she frowned slightly at the final verse:

No man can serve two masters; for either he will hate the one, and love the other, or else he will hold to one, and despise the other. You cannot serve God and Mammon.

Perhaps, thought Diane Verwoerd. But I'm not really serving Martin Humphries. I'm working for him. I'm getting rather wealthy off him. But I'm serving only myself, no one else.

Still, she cleared the wallscreen with a single sharp command to the computer. The Bible passage disappeared, replaced by a reproduction of a Mary Cassat painting of a mother and child.

DOSSIER:
JOYCE TAKAMINE

You had to have an education to be considered for a job at Selene. The lunar nation was hiring engineers and technicians, not fruit pickers. Joyce's passport to the Moon was a battered old palmcomp that her father had given her. Through it she could access virtually any class in any university on the net. She studied every night, even when she was so tired from picking that she could barely find the strength to open the palmcomp's scuffed plastic lid.

The other pickers complained that the flickering light kept them from sleeping, so Joyce moved outside the barracks and kept doggedly at her studies out in the open, under the stars. When she looked up at the Moon and saw Selene's beacon light, it seemed to her as if that laser's bright beam was calling to her.

Once a guy she briefly slept with stole her palmcomp; just walked off with it, as if he owned it. In a panicked fury, Joyce tracked him down at the next camp and nearly took his head off with a two-by-four. The owner's guards let her go, once she told them the whole story. They had no use for thieves, especially stupid ones who let a scrawny oriental girl cold cock them.

In three years, Joyce got her degree in computer systems analysis from California Coast University. She applied for an advertised job at Selene. She didn't get it. Four hundred and twenty-seven other people, most of them just as desperate and needy as Joyce, had applied for the same position.

The same day that she was turned down by Selene she got the message that both her parents had died in a freeway pileup during the earthquake that destroyed the shantytowns up in the hills above the drowned ruins of San Francisco.

CHAPTER 25

Nothing.

Fuchs scowled at the display screens that curved around his command chair, then looked out through the bridge's windows. No sign of *Waltzing Matilda*. Nothing here but the lumpy irregular shape of an asteroid tumbling slowly in the barren emptiness, dark and pitted and strewn with small boulders and rocks.

This was the last position that the IAA had for Big George's ship. *Matilda*'s telemetering had cut off here, at this location. But the ship was nowhere in sight.

Almost without consciously thinking about it, he put *Starpower* into a tight orbit around the little asteroid. Was George really here? He wondered. If he was he probably didn't linger very—

Then he saw an area on the 'roid where neat rectangular slabs had been cut out of the rock. George *had* been here! He had started to mine the asteroid. Turning up the magnification on his telescope to max, Fuchs saw that there was still some equipment standing on the surface. He left in a hurry, Fuchs realized, too much of a hurry to pick up all his gear.

It was a cutting laser, Fuchs saw, still standing silently at the edge of one of the cut-out rectangles. I must retrieve it, he said to himself. It could be evidence.

The easiest way to get it would be to suit up and go EVA. But with no one else in the ship, Fuchs decided against that. Instead, he maneuvered *Starpower* into an orbit that matched the asteroid's own spin, the tip of his tongue apprehensively between his teeth, then slowly, carefully, brought the big ship to within a dozen meters of the rocky surface.

Using the manipulator arms on *Starpower*'s equipment module,

Fuchs snatched the laser up off the asteroid and tucked it inside the cargo bay. He was soaked with perspiration by the time the job was done, but proud of his piloting.

Mopping his forehead, Fuchs resisted the temptation to call Ceres and ask if they had any fresh data on George's ship. No! he scolded himself. You must remain silent.

Maybe that's what George is doing, he thought. Gone silent, so no one can find him. Obviously he left in a big hurry. Most likely he was attacked, perhaps killed. But if he got away, now he's staying silent to keep his attacker from finding him again.

But what do I do now? Fuchs wondered.

He left the bridge and went to the galley. The brain needs nourishment, he said to himself. I can't think well on an empty stomach. He realized that his coverall shirt was sticky with perspiration. Honest work, he told himself. But it doesn't smell good.

But by the time he washed up and ate a packaged meal, he still had no clear idea of what he should do next.

Find George, he thought. Yes, but how?

Back to the bridge he went and called up the search and rescue program from the computer files. "Aha!" he said aloud. Expanding spiral.

Standard operational procedure for a search mission was to fly an expanding spiral out from the last known position of the lost spacecraft. The one thing that worried Fuchs, though, was that George might have gone batting off at a high angle from the ecliptic. While the major planets orbited within a few degrees of the ecliptic path, plenty of asteroids roamed twenty or thirty degrees above or below that plane. Suppose George had gone angling away at high thrust? Fuchs knew he'd never find him then.

As it was, the Belt was so huge that even if George stuck close to the ecliptic, he could be halfway to hell by now. A few days at high thrust could push a ship all the way back to Earth. Or out past Jupiter.

Still, there was nothing more that Fuchs could do but fly his expanding spiral, and sweep with his radar at high angles above and below his position while he moved away from the asteroid.

He set the course, then got into his spacesuit to slither down the long buckyball cable that connected *Starpower*'s habitation unit with the equipment module. The hollow cable was big enough for a person to squeeze through, but it was not pressurized. You had to wear a suit, and that made crawling along the kilometer-long cable a long, arduous chore. Still, Fuchs had nothing else to do, and he wanted to see the laser that George had left behind.

• • •

Dorik Harbin was searching, too.

He had picked up *Starpower*'s telemetry signals within hours of Fuchs's leaving Ceres and tracked the departing ship from a safe distance.

Before the day was out, however, the telemetry signal had abruptly cut off. Harbin debated moving close enough to the ship to sight it visually, but before he could make up his mind to do that, the telemetry came back on and showed that *Starpower* was moving again, cutting diagonally across the Belt at high thrust.

Where could he be going? Harbin asked himself. He must have a specific destination in mind, going at that velocity.

He matched *Starpower*'s course and speed, staying far enough behind the departing spacecraft that he wouldn't be spotted. Even if Fuchs was cautious enough to probe behind him with radar, the beam would be so scattered by his own engine's exhaust that he'd never see me, Harbin knew. He stayed within the shadow of Fuchs's exhaust cloud and trailed *Starpower*—he thought. Actually he was following Fuchs's escape pod.

Again he thought of Grigor's comment: destroy *Starpower* and all this hunting and killing might be finished. I'll get my money and a considerable bonus, Harbin thought. I can go back to Earth and find a safe area and live like an emir for the rest of my life.

Where would the best place be, on Earth? I want a warm climate, safe from the rising sea levels, no earthquakes, stable government. A wealthy country, not one where half the population is starving and the other half plotting revolution. Canada, perhaps. Or Australia. They have very tight restrictions of immigration, but with enough money a man can go wherever he wants. Maybe Spain, he thought. Barcelona is still livable, and Madrid hasn't had a food riot in years.

CHAPTER 26

Hiring reliable people was Amanda's biggest headache. She worried about her husband sailing all alone out into the Belt, trying like so many others to strike it rich. Or was he? Her greatest fear was that Lars was out seeking revenge on Humphries by attacking HSS ships. Even if he didn't get killed he'd become an outlaw, a pariah.

She tried to force such thoughts out of her mind as she worked at restarting their supply business on the insurance money from the fire.

Labor was at a premium on Ceres. Most of the people who came out to the Belt went prospecting, intent on finding a rich asteroid and becoming wealthy from its ores. Even the experienced hands who had learned from bitter experience that most prospectors barely broke even, while the big corporations raked in the profits from selling ores, still went out time and again, always seeking the "big one" that would make their fortunes. Or they worked as miners, taking the ores from asteroids either as corporate employees or under contract to one of the big corporations. Miners didn't get rich, but they didn't starve, either.

Amanda had taken courses in economics at college. She understood that the more asteroids were mined, the more plentiful their metals and minerals, the lower their value. A corporation like Astro or HSS could afford to work on a slim profit margin, because they handled such an enormous volume of ores. A lone prospector had to sell at market prices, and the price was always far below their starry-eyed dreams.

She frowned as she dressed for another day of work. Then why is Lars out there, prospecting? He knows the odds as well as anyone does. And why hasn't he sent any messages to me? He warned me that he wouldn't, but I thought that after a few days he'd at least tell me he's all right.

The answer was clear to her, but she didn't want to believe it. He's not prospecting. He's out there on some insane kind of mission to get even with Martin. He wants to fight back—one man against the most powerful corporation in the solar system. He'll get himself killed, and there's nothing I can do about it.

That was what hurt her the most, that feeling of utter impotence, the knowledge that there was no way she could protect, or even help, the man she loved. He's gone away from me, she realized. Not merely physically; Lars has moved away from me, away from our marriage, away from our relationship. He's let his anger override our love. He's after vengeance now, no matter what it costs.

Fighting back the tears in her eyes, she booted up her computer and took up where she'd left off the previous night, searching for people willing to work in the warehouse. In her desperation she had even sent a call to Pancho, back Earthside. Now, as the wallscreen sprang to life, she saw that Pancho had replied.

"Show Pancho Lane's message," she commanded the computer.

Pancho's angular, mocha-skinned face grinned at her. She appeared to be in an office somewhere in the tropics. Probably Astro's corporate headquarters in Venezuela.

"Got your sad story, Mandy. I can 'preciate how tough it is to get reliable people to work in your warehouse. Wish I could ship you a couple of my folks, but nobody with a decent job here is gonna go peacefully out to Ceres unless they got asteroid fever and think they're gonna become zillionaires in six weeks."

Hunching closer to the camera, Pancho went on, "Lemme warn you about one thing, though: some of the people who might agree to work for you could be HSS plants. Screen ever'body real careful, kid. There's skunks in the woodworks, I bet."

Amanda shook her head wearily. As if I didn't have enough to worry about, she thought.

Pancho leaned back again and said, "I'm off to Lawrence, Kansas. Got a meeting with an international consortium of universities to work out a deal to build a research station in Jupiter orbit. Might be some college kids looking for jobs. Lord knows there's enough unemployment around. I'll see what I can find for you. In the meantime, watch your butt. That ol' Humper still wants to take over Astro, and you'n'Lars are standing in his way."

With a cheerful wave, Pancho signed off. Amanda felt like crawling back into bed and staying there until Lars returned.

If he returned at all.

•　•　•

How long should I search? Fuchs asked himself. It's been three days now, and no sign of George. No sign of anything.

He had known, intellectually, that the Belt was almost entirely empty space. Even in his freshman astronomy course he remembered it being compared to a big, empty theater that contained only a few specks of dust floating in its vast volume. Now he felt the reality of it. Staring out the windows in the bridge of *Starpower*, studying the screens that displayed the radar scans and telescopic views, he saw that there was nothing out there, nothing but empty space, darkness and eternal silence.

He thought of how Columbus's crew must have felt, alone out in the middle of the Atlantic without even a bird in sight; nothing but empty sea and emptier sky.

Then the comm unit chirped.

Fuchs was startled by the unexpected noise. He turned in the command chair and saw that the communications display showed an incoming message had been received on the optical comm system.

An optical signal? Puzzled, he commanded the comm computer to display the message.

The screen flashed into a harsh jumble of colors while the speakers rasped with hisses and squeaks. Only random noise, Fuchs thought. Probably a solar flare or a gamma burster.

But the other sensors showed no evidence of a solar flare and, once he though about it, Fuchs wondered if a gamma-ray burst would not have registered on the optical receiver.

He ordered the navigation program to move *Starpower* back to the area where the optical signal had been detected. Turning a ship of *Starpower*'s mass was no simple matter. It took time and energy. But at last the nav computer reported it was done.

Nothing. The comm system remained silent.

It was a fluke, Fuchs told himself. An anomaly. Still, *something* must have caused it, and he felt certain that it wasn't an internal glitch in the communications equipment. Nonsense, snapped the reasoning part of his brain. You're convinced because you want it to be a signal. You're letting your hopes overbalance your good sense.

Yes, that's true, Fuchs admitted to himself. But he ordered the nav system to move *Starpower* along the vector that the spurious signal had come from.

Hoping that his gut feeling was closer to the mark than his rational mind, Fuchs followed that course for an hour, then two, then—

The comm screen lit up with a weak, grainy picture of what looked to Fuchs like a bald, emaciated Asian.

"This is the *Waltzing Matilda*. We are disabled and unable to control our course. We need help urgently."

Fuchs stared at the streaky, weak image for several slack-jawed moments, then flew into a flurry of activity, trying to pin down *Matilda*'s location and move his own ship to her as quickly as possible while getting off a signal to her on every channel his comm system could transmit on.

Dorik Harbin was furious.

It's a decoy! he raged. A stupid, sneaking decoy! And you fell for it. You followed it like an obedient puppy halfway to hell!

He had maneuvered *Shanidar* slightly away from the exhaust wake of what he'd thought was *Starpower* more out of boredom than any intelligent reason. He'd been following the ship's telemetry signals for several days, intent on finding where it was heading. His standing orders from Grigor were to wait until a ship takes up orbit around a particular asteroid, then destroy it. Harbin knew without Grigor telling him that HSS then claimed the asteroid for itself.

But after several days his quarry showed no indication of searching for an asteroid. It simply puttered along at low thrust, like a tourist boat showing off the local sights. Except there were no tourists out here and no sights to show; the Belt was cold and empty.

Now Harbin could see clearly in his screens that what he'd been following was not *Starpower* at all but a crew emergency vehicle, a miserable escape pod.

This was no accident. Fuchs had deliberately set him up while he went off in some other direction. Where? Grigor would not be happy to learn that he'd failed. Harbin swore to himself that he would find Fuchs and destroy the cunning dog.

If he reversed his course it would cost so much of his propellant that he'd need another topping off within a few days. And the nearest HSS ship was at least three days off. Harbin searched his sensor screens. What he needed was a fair-sized rock close enough . . .

He found one, an asteroid that had enough mass for the maneuver he had in mind. Too small for a slingshot move, but Harbin eased close to the twelve-kilometer-long rock and put *Shanidar* into a tight orbit around it. He checked his nav computer twice before setting up the program. At precisely the proper instant he fired his thrusters, and *Shanidar* shot away from the unnamed asteroid in the direction Harbin wanted, at a fraction of the propellant loss that a powered turnaround would have cost.

Now he sped back toward the region where *Starpower* had fired off its decoy. That was easy to calculate: it had to be where *Starpower*'s telemetry signals went off for a few hours. That's when the clever dog transferred his transmitter to the escape pod. He's been running silent ever since.

Or maybe not, Harbin reasoned. He might be communicating with Ceres on another channel. Or perhaps signaling some other ship.

So Harbin kept all his communications receivers open as he raced back to the area where Fuchs had fooled him into following the decoy.

Chance favors the prepared mind. After two days of running at full thrust, Harbin picked up the distant, weak signal of Fuchs answering *Waltzing Matilda*'s distress call.

So that's where he's going. Harbin nodded to himself, satisfied that now he could destroy *Starpower* and finish the job on *Waltzing Matilda*.

WALTZING MATILDA

George had drifted to sleep in the copilot's chair, leaving Nodon to monitor the control console. There wasn't much to monitor. They were still drifting helplessly, alone, slowly starving.

"I have a signal!" Nodon exulted.

His shout roused George from a dream about dining with a beautiful woman in the Earthview restaurant back in Selene. Groggy with sleep, George knuckled his eyes, wondering which was more important in his dream, the woman or the tucker.

"What signal?" he mumbled.

Nodon was quivering with excitement. "Look!" He pointed a bony, shaking finger at the comm screen. "Look!"

George blinked several times. By crikes, there was Lars Fuchs's dour, dead-serious face on the screen. George had never seen anyone more beautiful.

"I have received your distress call and am proceeding at full thrust to your position. Please home on my beacon and keep repeating your signal so my nav system can maintain an accurate track on you."

Nodon's fingers were already dancing across the keyboard on the control console.

"Ask 'im how long it'll take him to reach us," George said.

"I have already fed the data into the computer." Nodon tapped a few more keystrokes. "Ah. Here is the answer. Fifty-two hours."

"A little more'n two days." George broke into a shaggy smile. "We can hold up for two more days, can't we mate?"

"Yes! Certainly!"

CHAPTER 27

Harbin listened intently to the messages that Fuchs was beaming out. Coldly, he thought, If the fool kept himself restricted to laser signals I wouldn't have been able to detect him. Radio signals expand through space like a swelling balloon. Like a flower opening up to the sun. A blossom of death, he realized.

He knew that he had to conserve his propellant supply; it was already low enough to be of concern. Not a danger, not yet, but he couldn't roar out to his prey at full thrust, not if he wanted to have enough propellant to get back to an HSS tanker. But there was no rush. Let Fuchs rescue whoever is left alive on *Matilda*. I'll simply cruise toward them and intercept *Starpower* on its way back to Ceres.

He kept his communications receivers open, and soon heard Fuchs reporting excitedly back to Ceres that he had located *Waltzing Matilda* and its two crewmen were still alive. Not for long, Harbin thought.

Then a new thought struck him. It was not all that unusual for a prospector's ship to disappear out in the lonely vastness of the Belt. He had destroyed several of them; others had failed without his help. A single ship like *Waltzing Matilda* could wink out of contact, never to be heard from again, and no one would know the cause. Of course, there were grumbles about piracy here and there, but no one really took that seriously.

On the other hand, if *Matilda*'s crew is alive, they will be able to tell what actually happened to them. They'll inform the IAA that they were deliberately attacked and left for dead. I can't allow them to survive.

But on the *other* other hand, Harbin mused on, how will it look if the ship that rescues *Matilda*'s crew also disappears? That will raise the rumbles of piracy to the level of a major investigation.

He shook his head, trying to clear his thoughts. *I'm out here alone; I can't call back to Grigor or anyone else for instructions. I've got to make the decision here and now.*

It took him less than a minute to decide. *Let* Starpower *rescue* Matilda's *crew and then destroy the lot of them. Perhaps I can kill them before they can blab their whole story to Ceres or the IAA.*

Amanda's heart clutched in her chest when she answered the INCOMING MESSAGE signal on her computer and Lars's image took shape on her wallscreen.

He looked tense; there were dark circles under his eyes. But his normally severe, gloomy face was smiling widely.

"I've found them! George and his crewman. They're alive and I'm going to pick them up."

"What happened to them?" Amanda asked, forgetting that her husband was too far away for interactive conversation.

"Their ship is disabled," Fuchs was saying, "but they are both uninjured. That's all I know at the moment. I'll send more information after I've taken them aboard my ship."

The screen went blank, leaving Amanda awash in a thousand questions. But none of them mattered to her. *Lars is all right and he's not doing anything dangerous. He's going to rescue George and his crewman and then he'll come back here, back to me.*

She felt enormously relieved.

The airlock compartment felt cramped, crowded once George and his crewman came through the hatch in their bulky spacesuits. And as soon as they started pulling off their suits, Fuchs nearly gagged from the stench.

"You both need showers," he said, as delicately as he could manage.

George grinned sheepishly through his wildly tangled beard. "Yeah. Guess we don't smell so sweet, eh?"

The Asian said nothing, but looked embarrassed. He was only a youngster, Fuchs saw.

As Fuchs led them along the passageway to the lav, George said cheerfully, "Hope you've got a full larder."

Fuchs nodded, resisting the urge to hold his nose. Then he asked, "What happened to you?"

Shooing the silent Nodon into the shower stall, George answered, "What happened? We were attacked, that's what happened."

"Attacked?"

"Deliberately shot to pieces by a bloke with a high-power laser on his ship."

"I knew it," Fuchs muttered.

Nodon discreetly stepped into the shower stall before peeling off his coveralls. Then they heard the spray of water, saw tendrils of steamy air rising from the stall.

"I guess we're not the first to be chopped," said George. "*Lady of the Lake. Aswan* . . . four or five others, at least."

"At least," Fuchs agreed. "We'll have to inform the IAA of this. Maybe now they'll start a real investigation."

"Dinner first," George said. "Me stomach's growlin'."

"A shower first," Fuchs corrected. "Then you can eat."

George laughed. "Suits me." Raising his voice, he added, "If we can get a certain Asian bloke out of the fookin' shower stall."

Harbin was glistening with perspiration as he exercised on the ergonomics bike. *Shanidar* was cruising at one-sixth g, the same grav level as the Moon, but Harbin's military upbringing unsparingly forced him to maintain his conditioning to Earth-normal standards. As he pedaled away and pumped at the hand bars, he watched the display screen on the bulkhead in front of him.

It was a martial arts training vid, one that Harbin had seen dozens of times. But each time he picked up something new, some different little wrinkle that he had overlooked before or forgotten. After his mandatory twenty klicks on the bike, he would rerun the vid and go through its rigorous set of exercises.

But his mind kept coming back to the central problem he faced. How can I prevent Fuchs from informing Ceres of what happened to *Waltzing Matilda*? He's already sent one brief message to his wife. Once he beams out their whole story the IAA will launch a full investigation.

He almost smiled. If that happens, my career in piracy is finished. Grigor's superiors might even decide that it would be safer to terminate me than to pay me off.

It's imperative, then, that I silence *Starpower* as quickly as possible. But how? I can't jam their transmissions; I don't have the proper equipment aboard.

I could accelerate, get to them at top speed, knock them out before they get a message back to Ceres. But then I'd be too low on fuel to get back to a tanker. I'd have to signal Grigor to send a tanker to me.

And what better way to be rid of me than to let me drift alone out here until I starve to death or the recyclers break down? That way Grigor and his HSS bosses get total silence, for free.

With a grim shake of his head, Harbin decided he would continue on his present course and speed. He'd catch up to *Starpower* and destroy the ship. Fuchs would die. Harbin only hoped that he could finish the job before Fuchs told Ceres what was going on.

That's in the lap of the gods, he thought. It's a matter of chance. A quatrain from the *Rubaiyat* came to him:

Ah, Love! could thou and I with Fate conspire
To grasp this sorry Scheme of Things entire,
Would not we shatter it to bits—and then
Re-mould it nearer to the Heart's Desire!

Yes, Harbin thought. That would be pleasant, to shatter this world to bits and rebuild it into something better. To have a woman to stand beside me, to love me, to be my heart's desire.

But that is fantasy, he told himself sternly. Reality is this godforsaken emptiness, this dreary ship. Reality is studying ways to kill.

With a deep, heartfelt breath, he said silently, Reality is this damned bike, going nowhere but taking all my energy to get there.

CHAPTER 28

Fuchs sat in the galley, nearly stunned with amazement as he watched George wolf down enough food to feed an ordinary man for a week. The crewman, Nodon, ate more sparingly but still put away a good pile of rations.

". . . then after he slagged our antennas," George was saying through a mouthful of veggieburger and reconstituted potatoes, "he zapped the fookin' thruster nozzle and for good measure popped our propellant tanks."

"He was very thorough," Fuchs said.

George nodded. "I figure he musta thought we were still inside the hab module. Nodon and me played doggo until he left. By then, old *Matilda* was driftin' in the general direction of Alpha Centauri."

"He assumed you were dead."

"Or as good as."

"You've got to tell all this to the IAA," said Fuchs.

"If we'd'a had our cutting laser on board I would've shot back at th' bastard. He caught us with the laser sittin' on the 'roid and our power pack bein' recharged."

"I have your laser," Fuchs said. "It's in the cargo bay."

Nodon looked up from his food. "I will check it out."

"You do that," George agreed. "I'll call up the IAA people in Selene."

"No," said Fuchs. "We'll call IAA headquarters on Earth. This story must be told to the top people, and quickly."

"Okay. Soon's I polish off some dessert. Whatcha got in the freezer?"

Turning to Nodon, Fuchs said, "I'm carrying a cutting laser, too. It's stored in the cargo bay, along with yours."

The Asian asked softly, "Do you want me to connect them both to power sources?"

Fuchs saw calm certainty in the young man's hooded brown eyes. "Yes, I think it might be wise to have them both operational."

George caught their meaning as he got up and stepped to the freezer. "How're you gonna fire 'em from inside the cargo bay, mate?"

"Open the hatches, obviously," said Fuchs.

"Better wear a suit, then."

Nodon dipped his chin in silent agreement.

"You both think he'll be back, then," said Fuchs.

"Perhaps," Nodon answered.

"Better to be ready if and when," George said, as he scanned the inventory list on the freezer's display screen. "I don't wanna be caught with me pants down again. Could be fatal."

Diane Verwoerd could see that her boss was getting cold feet. Martin Humphries looked uncomfortable, almost nervous, as she entered the spacious living room of his mansion.

"How do I look?" he asked her, something he never did ordinarily.

He was dressed in a full-fledged tuxedo, complete with a bow tie and plaid cummerbund. She smiled, suppressing the urge to tell him he looked like a chubby penguin.

"You look very debonair," she said.

"Damned silly business. You'd think that after a couple of centuries they'd figure out something better to wear for formal occasions."

"I'm impressed that you knotted the tie so perfectly."

He frowned at her. "It's pre-tied and you know it. Don't be cute."

Verwoerd was wearing a floor-length sheath of glittering silver, its long skirt slit nearly to the hip.

"Stavenger didn't invite me to the damned opera out of the goodness of his heart," Humphries complained as they headed for the door. "He wants to pump me about something and he thinks I'll be off my guard in a social setting."

"Cocktails and dinner, and then *Il Trovatore*," Verwoerd murmured. "That's enough to relax you to the point of stupefaction."

"I hate opera," he grumbled as he opened the door.

Stepping out into the garden behind him, Verwoerd asked, "Then why did you accept his invitation?"

He glared at her. "You know why. Pancho's going to be there. Stavenger's got something up his sleeve. He may be officially retired but he still runs Selene, the power behind the throne. He lifts an eyebrow and everybody hops to do what he wants."

As they walked through the lush shrubbery and trees that filled the grotto, Verwoerd said, "I wonder what it is that he wants now?"

Humphries threw a sour glance at her. "That's what I pay you to find out."

The cocktail reception was out in the open, under the dome of the Grand Plaza next to the amphitheater that housed all of Selene's theatrical productions. When Humphries and Verwoerd arrived, Pancho Lane was standing near the bar deep in earnest conversation with Douglas Stavenger.

Nearly twice Humphries's age, Doug Stavenger still looked as young and vigorous as a thirty-year-old. His body teemed with nanomachines that kept him healthy and youthful. Twice they had saved him from death, repairing damage to his body that ordinarily would have been lethal.

Stavenger was not an ordinary man. His family had founded the original Moonbase, built it from a struggling research station into a major manufacturing center for nanomachine-built spacecraft. Stavenger himself had directed the brief, sharp battle against the old U.N. that established the lunar settlement's independence from Earthside government. He had chosen the name Selene.

Towing Verwoerd on his arm, Humphries pushed through the chatting crowd of tuxedoed men and bejeweled, gowned women to join Stavenger and Pancho. He nearly pushed himself between them.

"Hello, Martin," Stavenger said, with an easy smile. He was handsome, his face somewhere between rugged and pretty, his skin slightly lighter than Pancho's, a deep golden tan. It always surprised Humphries to see that Stavenger was considerably taller than himself; the man's compact, broad-shouldered build disguised his height effectively.

Without bothering to introduce Verwoerd, Humphries said, "It looks like you got half of Selene to come out tonight."

Stavenger laughed lightly. "The other half is performing in the opera."

Humphries noticed the way the two women eyed each other from crown to toe, sizing up one another like a pair of gladiators entering the arena.

"Who's your friend?" Pancho asked. Her gown was floor-length, too, and as deeply black as the men's tuxes. Her short-cropped hair was sprinkled with something glittery. The diamond necklace and bracelet that she wore probably came from asteroidal stones, Humphries guessed.

"Diane Verwoerd," Humphries said, by way of introduction, "Pancho Lane. You already know Doug, here, don't you?"

"By reputation," Verwoerd said, smiling her brightest. "And it's good to meet you, at last, Ms. Lane."

"Pancho."

Stavenger said, "Pancho's trying to talk me into investing in a research station to be set up in Jupiter orbit."

So that's it, Humphries said to himself.

"Selene's made a pocketful of profits out of building spacecraft," Pancho said. "You can make even more from bringing fusion fuels back from Jupiter."

"She makes a good case," Stavenger said. "What do you think of the idea, Martin?"

"I'm on record against it," Humphries snapped. As if he doesn't know that, he growled inwardly.

"So I'd heard," Stavenger admitted.

Three-note chimes sounded. "Time for dinner," Stavenger said, offering Pancho his arm. "Come on, Martin, let's talk about this while we eat."

Humphries followed him toward the tables that had been set up on the manicured grass outside the amphitheater. Verwoerd walked beside him, convinced that the four of them would be talking about this Jupiter business all through the opera, even the Anvil Chorus.

Which was all right with her. She loathed *Il Travotore*.

CHAPTER 29

With Nodon working in the cargo bay, Fuchs finally got George out of the galley and into the bridge.

"You must tell everything that happened to the IAA," Fuchs said, setting himself in the command chair.

George took the copilot's seat; overflowed it, actually. He may have been hungry, Fuchs thought, but he hasn't lost much weight.

"Be glad to, mate," George said amiably. "Just get 'em on the horn."

Fuchs instructed the comm computer to call Francesco Tomasselli at IAA headquarters in St. Petersburg.

"Oh-oh," said George.

Fuchs saw that he was pointing at the radar display. A single blip showed in the upper right corner of the screen.

"He's here," George said.

"It could be a rock," Fuchs heard himself say, even though he didn't believe it.

"It's a ship."

Fuchs tapped on his command keyboard. "A ship," he agreed, after a few moments. "And it's on an intercept course."

"I'd better get into a suit and back to the cargo bay with Nodon. You suit up, too."

As he followed George down to the airlock compartment where the spacesuits were stored, Fuchs heard the comm unit's synthesized voice said, "Signor Tomasselli is not available at this time. Do you want to leave a message?"

· · ·

Fifteen minutes later he was back in the bridge, feeling like a medieval knight in armor, wearing the cumbersome spacesuit.

The blip was centered in the radar display now. Fuchs peered through the window, but could see nothing in the dark emptiness out there.

"He still approaching?" George's voice rasped in his helmet earphones.

"Yes."

"We got your laser connected to the main power supply. Ours is down, something's buggered it up."

"But the one is working?"

"Yeah. Swing the ship around so we can get a clear view of 'im."

"George," Fuchs said, "suppose it's not the ship that attacked you?"

A half-moment of silence, then, "You think somebody else just happened to drop by? Not bloody likely."

"Don't shoot at him unless he fires on us first," Fuchs said.

George grumbled, "You sound like some bleedin' Yank. 'Don't fire until you see the whites of their eyes.'!"

"Well, we shouldn't—"

The comm screen suddenly flashed brightly, then went blank. With gloved fingers Fuchs tapped out a diagnostic command.

"I think he's hit our main antenna," he said to George.

"Turn the bloody ship so I can shoot back!"

The air pressure alarm started shrilling, and Fuchs heard the safety hatch at his back slam shut.

"He's punctured the hull!"

"Turn, dammit!"

Hoping the controls still worked, Fuchs heard a startled voice in his head say, *Mein gott,* we're in a space battle!

This might work out after all, Harbin told himself.

His first shot had disabled *Starpower*'s main communications antenna. And just in time, too. Fuchs had already put in a call to the IAA back Earthside.

His second shot had holed their habitation module, he was certain. They were swinging their ship around, trying to protect the hab module by moving it behind their cargo bay. Harbin studied the schematics of *Starpower* while he waited for his laser to recharge.

No sense wasting time or energy. Hit the propellant tanks, drain them dry and then leave them to drift helplessly deeper into the Belt.

He shook his head, though. No, first I've got to disable their antennas. All of them. They could scream their heads off to the IAA while I'm puncturing their tanks. They could tell the whole story before they drift away and starve to death. If they had any sense, they'd be broadcasting on all frequencies now. They must be panicked, too terrified to think clearly.

You have much to be terrified of, Harbin said silently to the people aboard *Starpower*. The angel of death is breathing upon you.

"What's he doin'?" George asked.

"He's hit us several times," Fuchs replied into his helmet microphone. "He seems to be concentrating on the hab module."

"Goin' for the antennas, just like he did to us."

"The antennas?"

"So we can't call for help."

Fuchs knew that was wrong. What good would it do us to call for help? It would take ten minutes or more for our signal to reach Ceres. How could anyone possibly help us?

"I can see him!" Nodon shouted.

"Now we can shoot back at 'im," George said excitedly. "Hold us steady, dammit."

Working the reaction jets that controlled the ship's attitude, Fuchs's mind was racing. He's not worried about our calling for help, he realized. He doesn't want us to tell anyone that we're under attack. He wants us to simply disappear, another ship mysteriously lost out in the Belt. If we get a distress call off then everyone will know that ships are being deliberately destroyed. Everyone will know that Humphries is killing people.

He called up the comm system diagnostics. Every last antenna was gone, nothing but a string of baleful red lights glowering along the display screen.

What can we do? Fuchs asked himself. What can we do?

George blinked at the sweat that stung his eyes maddeningly.

"Are you ready?" he shouted at Nodon, even though the spacesuited crewman was hardly three meters from him. They were standing on either side of the bulky cutting laser, a collection of tubes and vanes and piping that looked too complicated to possibly work correctly. Yet George saw Nodon nod, tight-lipped, inside his bubble helmet.

"Ready," he said.

George glanced at the control board, leaning slightly canted against the curving bulkhead of the cargo bay. All the lights in the green, he saw. Good. Looking up through the open cargo bay hatch he could see the distant speck of the attacking ship, a cluster of gleaming sunlit crescents against the dark depths of infinity.

"Fire!" George said, leaning on the red button so hard he forced himself up off the metal deck. He raised a gloved hand to the overhead and pushed gently, felt his boots touch the deck plates again.

The cutting laser was a continuous wave device, designed to slice through rock. Its aiming system was so primitive that George had to sight the thing by eye. Its infrared beam was invisible, and the red beam of the low-power guide laser disappeared in the emptiness of space. In the vacuum of the cargo bay there was no sound, not even a vibration that George could feel.

"Are we hitting him?" Nodon asked, his voice pitched high.

"How the fook should I know?" George snapped. "I'm not even sure the fookin' kludge is workin'."

"It's working! Look at the panel."

It's working, all right, George saw. But is it doing any good?

The first hint that *Starpower* was firing back at him came when Harbin's control board suddenly sprung a half-dozen amber warning lights. Without hesitation, he hit the maneuvering jets to jink *Shanidar* sideways. It ruined his own shot, but it moved him out of harm's way. Temporarily.

Frowning at the displays, Harbin saw that one of his propellant tanks had been ruptured. He looked up at *Starpower* hanging out there and saw the big hatch of the ship's cargo bay was open. They must have a laser in there, probably a cutting laser they use for mining. And they're shooting at me with it.

He maneuvered *Shanidar* away from the open cargo hatch while checking his ship's systems. Fortunately, the propellant tank they holed was almost empty anyway. Harbin could afford to jettison it. Yet as he did, he began to worry that they might hit remaining tanks before he had the chance to finish them off.

Staring at the dumbbell shape of *Starpower* rotating slowly against the distant, uncaring stars, Harbin's chiseled features twisted into a cruel smile.

"Kill or be killed," he whispered to himself.

CHAPTER 30

I t took only a few days of running Helvetia Ltd. by herself for Amanda to come to the conclusion that she didn't need to hire a replacement for Niles Ripley. I can do the systems management job myself, she realized.

With the habitat more than halfway finished, what was needed was a general overseer, a straw boss who understood the various engineering fields that contributed to the ongoing construction program. Amanda had learned a good deal of the technical skills in her training and experience as an astronaut. The only question in her mind was whether she had the strength, the backbone, to boss a gaggle of construction technicians.

Most of them were men, and most of the men were young and full of testosterone. In general, men outnumbered women in Ceres by six to one. The balance on the construction project actually was better: three men to each woman on the team, Amanda saw as she carefully reviewed the personnel files.

Sitting at her desk, she thought, If Lars were here there would be no problem. But if Lars were here he would take over the task, or hire someone to do it. Shaking her head, Amanda told herself, It's up to you, old girl. You've got to do this for Lars, for all the people living here in Ceres.

Looking into the mirror over the dresser of their one-room quarters, Amanda realized, No. Not merely for them. You've got to do this for yourself.

She got to her feet and surveyed herself in the mirror. It's the same old problem: the men will see me as a sex object and the women will see me as competition. That has some advantages, of course, but in this case the drawbacks outweigh the advantages. Time for baggy sweaters and shapeless slacks. Minimal makeup and keep your hair pinned up.

I can do it, she told herself. I can make Lars proud of what I accomplish.

She set a goal for herself: I'll handle this project so well that when Lars returns he'll want me to stay with it to completion.

Despite her best control, though, she could not avoid hearing a fearful voice in her mind that said, *If* Lars returns.

"He's coming closer!" Nodon shouted.

Wincing inside his bubble helmet, George hollered, "I can see that! And I can fookin' hear you, too. No need to yell."

The two spacesuited men tugged at the big aiming mirrors of the cutting laser, clumsy in their suits as they tried to slew the coupled pair of copper slabs on their mounting. The mirror assembly moved smoothly enough; pointing it precisely was the problem. It had been designed for slicing ore samples out of asteroids, not hitting pinpoint targets that were moving.

"Lars, you've gotta rotate us so we can keep 'im in our sights," George called to the bridge.

"I'm doing my best," Fuchs snapped. "I've got to do it all by hand. The steering program wasn't designed for this."

George tried to squint along the output mirrors' focusing sight and bumped the curving front of his helmet against the device. Cursing fluently, he sighted the laser as best he could.

"Hold us there," he said to Fuchs. "Bastard's coming straight at us now."

"Tell me when to fire," Nodon said, hunching over the control board.

"Now," George said. "Fire away."

He strained his eyes to see if the beam was having any effect on the approaching ship. We can't miss him, not at this range, George thought. Yet nothing seemed to be happening. The attacking ship bored in closer. Suddenly it jerked sideways and down.

"He's maneuvering!" Nodon stated the obvious.

"Shut down the laser," George commanded. To Fuchs, up on the bridge, he yelled, "Turn us, dammit! How'm I gonna hit him if we can't keep the fookin' laser pointin' at him?"

Another string of red lights sprang up across Harbin's control panel. The propellant tanks. He's sawing away at them.

He was in his spacesuit now. Once he'd realized that *Starpower* was shooting back at him he'd put on the suit before bringing *Shanidar* back into the battle.

His steering program was going crazy. The swine had hit a nearly-full tank, and propellant spurting from the rip in it was acting as a thruster jet, pushing him sideways and down from the direction he wanted to go. He had to override the unwanted thrust manually; no time to reprogram the steering to compensate for it. Besides, by the time he could reprogram the stupid computer, the tank would be empty and there'd be no more thrust to override.

In a way, though, the escaping propellant helped. It jinked *Shanidar* in an unexpected burst, making it difficult for the enemy to keep their laser trained on him.

But I can't afford to lose propellant! Harbin raged silently. They're killing me.

The amphetamines he sometimes took before going into battle were of no use to him now. He was keyed up enough, stimulated to a knife-edge of excitement. What he needed was something to calm him down a little, stretch out time without dulling his reflexes. He had a store of such medications aboard his ship. But inside his spacesuit, his cache of drugs was out of reach, useless to him.

I don't need drugs, he told himself. I can beat them on my own.

He called up the highest magnification his optical sensors could give and focused on the area where he'd briefly seen the red telltale light of their guide laser. That's where the danger is. If I can see the beam of their aiming laser, they can hit me with the infrared cutter.

Swiftly, he came to a plan of action. Fire the thrusters so that I jet up and across their field of view. As soon as I see the light of their guide laser I fire at them. I can get off a pulse and then be up past their field of view before they can fire back. Once I've disabled their laser I can chop them to pieces at my leisure.

With the semicircle of display screens curving around him, Fuchs saw the attacking spacecraft spurt down and away from them, a ghostly issue of gas glinting wanly in the light of the distant Sun. He could see a long thin slit slashed across one of the ship's bulbous propellant tanks.

"You've hit him, George!" Fuchs said into his helmet microphone. "I can see it!"

George's reply sounded testy. "So swing us around so's I can hit 'im again!"

Fuchs tapped at the control keyboard, wishing he was more adept at maneuvering a spacecraft. *Starpower* was not built for graceful turns. Pancho was right, he remembered. We turn slow and ugly.

In the cargo bay, George stared out at emptiness.

"Where the fook is he?" he wailed.

"Still below your line of sight," came Fuchs's answer in his earphones.

"So turn us toward him!"

Nodon said, "The cooling system needs more time to recover. We have inadequate coolant flow."

"Just need a few seconds, mate," said George, "once we get 'im back in our sights."

He stepped up to the lip of the cargo hatch and looked down in the direction he had last seen the attacking vessel.

"There he is!" George saw. "Comin' our way again."

The attacker was zooming up swiftly. George turned back toward the laser. "Fire her up!" he yelled to Nodon.

"Firing!" Nodon shouted back.

A blinding flash of light stunned George. He felt himself toppling head over heels and then something slammed into him so hard it spun him like an unbalanced gyroscope. Through blurry, tear-filled eyes he saw a spacesuited arm fly past, geysering blood where it had been severed, just above the elbow, rotating over and over as it dwindled out of his view. He heard someone bellowing in pain and rage and realized it was himself.

I'm a dead man, Harbin told himself.

Strangely, the knowledge did not seem to frighten him. He sat back in his spacesuit, relaxed now that the tension of battle had drained out of him.

They've killed me, he thought. I wonder if they know it.

His plan to silence the enemy's laser had worked, after a fashion. He'd popped up into their field of view and fired off a full-energy burst as soon as he saw the red dot of their guide laser. They couldn't have revved up their laser in time to hit him, he was certain of that.

Not unless they already had their laser cooking and he'd walked right into their beam. Which is exactly what had happened.

Harbin knew he had knocked out their laser with his one quick shot. But in doing so he had sailed *Shanidar* across the continuous beam of their mining laser. It had carved a long gash through two of the remaining propellant tanks and even sliced deeply into the habitation module itself.

I'll have to stay inside this damned suit, he growled to himself. For how long? Until the air runs out. Hours, perhaps a day or so. No longer than that.

He pulled himself out of the command chair, thinking, Of course, I could tap into the ship's air tanks. If the recycler hasn't been damaged, the air could last for months, even a year or more. I'd starve before I asphyxiated.

But what would be the point? I'm drifting, too low on propellant to reach a tanker or any other help. Leaning forward slightly so he could check the control displays through his suit helmet, he saw that the ship's power generator was unscathed. He would have enough electrical power to keep his systems going. He could even patch the hab module's hull, bring the air pressure back to normal, and get out of the suit.

To what avail? To drift helplessly through the Belt until I starve.

You could call the nearest tanker and ask for a retrieval, he told himself. The computer has their positions in its memory and you could contact them with a tight-beam laser signal.

Would they come to my rescue? Not before they checked with HSS headquarters. Grigor will not be happy to learn that I failed to eliminate *Starpower*. By now Fuchs and his friends are probably screaming their heads off to the IAA. Would Grigor tell them to rescue me, or would he decide that it's better if I just quietly die?

Quietly. Harbin smiled. That's the key. *Do not go gentle into that good night,* he quoted silently. *Rage, rage against the dying of the light.*

On a clear channel, he put through a call to Grigor.

CHAPTER 31

eorge awoke to see Fuchs and Nodon staring down at him, Fuchs looking grim, irritated. Nodon was wide-eyed with fright. Strange to see him with those fierce carvings in his face looking so scared, George thought.

"So I'm not in heaven, then," he said, trying to grin. His voice sounded strained, terribly weak.

"Not yet," Fuchs growled.

George realized he was lying in one of *Starpower*'s privacy cubicles, his spacesuit removed. Either they've got me tied down or I'm so fookin' feeble I can't move.

"What happened?" he asked.

Nodon glanced at Fuchs, then licked his lips and said, "The laser blast shattered our laser. The mirror assembly broke loose and . . . and took off your arm."

He said the last words all in a rush, as if ashamed of them. George looked down, surprised at how much effort it took to twist his head, and saw his left arm ended just short of the elbow. The stump was swathed in plastic spray-bandage.

He felt more fuddled than shocked. Just the barest tendril of pain, now that he thought about it. Not scared. No worries. They must have me doped up pretty good.

"The rest of your arm is in the freezer," Fuchs said. "We're heading back to Ceres at high thrust. I will alert Kris Cardenas."

George closed his eyes and remembered seeing the spacesuited arm spiraling out the cargo hatch.

He looked at Nodon. "You shut off the bleedin', huh?"

The younger man bobbed his head up and down.

"And closed off the suit arm," George added.

Fuchs said, "He also went out EVA and recovered your arm. I thought for a few minutes that we would lose him altogether."

"Did you now?" George said, feeling stupid, muffled. "Thanks, mate."

Nodon looked embarrassed. He changed the subject. "You must have hit the other ship a damaging blow. It left at high speed."

"That's good."

"We'll be in Ceres in another fourteen hours," said Fuchs.

"That's good." George couldn't think of anything else to say. Somewhere, in a deep recess of his mind, he knew that he should be screaming. *Prosthetics be damned, I've lost my fookin' arm!*

But the drugs muted his emotional pain as well as the physical. Nothing really seemed to matter. All George wanted was for them to leave him alone and let him sleep.

Fuchs seemed to understand, thank god. "You rest now," he said, his tight slash of a mouth turned down bitterly. "I have a long report to send to the IAA as soon as we can repair one of the antennas."

"Not this Fuchs person again," complained Hector Wilcox.

Erek Zar and Francesco Tomasselli were sitting in front of Wilcox's desk, Zar looking decidedly uncomfortable, Tomasselli almost quivering with righteous indignation.

Wilcox's office was imposing, as befitted the Counsel General of the International Astronautical Authority. Slim, sleek, impeccably clothed in a somber charcoal business suit and dapper pearl-gray tie that nicely set off his silvery hair and trim moustache, Wilcox looked every centimeter the successful administrator, which he believed himself to be. He had arbitrated many a corporate wrangle, directed teams of bureaucrats to generate safety regulations and import duties on space manufactures, and climbed the slippery slope of the IAA's legal department until he sat at its very top, unchallenged and hailed by his fellow bureaucrats as an example of patience, intelligence and—above all—endurance.

Now he had a charge of piracy to deal with, and it unsettled him to his very core.

"He sent in a complete report," Tomasselli said, lean and eager, his dark eyes flashing.

Zar interrupted. "Fuchs claims his ship was attacked."

"He *reports*," Tomaselli resumed, laying emphasis on the word, "not only that his own ship was attacked, but another as well, and one of the men seriously injured."

"By a pirate vessel."

Zar's ruddy, fleshy face colored deeper than usual. "That's what he claims."

"And the evidence?"

"His ship is damaged," Tomasselli said before Zar could open his mouth. "He is bringing the injured man to Ceres."

"Which ships are we talking about?" Wilcox asked, clear distaste showing on his lean, patrician face.

Zar put out a hand to silence his underling. "Fuchs's ship is named *Starpower*. The other ship that he claims was attacked is *Waltzing Matilda*."

"Is that one on its way to Ceres, too?"

"No," Tomasselli jumped in. "They had to abandon it. The three of them are coming in on *Starpower*: Fuchs and the two men from *Waltzing Matilda*."

Wilcox gave the Italian a sour look. "And Fuchs has charged Humphries Space Systems with piracy?"

"Yes," said both men simultaneously.

Wilcox drummed his fingers on his desktop. He looked out his window at the St. Petersburg waterfront. He wished he were in Geneva, or London, or anywhere except here in this office with these two louts and this ridiculous charge of piracy. Piracy! In the twenty-first century! It was ludicrous, impossible. Those rock rats out in the Asteroid Belt have their private feuds and now they're trying to drag the IAA into it.

"I suppose we'll have to investigate," he said gloomily.

"Fuchs has registered a formal charge," said Tomasselli. "He has requested a hearing."

Which I will have to preside over, Wilcox said to himself. I'll be a laughingstock, at the very least.

"He should arrive at Ceres in a few hours," Zar said.

Wilcox looked at the man's unhappy face, then turned his gaze to the eager, impetuous Tomasselli.

"You must go to Ceres," he said, pointing a long, manicured finger at the Italian.

Tomasselli's eyes brightened. "I will conduct the hearing there?"

"No," Wilcox snapped. "You will interview this man Fuchs and the others with him, and then bring the three of them back here, under IAA custody. Bring two or three Peacekeeper troopers with you."

"Peacekeepers?" Zar asked.

Wilcox gave him a wintry smile. "I want to show that the IAA is taking this situation quite seriously. If these men believe they have been attacked by pirates, then they should have some visible protection, don't you agree?"

"Oh! Yes, of course."

Tomasselli said, "One of the men is seriously injured, and all three of them have been living in low gravity for so long that they could not return to Earth unless they spend several weeks in reconditioning exercises."

Wilcox let a small hiss escape his lips, his only visible sign of displeasure so far. Yet he knew that his control was on the fragile brink of crumbling into towering anger.

"Very well, then," he said icily. "Bring them to Selene."

"I will conduct the hearing there?" Tomasselli asked eagerly.

"No," Wilcox replied. "*I* will conduct the hearing there."

Zar looked stunned. "You'll go to Selene?"

Drawing himself up on his dignity, Wilcox replied, "I have not risen this far in the service of the International Astronautical Authority by avoiding the difficult tasks."

It was a bald-faced lie, but Wilcox almost believed it to be true, and Zar was willing to accept whatever his superior told him.

CHAPTER 32

George could tell from the look on Dr. Cardenas's face that the news was not good.

Fuchs and Nodon had rushed him to Ceres's minuscule infirmary as soon as they had landed, Nodon carrying the insulated plastic box that held George's severed arm. Half the population of the asteroid had also tried to crowd into the infirmary, some out of morbid curiosity, most because they heard that Big George had been injured and they knew and liked the red-haired Aussie. Cardenas had firmly shooed all of the bystanders into the tunnel outside, except for Amanda.

Fuchs embraced his wife, and she threw her arms around his neck and kissed him solidly.

"You're all right, Lars?" she asked.

"Yes. Fine. Not a scratch."

"I was so worried!"

"It's George who was hurt. Not me."

Cardenas put George through the diagnostic scanners, then took the container from Nodon and disappeared into the lab that adjoined the infirmary, leaving George sitting up on one of the three infirmary beds, surrounded by Amanda, Fuchs, and Nodon.

"You really were attacked by another ship?" Amanda asked, still not quite believing it could be possible.

George held up the stump of his left arm. "Wasn't termites did this," he said.

"I've sent in a full report of the attack to IAA headquarters," said Fuchs.

Amanda replied, "They've sent a confirmation back. One of their administrators is coming out here to bring you and George and," she glanced at Nodon, whom she'd just met, "and you, Mr. Nodon, to Selene for a hearing before the chief of the IAA legal department."

"A hearing!" Fuchs exulted. "Good!"

"At Selene."

"Even better. We'll beard Humphries in his own den."

"Can George travel?" Amanda asked.

"Why not?" George asked back.

That was when Cardenas came back into the infirmary, her expression dark and grave.

George immediately saw the situation. "Not good news, eh?"

Cardenas shook her head. "The arm's deteriorated too far, I'm afraid. Too much damage to the nerves. By the time we get you back to Selene, the deterioration will be even worse."

"Can't you stitch it back on here?" George asked.

"I'm not that good a surgeon, George. I'm not even a physician, really, I'm just pretending to be one."

George leaned back on the bed. It was hard to tell what was going on behind his shaggy, matted beard and overgrown head of hair.

"They have regeneration specialists at Selene. With some of your stem cells they'll be able to regrow your arm in a few months."

"Can you do it with nanomachines?" Amanda asked.

Cardenas shot her a strangely fierce look: part anger, part guilt, part frustration.

"Regeneration could be done with nanotherapy," she said tightly, "but I couldn't do it."

Fuchs said, "But you are an expert in nanotechnology. A Nobel laureate."

"That was long ago," Cardenas said. "Besides, I swore that I wouldn't engage in any nanotech work again."

"Swore? To whom?"

"To myself."

"I don't understand."

Cardenas was obviously struggling with herself. After a few heartbeats she said, "This isn't the time to tell you the sad story of my life, Lars."

"But—"

"Go to Selene. They have regeneration experts there, George. They'll grow your arm back for you."

George shrugged good-naturedly. "Long as they don't grow it back before our hearing." He waved his stump. "I want those IAA bludgers t'see what the bastards did to me."

Fuchs patted George's good shoulder. "And I want Humphries to be there to see it."

Fuchs and Amanda spent that night making love. No words, no talk about what had happened or discussions about what the future might bring. Nothing but animal heat and passion.

Lying beside her afterward, their room lit only by the dimmed numerals of the digital clock, Fuchs realized he had made love to Amanda as if he would never see her again. He had learned something in that battle out in space: His first brush with imminent death had taught him that he had to live life as if it would end in an instant.

I have no future, he told himself in the silence of their darkened room. As long as I'm in this war against Humphries I cannot hope for anything. I must live moment by moment, expecting nothing, ready to accept whatever comes next and deal with it. Only then can I escape the fear; only by shutting out the future can I cope with the present.

Briefly he thought about the frozen zygotes they had waiting in Selene. If I'm killed, Fuchs reflected, at least Amanda will be able to bear our child—if she wants to.

Amanda, lying beside him, pretended to sleep. But she was thinking too. What can Lars accomplish by this hearing with the IAA? Even if they find Humphries responsible for the attacks on all those ships, what can they do about it? Whatever happens, it will only make Martin even more enraged against Lars.

If only Lars would give this up, forget this war of his. But he won't. He'll keep on fighting until they kill him. He'll keep on fighting until he's as murderous and hateful as they are. He'll never stop, no matter how I beg him. He's moving away from me, becoming a stranger to me. Even in bed, he's not the same person anymore.

CHAPTER 33

S o he's getting a hearing with the IAA," Humphries said as he mixed himself a vodka and tonic.

The bar in his palatial home was a sizable room that also served as a library. Bookshelves ran up to the ceiling along two walls, and a third wall had shelves full of video disks and cyberbook chips stacked around a pair of holowindows that showed slowly-changing views of extraterrestrial scenery.

Humphries paid no attention to the starkly beautiful Martian sunset or the windswept cloud deck of Jupiter. His mind was on Lars Fuchs.

"The hearing will be held in the IAA offices here in Selene," said Diane Verwoerd. Seated on a plush stool at the handsome mahogany bar, she nursed a long slim glass of sickly greenish Pernod and water.

Verwoerd was the only other person in the room with Humphries. She was still in her office clothes: a white sleeveless turtleneck blouse under a maroon blazer, with dark charcoal slacks that accentuated her long legs. Humphries had already changed to a casual open-necked shirt and light tan chinos.

"Is he bringing his wife with him?" Humphries asked as he stepped out from behind the bar.

"Probably." Verwoerd swiveled on her stool to follow him as he paced idly along the rows of leather-bound books.

"You don't know for certain?"

"I can find out easily enough," she said.

Humphries muttered, "He wouldn't leave her alone on that rock."

"It didn't do you any good the last time he brought her here."

He shot her a venomous look.

"We have something else to worry about," Verwoerd said. "This man Harbin."

Humphries's expression changed. It didn't soften: it merely went from one object of anger to another.

"That's why you wanted to talk to me alone," he said.

She raised a brow slightly. "That's why I agreed to have a drink with you, yes."

"But not dinner."

"I have other plans for dinner," she said. "Besides, you should be thinking about Harbin. Thinking hard."

"What's the situation?"

She took a sip of her drink, then placed the glass carefully on the bar. "Obviously, he failed to eliminate Fuchs."

"From what I've heard, Fuchs nearly eliminated him."

"His ship was damaged and he had to break off his attack on *Starpower*. Apparently Fuchs was expecting him; at least, that's what Harbin believes."

"I don't care a termite fart's worth for what he believes. I'm paying him for results and he's failed. Now I'm going to have the idiotic IAA to deal with."

Humphries kicked at an ottoman that was in his way and sat heavily on the sofa facing the bar. His face was an image of pure disgust.

"You have Harbin to deal with, too."

"What?" He looked up sharply at her. "What do you mean?"

"He knows enough to hurt you. Badly."

"He's never seen me. He dealt entirely with Grigor."

With deliberate patience, Verwoerd said, "If Harbin tells the IAA what he's been doing, do you think they'll lay the blame in Grigor's lap or yours?"

"They can't—"

"Don't you think they're intelligent enough to realize that Grigor would never authorize attacks on prospectors' ships unless you ordered them?"

Humphries looked as if he wanted to throw his drink at her. It's dangerous being the messenger, Verwoerd told herself, when you bring bad news.

"You'll have to eliminate Harbin, then," he said. "Maybe Grigor, too."

And then me? Verwoerd asked herself. Aloud, she replied, "Harbin's thought of that possibility. He claims he's sent copies of his ship's log to a few friends on Earth."

"Nonsense! How could he—"

"Tight-beam laser links. Coded data. It's done every day. It's the way he communicated with our own tankers out there in the Belt."

"Send messages all the way back to Earth?"

Verwoerd took up her drink again. "It's done every day," she repeated.

"He's bluffing," Humphries mumbled.

She got off the stool and stepped toward the sofa where he was sitting. Nudging the ottoman into position with one foot, she sat on it and leaned toward him, arms on her knees, drink in both hands.

"Even if he's bluffing, it's too big a risk to take. Eliminating him won't be easy. He's a trained fighter and he's tough."

"He's coming here to Selene on an HSS vessel, isn't he?" Humphries pointed out. "The crew can get rid of him."

Verwoerd sighed like a schoolteacher facing a boy who hadn't done his homework. "Then you'd have half a dozen people who'd have something on you. Besides, I don't think the entire crew could take him. As I said, he's trained and he's tough. Things could get quite messy if we try to take him out."

"Then what do you recommend?" he asked sullenly.

"Let me deal with him. Personally."

"You?"

She nodded. "Keep Grigor out of this. Harbin is most likely worried that we want to take him out, especially since he failed with Fuchs and he knows enough to hang us all. Let me show him that it's not that way. I'll offer him a bonus, send him back to Earth with a fat bank account."

"So he can blackmail me for the rest of his life."

"Yes, of course. That's exactly what he'll think. And we'll let him go on thinking that until he's living it up on Earth and his guard is down."

A crooked smile slowly curled across Humphries's lips.

"Delilah," he murmured.

Verwoerd saw that he was satisfied with her plan. She took a long swallow of the licorice-flavored Pernod, then agreed, "Delilah."

Humphries's smile turned sardonic. "Are you going to fuck him, too?"

She made herself smile back. "If I have to."

But she was thinking, You don't know whose hair is going to get trimmed, Martin. And there's more than one way to screw a man; even you.

Fuchs had dreaded this moment. He knew it had to come, though. There was no way around it. The IAA official was due to arrive at Ceres in another few hours.

He started packing his travel bag for the trip to Selene. When Amanda took her bag from the closet and laid it on the bed beside his, he told her that he was going without her.

"What do you mean?" Amanda asked, obviously startled by his decision.

"Precisely what I said. George, Nodon and I are going. I want you to remain here."

She looked puzzled, hurt. "But, Lars, I—"

"You are *not* going with me!" Fuchs said sharply.

Shocked at his vehemence, Amanda stared at him openmouthed as if he had slapped her in the face.

"That's final," he snapped.

"But, Lars—"

"No buts, and no arguments," he said. "You stay here and run what's left of the business while I'm in Selene."

"Lars, you can't go without me. I won't let you!"

He tried to stare her down. This is the hardest part, he realized. I've got to hurt her, there's no other way to do this.

"Amanda," he said, trying to sound stern, trying to keep his own doubts and pain out of his voice, out of his face. "I have made up my mind. I need you to remain here. I'm not a little boy who must bring his mother with him wherever he goes."

"Your mother!"

"Whatever," he said. "I'm going without you."

"But why?"

"Because that's what I want," he said, raising his voice. "I know that you think I'd be safer if you were with me, that Humphries won't attack me if he believes you might be hurt, too. Poppycock! I don't need your protection. I don't want it."

She burst into tears and fled to the lavatory, leaving him standing by the bed in agony.

If he's going to try to kill me, it won't matter to him whether Amanda's with me or not. The closer I get to hurting him, the more desperate he becomes. She'll be safer here, among friends, among people who know her. He wants to kill me, not her. I'll face him without her. It will be better that way.

He was certain he was right. If only he couldn't hear her sobbing on the other side of the thin door.

Hector Wilcox felt extremely uneasy about going to the Moon. His flight from the spaceport at Munich had been terrifying, despite all the reassurances of the Astro Corporation employees. Their stout little Clippership looked sturdy enough when he boarded it. The flight attendant who showed him to his seat went on at length about the ship's diamond structure hull and the reliability records that Clipperships had run up. All well and good, Wilcox thought. He strapped himself firmly into his seat and, fortified by several whiskies beforehand and a medicinal patch plastered on the inside of his elbow to ward against spacesickness, he gripped the seat's armrests and listened with growing apprehension to the countdown.

Takeoff terrified him. It was like an explosion that jolted every bone in his body. He felt squashed down in his seat, then before he could utter a word of complaint he was weightless, floating against the straps of his safety harness, his stomach rising up into his throat despite the medicine patch. Swallowing bile, he reached for the retch bags tucked into the pouch on the seat back in front of him.

By the time the Clippership had docked with the space station, Wilcox was wishing that he'd insisted on holding the damnable hearing on Earth. There were plenty of smiling, uniformed Astro personnel to help him out of the Clippership and into the transfer vehicle that would go the rest of the way to the Moon. Groaning in zero gravity, Wilcox allowed them to haul him around like a helpless invalid and tuck him into a seat on the transfer ship that was far less comfortable then the Clippership's had been.

At least there was some feeling of gravity when the transfer vehicle started its high-thrust burn Moonward. But that dwindled away all too soon, and for the next several hours Wilcox wondered if he was going to survive this journey.

Gradually, though, he began to feel better. His stomach didn't feel so queasy; the pressure behind his eyes eased off. If he didn't turn his head or make any sudden moves, zero gravity was almost pleasurable.

Once they landed at Selene's Armstrong spaceport, the light lunar gravity gave Wilcox a renewed sense of up-and-down. He was able to unstrap and get out of his chair without help. He stumbled at first, but by the time he had been checked through customs and rented a pair of weighted boots, he felt almost normal.

The soothing elegance of the Hotel Luna's lobby helped Wilcox to feel even more at home. Quiet luxury always pleased him, and although the lobby was slightly tatty here and there, the general tone and atmosphere of the place was reassuring. The local IAA flunkies had taken the best suite in Selene's only hotel for him. Spare no expense, Wilcox thought as he looked around the sumptuous sitting room, so long as it's coming out of the taxpayers' pocketbook and not mine. An assistant manager brought him to the suite, unpacked his bags for him, and even politely refused the tip Wilcox proferred. The hotel staff had prepared everything for him, including a well-stocked bar. One good jolt of whisky and Wilcox felt almost normal again.

There was a tap on the door, and before Wilcox could say a word, the door slid open and a liveried servant pushed in a rolling table laden with covered dishes and a half-dozen bottles of wine.

Surprised, Wilcox began to protest, "I didn't order—"

Then Martin Humphries walked into the suite, all smiles.

"I thought you'd appreciate a good meal, Hector," said Humphries. "This is from my own kitchen, not the regular hotel fare." Gesturing toward the bottles, he added, "From my own cellar, too."

Wilcox broke into a genuinely pleased smile. "Why, Martin, for goodness' sake. How kind of you."

As the waiter silently set out their dinner, Humphries explained, "We shouldn't be seen in a public restaurant together, and I couldn't invite you down to my home without it seeming improper. . . ."

"Quite so," Wilcox agreed. "Too many damnable snoops willing to believe the worst about anyone."

"So I decided to bring dinner to you. I hope you don't mind."

"Not at all! I'm delighted to see you again. How long has it been?"

"I've been living here in Selene for more than six years now."

"Has it been that long?" Wilcox brushed his moustache with a fingertip. "But, eh . . . aren't we running the risk of seeming impropriety? After all, with the hearing coming up—"

"No risk at all," Humphries said smoothly. "This man is a loyal employee of mine, and the hotel people can be relied on to be discreet."

"I see."

"You can't be too careful these days, especially a man in such a high position of trust as you are."

"Rather," said Wilcox, smiling as he watched the waiter open the first bottle of wine.

CHAPTER 34

Dorik Harbin looked around the spare one-room apartment. Good enough, he thought. He knew that in Selene, the lower the level of your living quarters, the more expensive. It was mostly nonsense: you were just as safe five meters below the Moon's surface as you were at fifty or even five hundred. But people let their emotions rule them, just as on Earth they paid more for an upper floor in a condo tower, even though the view might be nothing more than another condo tower standing next door.

He had been tense during the flight in from the Belt. After leaving the crippled *Shanidar* with an HSS tanker, he had received orders from Grigor to report to Selene. They provided him with a coffin-sized berth on an HSS freighter that was hauling ores to the Moon. Harbin knew that if they were going to assassinate him, this would be the time and place for it.

Apparently Grigor and his superiors believed his claim that he had sent complete records of *Shanidar*'s campaign of destruction to several friends on Earth. Otherwise they would have gotten rid of him, or tried to. Harbin had no friends on Earth or anywhere else. Acquaintances, yes, several people scattered here and there that he could trust a little. No family; they had all been killed while he was still a child.

Harbin had sent a rough ship's log from *Shanidar* to three persons he had known for many years: one had been the sergeant who had trained him in the Peacekeepers, now retired and living in someplace called Pennsylvania; another, the aged imam from his native village; the third was the widow of a man whose murder he had avenged the last time he had visited his homeland.

The instructions he had sent with the logs—a request, really—were to give the data to the news media if they learned that Harbin had died. He knew that if Grigor received orders to kill him, no one on Earth would likely hear of his death. But the faint possibility that *Shanidar*'s log might be revealed to the public was enough to stay Grigor's hand. At least, Harbin estimated that it was so.

It would have been easier to keep his murder quiet if they'd killed him on the ship coming in, Harbin thought. The fact that he was now quartered in this one-room apartment in Selene told him that they did not plan to kill him. Not yet, at least.

He almost relaxed. The room was comfortable enough: nearly spacious, compared to the cramped quarters of a spacecraft. The freezer and cupboards were well stocked; Harbin decided to throw everything in the recycler and buy his own provisions in Selene's food market.

He had his head under the sink, checking to see if there were any unwanted attachments to his water supply, when he heard a light tap at his door.

Grigor, he thought. Or one of his people.

He got to his feet, closed the cabinet, and walked six steps to the door, feeling the comfortable solidity of the electrodagger strapped to the inside of his right wrist, beneath the loose cuff of his tunic. He had charged the battery in the dagger's hilt as soon as he had entered the apartment, even before unpacking.

He glanced at the small display plate beside the door. Not Grigor. A woman. Harbin slowly slid the accordion door back, balanced on the balls of his feet, ready to spring aside if this woman pointed a weapon at him.

She looked surprised. She was almost Harbin's own height, he saw: slim, with smoky dark skin and darker hair curling over her shoulders. She wore a sleeveless sheer sweater that revealed little but suggested much. Form-fitting slacks and soft, supple-looking boots.

"You are Dorik Harbin?" she asked, in a silky contralto voice.

"Who are you?" he countered.

"Diane Verwoerd," she said, stepping into the room, forcing Harbin to swing back from the doorway so she could enter. "I'm Martin Humphries's personal assistant."

Diane looked him up and down and saw a tall, lean, *hard*-looking man with a fierce dark beard and a world of suspicion in his cold blue eyes. Strange, startling eyes, she thought. Dead man's eyes. Killer's eyes. He was wearing ordinary coveralls that looked faded from long use, but clean and crisp as a military uniform. A strong, muscled body beneath the clothes, she judged. An impressive man, for a hired killer.

"I was expecting Grigor," Harbin said.

"I hope you're not disappointed," she said, heading for the couch across the room.

"Not at all. You said you are Mr. Humphries's personal assistant?"

She sat and crossed her long legs. "Yes."

"Will I meet him?"

"No. You will deal with me."

He did not reply. Instead, Harbin went to the refrigerator and took out a bottle of wine. She watched him open it, then search in the cabinet above the sink for wine glasses. Is he using this time to think of what he should say? Verwoerd asked herself. Finally he pulled out two simple tumblers and splashed some wine into them.

"I arrived only a few hours ago," he said, handing her one glass, then pulling up the desk chair to sit facing her. "I don't know where things are yet."

"I hope this room is comfortable for you," she said.

"It will do."

She waited for him to say more, but he simply studied her with those icepick blue eyes. Not undressing her. There was nothing sexual in it. He was . . . she tried to find the right word: *controlled*. That's it: he's completely under control. Every gesture, every word he speaks. I wonder what he looks like beneath the beard, Verwoerd thought. Is he the ruggedly handsome type, or does the beard hide a weak chin? Ruggedly handsome, she guessed.

The silence stretched. She took a sip of the wine. Slightly bitter. Perhaps it will improve after it's breathed a while. Harbin did not touch his wine; he simply held the glass in his left hand and kept his eyes riveted on her.

"We have a lot to discuss," she said at last.

"I suppose that's true."

"You seem to be afraid that we want to get rid of you."

"That's what I would do if I were in your position. I'm a liability to you now, isn't that so?"

He's brutally frank, she thought. "Mr. Harbin, please let me assure you that we have no intention of causing you harm."

He smiled at that, and she saw strong white teeth behind the dense black beard.

"In fact, Mr. Humphries has told me to give you a bonus for the work you've done."

He gave her a long, hard look, then said, "Why don't we stop this fencing? You wanted me to kill Fuchs and I failed. Now he's here in Selene ready to testify that you're behind the attacks on prospectors' ships. Why should you pay me a bonus for that?"

"We'll pay for your silence, Mr. Harbin."

"Because you know that if you kill me the ship's log will go to the news media."

"We have no intention of killing you." Verwoerd nodded toward his untouched glass. "You can drink all the wine you want."

He put the tumbler down on the thinly carpeted floor. "Ms. Verwoerd—"

"Diane," she said, before she had a chance to think about it.

He tilted his head slightly. "Diane, then. Let me explain how this looks to me."

"Please do." She noted that he did not tell her to use his first name.

"Your corporation hired me to scare the independent prospectors out of the Belt. I knocked off several of their ships, but this man Fuchs caused a fuss. Then you instructed me to get rid of Fuchs, and this I failed to do."

"We are disappointed, Mr. Harbin, but that doesn't mean there's any reason for you to fear for your safety."

"Doesn't it?"

"We'll handle this hearing. In a way, it's an opportunity for us to deal with Fuchs in a different manner. Your part of this operation is finished. All we want to do is pay you off and thank you for your work. I know it wasn't easy."

"People like you don't come to people like me for easy jobs," Harbin said.

He's not afraid, Verwoerd saw. He's not frightened or disappointed or angry. He's like a block of ice. No visible emotions. No, she corrected herself. He's more like a panther, a lithe, deadly predator. Every muscle in his body under control, every nerve alert and ready. He could kill me in an instant if he wanted to.

She felt strangely thrilled. I wonder what he would be like if I could break through that control of his. What would it be like to have all that pent-up energy inside me? Not now. Later, she commanded herself. After the hearing is over. If we come out of the hearing okay, then I can relax with him. If we don't . . . I'd hate to be the one sent to terminate him. If it comes to that, we'll need a team of people for the job. A team of very good people.

Then she thought, Why think about terminating him? Use him!

Can I make him loyal to me? she asked herself. Can I use him for my personal agenda? Smiling inwardly, she thought, It could be fun. It could be very pleasurable.

Aloud, she said, "There is one more task you could do for us before you . . . eh, retire."

"What is that?" he asked, his voice flat, his eyes riveted on hers.

"You'll have to go to Ceres. I can arrange a high-thrust flight for you. But it must be very quiet; no one is to know. Not even Grigor."

He stared at her for long, intense moment. "Not even Grigor?" he muttered.

"No. You will report directly to me."

Harbin smiled at that, and she wondered again how he would look without his beard.

"Do you ever shave?" she asked.

"I was going to, when you knocked at my door."

Hours later, sticky and sweaty in bed beside him, Diane grinned to herself. Being Delilah was thoroughly enjoyable.

Harbin turned to her and slid a hand across her midriff. "About this business on Ceres," he said, surprising her.

"Yes?"

"Who do I have to kill?"

CHAPTER 35

Much to Hector Wilcox's misgiving, Douglas Stavenger inserted himself into the hearing. Two days before the hearing was to begin, Stavenger invited Wilcox to dinner at the Earthview restaurant. Wilcox knew it was not a purely social invitation. If the youthful founder of Selene wanted to be in on the hearing, there was nothing the IAA executive could do about it without raising hackles.

Stavenger was very diplomatic, of course. He offered a conference room in Selene's offices, up in one of the towers that supported the dome of the Grand Plaza. The price of his hospitality was to allow him to sit in on the hearing.

"It'll be pretty dull stuff, mostly," Wilcox warned, over dinner his second night on the Moon.

"Oh, I don't think so," said Stavenger, with the bright enthusiasm of a youth. "Anything involving Martin Humphries is bound to be interesting."

So that's it, Wilcox said to himself as he picked at his fruit salad. He's following Martin's trail.

"You know, Mr. Humphries won't be present at the hearing," he said.

"Really?" Stavenger looked surprised. "I thought that Fuchs was accusing him of piracy."

Wilcox frowned his deepest. "Piracy," he sneered. "Poppycock."

Stavenger smiled brightly. "That's what the hearing is for, isn't it? To determine the validity of the charge?"

"Oh, yes, of course," said Wilcox hastily. "To be sure."

Fuchs had not slept well his first two nights in Selene, and the night before the hearing began he expected to be too jumpy to sleep at all, but strangely, he slept soundly the whole night through. Pancho had come up to Selene and treated him to a fine dinner at the Earthview Restaurant. Perhaps the wine had something to do with my sleeping, he told himself as he brushed his teeth that morning.

He had dreamed, he knew, but he couldn't remember much of his dreams. Amanda was in them, and George, and some vague dark looming danger. He could not recall any of the details.

When his phone chimed he thought it must be Pancho, ready to pick him up and go with him to the hearing room.

Instead, the wallscreen showed Amanda's beautiful face. Fuchs felt a rush of joy that she had called. Then he saw that she looked tired, concerned.

"Lars, darling, I'm just calling to wish you well at the hearing and to tell you that I love you. Everything here is going quite well. The prospectors are giving us more business than we can handle, and there hasn't been a bit of trouble from any of the HSS people."

Of course not, Fuchs thought. They don't want to raise any suspicions while this hearing is going on.

"Good luck in the hearing, darling. I'll be waiting for you to call and tell me how it turned out. I miss you. I love you!"

Her image winked out, the wallscreen went blank. Fuchs glanced at the clock on his bed table, then swiftly ordered the computer to reply to her message.

"The hearing begins in half an hour," he said, knowing that by the time Amanda heard his words the meeting would almost be starting. "I'm sorry I didn't bring you with me. I miss you, too. Terribly. I'll call as soon as the hearing ends. And I love you, too, my precious. With all my heart."

The phone chimed again. This time it was Pancho. "Rise and shine, Lars, ol' buddy. Time to get this bronco out of the chutes."

Fuchs was disappointed that Humphries did not show up for the hearing. On thinking about it, though, he was not surprised. The man is a coward who sends others to do his dirty work for him, he thought.

"Hey, look," Pancho said as they entered the conference room. "Doug Stavenger's here."

Stavenger and half a dozen others were sitting in the comfortable wheeled chairs arranged along one wall of the room. The conference table had been moved to the rear wall and set out with drinks and finger foods. A smaller table was at the other side of the room, flanked by two chairs already occupied by men in business suits. One of them was overweight, ruddy, red-haired; the other looked as lean and jittery as a racing greyhound. They each held palmcomps in their laps. The wallscreen behind the table showed the black and silver logo of the International Astronautical Society. Two clusters of chairs had been arranged in front of the table. George and Nodon were already seated there. Fuchs saw that the other set was fully occupied by what he presumed to be HSS personnel.

"Good luck, buddy," Pancho whispered, gesturing Fuchs toward the chairs up front. She went back to sit beside Stavenger.

Wondering idly who was paying for the food and drink that had been set out, Fuchs took the chair between Big George and Nodon. He had barely sat down when one of the men seated up front announced, "This hearing will come to order. Mr. Hector Wilcox, chief counsel of the International Astronautical Authority, presiding."

Everyone got to their feet, and a gray-haired distinguished-looking gentleman in a Saville Row three-piece suit came in from the side door and took his place behind the table. He put a hand-sized computer on the table and flicked it open. Fuchs noticed that an aluminum carafe beaded with condensation and a cut crystal glass rested on a corner of the table.

"Please be seated," said Hector Wilcox. "Let's get this over with as efficiently as we can."

It begins, Fuchs said to himself, his heart thudding under his ribs, his palms suddenly sweaty.

Wilcox peered in his direction. "Which of you is Lars Fuchs?"

"I am," said Fuchs.

"You have charged Humphries Space Systems with piracy, have you not?"

"I have not."

Wilcox's brows shot toward his scalp. "You have not?"

Fuchs was amazed at his own cheek. He heard himself say, "I do not charge a corporation with criminal acts. I charge a person, the man who heads that corporation: Martin Humphries."

Wilcox's astonishment turned to obvious displeasure.

"Are you implying that the acts you call piracy—which have yet to be established as actually occurring—were deliberately ordered by Mr. Martin Humphries?"

"That is precisely what I am saying, sir."

On the other side of the makeshift aisle, a tall, dark-haired woman rose unhurriedly to her feet.

"Your honor, I am Mr. Humphries's personal assistant, and on his behalf I categorically deny this charge. It's ludicrous."

Big George hopped to his feet and waved the stump of his arm over his head. "Y'call this ludicrous? I di'n't get this pickin' daisies!"

"Order!" Wilcox slapped the table with the flat of his hand. "Sit

down, both of you. I will not have outbursts in this hearing. We will proceed along calm, reasoned lines."

Verwoerd and George resumed their seats.

Pointing a bony finger at Fuchs, Wilcox said, "Now, sir, if you have
evidence to sustain a charge of piracy, let us hear it. We'll look into the
responsibility for such acts after we ascertain that they have actually
happened."

Fuchs slowly rose, feeling a trembling anger in his gut. "You have the
transcription of the battle between my ship, *Starpower*, and the ship that
attacked us. You have seen the damage inflicted on *Starpower*. Mr.
Ambrose, here, lost his arm in that battle."

Wilcox glanced over his shoulder at the ruddy-faced IAA flunky, who
nodded once. "Noted," he said to Fuchs.

"That same ship earlier attacked Mr. Ambrose's ship, *Waltzing
Matilda*, and left him and his crewman for dead."

"Do you have any evidence for this, other than your unsupported
word?" Wilcox asked.

"*Waltzing Matilda* is drifting in the Belt. We can provide approximate
coordinates for a search, if you wish to undertake it."

Wilcox shook his head. "I doubt that such a search will be necessary."

"Earlier," Fuchs resumed, "several others vessels were attacked: *The
Lady of the Lake, Aswan, The Star*—"

Verwoerd called from her chair, "There is no evidence that any of
those ships were attacked."

"They disappeared without a trace," Fuchs snapped. "Their signals
cut off abruptly."

With a smile, Verwoerd said, "That is not evidence that they were
attacked."

"Quite so," said Wilcox.

"In most of those cases, the asteroids that those ships claimed were
later claimed by Humphries Space Systems," Fuchs pointed out.

"What of it?" Verwoerd retorted. "HSS ships have laid claim to many
hundreds of asteroids. And if you examine the record carefully, you will
see that four of the six asteroids in question have been claimed by entities
other than HSS."

Wilcox turned toward the lean assistant on his left. The man nodded
hastily and said, "Three of them were claimed by a corporation called
Bandung Associates and the fourth by the Church of the Written Word.
None of these entities are associated with HSS; I checked thoroughly."

"So what this hearing boils down to," Wilcox said, turning back to
Fuchs, "is your assertion that you were attacked."

"For that I have evidence, and you have seen it," Fuchs said, boiling inside.

"Yes, yes," said Wilcox. "There's no doubt that you were attacked. But attacked by whom? That's the real question."

"By a ship working for HSS," Fuchs said, feeling he was pointing out the obvious. "Under the orders of Martin Humphries."

"Can you prove that?"

"No employee of HSS would take such a step without the personal approval of Humphries himself," Fuchs insisted. "He even had one of my people killed, murdered in cold blood!"

"You are referring to the murder of a Niles Ripley, are you not?" asked Wilcox.

"Yes. A deliberate murder to stop our construction of the habitat we're building—"

Verwoerd interrupted. "We concede that Mr. Ripley was killed by an employee of Humphries Space Systems. But it was a private matter; the killing was neither ordered nor condoned by HSS. And Mr. Fuchs personally dispatched the killer, in a violent act of vigilantism."

Wilcox fixed Fuchs with a stern gaze. "Frontier justice, eh? It's too bad that you executed him. His testimony might have supported your case."

Feeling exasperated, Fuchs said, "Who else would benefit from all these criminal acts?"

With a wry smile, Wilcox said, "I was hoping you could tell me, Mr. Fuchs. That's why we've gone to the expense and trouble of holding this hearing. Who is responsible here?"

Fuchs closed his eyes briefly. I don't want to bring Amanda into this. I don't want to make this seem like a personal feud between Humphries and me.

"Do you have anything else to offer, Mr. Fuchs?"

Before he could reply, George got to his feet again and said, very calmly, "Everybody on Ceres knows that Humphries is tryin' to squeeze Fuchs out of the Belt. Ask anybody."

"Mr . . ." Wilcox glanced down at his computer screen. "Ambrose, is it? Mr. Ambrose, what 'everybody knows' is not evidence in a court of law. Nor in this hearing."

George sat down, mumbling to himself.

"The fact is," Fuchs said, struggling to keep from screaming, "that someone is killing people, someone is attacking prospectors' ships, *someone* is committing terrible crimes in the Asteroid Belt. The IAA must take action, must protect us . . ." He stopped. He realized he was begging, almost whining.

Wilcox leaned back in his chair. "Mr. Fuchs, I quite agree that your frontier is a violent, lawless place. But the International Astronautical Authority has neither the power nor the legal authority to serve as a police force across the Asteroid Belt. It is up to the citizens of the Belt themselves to provide their own protection, to police themselves."

"We are being systematically attacked by Humphries Space Systems personnel!" Fuchs insisted.

"You are being attacked, I grant you," Wilcox responded, with a sad, condescending smile. "Most likely by renegades from among your own rough and ready population. I see no evidence linking Humphries Space Systems to your problems in any way, shape or manner."

"You don't want to see!" Fuchs raged.

Wilcox stared at him coldly. "This hearing is concluded," he said.

"But you haven't—"

"It's finished," Wilcox snapped. He stood up, grabbed his computer, clicked its lid shut and tucked it into his jacket pocket. Then he turned and strode out of the room, leaving Fuchs standing there, frustrated and furious.

CHAPTER 36

Straining to keep a satisfied smile off her face, Diane Verwoerd led the squad of Humphries employees out of the hearing room, leaving Fuchs and his two friends standing there in helpless, confused frustration.

Out in the corridor she made polite small talk with Douglas Stavenger and Pancho Lane as they left, looking disappointed at the outcome of the hearing. Verwoerd knew that Pancho was Humphries's chief opponent on the board of Astro Corporation, and that Humphries would not be satisfied until he had full control of Astro. Which means, she told herself, that once we've finally gotten rid of Fuchs, Pancho is next.

She hurried to the power stairs that led down to her office. Once there, alone, she put through a tight-beam laser call to Dorik Harbin. He should be arriving at Ceres in another hour or so, she knew.

It took nearly twenty minutes before his face appeared on her wallscreen: smolderingly handsome without the beard, his chin firm and hard, his eyes icy blue, intent.

"I know you can't reply to this before you land," she said to Harbin's image. "But I wanted to wish you good luck and tell you that . . . well, I'm counting the minutes until you get back here to me."

She took a deliberate breath, then added, "I've made arrangements with the HSS people at Ceres. The drugs you need will be there, waiting for you."

Verwoerd cut the connection. The screen went dark. Only then did she smile. Keep him personally bound to you, she told herself. Use his weaknesses; use his strengths. He's going to be very valuable, especially if you ever have to protect yourself from Martin.

She turned and studied her reflection in the mirror on the far wall of her office. Delilah, she said to herself, and laughed.

"So whattawe do now?" George asked as he, Fuchs and Nodon made their way down the power stairs.

Fuchs shook his head miserably. "I don't know. This hearing was a farce. The IAA has given Humphries a free hand to do whatever he wants."

"Looks that way," George agreed, scratching at his beard.

Nodon said nothing.

"Amanda," Fuchs said. "I must tell her what's happened. I must tell her that I've failed."

Harbin looked over the eight men that had been assigned to his command. A ragtag bunch, at best. Roughnecks, hoodlums, petty thugs. Not one of them had a scrap of combat training or true military discipline. But then, he remembered, this isn't really a military operation. It's a simple theft, nothing more.

He had spent the high-g flight from Selene studying the plan and background information Diane had given him, but he had expected reliable men to work under him, not a gaggle of hooligans. Steeling himself to his task, Harbin silently repeated the mantra that the workman does not blame his tools, and the warrior must fight with what he has at hand. The first task is to instill these morons with some purpose other than cracking skulls and making money.

Harbin assumed that none of the louts assigned to him gave a damn about what had happened to the hotheaded Tracy Buchanan, but the doctrine that his old sergeant had drilled into him asserted that it was beneficial to a unit's cohesion and teamwork to build group solidarity in any way possible.

So he said to them, "You remember what that man Fuchs did to Trace Buchanan?" It was purely a rhetorical question.

They nodded unenthusiastically. Buchanan had been a bully and a fool; he did not have friends, only associates who were afraid to make him angry. None of them mourned the late Mr. Buchanan.

But Harbin felt he had to whip up some enthusiasm among his eight underlings. He had brought them together in the cramped little office at the HSS warehouse: eight men who had been flown to Ceres specifically because they could follow orders and weren't strangers to mayhem.

"Okay," Harbin told them. "Tonight we even the score. Tonight we hit Fuchs's warehouse and clean it out once and for all."

"I got a better idea," said Santorini.

Harbin felt the old anger simmering inside him. Santorini had the intelligence of a baboon. "What is it?"

"You wanna get even with Fuchs, why don't we do his wife?"

The others all grinned at the thought.

Are these the best that Diane could hire? Harbin asked himself. Or did somebody in her office merely scrape a few barroom floors and send these specimens here to Ceres?

"Our orders are to leave her strictly alone," he said sharply. "Those orders come from the top. Don't even go near her. Understand? Anybody who even looks in her direction will be in deep shit. Is that clear?"

"Somebody up there likes her," one of the lunks said.

"Somebody up there's got the hots for her," agreed the goon next to him.

Harbin snarled, "That *somebody* will fry your testicles and then feed them to you in slices if you don't follow orders. Our job is to hit the warehouse. We go in, we do the job, and then we leave. If we do it right you can all go back to Earth with a big fat bonus in our accounts."

"Plenty of slash back home."

"Yeah, 'specially if you got money."

Harbin let them think about how they were going to enjoy their bonuses. Get them away from thinking about Fuchs's wife. Diane had been very specific about that. She is not to be harmed or even threatened. Not in any way, shape, or form.

The warehouse was something else.

"Where the hell have you been?" Humphries snapped.

Verwoerd allowed herself a small smile. "I took a long lunch. A victory celebration."

"The whole damned afternoon?"

Humphries was sitting in the mansion's dining room, alone at one end of the long rosewood table, the remains of his dinner before him. He did not invite his assistant to sit down with him.

"I expected you here as soon as the hearing ended."

"You got the news without me," she said coolly. "In fact, you knew how the hearing would turn out before it ever started, didn't you?"

His frown deepened. "You're pretty damned sassy this evening."

"Fuchs is on his way back to Ceres," she said. "By the time he gets there he won't have a warehouse. His company will be broke, he'll be ruined, and you'll be king of the Asteroid Belt. What more do you want?"

She knew what he wanted. He wanted Amanda Cunningham Fuchs. For that, though, it won't be enough to ruin Fuchs, she thought. We'll have to kill the man.

Humphries's frown dissolved slowly, replaced by a sly smile. "So," he asked, "what are you doing for sex now that you've sent your soldier boy off to Ceres?"

Verwoerd tried to keep the surprise off her face. *The sneaking bastard has been keeping me under surveillance!*

"You bugged his quarters," she said coldly.

Grinning, Humphries said, "Would you like to see a replay?"

It took her a moment to get her emotions under control. Finally she managed to say, "He's an interesting man. He quotes Persian poetry."

"In bed."

Still standing, Verwoerd stared down at him for a long moment, then conceded the point with a curt nod, thinking, *He probably has my apartment bugged, too! Does he know about Bandung Associates?*

But Humphries seemed more amused than annoyed. "I have a proposition for you."

Guardedly, she asked, "What kind of a proposition?"

"I want you to bear my child."

She could feel her eyes go round. "What?"

Laughing, Humphries leaned back in the cushioned dining room chair and said, "You won't go to bed with me, the least you can do is carry my child for me."

She pulled out the chair closest to her and sank slowly into it.

"What are you saying?" she asked.

Almost offhandedly, Humphries said, "I've decided to have a child. A son. My medical experts are picking the best possible egg cells for me to inseminate. We're going to clone me. My son will be as close to me as modern biological science can make him."

"Human cloning is outlawed," Verwoerd murmured.

"In most nations on Earth," Humphries conceded. "But even on Earth there are places where a man of means can have himself cloned. And here in Selene, well—why not?"

Another little Martin Humphries, Verwoerd thought. But she said nothing.

"The cloning procedure is still a bit dicey," he went on, as casually as a man discussing the stock market, "but my people should be able to produce some viable fertilized eggs and get a few women to carry them."

"Then why do you want me?"

He waved a hand. "You're a very good physical specimen; you ought to make a good home for my clone. Besides, it's rather poetic, don't you think? You won't have sex with me, but you'll bear my son. That boy-toy of yours isn't the only one with a poetic soul."

"I see," Verwoerd said, feeling slightly numbed by his cheerful arrogance.

"What I need is several wombs to carry the zygotes to term. I've decided you'd be perfect for the job. Young, healthy, and all that."

"Me."

"I've gone through your medical records and your family history," Humphries said. "You might say that I know you inside out."

She was not amused.

"You carry my son to term," he said, his smile fading, his tone more commanding. "You'll get a very sizable bonus. I'll even transfer a couple more of my asteroids to your Bandung Associates."

The pit of her stomach went hollow.

"Did you think you could embezzle three very profitable asteroids from me without my finding out about it?" Humphries asked, grinning with satisfaction.

Verwoerd knew it was hopeless. She felt glad that she had Dorik on her side.

CHAPTER 37

As they pulled up their convoy of four minitractors to the entrance of the Helvetia warehouse, Harbin saw that there were only two people on duty there, and one of them was a woman, gray-haired and grandmotherly, but with a hard, scowling face. She was stocky, stumpy, built like a weightlifter.

"What do you guys want?" she demanded as Harbin got down from the lead tractor.

"Don't give us a hard time, grandmother," he said gently. "Just relax and do what you're told."

A face-to-face job like this was far different from shooting up spacecraft in the dark emptiness of the Belt. That was like a game; this was blood. Be still, he commanded silently. Don't make me kill you. But he felt the old rage building up inside him: the manic fury that led to death.

"What are you doing here?" the woman repeated truculently. "Who the hell are you assholes?"

Working hard to keep his inner rage under control, Harbin waved his undisciplined team into the Helvetia warehouse. They all wore breathing masks, nothing unusual in the dusty tunnels of Ceres. They also wore formfitting shower caps that had been ferried in all the way from Earth; with the caps on, no one could see a man's hair color or style. Harbin also made certain none of his crew had any name tags or other identification on themselves. If Tracy Buchanan had taken that simple precaution he would undoubtedly still be alive now, Harbin thought.

"What's this goddam parade of tractors for?" the woman demanded.

She was wearing a breathing mask, too. So was the skinny kid standing a few paces down the shadowy aisle of tall shelves.

"We're here to empty out your warehouse," Santorini said, strutting up to her.

"What the hell do you mean?" the woman asked angrily, reaching for the phone console.

Santorini swatted her to the floor with a backhand smack. The kid back in the stacks threw up his hands in the universal sign of surrender.

"Come on," Santorini said, waving to the rest of them.

Harbin nodded his approval. They started to move in. The kid stood absolutely still, frozen in terror from the look on his ashen face. Santorini kicked him in the stomach so hard he bounced off the shelving and collapsed groaning to the floor.

"How's that for martial arts?" Santorini shouted over his shoulder as the others revved up the minitractors and trundled into the warehouse, raising billows of black dust.

Swaggering little snot, Harbin thought, looking at the woman Santorini had knocked down. Her lip was bloody, but the look in her eyes proclaimed pure malevolent fury. She struggled to her feet, then lurched toward the phone console.

Harbin grabbed her by one shoulder. "Be careful, grandmother. You could get hurt."

The woman growled and swung her free fist into Harbin's temple. The blow surprised more than hurt him, but it triggered his inner anger.

"Stop it," he snarled, shaking her.

She aimed a kick at his groin. Harbin twisted sideways to catch it on his hip but it still hurt. Without thinking he slid the electrodagger out of its sheath on his wrist and slit her throat.

The old woman gurgled blood and collapsed to the floor like a sack of wet cement.

Fuchs's black mood of frustration and anger deepened into an even darker pit of raging fury as he and Nodon boarded the Astro Corporation ship *Lubbock Lights* bound for Ceres. They had said a lingering goodbye to George at the Pelican Bar the night before.

"I'll be back at the Belt as soon's me arm grows back," George had promised several times, over many beers.

Pancho had bought all their rounds, drinking with them in gloomy comradeship.

Now, with a thundering headache and a towering hatred boiling inside him, Fuchs faced the four-day journey back to Ceres with the exasperation of a caged jungle beast.

When the message came in from Amanda he nearly went berserk.

He was in his privacy compartment, a cubicle barely large enough to hold a narrow cot, trying to sleep. Each time he closed his eyes, though, he saw Martin Humphries sneering at him. And why not? Fuchs raged at himself. He has gotten away with murder. And piracy. No one can stop him; no one will even stand up to him except me, and I'm powerless: a pitiful, impotent, useless fool.

For hours he tossed on the cot, clad only in a pair of shorts, sweating, his hair matted, his jaw stubbled with a two-day growth of beard. Stop this fruitless nonsense! he raged at himself. It's useless to pound your head against a wall. Think! Prepare! If you want revenge on Humphries you must out-think him, you must make plans that are crystal clear, a strategy that will crush him once and for all. But each time he tried to think clearly, logically, his anger rose like a tide of red-hot lava, overwhelming him.

The phone buzzed. Fuchs sat up on the cot and told the computer to open the incoming message.

Amanda's face filled the screen on the bulkhead at the foot of the cot. She looked tense, even though she tried to smile.

"Hello, dear," she said, brushing at a stray lock of hair that had fallen across her forehead. "I'm fine, but they've looted the warehouse."

"What? Looted?"

She couldn't hear or see him, of course. She had sent the message a good fifteen minutes earlier.

"They killed Inga. Out of pure bloodthirsty spite, from what Oscar told me. You remember him, Oscar Jiminez. He's the young boy I hired to help handle the stock."

She's terrified, Fuchs realized, watching the lines of strain on her face, listening to her ramble on.

"They came in during the night shift, when only Inga and Oscar were there, about nine or ten of them, according to Oscar. They beat him and slit Inga's throat. The man who did it laughed about it. Then they emptied the warehouse. Every box, every carton, every bit of stock we had. It's all gone. All of it."

Fuchs's teeth were grinding together so furiously his jaw began to ache. Amanda was trying hard to keep from crying.

"I'm perfectly fine," she was saying. "This all happened late last night. The morning shift found Inga on the floor in a pool of blood and Oscar tied and gagged all the way in the rear of the warehouse. And—and that's the whole story. I'm all right, no one's bothered me at all. In fact, everyone seems to be very protective of me today." She brushed at her hair again. "I suppose that's all there is to say, just at this moment. Hurry home, darling. I love you."

The screen went blank. Fuchs pounded a fist against the unyielding bulkhead and roared a wordless howl of frustration and rage.

He leaped off the cot and ripped open the flimsy sliding door of his cubicle. Still clad in nothing but his shorts he stormed up the ship's passageway to the bridge.

"We must get to Ceres as fast as possible!" he shouted to the lone crewwoman sitting in the command chair.

Her eyes popped wide at the sight of him.

"Now! Speed up! I have to get to Ceres before they murder my wife!"

The woman looked at Fuchs as if he were a madman, but she summoned the captain, who came onto the bridge wrapped in a knee-length silk robe, rubbing sleep from his eyes.

"My wife is in danger!" Fuchs bellowed at the captain. "We must get to Ceres as quickly as possible!"

It was maddening. Fuchs babbled his fears to the captain, who finally understood enough to put in a call to IAA mission control for permission to increase the ship's acceleration. It took nearly half an hour for a reply to come back from IAA headquarters on Earth. Half an hour while Fuchs paced up and down the bridge, muttering, swearing, wondering what was happening at Ceres. The captain suggested that they both put on some clothes, and went back to his quarters. Nodon appeared, then left without a word and returned minutes later carrying a pair of coveralls for Fuchs.

Tugging them on and sealing the Velcro closures, Fuchs asked the crewwoman to open a communications channel to Ceres. She did so without hesitation.

"Amanda," he said, "I'm on the way. We are asking for permission to accelerate faster, so I might be able to reach you before our scheduled arrival time. I'll let you know. Stay in your quarters. Ask some of the people who work for us to act as guards at your door. I'll be there as soon as I can, darling. As soon as I can."

By the time the captain returned to the bridge, face washed, hair combed, and wearing a crisp jumpsuit with his insignia of rank on the cuffs, the answer arrived from IAA control.

Permission denied. *Lubbock Lights* will remain at its current velocity vector and arrive at Ceres in three and a half more days, as scheduled.

Trembling, Fuchs turned from the robotlike IAA controller's image on the screen to the uniformed captain.

"I'm sorry," said the captain, with a sympathetic shrug of his shoulders. "There's nothing I can do."

Fuchs stared at the man's bland, scrubbed face for half a moment, then smashed a thundering right fist into the captain's jaw. His head snapped back and blood flew from his mouth as he buckled to the deck. Turning on the gape-mouthed crew woman, Fuchs ordered, "Maximum acceleration. *Now!*"

She glanced at the unconscious captain, then back at Fuchs. "But I can't—"

He ripped an emergency hand torch from its clips on the bulkhead and brandished it like a club. "Get away from the controls!"

"But—"

"Get out of that chair!" Fuchs bellowed.

She jumped to her feet and stepped sideways, slipping along the curving control panel, away from him.

"Nodon!" Fuchs called.

The young Asian stepped through the open hatch. He glanced nervously at the captain lying on the deck, then at the frightened crewwoman.

"See that no one enters the bridge," Fuchs said, tossing the hand torch to him. "Use that on anyone who tries to get in here."

Nodon gestured the woman toward the hatch as Fuchs sat in the command chair and studied the control board. Not much different from *Starpower* or the other vessels he'd been on.

"What about the captain?" the crewwoman asked. He was groaning softly, his legs starting to move a little.

"Leave him here," said Fuchs. "He'll be all right."

She left and Nodon swung the hatch shut behind her.

"Lock it," Fuchs ordered.

The captain sat up, rubbed at the back of his neck, then looked up blearily at Fuchs sitting at the controls.

"What the hell do you think you're doing?" the captain growled.

"I'm trying to save my wife's life," Fuchs answered, pushing the ship's acceleration to its maximum of one-half normal Earth gravity.

"This is piracy!" the captain snapped.

Fuchs swung around in the command chair. "Yes," he said tightly. "Piracy. There's a lot of it going around, these days."

CHAPTER 38

H e's *what?*" Hector Wilcox did not believe his ears.

Zar looked stunned as he repeated, "He's taken over the *Lubbock Lights*. He's accelerating at top speed to Ceres. Our flight controllers have ordered him to cease and desist, but he's paying no attention to them."

Wilcox sagged back in his desk chair. "By god, the man's committed an act of piracy."

"It would seem so," Zar agreed cautiously. "According to our people on Ceres, someone broke into Fuchs's warehouse and cleaned out everything. They murdered one of the people working there. A woman."

"His wife?"

"No, an employee. But you can understand why Fuchs wants to reach Ceres as quickly as he can."

"That doesn't justify piracy," Wilcox said sternly. "As soon as he arrives at Ceres, I want our people there to arrest him."

Zar blinked at his boss. "They're only flight controllers, not policemen."

"I don't care," Wilcox said sternly. "I won't have people flouting IAA regulations. This is a matter of principle!"

Diane Verwoerd had spent most of the morning combing her apartment for bugs. She found none, which worried her. She felt certain that Humphries had bugged her place; how else would he know what she was doing? Yet she could find no hidden microphones, no microcameras tucked in the ventilator grills or anywhere else.

Could Martin have been guessing about Bandung Associates? She had thought she'd covered her trail quite cleverly, but perhaps naming her dummy corporation after the city in which her mother had been born wasn't so clever, after all.

Whatever, she decided. Martin knows that I've winkled him out of several choice asteroids and he's willing to let that pass—if I carry his cloned baby for him.

She shuddered at the thought of having a foreign creature inserted into her womb. It's like the horror vids about alien invaders we watched when we were kids, she thought. And she had heard dark, scary stories about women who carried cloned fetuses. It wasn't like carrying a normal baby. The afterbirth bloated up so hugely that it could kill the woman during childbirth, they said.

But the rational part of her mind saw some possible advantages. Beyond the monetary rewards, this could put me in a position of some power with Martin Humphries, she told herself. The mother of his clone. That puts me in a rather special position. A very special position, actually. I might even gain a seat on his board of directors, if I play my cards well.

If I live through it, she thought, shuddering again.

Then she thought of Harbin. Beneath all that steely self-control was a boiling hot volcano, she had discovered. If I play him correctly, he'll sit up and roll over and do any other tricks I ask him to perform. A good man to have at my side, especially if I have to deal with Martin after the baby is born.

The baby. She frowned at the thought, wondering, Should I tell Dorik about it? Eventually, I'll have to. But not now. Not yet. He's too possessive, too macho to accept the fact that I'll be carrying someone else's baby while I'm letting him make love to me. I'll have to be very careful about the way I handle that little bit of news.

She walked idly through her apartment, thinking, planning, staring at the walls and ceilings as if she could make the electronic bugs appear just by sheer willpower. Martin's snooping on me. She felt certain of it. He certainly got his jollies watching me do it with Dorik.

With a reluctant sigh she decided she would have to call in some expert help to sweep the apartment. The trouble is, she told herself, all the experts I know are HSS employees. Can I get them to do the job right?

Then she thought of an alternative. Doug Stavenger must know some experts among Selene's permanent population. I'll ask Stavenger to help me.

Both of the IAA flight controllers were waiting at the cave that served as a reception area at Ceres's spaceport when Fuchs returned. He had left *Lubbock Lights* in orbit around the asteroid, turned the ship back to its captain, and ridden a shuttlecraft down to the surface. The two controllers left their posts in the cramped IAA control center and went to the reception area to meet him.

As Fuchs stepped out of the pressurized tunnel that connected the shuttlecraft to the bare rock cave, the senior controller, a thirtyish woman of red hair and considerable reputation among the men who frequented the Pub, cleared her throat nervously and said:

"Mr. Fuchs, the IAA wants you to turn yourself in to the authorities to face a charge of piracy."

Fuchs ignored her and started for the tunnel that led to the underground living quarters. She glanced at her partner, a portly young man with a round face, high forehead, and long ponytail hanging halfway down his back. They both started after Fuchs.

He said, "Mr. Fuchs, please don't make this difficult for us."

Kicking up clouds of dark gray dust as he shuffled into the tunnel, Fuchs said, "I will make it very easy for you. Go away and leave me alone."

"But, Mr. Fuchs—"

"I have no intention of turning myself in to you or anyone else. Leave me alone before you get hurt."

They both stopped so short that swirling clouds of dust enveloped them to their knees. Fuchs continued shambling down the tunnel, heading for his quarters and his wife.

He was no longer the raging, bellowing puppet yanked this way and that by strings that Martin Humphries controlled. His fury was still there, but now it was glacially cold, calm, calculating. He had spent the hours in transit to Ceres calculating, planning, preparing. Now he knew exactly what he had to do.

There was no guard at his door. Hands trembling, Fuchs slid it open. And there was Amanda sitting at the work desk, her eyes wide with surprise.

"Lars! No one told me you had arrived!" She jumped out of her chair and threw her arms around his neck.

"You're all right?" he asked, after kissing her. "No one has tried to harm you?"

"I'm fine, Lars," she said. "And you?"

"I've been charged with piracy by the IAA. They probably want me to turn around and return to Selene for a trial."

She nodded gravely. "Yes, they sent me a message about it. Lars, you didn't need to take over the ship. I'm quite all right."

Despite everything, he grinned at her. Feeling her in his arms, most of his fears dissolved. "Yes," he breathed, "you're more than all right."

Amanda smiled back at him. "The door's still open," she pointed out.

He stepped away from her, but instead of closing the door, went to the desk. The wallscreen showed a form letter from their insurance carrier. Fuchs scanned it as far as the line telling them that their policy had been terminated, then blanked the screen.

"I've got to go to the warehouse," he said. "Nodon will be waiting there for me."

"Nodon?" Amanda asked. "George's crewman?"

"Yes," said Fuchs as he called up Helvetia's personnel file. "He was with us at the farce of a hearing in Selene."

"I know."

Looking up at her, he asked, "Which of these people witnessed Inga's murder?"

"Oscar Jiminez," Amanda said, pulling up the room's other chair to sit beside him.

"I must speak to him," Fuchs said. He got up from his chair and went to the door, leaving Amanda sitting there alone.

Nodon was waiting for him at the warehouse. Feeling uneasy, irritable, Fuchs called Jiminez and two other Helvetia employees, both men, both young. When they all arrived at the warehouse's little office area, the place felt crowded and suddenly warm from the press of their bodies. Jiminez, skinny and big-eyed, stood between the two other men.

"In a day or two," Fuchs told them, "we're going to the HSS warehouse and take back the material they stole from us."

The men looked nervously at one another. "And we're going to administer justice to the men who murdered Inga," he added.

"They've gone," Jiminez said, in a voice pitched high with tension.

"Gone?"

"The day after the raid on our warehouse," said one of the older men. "Nine HSS employees left on one of their ships."

"Where is it bound?" Fuchs demanded. "Selene?"

"We don't know. Maybe it's going to Earth."

"We'll never get them once they reach Earth," Fuchs muttered.

"They brought in another bunch on the ship that took them away," said the other man, a trim-looking welterweight with a military buzz cut and jewelry piercing his nose, both eyebrows and earlobes.

"I suppose they are guarding the HSS warehouse," Fuchs said, glancing at Nodon, who remained silent, taking it all in.

The young man nodded.

"Very well, then," Fuchs said. He took a deep breath. "This is what we're going to do."

DOSSIER:
JOYCE TAKAMINE

I t's not what you know," he told her, time and again. "It's who you know."

Joyce "graduated" from picking to helping run one of the big farm management companies. Armed with her degree in computer analysis, she had worked up the courage to ask the young man running the company's local office for a job. He offered to discuss the possibilities over dinner, in his mobile home. They ended the evening in his bed. She got the job and lived for the next two years with the young man, who constantly reminded her about "the great American know-who."

When Joyce took his advice and left him for an older man who happened to be an executive with Humphries Space Systems, the young man was shocked and disillusioned.

"But it's what you've been telling me to do all along," Joyce reminded him.

"Yeah," he admitted, crestfallen. "I just didn't think you'd take my advice so literally."

Joyce stayed with the executive only long enough to win a position at HSS's corporate offices in Selene. She left the tired old Earth at last, and moved to the Moon.

CHAPTER 39

Two days passed.

Amanda spent the time trying to find out what her husband was up to, to no avail. It was clear to her that Lars was planning something; he was putting together some scheme to fight back against Humphries. But he would not tell her a word of it.

Lars is a different man, she knew. I hardly recognize him. He's like a caged animal, pacing, waiting, planning, looking for a way to break free. He's dead set on wreaking vengeance on the people who looted his warehouse and killed Inga, but he won't reveal his thinking to me.

In bed he relaxed a little, but still he kept his own counsel. "The only law out here is the law we enforce for ourselves," he said in the darkness as he lay next to her. "If we don't fight back he'll turn us all into his slaves."

"Lars, he's hired trained mercenaries. Professional killers," Amanda pleaded.

"Scum," her husband answered. "I know how to deal with scum."

"They'll kill you!"

He turned to her, and she could feel the heat radiating from his body. "Amanda, my darling, they are going to kill me anyway. That's what he wants. Humphries wants me dead and he won't be satisfied until I'm killed and you're at his mercy."

"But if you'd only—"

"Better for me to strike at him when and where he doesn't expect it," Fuchs said, reaching for her. "Otherwise, we just wait here like sheep ready to be slaughtered."

"But what are you going to do? What do you—"

He silenced her with a finger on her lips. "Better that you don't know, my darling. You can't be any part of this."

Then he made love to her ardently, furiously. She reveled in his passion, but she found that not even the wildest sex could divert him from his aim. He was going to attack HSS, attack Humphries, extract vengeance for the killings that had been perpetrated. He was going to get himself killed, she was certain.

His singlemindedness frightened Amanda to the depths of her being. *Nothing can move him a centimeter away from this,* she realized. *He's rushing toward his own death.*

The morning of the third day she found an incoming message from IAA headquarters on Earth. A ship had been dispatched to Ceres, carrying a squad of Peacekeeper troops. Their assignment was to arrest Lars Fuchs and return him to Earth for trial on a charge of piracy.

Fuchs smiled grimly when she showed him the message.

"Piracy." He practically spat the word. "*He* destroys ships and loots and murders and they say I have no proof. Me they accuse of piracy."

"Go with them," Amanda urged. "I'll go with you. You can tell them that you were in a state of emotional distress. Surely they'll understand—"

"With Humphries pulling the strings?" he snapped. "They'll hang me."

It was hopeless, Amanda admitted.

Fuchs sat in the empty Helvetia warehouse, going over his plan with Nodon.

"It all hinges on the people you've recruited," he said.

Nodon dipped his chin once in acknowledgment.

The two men were sitting at the desk just off the entrance to the warehouse, in a pool of light from a single overhead fluorescent shining in the otherwise darkened cave. The shelves were empty. No one else was there. Beyond the entrance, the tunnel led in a slight downward slope toward the living quarters and life support equipment; in the other direction, to the HSS warehouse and the reception area where incoming personnel and freight arrived and outgoing flights departed.

"You're certain these men are reliable?" Fuchs asked for the twelfth time that evening.

"Yes," Nodon replied patiently. "Men and women both; most of them are from families I have known for many years. They are honorable persons and will do what you command."

"Honorable," Fuchs murmured. Honor meant that a person would take your money and commit mayhem, even murder, to earn that pay. I'm hiring mercenary killers, he told himself. Just as Humphries has. To fight evil you have to do evil things yourself.

"They understand what they must do?"

Nodon allowed himself a rare smile. "I have explained it all to them many times. They may not speak European languages very well, but they understand what I have told them."

Fuchs nodded, almost satisfied. Through Nodon he had hired six Asians, four men and two women. Pancho had allowed them to ride to Ceres on an Astro freighter, and now they waited aboard the half-finished habitat orbiting the asteroid. As far as Pancho or anyone else was concerned, they had been recruited to restart construction of the habitat. Only Fuchs and Nodon—and the six themselves—knew better.

"All right," Fuchs said, struggling against the surge of doubts and worries that churned in his guts. "At midnight, then."

"Midnight," Nodon agreed.

With a sardonic smile, Fuchs added, "We've got to get this over and done with before the Peacekeeper troops arrive."

"We will," Nodon said confidently.

Yes, Fuchs thought, this will be over and done with in a few hours, one way or the other.

The nearest thing to a restaurant on Ceres was the Pub, where mechanical food dispensers standing off in one corner offered packaged snacks and even microwavable full meals, of a sort.

Fuchs made a point of taking Amanda out to dinner that night. The Pub was usually noisy but this particular evening the crowd was hushed; everyone seemed tense with expectation.

That worried Fuchs. Had news of his planned attack leaked out? Humphries's people could be waiting for him; he could be leading his men into a trap. He mulled over all the possibilities as he picked listlessly at his dinner.

Amanda watched him with worried eyes. "You haven't been eating right ever since you came back from Selene," she said, her tone more concerned than accusatory.

"No, I suppose I haven't." He tried to make a careless shrug. "I sleep well, though. Thanks to you."

Even in the dim lighting he could see her cheeks flush. "Don't try to change the subject, Lars." But she was smiling as she spoke.

"Not at all. I merely—"

"Do you mind if I sit with you?"

They looked up and saw Kris Cardenas holding a dinner tray in both hands.

"No, of course not," said Amanda. "Do join us."

Cardenas put her tray on their table. "The place is crowded tonight," she said as she sat on the vacant chair between them.

"But awfully quiet," Amanda said. "It's as if everyone here is attending a funeral."

"The Peacekeepers are due to arrive tomorrow," Cardenas said, jabbing a fork into her salad. "Nobody's happy with the thought."

"Ah, yes," said Fuchs, feeling relieved. "That's why everyone is so morose."

"They're worried it's the first step in a takeover," Cardenas said.

"Takeover?" Amanda looked startled at the idea. "Who would take control of Ceres? The IAA?"

"Or the world government."

"The world government? They don't have any authority beyond geosynchronous Earth orbit."

Cardenas shrugged elaborately. "It's their Peacekeepers that arrive tomorrow."

"Looking for me," Fuchs said unhappily.

"What do you intend to do?" Cardenas asked.

Looking squarely at Amanda, Fuchs said, "I'm certainly not going to fight the Peacekeepers."

Cardenas chewed thoughtfully for a few moments, swallowed, then said, "We did at Selene."

Shocked, Amanda asked, "What are you suggesting, Kris?"

"Nothing. Nothing at all. I'm just saying that six Peacekeeper troops in their nice little blue uniforms aren't enough to force you to go back Earthside with them, Lars. Not if you don't want to go."

"You mean we should fight them?" Amanda said, her voice hollow with fright.

Cardenas leaned closer and replied, "I mean that I could name a hundred, a hundred and fifty rock rats here who'd protect you against the Peacekeepers, Lars. You don't have to go with them if you don't want to."

"But they're armed! They're trained soldiers!"

"Six soldiers against half the population of Ceres? More than half? Do you think they'd fire on us?"

Amanda looked at Fuchs, then back to Cardenas. "Wouldn't they just send more troops, if these six were turned away?"

"If they tried that, I'm willing to bet that Selene would step in on our side."

"Why would Selene—?"

"Because," Cardenas explained, "if the world government takes over Ceres, Selene figures they'll be next. They tried it once, remember."

"And failed," Fuchs said.

"There are still nutcases Earthside who think their government should control Selene. And every human being in the whole solar system."

Fuchs closed his eyes, his thoughts spinning. He had never had the faintest inkling that Selene could become involved in his fight. This could lead to war, he realized. An actual war, bloodshed and destruction.

"No," he said aloud.

Both women turned toward him.

"I will not be the cause of a war," Fuchs told them.

"You'll surrender to the Peacekeepers tomorrow, then?" Cardenas asked.

"I will not be the cause of a war," he repeated.

After dinner, Fuchs led Amanda back to their quarters. She leaned heavily on his arm, yawning drowsily.

"Lord, I don't know why I feel so sleepy," she mumbled.

Fuchs knew. He had worried, when Cardenas sat at their table, that he wouldn't be able to slip the barbiturate into his wife's wine. But he had gotten away with it, Kris hadn't noticed, and now Amanda was practically falling asleep in his arms.

She was far too gone to make love. He helped her to undress; by the time she lay her head on the pillow she was peacefully unconsciousness.

For a long time Fuchs gazed down at his beautiful wife, tears misting his eyes.

"Good-bye, my darling," he whispered. "I don't know if I will ever see you again. I love you too much to let you risk your life for my sake. Sleep, my dearest."

Abruptly he turned and left their apartment, carefully locking the door as he stepped out into the tunnel. Then he headed for the warehouse and his waiting men.

CHAPTER 40

Oscar Jiminez was clearly worried as Fuchs led Nodon and four others of his employees up the tunnel toward the HSS warehouse.

"There's only six of us," he said, his voice low and shaky as he shuffled along the dusty tunnel beside Fuchs. "I know it's after midnight, but they've probably got at least ten guys in the warehouse."

Fuchs and Nodon carried hand lasers, fully charged. The others held clubs of asteroidal steel, pulled from the empty Helvetia warehouse shelves. All of them wore breathing masks to filter out the dust they were raising as they marched purposefully up the tunnel.

"Don't worry," Fuchs assured him calmly. "You won't have to fight. If all goes as I've planned, there won't be a fight."

"But then why—"

"I want you to identify the man who murdered Inga."

"He won't be there," the teenager said. "They took off. I told you."

"Perhaps. We'll see."

"Anyway, they were wearing breathing masks and some kind of hats. I couldn't identify the guy if I saw him."

"We'll see," Fuchs repeated.

Fuchs stopped them at one of the safety hatches that stood every hundred meters or so along the tunnel. He nodded to one of the men, a life support technician, who pried open the cover of the hatch's set of sensors.

Fuchs motioned his men through the open hatch as the technician fiddled with the sensors.

"Got it," he said at last.

An alarm suddenly hooted along the tunnel. Fuchs twitched involuntarily even though he had expected the blaring noise. The technician scurried through the hatch just before it automatically slammed shut.

"Hurry!" Fuchs shouted, and he started racing up the tunnel.

A half-dozen bewildered HSS men were out in the tunnel in front of the entrance to their warehouse, looking up and down as if searching for the source of the alarm. They were clad in light tan coveralls bearing the HSS logo; none of them wore breathing masks.

"Hey, what's going on?" one of them yelled as he saw Fuchs and the others rushing toward them, raising billows of dust.

Fuchs pointed his laser at them. It felt clumsy in his hand, yet reassuring at the same time.

"Don't move!" he commanded.

Five of the six froze in place. Two of them even raised their hands above their heads.

But the sixth one snarled, "What the fuck do you think you're doing?" and started to duck back inside the warehouse entrance.

Quite deliberately, Fuchs shot him in the leg. The laser cracked once, and the man yowled and went down face-first into the dust, a smoking charred spot on the thigh of his coveralls. A part of Fuchs's mind marveled that there was no recoil from the laser, no smoke or smell of gunpowder.

They herded the six men inside the warehouse, two of them dragging their wounded companion. Two more HSS men were at the desktop computer, trying to determine what was causing the alarm signal when all the life support systems were solidly in the green. Completely surprised, they raised their hands above their heads when Fuchs trained his laser on them.

They looked disgruntled once they realized that they were prisoners. Fuchs made them sit on the floor, hands on their knees.

Four minitractors were sitting just inside the warehouse entrance. Fuchs detailed four of his men to rev them up; then they went through the aisles, pulling down anything that looked as if it had come from the Helvetia warehouse and loading it onto the tractors.

"There'll be a couple dozen more of our people on their way up here," said the man Fuchs had shot. He sat with his companions, both hands clutching his thigh. Fuchs could not see any blood seeping from his wound. The laser pulse cauterizes as it burns through the flesh, he remembered.

"No one will come here," he said to the wounded man. "The alarm sounded only in this section of the tunnel. Your friends are sleeping peacefully in their quarters."

Finally the laden tractors were parked out in the tunnel, heaped high with crates and cartons that bore the Helvetia imprint.

"I think that's everything," said one of Fuchs's men.

"Not quite," Fuchs said. Turning to Jiminez, he asked, "Do you recognize any of these men?"

The youngster looked frightened. He shook his head. "They were wearing breathing masks, like I told you. And funny kind of hats."

"This one, maybe?" Fuchs prodded the shoulder of the man he had shot.

"I don't know!" Jiminez whined.

Fuchs took a deep breath. "All right. Take the tractors back to our warehouse."

Jiminez dashed out into the tunnel, plainly glad to get away.

"You think you're going to get away with this?" the wounded man growled. "We're gonna break you into little pieces for this. We'll make you watch while we bang your wife. We're gonna make her—"

Fuchs wheeled on him and kicked him in the face, knocking him onto his back. The others scuttled away. Nodon shouted, "Don't move!" and leveled his laser at them.

Frenzied with rage, Fuchs rushed to one of the storage bins lining the wall and yanked out a length of copper wire. Tucking his laser back into its belt pouch, he wrapped one end of the wire several times around the groaning, half-conscious man's neck, then dragged him toward the high stacks of shelving, coughing and sputtering blood from his broken teeth.

The others watched, wide-eyed, while Fuchs knotted the wire at the man's throat, then tossed the other end of it around one of the slim steel beams supporting the shelving. He yanked hard on the wire and the wounded man shot up into the air, eyes bulging, both hands struggling to untie the wire cutting into his neck. He weighed only a few kilos in Ceres's light gravity, but that was enough to slowly squeeze his larynx and cut off his air.

Blazing with ferocity, Fuchs whirled on the other HSS men, who sat in the dust staring at their leader thrashing, choking, his legs kicking, a strangled gargling inhuman sound coming from his bleeding mouth.

"Watch!" Fuchs roared at them. "Watch! This is what happens to any man who threatens my wife. If any of you even *looks* at my wife I'll tear your guts out with my bare hands!"

The hanging man's struggles weakened. He lost control of his bladder and bowels in a single burst of stench. Then his arms fell to his sides and he became still. The men on the floor stared, unmoving, open-mouthed. Even Nodon watched in terrible fascination.

"Come," Fuchs said at last. "We're finished here."

CHAPTER 41

Diane Verwoerd was in bed with Dorik Harbin when her phone buzzed and the wallscreen began blinking with PRIORITY MESSAGE in bright yellow letters.

She disentangled herself from him and sat up.

"It's almost two," he grumbled. "Aren't you ever off-duty?"

But Diane was already staring at the frightened face of her caller and listening to his breathless, almost incoherent words. Then the screen showed a man hanging by the neck, eyes bulging, tongue protruding from his mouth like an obscene wad of flesh.

"Great god," said Harbin.

Verwoerd slipped out of bed and began to get dressed. "I'll have to tell Martin about this personally. This isn't the kind of news you relay by phone."

She found Humphries still awake and alone in the big mansion's game room.

"We have troubles," she said as she entered the room.

He was bent over the pool table, cue in hand. Humphries had spent many long hours learning how to shoot pool on the Moon. The one-sixth gravity only subtly affected the way the balls rolled or caromed. A visitor could play a few rounds and think nothing was different from Earth. That's when Humphries would offer a friendly wager on the next game.

"Troubles?" he said, intent on his shot. He made it; the balls clicked and one of the colored ones rolled to a corner pocket and dropped neatly in. Only then did Humphries straighten up and ask, "What troubles?"

"Fuchs raided the warehouse and killed one of the men there. Hanged him."

Humphries's eyes widened. "Hanged him? By the neck?"

"The others have quit," Verwoerd went on. "They want no part of this fight."

He snorted disdainfully. "Cowardly little shits."

"They were hired to bully people. They never thought that Fuchs would fight back. Not like this."

"I suppose they expect me to pay for their transport back to Earth," Humphries groused.

"There's more."

He turned and stacked his cue in its rack. "Well? What else?"

"Fuchs has stolen an Astro ship, the *Lubbock Lights*. He's left—"

"How the hell could he steal a ship?" Humphries demanded angrily.

Verwoerd kept the pool table between them. "According to the captain—"

"The same limp spaghetti that allowed Fuchs to commandeer his ship on the way in to Ceres?"

"The same man," Verwoerd replied. "He reported to the IAA that a half-dozen Asians boarded the ship under the pretense of loading ores. They were armed and took control of the ship. Then Fuchs came up from Ceres with another Oriental, apparently the man who was with him when he was here for the hearing. They packed the captain and regular crew into the shuttlecraft and sent them back down to Ceres."

"Son of a bitch," Humphries said fervently.

"By the time the Peacekeepers arrived, Fuchs was gone."

"In one of Pancho's ships." He grinned. "Serves her right."

Verwoerd pursed her lips, weighing the dangers of antagonizing him further against the pleasures of yanking his chain a little bit. "If possession is nine-tenths of the law," she said slowly, "then it's mostly his ship now, not Astro's."

He glared at her, fuming. She kept her expression noncommittal. A smile now could set off a tantrum, she knew.

He stood in angry silence for several long moments, face flushed, gray eyes blazing. Then, "So those pansies you hired to clean out Fuchs want to quit, do they?"

"Actually, Grigor hired them," Verwoerd said. "And, yes, they want out. Fuchs made them watch while he hanged their leader."

"And Amanda? She went with him?"

With a shake of her head, Verwoerd answered, "No, she's still on Ceres. Apparently Fuchs's people took back most of the items that were looted from their warehouse."

"He left her on Ceres? Alone?"

"He hanged the man because he made some crack about her. Nobody's going to go near her, believe me."

"I don't want anybody to go near her," Humphries snapped. "I want her left strictly alone. I've given orders about that!"

"No one's harmed her. No one's threatened her."

"Until this asshole opened his big mouth in front of Fuchs."

"And he strung him up like a common criminal."

Humphries leaned both hands on the rim of the pool table and hung his head. Whether he was overwhelmed with sorrow or anger or the burden of bad news, Verwoerd could not tell.

At last he lifted his head and said crisply, "We need someone to go after Fuchs. Someone who isn't afraid of a fight."

"But nobody knows where he's gone," Verwoerd said. "It's an awfully big area, out there in the Belt. He's not sending out a tracking beacon. He's not even sending telemetry data. The IAA can't find him."

"He'll run out of fuel sooner or later," Humphries said. "He'll have to come back to Ceres."

"Maybe," she said, uncertainly.

Pointing a finger at her as if he were pointing a pistol, Humphries said, "I want somebody out there who can find him. And kill him. I want somebody who knows how to fight and isn't afraid of being shot at."

"A professional soldier," Verwoerd said.

Humphries smiled thinly. "Yes. Like your boy-toy."

She had known from the moment she'd heard about Fuchs's actions that it would come down to this. "I agree," she said, keeping her voice even, emotionless. "Harbin would be perfect for this task. But . . ." She let the word dangle in the air between them.

"But?" Humphries snapped. "But what?"

"He'll want to be paid a lot more than he's been getting."

He stared at her for a moment. "Are you representing him now? Are you his goddamned agent?"

She made herself smile at him. "Let's just say that I know him a lot better than I did a few weeks ago."

CHAPTER 42

As they sped away from Ceres on *Lubbock Lights,* Fuchs familiarized himself with the crew that Nodon had recruited. Silent, blank-faced Asians, Mongols, descendents of Genghis Khan. They didn't look particularly ferocious; they looked more like kids, students, fugitives from some high-tech training school. But they apparently knew their way around a fusion-powered spacecraft.

All the fusion ships were built along two or three basic designs, Fuchs knew. *Lubbock Lights* was a freighter, but now he had armed the vessel with three mining lasers taken from his own warehouse.

Once they were well under way, accelerating through the belt at a lunar one-sixth g, Fuchs called his crew into the galley. The seven of them crowded the little space, but they stood respectfully before him, their dark eyes showing no trace of emotion.

"You realize that we are outlaws now," he began, without preamble. "Pirates. There is no turning back."

Nodon spoke up. "We will follow you, sir. For us there is no other choice."

Fuchs looked from one face to another. Young, all of them. Some with facial tattoos, all of them pierced here and their with plain metal adornments. Already embittered by the way the world had treated them. Nodon had given him their backgrounds. They had all come from poor families who struggled to send their children to university where they could learn how to become rich. All six of them had studied technical subjects, from computer design to electrical engineering to environmental sciences. All six of them had been told, upon graduation, that there were no jobs for them. The world was crumbling, their home cities were being abandoned because of drought and disastrous storms that flooded the parched valleys and washed away the farmlands instead of nourishing them. All six of their families became part of the huge, miserable, starving army of the homeless, wandering the stark, bitter land, reduced to begging or stealing or giving up to die on the roadside.

These are the statistics that I've read about, Fuchs realized. Ragged scarecrows who have lost their place in society, who have lost their families and their futures. The desperate ones.

He cleared his throat and resumed, "One day, I hope, we will be able to return to Earth as wealthy men and women. But that day may never come. We must live as best as we can, and accept whatever comes our way."

Nodon said gravely, "That is what each of us has been doing, sir, for more than a year. Better to be here and fight for our lives than to be miserable beggars or prostitutes, kicked and beaten, dying slowly."

Fuchs nodded. "Very well, then. We will take what we need, what we want. We will not allow others to enslave us."

Brave words, he knew. As Nodon translated them to the crew, Fuchs wondered if he himself truly believed them. He wondered which of these blank-faced strangers would turn him in for a reward. He decided that he would have to protect his back at all times.

The Asians spoke among themselves in harsh whispers. Then Nodon said, "There is one problem, sir."

"A problem?" Fuchs snapped. "What?"

"The name of this ship. It is not appropriate. It is not a fortunate name."

Fuchs thought, It's a downright silly name. *Lubbock Lights*. He had no idea who had named the ship or why.

"What do you propose?" he asked.

Nodon glanced at the others, then said, "That is not for us to say, sir. You are the captain; you must make the decision."

Again, Fuchs looked from face to impassive face. Young as they were, they had learned to hide their feelings well. What's going on behind their masks? he wondered. Is this a test? What do they expect from me? More than a name for this ship. They're watching, judging, evaluating me. I'm supposed to be their leader; they want to see the quality of my leadership.

A name for the ship. An appropriate, fortunate name.

A single word escaped his lips. *"Nautilus."*

They looked puzzled. At least I've broken their shell a little, Fuchs thought.

He explained, "The *Nautilus* was a submarine used by its captain and crew to destroy evil ships and wreak vengeance on wrongdoers."

Nodon frowned a little, then translated to the others. There was a little jabbering back and forth, but after a few moments they were all bobbing their heads in agreement. A couple of them even smiled.

"*Nautilus* is a good name," said Nodon.

Fuchs nodded. "*Nautilus* it will be, then." He had no intention of telling them that the vessel was fictional, or how it—and its captain—came to their end.

Amanda woke up with a headache throbbing behind her eyes. She turned and saw that Lars was not in bed with her. And the wallscreen showed seven messages waiting. Strange that there was no sound from the phone. Lars must have muted it, she thought.

Sitting up in the bed, she saw that he was not in the one-room apartment. Her heart sank.

"Lars," she called softly. There was no answer. He's gone, she knew. He's gone from me. For good, this time.

The first message on the list was from him. Barely able to speak the command, her voice trembled so badly, she told the computer to put it on the screen.

Lars was sitting at the desk in the warehouse, looking as grim as death. He wore an old turtleneck shirt, dead black, and shapeless baggy slacks. His eyes were unfathomable.

"Amanda, my dearest," he said, "I must leave you. By the time you get this message I will be gone. There is no other way, none that I can see. Go to Selene, where Pancho can protect you. And no matter what you hear about me, remember that I love you. No matter what I have done or will do, I do it because I love you and I know that as long as you are near me your life is in danger. Good-bye, darling. I don't know if I'll ever see you again. Good-bye."

Without realizing it, she told the computer to rerun his message. Then again. But by then she couldn't see the screen for the tears that filled her eyes.

FOURTEEN MONTHS LATER

CHAPTER 43

She used her maiden name now: Amanda Cunningham. It wasn't that she wanted to hide her marriage to Lars Fuchs; everybody on Ceres, every rock rat in the Belt knew she was his wife. But ever since Fuchs had taken off into the depths of space, she had worked on her own to establish herself and to achieve her goals.

She sold off Helvetia, Ltd., to Astro Corporation for a pittance. Pancho, for once, outmaneuvered Humphries and convinced the Astro board of directors that this was a bargain they could not refuse.

"Besides," Pancho pointed out to the board, staring straight at Humphries across the table from her, "we should be competing out there in the Belt. It's where the natural resources are, and that's where the real wealth comes from."

Glad to be rid of Helvetia, Amanda watched Pancho begin to develop the warehouse into a profitable facility for supplying, repairing and maintaining the ships that plied the Belt. She lived off the income from the Astro stock that she had acquired from the sale, and concentrated her efforts on another objective, one that had originally been Lars's goal: his idea of getting the rock rats to form some kind of government for themselves so they could begin to establish a modicum of law and order on Ceres. The independent-minded prospectors and miners had been dead-set against any form of government, at first. They saw laws as restrictions on their freedom; order as strangling their wild times when they put in at Ceres for R&R.

But as more and more ships were attacked they began to understand how vulnerable they were. A war was blazing across the Belt, with HSS attacking the independents, trying to drive them out of the Belt, while

Fuchs singlehandedly fought back against HSS ships, swooping out of nowhere to cripple or destroy them.

In Selene, Martin Humphries howled with frustrated anger as his costs for operating in the Belt escalated over and again. It became increasingly expensive to hire crews to work HSS ships, and neither the IAA nor Harbin nor any of the other mercenaries that Humphries hired could find Fuchs and kill him.

"They're helping him!" Humphries roared time and again. "Those goddamned rock rats are harboring him, supplying him, helping him to knock off my ships."

"It's worse than that," Diane Verwoerd retorted. "The rock rats are arming their ships now. They're shooting back—ineptly, for the most part. But it's getting more dangerous out there."

Humphries hired still more mercenaries to protect his ships and seek out Lars Fuchs. To no avail.

The people who, like Amanda, actually lived on Ceres—the maintenance technicians and warehouse operators and shopkeepers, bartenders, even the prostitutes—they gradually began to see that they badly needed some kind of law and order. Ceres was becoming a dangerous place. Mercenary soldiers and outright thugs swaggered through the dusty tunnels, making life dangerous for anyone who got in their way. Both HSS and Astro hired "security" people to protect their growing assets of facilities and ships. Often enough the security people fought each other in the tunnels, the Pub, or the warehouses and repair shops.

Big George Ambrose returned to Ceres, his arm regrown, with a contract to work as a technical supervisor for Astro.

"No more mining for me," he told his friends at the Pub. "I'm a fookin' executive now."

But he brawled with the roughest of them. Men and women alike began to carry hand lasers as sidearms.

At last, Amanda got most of Ceres's population to agree to a "town meeting" of every adult who lived on the asteroid. Not even the Pub was big enough to hold all of them, so the meeting was held electronically, each individual in their own quarters, all linked through the interactive phone system.

Amanda wore the turquoise dress she had bought at Selene as she sat at the desk in her quarters and looked up at the wallscreen. Down in the comm center, Big George was serving as the meeting's moderator, deciding who would talk to the group, and in which order. He had promised, at Amanda's insistence, that everyone who wanted to speak would get his or her turn. "But it's goin' t'be a bloody long night," he predicted.

It was. *Everyone* had something to say, even though many of them repeated ideas and positions already discussed several times over. Through the long, long meeting—sometimes strident, often boring— Amanda sat and carefully listened to each and every one of them.

Her theme was simple: "We need some form of government here on Ceres, a set of laws that we can all live by. Otherwise we'll simply have more and more violence until the IAA or the Peacekeepers or some other outside group comes in and takes us over."

"More likely it'd be HSS," said a disgruntled-looking prospector, stuck on Ceres temporarily while his damaged ship was being repaired. "They've been trying to take us over for years now."

"Or Astro," an HSS technician fired back.

George cut them both off before an argument swallowed up the meeting. "Private debates can be held on another channel," he announced cheerfully, turning the screen over to the lean-faced, sharp-eyed Joyce Takamine, who demanded to know when the habitat was going to be finished so they could move up to it and get out of this dust-filled rathole.

Amanda nodded sympathetically. "The habitat is in what was once called a Catch–22 situation," she replied. "Those of us who want it finished so we can occupy it, haven't the funds to get the work done. Those who have the funds—such as Astro and HSS—have no interest in spending them on completing the habitat."

"Well, somebody ought to do something," Takamine said firmly.

"I agree," said Amanda. "That's something that we could do if we had some form of government to organize things."

Nearly an hour later, the owner of the Pub brought up the key question. "But how're we gonna pay for a government and a police force? Not to mention finishing the habitat. That'll mean we all hafta pay taxes, won't it?"

Amanda was ready for that one. In fact, she was glad the man had brought it up.

Noting that the message board strung across the bottom of her wallscreen immediately lit up from one end to the other, she said sweetly, "We will not have to pay taxes. The corporations can pay instead."

George himself interjected the question everybody wanted to ask. "Huh?"

Amanda explained, "If we had a government in place, we could finance it with a very small tax on the sales that HSS and Astro and any other corporation makes here on Ceres."

It took a few seconds for George to sort out all the incoming calls and flash the image of a scowling prospector onto her wallscreen.

"You put an excise tax on the corporations and they'll just pass it on to us by raising their prices."

Nodding, Amanda admitted, "Yes, that's true. But it will be a very small rise. A tax of one percent would bring in ten thousand international dollars for every million dollars in sales."

Without waiting for the next questioner, Amanda continued, "HSS alone cleared forty-seven million dollars in sales last week. That's nearly two and a half a billion dollars per year, which means a tax of one percent would bring us more than twenty-four million in tax revenue from HSS sales alone."

"Could we finish the habitat on that kind of income?" asked the next caller.

Amanda replied, "Yes. With that kind of assured income, we could get loans from the banks back on Earth to finish the habitat, just the same as any government secures loans to finance its programs."

The meeting dragged on until well past one A.M., but when it was finished, Amanda thought tiredly that she had accomplished her objective. The people of Ceres were ready to vote to form some kind of a government.

As long as Martin Humphries doesn't move to stop us, she reminded herself.

CHAPTER 44

Lars Fuchs stood spraddle-legged behind the pilot's chair on the bridge of *Nautilus*, carefully studying the screen's display of what looked like an HSS freighter.

According to the communications messages to and from the ship, she was the *W. Wilson Humphries,* the pride of Humphries Space Systems' growing fleet of ore carriers, named after Martin Humphries's late father. She was apparently loaded with ores from several asteroids, heading out of the Belt toward the Earth/Moon system.

Yet Fuchs felt uneasy about approaching her. Fourteen months of hiding in the Belt, of taking his supplies and fuel from ships he captured, of sneaking quick visits aboard friendly independent ships now and then, had taught him wariness and cunning. He was leaner now, still built like a miniature bull but without a trace of fat on him. Even his face was harder, his square jaw more solid, his thin slash of a mouth set into a downturned scowl that seemed permanent.

He turned to Nodon, who was handling the communications console on the bridge.

"What's the traffic to and from her?" he asked, jabbing a thumb toward the visual display.

"Normal telemetry," Nodon replied. "Nothing more at present."

To the burly young woman in the pilot's chair Fuchs said, "Show me the plot of her course over the past six weeks." He spoke in her own Mongol dialect now; haltingly, but he was learning his crew's language. He did not want them to be able to keep secrets from him.

One of the auxiliary screens lit up with thin, looping curves of yellow set against a sprinkling of green dots.

Fuchs studied the display. If it was to be believed, that yellow line represented the course that the Humphries ship had followed over the past six weeks, picking up loads of ore at five separate asteroids. Fuchs did not believe it.

"It's a fake," he said aloud. "If she'd really followed that plot she'd be out of propellant by now and heading for a rendezvous with a tanker."

Nodon said, "According to their flight plan, they will increase acceleration in two hours and head inward to the Earth/Moon system."

"Not unless they've refueled in the past few days," Fuchs said.

"There is no record of that. No tankers in the vicinity. No other ships at all."

Fuchs received brief snippets of intelligence information from the friendly ships he occasionally visited. Through those independent prospectors he arranged a precarious line of communications back to Ceres by asking them to tell Amanda what frequency he would use to make his next call to her. His calls were months apart, quick spurts of ultracompressed data that told her little more than the fact that he was alive and missed her. She sent similar messages back by tight laser beam to predesignated asteroids. Fuchs was never there to receive them; he left a receiving set on each asteroid ahead of time that relayed the message to him later. He had no intention of letting Humphries's people trap him.

But now he felt uneasy about this supposed fat, dumb freighter. It's a trap, he heard a voice in his mind warning him. And he remembered that Amanda's latest abbreviated message had included a piece of information from Big George to the effect that Humphries's people were setting up decoy ships, "Trojan horses," George called them, armed with laser weapons and carrying trained mercenary troops whose mission was to lure Fuchs into a fatal trap.

"George says it's only a rumor," Amanda had said hastily, "but it's a rumor that you should pay attention to."

Fuchs nodded to himself as he stared at the image of the ship on the display screen. Some rumors can save your life, he thought.

To the woman piloting the ship he commanded, "Change course. Head back deeper into the Belt."

She wordlessly followed his order.

"We leave the ship alone?" Nodon asked.

Fuchs allowed the corners of his mouth to inch upward slightly into a sour smile, almost a sneer. "For the time being. Let's see if the ship leaves us alone once we've turned away from it."

Sitting in the command chair on the bridge of *W. Wilson Humphries*, Dorik Harbin was also watching the display screens. He clenched his teeth in exasperation as he saw the ship that had been following them for several hours suddenly veer away and head back into the depths of the Belt.

"He suspects something," said his second-in-command, a whipcord-lean Scandinavian with hair so light she seemed almost to have no eyebrows. She had a knack for stating the obvious.

Wishing he were alone, instead of saddled with this useless crew of mercenaries, Harbin muttered, "Apparently."

The crew wasn't useless, exactly. Merely superfluous. Harbin preferred to work alone. With automated systems he had run his old ship, *Shanidar,* by himself perfectly well. He could go for months alone, deep in solitude, killing when the time came, finding solace in his drugged dreaming.

But now he had a dozen men and women under his command, his responsibility, night and day. Diane had told him that Humphries insisted on placing troops in his decoy ships; he wanted trained mercenaries who would be able to board Fuchs's ship and carry back his dead body.

"I tried to talk him out of it," Diane whispered during their last night together, "but he won't have it any other way. He wants to see Fuchs's dead body. I think he might have it stuffed and mounted as a trophy."

Harbin shook his head in wonder that a man with such obsessions could direct a deadly, silent war out here among the asteroids. Well, he thought, perhaps only a man who is obsessed can direct a war. Yes, he answered himself, but what about the men who do the fighting? And the women? Are we obsessed, too?

What difference? What difference does any of it make? How did Kayyam put it?

The Worldly Hope men set their Hearts upon
Turns Ashes—or it prospers; and anon,
Like Snow upon the Desert's dusty face
Lighting a little Hour or two—is gone.

What difference do our own obsessions make? They turn to ashes or prosper. Then they melt like snow upon the desert. What difference? What difference?

He heard his second-in-command asking, "So what are we going to do? He's getting away."

He said calmly, "Obviously, he doesn't believe that we're carrying ores back to Earth. If we turn around and chase him we'll simply be proving the point."

"Then what do we do?" the Scandinavian asked. The expression on her bony, pale face plainly showed that she wanted to go after the other ship.

"We continue to behave as if we are an ore-carrier. No change in course."

"But he'll get away!"

"Or come after us, once we've convinced him that we're what we pretend to be."

She was clearly suspicious of his logic, but murmured, "We play cat and mouse, then?"

"Yes," said Harbin, glad to have satisfied her. It didn't seem to matter to her which one of the two ships was the cat and which the mouse.

In Selene, Douglas Stavenger stood by his office window, watching the kids out in the Grand Plaza soaring past on their plastic wings. It was one of the thrills that could only be had on the Moon, and only in an enclosed space as large as the Grand Plaza that was filled with breathable air at normal Earthly pressure. Thanks to the light gravity, a person could strap wings onto her arms and take off to fly like a bird on nothing more than her own muscle power. How long has it been since I've done that? Stavenger asked himself. The answer came to him immediately: too blasted long. He chided himself, For a retired man, you don't seem to have much fun.

Someone was prodding the council to allow him to build a golf course out on the floor of Alphonsus. Stavenger laughed at the idea, playing golf in space suits, but several council members seemed to be considering it quite seriously.

His desk phone chimed, and the synthesized voice announced, "Ms. Pahang is here."

Stavenger turned to his desk and touched the button that opened his door. Jatar Pahang stepped through, smiling radiantly.

She was the world's most popular video star, "The Flower of Malaya," a tiny, delicate, exotic woman with lustrous dark eyes and long, flowing, midnight-black hair that cascaded over her bare shoulders. Her dress shimmered in the glareless overhead lights of Stavenger's office as she walked delicately toward him.

Stavenger came around his desk and extended his hand to her. "Ms. Pahang, welcome to Selene."

"Thank you," she said in a voice that sounded like tiny silver bells.

"You're even more beautiful than your images on-screen," Stavenger said as he led her to one of the armchairs grouped around a small circular table in the corner of his office.

"You are very gracious, Mr. Stavenger," she said as she sat in the chair. Her graceful frame made the chair seem far too large for her.

"My friends call me Doug."

"Very well. And you must call me Jatar."

"Thank you," he said, sitting beside her. "All of Selene is at your feet. Our people are very excited to have you visit us."

"This is my first time off Earth," she said. "Except for two vids we made in the *New China* space station."

"I've seen those videos," Stavenger said, grinning.

"Ah. I hope you enjoyed them."

"Very much," he said. Then, pulling his chair a bit closer to hers, he asked, "What can I do, personally, to make your visit more . . . productive?"

She glanced at the ceiling. "We are alone?"

"Yes," Stavenger assured her. "No listening devices here. No bugs of any kind."

She nodded, her smile gone. "Good. The message I carry is for your ears alone."

"I understand," said Stavenger, also fully serious.

Jatar Pahang was not only the world's most popular video star; she was also the mistress of Xu Xianqing, chairman of the world government's inner council, and his secret envoy to Stavenger and the government of Selene.

CHAPTER 45

The art of governing, thought Xu Xianqing, is much like the art of playing the piano: never let your left hand know what your right hand is doing.

It had been a long, treacherous road to the leadership of the world government. Xianqing had left many friends, even members of his own family, by the wayside as he climbed to the shaky pinnacle of political power. The precepts of K'ung Fu-Tzu had been his nominal moral guide; the writings of Machiavelli his actual handbook. During his years of struggle and upward striving, more than once he marveled inwardly that he—or anyone—bothered even to try. Why am I driven to climb higher and higher? he asked himself. Why do I take on such pains, such risks, such unending toil?

He never found a satisfactory answer. A religious man might have concluded that he had been chosen for this service, but Xianqing was not a man of faith. Instead, he considered himself a fatalist, and reasoned that the blind forces of history had somehow pushed him to his present pinnacle of authority and power.

And responsibility. Perhaps that was the true, ultimate answer. Xianqing understood that with the power and authority came responsibility. The planet Earth was suffering a cataclysm unmatched in all of human history. The climate was changing so severely that no one could cope with the sudden, disastrous floods and droughts. Earthquakes raged. Cities were drowned by rising waters. Farmlands were parched by shifting rainfall patterns, then washed away by savage storms. Millions had already died, and hundreds of millions more were starving and homeless.

In many lands the bewildered, desperate people turned to fundamentalist faiths for help and strength. They traded their individual liberties for order and safety. And food.

Yet, Xianqing knew, the human communities on the Moon and in the Asteroid Belt lived as if the travails of their brethren on Earth meant nothing to them. They controlled untold wealth: energy that Earth's peoples desperately needed, and natural resources beyond all that Mother Earth could provide its wretched and despairing children.

The giant corporations sold fusion fuels and solar energy to the wealthy of Earth. They sold metals and minerals from the asteroids to those who could afford it. How can I convince them to be more generous, to be more helping? Xianqing asked himself every day, every hour.

There was only one way that he could see: Seize control of the riches of the Asteroid Belt. The fools who plied that dark and distant region, the prospectors and miners and their corporate masters, were fighting among themselves. The ancient crime of piracy had reappeared out there among the asteroids. Murder and violence were becoming commonplace.

The world government could send an expedition of Peacekeepers to Ceres to restore order, Xianqing thought. We could stop the mayhem and bring peace to the region. And thereby, we could gain control of those precious resources. The prospectors and miners would grumble, of course. The corporations would howl. But what could do they do in the face of a *fait accompli*? How could they protest against the establishment of law and peace along that murderous frontier?

One thing barred such a prospect: Selene.

The people of the lunar community had fought for their independence and won it. They would not sit back and allow the world government to seize the Asteroid Belt. Would they fight? Xianqing feared that they would. It would not be difficult for them to attack spacecraft that were launched from Earth. We live in the bottom of a gravity well, Xianqing knew. While our vessels fight their way into space, Selene could destroy them, one by one. Or worse yet, cut off all supplies of energy and raw materials from space. Earth would be reduced to darkness and impotence.

No, direct military intervention in the Belt would be counterproductive—unless Selene could be neutralized.

So, Xianqing decided, if I cannot be a conqueror, I will become a peacemaker. I will lead the effort to resolve the fighting in the Asteroid Belt and gain the gratitude of future generations.

His first step was to contact Douglas Stavenger, in secret, through his beautiful mistress.

CHAPTER 46

"This isn't going to work, Lars," said Boyd Nielson.

Fuchs muttered, "That's my worry, not yours."

"But some of those people down there are just construction workers," Nielson pleaded. "Some of them are friends of ours, for god's sake!"

Fuchs turned away. "That can't be helped," he growled. "They shouldn't be working for Humphries."

Nielson was an employee of Humphries Space Systems, commander of the ore freighter *William C. Durant,* yet he had been a friend of Fuchs's in the early days on Ceres, before all the troubles began. Fuchs had tracked the *Durant* as the ship picked its way from one asteroid to another, loading ores bound back to the Earth/Moon system. With a handful of his crew, Fuchs had boarded Nielson's ship and taken it over. Faced with a half-dozen fierce-looking armed men and women, there was no fight, no resistance from Nielson or his crew. With its tracking beacon and all other communications silenced, Fuchs abruptly changed *Durant*'s course toward the major asteroid Vesta.

"Vesta?" Nielson had asked, puzzled. "Why there?"

"Because your employer, the high-and-mighty Mister Martin Humphries, is building a military base there," Fuchs told him.

Fuchs had heard the rumors in the brief flurries of communications he received from Amanda, back at Ceres. HSS people were building a new base on Vesta. More armed ships and mercenaries were going to use the asteroid as the base from which they would hunt down Lars Fuchs and kill him.

Fuchs decided to strike them first. He ordered the compliant Nielson to contact Vesta and tell them that *Durant* had been damaged in a fight with Fuchs's ship and needed to put in for repairs.

But now, as the two men stood at the command console on *Durant*'s bridge and Nielson finally understood what Fuchs was going to do, he began to feel frightened. He was a lean, wiry redhead with a pointed chin and teeth that seemed a size too big for his jaw. Nielson's crew were all locked in their privacy cubicles. Nodon and the other Asians were at the ship's controls. Nielson was not the nervous type, Fuchs knew, but as they approached Vesta he started to perspire visibly.

"For the love of mercy, Lars," he protested.

"Mercy?" Fuchs snapped. "Did they show mercy to Niles Ripley? Did they show mercy to any of the people in the ships they destroyed? This is a war, Boyd, and in a war there is no mercy."

The asteroid looked immense in the bridge's main display screen, a massive dark sphere, pitted with numberless craters. Spreading across one of the biggest of the craters, Fuchs saw, was a tangle of buildings and construction equipment. Scorch marks showed where shuttlecraft had landed and taken off again.

"Three ships in orbit," Fuchs noted, eyes narrowing.

"Might be more on the other side, too," said Nielson.

"They'll all be armed."

"I imagine so." Nielson looked distinctly uncomfortable. "We could all get killed."

Fuchs nodded, as if he had made a final calculation and was satisfied with the result.

To Nodon, sitting in the pilot's chair, Fuchs said, "Proceed as planned." Turning to Nielson, "You should ask them for orbital parameters."

Nielson's left cheek ticked once. "Lars, you don't have to do this. You can get away, go back to your own ship, and no harm done."

Fuchs glowered at him. "You don't understand, do you? I *want* to do harm."

Standing on the rim of the unnamed crater in his dustcaked spacesuit, Nguyan Ngai Giap surveyed the construction work with some satisfaction. Half a dozen long, arched habitat modules were in place. Front loaders were covering them with dirt to protect them against radiation and micrometeor hits. They would be ready for occupation on time, and he had already reported back to HSS headquarters at Selene that the troops could be sent on their way. The repair facilities were almost finished, as well. All was proceeding as planned.

"Sir, we have an emergency," said a woman's voice in his helmet earphones.

"An emergency?"

"An ore freighter, the *Durant*, is asking permission to take up orbit. It needs repairs."

"*Durant?* Is this an HSS vessel?" Giap demanded.

"Yes, sir. An ore freighter. They say they were attacked by Fuchs's ship."

"Give them permission to establish orbit. Alert the other ships up there."

"Yes, sir."

Only after he had turned his attention back to the construction work did Giap wonder how *Durant* knew of this facility. HSS vessel or not, this base on Vesta was supposed to be a secret.

"Freighter approaching," called the crewman on watch in *Shanidar*'s bridge.

Dorik Harbin hardly paid any attention. After the fruitless attempt to decoy Fuchs with the fake ore freighter, he had returned to the repaired and refurbished *Shanidar*, waiting for him in a parking orbit around Vesta. As soon as refueling was completed, Harbin could resume his hunt for Lars Fuchs. *Shanidar*'s crew had been disappointed that they had put in at Vesta instead of Ceres, where they could have spent their waiting time at the asteroid's pub or brothel. Let them grumble, Harbin said to himself. The sooner we get Fuchs the sooner all of us can leave the Belt for good.

He thought of Diane Verwoerd. No woman had ever gained a hold on his emotions, but Diane was unlike anyone he had ever known before. He had had sex with many women, but Diane was far more than a bedmate. Intelligent, understanding, and as sharply driven to get ahead in this world as Harbin was himself. She knew more about the intrigues and intricacies of the corporate world than Harbin had ever guessed at. She would be a fine partner in life, a woman who could stand beside him, take her share of the burden and then some. And the sex was good, fantastic, better than any drug.

Do I love her? Harbin asked himself. He did not understand what love truly was. Yet he knew that he wanted Diane for himself: she was his key to a better world, she could raise him above this endless circle of mercenary killing that was his life.

He also knew that he would never have her until he found this elusive madman Fuchs and killed him.

"She's carrying a heavy load of ores," the crewman noticed.

Harbin turned his attention to the approaching ore freighter in the display screen on his bridge. Damaged in a fight with Fuchs, her captain had said. But he could see no signs of damage. Maybe they're hidden by that pile of rocks she's carrying, he thought. More likely the frightened rabbit raced away from the first sign of trouble and scurried here for protection.

Harbin's beard had grown thick again over the months he had been chasing Fuchs across the Belt. He scratched at it idly as a new thought crossed his mind. How did this ore freighter know that we are building a base here? It's supposed to be a secret. If every passing tugboat knows about it, Fuchs will hear of it sooner or later.

What difference? Harbin asked himself. Even if he knows about it, what can he do? One man in one ship, against a growing army. Sooner or later we'll find him and destroy him. It's only a matter of time. And then I can return to Diane.

As he watched the display screen, he noticed that the approaching freighter didn't seem to be braking into an orbit. Instead, it was accelerating. Rushing toward the asteroid.

"It's going to crash!" Harbin shouted.

Maneuvering a spinning spacecraft with pinpoint accuracy was beyond the competence of any of Fuchs's people. Or of Nielson's crew. But to the ship's computer it was child's play: simple Newtonian mechanics, premised on the first law of motion.

Fuchs felt the ship's slight acceleration as *Durant* followed the programmed course. Standing spread-legged on the bridge, he saw the rugged, pitted surface of the asteroid rushing closer and closer. He knew they were accelerating at a mere fraction of a g, but as he stared at the screen it seemed as if the asteroid was leaping up toward them. Will we crash? he asked himself. What of it? came his own mind's answer. If we die that's the end of it.

But as *Durant* accelerated silently toward the asteroid, its maneuvering jets fired briefly and the clamps holding nearly fifteen hundred thousand tons of asteroidal ores let go of their burden. The ship jinked slightly and slipped over the curve of the asteroid's massive dark rim, accelerating toward escape velocity. The jettisoned ores spread into the vacuum of space like a ponderous rock slide, pouring down slowly toward the crater where the HSS base was being built.

In that vacuum, a body in motion stays in motion unless some outside force deflects it. In Vesta's minuscule gravity, the rocks actually weighed next to nothing. But their mass was still nearly fifteen hundred thousand tons. They fell gently, leisurely, toward the asteroid's surface, a torrent of death moving with the languid tumbling motion of a nightmare.

"Sir? Incoming call from *Shanidar*." The woman's voice in Giap's earphones sounded strained, almost frightened.

Without waiting for him to tell her, she connected Harbin. "That ship is on a collision course with—no, wait. It's released its cargo!"

It was difficult to look up from inside the spacesuit helmet, but when Giap twisted his head back and slightly sideways, all he could see was a sky full of immense dark blobs blotting out the stars.

He heard Harbin's tense, strained voice, "Break us out of orbit!"

Then the ground jumped so hard he was blasted completely off his feet and went reeling, tumbling into an all-engulfing billow of black dust.

Aboard *Shanidar*, Harbin watched in horror as the rocks dropped ever-so-softly toward the construction site in the crater. The ore freighter was masked by them and heading over the curve of the asteroid's bulk. The men and women down in that crater were doomed, condemned to inexorable death.

"Break us out of orbit!" he shouted to the woman in the pilot's chair.

"Refueling isn't completed!"

"Forget the mother-humping refueling!" he yelled. Pounding the intercom key on the console before him, he called to the crew, "Action stations! Arm the lasers! *Move!*"

But he knew it was already too late.

With nothing to impede their motion the landslide of rocks glided silently through empty space until they smashed into the surface of Vesta. The first one missed the buildings but blasted into the rim of the crater, throwing up a shower of rocky debris that spread leisurely across the barren landscape. The next one obliterated several of the metal huts dug halfway into the crater floor. Then more and more of them pounded in, raising so much dust and debris that Harbin could no longer see the crater at all. The dust cloud rose and drifted, a lingering shroud of destruction and death, slowly enveloping the entire asteroid, even reaching out toward his ship. Harbin unconsciously expected it to form a mushroom shape, as nuclear bombs did on Earth. Instead the cloud simply grew wider and darker, growing as if it fed on the asteroid's inner core. Harbin realized it would hang over the asteroid for days, perhaps weeks, a dark pall of death.

By the time *Shanidar* had broken out of orbit, the ore freighter was long gone. The damnable dust cloud even interfered with Harbin's attempts to pick it up on a long-range radar sweep.

CHAPTER 47

H e *what?*" Martin Humphries screamed.

"He wiped out the base on Vesta," Diane Verwoerd repeated. "All fifty-two people on the surface were killed."

Humphries sank back in his desk chair. He had been on the phone negotiating a deal to sell high-grade asteroidal nickel-iron to the government of China when she had burst into his office, tight-lipped and pale with shock. Seeing the expression on her face, Humphries had fobbed the Chinese negotiator off onto one of his underlings in Beijing as politely as possible, then cut the phone link and asked her what was the matter.

"Wiped out the entire base?" he asked, his voice gone hollow.

"One of our ships in orbit around Vesta got caught in the dust cloud and—"

"What dust cloud?" Humphries demanded irritably.

Verwoerd sank into one of the chairs in front of his desk and explained as much as she knew of Fuchs's attack. Humphries had never seen her look so stunned, so upset. It intrigued him.

"Fifty-two people killed," she murmured, almost as if talking to herself. "And the crew of the ship that was damaged by the dust cloud . . . four of them died when their life support system broke down."

Humphries calmed himself, then asked, "And Fuchs got away?"

"Yes," she said. "Harbin tried to give chase, but he was too low on fuel. He had to turn back."

"So he's still out there, hatching more mischief."

"Mischief?" She looked squarely at him. "This is more than mischief, Martin. This is a massacre."

He nodded, almost smiled. "That's right. That's exactly what it was. A deliberate massacre."

"You look as if you're pleased about it."

"We can make it work in our favor," Humphries said.

"I don't see—"

"Those rock rats have been helping Fuchs, giving him fuel and food, giving him information about our ships' schedules and destinations."

"Yes," she said. "Obviously."

"*Somebody* told him about the base on Vesta."

"Obviously," Verwoerd repeated.

"And now he's killed a couple of dozen of his own people. Rock rats. Construction workers. Right?"

She took a deep breath, straightened up in the chair. "I see. You think they'll turn against him."

"Damned right."

"What if they turn against *you*?" Verwoerd asked. "What if they decide that working for HSS is too dangerous, no matter how good the pay?"

"That's where we play our trump card," Humphries said. "Stavenger's been putting out feelers about arranging a peace conference. Apparently the world government's sticking its nose into the situation and Stavenger wants to head them off."

"A peace conference?"

"Humphries Space Systems, Astro, Selene . . . even the world government will send a representative. Slice up the Asteroid Belt neat and clean, so there's no more fighting."

"Who'll represent the rock rats?"

He laughed. "What do we need them for? This is strictly among the major players. The big boys."

"But it's about them," Verwoerd countered. "You can't divide up the Asteroid Belt between HSS and Astro without including them."

With a shake of his head, Humphries said, "You don't understand history, Diane. Back in the twentieth century there was a big flap in Europe over some country called Czechoslovakia. It doesn't even exist anymore. But at that time, Germany wanted to take it over. England and France met with the Germans in Munich. They decided what to do with Czechoslovakia. The Czechs weren't included in the conference. No need for them; the big boys parceled it all out."

Verwoerd shot back, "And a year later all Europe was at war. I know more history than you think. You can't have a conference about parceling out the Belt without having the rock rats in on it."

"Can't we?"

"You'll be throwing them into Fuchs's arms!"

Humphries frowned at that. "You think so?" he asked.

"Of course."

"H'mm. I hadn't thought of that. Maybe you're right."

Verwoerd leaned toward him slightly. "But if you included the rock rats, got them to send a representative to the conference—"

"We'd be making them a party to the crime," Humphries finished for her.

"And the only outsider, the only one who doesn't agree to the settlement, would be Fuchs."

"Right!"

"He'd be isolated," Verwoerd said. "Really alone. He'd have to give up. Nobody would help him and he'd be forced to quit."

Humphries clasped his hands behind his head and leaned far back in his big, comfortable chair. "And he'd also have to face trial for killing all those people on Vesta. I love it!"

CHAPTER 48

Much to his surprise, George Ambrose was elected "mayor" of Ceres.

His official title was Chief Administrator. The election came about once the inhabitants of Ceres reluctantly admitted that they needed some form of government, if only to represent them against the growing mayhem that was turning the Belt into a war zone. Fuchs's destruction of the Vesta base was the last straw; more than two dozen residents of Ceres had been killed in the attack.

Amanda tried to distance herself from her estranged husband's offense by throwing herself into the drive to bring some form of law and order to Ceres. She worked tirelessly to craft a government, searching databases for months to find governmental organizations that might fit the needs of the rock rats. Once she had put together a proposed constitution, the rock rats grumbled and fussed and ripped it to shreds. But she picked up the pieces and presented a new document that addressed most of their complaints. With great reluctance, they voted to accept the new government—as long as it imposed no direct taxes on them.

Staffing the government was simple enough: there were enough clerks and technical supervisors on Ceres to handle the jobs. Many of them were delighted with the prospect of getting an assured salary, although Amanda made certain that each bureaucrat had to satisfy a strict performance review annually to hold onto the job.

Then came the selection of a governing board. Seven people were chosen at random by computer from the permanent residents of Ceres. No one was allowed to refuse the "honor." Or the responsibility. Amanda was not selected by the computerized lottery, which disappointed her. George was, which disappointed him even more.

At their first meeting, the board elected George their chief, over his grudging protests.

"I won't fookin' shave," he warned them.

"That's all right, George," said one of the young women on the board. "But could you just tone down your language a little?"

Thus it was that Big George Ambrose, now the reluctant "mayor" of the rock rats, became their representative in the conference that took place at Selene, where he had once lived as a fugitive and petty thief.

"I'm not goin' by meself," George insisted. "I'll need some backup."

The governing board decided they could afford to send two assistants with George. His first real decision as the newly-elected Chief Administrator of Ceres was to pick the two people who would go with him. His first choice was easy: Dr. Kris Cardenas.

As he tussled in his mind over who the other appointee should be, Amanda surprised him by volunteering for the post.

She popped into his "office"—actually nothing more than his everyday living quarters—and told him that she wanted to be part of the delegation to Selene.

"You?" George blurted. "How come?"

Amanda looked away from his eyes. "I've done as much work to create this government as anyone. More, in fact. I deserve to go."

George said warily, "This won't be a fookin' vacation, y'know."

"I understand that."

He offered her his best chair, but she shook her head and remained standing in the middle of his one-room residence. She seemed calm, and very determined. The place is pretty messy, George thought: bed's not made, plates in the sink. But Amanda simply stood there staring off into infinity, seeing—what? George wondered.

"Humphries is there, in Selene," he said.

Amanda nodded, her face expressionless, frozen, as if she were afraid to show any emotion at all.

"Lars won't like you goin'."

"I know," she said, her voice almost a whisper. "I've thought it all out, George. I must go with you. But I don't want Lars to know. Please don't tell him."

Scratching his beard, trying to sort out what she was saying, George asked, "How can I tell 'im? The only way I get any word to him is through you."

"I've got to go with you, George," Amanda said, almost pleading now. "Don't you see? I've got to do whatever I can to put an end to this fighting. To save Lars before they find him and kill him!"

George nodded, finally understanding. At least, he thought he did.

"All right, Amanda. You can come with us. I'll be glad to have you."

"Thank you, George," she said, smiling for the first time. But there was no happiness in it.

Amanda had wrestled with her conscience for two days before asking George to let her go with him to Selene. She knew that Lars would not want her to be so near to Humphries, especially without him there to protect her. She herself did not fear Humphries any longer; she felt that she could handle him. Martin wouldn't hurt me, she told herself. Besides, George and Kris will be there to chaperone me.

What worried her was Lars's reaction. He would be dead-set against her going to Selene, to Humphries's home territory. So, after two days of inner turmoil, Amanda decided to go. Without telling Lars.

A total of twenty-two ships made rendezvous above the ruined base on Vesta. The dust cloud from Fuchs's attack had finally settled, but Harbin could see nothing of the base, not even the crater in which it had been situated. It was all obliterated by a new set of overlapping craters, fresh, sharp, raw-looking circular scars on the asteroid's dark surface. They reminded Harbin of the scars left on sperm whales by the suckers of giant squids' tentacles.

With no little bit of irony, Dorik Harbin considered his position as he stood on the bridge of *Shanidar*. A man who treasured his solitude, who had never wanted to be dependent on anyone else, now he was the commander of an entire fleet of spacecraft: attack ships, tankers, even surveillance drones that were spreading across the Belt seeking one infinitesimal speck in all that dark emptiness: Lars Fuchs.

Although he far preferred to work alone, Harbin had been forced to admit that he could not find Fuchs by himself. The Belt was too big, the quarry too elusive. And, of course, Fuchs was aided covertly by other rock rats who gave him fuel and food and information while they secretly applauded his one-man war against Humphries Space Systems. Probably Astro Corporation was also helping Fuchs. There was no evidence of it, Harbin knew; no outright proof that Astro was supplying the renegade with anything more than gleeful congratulations on his continuing attacks.

But Humphries himself was certain that Astro was behind Fuchs's success. Diane had told Harbin that Humphries was wild with rage, willing now to spend every penny he had to track down Fuchs and eliminate him, once and for all. This armada was the result: its cost to Humphries was out of all proportion to the damage that Fuchs had done, but Humphries wanted Fuchs destroyed, no matter what the cost, Diane said.

Diane. Harbin reflected soberly that she had become a part of his life. *I've become dependent on her,* he realized. Even with the distance between them, she protected him against Humphries's frustrated anger. She was the one who had convinced Humphries to give Harbin command of this all-out campaign against Fuchs. She was the one who would be waiting for him when he returned with Fuchs's dead body.

Well, he thought as he surveyed the display screens showing a scattering of his other ships, *now I have the tools I need to finish the job. It's only a matter of time.*

The surveillance probes were already on their way to quarter the Belt with their sensors. Harbin gave the orders to his fleet to move out and start the hunt.

Satisfaction showed clearly on Martin Humphries's face as he sat down at the head of the long dining table in his mansion. Diane Verwoerd was the only other person at the table, already seated at his right.

"Sorry I'm late for lunch," Humphries said, nodding to the servant waiting to pour the wine. "I was on the phone with Doug Stavenger."

Verwoerd knew her boss expected her to ask what the call was about, but she said nothing.

"Well, he's done it," Humphries said at last, just a little bit nettled. "Stavenger's pulled it off. We're going to have a peace conference right here at Selene. The world government's agreed to send their number-two man, Willi Dieterling."

Diane Verwoerd made herself look impressed. "The man who negotiated the Middle East settlement?"

"The very same," said Humphries.

"And the rock rats are sending a representative?" she prompted.

"Three people. That big Australian oaf and two assistants."

"Who'll represent Astro?"

"Probably Pancho," he said lightly. "She's the real power on the board these days."

"It should be interesting," said Verwoerd.

"It should be," Humphries agreed. "It certainly should."

Lars Fuchs scowled at his visitor. Yves St. Claire was one of his oldest and most trusted friends; Fuchs had known the Quebecois since their university days together in Switzerland. Yet now St. Claire was stubbornly refusing to help him.

"I need the fuel," Fuchs said. "Without it, I'm dead."

The two men stood in *Nautilus*'s cramped galley, away from the crew. Fuchs had given them orders to leave him alone with his old friend. St. Claire stood in front of the big freezer, his arms folded obstinately across his chest. When they had been students together he had been slim and handsome, with a trim little pencil moustache and a smooth line of patter for the women, despite his uncouth accent. In those days his clothes had always been in the latest fashion; his friends joked that he bankrupted his family with his wardrobe. During his years of prospecting in the Belt, however, he had allowed himself to get fat. Now he looked like a prosperous middle-aged bourgeois shopkeeper, yet his carefully draped tunic of sky blue was designed to minimize his expanding waistline.

"Lars," said St. Claire, "it is impossible. Even for you, old friend, I can't spare the fuel. I wouldn't have enough left to get back to Ceres."

Fuchs, dressed as usual in a black pullover and baggy slacks, took a long breath before answering.

"The difference is," he said, "that you can send out a distress call and a tanker will come out for you. I can't."

"Yes, a tanker will come out for me. And do you know how much that will cost?"

"You're talking about money. I'm talking about my life."

St. Clair made a Gallic shrug.

Since the attack on Vesta Fuchs had survived by poaching fuel and other supplies from friendly prospectors and other ships plying the Belt. A few of them gave freely; most were reluctant and had to be convinced. Amanda regularly sent out schedules for the prospectors, miners, tankers and supply vessels that left Ceres. Fuchs planted remote transceivers on minor asteroids, squirted the asteroids' identification numbers to Amanda in bursts of supercompressed messages, then picked up her information from the miniaturized transceivers the next time he swung past those rocks. It was an intricate chess game, moving the transceivers before Humphries's snoops could locate them and use them to bait a trap for him.

Humphries's ships went armed now, and seldom alone. It was becoming almost impossibly dangerous to try to hit them. Now and again Fuchs commandeered supplies from Astro tankers and freighters. Their captains always complained and always submitted to Fuchs's demands under protest, but they were under orders from Pancho not to resist. The cost of these "thefts" was submicroscopic in Astro's ledgers.

Despite everything, Fuchs was badly surprised that even his old friend was being stubborn.

Trying to hold on to his temper, he said placatingly, "Yves, this is literally a matter of life and death to me."

"But it is not necessary," St. Clair said, waving both hands in the air. "You don't need to—"

"I'm fighting your fight," Fuchs said. "I'm trying to keep Humphries from turning you into his vassals."

St. Clair cocked an eyebrow. "Ah, Lars, *mon vieux.* In all this fighting you've killed friends of mine. Friends of ours, Lars."

"That couldn't be helped."

"They were construction workers. They never did you any harm."

"They were working for Humphries."

"You didn't give them a chance. You slaughtered them without mercy."

"We're in a war," Fuchs snapped. "In war there are casualties. It can't be helped."

"*They* weren't in a war!" said St. Clair, with some heat. "I'm not in a war! You're the only one who is fighting this war of yours."

Fuchs stared at him. "Don't you understand that what I'm doing, I'm doing for you? For all the rock rats?"

"Pah! Soon it will be all over, anyway. There is no need to continue this . . . this vendetta between you and Humphries."

"Vendetta? Is that what you think I'm doing?"

Drawing in a deep, deliberate breath, St. Clair said more reasonably, "Lars, it is finished. The conference at Selene will put an end to this fighting."

"Conference?" Fuchs blinked with surprise. "What conference?"

St. Clair's brows rose. "You don't know? At Selene. Humphries and Astro are meeting to discuss a settlement of their differences. A peace conference."

"At Selene?"

"Of course. Stavenger himself arranged it. The world government has sent Willi Dieterling. Your own wife will be there, one of the representatives from Ceres."

Fuchs felt an electric shock stagger him. "Amanda's going to Selene?"

"She is on her way, with Big George and Dr. Cardenas. Didn't you know?"

Amanda's going to Selene, thundered in Fuchs's mind. To Selene. To Humphries.

It took him several moments to focus his attention again on St. Clair, still standing in the galley with him, a bemused little smile on his lips.

"You didn't know?" St. Clair asked again. "She didn't tell you?"

His voice venomously low, Fuchs said, "I'm going to take the fuel I need. You can call for a tanker after I've left the area."

"You will steal it from me?"

"Yes," said Fuchs. "That way you can make a claim to your insurance carrier. You're insured for theft, aren't you?"

DOSSIER:
JOYCE TAKAMINE

J oyce was quite content living on the Moon. She lived alone, not celibate, certainly, but not attached to anyone, either. She had achieved most of what she had dreamed of, all those long hard years of her youth.

She was a mature woman now, lean and stringy, hardened by years of physical labor and cold calculation, inured to clambering up the ladder of life by grabbing for any rung she could reach. Now that she was at Selene, with a well-paying job and a secure career path, she felt that she could relax and enjoy life for the first time.

Except—she soon felt bored.

Life became too predictable, too routine. Too safe, she finally realized. There's no challenge to this. I can run my office blindfolded. I see the same people socially every time I go out. Selene's just a small town. Safe. Comfortable. Boring.

So she transferred to the Humphries operation on Ceres, much to her supervisor's shock, and rode out to the Belt.

Ceres was even smaller than Selene, dirty, crowded, sometimes dangerous. Joyce loved it. New people were arriving and departing all the time. The Pub was rowdy, raucous. She saw Lars Fuchs kill a man there, just jam a power drill into the guy's chest like an old-fashioned knight's spear. The guy had admitted to killing Niles Ripley, and he tried to shoot Fuchs right there at the bar.

She served on the jury that acquitted Fuchs and, when the people of Ceres finally started to pull together a ragtag kind of government, Joyce Takamine was one of those selected by lottery to serve on the community's first governing council. It was the first time she had won anything.

CHAPTER 49

Humphries gave a party in his mansion for the delegates to the peace conference. Not a large, sumptuous party; just an intimate gathering of the handful of men and women who would meet the next morning in a discreet conference room in Selene's office tower, up in the Grand Plaza.

Pancho Lane was the first guest to arrive. Humphries greeted her in the sprawling living room of his home, with Diane Verwoerd at his side. Diane wore a glittering floor-length sheath of silver, its neckline plunging almost to her waist. Pancho was in a lavender cocktail dress accented with big copper bangle earrings and hoops of copper at her wrists and throat.

Humphries, wearing a collarless burgundy jacket over a space-black turtleneck shirt and charcoal slacks, smirked to himself. Pancho had learned a lot in her years on the Astro board, but she was still gawky enough to show up at the party precisely on time, rather than fashionably late.

Soon enough the other guests began to arrive, and Humphries's servants showed them into the lavishly furnished living room. Willi Dieterling came in with two younger men flanking him; his nephews, he told Humphries as they exchanged introductions.

"May I congratulate you, sir," Humphries said, "on your successful resolution of the Mideast crisis."

Dieterling smiled in a self-deprecating manner and touched his trim gray beard with a single finger. "I cannot take all the credit," he said softly. "Both sides had run out of ammunition. My major accomplishment was to get the arms dealers to stop selling to them."

Everyone laughed politely.

Dieterling went on, "With the Mediterranean threatening to flood Israel and the Tigris–Euphrates rivers washing away half of Iraq, both sides were ready to cooperate."

"Still," Humphries said as a waiter brought a tray of champagne flutes, "your accomplishment is something that—"

He stopped and stared past Deiterling. Everyone turned toward the doorway. There stood Big George Ambrose with his shaggy red hair and beard, looking painfully ill at ease in a tight-fitting dinner jacket. On one side of him was Kris Cardenas, in Selene for the first time in more than six years. On George's other side was Amanda, in a plain white sleeveless gown, accented with a simple necklace and bracelet of gold links.

Humphries left Dieterling and the others standing there and rushed to Amanda.

His mouth went dry. He had to swallow hard before he could croak out, "Hello."

"Hello, Martin," said Amanda, unsmiling.

He felt like a tongue-tied schoolboy. He didn't know what to say.

Pancho, of all people, rescued him. "Hi, Mandy!" she called cheerfully, walking toward them. "Good to see ya."

Humphries felt almost grateful as Pancho introduced Amanda, Cardenas, and Big George to Dieterling and his nephews. Then Doug Stavenger came in, with his wife, and the party was complete.

While his guests sipped champagne and chatted, Humphries called one of the waiters over and instructed him to change the seating in the dining room. He wanted Amanda at his right hand.

Two minutes later his butler came up to him and whispered in his ear, "Sir, Doctor Dieterling is supposed to be sitting at your right. Diplomatic protocol—"

"Protocol be damned!" Humphries hissed. "Rearrange the seating. Now!"

The butler looked alarmed. Verwoerd stepped in and said, "Let me take care of it."

Humphries nodded to her. She and the butler headed off to the dining room. Humphries turned back to Amanda. She seemed to glow like a goddess among the chattering mortals arrayed around her.

Dinner was long and leisurely. Humphries was certain that the conversation was sophisticated, deeply significant, a fine way for the delegates to tomorrow's meeting to get to know each other. Bursts of laughter showed that considerable wit sparkled around the table. Humphries heard not a word. All he could see was Amanda. She smiled now and then, but not at him. She chatted with Dieterling, seated on her other side, and with

Stavenger, who was across the table from her. She said hardly a word to Humphries and he found it difficult to talk to her, especially with all these others surrounding him.

After-dinner drinks were served in the library-cum-bar. As midnight tolled on the antique grandfather clock in the corner, the guests began to make their farewells. Amanda left with Cardenas and Big George. Pancho stayed until everyone else had gone.

"First in, last out," she said, once she finally put her glass down on the bar. "I never want to miss anything."

Humphries let Verwoerd escort Pancho to the door. He stepped behind the bar and poured himself a stiff single-malt, neat.

Verwoerd returned, a subtle smile creasing her sultry lips. "She's even more beautiful in person than her on-screen image."

"I'm going to marry her," Humphries said.

Verwoerd actually laughed. "Not until you get up the nerve to speak to her, I should think."

Anger flared in his gut. "Too many people around. I can't say anything meaningful to her in a crowd like that."

Still smirking, Verwoerd said, "She didn't have much to say to you, either."

"She will. I'll see to that."

Picking up her half-finished drink from the bar, Verwoerd said, "I noticed that the other woman didn't have much to say to you, either."

"Doctor Cardenas?"

"Yes."

"We've had our . . . differences, in the past. When she lived here at Selene."

"She used to run the nanotech lab, didn't she?"

"Yes." Kris Cardenas had been shut out of her lab because of Humphries. He was certain that Verwoerd knew it; the feline smile on her face told him that she knew and was enjoying his discomfort over it. And his inability to say more than a few words to Amanda. She's *enjoying* watching me turn myself into knots over the woman I love, he fumed silently.

"It'll be interesting to see what they have to say tomorrow, if anything," Verwoerd mused.

"Tomorrow?"

"At the conference."

"Oh, yes. The conference."

"I'm looking forward to it," said Verwoerd.

"You won't be there."

Her eyes went wide for just a flash of a second, then she regained control of herself.

"I won't be at the conference? Why not?"

"Because you'll be in the medical lab. It's time for you to be implanted with my clone."

Verwoerd's self-control crumpled. "Now? You're going to do that now, with the conference and—"

He had just made up his mind. Seeing the smug superiority on her face had decided him. It's time to show her who's in charge here; time to make her realize she's here to do my bidding.

"Now," Humphries said, enjoying her shock and confusion. "I'm going to marry Amanda and you're going to carry my baby."

CHAPTER 50

So it boils down to this, Dorik Harbin said to himself as he read the message on his screen. All this effort and maneuvering, all these ships, all the killing, and it comes down to a simple little piece of treachery.

He sat in his privacy cubicle and stared at the screen. Some flunky who had once worked for Fuchs had sold out. For a despicably small bribe he had hacked into Fuchs's wife's computer files and found out where Fuchs had planted communications transceivers. Those little electroptics boxes were Fuchs's lifeline, his link to information on where and when he could find the ships he preyed upon.

Harbin smiled tightly, but there was no joy in it. He opened a comm channel to his ships and began ordering them to the asteroids where Fuchs's transceivers lay. Sooner or later he would show up at one of those rocks to pick up the latest intelligence information from his wife. When he did, there would be three or four of Harbin's ships waiting for him.

Harbin hoped that Fuchs would come to the asteroid where he himself planned to lie in wait.

It will be good to finish this fight personally, he told himself. Once it's over, I'll be wealthy enough to retire. With Diane.

Diane Verwoerd spent a sleepless night worrying about the ordeal she faced. I'll bear Martin's child without really being impregnated by him. I'll be a virgin mother, almost.

The humor of the situation failed to ease her fears. Unable to sleep, she went to her computer and searched for every scrap of information she could locate about cloning: mammals, sheep, pigs, monkeys, apes—humans. Most nations on Earth forbade human cloning. The ultraconservative religious organizations such as the New Morality and the Sword of Islam jailed and even executed scientists for merely doing research in cloning. Yet there were laboratories, private facilities protected by the very wealthy, where such experiments were done. Most attempts at cloning failed. The lucky ones suffered spontaneous abortions early. Less lucky women died in childbirth, or gave birth to stillborns.

My chances for presenting Martin with a healthy son are about one in a hundred, Verwoerd saw. My chances for dying are better than that.

She shuddered, but she knew she would go through with it. Because being the mother of Martin Humphries's son was worth all the risk to her. I'll get a seat on the board of directors for this. With Dorik to protect me, there's no telling how far I can go.

Humphries awoke that morning and smiled. It's all coming together nicely, he told himself as he got out of bed and padded into his tiled lavatory. Amanda's here without Fuchs. By the time the conference is over he'll be totally cut off from her and everybody else. I'll have the chance to show her what kind of life she can have with me.

The mirror above the sink showed him a puffy-faced, bleary-eyed unshaven image. Will she want me? he asked himself. I can give her everything, everything a woman could possibly desire. But will she turn me down again? Will she stick with Fuchs?

Not when the man is dead, he thought. Then she'll have no choice. The competition will be over.

His hands trembled as he reached for his electric toothbrush. Frowning at this weakness, Humphries opened his medicine cabinet and rummaged through the vials lined up there in alphabetical order. A cure for every malady, he said to himself. Most of them were recreational drugs, cooked up by some of the bright researchers he kept on his payroll. I need something to calm me down, Humphries realized. Something to get me through this conference without losing my temper, without making Amanda afraid of me.

As he pawed through the medicine cabinet, the image of Diane Verwoerd's troubled, frightened face flashed in his mind. I wiped her superior smile away, he thought, relishing the memory of her surprise and fear. He tried to remember how many women had carried clones of his, all to no avail. Several had died; one had produced a monstrosity that lived less than a day. Diane's strong, he told himself. She'll come through for me. And if she doesn't—he shrugged. There are always other women for the job.

He found the little blue bottle that he was looking for. Just one, he said silently; just enough to get me through the meeting on an even keel.

Later on, I'll need something else, something stimulating. But not yet. Not this morning. Later, when Amanda's here with me.

Pancho dressed carefully for the conference in a pumpkin orange silk blouse and slacks with a neat patchwork jacket embellished with highlights of glitter. This is an important conference and I'm representing Astro Corporation, she told herself. Better look like a major player. She thought she would be the first one to show up for the conference, but when she got there Doug Stavenger was already standing by the big window that swept along one wall of the spacious room, looking relaxed in an informal cardigan jacket of teal blue.

"Hello," he called cheerfully. Gesturing toward the side table laden with coffee urns and pastries, he asked, "Have you had your breakfast?"

"I could use some coffee," Pancho said, heading for the table.

The conference room was part of the suite of offices that Selene maintained in one of the twin towers that supported the expansive dome of the Grand Plaza. Gazing through the window down into the Plaza itself, Pancho saw the lovingly maintained lawn and flowering shrubbery, the fully-leafed trees dotting the landscape. There was the big swimming pool, built to attract tourists, and the outdoor theater with its gracefully curved shell of lunar concrete. Not many people on the walks this early in the morning, she noticed. Nobody in the pool.

Stavenger smiled at her. "Pancho, are you seriously going to try to hammer out your differences with Humphries, or is this conference going to be a waste of time?"

Pancho grinned back at him as she picked up a coffee cup and started to fill it with steaming black brew. "Astro is willing to agree to a reasonable division of the Belt. We never wanted a fight; it was Humphries who started the rough stuff."

Stavenger pursed his lips. "I guess it all depends, then, on how you define the word 'reasonable.'"

"Hey, look," Pancho said. "There's enough raw materials in the Belt to satisfy ever'body. Plenty for all of us. It's Humphries who wants to take it all."

"Are you talking about me, Pancho?"

They turned and saw Humphries striding through the door, looking relaxed and confident in a dark blue business suit.

"Nothing I haven't said to your face, Humpy, old buddy," Pancho replied.

Humphries raised an eyebrow. "I'd appreciate it if you referred to me as Mr. Humphries when the other delegates get here."

"Sensitive?"

"Yes. In return for your consideration I'll try to refrain from using phrases such as 'guttersnipe' or 'grease monkey.'"

Stavenger put a hand to his forehead. "This is going to be a lovely morning," he groaned.

Actually, the conference went along much more smoothly than Stavenger had feared. The other delegates arrived, and Humphries turned his attention to Amanda, who smiled politely at him but said very little. He seemed almost to be a different person when Fuchs's wife was near: polite, considerate, earnestly trying to win her admiration, or at least her respect.

Stavenger called the meeting to order, and everyone took seats along the polished oblong conference table. Pancho behaved like a proper corporate executive and Humphries was affable and cooperative. Each of them made an opening statement about how they wanted nothing more than peace and harmony in the Asteroid Belt. Willi Dieterling then said a few brief words about how important the resources of the Belt were to the people of Earth.

"With so many millions homeless and hungry, with so much of our global industrial capacity wiped out, we desperately need the resources from the Belt," he pleaded. "This fighting is disrupting the supply of raw materials that we need to recover from the climate catastrophe that has brought civilization to its knees."

Stavenger pointed out, "The people of Selene are ready to help as much as we can. We have industrial capacity here on the Moon, and we can help you to build factories and power-generation stations in Earth orbit."

It was Big George who ended the platitudes.

"We all want peace and brotherhood," he began, "but the painful truth is that people are killin' each other out in the Belt."

Dieterling immediately replied, "The world government is prepared to offer Peacekeeping troops to you to help you maintain order in the Belt."

"No thanks!" George snapped. "We can maintain order for ourselves—" he turned to look squarely at Humphries "—if the corporations'll stop sending killers to us."

"Corporations, plural?" Pancho asked. "Astro hasn't sent any killers to the Belt."

"You've sent your share of goons, Pancho," said George.

"To protect our property!"

Humphries made a hushing motion with both hands. "I presume you're both referring to certain actions taken by employees of Humphries Space Systems."

"Fookin' right," George blurted.

With all eyes on him, Humphries said calmly, "It's perfectly true that some of the people my corporation sent to Ceres have been . . . well, roughnecks."

"Murderers," George muttered.

"One man committed a murder, true enough," Humphries conceded. "But he acted on his own. And he was punished for it swiftly enough."

"By Lars Fuchs, I understand," said Dieterling.

Humphries nodded. "Now we're getting down to the crux of the problem."

"Wait a minute," George interjected. "Let's not start dumpin' on Lars. Plenty of ships have been knocked off out in the Belt, and it was HSS that started it."

"That's not true," Humphries said.

"Isn't it? I was fookin' attacked by one of your butcher boys. Took me arm off. Remember?"

"We went through an IAA hearing over that. No one was able to prove it was one of my ships that attacked you."

"That doesn't mean it wasn't one of 'em, does it now?"

Stavenger broke into the budding argument. "Unless we have concrete evidence, there's no use throwing accusations around."

George glowered at him, but said nothing.

"We do have concrete evidence," Humphries resumed, with a swift glance at Amanda, "that Lars Fuchs has attacked ships, killed men, stolen supplies, and now he's wiped out a base we were building on Vesta in a totally unwarranted and premeditated attack. He's killed several dozen people. He's the reason for all this violence out in the Belt and until he's caught and put away, the violence will continue."

Absolute silence. Not one of the men or women seated around the conference table said a word in Fuchs's defense. Not even Amanda, Humphries noted with unalloyed delight.

CHAPTER 51

The asteroid had no name. In the catalogue files it was merely 38–4002. Barely a kilometer long and half that at its widest, it was a dark carbonaceous body, a loose aggregation of pebble-sized chondrules, more like a beanbag than a solid rock. Fuchs had left one of his transceivers there weeks earlier; now he was returning to the asteroid to retrieve it and see what information Amanda had been able to beam to him.

She's gone to Selene, he kept repeating in his mind. To a conference. To Humphries. Without telling me. Without mentioning a word of it. He saw St. Claire's face again as the man told him the news, almost smirking. *Your wife didn't tell you?* he heard St. Claire ask, again and again. *She never even mentioned it to you?*

It's probably in the messages waiting for me, Fuchs told himself. Amanda must have put it into the latest batch of messages just before she left for Selene. For Humphries's home. His guts knotted like fists every time he thought of it.

Why didn't she tell me beforehand? he raged silently. Why didn't she discuss this with me before she decided to go? The answer seemed terribly clear: Because she didn't want me to know she was going, didn't want me to know she would be seeing Humphries.

He wanted to bellow his rage and frustration, wanted to order his crew to race to Selene, wanted to take Amanda off the ship that was carrying her to the Moon and keep her safely with him. Too late, he knew. Far too late. She's gone. She's there by now. She's left me.

Nautilus's propellant tanks were full. Fuchs felt a slight pang of conscience about taking the hydrogen and helium fuels from his onetime friend St. Claire, but he had no choice. He had left St. Claire on less than friendly terms, but nevertheless the Quebecois waited six full hours before putting in an emergency call for a tanker, as Fuchs had ordered him to do.

Shaking his head as he sat in the command chair on *Nautilus*'s bridge, Fuchs wondered at how the human mind works. *St. Claire knew I wouldn't harm him. Yet he waited the full six hours before calling for help, giving me plenty of time to get safely away. Is he still my friend, despite everything? Or was he afraid I'd come back and fire on him?* Pondering the question, Fuchs decided, most likely St. Claire was simply playing it safe. *Our friendship is dead, a casualty of this war. I have no friends.*

I have no wife, either. I've driven her away. Driven her into Humphries's territory, perhaps into his arms.

The Asian navigator seated to one side of the bridge said to the woman who was piloting the ship, "The rock is in visual range." He spoke in their native Mongol dialect, but Fuchs understood them. *It's not a rock,* he corrected silently. *It's an aggregate.*

Glad to have something else to occupy his mind, Fuchs commanded his computer to put the telescopic view of the asteroid on his console screen. It was tumbling slowly along its long axis, end over end. As they approached the 'roid, Fuchs called up the computer image that showed where they had planted the transceiver.

He hunched forward in his chair, studying the screen, trying to drive thoughts of Amanda out of his mind. It showed the telescope's real-time image of the asteroid with the computer's grid map superimposed over it. *Strange,* he thought. *The contour map doesn't match the visual image any more. There's a new lump on the asteroid, not more than fifty meters from where the transceiver should be sitting.*

Fuchs froze the image and peered at it. *The asteroids are dynamic,* he knew. *They're constantly being dinged by smaller chunks of rock. An aggregate like this 'roid wouldn't show a crater, necessarily. It's like punching your fist into a beanbag chair: it just gives and reforms itself.*

But a lump? What would cause a lump?

He felt an old, old fervor stirring inside him. Once he had been a planetary geochemist; he had first come out to the Belt to study the asteroids, not to mine them. A curiosity that he hadn't felt in many years filled his mind. *What could raise a blister on a carbonaceous chondritic asteroid?*

Dorik Harbin was half a day's journey distant from the carbonaceous asteroid, even at the 0.5 g acceleration that was *Shanidar*'s best speed. He had dropped his ship into a grazing orbit around the jagged, striated body of nickel-iron where Fuchs had left one of his transceivers. His navigator was still sweating and wide-eyed with apprehension. His pale blond Scandinavian second-in-command had warned him several times that they were dangerously close to crashing into the rock.

But Harbin wanted to be so close that an approaching ship would not spot him. He wished this chunk of metal was porous, like the carbonaceous rock where one of Fuchs's other transceivers had been found. The crew there had simply detached their habitation module from the rest of their ship and buried it under a loose layer of rubble. Then the remainder of the ship, crewed only by a pilot and navigator, flew out of range. If Fuchs showed up there, all he would see would be an innocent pile of dirt. A Trojan horse, Harbin thought grimly, that would disgorge half a dozen armed troops while calling all of Harbin's armada to close the trap.

The Scandinavian was clearly unhappy orbiting mere meters from the scratched and pitted surface of the asteroid. "We are running the danger of having the hull abraded by the dust that hovers over the rock," she warned Harbin.

He looked into her wintry blue eyes. So like my own, he thought. Her Viking ancestors must have invaded my village some time in the past.

"It's dangerous!" she said sharply.

Harbin made himself smile at her. "Match our orbit to the rock's intrinsic spin. If Fuchs comes poking around here, I don't him to see us until it's too late for him to get away."

She started to protest, but Harbin cut her off with an upraised hand. "Do it," he said.

Clearly unhappy, she turned and relayed his order to the navigator.

"Let's break for lunch," said Doug Stavenger.

The others around the conference table nodded and pushed their chairs back. The tension in the room cracked. One by one, they got to their feet, stretched, took deep breaths. Stavenger heard vertebrae pop.

Lunch had been laid on in another conference room, down the hall. As the delegates filed out into the corridor, Stavenger touched Dieterling's arm, detaining him.

"Have we accomplished anything?" he asked the diplomat.

Dieterling glanced at the doorway, where his two nephews stood waiting for him. Then he turned back to Stavenger. "A little, I think."

"At least Humphries and Pancho are talking civilly to each other," Stavenger said, with a rueful smile.

"Don't underestimate the benefits of civility," said Dieterling. "Without it, nothing can be done."

"So?"

With a heavy shrug, Dieterling answered, "It's clear that the crux of the problem is this man Fuchs."

"Humphries certainly wants him out of the way."

"As long as he is rampaging out there in the Belt there can be no peace."

Stavenger shook his head. "But Fuchs started his . . . rampage, as you call it, in reaction to the violence that Humphries's people began."

"That makes no difference now," Dieterling said, dropping his voice almost to a whisper. "We can get Humphries and Ms. Lane to let bygones be bygones and forget the past. No recriminations, no acts of vengeance. They are willing to make a peaceful settlement."

"And stick to it, do you think?"

"Yes. I'm certain of it. This war is becoming too expensive for them. They want it ended."

"They can end it this afternoon, if they want to."

"Only if Fuchs is stopped," Dieterling said. "He is the wild card, the terrorist who is beyond ordinary political control."

Stavenger nodded glumly. "He's got to be stopped, then. Dammit."

Humphries stepped into the washroom, relieved himself of a morning's worth of coffee, then washed up and popped another tranquilizing pill. He thought of them as tranquilizers, even though he knew they were much more than that.

As he stepped out into the corridor, Amanda came out of the ladies' room. His breath caught in his throat, despite the pill. She was dressed in a yellow pant suit that seemed faded from long use, yet in Humphries's eyes she glowed like the sun. No one else was in sight; the others must have all gone into the room where lunch was laid out.

"Hello, Amanda," he heard himself say.

Only then did he see the cold anger in her eyes.

"You're determined to kill Lars, aren't you?" she said flatly.

Humphries licked his lips before replying, "Kill him? No. Stop him. That's all I want, Amanda. I want him to stop the killing."

"Which you started."

"That doesn't matter anymore. He's the problem now."

"You won't rest until you've killed him."

"Not—" He had to swallow hard before he could continue. "Not if you'll marry me."

He had expected her to be surprised. But her eyes did not flicker, the expression on her utterly beautiful face did not change one iota. She simply turned and headed up the corridor, away from him.

Humphries started to after her, but then he heard Stavenger and Dieterling coming up the hall behind him. Don't make an ass of yourself in front of them, he told himself sternly. Let her go. For now. At least she didn't say no.

CHAPTER 52

As Fuchs studied the image of asteroid 38–4002, Nodon ducked through the hatch and stepped into the bridge. Fuchs heard him ask the pilot if the long-range scan showed any other ships in the area.

"None," said the pilot.

What could raise a lump on a beanbag collection of pebbles? Fuchs asked himself for the dozenth time. *Nautilus* was approaching the asteroid at one-sixth g; they would have to start a braking maneuver soon if they were going to establish an orbit around it.

Wishing he had a full panoply of sensors to play across the asteroid's surface, Fuchs noted again that there were several noticeable craters on its surface, but none of them had the raised rims that formed when a boulder crashed into a solid rock. No, this is a collection of nodules, he thought, and the only way to build a blister like that is for something to push the pellets up into a mound.

Something. Then it hit him. Or some*one*.

He turned in his chair and looked up at Nodon. "Warm up laser number one," he commanded.

Nodon's big eyes flashed, but he nodded silently and left the bridge.

Turning back to the image of the approaching asteroid, Fuchs reasoned, If something natural pushed up that mound, then there should be a depression next to it, from where the pebbles were scooped up. But there isn't. Why not? Because something is buried under that mound. Because someone dug a hole in that porous pile of rubble and buried something in it.

What?

"Cut our approach velocity in half," he said to the pilot. The Asian complied wordlessly.

Several minutes later, Nodon called from the cargo bay, "Laser number two is ready."

"Number two?" Fuchs replied sharply. "What happened to number one?"

"Its coolant lines are being flushed. Routine maintenance."

"Get it on line," Fuchs snapped. "Get number three on line, too."

"Yes, sir." Fuchs could hear Nodon speaking in rapid dialect to someone else down in the cargo bay.

"Slave number two to my console," Fuchs ordered.

He began to reconfigure his console with fingertip touches on its main display screen. By the time he had finished, the laser was linked. He could run it from the bridge.

He put the asteroid on-screen and focused on that suspicious mound of rubble. He saw the red dot of the aiming laser sparkling on the dark, pebbly ground and walked it to the middle of the mound. Then, with a touch of a finger, he fired the high-power laser. Its infrared beam was invisible to his eyes, but Fuchs saw the ground cascade into a splash of heat, a miniature fountain of red-hot lava erupting, spraying high above the asteroid's surface.

His face set in a harsh scowl, Fuchs held the cutting laser's beam on the spewing geyser of molten rock. Ten seconds. Fifteen. Twenty. . . .

The mound erupted. Half a dozen spacesuited figures scurried in all directions like cockroaches startled out of their nest, stumbling across the rough surface of the asteroid.

"I knew it!" Fuchs shouted. The three Asians on the bridge turned toward him.

Nodon called from the cargo bay, "They were waiting for us to pick up the transceiver!"

Fuchs ignored them all. He swung the laser toward one of the figures. The man had tripped and sprawled clumsily in the minuscule gravity of the little asteroid, then when he tried to get up, he had pushed himself completely off the ground. Now he floated helplessly, arms and legs flailing.

Fuchs walked the laser beam toward him, watched its molten path as it burned across the asteroid's gravelly surface.

"Waiting to trap me, were you?" he muttered. "You wanted to kill me. Now see what death is like."

For an instant he wondered who was inside that spacesuit. What kind of a man becomes a mercenary soldier, a hired killer? Is he like my own crew, the castoffs, the abandoned, so desperate that they'll do anything, follow anyone who can give them hope that they'll live to see another day? Fuchs watched the spacesuited figure struggling, arms and legs pumping frantically as he drifted farther off the asteroid. He certainly had no experience in microgravity, Fuchs saw. And his comrades are doing nothing to help him.

You're going to die alone, he said silently to the spacesuited figure.

Yet he turned off the cutting laser. His hand had touched the screen icon that deactivated its beam before his conscious mind understood what he had done. The red spot of the low-power aiming laser still scintillated on the asteroid's surface. Fuchs moved it to shine squarely on the flailing, contorted body of the mercenary.

Kill or be killed, he told himself. It took an effort, though, to will his hand back to the high-power laser's firing control. He held it there, poised a bare centimeter above it.

"Two ships approaching at high acceleration," called the pilot. "No, four ships, coming in from two different directions."

Fuchs knew he couldn't murder the man. He could not kill him in cold blood. And he knew that their trap had worked.

It all fell in on him like an avalanche. They knew where the transceivers were hidden. Someone had told them. Someone? Only Amanda knew where the transceivers were located. She wouldn't betray him, Fuchs told himself. She wouldn't. Someone must have ferreted out the information somehow. And then sold it to Humphries.

"Six ships," called the pilot, sounding frightened. "All approaching at high g."

Trapped. They were waiting for me to show up. Six ships.

Nodon's voice came over the intercom. "Lasers one and three ready to fire."

I'll get them all killed if I try to fight back, Fuchs realized. It's me that Humphries wants, not my crew.

Suddenly he felt tired, bone tired, soul weary. It's over, he realized. All this fighting and killing and what has it gained me? What has it gained anyone? I've walked my crew into a trap, like a fool, like a wolf caught in the hunter's net. It's over. It's finished. And I've lost everything.

With a feeling of resignation that overwhelmed him, Fuchs touched the communications key and spoke, "This is Lars Fuchs aboard the *Nautilus*. Don't fire. We surrender."

Harbin heard the defeat in Fuchs's voice. And he cursed Martin Humphries for saddling him with this oversized armada and company of troops. I could have done this by myself, he thought. Given the information about where he planted his transceivers, I could have trapped him by myself, without all these others—all these witnesses.

By himself, Harbin would have sliced Fuchs's ship into bits and killed everyone aboard it. Then he would have carried Fuchs's dead body back to Diane and her boss, so Humphries could glory in his triumph and Harbin could claim the immense bonus that would be rightfully his. Then he would take Diane for himself and leave Humphries to gloat over his victory.

But there were more than a hundred men and women aboard this fleet that Humphries had insisted upon. It was nonsense to believe that each of them would remain quiet if Harbin killed Fuchs after the man had surrendered. It would be too big a story, too much temptation. Someone would cash out to the news media, or to spies from Humphries's competitors in Astro Corporation.

No. Against his instincts, against his judgment, Harbin knew he had to accept Fuchs's surrender and bring the man and his crew back to Ceres. Then he smiled grimly. Perhaps once he's on Ceres something might happen to him. After all, the man's made many enemies there. They might even put him on trial and execute him legally.

CHAPTER 53

The implantation procedure was not as draining as Diane feared it would be.

She had insisted that all the attending personnel be women, and Selene's medical staff had complied with her demand. They were smiling, soothing, soft-spoken. After an injection of a tranquilizer, they wheeled Diane into the little room where the procedure would take place. The room felt cold. A plastic container sat on the table where the instruments were laid out, steaming icy white vapor. The frozen embryo was in there, Diane realized, her thoughts getting fuzzy from the injection.

It's like being put on the rack by the Spanish Inquisition, she thought. The instruments of torture lay in a neat row beside her. Bright lights glared down at her. The torturers gathered around her, masked and gowned, their hands gloved in skin-thin plastic.

She took a deep breath as they gently placed her feet in the stirrups.

"Just try to relax," said a soothing woman's voice.

Good advice, Diane thought. Just try.

Humphries was seated up near the head of the table, one chair down from Stavenger. Dieterling was at his left, Pancho Lane across the table from him, and Big George Ambrose at his right. Humphries did not relish being next to the big Aussie; the shaggy redhead was intimidating even when he was doing nothing more than sitting quietly and listening to the others wrangle.

Amanda was on George's other side. Humphries couldn't even glance at her without leaning around the Australian and being obvious about it.

"The essence of agreement is compromise," Dieterling was saying for the *n*th time. "And compromise is impossible without trust."

Dieterling expects the Nobel Peace Prize for his work in the Middle East, Humphries thought. It won't matter much what he accomplishes or fails to accomplish here. But he's so damned *earnest*. You'd think his own life hinges on what we're doing today.

Pancho, across the table, eyed Humphries for a moment, then said to Dieterling, "Astro's willing to compromise. I've been sayin' all along that there's so much natural wealth out in the Belt that there's plenty for ever'-body. What we need is an agreement about who gets what."

Stavenger shook his head. "I don't think you can carve up the Belt the way Spain and Portugal divided up the New World back in the sixteenth century."

"Yeah," Big George agreed. "What about the independents? You can't give the whole fookin' Belt to the corporations."

"What is required," Dieterling said, "is an agreement to forgo the use of violence; an agreement to proceed peacefully and respect the rights of others."

Humphries's phone buzzed in his jacket pocket. Ordinarily he would have been annoyed at the interruption, but at this point he welcomed it.

"Please excuse me," he said, plucking the phone from his pocket. "This must be extremely important. I gave orders that I wasn't to be disturbed."

Stavenger spread his hands. "This is a good time for a short break, I think."

Humphries strode off to a corner of the conference room as the others all got up from their chairs.

Tucking the phone's little speaker into his earlobe, Humphries flicked the device open and saw URGENT—PRIORITY 1 printed across its tiny screen.

"Proceed," he said softly.

Dorik Harbin's dark bearded face formed on the screen. "Sir, we have captured the man Fuchs and his entire crew. We are on the way back to Ceres with them in custody."

Kill him! Humphries wanted to cry. Instead, his eyes scanned the conference room. The others were standing at the refreshments table. Amanda was nowhere in sight; probably gone to the rest room, he thought.

Knowing that his response would not reach Harbin for nearly a half-hour, Humphries said tightly, "Good work. Make certain you don't lose him. If he tries to get away, or if anyone tries to free him, take appropriate action."

Appropriate action, Grigor had assured him, was the euphemistic code phrase that meant, *kill the sonofabitch if he twitches an eyebrow.*

Humphries closed the phone and slipped it back into his jacket. His pulse was thudding in his ears; he tasted salty perspiration on his upper lip. It's over, he thought, trying to calm himself. It's finished. I've got him, and now I'm going to get Amanda!

He stayed in the far corner of the room as the others slowly came back to their seats. Amanda returned, looking calm, even dignified. She's grown over the years, Humphries realized. She's become much more sure of herself, much more mature. Stavenger glanced his way, and Humphries—working hard to suppress a grin and look serious—slowly walked to his own chair.

Instead of sitting, though, he gripped the back of the chair and said, "I have an announcement to make."

They all looked up at him. Even Amanda.

"The one sticking point in our discussion today has been the one-man guerilla war of Lars Fuchs."

Dieterling and several others nodded.

"That problem has been resolved," Humphries said, looking squarely at Amanda. For an instant she looked startled, frightened, but she recovered quickly and looked squarely into his eyes.

"Lars Fuchs is in custody. He's aboard one of my ships and heading back to Ceres. I presume he'll stand trial there for piracy and murder."

Absolute silence fell across the conference table. Then Amanda slowly got up from her chair.

"Excuse me, please," she said. "I must try to contact my husband." She turned and headed for the door.

Pancho started to get out of her chair, but thought better of it and sat down again. "Okay, then," she said, as Amanda left the conference room. "We got nothin' in the way of making an agreement we can all live with."

Humphries nodded, but he was thinking, There's nothing in our way except Fuchs. But he's not going to interfere with my plans any more. He's not going to live much longer.

CHAPTER 54

Will you release my crew once we reach Ceres?" Fuchs asked dully, mechanically.

Harbin replied, "That's not up to me. That decision will be made—"

"By Martin Humphries, I know," said Fuchs.

Harbin studied the man. They were sitting at the small table in *Shanidar*'s galley, the only space in the ship where two people could converse in privacy. The hatch to the bridge was shut, by Harbin's orders. Fuchs had looked utterly weary, dispirited, when he had first been brought aboard *Shanidar*. The look of defeat: Harbin had seen it before. A man stops fighting when he becomes convinced that no hope is left; victory begins when the enemy's will to resist crumbles. But now, after a decent meal and a few hours to adjust his thinking to his new situation, Fuchs seemed to be regaining some spark of resistance.

He was a powerfully-built man, Harbin saw, despite his smallish stature. Like a badger, or—what was that American creature? A wolverine, he remembered. Small but deadly. Sharp teeth and utter fearlessness.

For a few moments Harbin contemplated what would happen if Fuchs tried to attack him. He had no doubt that he could handle the man, despite Fuchs's apparent strength and potential ferocity. It would simplify everything if I had to kill him in self-defense, Harbin thought. Perhaps I can goad him into attacking me. His wife is apparently a sore point with him.

But then Harbin thought, To be convincing, I'd need at least one witness. That would be self-defeating. With another person in the room Fuchs probably would be smart enough to keep his hands to himself. If I tried to goad him, the witness would witness that, too.

Fuchs broke into his thoughts with, "Where is my crew? What have you done with them?"

"They've been placed aboard my other ships," Harbin said. "No more than two to a ship. It's safer that way; they won't be tempted to try anything foolish."

"I expect them to be treated properly."

Harbin bobbed his head once. "As long as they behave themselves they will be fine."

"And I want them released when we get to Ceres."

Barely suppressing a smile at Fuchs's growing impudence, Harbin said, "As I told you, that decision will be made by higher authority."

"I take full responsibility for everything that's happened."

"Naturally."

Fuchs lapsed into silence for a few moments. Then he said, "I suppose I'll have to speak to Humphries directly, sooner or later."

Harbin answered, "I doubt that he'll want to speak to you."

"About my crew—"

"Mr. Fuchs," Harbin said, getting to his feet, "the fate of your crew is something that neither you nor I have the power to decide."

Fuchs rose also, barely reaching Harbin's shoulder.

"I think it would be best," Harbin said, "if you remained in your privacy cubicle for the rest of the flight. We'll be at Ceres in less than thirty-six hours. I'll have your meals brought to you."

Fuchs said nothing, but let Harbin lead him down the passageway to the cubicle they had assigned him. There was no lock on the sliding door, which was so flimsy that a lock would have been useless anyway. Fuchs realized that Harbin had been clever to break up his crew and parcel them out among the other ships in his fleet.

I'm alone here, he thought as Harbin gestured him into the cubicle. The door slid closed. Fuchs sat heavily on the hard springless cot. Like Samson captured and blinded by the Philistines, he told himself. Eyeless in Gaza.

At least I wasn't sold out by Amanda. She'd never be a Delilah, never betray me. Never.

He desperately wanted to believe that.

"The essence of our agreement, then," said Stavenger, "is that both Astro and Humphries Space Systems disband their mercenary forces and allow the independent prospectors to operate without harassment."

"And without placing any controls on the prices for ores," Humphries added, with a satisfied nod.

"No price controls," Pancho agreed.

Dieterling said, "Pardon my bluntness, but don't you feel that your refusal to accept price controls is blatantly selfish?"

"Not at all," snapped Humphries.

"Works the other way around, Willi," Pancho said, quite seriously. "Supply and demand works in favor of the buyer, not the seller."

"But you buy the ores from the prospectors—"

"And sell the refined metals to you," Humphries pointed out.

Frowning slightly, Dieterling muttered, "I'm not an economist. . . ."

"I think a free market works in Selene's favor," Stavenger said. "And Earth's."

Pancho hunched forward in her chair. "See, if you leave the market open, then the more ores the prospectors locate the lower the price'll go. Supply and demand."

"But Earth needs vast amounts of those raw materials," Dieterling said.

Stavenger put a hand on the diplomat's sleeve, gently. "Doctor Dieterling, I don't think you have any idea of how enormous the resources in the Asteroid Belt are. There are trillions of tons of high-grade ores out there. Hundreds of trillions of tons. We've only begun to scratch the surface, so far."

"Price controls would work in favor of the prospectors, not the ultimate consumers on Earth," Humphries said firmly.

"Or Selene," added Stavenger.

Still worrying that uncontrolled prices for asteroidal ores would somehow work against Earth's best interests, Dieterling reluctantly agreed to drop the issue and allow Astro and HSS to draft an agreement. The International Astronautical Authority would be empowered to adjudicate claims against one corporation or the other.

"There's one remaining problem," Stavenger pointed out, just as everyone was getting ready to call the conference a success.

Humphries, halfway out of his chair, grumbled, "What now?"

"Enforcement," Stavenger said. "There's nothing in the draft agreement about enforcing the peace."

Sitting down again, Humphries asked, "You don't trust us to live up to the terms we agree to?"

Pancho grinned. "I know you can trust Astro."

"Sure we can," Stavenger replied, grinning back at her. "But I'd prefer to see something on paper."

George spoke up. "We'll enforce the peace," he said.

Everyone turned to him.

"You?" Humphries scoffed. "The rock rats?"

"We've got a government now, or the beginnings of one," George said. "We'll police Ceres. Any complaints from the prospectors, we'll handle 'em."

"How could you—"

"Everything goes through Ceres," George explained. "That's where the ships get fitted out and supplied. We hold the water taps, mate. And the food cupboards and fuel tanks and even the foo—the bleedin' oxygen for breathin'. We'll keep law and order for ya. It's in our own best interests."

Dieterling turned back to Stavenger. "Could that work?"

"We can make it work," said Kris Cardenas, sitting across the table from George.

Stavenger had a strange expression on his face. "This means that the rock rats will have political control of the Belt."

"Which is the way it should be," Cardenas said firmly. "We're the people who live there, we ought to be able to control our own destiny."

Looking from her to Stavenger and back again, Dieterling said, "That is a great deal of power. The entire Asteroid Belt . . ."

"We can handle it," George said, totally serious. "Like Kris here said, it's the way things oughtta be."

CHAPTER 55

The conference ended at last. As the delegates got up from the table and made their way to the door, Humphries remained seated, hands clasped on the tabletop, deep in thought.

"Ain't you goin' home?" Pancho asked as she came around the table.

"In a while," Humphries said. "Not right this moment."

Stavenger was going through the doorway with Dieterling and his two nephews. Big George and Dr. Cardenas were already gone; George had been the first out the door, like a schoolboy racing away from the classroom once the bell has rung.

"I don't think Mandy'll be comin' back here," Pancho said.

Humphries made himself smile up at her. "We'll see."

"Suit yourself," Pancho said.

Humphries watched her saunter out the door, leaving him alone in the conference room. So we'll have peace in the Belt, he said to himself. And the rock rats will enforce it. Sure they will.

He got to his feet and went to the slim little podium that had been wheeled into a corner of the room. The audio–visual controls on its surface were simple enough. With a touch of his finger, Humphries lit up the wallscreen at the other end of the conference room. It showed Selene's logo: the androgynous outline of a human being against the full Moon. Scrolling idly through the computer's stored images, he stopped when a map of the Belt came up: the wild tangle of orbits looked like a long-exposure view of a mad raceway.

So we won't bother the independents anymore, Humphries said to himself. We won't call down the wrath of the rock rats and their fledgling government. We won't have to. All the independents will be selling to me or to Astro; there's no third choice. They'll all fall into line now.

He drew in a breath, thinking, Now the fight's between Astro and HSS. Now the *real* war begins. And when it's over, I'll have Astro in my pocket and total control of the Belt. Total control of the whole fricking solar system and everyone in it!

As if on cue, Amanda entered the conference room.

Humphries stared at her. Somehow she looked different: still the most beautiful woman he had ever seen, the most desirable. Yet there was something else about her now, something that almost unnerved him. She looked back at him, her eyes steady, dry. She's not shedding any tears for her husband, Humphries told himself.

"They won't let me speak to him," Amanda said, her voice so soft he could barely make out the words. She walked along the length of the conference table toward Humphries.

"He's too far out for a two-way conversation," he said.

"I put through a call to him and they wouldn't even accept it. They told me he's not allowed to receive any messages from anyone."

"He's being held incommunicado."

"On your orders."

"Yes."

"You intend to kill him, don't you?"

Humphries evaded her unwavering blue eyes. "I imagine they'll put him on trial at Ceres. He's killed a lot of people."

"Will he live long enough to face a trial?" Amanda asked, her voice flat, calm, not accusative so much as resigned.

Uncomfortably nervous, Humphries shifted his weight from one foot to another. "He's a violent man, you know. He might try to escape custody."

"That would be convenient, wouldn't it? Then he could be killed while trying to escape."

Humphries came around the podium and stepped toward her, reaching his arms out to her.

"Amanda," he said, "it's all over. Fuchs has dug his own grave and—"

"And you're going to see that he goes into it."

"It's not my doing!" At that moment he almost felt that it was true.

Amanda simply stood there, unmoving, unmoved, her arms at her sides, her eyes focused on him, searching for something, something. He wished he knew what it was.

"What do you want from me?" he asked her.

For a moment she said nothing. Then, "I want your promise that you won't allow him to be harmed in any way."

"The rock rats are going to put him on trial for murder."

"I understand that," Amanda said. "I still want your promise that *you* won't do anything to harm him."

He hesitated, then asked coldly, "And what will you do in exchange for my promise?"

"I'll go to bed with you," Amanda said. "That's what you want, isn't it?"

"No!" he blurted. Almost pleading, he said, "I want to marry you, Amanda. I love you! I want to give you . . . everything you've ever wanted."

She waited a heartbeat, then said, "All I want is Lars's safety."

"And not me?"

"I owe it to Lars. All this has happened because of me, hasn't it?"

He wanted to lie, wanted to tell her that everything he had done he had done for her and for her alone. But he couldn't. Facing her, so close to her, he could not lie.

"You were a part of it, Amanda. But only a part. Something like this would have happened anyway."

"But Lars wouldn't have been caught in the middle of it, would he?"

"Probably not," Humphries agreed.

"Then I'll marry you, if that's what you want. In exchange for your promise to leave Lars alone."

Humphries's throat felt dry, parched. He nodded mutely.

"Now you have everything *you* want, don't you?" Amanda said. There was no rancor in it. No trace of anger or bitterness. At last Humphries understood what was different about her, what had changed. She's not the innocent, naive girl she once was. Those blue eyes are unsmiling now, calculating.

He couldn't find words. He wanted to make her feel better about this, wanted to make her smile. But he couldn't find any words.

"That is what you want, isn't it?" Amanda insisted.

"Not like this," he said, finding his voice. And it was the truth. "Not as part of a . . . an arrangement."

Amanda shrugged slightly. "This is the way it is, Martin. There's nothing either one of us can do to change it. I'll marry you if you swear that you won't harm Lars."

He licked his lips. "He'll still have to face trial on Ceres. I can't stop that."

"I know," she said. "I accept that."

"All right, then."

"I want to hear you say it, Martin. I want your promise, here and now."

Drawing himself up to his full height, Humphries said, "Very well. I promise you, Amanda, that I will do nothing to harm Lars Fuchs in any way."

"You won't give anyone orders to hurt him."

"I swear to you, Amanda."

The breath seemed to sag out of her. "All right, then. I'll marry you as soon as a divorce can be arranged."

Or as soon as you become a widow, Humphries thought. Aloud, he said, "Now it's your turn to make a promise, Amanda."

Alarm flashed in her eyes momentarily. Then she understood. "I see. Yes, I promise that I will be your loving wife, Martin. This won't be merely a marriage of appearances."

Before he could take her hands in his, she turned and walked out of the conference room, leaving him standing alone. For a few moments he felt rejected, wronged, almost angry. But slowly it dawned on him that Amanda had agreed to marry him, to love him. It wasn't the romantic perfection he had fantasized about over all the years, but she had promised to marry him! All right, she's upset about it now. I've forced her into it and she doesn't like that. She feels an obligation to Fuchs. But that will change. In time, she'll accept it. She'll accept me. She'll love me. I know she will.

Suddenly Humphries was laughing out loud, dancing around the conference table like a manic teenager. "I've got her!" he shouted to the ceiling. "I've got everything I've ever wanted! The whole miserable solar system is in my grasp!"

Big George thought they were lucky to snag a ride aboard an HSS ship heading for Ceres on a high-energy trajectory.

"We'll be there in four days," he said to Kris Cardenas as they picked meal packages from the galley's freezer.

Cardenas was more skeptical about their luck. "Why is Humphries sending this ship to Ceres on a high-g burn? It's practically empty. We're the only passengers and there isn't any cargo, far as I can tell."

Sliding his dinner into the microwave, George said, "From what the crew's buzzin', they're goin' out to pick up the bloke who captured Lars."

Comprehension lit Cardenas's cornflower-blue eyes. "So that's it! A triumphal return for the conquering hero."

"It isn't funny, Kris. We've gotta put Lars on trial, y'know. He's killed people."

"I know," she said despondently.

The microwave bell chimed.

"George," she asked, "isn't there some way we can save Lars's neck?"

"Sure," he said, pulling out the tray. "Sentence 'im to life at hard labor. Or maybe pop 'im into a cryonic freezer for a hundred years or so."

"Be serious," Cardenas said.

George sat at the galley's little table and unwrapped his steaming tray. "Dunno what we can do except give him as fair a trial as we can. He's made a lot of enemies, y'know."

She slammed her tray back into the freezer and sat glumly beside him. "I wish there were some way we could save him."

Already digging into his dinner, George tried to change the subject. "We'll do what we can for Lars. But, y'know, I been thinkin' . . . why can't you develop nanomachines to take the ores outta the asteroids right there on the spot and refine 'em? That'd make it a snap to mine 'em."

"It would throw almost all the miners out of work."

"Maybe so," George admitted. "But what if we let 'em buy shares of the nanotech operation? That way they could become fookin' capitalists instead o' grubbin' away at the rocks."

Harbin personally escorted Fuchs from *Shanidar* to the underground settlement on Ceres. Fuchs was not handcuffed or fettered, but he knew he was a prisoner. Harbin brought two of his biggest men with him; he was taking no chances.

As they rode the ungainly shuttlecraft down to the asteroid's surface, Fuchs spotted the still-unfinished habitat rotating lazily across the star-flecked sky. Will they ever finish it? He asked himself. Will they ever be able to live the way I wanted Amanda and me to live?

Amanda. The thought of her sapped all the strength from him. At least she will be safe, Fuchs thought. Yes, came a mocking voice from within his mind. She'll be quite safe once she's married Humphries. The old anger surged for a moment, but it faded away, replaced with the hopelessness of his situation. He's won her and I've lost, he knew.

As they stepped through the airlock and into the reception area, Fuchs saw a group of four women and three men waiting for him. He recognized them all: former neighbors, former friends.

"We'll take him from here," said Joyce Takamine, her gaunt, pinched face blankly expressionless. She would not look Fuchs in the eyes.

"Take him where?" Harbin demanded.

"He's under house arrest," Takamine replied stiffly, "pending the return of our Chief Administrator. He's going to stand trial for piracy and murder."

Harbin nodded his agreement and allowed them to lead Fuchs away. It's finished, he told himself. I've done my job. Now for the rewards.

He led his two men to the Humphries office, only a short walk through the dusty tunnel. There a smiling young woman got up from her metal desk and personally escorted the trio to quarters deeper inside the warren of tunnels and cubicles. The two men had to share one room; Harbin got a private apartment. It was still just one room, but it was his alone. Someone had even brought his travel bag and placed it on the bed.

A message from Diane was waiting for him.

She should have looked happy, jubilant, Harbin thought, rejoicing in their victory, his triumph. Instead, her face looked serious, almost grave, in the wallscreen image.

"Dorik, I've set up a high-g flight for you. I want you here at Selene as soon as you can get here. Now that you've taken Fuchs, there's a lot we have to do, a lot of changes in both our lives. I'll tell you all about it when you get here."

The screen went blank. Harbin stared at it for a few moments, thinking, Not a word of congratulations. Not a syllable of warmth. Well, she's never said she loves me.

He went to the bed and sat on it, suddenly tired. I never expected love, he told himself. Then he realized, Not until now. He opened his travel bag and searched through it for the pills that would bring him peace—at least for a little while.

CHAPTER 56

Humphries spent the morning making arrangements for his wedding. He had his legal department send a notice of Amanda's divorce suit to Fuchs at Ceres. That ought to put the icing on his cake, he though delightedly. Maybe he'll commit suicide once he gets the news and spare us all the trouble of putting him on trial. Then he decided to buy the Hotel Luna and refurbish it so it would look properly gleaming for his wedding. It won't be a big affair, he thought, just a few dozen friends. And the most important of my business associates, of course. It's got to be first-class all the way. What was that old word the English used, long ago? Posh. That's it. I want this wedding to be small, intimate, and very posh.

Amanda will probably invite Pancho, he realized. So what? I wonder how much family she has back on Earth. I'll bring them all up here. Why not? I'm going to shower her with so much kindness and luxury that she'll fall in love with me whether she wants to or not.

By lunch time he was still grinning and whistling to himself. He ate at his desk, casually running down the past two days of activities reports. He stopped when he saw that Diane had authorized a high-energy flight to Ceres. The only passengers aboard the vessel were Ambrose and Dr. Cardenas.

Why would she do that? he wondered.

And then he remembered, She went through the implantation procedure yesterday. And she still got up and ordered a special flight for those two rock rats?

His mood only slightly dimmed, he called Verwoerd on the phone.

"I'm going to take a stroll through the garden," he said when her image appeared on the wallscreen. "Are you up to joining me?"

"I'm trying to catch up on what I missed yesterday," she said guardedly.

"That can wait. A walk in the fresh air will be good for you."

She hesitated a fraction of a second, then capitulated. With a nod, she said, "I'll meet you at your front door."

He expected that she would show some strain from the procedure she'd been through, but to Humphries's eye Diane Verwoerd looked no different than before the implantation.

"The procedure went well?" he asked as they stepped along the brick path that wound through lushly thick bushes of coral pink oleanders and scarlet azaleas.

She gave him a sidelong glance. "The report should be on file."

"I've seen the report," he replied testily. "I want to know how you feel."

"Oh," said Verwoerd. "Concerned for the mother of your son?"

"That's right."

She stayed silent for a few steps, then said at last, "I'm fine. Mother and fetus in good condition."

"Good."

"By the way, let me offer my congratulations."

He couldn't help breaking into a smile. "About Amanda? Thank you."

They passed a little bench of lunar stone. Verwoerd asked, "Now that you'll be able to make a baby the old-fashioned way, do you still want me to go to term?"

"Of course I do," he snapped. "That's my son you're talking about."

"Your clone."

"I wouldn't have you abort him. I can have more than one child."

"But this one," she patted her stomach lightly, "carries your genes and nobody else's."

"Damned right."

"He won't be exactly like you, you know," Verwoerd said, a teasing smile playing across her lips. "Genetically, he'll be identical, but he'll be affected by the enzymes of my body and—"

"I know all that," Humphries interrupted.

"I'm sure you do."

He glared at her. "You're downright sassy today, aren't you?"

"And why shouldn't I be, Martin? I'm carrying your child. You're going to reward me very handsomely for that, aren't you?"

"If the boy is healthy when he's born."

"No, I don't want to wait until then. I want my payoff now. I want a seat on the board of directors. I've earned it. And I'll be a lot better at it than most of those fossils."

Power, Humphries thought. She's after power. Aloud, he asked, "Is that all?"

"I want money, too. I want a lot of money, Martin. I know you can afford it."

He stopped walking and planted his fists on his hips. "Since when do you call me by my given name?"

She smiled saucily. "I'm taking a very large risk for this fetus of yours. I think that works out to a first-name relationship, don't you?"

"No, I don't."

"Very well then, we'll keep everything strictly on a business level, *Mister* Humphries. I want ten million a year, for life."

"Ten mil—" He barked out a bitter laugh. "You're dreaming. I could get a hundred women to do what you're doing and it wouldn't cost me a fraction of that."

Verwoerd began walking along the brick path again, slowly. Humphries had no choice but to follow her.

"Yes, I'm sure you could buy a surrogate mother for your clone on the cheap. But I'm worth ten million. Even more, in fact."

"Are you?" he asked sullenly, realizing now where she was heading.

"I know a lot about you, about what you've done in the Belt. I've been a faithful employee, *Mister* Humphries, And I've kept my mouth shut. But continued silence will cost you ten million per year. You can set up a trust fund; I'll handle the details for you."

Strangely, Humphries felt no anger. He almost admired her audacity. "So it's come to this," he said.

"Yes, it has."

With a slow, disappointed shake of his head, Humphries said, "I was afraid you'd get delusions of grandeur. This isn't the first time an employee of mine had tried to extort money from me."

"Don't you think I'm worth ten mil per year?" she asked, rank impudence on her smiling lips.

Before he could think of an appropriate reply, Verwoerd added, "And don't think you can conveniently get rid of me. I'm not going to have an accident, Martin. I have a very good insurance policy against accidents of all kinds."

Then it dawned on him. "So that's why you're rushing Harbin back here."

She nodded. "Dorik's my insurance policy. If you attempt any violence against me, he'll kill you. He's good at it. Ask Grigor; Grigor's ter-rified of him."

"Is he?"

"Yes. And for good reason. You should be terrified of him, too, if you think you can get rid of me. It's cheaper to pay the ten million, Martin. That covers both of us, Dorik and me together."

"A real bargain," Humphries growled.

CHAPTER 57

It was maddening. All day long Lars Fuchs paced his one-room apartment like a caged tiger, to the door, turn around, to the far wall where the wallscreen stood blank and mute. Again and again: the door, then past the bed where he and Amanda had slept together, made love together . . .

He wanted to scream. He wanted to pound the walls, smash down the flimsy door and run through the dusty tunnels until someone shot him down and put an end to it all.

He recalled the phrase the Americans used: cruel and unusual punishment. To be put under house arrest, to be locked in the room that had for so many years been his home, to know that his wife was millions of kilometers away and preparing to marry the man who had ruined his life—better to be dead, better to be out of this endless torture.

He caught a glimpse of himself in the mirror over the bureau and saw a man he hardly recognized, clothes wrinkled and sweat-stained, hair unkempt, jowly face unshaved. He stopped pacing and stared at the image in the mirror: a man steeped in self-pity, wallowing in defeat.

No, he said to himself. I won't let it end this way. They've taken everything from me, but they won't take my self-respect. No one can do that except I myself.

He tore off his sweaty clothes and stepped into the shower. When the spray turned on automatically, he thought about his water allotment, but then he decided, To hell with it; a condemned man has the right to a decent wash. But as the steamy mist enveloped him he thought of the times when he and Amanda had squeezed into the narrow stall together. It took all his strength to keep from crying.

Freshly dressed and shaved, he asked the phone to call George

Ambrose. Less than a quarter-hour later, Big George rapped once on his
door and slid it back.

"Hullo, Lars," the big Aussie said, looking slightly shamefaced. "You
wanted to see me?"

Fuchs saw that an armed guard stood out in the tunnel; even with his
breathing mask on he recognized the guard as Oscar Jiminez.

"Step in, by all means," Fuchs said, trying to sound brave. "I welcome a break in the monotony."

George slid the door shut again and stood uneasily by it. "I di'n't
think how the hours must drag for you, havin' to stay in here."

"The only communication I've had from outside was a notice from
Humphries's lawyers that Amanda is suing for a divorce."

"Aw, cripes, Lars," George said, crestfallen, "I'm sorry about that."

"I didn't contest it," Fuchs went on, almost enjoying the obvious guilt
on George's bearded face. "What difference does it make? I'm going to
be executed soon, am I not?"

George's expression turned even gloomier. "Well, we're settin' up a
trial for you. You're gonna need to have somebody to act as your defense
counsel."

"I don't want a trial." Fuchs was surprised to hear himself say it.

"Neither do I, mate, but we've gotta have it."

"You don't understand, George. I waive my right to a trial . . . as long
as my crew is exonerated and allowed to go free. I take full responsibility
for everything."

"Let your crew go?" George scratched at his beard thoughtfully.

"I gave the orders. They didn't know that my orders would kill the
people on Vesta."

"You take full responsibility?"

"Absolutely."

"And you admit you killed the construction team on Vesta? Deliberately?"

"I'd do it again," Fuchs said fervently, "if the same situation arose."

George blew out a huge breath. "Guess we won't need a trial, then."

"You'll let my crew go free?"

"I'll hafta run it past the rest of the council, but, yeah, I don't see any
point in holdin' them if you're willing to take all the blame."

"I take all the blame," Fuchs said.

"Okay, then," said George. "I guess the only question left is whether
you want a blindfold or not."

Martin Humphries didn't wait for Dorik Harbin to arrive at Selene. He
ordered an HSS spacecraft to fly him to a rendezvous with the vessel

Harbin was on. He grimaced when he thought about the expense, but he wanted to see this mercenary soldier, this hired killer, without Verwoerd involved.

Even though he had studied Harbin's personnel file to the last detail, Humphries was still surprised when he finally met the man. He's like some prowling jungle cat, Humphries thought as soon as he entered Harbin's compartment. Even in the stark cramped shipboard cubicle, Harbin reminded him of a panther, restless energy pent beneath a sleekly muscled hide.

He was definitely handsome, in a rugged, almost cruel way. Harbin had shaved off his beard and put on a long-sleeved shirt and khaki slacks for his meeting with Humphries. The clothes were creased so sharply they might as well have been a military uniform. Humphries felt decidedly civilian in his casual turtleneck pullover and whipcord trousers.

They shook hands and murmured polite greetings to one another. Harbin invited Humphries to sit on the cubicle's sole chair, a plastic recliner, then sat on the edge of the bunk, rigid as if at attention. Even sitting down he looks as if he's ready to leap at his prey, Humphries thought.

"I brought you a gift," Humphries said genially, pointing to the compartment's blank wallscreen. "Authorization for any, uh . . . medications you might need."

"You mean drugs," Harbin said.

"Yes. Recreational, stimulants—anything you want, my pharmacists at Selene will produce them for you."

"Thank you."

"Think nothing of it," said Humphries.

Then there was silence. Harbin simply sat there, appraising Humphries with his spooky ice-blue eyes. I've got to be very careful with this man, Humphries realized. He's like a vial of nitroglycerine: handle him the wrong way and he'll explode.

At last Humphries cleared his throat and said, "I wanted to meet you personally, to congratulate you on a job well done."

Harbin said nothing.

"You've earned a sizable bonus."

"Thank you."

"That business about sending copies of your logs to several friends on Earth," Humphries went on, "was very clever. It shows a lot of intelligence on your part."

Harbin's expression changed minutely. A hint of curiosity flickered in his eyes.

"Very clever," Humphries continued. "But really unnecessary. You have nothing to fear from me. I'm grateful to you, and I don't turn on the people who do their jobs well. Ask Grigor. Ask anyone."

Harbin seemed to think it over for a moment. Then, "I was being cautious."

"I understand. In a way, I even agree with you. If I'd been in your position, I probably would have done the same thing, more or less."

"You mentioned a bonus."

"One million international dollars, paid to any bank you name."

Harbin didn't move a millimeter, but he seemed somehow to stiffen, like an animal that suddenly senses danger.

"I had expected more," he said.

"Really? I think a million is very generous."

"Diane said there would be more."

There! Humphries cheered silently. He's brought up her name.

"Diane? Diane Verwoerd?"

"Your personal assistant, yes."

"She has no authority to make you an offer that I haven't approved," Humphries said sternly.

"But she told me . . ." Harbin's voice trailed off in confusion.

Humphries made himself smile understandingly. "Diane sometimes exceeds her authority." With a sly wink, he went on, "That's the trouble with a woman. If they share your bed they start behaving as if they own you."

"Share your bed?"

"Didn't you know? She didn't tell you? For god's sake, the woman's carrying my baby."

Harbin rose slowly to his feet. "Carrying . . . your baby?"

Trying to keep from showing fear, Humphries sat where he was and said innocently, "We just found out about it a few days ago. She's pregnant, all right. We've been sending the happy news to all our friends. I'm surprised she didn't tell you."

CHAPTER 58

The drugs only made it worse. Harbin selected carefully among the narcotics available from Humphries's supplier, but he could not eradicate the thought of Diane betraying him. For two days after his arrival in Selene he lay in the apartment Humphries had provided him, trying to smother the pictures that played in his head. The drugs distorted his visions, twisted them and made them physically painful, but they did not bring the peace and oblivion that he sought. Just the opposite. They sharpened the knives that twisted in his flesh; they drove the daggers deeper inside him.

She's been sleeping with him! She's allowed herself to get pregnant by him! All the time she was with me, she was mocking me, manipulating me to do what she wanted, what they *wanted me to do. She's played me for a fool and she thought she could get away with it.*

At last he could stand it no longer. Close to midnight, he lurched out of his apartment into the corridors that honeycombed Selene, bleary-eyed, unshaven, still in the clothes he had slept in for the past two nights. He shambled along the nearly empty corridors, heading for Diane's quarters.

Sleeping alone in his giant bed, Humphries was awakened by the buzz of his private phone. Grumbling, he sat up and told the computer to put his caller on-screen.

The wallscreen showed Grigor's somber lean face.

"He's left the apartment," Grigor said without preamble.

Humphries nodded and cut the connection. Wide awake now, he bunched the pillows behind him and sat back comfortably, then commanded the computer to show the display from the picocameras built into

Diane Verwoerd's apartment. She had searched her quarters several times, seeking the bugs, Humphries knew. But no one had found the microscopic cameras built into the apartment's wiring.

Four dark pictures quartered Humphries's bedroom wallscreen, one view of each room in Diane's apartment: sitting room, bedroom, kitchen, lavatory. He switched to infrared mode and saw that she was lying asleep in her bed. For two days she had searched Selene for Harbin and not found him. Humphries had secreted the mercenary far from her prying eyes. And fed the man with drugs that heightened his normal sense of betrayal, elevated his anger into homicidal fury. Years earlier chemists had developed hallucinogenic PCPs such as angel dust out of the primitive natural amphetamines. What Humphries's people were feeding Harbin was far more sophisticated, fine-tuned to turn him into a raging maniac.

Now Humphries sat back in his bed and waited for the conclusion of this little drama that Diane Verwoerd had brought upon herself. Try to force me to knuckle under to you, will you? Blackmail me? Threaten me? Well, now you'll get what you deserve, you little slut.

Harbin found her door at last. He hesitated a moment, head swimming, fist poised to rap on the door. And give her a chance to call for help? Give her a chance to hide her latest lover?

He forced the lock on the sliding door easily and stepped inside her shadowy living room. It took a few moments for his eyes to adjust to the darkness, then he padded silently to her bedroom door. Something smelled rank, foul, and he realized it was his own body odor. She's done this to me, he told himself. She's made me into a pig.

Like Circe, he thought, peering into the shadows to make out her sleeping form on the bed. The enchantress who turns men into swine.

She was alone, he saw. He moved to the night table and switched on the lamp.

Diane awoke slowly, blinked up at him, then smiled.

"Dorik, where have you been? I've looked everywhere for you."

Then she saw the murderous look on his unshaved face. She sat up and let the covers slip to her waist.

"What's the matter? What's wrong? You look *terrible*."

He stared down at her. How many times had he caressed those breasts? How many other men had shared her body?

"Dorik, what's happened?"

His voice, when he found it, was little more than a croak. "Are you pregnant?"

The shock on her face was all the answer he needed. "I was going to tell you—"

"With Humphries' baby?"

"Yes, but—"

She got no farther. He seized her by the throat and pulled her off the bed, squeezing hard with both hands. She flailed her arms pitifully as he throttled her. Her eyes glazed, her tongue bulged out of her gagging mouth. Still crushing her larynx with one hand, Harbin grabbed her protruding tongue with the other, dug his nails into it and pulled it out of her lying mouth. Her shriek of pain drowned in the blood gushing from her mouth. Harbin relaxed his grip on her throat just enough to let her strangle on her own blood, gurgling, moaning, her hands sliding down his arms until her arms hung limp and dead.

Watching from his bed, Humphries felt his guts churn and heave. He lurched to his feet and staggered to the lavatory, Diane's last bubbling moans lost in his own retching agony. By the time he had wiped his face and stumbled back into his bedroom, the wallscreen showed Harbin on his knees, sobbing inconsolably, Diane lying on the floor beside him, her face spattered with blood, her eyes staring sightlessly.

He ripped her tongue out! Humphries said to himself, gagging again. My god, he's a monster!

Crawling back into bed, he switched off the camera view and called Grigor, who was waiting patiently in his office.

"Diane Verwoerd's had a heart attack," Humphries said to his security chief, struggling to keep his voice even. "A fatal one. Get a reliable crew to her apartment to clean the place up and take care of the body."

Grigor nodded once. "And Harbin?"

"Get him tranquilized and tucked away in a safe place. Better bring a team. He won't trank easily."

"Wouldn't it be better to silence him?"

Humphries laughed bitterly. "With this hanging over him? He's silenced, believe it. And he's still available to do whatever I need him to do."

"Still . . ."

"I'll find plenty of work for him, don't worry," Humphries said. "Just keep him away from me. I don't want him in the same room with me, ever again." He thought a moment, then added, "I don't want him on the same *planet* with me."

CHAPTER 59

L ars Fuchs looked up in surprise when he heard the knock at his door. He shut down the drama he'd been watching—Sophocles' *Antigone*—and called out, "Come in."

It was George again, looking grim.

Fuchs rose from his chair. "To what do I owe this honor?"

"Time to go," George said.

Even though he knew this moment was inevitable, Fuchs felt startled. His insides went hollow.

"Now?"

"Now," said George.

There were two armed men outside his door, both strangers to Fuchs. He walked stolidly beside George up the dusty tunnel, trying to suppress the irritation that rasped in his lungs and throat. He couldn't do it, and broke into a racking cough.

"Shoulda brought masks," George mumbled.

"What difference does it make?" Fuchs asked, as he tried to bring his coughing under control.

George hacked a bit, too, as they walked along the tunnel. Fuchs realized the were headed upward, toward the airlock that opened onto the surface. Maybe that's how they'll execute me, he thought: toss me outside without a suit.

But they stopped short of the airlock. George ushered Fuchs into a sizable chamber while the two armed guards stayed out in the dust.

Fuchs saw that his former crew were all there. They all turned toward him.

"Nodon . . . Sanja . . . you're all right, all of you?"

The six of them nodded and even smiled. Nodon said, "We are quite all right, Captain sir."

"They're leavin'," George said. "Your ship's been refitted and fueled up. They're headin' out into the Belt."

"Good," Fuchs said. "I'm glad."

"And you're goin' with them," George added, his shaggy face deeply creased with a worried frown.

"Me? What do you mean?"

George took a heavy breath, then explained, "We're not goin' to execute you, Lars. You're bein' exiled. For life. Get out and don't come back. Ever."

"Exiled? I don't understand."

"We talked it over, me an' the council. We decided to exile you. That's it."

"Exile," Fuchs repeated, stunned, unable to believe it.

"That's right. Some people won't like it, but that's what we fookin' decided."

"You're saving my life, George."

"If you call flittin' out in the Belt like a bloody Flyin' Dutchman savin' your life, then, yeah, that's what we're doin'. Just don't ever try to come back here, that's all."

For weeks Fuchs had been preparing himself mentally to be executed. He realized now that his preparations had been nothing short of a pitiful sham. An enormous wave of gratitude engulfed him. His knees felt watery; his eyes misted over.

"George . . . I . . . what can I say?"

"Say good-bye, Lars."

"Good-bye, then. And thank you!"

George looked decidedly unhappy, like a man who had been forced to make a choice between hideous alternatives.

Fuchs went with his crew to the airlock, suited up, and climbed into the shuttlecraft that was waiting to take them to *Nautilus,* hanging in orbit above Ceres.

Half an hour later, as he sat in the command chair on *Nautilus's* bridge, Fuchs sent a final message to Big George:

"Finish the habitat, George. Build a decent home for yourselves."

"We will," George answered, his red-bearded face already small and distant in the ship's display screen. "You just keep yourself outta trouble, Lars. Be a good rock rat. Stay inside the lines."

It was only then that Fuchs began to understand what exile meant.

CHAPTER 60

It was the biggest social event in the history of Selene. Nearly two hundred wedding guests assembled in the garden outside Humphries's mansion.

Pancho Lane wore a pale lavender mid-calf silk sheath that accented her slim, athletic figure. Sapphires sparkled at her earlobes, wrists, and her long, graceful throat. Her tightly curled hair was sprinkled with sapphire dust.

"You look like a fookin' million dollars on the hoof," said Big George.

Pancho grinned at the Aussie. He looked uncomfortable, almost embarrassed, in a formal suit of dead black and an old-fashioned bow tie.

"The way I figure it," she said, "if I've got to play the part of a corporate bigwig, I should at least look like one."

"Pretty damned good," said George.

"You don't look too bad yourself," Pancho said.

"Come on," George said. "We'd better find our seats."

Every aspect of the wedding was meticulously controlled by Humphries's people. Each white folding chair set up on the garden's grass had a specific guest's name stenciled on its back, and each guest had been given a specific number for the reception line after the ceremony.

Almost as soon as they sat down, Kris Cardenas joined Pancho and George, looking radiantly young in a buttercup-yellow dress that complemented her golden hair.

"Amanda's really going through with it," Cardenas said, as if she wished it weren't true.

"Looks that way," George replied, leaning forward in his chair and keeping his voice low. "Don't think she'd let things get this far and then back out, do you?"

"Not Mandy," said Pancho, sitting between George and Cardenas. "She'll go through with it, all right."

"I feel bad for Lars," Cardenas said.

Pancho nodded. "That's why Mandy's marrying Humphries; to keep Lars alive."

"Well, he's alive, at least," said George. "Him and 'is crew are out in the Belt someplace."

"Prospecting?"

"What else can they do? If he tries to put in here at Selene or any-where on Earth they'll arrest 'im."

Cardenas shook her head. "It doesn't seem fair, exiling him like that."

"Better than killin' him," said George.

"I suppose, but still . . ."

"It's done," George said, with heavy finality. "Now we've got to look forward, to the future."

Pancho nodded agreement.

"I want you," George said to Cardenas, "to start figurin' out how we can use nanos for mining."

Cardenas stiffened slightly. "I told you that I don't think it's a good idea."

"Stuff it," George snapped. "It's a great idea and you know it. Just because—"

The live orchestra that Humphries had brought to Selene for the occasion began to play the wedding march. Everyone got to their feet and turned to see Amanda, in a white floor-length gown, starting down the aisle several paces ahead of the other women in their matching aqua gowns. Amanda walked alone and unsmiling, clutching a bouquet of white orchids and pale miniature roses in both hands.

It won't be that bad a life, Amanda was telling herself as she walked slowly up the aisle to the tempo of the wedding march. Martin isn't a monster; he can be positively sweet when he wants to. I'll simply have to keep my wits about me and stay in command of the situation.

But then she thought of Lars and her heart melted. She wanted to cry, but knew she shouldn't, mustn't. A bride is supposed to smile, she thought. A bride is supposed to be radiantly happy.

Martin Humphries was standing at the makeshift altar up at the head of the aisle. Two hundred-some guests were watching Amanda as she walked slowly, in measured tread, to him. Martin was beaming, looking resplendent in a tuxedo of deep burgundy velvet, standing there like a triumphant champion, smiling at her dazzlingly.

The minister had been flown to Selene from Martin's family home in

Connecticut. All the other members of the bridal party were strangers to Amanda.

As the minister started to speak the words of the ceremony, Amanda thought of the fertilized embryos that she and Lars had left frozen in the clinic in Selene. The zygotes were Lars's children, his offspring. And hers.

She glanced at Martin, who would be her legal husband in a few moments. I'll have sex with him, Amanda thought. Of course. That's what he wants. That's what he expects. And I'll give him everything he expects. Everything.

But when I bear a child, it will be Lars's baby, not Martin's. I'll see to that. Martin will never know, but I will. I'll bring Lars's son into the world. That's what I'll do.

When Amanda had to say, "I do," she smiled for the first time.

Martin Humphries stood beside the most splendidly beautiful woman in the solar system and knew that she would be his and his alone for as long as he wanted her.

I've got everything I want, he told himself. Almost. He had seen Pancho among the wedding guests, standing there with that big red-headed oaf and Dr. Cardenas. Amanda had invited them, they were her friends. Humphries thought he himself would have invited Pancho, just to let her watch him take possession of Amanda.

Pancho thinks the war's over. We have the rock rats under control and the fight between Astro and me can be channeled into peaceful competition. He almost laughed aloud. Amanda glanced at him. She probably thinks I'm smiling for her, Humphries thought. Well, I am. But there's more to it than that. Much more.

I'll have a son with Amanda. The clones will come to term soon and I'll pick the best of the litter, but I'll have a natural son with Amanda, as well. The old-fashioned way. I'll make her forget about Fuchs. I'll drive him out of her memory completely, one way or the other.

Fuchs is finished. They may have let him loose, but he's a dead man anyway. He can't do anything to hurt me now. He's an exile, alone and without friends to help him. I promised Amanda that I wouldn't harm him and I won't have to. He's out of my way now and the rock rats are under control. Now the real battle against Astro can begin. I'll take control of Astro Corporation, and the Belt, and the whole goddamned solar system.

At that moment the minister asked Humphries if he would take Amanda Cunningham as his lawful wedded wife.

His answer to that question, and to his own ambitions, was, "I will!"

EPILOGUE

Dorik Harbin writhed and groaned in his drugged sleep as he rode the fusion ship out to the Belt again. Humphries's psychologists had done their best with him, but his dreams were still tortured by visions of Diane dying at his feet. Their drugs couldn't erase the memory; sometimes they made it worse, distorted: sometimes it was Harbin's mother drowning on her own blood while he stood helplessly watching.

When he awoke the visions of her death still haunted him. He heard her last gurgling moans, saw the utter terror in her eyes. She deserved to die, he told himself as he stared out the spacecraft's thick quartz port at the star-flecked emptiness beyond the ship's hull. She lied to me, she used me, laughed at me. She deserved to die.

Yes, said the voice in his mind that he could never silence. Everyone deserves to die. Including you.

He grimaced, and remembered Khayyam's quatrain:

One Moment in Annihilation's Waste,
One Moment, of the Well of Life to taste—
The Stars are setting and the Caravan
Starts for the Dawn of Nothing—Oh, make haste!

Deep in the Asteroid Belt, Lars Fuchs sat uneasily in the command chair of *Nautilus,* staring into the bleak emptiness outside.

This ship is my whole world now, he told himself. This one ship and these six strangers who crew it. Amanda is gone; she is dead to me. All my friends, my whole life, the woman I love—all dead and gone.

He felt like Adam, driven out of the garden of Eden, kept from returning by an angel with a flaming sword. I can never return. Never. I'll spend the rest of my days out here in this desert. What kind of a life do I have to look forward to?

The answer came to his mind immediately. Martin Humphries has everything I worked for. He possesses my wife. He's driven me into exile. But I will get back at him. No matter how long it takes; no matter how powerful he is. I will have my revenge.

Not like Adam. Not like that sniveling weakling. No, he told himself. Like Samson. Betrayed, blinded, chained and enslaved. Eyeless in Gaza. Yet he prevailed. Even at the cost of his life he had his vengeance. And I will have mine.

THE SILENT WAR

To the memory of Stephen Jay Gould,
scientist, writer, baseball fan,
and an inspiration to all thinking people

Everything is very simple in war, but
the simplest thing is difficult. . . . War is
the province of uncertainty; three-fourths
of the things on which action in war is
based lie hidden in the fog of a greater or
lesser certainty.

—Carl von Clausewitz,
On War

ASTEROID 67-046

I was a soldier," he said. "Now I am a priest. You may call me Dorn."

Elverda Apacheta could not help staring at him. She had seen cyborgs before, but this . . . person seemed more machine than man. She felt a chill ripple of contempt along her veins. How could a human being allow his body to be disfigured so?

He was not tall; Elverda herself stood several centimeters taller than he. His shoulders were quite broad, though; his torso thick and solid. The left side of his face was engraved metal, as was the entire top of his head: like a skullcap made of finest etched steel.

Dorn's left hand was prosthetic. He made no attempt to disguise it. Beneath the rough fabric of his shabby tunic and threadbare trousers, how much more of him was metal and electrical machinery? Tattered though his clothing was, his calf-length boots were polished to a high gloss.

"A priest?" asked Martin Humphries. "Of what church? What order?"

The half of Dorn's lips that could move made a slight curl. A smile or a sneer, Elverda could not tell.

"I will show you to your quarters," said Dorn. His voice was a low rumble, as if it came from the belly of a beast. It echoed faintly off the walls of rough-hewn rock.

Humphries looked briefly surprised. He was not accustomed to having his questions ignored. Elverda watched his face. Humphries was as handsome as regeneration therapies and cosmetic nanomachines could make a person appear: chiseled features, straight of spine, lean of limb, athletically flat midsection. Yet his cold gray eyes were hard, merciless.

And there was a faint smell of corruption about him, Elverda thought. *As if he were dead inside and already beginning to rot.*

The tension between the two men seemed to drain the energy from Elverda's aged body. "It has been a long journey," she said. "I am very tired. I would welcome a hot shower and a long nap."

"Before you see it?" Humphries snapped.

"It has taken us more than a week to get here. We can wait a few hours more." Inwardly she marveled at her own words. *Once she would have been all fiery excitement. Have the years taught you patience? No,* she realized. *Only weariness.*

"Not me!" Humphries said. Turning to Dorn, "Take me to it now. I've waited long enough. I want to see it now."

Dorn's eyes, one as brown as Elverda's own, the other a red electronic glow, regarded Humphries for a lengthening moment.

"Well?" Humphries demanded.

"I am afraid, sir, that the chamber is sealed for the next twelve hours. It will be imposs—"

"Sealed? By whom? On whose authority?"

"The chamber is self-controlled. Whoever made the artifact installed the controls, as well."

"No one told me about that," said Humphries.

Dorn replied, "Your quarters are down this corridor."

He turned almost like a solid block of metal, shoulders and hips together, head unmoving on those wide shoulders, and started down the central corridor. Elverda fell in step alongside his metal half, still angered at his self-desecration. Yet despite herself, she thought of what a challenge it would be to sculpt him. *If I were younger,* she told herself. *If I were not so close to death. Human and inhuman, all in one strangely fierce figure.*

Humphries came up on Dorn's other side, his face red with barely suppressed anger.

They walked down the corridor in silence, Humphries's weighted shoes clicking against the uneven rock floor. Dorn's boots made hardly any noise at all. *Half-machine he may be,* Elverda thought, *but once in motion he moves like a panther.*

The asteroid's inherent gravity was so slight that Humphries needed the weighted footgear to keep himself from stumbling ridiculously. Elverda, who had spent most of her long life in low-gravity environments, felt completely at home. The corridor they were walking through was actually a tunnel, shadowy and mysterious, or perhaps a natural chimney vented through the metallic body by escaping gases eons ago when the asteroid was still molten. Now it was cold, chill enough to make Elverda *shudder. The rough ceiling was so low she wanted to stoop, even though the rational side of her mind knew it was not necessary.*

Soon, though, the walls smoothed out and the ceiling grew higher. Humans had extended the tunnel, squaring it with laser precision. Doors lined both walls now and the ceiling glowed with glareless, shadowless light. Still she hugged herself against the chill that the two men did not seem to notice.

They stopped at a wide double door. Dorn tapped out the entrance code on the panel set into the wall, and the doors slid open.

"Your quarters, sir," he said to Humphries. "You may, of course, change the privacy code to suit yourself."

Humphries gave a curt nod and strode through the open doorway. Elverda got a glimpse of a spacious suite, carpeting on the floor and hologram windows on the walls.

Humphries turned in the doorway to face them. "I expect you to call for me in twelve hours," he said to Dorn, his voice hard.

"Eleven hours and fifty-seven minutes," Dorn replied.

Humphries's nostrils flared and he slid the double doors shut.

"This way." Dorn gestured with his human hand. "I'm afraid your quarters are not as sumptuous as Mr. Humphries's."

Elverda said, "I am his guest. He is paying all the bills."

"You are a great artist. I have heard of you."

"Thank you."

"For the truth? That is not necessary."

I was a great artist, Elverda said to herself. Once. Long ago. Now I am an old woman waiting for death.

Aloud, she asked, "Have you seen my work?"

Dorn's voice grew heavier. "Only holograms. Once I set out to see The Rememberer *for myself, but—other matters intervened."*

"You were a soldier then?"

"Yes. I have only been a priest since coming to this place."

Elverda wanted to ask him more, but Dorn stopped before a blank door and opened it for her. For an instant she thought he was going to reach for her with his prosthetic hand. She shrank away from him.

"I will call for you in eleven hours and fifty-six minutes," he said, as if he had not noticed her revulsion.

"Thank you."

He turned away, like a machine pivoting.

"Wait," Elverda called. "Please—how many others are here? Everything seems so quiet."

"There are no others. Only the three of us."

"But—"

"I am in charge of the security brigade. I ordered the others of my command to go back to our spacecraft and wait there."

"And the scientists? The prospector family that found this asteroid?"

"They are in Mr. Humphries's spacecraft, the one you arrived in," said Dorn. "Under the protection of my brigade."

Elverda looked into his eyes. Whatever burned in them, she could not fathom.

"Then we are alone here?"

Dorn nodded solemnly. "You and me—and Mr. Humphries, who pays all the bills." The human half of his face remained as immobile as the metal. Elverda could not tell if he were trying to be humorous or bitter.

"Thank you," she said. He turned away and she closed the door.

Her quarters consisted of a single room, comfortably warm but hardly larger than the compartment on the ship they had come in. Elverda saw that her meager travel bag was already sitting on the bed, her worn old drawing computer resting in its travel-smudged case on the desk. She stared at the computer case as if it were accusing her. I should have left it home, she thought. I will never use it again.

A small utility robot, hardly more than a glistening drum of metal and six gleaming arms folded like a praying mantis's, stood mutely in the farthest corner. Elverda studied it for a moment. At least it was entirely a machine; not a self-mutilated human being. To take the most beautiful form in the universe and turn it into a hybrid mechanism, a travesty of humanity. Why did he do it? So he could be a better soldier? A more efficient killing machine?

And why did he send all the others away? she asked herself while she opened the travel bag. As she carried her toiletries to the narrow alcove of the lavatory, a new thought struck her. Did he send them away before he saw the artifact, or afterward? Has he even seen it? Perhaps . . .

Then she saw her reflection in the mirror above the wash basin. Her heart sank. Once she had been called regal, stately, a goddess made of copper. Now she looked withered, dried up, bone thin, her face a geological map of too many years of living, her flight coveralls hanging limply on her emaciated frame.

You are old, she said to her image. Old and aching and tired.

It is the long trip, she told herself. You need to rest. But the other voice in her mind laughed scornfully. You've done nothing but rest for the entire time it's taken to reach this piece of rock. You are ready for the permanent rest; why deny it?

She had been teaching at the University of Selene, the Moon being the closest she could get to Earth after a long lifetime of living in low-gravity *environments. Close enough to see the world of her birth, the only world of life and warmth in the solar system, the only place where a person could walk out in the sunshine and feel its warmth soaking your bones, smell the fertile earth nurturing its bounty, feel a cool breeze plucking at your hair.*

But she had separated herself from Earth permanently. She had stood on the ice crags of Europa's frozen ocean; from an orbiting spacecraft she had watched the surging clouds of Jupiter swirl their overpowering colors; she had carved the kilometer-long rock of The Rememberer. *But she could no longer stand in the village of her birth, at the edge of the Pacific's booming surf, and watch the soft white clouds form shapes of imaginary animals.*

Her creative life was long finished. She had lived too long; there were no friends left, and she had never had a family. There was no purpose to her life, no reason to do anything except go through the motions and wait. She refused the rejuvenation therapies that were offered her. At the university she was no longer truly working at her art but helping students who had the fires of inspiration burning fresh and hot inside them. Her life was one of vain regrets for all the things she had not accomplished, for all the failures she could recall. Failures at love; those were the bitterest. She was praised as the solar system's greatest artist: the sculptress of The Rememberer, *the creator of the first great ionospheric painting,* The Virgin of the Andes. *She was respected, but not loved. She felt empty, alone, barren. She had nothing to look forward to; absolutely nothing.*

Then Martin Humphries swept into her existence. A lifetime younger, bold, vital, even ruthless, he stormed her academic tower with the news that an alien artifact had been discovered deep in the Asteroid Belt.

"It's some kind of art form," he said, desperate with excitement. "You've got to come with me and see it."

Trying to control the long-forgotten yearning that stirred within her, Elverda had asked quietly, "Why do I have to go with you, Mr. Humphries? Why me? I'm an old wo—"

"You are the greatest artist of our time," he had answered without an eyeblink's hesitation. "You've got to see this! Don't bullshit me with false modesty. You're the only other person in the whole whirling solar system who deserves to see it!"

"The only other person besides whom?" she had asked.

He had blinked with surprise. "Why, besides me, of course."

So now we are on this nameless asteroid, waiting to see the alien artwork. Just the three of us. The richest man in the solar system. An elderly artist who has outlived her usefulness. And a cyborg soldier who has cleared everyone else away.

He claims to be a priest, Elverda remembered. A priest who is half machine. She shivered as if a cold wind surged through her.

A harsh buzzing noise interrupted her thoughts. Looking into the main part of the room, Elverda saw that the phone screen was blinking red in rhythm to the buzzing.

"Phone," she called out.

Humphries's face appeared on the screen instantly. "Come to my quarters," he said. "We have to talk."

"Give me an hour. I need—"

"Now."

Elverda felt her brows rise haughtily. Then the strength sagged out of her. He has bought the right to command you, she told herself. He is quite capable of refusing to allow you to see the artifact.

"Now," she agreed.

Humphries was pacing across the plush carpeting when she arrived at his quarters. He had changed from his flight coveralls to a comfortably loose royal blue pullover and expensive genuine twill slacks. As the doors slid shut behind her, he stopped in front of a low couch and faced her squarely.

"Do you know who this Dorn creature is?"

Elverda answered, "Only what he has told us."

"I've checked him out. My staff in the ship has a complete file on him. He's the butcher who led the Chrysalis *massacre, six years ago."*

"He . . ."

"Eleven hundred men, women and children. Slaughtered. He was the man who commanded the attack."

"He said he had been a soldier."

"A mercenary. A cold-blooded murderer. He worked for me once, long ago, but he was working for Yamagata then. The Chrysalis *was the rock rats' habitat. When its population refused to give up Lars Fuchs, Yamagata put him in charge of a squad to convince them to cooperate. He killed them all; slashed the habitat to shreds and let them all die."*

Elverda felt shakily for the nearest chair and sank into it. Her legs seemed to have lost all their strength.

"His name was Harbin then. Dorik Harbin."

"Wasn't he brought to trial?"

"No. He ran away. Disappeared. I always thought Yamagata helped to hide him. They take care of their own, they do. He must have changed his name afterwards. Nobody would hire the butcher, not even Yamagata."

"His face . . . half his body . . ." Elverda felt terribly weak, almost faint. "When . . . ?"

"Must have been after he ran away. Maybe it was an attempt to disguise himself."

"And now he is working for you again." She wanted to laugh at the irony of it, but did not have the strength.

"He's got us trapped on this chunk of rock! There's nobody else here except the three of us."

"You have your staff in your ship. Surely they would come if you summoned them."

"His security squad's been ordered to keep everybody except you and me off the asteroid. He gave those orders."

"You can countermand them, can't you?"

For the first time since she had met Martin Humphries, he looked unsure of himself. *"I wonder,"* he said.

"Why?" Elverda asked. *"Why is he doing this?"*

"That's what I intend to find out." Humphries strode to the phone console. *"Harbin!"* he called. *"Dorik Harbin. Come to my quarters at once."*

Without even a microsecond's delay the phone's computer-synthesized voice replied, *"Dorik Harbin no longer exists. Transferring your call to Dorn."*

Humphries's gray eyes snapped at the phone's blank screen.

"Dorn is not available at present," the phone's voice said. *"He will call for you in eleven hours and thirty-two minutes."*

"What do you mean, Dorn's not available?" Humphries shouted at the blank phone screen. *"Get me the officer on watch aboard the Humphries Eagle."*

"All exterior communications are inoperable at the present time," replied the phone.

"That's impossible!"

"All exterior communications are inoperable at the present time," the phone repeated, unperturbed.

Humphries stared at the empty screen, then turned slowly toward Elverda Apacheta. *"He's cut us off. We're trapped in here."*

SIX YEARS EARLIER

SELENE: ASTRO CORPORATION HEADQUARTERS

Pancho Lane tilted back in her sculpted chair, fingers steepled in front of her face, hiding any display of the suspicion she felt for the man sitting before her desk.

One of the two major things she had learned in her years as chief of Astro Corporation was to control her emotions. Once she would have gotten out of her chair, strode around the desk, hauled this lying turkey buzzard up by the scruff of his neck and booted his butt all the way back to Nairobi, where he claimed to come from. Now, though, she simply sat back in cold silence, hearing him out.

"A strategic alliance would be of great benefit to both of us," he was saying, in his deeply resonant baritone. "After all, we are going to be neighbors here on the Moon, aren't we?"

Physically, he was a hunk and a half, Pancho admitted to herself. If he's here as bait, at least they sent something worth biting on. Strong, broad cheekbones and a firm jawline. Deeply dark eyes that sparkled at her when he smiled, which he did a lot. Brilliant white teeth. Skin so black it almost looked purple. Conservative gray business cardigan, but under it peeped a colorfully patterned vest and a soft yellow shirt opened at the collar to reveal a single chain of heavy gold.

"Your base is going to be more'n four thousand kilometers from here, way down at Aitken Basin."

"Yes, of course," he said, with that dazzling smile. "But our base at Shackleton will be only about a hundred klicks from the Astro power facility down in the Malapert Range, you see."

"The Mountains of Eternal Light," Pancho murmured, nodding. The Japanese called them the Shining Mountains. Down near the lunar south pole there were several peaks so tall that they were perpetually in sunlight. Astro had established a solar power center there, close to the deposits of frozen water.

"The facility that we are building will be more than a mere base," the Nairobi representative added. "We intend to make a real city at Shackleton Crater, much like Selene."

"Really?" Pancho said, keeping her expression noncommittal. She had just been informed, a few minutes earlier, that another Astro freighter had disappeared out in the Belt: the second one in as many weeks. Humphries is at it again, she thought, nibbling away. And if this guy isn't a stalking horse for Humphries, I'll be dipped in deep dung.

The other major thing that Pancho had learned was to maintain herself as physically youthful as possible. Rejuvenation therapies that were once regarded as expensive extravagances for the vain and video personalities were now commonplace, especially among the viciously competitive power brokers of the giant corporations. So Pancho looked, physically, much as she had when she'd been thirty: tall, leggy and slim. She had even had the tattoo on her buttocks removed, because board room politics sometimes evolved into bedroom antics, and she didn't want a teenaged misjudgment to become a whispered rumor. She hadn't done anything about her face, though, which she considered to be forgettably ordinary except for its unfortunate stubborn, square jaw. Her only concession to the years was that she'd allowed her closely cropped hair to go totally white. The beauticians told her it made a stunning contrast to her light mocha skin.

Pancho made a point of going counter to the fashionable styles of the moment. This season the emphasis was on bulky pullovers and heavy-looking sweaters with strategic cutouts to make them interesting to the eye. Instead, Pancho wore a tailored pantsuit of pale ivory, which accented her long, lean figure, with highlights of asteroidal jewelry at her wrists and earlobes. Her office wasn't particularly large, as corporate suites went, but it was sumptuously decorated with modern furniture, paintings that Pancho had personally commissioned, and holowindows that could display scenery from half a dozen worlds.

"Pardon me for asking a foolish question, I've never been to the Moon before. Is that real wood paneling?" her visitor asked, wide-eyed.

Aw, come on, Pancho groused silently. You can't be that much of a rube.

"And your desk, too? Did you have it flown all the way here to the Moon?"

"In a sense," Pancho answered evenly, wondering how much of this guy's naïveté was an act. "Our biotech division sent up a shipload of gengineered bacteria that produce cellulose. Same things tree do, at the cellular level."

"I see," he said, his voice still somewhat awed. "The bacteria produce bioengineered wood for you."

Pancho nodded. "All we bring up from Earth is a small sample of bugs, and they reproduce themselves for us."

"Marvelous. Nairobi Industries doesn't have a biotechnology division. We are only a small corporation, compared to Astro or Humphries Space Systems."

"Well, we all had to start at the beginning," Pancho said, thinking that it sounded fatuous.

Her visitor didn't seem to notice. "However, in exchange for help in building our base here on the Moon we offer a unique entry into the growing markets of Africa and the Indian subcontinent."

The Indian subcontinent, Pancho thought grimly; between their nukes and their biowar there isn't much left for those poor bastards. And Africa's still a mess, pretty much.

"We are also developing strong ties with Australia and New Zealand," he went on. "They still hesitate to deal with Africans, but we are overcoming their prejudices with sound business opportunities for them."

Pancho nodded. This guy's a stalking horse, all right. Whoever he's really working for thinks he's damned smart sending a black man to make this offer. Thinks I'll get all gooey and not see past the trap they're setting up.

Humphries. It's gotta be Martin Humphries, she reasoned. The old Humper's been after Astro for years. This is just his latest maneuver. And he's started knocking off our freighters again.

As if he could read her thoughts, the Nairobi representative added, in a confidential near-whisper, "Besides, an alliance between your corporation and mine will outflank Humphries Space Systems, so to speak. Together, we could take a considerable amount of market share away from HSS."

Pancho felt her eyebrows hike up. "You mean the asteroidal metals and minerals that Earthside corporations buy."

"Yes. Of course. But Selene imports a good deal from Humphries's mining operations in the Belt, too."

The big struggle, Pancho knew, was to control the resources of the Asteroid Belt. The metals and minerals mined from the asteroids were feeding Earthside industries crippled by the environmental disasters stemming from the greenhouse cliff.

"Well," said the Nairobi executive, with his gleaming smile, "that's just about the whole of it. Does it strike any interest in you?"

Pancho smiled back at him. "'Course it does," she said, thinking about how the kids she grew up with in west Texas would cross their fingers when they fibbed. "I'll give it a lot of thought, you can believe me."

"Then you'll recommend a strategic alliance to your board?"

She could see the eagerness on his handsome young face.

Keeping her smile in place, Pancho replied, "Let me think it over, get my staff to run the numbers. Then, if everything checks out, I'll certainly bring it up before the board."

He fairly glowed with pleasure. Pancho thought, Whoever sent this hunk of beefcake didn't pick him because he's got a poker face.

She got to her feet and he shot up so quickly that Pancho thought he'd bounce off the ceiling. As it was, he stumbled slightly, unaccustomed to the low lunar gravity, and had to grab a corner of her desk to steady himself.

"Easy there," she said, grinning. "You only weigh one-sixth of Earth normal here."

He made a shamefaced smile. "I forgot. The weighted boots aren't all that much help. Please forgive me."

"Nothing to it. Everybody needs a little time to get accustomed to lunar gee. How long will you be staying at Selene?"

"I leave tomorrow."

"You won't be talking to anybody from HSS?"

"No. Mr. Humphries has a reputation for swallowing up smaller corporations rather than helping them."

Maybe he's not from Humphries after all, Pancho thought.

She asked, "So you came up here just to see me?"

He nodded. "This alliance is very important to us. I wanted to speak to you about it face-to-face, not by videophone."

"Good thinking," Pancho said, coming around her desk and gesturing toward her office door. "That three-second lag in phone communication is enough to drive me loco."

He blinked. "Loco? Is that lunar slang?"

With a laugh, Pancho answered, "West Texas, for crazy."

"You are from Texas?"

"Long time ago."

Pancho played it cool, watching how he tried to maneuver their conversation into a dinner invitation before she could shoo him out of her office. He smelled good, she noticed. Some sort of cologne that reminded her of cinnamon and tangy spices.

Finally he got to it. "I suppose a person of your importance has a very full calendar."

"Yep. Pretty much."

"I was hoping we might have dinner together. Actually, I don't know anyone else in Selene City."

She made a show of pulling up her schedule on the wallscreen. "Dinner engagement with my PR director."

He looked genuinely crestfallen. "Oh. I see."

Pancho couldn't help smiling at him. "Hell, I can talk to her some other time. Let's have dinner together."

His smile grew even wider than before.

And he was good in bed, too, Pancho discovered. Great, in fact. But the next morning, once he was on his way back Earthside and Pancho had fed herself a breakfast of vitamin E and orange juice, she called her security director from her kitchen and told him to check the guy out thoroughly. If he's not from Humphries, maybe somebody else wants to move into the territory.

She chuckled to herself as she headed for her office that morning. She had forgotten the man's name.

TORCH SHIP *NAUTILUS*

The ship had once been a freighter with the unlikely name of *Lubbock Lights,* plying the Asteroid Belt, picking up ores mined by the rock rats and carrying them back to the factories in Earth orbit and on the Moon. Lars Fuchs and his ragtag crew of exiles had seized it and renamed it *Nautilus,* after the fictional submersible of the vengeance-seeking Captain Nemo.

Over the years, Fuchs had changed the spacecraft. It was still a dumbbell shape, rotating on a buckyball tether to provide a feeling of gravity for the crew. It still could carry thousands of tons of ores in its external grapples. But now it also bore five powerful lasers, which Fuchs used as weapons. And it was armored with thin layers of asteroidal copper fixed a few centimeters outside the ship's true hull, enough to absorb an infrared laser beam for a second or more. *Nautilus's* fusion propulsion system was among the most powerful in the Belt. Speed and maneuverability were important for a pirate vessel.

In the ship's cramped bridge Fuchs leaned over the back of the pilot's chair and scowled at the scanner display.

"It is a freighter, nothing more," said Amarjagal, his pilot. She was a stocky, stoic woman of Mongol ancestry who had been with Fuchs since he'd fled from the mining center at Ceres to take up this life of exile and piracy.

"With a crew pod?" Fuchs sneered.

Nodon, the ship's engineer, had also been part of Fuchs's renegade team since the earliest days. He was rail-thin, all bone and sinew, his head shaved bald, spiral scars of ceremonial tattoos swirling across both cheeks. A menacing black moustache drooped down to his jawline, yet his dark brown eyes were big and expressive, soulful.

"A crew pod means that the ship carries food," he pointed out as he studied the image on the display screen.

"And medical supplies," added Amarjagal.

"Both of which we could use," said Nodon.

Fuchs shook his head ponderously. "It could be a trap."

Neither of his crew replied. They glanced at each other but remained silent.

Fuchs wore a black pullover and shapeless black slacks, as usual. He was a short-limbed, barrel-chested little bear of a man, scowling with anger and implacable in his wrath. His broad, jowly face was etched with hatred, thin slash of a mouth set in a permanent glower, deepset eyes looking far beyond what the others saw. He looked like a badger, a wolverine, small but explosively dangerous.

For nearly a decade Lars Fuchs had been a pirate, an outcast, a renegade who cruised through the vast, silent emptiness of the Belt and preyed on ships owned by Humphries Space Systems.

Once he had considered himself the luckiest man in the solar system. A love-struck student riding the first crewed exploratory ship into the Asteroid Belt, he had actually married the most beautiful woman he'd ever seen, Amanda Cunningham. But then he became ensnarled in the battle over the riches of the Belt, one man pitted against Martin Humphries, the wealthiest person off-Earth, and his Humphries Space Systems' hired thugs. When the HSS mercenaries finally cornered him, Amanda begged Humphries to spare his life.

Humphries was merciful, in the cruelest manner imaginable. Fuchs was banished from Ceres, the only permanent settlement in the Belt, while Amanda divorced him and married Humphries. She was the price for Fuchs's life. From that time on, Fuchs wandered through the vast dark emptiness of the Belt like a Flying Dutchman, never touching down at a human habitation, living as a rock rat, sometimes prospecting among the asteroids in the farthest reaches of the Belt and digging metal ores and minerals to sell to refinery ships.

More often he swooped down on HSS freighters like a hawk attacking a pigeon, taking the supplies he needed from them, even stealing the ores they carried and selling them clandestinely to other rock rats plying the Belt. It was a pitiful way to maintain his self-respect, telling himself that he was still a thorn in Humphries's flesh. Merely a small thorn, to be sure, but it was the only thing he could do to keep his sanity. While he almost always attacked automated drone freighters toting their ores back toward the Earth/Moon system, often enough he hit ships that were crewed. Fuchs did not consider himself a killer, but there were times when blood was spilled.

As when he wiped out the HSS mercenaries' base on Vesta.

Now he frowned at the image of the approaching freighter, with its crew pod attached.

"Our supplies are very low," Nodon said in a soft voice, almost a whisper.

"They won't have much aboard," Fuchs muttered back.

"Enough for us and the rest of the crew for a few weeks, perhaps."

"Perhaps. We could grab more supplies from a logistics ship."

Nodon bowed his head slightly. "Yes, that is so."

Despite its name, the Asteroid Belt is a wide swath of emptiness between the orbits of Mars and Jupiter, populated by millions of tiny, cold, dark lumps of metal and rock tumbling around the Sun, leftover bits from the creation of the solar system. The largest, Ceres, is barely a thousand kilometers across. Most of the asteroids are the size of boulders, pebbles, dust motes. Trash, Fuchs thought. Chunks of matter that never became part of a true planet. Leftovers. God's garbage.

But the "garbage" was a treasure trove for desperate, needy humankind. Earth had been hit hard by climate change, a greenhouse cliff that struck suddenly, viciously, over a few decades. Glaciers melted down, ocean levels rose, coastal cities worldwide were flooded out, the global electrical power net collapsed, hundreds of millions lost their homes, their livelihoods, even their lives. Farmlands dried to dust in perpetual droughts; deserts were swamped with rain; monster storms lashed the frightened, starving refugees everywhere.

In the distant stretches of the Asteroid Belt there were metals and minerals beyond reckoning, raw materials to replace the lost mines of Earth. Factories built in orbit and on the Moon depended on those raw materials. The salvation of the battered, weary Earth lay in the resources and energy of space.

Fuchs gave all this hardly a thought. He concentrated on that freighter plying its way through the Belt, heading at a leisurely pace inward, toward Earth.

"If there's a crew aboard, why are they coasting on a Hohmann ellipse? Why not light their fusion drive and accelerate toward Earth?"

"Perhaps their engines malfunctioned," Amarjagal said, without looking up from her control board.

"She's not beaming out a distress call."

The pilot lapsed into silence.

"We could hail her," Nodon proposed.

"And let her know we're on her tail?" Fuchs snarled.

"If we can see her, she can see us."

"Then let her hail us."

"She isn't transmitting anything except a normal tracking beacon and telemetry data," said Amarjagal.

"What's her name and registration?"

The pilot touched a key on the board before her, and the information superimposed itself on the ship's image: *John C. Frémont,* owned and operated by Humphries Space Systems.

Fuchs sucked in a deep breath. "Get us out of here," he said, gripping the pilot's shoulder in his broad, thick-fingered hand. "That ship's a trap."

Amarjagal glanced at the engineer, sitting in the right-hand seat beside her, then obediently tapped in a course change. The ship's fusion engines powered up; *Nautilus* swung deeper into the Belt.

Aboard the *John C. Frémont,* Dorik Harbin watched the radar screen on his control panel, his ice-blue eyes intent on the image of Fuchs's ship dwindling into the vast emptiness of the Asteroid Belt.

His face was like a warrior of old: high cheekbones, narrow eyes, a bristling dark beard that matched the thick black thatch that tumbled over his forehead. His gray coveralls bore the HSS logo over the left breast pocket, and symbols of rank and service on the sleeves and cuffs; he wore them like a military uniform, immaculately clean and sharply pressed. Yet those glacier cold eyes were haunted, tortured. He only slept when he could no longer force himself to stay awake, and even then he needed sedatives to drive away the nightmares that screamed at him.

Now, though, he smiled—almost. He had tangled with Fuchs several times in the past, and the wily outlaw always escaped his grasp. Except once, and that had required a small army of mercenaries. Even then, Humphries had allowed Fuchs to get away alive. It was Fuchs's wife that Humphries was after, Harbin had learned.

But now Humphries had ordered Harbin to find Fuchs and kill him. Quietly. Out in the cold darkness of the Belt, where no one would know for many months, perhaps years, that the man was dead. So Harbin hunted his elusive quarry alone. He preferred being alone. Other people brought complications, memories, desires he would rather do without.

Harbin shook his head, wondering what schemes played through Humphries's mind.

Better not to know, he told himself. You have enough old crimes to fill your nightmares for the rest of your life. You don't need to peer into anyone else's.

SELENE: WINTER SOLSTICE PARTY

I t was the social event of the year. Everyone who meant anything in Selene City was invited and everyone who was invited dressed up and came to the party. Douglas Stavenger, the scion of the lunar nation's founding family, brought his wife. The ambassador from the Global Economic Council, Earth's world government in all but name, brought two of his four wives. Pancho Lane, head of the rival Astro Corporation, came unescorted. Nobuhiko Yamagata, head of the giant Japanese corporation, made a special trip to Selene for the occasion. Even Big George Ambrose, the shaggy red-maned chief of the rock rats' settlement at Ceres, traveled on a torch ship all the way from the Belt to be at Martin Humphries's Christmas party.

The invitations called it a Winter Solstice Party, artfully avoiding any religious sensitivities among the Moslems, Buddhists, Hindus and die-hard atheists on the guest list. Some of the Christian conservatives grumbled at the lack of proper piety, but then Martin Humphries never pretended to be a believer. Big George complained, with a mug of beer in each beefy paw, that back in his native Australia this time of the year marked the onset of winter darkness, not the gradually longer days that led to springtime.

One of the reasons for the full turnout was that Humphries gave the party in his palatial home, built deep in the lowest level of Selene City. He rarely invited anyone to his mansion, and curiosity—more than holiday good cheer—impelled many of the hundreds of guests.

Technically, the sprawling, low-roofed mansion was the property of the Humphries Trust Research Center, a legal fiction that was a monument to the ingenuity of Martin Humphries.

The airless surface of the Moon is exposed to temperature swings of four hundred degrees between sunlight and shadow, drenched in hard radiation from the Sun and deep space, and peppered with a constant infall of microscopic meteoroids. Human settlements are built underground, and the deeper below the surface, the more prestigious and expensive the habitation.

Humphries built his home in the deepest grotto below the original Moonbase, seven levels beneath the surface. He established an extensive garden that filled the grotto with the heady scents of roses and lilacs, irrigated by water manufactured from oxygen and hydrogen smelted out of the lunar surface rocks, lit by long strips of broad-spectrum lamps fixed to the rough rock ceiling to simulate sunshine. The garden was a little over one square kilometer in extent, slightly more than ten hectares. It cost a fortune to maintain this improbable paradise, with its showy azaleas and peonies always in bloom, its alders and white-boled birches and graceful fronds of frangipani. Flowering white and pink gardenia bushes grew tall as trees. Humphries had established a research trust to finance his garden, and had even gotten the government of Selene to accept the slightly absurd justification that it was a long-term study in maintaining a man-made ecology on the Moon.

The truth was that Humphries wanted to live on the Moon, as far away as he could get from his coldly crusty father and the storm-racked world of his birth. So he built a mansion in the middle of his underground Eden, half of it taken up by research laboratories and botanical workshops, the other half an opulent home for none other than Martin Humphries.

The residential half of the mansion was big enough to take a couple of hundred guests easily. The big living room accommodated most of them, while others roamed through the formal dining room and the art galleries and outdoor patios.

Pancho headed straight for the bar built into the book-lined library, where she found Big George Ambrose with one hand wrapped around a frosty-looking beer mug, deep in intent conversation with a slinky, low-cut blonde. George was unconsciously worming a finger of his free hand in his collar, obviously uncomfortable in a tux. Wonder who did the bow tie for him, Pancho asked herself. Or maybe it's a clip-on.

Grinning, Pancho worked her way through the chattering crowd and ordered a bourbon and ginger ale from one of the three harried-looking men working behind the bar. Dozens of conversations buzzed around her; laughter and the tinkle of ice cubes filled the big, beam-ceilinged room. Pancho leaned both her elbows against the bar and searched the crowd for Amanda.

"Hey, Pancho!" Big George had disentangled himself from the

blonde and pushed toward her, the crowd parting before him like sailboats scampering out of the way of a lumbering supertanker.

"How're the bots bitin', old gal?" George asked, in his surprisingly high, sweet tenor.

Pancho laughed. While she had worked for years to smother her West Texas accent as she climbed the slippery ladder of Astro Corporation, George's Aussie argot seemed to get thicker every time she saw him.

"Some bash, isn't it?" she shouted over the noise of the crowd.

George nodded enthusiastically. "'Nuff money in this room to finance a trip to Alpha Centauri."

"And back."

"How's it goin' with you, Panch?"

"No major complaints," she lied, unwilling to talk about the missing freighters. "What's new with the rock rats?"

"Closed down the last warehouse on Ceres," George said. "Everything's up in *Chrysalis* now."

"You finally finished the habitat?"

"Naw, it'll never be finished. We'll keep addin' to it, hangin' bits and pieces here and there. But we don't have to live down in the dust anymore. We've got a decent gravity for ourselves."

Searching the crowd as she spoke, Pancho asked, "A full one g?"

"One-sixth, like here. Good enough to keep the bones producin' calcium and all that."

"You seen Mandy?"

George's shaggy-bearded face compressed into a frown. "You mean Mrs. Humphries? Nope. No sign of her."

Pancho could hear the scorn in the big redhead's voice. Like most of the other rock rats, he loathed Martin Humphries. *Is he sore at Amanda for marrying the Hump?* Pancho wondered.

Before she could ask George about that, Humphries appeared in the doorway that led to the living room, clutching Amanda by the wrist at his side.

She was splendidly beautiful, wearing a sleeveless white gown that hung to the floor in soft folds. Despite its slack cut, anyone could see that Amanda must be the most beautiful woman in the solar system, Pancho thought: radiant blond hair, a face that would shame Helen of Troy, the kind of figure that makes men and even other women stare in unalloyed awe. With a slight grin, Pancho noticed that Amanda's hairdo, piled high atop her head, made her a centimeter or so taller than Humphries, even with the lifts he always wore in his shoes.

When Pancho had first met Humphries, more than a decade earlier, his face had been round and puffy, his body soft, slightly pot-bellied. Yet his eyes were hard, piercing gray chips of flint set into that bland face. Since he'd married Amanda, though, Humphries had become slimmer, straighter; his face thinned down, too. Pancho figured he had partaken liberally of nanotech therapies; no need for cosmetic surgery when nanomachines could tighten muscles, smooth skin, erase wrinkles. Those gray eyes of his were unchanged, though: brutal and ruthless.

"Can I have your attention, please?" Humphries called out in a strong baritone.

The room fell silent and everyone turned to face their host and hostess.

Smiling broadly, Humphries said, "If you can tear yourselves away from the bar for a minute, Amanda and I have an announcement to make, in the living room."

The guests dutifully trooped into the living room. Pancho and George lingered at the bar, then at last followed the others. George even put his beer mug down. The living room was packed now with women in opulent gowns and dazzling jewelry, men in formal black attire. Peacocks and penguins, Pancho thought. Only, the women are the peacocks.

Despite the room's great size it felt slightly uncomfortable with that many bodies pressed together, no matter how well they were dressed. Pancho's nostrils twitched at the mingled scents of perfume and perspiration.

Humphries led Amanda by the hand to the grand piano in the middle of the spacious room, then climbed up on its bench. Amanda stood on the floor beside him, smiling, yet to Pancho's eyes she looked uncomfortable, unhappy, almost frightened.

"My friends," Humphries began.

Friends my blistered butt, Pancho said to herself. He hasn't got any friends, just people he's bought or bullied.

"It's so good to see all of you here. I hope you're enjoying yourselves."

Some sycophant started clapping and in a flash the whole crowd was applauding. Even Pancho slapped her hands together a few times.

Humphries smiled and tried to look properly humble.

"I'm so glad," he said. "I'm especially happy to be able to tell you our good news." He hesitated a moment, savoring the crowd's obvious anticipation. "Amanda and I are going to have a son. The exact delivery date hasn't been determined yet, but it should be in late August."

The women cooed, the men cheered, then everybody applauded and shouted congratulations. Pancho was tall enough to see past the heads bobbing in front of her. She focused on Amanda. Mandy was smiling, sure enough, but it looked forced, without a trace of happiness behind it.

The crowd formed an impromptu reception line, each guest shaking

Humphries's hand and congratulating him and the expectant mother. When Pancho's turn came, she saw that Amanda's china-blue eyes looked bleak, miserable.

She had known Amanda since they'd both been astronauts working for Astro Corporation. Pancho had been there when Mandy had first met Lars Fuchs, and when Fuchs proposed to her. They were old friends, confidants—until Amanda had married Humphries. For the past eight years she had seen Mandy only rarely, and never alone.

"Congratulations, Mandy," Pancho said to her, grasping her hand in both of her own. Amanda's hand felt cold. Pancho could feel it trembling.

"Congratulate me, too, Pancho," said Humphries, full of smiles and good cheer. "I'm the father. She couldn't have done it without me."

"Sure," Pancho said, releasing Amanda's hand. "Congratulations. Good work."

She wanted to ask him why it had taken eight years, but held her tongue. She wanted to say that it didn't take skilled labor to impregnate a woman, but she held back on that, too.

"Now I've got everything a man needs to be happy," Humphries said, clutching Amanda's hand possessively, "except Astro Corporation. Why don't you retire gracefully, Pancho, and let me take my rightful place as chairman of the Astro board?"

"In your dreams, Martin," Pancho growled.

With a brittle smile, Humphries said, "Then I'll just have to find some other way to take control of Astro."

"Over my dead body."

Humphries' smile turned brighter. "Remember, you said that, Pancho. I didn't."

Frowning, Pancho left them and drifted off into the crowd, but kept an eye on Amanda. If I can just get her alone, without the Humper hanging onto her . . .

At last she saw Amanda disengage herself from her husband's hand and make her way toward the stairs that led up to their bedroom. She looked as if she were fleeing, escaping. Pancho slipped back through the bar, into the kitchen and past the busy, clanging, complaining crew that was already starting to clean up the plates and glasses, and went up the back stairs.

Pancho knew where the master suite was. More than eight years ago, before Mandy married Fuchs and the Humper was pursuing her fervently, Pancho had broken into Humphries's mansion to do a bit of industrial espionage for Astro Corporation. With the noise of the party guests filtering up from below, she slipped along the upstairs corridor and through the open double doors of the sitting room that fronted the master bedroom.

Holding her long skirt to keep it from swishing, Pancho went to the bedroom door and looked in. Amanda was in the lavatory; she could see Mandy's reflection in the full-length mirror on the open lavatory door; she was standing in front of the sink, holding a small pill bottle. The bedroom was mirrored all over the place, walls and ceiling. Wonder if the Humper still keeps video cameras behind the mirrors, Pancho asked herself.

"Hey, Mandy, you in there?" she called as she stepped into the plushly carpeted bedroom.

She could see Amanda flinch with surprise. She dropped the vial of pills she'd been holding. They cascaded into the sink and onto the floor like a miniature hailstorm.

"Jeeps, I'm sorry," Pancho said, coming up to the open lavatory door. "Didn't mean to scare you."

"It's all right, Pancho," said Amanda, her voice trembling almost as much as her hands. She began to scoop the pills out of the sink and tried to return them to the little bottle. She dropped as many as she got in.

Pancho knelt down and started scooping the oval, blood-red lozenges. No trademark embossed on them.

"What are these?" she asked. "Somethin' special?"

Leaning on the sink, trying to hold herself together, Amanda said, "They're rather like tranquilizers."

"You need tranquilizers?"

"Now and again," Amanda replied.

Pancho took the bottle from Amanda's shaking hands. There was no label on it.

"You don't need this shit," Pancho growled. She pushed past Amanda and started to pour the pills down the toilet.

"Don't!" Amanda screeched, snatching the bottle from Pancho's hands. "Don't you dare!"

"Mandy, this crap can't be any good for you."

Tears sprang into Amanda's eyes. "Don't tell me what's good for me, Pancho. You don't know. You have no idea."

Pancho looked into her red-rimmed eyes. "Mandy, this is me, remember? You can tell me whatever troubles you got."

Amanda shook her head. "You don't want to know, Pancho."

She clicked the bottle's cap back on after three fumbling tries, then opened the medicine chest atop the sink to return the bottle to its shelf. Pancho saw the chest was filled with pill bottles.

"Jeeps, you got a regular drug store," she murmured.

Amanda said nothing.

"You need all that stuff?"

"Now and again," Amanda repeated.

"But why?"

Amanda closed her eyes and took a deep, shuddering breath. "They help me."

"Help you how?"

"When Martin wants some special performances," Amanda said, in a voice so low that Pancho could barely hear her. "When he invites other women to help us in bed. When he wants me to take aphrodisiacs to enhance my response to him and his friends. Some of them are video stars, you know. You'd recognize them, Pancho. They're famous."

Pancho felt her jaw drop open.

"And when Martin brings one or two of his strange young male friends to join us, I really need pills to get through that. And for watching the videos he projects on the ceiling. And for trying to sleep without seeing all those nasty, horrible scenes over and over again . . ."

Amanda was sobbing now, tears streaming down her cheeks, her words incomprehensible. Pancho wrapped her long arms around her and held her tightly. She didn't know what to say except to whisper, "There, there. It'll be all right, Mandy. You'll see. It'll be all right."

After several minutes, Amanda pulled away slightly. "Don't you see, Pancho? Don't you understand? He'll kill Lars if I don't satisfy him. He's got me completely under his control. There's no way out for me."

Pancho had no response for that.

"That's why I agreed to have the baby, Pancho. He's promised to stop the sex games if I bear his son. I'll have to quit the drugs, of course. I'm already started on a detox program."

Pointing to the bottle of red capsules, Pancho said, "Yeah, I can see."

"I'm weaning myself off them," Amanda protested. "It's just that tonight . . . I need one."

"What the news nets would give for this story," Pancho muttered.

"You can't! You mustn't!" Desperate alarm flashed in her tear-filled eyes. "I only told you—"

Pancho gripped her quaking shoulders. "Hey, this is me, remember? I'm your friend, Mandy. Not a peep of this gets past that door."

Amanda stared at her.

"Not even if it could save Astro from being taken over by the Humper. This is between you and me, Mandy, nobody else. Ever."

Amanda nodded slowly.

"But I'll tell you one thing. I'd like to go downstairs and punch that smug sonofabitch so hard he'll never be able to smile again."

Amanda shook her head slowly, wearily. "If only it were that simple, Pancho. If only—"

The phone in the bedroom buzzed. Amanda took a deep breath and walked to the bed. Pancho swung the lavatory door halfway shut, hiding her from the phone camera's view.

"Answer," said Amanda.

Pancho heard Humphries's irritated voice demand, "How long are you going to stay up there? Some of the guests are starting to leave."

"I'll be down in a moment, Martin."

Amanda returned to the lavatory and began repairing the makeup on her face. Pancho thought that if the Humper even noticed she'd been crying, it wouldn't make any difference to him.

Then a new thought struck her. If Lars knew about this he'd kill Humphries. He'd fight his way past all the armies in the solar system to get to Humphries and rip his throat out.

SELENE: HOTEL LUNA RESIDENTIAL SUITE

Pancho could not sleep that night. She roamed the rooms and corridors of her residential suite, her mind in a turmoil over Amanda and Humphries.

It had taken Pancho years to realize that, as the top executive of one of the largest corporations in the solar system, she could afford luxuries. It wasn't until her younger sister left on the five-year expedition to Saturn that it finally hit her: Sis is on her own now, I'm not responsible for her anymore. I can start living any way I want to.

She changed her lifestyle, but only minimally. Her wardrobe improved, although not grandiosely so. She didn't become a party-goer; she *never* got mentioned in the tabloid shows. She still worked nearly every waking moment at her job as chief executive officer of Astro Corporation, still spent as much time in the factories and research labs as in the corporate offices and conference rooms, still knew each of the division heads and many of the lower-echelon managers on a first-name, drinking buddy basis.

Her one obvious change was her domicile. For years Pancho had lived with her sister in a pair of adjoining two-room units on Selene's third level. When she traveled to Earth she stayed at corporate-owned suites. After her sister left, Pancho spent several months feeling lonely, betrayed by the sister she had raised from infancy—twice, since Sis had died and been cryonically preserved for years while Pancho watched over her sarcophagus and waited for a cure for the cancer that took her first life.

Once Sis was revived from her liquid-nitrogen immersion, Pancho had to train her all over again to walk, to use the toilet, to speak, to live as an adult. And then the kid took off for distant Saturn with a team of scientists and their support personnel, starting her second life in independence, as far from her big sister as she could get.

Eventually Pancho realized that now she could live in independence, too. So she splurged for the first time in her life. She leased several units from the nearly bankrupt Hotel Luna and brought in contractors who broke through walls and floors to make her a spacious, high-ceilinged, thoroughly modern home that was perfectly suited to her personality. The double-height ceilings were a special luxury; no one else in Selene enjoyed such spaciousness, not even Martin Humphries in his palatial mansion.

Some said she was competing with Humphries, trying to show that she too could live in opulence. That thought had never occurred to Pancho. She simply decided to build the home of her dreams, and her dreams were many and various.

In every room, the walls and floors and ceilings were covered with smart screens. Pancho could change the décor, the ambiance, even the scent of a room with the touch of a button or the mere utterance of a word. She could live in the palace of the Caliph of Baghdad, or atop the Eiffel Tower, or deep in the fragrant pine forest of the Canadian Rockies, or even out in the flat dusty scrubland of her native west Texas.

This night, though, she walked on the barren, pockmarked surface of the Moon, as the cameras on the floor of the crater Alphonsus showed it in real time: silent, airless, the glowing blue and white crescent of Earth hanging in the black star-strewn sky.

Mandy doesn't want Lars to know what she's been going through, Pancho finally realized, because he'd go wild and try to kill Humphries, but Humphries's people would kill Lars long before he got anywhere near the Humper.

She stopped her pacing and stared out across the dark uneven floor of Alphonsus, dotted with smaller craterlets and cracked here and there by rilles. Maybe that's what Humphries wants. He promised Mandy he wouldn't try to kill Fuchs if Mandy married him, but now he's making her life so miserable that Lars'll come after him. And get himself killed.

That's just like the Humper. Make the other guy jump to his tune. He won't go after Lars; he'll make Lars come after him.

What'll Lars's reaction be when he finds out Mandy's going to have a baby? Will that be enough to set him off? Is that why Humphries impregnated Mandy? He's got one son already, somebody to carry on his gene line. Rumor is the kid's his clone, for cripes sake. Why's he need another son?

To kill Lars, that's why, Pancho answered herself.

What should I do about it? Should I do anything? Warn Lars? Try to help Mandy, show her she's got somebody she can depend on? Or just stay the hell out of the whole ugly mess?

Pancho gazed out at the tired, worn, slumped ringwall mountains of Alphonsus. They look like I feel, she said to herself. Weary. Worn down.

What should I do? Without thinking about it, she called out, "Décor scheme, deep space."

The lunar surface abruptly disappeared. Pancho was in the midst of empty space, stars and glowing nebulas and whirling galaxies stretching out into the blackness of infinity.

"Saturn vicinity," she called.

The ringed planet appeared before her eyes, hovering in emptiness, a splendid, eye-dazzling oblate sphere of delicate pastel colors with those impossible bright-white rings floating around its middle.

That's where Sis is, Pancho thought. Hundreds of millions of kilometers away.

Abruptly, she shook her head, as if to clear it. "Versailles, Hall of Mirrors," she called. And instantly was in the French palace, staring at her own reflections.

What should I do about Mandy? she asked herself again. Then a new thought struck her: What do I want to do?

Me. Myself. What do *I* want to do?

Once Pancho had been a roughneck astronaut, a tomboy who dared farther and played harder than all the others. But ever since her younger sister was struck down by cancer, so many years ago—so many lifetimes ago—Pancho had lived her life for others. Her sister. Then Dan Randolph came along, hired her as an astronaut and, as he lay dying, bequeathed his share of Astro Corporation to her. Ever since, she had been fighting Dan's fights, striving to hold Astro together, to make it profitable, to keep it out of Humphries's clutching paws. And now—Amanda?

What about me? she wondered. What do I want to be when I grow up?

She studied her reflection in the nearest mirror and saw beyond the floor-length party skirt and glittering lamé blouse, beyond the cosmetic therapies, to the gawky, gangling African-American from west Texas that lay beneath the expensive exterior. What do you want out of life, girl?

Her reflection shook its head at her. Doesn't matter. You inherited this responsibility from Dan Randolph. It's on your shoulders now. Mandy, Humphries, even this guy from Nairobi Industries, it's all part of the game you're in. Whether you like it or not. What you want doesn't matter. Not until this game is finished, one way or the other. Especially not now, with the Humper starting to peck away at Astro again. He's starting the war again. I thought it was all finished and over with eight years ago, but Humphries is starting again. Third freighter in as many weeks, according to this morning's report. He's only knocked off unmanned freighters so far, but this is just the beginning. He's probing to see how I'm gonna react.

And it's not just Humphries, either, Pancho reminded herself as she walked slowly along the mirrored corridor. It's the whole danged world. Earth's just starting to recover from the greenhouse cliff a li'l bit. Raw materials from the Belt are so blasted cheap they're providing the basis for an economic comeback. But if Humphries gets complete control of the Belt he'll jack up prices to wherever he wants 'em. He doesn't care about Earth or anybody besides himself. He wants a monopoly. He wants a goddam empire for himself.

You've got responsibilities, lady, she said to her reflection. You got no time to feel sorry for yourself.

"Acropolis," she commanded, striding back to her bedroom through colonnades of graceful fluted columns, the ancient city of Athens visible beyond them, lying in the hot summer sun beneath a sky of perfect blue.

Once in her bedroom Pancho made two phone calls: one to the investment firm in New York that she always used to check out potential business partners or rivals; the other was a personal call to Big George Ambrose, in his room in the very same Hotel Luna.

She was surprised when the phone's synthesized voice told her that George Ambrose had already left Selene; he was returning to Ceres.

"Find him, wherever he is," Pancho snapped at the phone. "I want to talk to him."

EARTH: CHOTA MONASTERY, NEPAL

The first thing Nobuhiko Yamagata did once he returned to Earth following Humphries's party was to visit his revered father, which meant an overnight flight in a corporate jet to Patna, on the Ganges, and then an arduous haul by tilt-rotor halfway up the snowy slopes of the Himalayas.

Saito Yamagata had founded the corporation in the earliest years of the space age and made it into one of the most powerful industrial giants in the world. It had been Saito's vision that built the first solar power satellites and established factories in Earth orbit. It had been Saito who partnered with Dan Randolph's Astro Corporation back in those primitive years when the frontier of human endeavor barely reached to the surface of the Moon.

When Nobuhiko was a young man, just starting to learn the intricacies of corporate politics and power, Saito was stricken with an inoperable brain tumor. Instead of stoically accepting his fate, the elder Yamagata had himself frozen, preserved cryonically in liquid nitrogen until medical science advanced enough to remove the tumor without destroying his brain.

Young Nobu, then, was in command of Yamagata Corporation when the greenhouse cliff plunged the world into global disaster. Japan was struck harder than most industrial nations by the sudden floods that inundated coastal cities and the mammoth storms that raged out of the ocean remorselessly. Earthquakes shattered whole cities, and tsunamis swept the Pacific. Many of the nations that sold food to Japan were also devastated by the greenhouse cliff. Croplands died in withering droughts or were carved away by roaring floods. Millions went hungry, and then tens of millions starved.

Still Saito waited in his sarcophagus of liquid nitrogen, legally dead yet waiting to be revived and returned to life.

Under Nobuhiko's direction, Yamagata Corporation retreated from space and spent every bit of its financial and technical power on rebuilding Japan's shattered cities. Meanwhile, he learned that he could use nanomachines to safely destroy the tumor in his father's brain; the virus-sized devices could be programmed to take the tumor apart, molecule by molecule. Nanotechnology was banned on Earth; fearful mobs and acquiescent politicians had driven the world's experts in nanotech off the Earth altogether. Nobu understood that he could bring his father's preserved body to Selene and have the nanotherapy done there. But he decided against it.

He did not stay his hand because of the horrendous political pressures that would be brought to bear on Yamagata Corporation for using a technology that was illegal on Earth, nor even because of the moral and religious outcry against such a step—although Nobuhiko publicly blamed those forces for his decision. In truth, Nobu dreaded the thought of his father's revival, fearing that his father would be displeased with the way he was running the corporation. Saito had never been an easy man to live with; his son was torn between family loyalty and his desire to keep the reins of power in his own hands.

In the end, family loyalty won. On the inevitable day when the corporation's medical experts told Nobu that his father's tumor could be safely removed without using nanomachines, Nobu felt he had no choice but to agree to the procedure.

The medical experts had also told him, with some reluctance, that although persons could be physically revived from cryonic suspension, their minds were usually as blank as a newborn baby's. Long immersion at cryogenic temperature erodes the synaptic connections in the brain's higher centers. No matter that the person was physically an adult, a cryonic reborn had to be toilet trained, taught to speak, to walk, to be an adult, all over again. And even then, the *mind* of the reborn would probably be different from the mind of the person who had gone into the cryonic suspension. Subtly different, perhaps, but Nobuhiko was warned not to expect his father to be exactly the same personality he'd been before he had died.

With some trepidation, Nobu had his father revived and personally supervised his father's training and education, wondering if the adult that finally emerged from all this would be the same father he had known. Gradually, Saito's mind returned. He was the same man. And yet not.

The first hint of Saito's different personality came the morning that the psychologists finally pronounced their work was finished. Nobu brought his father to his office in New Kyoto. It had once been Saito's office, the center of power for a world-spanning corporation.

Saito strode into the office alongside his son, beaming cheerfully until the door closed and they were alone.

He looked around curiously at the big curved desk, the plush chairs, the silk prints on the walls. "You haven't changed it at all."

Nobuhiko had carefully returned the office to the way it had been when his father was declared clinically dead.

Saito peered into his son's eyes, studied his face for long, silent moments. "My god," he said at last, "it's like looking into a mirror."

Indeed, they looked more like twin brothers than father and son. Both men were stocky, with round faces and deep-set almond eyes. Both wore western business suits of identical sky blue.

Saito threw back his head and laughed, a hearty, full-throated bellow of amusement. "You're as old as I am!"

Automatically, Nobu replied, "But not as wise."

Saito clapped his son on the shoulder. "They've told me about the problems you've faced. And dealt with. I doubt that I could have done better."

Nobu stood in the middle of the office. His father looked just as he remembered him. It was something of a shock for Nobu to realize that he himself looked almost exactly the same.

Feeling nervous, uncertain, Nobu gestured toward the sweeping curve of the desk. "It's been waiting for you, Father."

Saito grew serious. "No. It's your desk now. This is your office."

"But—"

"I'm finished with it," said Saito. "I've decided to retire. I have no intention of returning to work."

Nobu blinked with surprise. "But all this is yours, Father. It's—"

Shaking his head, Saito repeated, "I'm finished with it. The world I once lived in is gone. All the people I knew, all my friends, they're all gone."

"They're not all dead."

"No, but the years have changed them so much I would hardly recognize them. I don't want to try to relive a life that once was. The world moves on. This corporation is your responsibility now, Nobu. I don't want any part of it."

Stunned, Nobuhiko asked, "But what will you do?"

The answer was that Saito retired to a monastery high in the Himalayas, to a life of study and contemplation. Nobu could not have been more shocked if his father had become a serial killer or a child molester.

But even though he filled his days by writing his memoirs (or perhaps *because* he began to write his memoirs) Saito Yamagata could not entirely divorce himself from the corporation on which he had spent his first life. Whenever his son called him, Saito listened greedily to the events of the hour, then offered Nobuhiko the gift of his advice. At first Nobu was wary of his father's simmering interest in the corporation. Gradually, however, he came to cherish his father's wisdom, and even to rely upon it.

So now Nobuhiko flew to Nepal in a corporate tilt-rotor. Videophone calls were all well and good, but still nothing could replace a personal visit, face to face, where no one could possibly eavesdrop.

It was bitingly cold in the mountains. Swirls of snow swept around the plane when it touched down lightly on the crushed gravel pad outside the monastery's gray stone walls. Despite his hooded parka, Nobu was thoroughly chilled by the time a saffron-robed lama conducted him through the thick wooden door and into a hallway paneled with polished oak.

Saito was waiting for him in a small room with a single window that looked out on the snow-clad mountains. A low lacquered table and two kneeling mats were the only furniture, but there was a warm fire crackling in the soot-blackened fireplace. Nobu folded his parka neatly on the floor and stood before the fireplace, gratefully absorbing its warmth.

Wearing a kimono of deep blue, decorated with the flying crane emblem of the Yamagata family, his father waited in patient silence until Nobu grew uneasy and turned from the fireplace. Then Saito greeted his son with a full-bodied embrace that delighted Nobu even though it squeezed the breath out of him. Altitude and bear hugs did not mix well.

"You've lost a kilo or two," said the elder Yamagata, holding his son at arm's length. "That's good."

Nobuhiko dipped his chin in acknowledgment.

Saito slapped his bulging belly. "I've found them! And more!" He laughed heartily.

Wondering how his father could gain weight in a monastery, Nobu said, "I spoke with Martin Humphries. He apparently does not know that we are backing the Africans."

"And Astro?"

"Pancho Lane launched an investigation of Nairobi Industries. It has found nothing to tie us to them."

"Good," said Saito as he knelt slowly, carefully on one of the mats. It rustled slightly beneath his weight. "It's better if no one realizes we are returning to space operations."

"I still don't understand why we must keep our interest in Nairobi Industries a secret." Nobu knelt on the other mat, close enough to his father to smell the older man's aftershave lotion.

Saito patted his son's knee. "Humphries Space Systems and Astro Corporation are fighting for control of the Belt, aren't they? If they knew Yamagata will soon be competing against them, they might combine their forces against us."

Nobu shook his head. "Pancho Lane despises Humphries. And he feels the same about her."

With a knowing grin, Saito countered, "They might hate each other, but their personal feelings wouldn't stop them from uniting to prevent us from establishing ourselves in the Belt. Personal emotions take a back seat to business, son."

"Perhaps," Nobu conceded.

"Work through the Africans," Saito counseled. "Let Nairobi Industries establish a base on the Moon. That will be our foothold. The prospecting ships and ore carriers they send to the Asteroid Belt will return profits to Yamagata."

"One-third of our profits go to Humphries," Nobu reminded his father.

The hardest thing that Nobuhiko had been forced to tell his father was that Humphries had bought into Yamagata Corporation back in the days when the greenhouse cliff had struck so hard that the corporation was teetering on the edge of bankruptcy. Humphries owned a third of Yamagata Corporation, and was constantly scheming to gain more. It had taken every gram of Nobu's courage to tell his father that. He feared it would break the old man's heart.

Instead, Saito had accepted the news stoically, saying only, "Humphries took advantage of the situation."

With some heat, Nobu growled, "He took advantage of the catastrophes that struck Japan."

"Yes," Saito said, his voice a low rumble. "We'll have to do something about that, eventually."

Nobu had never felt so relieved, so grateful.

Now, Saito sat back on his heels and gazed out at the snowy mountains.

"Our first objective is to make certain that neither Humphries nor Astro Corporation learns that we aim to establish ourselves in the Belt."

Nobu nodded his acknowledgment.

"The best way to accomplish that," Saito went on, "is to keep them both busy fighting each other."

"We've already destroyed a few automated freighters of both corporations, as you suggested. Pancho Lane blames Humphries, of course, and he blames her."

"Good," Saito grunted.

"But they're not actually fighting. There's a bit of piracy in the Belt, mainly by the man Fuchs, but he is one lone madman, without support from anyone except a few of the rock rats."

"He may be the key to the situation, then."

"I don't understand how," said Nobu.

"Let me think about it," Saito replied. "Our objective remains to keep HSS and Astro focused on each other. Fuchs could be an important element in this. Properly exploited, he could help us to stir this simmering enmity between Pancho Lane and Martin Humphries into a major conflict."

"A major conflict?" Nobu asked, alarmed. "You mean actual fighting? War?"

"Business is a form of warfare, son. If Astro and Humphries fight each other out there in the Belt, it can only be to our benefit."

Nobuhiko left his father with his mind whirling. Set Humphries and Astro against each other. Yes, he decided, it would be in Yamagata Corporation's best interest to do so. And this exile Fuchs could be the pivot that moves the stone.

By the time he landed in the family's estate near New Kyoto, Nobuhiko was lost in admiration for the depth of his father's thought. A war between HSS and Astro. Nobu smiled. Living in a monastery hasn't softened the old man's heart. Or his brain.

HABITAT *CHRYSALIS*

Originally, the prospectors and miners who came out to the Belt lived inside the largest of the asteroids, Ceres. Honeycombed by nature with lava tubes and caves, Ceres offered solid rock protection against the hard radiation that constantly sleets through the solar system. But at less than half the size of Earth's Moon, the asteroid's minuscule gravity presented problems for long-term residents. Muscle and bone deteriorate in microgravity. And every movement in the asteroid's caves and tunnels, every footfall or hand's brush against a rock wall, stirred up fine, powdery, carbon-dark dust that lingered in the air, hovering constantly in the light gravity. The dust was everywhere. It irritated the lungs and made people cough. It settled in fine black coatings on dishes in cupboards, on furniture, on clothing hanging limply in closets.

It was Lars Fuchs who had started the ramshackle habitat that eventually was named *Chrysalis* by the rock rats. When he lived in Ceres with his wife, Amanda, before he was exiled and she divorced him to marry Humphries, Fuchs got his fellow rock rats to start building the habitat.

All the rock rats knew that Fuchs's real motive was to start a family. A habitat in orbit around Ceres, rotating to produce an artificial gravity, would be a much safer place to have babies. So they started buying stripped-down spacecraft and old junkers that had been abandoned by their owners. They connected them, Tinkertoy fashion, and slowly built a wheeled station in orbit around Ceres that could house the growing population of rock rats. It looked like a rotating junkyard, from the outside. But its interior was clean, efficient, and protected by the electromagnetic radiation shields that each individual ship had built into it.

By the time the residents of Ceres moved to their orbital habitat and named it *Chrysalis,* Fuchs had lost his one-man war against Humphries Space Systems, been exiled from the habitat he himself had originated, and lost his wife to Martin Humphries.

Big George Ambrose was thinking about that sad history while his torch ship approached Ceres. As he packed his toiletries in preparation for docking, he cast an eye at the wallscreen view of the habitat. *Chrysalis* was growing. A new ring was being built around the original circular collection of spacecraft. The new ring looked more like a proper habitat: the rock rats had enough money now to invest in real engineering and the same quality of construction that went into the space habitats in the Earth/Moon region.

One day we'll abandon the old clunker, George told himself, surprised at how rueful he felt about it. It's been a good home.

The big, shaggy-bearded, redheaded Aussie had started his career as an engineer at Moonbase, long before it became the independent nation of Selene. He had lost his job in one of the economic wobbles of those early days and became a fugitive, a non-person who lived by his wits in the shadowy black market of the "lunar underground." Then he'd run into Dan Randolph, who made George respectable again. By the time Randolph died, George was a rock rat, plying the dark and lonely expanse of the Belt in search of a fortune. Eventually he was elected chief administrator of Ceres. Now he was returning home from Humphries's winter solstice party.

He had spent the six days of his return voyage in a liaison with the torch ship's propulsion engineer, a delightful young Vietnamese woman of extraordinary beauty who talked about fusion rocket systems between passionate bouts of lovemaking. George had been flabbergasted by the unexpected affair, until he realized that she wanted a position on a prospecting ship and a fling with the chief of the rock rats' community looked to her like a good way to get one.

Well, thought George as he packed his one travel bag, it was fun while it lasted. He told her he'd introduce her to a few prospectors; some of them might need a propulsion engineer. Still, he felt sad about the affair. I've been manipulated, he realized. Then, despite himself, he broke into a rueful grin. She's pretty good at manipulatin', he had to admit.

Once his travel bag was zipped up, George instructed the ship's computer to display any messages waiting for him. The wall screen instantly showed a long list. He hadn't been paying attention to his duties for the past several days, he knew. Being chief administrator means bein' a mediator, a decision-maker, even a father/confessor to everyone and anyone in the fookin' Belt, he grumbled silently.

One message, though, was from Pancho Lane.

Surprised and curious, George ordered her message on-screen. The computer displayed a wavering, eye-straining hash of colored streaks. Pancho's message was scrambled. George had to pull out his personal palmcomp and hunt for the combination to descramble it.

At last Pancho's lean, lantern-jawed face filled with screen. "Hi George. Sorry we didn't get to spend more time together before you had to take off. Lemme ask you a question: Can you contact Lars if you need to? I might hafta talk to him."

The screen went blank.

George stared at it thoughtfully, wondering: Now why in all the caverns of hell would Pancho need to talk to Lars Fuchs?

HELL CRATER

Pancho always grinned when she thought about Father Maximilian J. Hell, the Jesuit astronomer for whom this thirty-kilometer-wide lunar crater had been named. Wily promoters such as Sam Gunn had capitalized on the name and built a no-holds-barred resort city at Hell Crater, complete with gambling casinos and euphemistically named "honeymoon hotels."

Astro Corporation had made a fair pocketful of profits from building part of the resort complex. But Pancho wasn't visiting Hell to check on corporate interests. She had received a message from Amanda to meet her at the medical center there. Mandy's message had come by a tortuously circuitous route, imbedded in a seemingly innocuous invitation to Selene's annual Independence Day celebration, sent by none other than Douglas Stavenger.

Ever since the Christmas party Pancho had been trying to see Amanda, to renew the friendship that had come to a screeching halt once Mandy had married Humphries. Amanda replied politely to each of Pancho's invitations, but somehow always had an excuse to postpone a meeting. Mandy never replied in real time; her messages were always recorded. Pancho studied Amanda's face each time, searching for some hint of how Mandy was and why she wouldn't—or, more likely, couldn't—get away from Humphries long enough to have lunch with an old pal.

So when Stavenger's video invitation popped up on Pancho's screen, she was staggered to see his youthful face morph into Amanda's features.

"Please meet me at the Fossel Medical Center, Pancho, next Wednesday at eleven-thirty."

Then her image winked out and Doug Stavenger's was smiling at her again. Pancho couldn't recapture Mandy's message, either. It was gone completely.

Curiouser and curiouser, Pancho thought as she rode the cable car from Selene. The cable lines were the cheapest and most efficient transportation system on the Moon. Rockets were faster, and there was a regular rocket shuttle between Selene and the growing astronomical observatory complex at Farside. But the cable cars ran up and over the Alphonsus ringwall mountains and out to Copernicus, Hell, and the other budding centers being built on the Moon's near side. There were even plans afoot to link Selene with the bases being built in the lunar south polar region by cable systems.

A corporate executive of Pancho's stature could have commandeered a car for herself, or even flown over to Hell in her own rocket hopper. But that wasn't Pancho's style. She enjoyed being as inconspicuous as possible, and found it valuable to see what the ordinary residents of Selene— the self-styled Lunatics—were thinking and doing. Besides, she didn't want to call the attention of Humphries's ever-present spies to the fact that she was going, literally, to Hell.

So she whizzed along twenty meters above the flat, pockmarked, rock-strewn surface of Mare Nubium, wondering what Amanda was up to. The cable car's interior was almost exactly like a spacecraft's passenger cabin, except that Pancho could feel it swaying slightly as she sat in her padded chair. Small windows lined each side of the cabin, and there was a pair of larger curving windows up forward, where tourists or romantics could get a broad view of the barren lunar landscape rushing past. What'd that old astronaut call it? Pancho asked herself. Then she remembered: "Magnificent desolation."

Those front seats were already taken, so Pancho slouched back in her chair and pulled out her palmcomp. Might's well get some work done, she told herself. But she couldn't help staring out at the mountains of the highlands rising beyond the horizon, stark and bare in the harsh unfiltered sunlight.

At last the car popped into the yawning airlock at Hell Crater. Pancho hurried through the reception center and out into the main plaza. The domed plaza was circular, which made it seem bigger than the plaza at Selene. Pancho marveled at the crowds that bustled along the shrubbery-lined walkways: elderly couples, plenty of younger singles, whole families with laughing, excited kids. Most of the tourists were stumbling in the low lunar gravity, even in the weighted boots they had rented. Despite the catastrophes that had smitten Earth, there were still enough people with enough wealth to make Hell a profitable resort.

Shaking her head ruefully as she walked toward the medical center, Pancho thought about how Hotel Luna back at Selene was practically bankrupt. It wasn't enough to a offer first-rate hotel facility on the Moon, she realized. Not anymore. But give people gambling, prostitution, and recreational drugs and they'll come up and spend their money. Of course, nobody accepted cash. All financial transactions were computerized, which helped keep everybody reasonably honest. For a modest percentage of the gross, the government of Selene policed the complex and saw to it that visitors got what they paid for, nothing more and nothing less. Even the fundamentalists among Selene's population appreciated the income that kept their taxes low, although they grumbled about the sinful disgrace of Hell.

As Pancho pushed through the lobby door of the Fossel Medical Center, she immediately saw that the center's clientele consisted almost entirely of two types: senior citizens with chronic complaints, and very beautiful prostitutes—men as well as women—who were required to have their health checked regularly. Pancho was wearing a well-tailored business suit, but still the "working women" made her feel shabby.

She strode up to the reception center, which was nothing more than a set of flat screens set into the paneling of the curved wall. Pancho picked the screen marked VISITORS and spoke her name slowly and clearly.

"You are expected in Room 21-A," said a synthesized voice, while the screen displayed a floor plan with Room 21-A outlined in blinking red. "Follow the red floor lights, please."

Pancho followed the lights set into the floor tiles and found 21-A without trouble. A couple of security people were in the corridor, a man at one end and a woman at the other, both dressed in ordinary coveralls, both trying to look unobtrusive. HSS flunkies, Pancho guessed.

When she opened the door and stepped into the room, though, she was surprised to see not Amanda, but Doug Stavenger.

"Hello, Pancho," he said, getting up from the chair on which he'd been sitting. "Sorry for all the cloak and dagger business."

The room was apparently a waiting area. Small, comfortably upholstered chairs lined its walls. A holowindow displayed a view of the Earth in real time. A second door was set into the back wall.

"I was expecting Mandy," said Pancho.

"She'll be here in a few minutes."

Doug Stavenger's family had created the original Moonbase, the lunar outpost that eventually grew into the nation of Selene. He had been the leader in Moonbase's brief, successful war against the old United Nations and their Peacekeeper troops, which established the lunar community's independence from Earth. Stavenger himself had chosen the name Selene for the fledgling lunar nation.

Although he was fully a generation older than Pancho, Stavenger looked no more than thirty: a handsome, solidly built middleweight whose tawny skin was only a shade lighter than Pancho's. His body was filled with therapeutic nanomachines that destroyed invading microbes, cleared away fats and arterial plaque, rebuilt his tissues to keep him physically youthful. They had saved his life, twice. Officially Stavenger had been retired for many years, although everyone knew he was still a political power broker in Selene. His influence was even felt in the Asteroid Belt and at the fusion-scooping operation in orbit around Jupiter. But he was exiled from Earth; the worldwide ban on nanotechnology meant that no nation on Earth would allow him within its borders.

"What're you doin' here?" Pancho asked as she sat in the chair next to Stavenger.

He hesitated a heartbeat, then replied, "I'll let Amanda tell you."

"What's she here for?"

Stavenger smiled sphinxlike.

If it had been anyone else Pancho would have fumed. She felt her brows knitting. "Some sort of game going on?"

Stavenger's smile faded. "Some sort, indeed."

The inner door swung open and Amanda stepped into the room. She was wearing the latest style of baggy blue-gray sweatshirt that stopped short of her rumpled, darker slacks so that her midriff was bare. In keeping with the current fashion, she had an animated decal sprayed around her waist: a procession of colorful elves and trolls, their endless marching powered by Amanda's body heat. Her golden hair was slightly disheveled. Even though she smiled at Pancho, the expression on her face seemed far less than happy. She looked pale, tense.

Stavenger got to his feet, but Pancho went like a shot to Amanda and wrapped her arms around her and held her close.

"Cripes almighty, Mandy, it's great to see you." *Without your sumbitch husband between us,* Pancho added mentally.

Amanda seemed to understand exactly how Pancho felt. She rested her head on Pancho's shoulder for a moment and murmured, "It's good to see you, too, Pancho."

They disentangled and sat down next to each other. Stavenger pulled a third chair over to sit facing them.

"The room's clean," he said. "Whatever we say here won't go beyond these walls. And all the other waiting rooms along this corridor are unoccupied."

Pancho realized that the security people out in the hallway were from Selene, not Humphries Space Systems.

"What's this all about?" she asked.

"I need to tell you something, Pancho," said Amanda.

"Must be important."

"Life or death," Stavenger muttered.

"Martin is planning some sort of move against Astro," Amanda said. "He's furious with you, Pancho. He believes you've been supplying Lars, helping him to prey on HSS ships."

"That's bullshit," Pancho snapped. "Hell, he's knocked off three of Astro's robot freighters in the past month. First one, I thought maybe Lars had done it, but not three."

"Lars wouldn't attack your ships, Pancho," Amanda said.

Stavenger agreed. "There's something in the wind, that's for sure. Someone's pumping money into this new African corporation."

"Nairobi Industries," said Pancho. "They're building a facility at Shackleton Crater, near the south pole."

"And Martin is backing them?"

"Either Humphries or a third player that's staying behind the scenes so far," said Stavenger.

"The Hump's always planning some sort of move," Pancho said lightly. "He's wanted to get his paws on Astro from the git-go."

"If he gains control of Astro Corporation, he'll have a monopoly on space operations from here to the Belt. He'll have the rock rats at his mercy."

"I think whatever Martin is planning could become violent," Amanda said. "He's rebuilding the base on Vesta that Lars destroyed. He's hiring a small army of mercenary troops."

Pancho had heard the same from her own intelligence people.

"But why is he going to all that expense?" Stavenger wondered aloud.

"To get control of Astro. To get control of everything," said Amanda.

"Including Lars," said Pancho.

"He's promised not to harm Lars," Amanda said. Without much conviction, Pancho thought.

"You believe him?"

Amanda looked away for a moment, then said bitterly, "I did once. I don't anymore."

Pancho nodded. "Neither do I."

"I thought we had this all settled eight years ago," Stavenger said. "You both agreed to stop the fighting."

"Astro's lived up the agreement," Pancho said.

"So has Humphries," replied Stavenger. "Until now."

"But why?" Pancho demanded again. "Why start all this crap again? Is he so damn crazy he really wants to be emperor of the whole solar system?"

"It's Lars," Amanda said. "He wants to kill Lars. He thinks I still love him."

"Do you?"

Amanda pressed her lips together tightly. Then she said, "That's why I'm here."

"Here? You mean this med center?"

"Yes."

"I don't understand, Mandy."

She took a deep breath. "The baby I'm carrying is Lars's, not Martin's."

Pancho felt as if someone had punched her in the solar plexus. "Lars's? How in hell did you—"

"We stored frozen zygotes years ago," said Amanda, "back when Lars and I first went out to the Belt on the old *Starpower*. We knew we could be exposed to dangerous radiation doses, so we fertilized some of my eggs and stored them at Selene."

"And now you've implanted yourself with one of 'em," Pancho said, her voice hollow.

Nodding slowly, Amanda said, "Martin thinks I'm carrying his son. But it's Lars's."

"If he finds out he'll kill you both."

"That's why I had it done here. Doug made the arrangements for me, brought together the proper medical personnel, even provided security."

Pancho glanced at Stavenger with new respect. "That's one way to spit in Humphries's eye," she muttered.

He shrugged. "I did it for Amanda, not to spite Humphries."

Yeah, sure, Pancho retorted silently.

Aloud, she said, "You're playin' with nitroglycerine, Mandy. If Humphries even suspects—"

Amanda silenced her with a flash of her eyes. "He won't rest until he's killed Lars," she said, her voice low but hard, determined. "But even if he does, I'll bear Lars's son."

Pancho let the breath sag out of her.

"It's the only way I can get back at him," Amanda said. "The only way I can express my love for Lars."

"Yeah, but if Humphries even suspects—"

"He won't," Stavenger said flatly. "Amanda's traveled here as part of my team, completely incognito."

"Only the three of us know about it," said Amanda.

"What about the medics?"

Stavenger answered, "They don't know who Amanda is. I fly the team up from Earth and then back again. They don't stay here."

"Only the three of us know about it," Amanda repeated.

Pancho nodded, but she thought about Ben Franklin's dictum: *Three people can keep a secret—if two of them are dead.*

LUNAR CABLE CAR 502

Pancho had to grin as she walked up to the cable car along with the other passengers returning to Selene. Above the car's front windows someone had stenciled the car's route in blood-red letters: TO HELL AND BACK. None of the other tourists or resident Lunatics seemed to pay any attention to the lettering. Pancho shook her head at their indifference to the unknown graffitist's sense of humor.

Amanda had left the Hell Crater complex as she had arrived, as part of Douglas Stavenger's small, private entourage. She had slipped a beige snood over her golden hair, and an equally bland, shapeless mid-calf coat over her dress. No one would see the parade of animated figures circling her waist. She blended in with the rest of Stavenger's people. Unless someone was specifically searching for her, no one would notice her among the others who boarded Stavenger's special cable car.

Pancho had decided not to go with them. The lantern-jawed face and tall, long-limbed figure of Astro Corporation's board chairwoman were known well enough that there was a small but real chance that she might be recognized by news reporters—or snoops from Humphries Space Systems. No sense taking unnecessary risks, she decided. So Pancho spent the rest of the afternoon playing in the casinos, enjoying herself. For an hour or so she piled up a considerable score on one of the computer games, but eventually the law of averages caught up with her. When she sank back to break-even, Pancho called it a day and strolled over to one of the better restaurants for a solitary dinner. Gambling was fun, she thought, but losing wasn't. And the longer you play, the better the odds favor the house.

She always ate too quickly when she was alone. Feeling full yet unsatisfied, Pancho made her way back to the cable car airlock. "To Hell and back," she muttered to herself as she climbed through the cable car's hatch and strapped herself into a seat up front. She looked forward to watching the lunar scenery whipping past, and besides, with her back to most of the other passengers there was less chance of her being recognized. I'll get a good look at the Straight Wall, she thought.

The overweight Asian-American who settled into the seat beside her, though, stared at her for a few moments after he clicked his safety harness over his bulky shoulders. Then, as the car jerked into motion and glided past the airlock doors, he said, "Pardon me, but aren't you Pancho Lane? I saw your picture in the financial news net a few days ago and . . ."

Pancho didn't have to say a word. She couldn't. The man prattled on nonstop about his own small company and his great admiration for an executive as lofty as Pancho and how he had come up to Selene from the big refugee center at SeaTac, in the States, to try to clinch a deal with Astro Corporation.

Pancho was almost grateful when the cable car suddenly lurched violently and then began to fall, slowly, with the inexorable horror of a nightmare, to crash nose-first into the dusty, cracked, crater-pocked ground.

Martin Humphries leaned back as his desk chair molded itself to the contours of his spine. He sat alone in his office, just off the master bedroom in his mansion, squinting at the string of numbers and accompanying text that hovered in midair above his wide, expansive desk. He steepled his fingers before his face as he studied the reports from his accounting department. Profits were down slightly, but he had expected that. Four ships had been lost in the past quarter, three of them automated ore freighters, one of them a logistics ship that had been seized, looted, and then gutted by Lars Fuchs. The crew had been set adrift in their escape pod. The attack had taken place close enough to Ceres for them to be rescued within forty-eight hours.

Humphries snapped his fingers and the report dissolved.

"Fuchs," he muttered. The sonofabitch is still out there in the Belt, drifting around like some Flying Dutchman, getting his pitiful little jolts out of knocking off HSS vessels. And that damned greasemonkey Pancho is helping him.

Humphries smiled to himself. Well, enjoy yourself while you can, Fuchs. The end is near. And meanwhile, I've got your ex-wife pregnant.

Pancho is a different problem. Tougher nut to crack. But I'll get her. I'll bleed Astro white until their board of directors boots her ass out the door. Then I'll offer them a merger deal that they can't afford to refuse. I'll take Astro Corporation; it's only a matter of time.

Getting up from the chair and walking slowly around his desk, Humphries laughed out loud. As soon as Amanda gets home from her shopping or whatever the hell she's doing today, I'll pop her into bed. Just because she's carrying my son doesn't mean I can't enjoy her.

"Holowindow," he called out, "give me a view of the Asteroid Belt."

The window on the left wall of the office immediately displayed a painting by Davis of a lumpy, potato-brown asteroid with a smaller chip of rock floating near it.

"No, a photo. Real-time telescopic view."

The holowindow went blank for a second, then showed a stretch of star-flecked darkness. One of the pinpoints of light was noticeably brighter than any of the others. The single word CERES flashed briefly next to it.

"He's out there somewhere," Humphries muttered to himself. "But not for much longer."

Humphries went back to his desk and called up the latest progress report from his special security detail in the Belt. The base on Vesta was complete, and twenty-four attack craft were on their way to take up stations around the Belt. All of HSS's freighters were being equipped with military crews and weapons. The costs were draining the corporation's profits, but sooner or later Fuchs would be found and destroyed.

In the meantime, Humphries thought, it's time to make my move against Astro. Time to take Pancho down. That greasemonkey's blocked my takeover of Astro long enough.

She doesn't understand the first principles of economics, Humphries told himself. Supply and demand. Astro is cutting our throats, undercutting our price for raw materials from the asteroids. And that damned guttersnipe will keep on undercutting me until I wipe her off the board completely. There isn't room for two players out in the Belt. The only way to make economic sense out there is to have just one corporation in charge of everything. And that one's got to be Humphries Space Systems.

Yet his thoughts returned to Fuchs. I've given the sonofabitch eight years. I promised Amanda I wouldn't harm him, and for eight years I've lived up to that promise. And what has Fuchs done? He sticks it to me every time he can. Instead of being grateful that I didn't kill him, he kicks me in the balls every chance he gets. Well, eight years is long enough. It's damned expensive trying to track him down, but I'm going to *get* that bastard, the sooner the better.

He's smart, though. Clever enough to hide out in the Belt and let his fellow rock rats help him. And Pancho, too; she's helping him all she can. I've got to get him out of hiding. Out into the open, where my people can destroy him.

Maybe the news that Amanda is pregnant will bring him out, goad him into making a mistake.

Looking at his own faint reflection in the holowindows, Humphries thought, I'd like to see the expression on his shitty face when he finds out Amanda's carrying my son.

MARE NUBIUM

Passengers screamed as the cablecar plunged in lunar slow motion toward the ground, twenty meters below. It was like a nightmare. Strangely, Pancho felt no fear, only an odd sort of fascination. While she watched the ground coming up toward the car's windows she had time to think, If the windows crack we'll lose our air and die in less than a minute.

The cable car's nose plowed into the ground with a grinding, screeching groan. Pancho was thrown painfully against the shoulder straps of her safety harness, then banged the back of her head against her seat's headrest.

For a second or two there was complete silence. Then people began to moan, sob. Pancho's head buzzed painfully. Automatically, she started to unclick the safety harness. The Asian-American seated next to her was already out of his straps.

"You okay?" he asked.

Pancho nodded tentatively. "I think so."

"They designed these cars to withstand a crash," he said.

"Yeah."

"They'll have a rescue team here shortly. There's enough air to keep us breathing for several hours, plus emergency tanks."

Pancho stared at him. "Sounds like you swallowed the emergency procedures book."

He grinned weakly, looking slightly ashamed. "I'm always a little nervous about traveling, so I read everything I can find about the vehicles I'm going to travel in."

Pancho tapped on the glassteel window. "Ain't even cracked."

"Good thing. There's no air outside."

"What's going to happen?" a woman's voice demanded sharply.

Pancho turned in her seat. The car's floor slanted upward, but otherwise everything inside seemed close to normal. A couple of the passengers had even stood up, legs a little shaky, looking around with wide, staring eyes.

"Better to stay in your seats," Pancho said, in her most authoritative voice. "The car's got an automatic emergency beacon. They've prob'ly already started a rescue team from Selene."

"How long will it take?"

"Will our air hold out?"

"The lights are dimmer, aren't they?"

"We must be on battery power," said the Asian-American. "The batteries are designed to last for six hours or more."

"Six hours? You mean we'll be stuck here for six hours?"

"No, it's just—"

The speakers set in to the overhead suddenly announced, "Cable car five-oh-two, this is the Safety Office headquarters. We will be launching a rescue hopper in less than thirty minutes. What is your situation, please?"

A babble of voices rose from the passengers, some frightened, some angry.

"*Shut Up!*" Pancho commanded. Once they were stilled, she said loudly and clearly, "We've crashed, but we're intact. All systems functioning. No major injuries."

"My back is hurt!" a woman said.

"I think I sprained my wrist," said one of the male passengers.

The loudspeakers replied, "We'll have a medic aboard the rescue hopper. Please stay calm. Help is on the way."

Pancho sat on her seat's armrest so she could look up the car's central aisle at the other passengers. They had all gotten back into their seats. No blood in sight. They looked shaken; a few of them were definitely angry, glaring.

"How long is this going to take?" one of the men asked no one in particular. "I've got a flight back to Kansas City to catch."

Pancho smiled inwardly. If they're in good enough shape to complain, she thought, we've got no major problems. Then she added, As long as the rescue team gets here before the batteries go flat.

The Asian-American pressed his fingertips against the curved inner wall of the car's hull. "Diamond construction," he said, as much to himself as to Pancho. "Built by nanomachines."

It sounded to Pancho as if he were trying to reassure himself. Then she noticed that he had a plastic packet in his lap. It contained two breathing masks and a small tank of compressed oxygen.

Lordy lord, Pancho thought. He really came prepared for a calamity.

LOGISTICS SHIP *ROEBUCK*

I still don't like it," said Luke Abrams as he studied the radar display.

"You'll like the money," replied his partner, Indra Wanmanigee.

Abrams shot her a sour look. They were sitting side by side in the cockpit of *Roebuck*'s crew module. Normally the ship carried supplies from the habitat in orbit around Ceres to the miners and prospectors scattered around the Belt. This time, however, they were sailing deeper into the Belt than normal. And instead of supplies, *Roebuck* carried a team of mercenaries, armed with a pair of high-power lasers.

Tired of eking out a living as a merchant to the rock rats, Wanmanigee had made a deal with Humphries Space Systems to use *Roebuck* as a Trojan horse, drifting deep into the Belt in the hope that Lars Fuchs would intercept the ship to raid it for supplies. Fuchs would find, of course, not the supplies he and his crew wanted, but trained mercenaries who would destroy his ship and kill him. The HSS people offered a huge reward for Fuchs's head, enough to retire and finally get married and live the rest of her life like a maharanee and her consort.

"I still don't like it," Abrams muttered again. "We're sitting out here like a big, fat target. Fuchs could gut our crew module and kill us both with one pop of a laser."

"He hardly ever kills independents," she replied mildly. "More likely he will demand to board us and steal our cargo."

Abrams grumbled something too low for her to understand. She knew he worried about the six roughnecks living in the cargo hold. There were two women among them, but still Abrams feared that they might take her into their clutches. Wanmanigee kept to the crew module; the only mercenary she saw was their captain—a handsome brute, she thought, but she wanted no man except her stoop-shouldered, balding, potbellied, perpetually worried Abrams. She could control him, and he genuinely loved her. No other man would be worth the trouble, she had decided years earlier.

Suddenly Abrams sat up straighter in his copilot's chair. "I've got a blip," he said, tapping a fingernail against the radar screen.

Aboard *Nautilus* Lars Fuchs sat in his privacy cubicle, staring bitterly at Big George's image on the screen above his bunk.

Over the years of his exile, Fuchs had worked out a tenuous communications arrangement with Big George, who was the only man outside of his ship's crew that Fuchs trusted. It was George who had commuted Fuchs's death sentence to exile; the big Aussie with the brick-red hair and bushy beard had saved Fuchs's life when Humphries had been certain that he'd seen the last of his adversary.

Fuchs planted miniaturized transceivers on tiny, obscure asteroids. From time to time, George squirted a highly compressed message to one of those asteroids by tight-beam laser. Each coded message ended with the number designation of the asteroid to which the next message would be beamed. In this way Fuchs could be kept abreast of the news from the rest of civilization. It was a halting, limping method of communication; the news reports Fuchs received were always weeks out of date, sometimes months. But it was his only link to the rest of the human race, and Fuchs was grateful to Big George for taking the trouble and the risk to do it.

Now, though, as he glowered at George's unhappy countenance, Fuchs felt considerably less than grateful.

"That's what his fookin' party was for," George was saying, morosely. "He got up on the fookin' piano bench to tell all those people that he was gonna be a father. Pleased as a fat snake, he looked."

Fuchs wiped George's image off the screen and got up from his chair. His compartment was only three strides across, and he paced from one side of it to the other twice, three times, four . . .

It was inevitable, he told himself. She's been married to him for eight years. She's been in his bed every night for all that time. What did you expect?

Yet a fury boiled within him like raging molten lava. This is Humphries's way of taunting me. Humiliating me. He's showing the whole world, the whole solar system, that he's the master. He's taken my wife and made her pregnant with his son. The bastard! The crowing, gloating, boasting filthy swine of a bastard! I've been fighting him for all these years and he fights back by stealing my wife and making her bear his son. The coward! The gutless shit-hearted spineless slimy coward.

His hands balled into fists, Fuchs advanced to the blanked screen, the image of George's shaggy-maned face still burning in his eyes. He had to hit something, anything, had to release this fury somehow, *now,* before it exploded inside him.

"Contact," sang Nodon's voice over the intercom. "We have radar contact with a vessel."

Fuchs's head jerked to the speaker built into the bulkhead.

"It appears to be a logistics ship," Nodon added.

Fuchs's lips curled into a humorless smile. "I'm coming up to the bridge," he said.

By the time he got to the compact, equipment-crammed bridge, Nodon had the approaching logistics ship on the main screen. Amarjagal was in the pilot's seat, silent and dour as usual. Fuchs stood behind her and focused his attention on the ship.

"What's a logistics ship doing this deep in the Belt?" he wondered aloud.

Nodon shifted his big, liquid eyes from the screen to Fuchs, then back again. "Perhaps it is off course," he suggested.

"Or a decoy," Fuchs snapped. "Any other ships in sight?"

"Nosir. The nearest object is a minor asteroid, less than a hundred meters across."

"Distance?"

"Four hundred kilometers. Four thirty-two, to be precise."

"Could it be another ship, disguised?"

Amarjagal spoke up. "There could be a ship behind it. Or even sitting on it."

The communications receiver's light began blinking amber.

"They're trying to speak to us," Nodon said, pointing to the light.

"Listen, but don't reply," Fuchs commanded.

"This is the *Roebuck,*" the comm speaker announced. A man's voice; it sounded a little shaky to Fuchs. He's excited, maybe nervous.

"We have a full cargo of supplies for you. Be willing to accept credit if you don't have hard goods to trade."

"Is *Roebuck* an HSS vessel?" Fuchs asked Nodon.

His fingers flicked across the keyboard set into the control panel. "Nosir. It is registered as an independent."

"Are the lasers ready?"

Pointing to the green lights of the weapons board, Nodon replied, "Yessir. The crews are all in place."

In *Roebuck*'s cargo bay the team of trained mercenaries was already in their spacesuits and warming up the laser weapons.

"Don't open the hatches until I give the word," their captain said from his post on the catwalk that ran around the interior of the spacious bay. "I don't want to give Fuchs any hint that we're ready to fry his ass."

Fuchs rubbed his broad, stubbled chin as he stared at the image of the logistics vessel on the bridge's main screen.

"Why would an independent logistics ship be this deep in the Belt?" he repeated. "There aren't any miners or prospectors out here."

"Except us," agreed Amarjagal.

"Fire number one at their cargo bay," Fuchs snapped.

Nodon hesitated for a fraction of a moment.

"Fire it!" Fuchs roared.

The first laser blast did little more damage than puncturing the thin skin of *Roebuck*'s cargo bay hull. As the air rushed out of the bay, their space-suited commander gave the order to open the hatches and begin firing back at *Nautilus*.

In the cockpit Abrams felt cold sweat break out all over his body. "He's shooting at us!"

Wanmanigee tensed, too. "We should get into our space suits! Quickly!"

Those were her last words.

His eyes glued to the main screen, Fuchs saw *Roebuck*'s cargo bay hatches open.

"They're firing back," reported Amarjagal, her voice flat and calm.

"All weapons fire," Fuchs said. "Tear her to shreds."

It was a totally unequal battle. *Roebuck*'s laser beams splashed off *Nautilus*'s copper armor shields. *Nautilus*'s five laser weapons slashed through *Roebuck*'s thin hull, shredding the cargo bay and crew pod within seconds. Fuchs saw several space-suited figures tumble out of the wreckage.

"Cease firing," he said.

Jabbing a finger at the image of the space-suited people floating helplessly, Nodon asked, "Shall we pick them up?"

Fuchs sneered at him. "Do you want to share your rations with them?"

Nodon hesitated, obviously torn.

"And if we take them aboard, what do we do with them? How do we get rid of them? Do you think we can cruise back to Ceres and land them there?"

Nodon shook his head. Still, he turned back to watch the helpless figures floating amidst the wreckage of what had been a vessel only a few moments earlier. His finger hovered over the communications keyboard.

"Don't tap into their frequency," Fuchs commanded. "I don't want to hear them begging."

For several moments Fuchs and his bridge crew watched the figures slowly, silently drifting. They must be screaming for help, Nodon thought. Beseeching us for mercy. Yet we will not hear them.

At last Fuchs broke the silence. "One-third g acceleration," he ordered. "Back on our original course. Let's find a real logistics ship and fill up our supplies."

"But . . ."

"They're mercenaries," Fuchs snapped. "Hired killers. They came out here to kill us. Now they'll be dead. It's no great loss."

Nodon's face still showed his desolation. "But they'll die. They'll float out there . . . forever."

"Think of it this way," Fuchs said, his voice iron-hard. "We've added a few more minor asteroids to the Belt."

SELENE: ASTRO CORPORATION HEADQUARTERS

S abotaged." Pancho knew it was true, even though she did not want to believe it.

Doug Stavenger looked grim. He sat tensely before Pancho's desk, wearing light tan slacks and a micromesh pullover. Only the slight sparkling in the air around him betrayed the fact that his image was a hologram; otherwise he looked as solid and real as if he were actually in Pancho's office, instead of his own office, up in one of the towers that supported the Main Plaza's dome.

"It could have been worse," he said. "A solar storm broke out just hours after you were rescued. We had to suspend all surface operations because of the radiation. If it had come a little earlier you would have fried out there in the cable car."

"Nobody can predict solar flares that fine," Pancho said.

"No, I suppose not."

"But—sabotage?" she repeated.

"That's what our investigation showed," Stavenger replied. "Whoever did it wasn't even very subtle about it. They used an explosive charge to knock out the trolley wheels that the cable car rides on. The blast damaged one of the poles, too."

Pancho leaned both elbows on her desk. "Doug, are you telling me we've got terrorists in Selene now?"

Stavenger shook his head. "I don't believe so."

"But who would want to knock out a cable car? That's the kind of random violence a terrorist would do. Or a nutcase."

"Or an assassin."

Pancho's insides clenched. There it was. The same conclusion her own security people had swiftly come to. Yet she heard herself ask, "Assassin?"

"Selene's security investigators think somebody was trying to kill you, Pancho."

And twenty-three other people who happened to be aboard the car, she added silently.

Stavenger asked, "What do your own security people think?"

"Exactly the same," she replied.

"I'm not surprised," said Stavenger.

"Neither am I, I guess," she said. Then she admitted, "I just didn't want to believe that he'd try to kill me."

"He?"

"Humphries. Who else?"

And she remembered their exchange at Humphries's party:

"Why don't you retire gracefully, Pancho, and let me take my rightful place as chairman of the Astro board?"

"In your dreams, Martin."

"Then I'll just have to find some other way to take control of Astro."

"Over my dead body."

"Remember, you said that, Pancho. I didn't."

The sonofabitch! Pancho thought.

Stavenger took a deep breath. "I don't want you fighting here in Selene."

Pancho understood his meaning. If Astro and Humphries are going to war, let it be out in the Belt.

"Doug," she said earnestly, "I don't want a war. I thought we had ended all that eight years ago."

"So had I."

"The sumbitch wants control of Astro, and he knows I won't step aside and let him take over."

"Pancho," said Stavenger wearily, rubbing a hand across his eyes, "Humphries wants control of the Belt and all its resources. That seems clear."

"And if he gets the Belt, he'll have control of the whole solar system. And everybody in it."

"Including Selene."

Pancho nodded. "Including Selene."

"I can't allow that to happen."

"So what're you going to do about it, Doug?"

He spread his hands in a gesture of uncertainty. "That's just it, Pancho. I don't know what I can do. Humphries isn't trying to take political control of Selene. He's after economic power. He knows that if he controls the resources of the Belt, he'll have Selene and everyone else under his thumb. He can let us continue to govern ourselves. But we'll have to buy our water and most of our other raw materials from him."

Pancho shook her head. Once Selene had been virtually self-sufficient, mining water from the deposits of ice at the lunar poles, and using the raw materials scraped from the Moon's surface layers of regolith. Selene even exported fusion fuels to Earth and supplied the aluminum and silicon for building solar power satellites in Earth orbit.

But once Selene's government decided to allow limited immigration from the devastated Earth, the lunar nation's self-sufficiency ended. Selene became dependent on the metals and minerals, even the water, imported from the asteroids. And the trickle of immigration from Earth had become an ever-increasing stream, Pancho knew.

"What're you going to do?" Pancho repeated.

Looking decidedly unhappy, Stavenger said, "I'll have a talk with Humphries. Not that it'll do much good, I expect."

Pancho heard his unspoken words. It's up to me to stop Humphries, she realized. I've got to fight him. Nobody else can.

"Okay," she said to Stavenger. "You talk. I'll act."

"No fighting here," Stavenger snapped. "Not here."

"Not here, Doug," Pancho promised. Already in her head she was starting to figure how much it would cost to go to war against Humphries Space Systems out in the Asteroid Belt.

Flying in the rattling, roaring helicopter from SeaTac Aerospaceport, the Asian-American who had been assigned to make certain that Pancho Lane survived the sabotage of the cable car looked forward to returning to his home in the mountains of Washington State's Olympic peninsula. His family would be waiting for him, he knew. So would the fat stipend from Yamagata Corporation.

The helicopter touched down on the cleared gravel area at the foot of the path that led up to his cabin. Strangely, no one was there to greet him. Surely his wife and children heard the copter's throbbing engines. He walked to the edge of the helipad, clutching his travel bag in one hand, squinting in the miniature sandstorm of gravel and grit from the helicopter's swirling rotors.

From the gravel pad he could see downslope to the drowned city of Port Townsend and the cluster of scuba-diving camps huddled around it. On a clear day, he could gaze through binoculars at the shattered remains of Seattle's high-rise towers poking up above the waters of Puget Sound.

It had been a curious assignment, he thought. Fly to the Moon as a tourist—at a cost that would have emptied his life savings—and ride in a certain cable car at a certain time, carrying emergency survival equipment to make certain that Ms. Lane would not be killed by the "accident."

He shrugged his heavy shoulders as he watched the helicopter dwindle into the cloudy sky, then turned and headed up the winding path toward his home.

He never saw his wife and children, who lay in their bloody beds, each of them shot through the head. Two men grabbed him as he stepped through the front door of his cabin and put a gun to his temple. By the time the local police arrived on the scene, several days later, it seemed obvious to them that the man had slaughtered his family and then committed suicide.

"He must've gone nuts," said the police chief. "It happens. A guy just snaps, for no apparent reason."

Case closed.

At Selene, the maintenance technician who had planted the tiny explosive device that knocked the car off its cable was also found dead: of an overdose of narcotics. His papers showed that although he was an employee of Selene's maintenance department, he had recently received a sizeable amount of money from some unknown benefactor. The money was untraceable; apparently he had used it to buy the drugs that killed him.

Rumors quickly bruited through Selene that the money had come from Humphries Space Systems. There was no hint that it had actually been provided by Yamagata Corporation.

HUMPHRIES MANSION

Somebody tried to kill Pancho?" Martin Humphries could barely hide his elation. "You mean there's somebody else who wants that guttersnipe offed?"

Grigor Malenkovich was not smiling. Humphries sometimes wondered if the man knew how to smile. The chief of HSS's security department, Grigor was a lean, silent man with thinning dark hair combed straight back from his forehead, and dark, probing eyes. He said little, and moved like a furtive shadow. He habitually wore suits of slate gray. He could fade into a crowd and remain unnoticed by all except the most discerning eye. Humphries thought of him as the ultimate bureaucrat, functioning quietly, obeying any order without question, as inconspicuous as a mouse, as dangerous as a plague bacillus.

He stood before Humphries's desk, sallow-faced, humorless.

"You are being blamed for the attempt on her life," he said, his voice low and soft as a lullaby.

"Me?"

Grigor nodded wordlessly.

"I didn't order her killed," Humphries snapped. "If you freelanced this—"

"Not me," said Grigor. "Nor anyone in my department."

"Then who?"

Grigor shrugged.

"Find out," Humphries commanded. "I want to know who tried to kill Pancho. Maybe I'll give him a reward."

"This is not funny, sir," Grigor replied. "An order has gone out from Astro Corporation headquarters to arm Astro's vessels in the Belt."

Humphries could feel his cheeks flush with anger. "That damned greasemonkey! She wants a war, does she?"

"Apparently she believes that you want one."

Humphries drummed his fingers on his desktop. "I don't," he said at last. "But if she wants to fight, by god I'll flatten her! No matter what it costs!"

Long after Grigor had left his office, Humphries's phone said in its synthesized voice, "Incoming call from Douglas Stavenger."

Humphries glared at the phone's blinking amber light. "Tell him I'm not available at present. Take his message."

Humphries knew what Stavenger's message would be. He wants to be the peacemaker again, just as he was eight years ago. But not this time, Humphries decided. Pancho wants to go to war, and I'm going to accommodate her. I'll get rid of her and take control of Astro in one swoop.

What was it that German said, he wondered silently, the guy who wrote about war? Then he remembered: War is a continuation of politics by other means.

Other means. Humphries smiled, alone in his office, and told his phone to instruct Grigor to contact that mercenary, Dorik Harbin. He's a one-man Mongol horde, Humphries remembered. A madman, when he's high on drugs. Time to get him onto Pancho's trail.

Amanda kept her eyes closed and her breathing deep and regular. Humphries lay beside her in their sumptuous bedroom, twitching slightly in his sleep. Nightmares again, she thought. He's such a powerful and commanding person all day long, demanding and imperious, but when he sleeps he whimpers like a whipped little boy.

She couldn't hate Martin Humphries. The man was driven by inner demons that he allowed no one to see, not even his wife. He was alone in his torments, and he kept a high wall of separation around the deepset fears that haunted his dreams. Even his sexual excesses were driven by a desperate need to prove himself master of his world. He says he does it to excite me, Amanda told herself, but we both know it's really to control me, to make me obey him, to prove that he's my master.

At least that's ended, she thought. For the time being. He won't do anything that might harm my baby.

If he knew it wasn't his. If he knew this life growing inside me is Lars's son, Martin would kill me and the child both. He mustn't know! He mustn't find out!

It had been simple enough to hack into Humphries's medical records and replace his genetic profile with Lars's. Amanda had done that herself, no accomplices, no chance of anyone revealing to her husband what she had done. To the doctors and medical technicians in Humphries's employ the baby's genetic profile seemed consistent with those of its parents. And it was.

Yet she knew it would be bad enough, once the baby was born. Humphries wanted a perfect child, healthy and intelligent. His six-year-old son was like that: bright, athletic, talented, strong.

The baby Amanda was carrying would not be so.

"It's a rather minor defect," the doctor had told her, after her examination at the Hell medical center. The somber expression on his face said it was worse than minor. "Thank god that the genetic screening revealed it. We can prepare for it and take steps to control his condition."

A minor genetic defect. The baby would be born with a form of chronic anemia. "It can be controlled with proper medication," said the doctor, trying to reassure Amanda. "Or we could replace the defective gene, if you choose to undergo the procedure."

They could operate on the fetus while it's in my womb, Amanda was told. But that would mean a major medical procedure and I'd never be able to keep that secret from Martin. Just getting the genetic screening tests done was difficult enough. If it weren't for Doug Stavenger's help I wouldn't have been able to do it.

"It might be just a random mutation," said the doctor, trying to look optimistic. "Or perhaps there was some chromosomal damage due to the zygote's long immersion in liquid nitrogen. We just don't know enough about the long-term effects of cryogenic temperatures."

It's the drugs, she knew. All those years and all those uppers and aphrodisiacs and designer specials. They must have done the damage, carried to the poor helpless embryo through my bloodstream. My son will pay for my weakness.

So the baby will be born with chronic anemia, Amanda thought. Martin will just have to accept that. He'll be unhappy about it, but he'll have to accept it. As long as he believes it's his son he'll do whatever is necessary for the baby.

The doctor had hesitated and stammered until he finally worked up the courage to suggest, "There's nanotechnology, of course, should you choose to use it. It's banned on Earth, and I couldn't recommend it there. But here on the Moon you might be able to use nanotherapy to correct the baby's faulty gene. And your own."

Amanda thanked him for being so open. But she knew that nanotherapy was impossible for her. Martin would find out about it. Not even Doug Stavenger could keep it a secret if she went to the nanotech lab in Selene. The news that Martin Humphries's wife wanted nano-therapy for her unborn child would flash to Martin's ears with the speed of light.

The only nanotechnologist Amanda could trust was Kris Cardenas, and she'd been living in Ceres for years in self-imposed exile from Selene. Now she was on the Saturn mission, going even farther away. No, nanotherapy is out, Amanda swiftly decided. I've got to handle this without using nanotech.

I've got to protect my baby, she said to herself as she lay in the darkness next to her sleeping, dreaming husband. I've got to protect him from Martin.

Which means I've got to live through the birth. Unconsciously, Amanda clenched her fists. Women don't die in childbirth. That hasn't happened in years, not in a century or more. Not in a modern medical facility. Not even women with weak hearts.

She had known that the years of living in low-gravity environments had taken a toll on her heart. All those years living in Ceres, practically zero gravity. Even here on the Moon it's only one-sixth g. Bad for the heart. Deconditions the muscles. It's so easy to enjoy low g and let yourself go.

Amanda had exercised regularly, mainly to keep her figure. Martin had married a beautiful woman and Amanda worked hard over the years to remain youthfully attractive. But it wasn't enough to strengthen her heart.

"Perhaps you should consider aborting this pregnancy," the doctor had suggested, as tentatively as a man suggesting heresy to a bishop. "Work to get your heart into proper condition and then try to have a baby again."

"No," Amanda had replied softly. "I can't do that."

The doctor had thought she had religious scruples. "I know abortion is a serious issue," he had told her. "But even the Catholics permit it now, as long as it's not simply to terminate an illegitimate pregnancy. I can provide medical justification—"

"Thank you," Amanda had said, "but no. I can't."

"I see." The doctor had sighed like a patient father faced with an intractable child. "All right, then we can use an auxiliary heart pump during the delivery."

It's very simple, he had explained. Standard procedure. A temporary ventricular assist pump, a slim balloon on the end of a catheter is inserted into the femoral artery in the thigh and worked up into the lower aorta. It provides extra cardiovascular pumping power, takes some of the workload off the heart during labor.

Amanda had nodded. When I go for my prenatal checkup at the hospital here in Selene, they'll find out about my heart and make the same recommendation. Martin will know about it but that's perfectly all right.

He'll call in the best cardiovascular experts. That's fine, too. As long as no one realizes I've switched Martin's genetic profile for Lars's. That's what I've got to avoid. Martin thinks his genes are perfect. He's got a six-year-old son to prove it.

We've already done a genetic screen on me, of course. I passed that test. It's just the baby, my poor helpless little baby, that has a problem.

I've got to make certain that Martin doesn't know. He mustn't find out.

Amanda lay in her bed for hours while Humphries thrashed and moaned in his sleep next to her. She stared at the darkened ceiling, watched the digital clock count the minutes and hours. At last, well after four A.M., still wide awake, she sat up and softly slipped out of bed. On bare feet she tiptoed across the thick carpeting past the lavatory, into the walk-in closet that was lined with the finest clothes money could buy. Only after she had gently closed the closet door did she grope for the light switch on the wall. Months earlier she had disconnected the sensor that automatically turned on the overhead lights. Squinting in the sudden brightness, she stepped deeper into the closet, ignoring the gowns and frocks and slacks and precious blouses. She went to one of the leather handbags hanging in the rear of the closet and, after rummaging in it for a few moments, came out with a handful of soft blue gelatin capsules.

Tranquilizers, Amanda told herself. They're nothing more than good, strong tranquilizers. I need them, if I want to get any sleep at all. She stared at the capsules in her palm; her hand was shaking so hard she feared she would drop them. She closed her fingers around them. They won't hurt the baby. They can't, that's what the chemist told me. And I need them. I need them badly.

ASTEROID VESTA

Dorik Harbin hid the discomfort he felt from all the others, but he could not hide it from himself. A man who preferred solitude, a lone wolf who tracked his prey silently, without help, he now was in command of nearly five hundred men and women, mercenaries hired by Humphries for the coming assault against Astro Corporation.

Most of them were engineers and technicians, not warriors. They were building a base on Vesta, burrowing deep into the asteroid's rocky body, tunneling out hardened silos to hold missiles that could blast approaching ships out of the sky. Harbin remembered HSS's first attempt to build a base on Vesta's surface. Fuchs had wiped it out with a single blow, dropping a freighter's load of asteroidal ores that smashed buildings and people in a deadly avalanche of falling rocks.

So now we dig, Harbin said to himself as he glided down one of the dusty tunnels toward the smoothed-out cave that would be his headquarters. He wore a real uniform now, complete with epaulets on his shoulders and an uncomfortable high choke of a collar. And insignias of rank. Harbin was a colonel now, with four-pointed stars at his throat and cuffs to show it. The emblems disturbed Harbin. They reminded him of crosses. He'd seen too many crosses over the years, in churches and more often in cemeteries.

Humphries paid someone to design these stupid uniforms, he knew. He also knew that a man's ability to command comes from what is in his head and in his guts, not from fancy uniforms and polished boots.

But Humphries pays the bills, Grigor constantly reminded him. And Humphries is in a sweat to complete this base and begin the assault that will wipe Astro out of the Belt.

But Fuchs is still out there, somewhere, hiding himself deep in the dark emptiness of the Belt. It's a mistake to stop hunting him, Harbin thought. Humphries thinks that once he's eliminated Astro, Fuchs will fall into his lap easily enough. But I wonder. The man is wily, tough, a survivor. He's dangerous, too dangerous to be permitted to live.

Despite its being the third-largest of all the asteroids, Vesta is still only slightly more than five hundred kilometers across. Its gravity is minuscule. Harbin and all the others working inside the tunnels and caves had to wear uncomfortable breathing masks and goggles clamped to their faces constantly because every step they took stirred up fine powdery dust that hung in the air endlessly, floating in the infinitesimal gravity like an eternal, everlasting mist. Still, the people he passed as he glided along the tunnel all snapped salutes at the stars on his uniform. Harbin dutifully returned each salute even though he loathed the necessity.

At least his office was clean. It was a small chamber carved by plasma torches out of the metallic rock and then sprayed with thick layers of plastic to hold down the dust. With the air blowers working, Harbin could take off his goggled mask and breathe normally once the door to the tunnel outside was shut.

The office was little more than a bare cubicle containing a desk and a few chairs. No decorations on the walls. Nothing to remind Harbin of his past. Even the desk drawers were mostly empty, except for the locked one that contained his medications. He slumped tiredly onto his desk chair and commanded his computer to display the day's incoming messages. I shouldn't be sitting behind a desk, he told himself. I should be in a ship, tracking down Fuchs. It's a mistake to let him live.

Then he smiled bitterly at himself. Not that I've been so successful at getting him. Fuchs is a wily old badger, Harbin admitted to himself. Almost, he admired the man.

The list of incoming messages took form in the air above Harbin's desk. Most of them were routine, but there was one from Grigor, Harbin's direct superior in the HSS chain of command, the only man between him and Martin Humphries himself.

Harbin told the computer to display Grigor's message.

Grigor's gloomy image appeared immediately. He was seated at his own desk. It was as if Harbin were looking into the man's office. To his surprise, the dour, cold-eyed chief of HSS security was actually smiling; it looked as if it pained him to stretch his thin lips that way.

"I have good news for you, Dorik," said Grigor, almost jovially. "A dozen attack ships are on their way to you, plus supply and logistics vessels. They are not sailing together, of course. That would attract unwelcome attention from Astro and even from the International Astronautical

Authority. But they will start arriving at your base within the week. A detailed schedule of their courses, cargoes and arrival times are attached to this message."

Harbin stopped Grigor's message and checked the attachment. Impressive. Within two weeks he would have a small armada of warships, ready to ravage the Belt.

He turned Grigor back on. "From the reports you've been sending, I can see that the base will be fully operational within three weeks or less. Mr. Humphries wants to make absolutely certain that the base is protected properly. He wants to take no chances that Fuchs or anyone else will attack it before it is completed. Therefore, you are to use the attack vessels as a defensive screen around Vesta. Keep them in orbit around the asteroid and keep them on high alert, prepared to intercept any unauthorized vessel. Is that clear?"

The question was rhetorical, of course. Harbin wouldn't be able to get a reply to Grigor at Selene for a half-hour or more.

"One final order," Grigor went on, without waiting for a reply. "Once the entire battle fleet has been assembled, you will hold it in readiness until an attack plan is sent to you through me. Mr. Humphries wants no moves made until he has approved a complete campaign plan."

Then Grigor smiled again, obviously forced. "Of course, we will expect your inputs for the plan. We won't finalize it until you have made your contribution."

The image winked off and Harbin was staring at the empty chairs in front of his desk once again.

"A plan of campaign," he muttered to himself. Humphries thinks he's a field marshal now, planning battle strategy. Harbin groaned inwardly. He's amassing all these weapons, all these people, and he's sitting back in the safety of that underground mansion of his, playing armchair general. I'll have to follow his orders, no matter how stupid they might be.

Harbin scrupulously avoided sexual liaisons with any of the people under his command. A commander doesn't take advantage of his troops, he told himself sternly. Besides, he had medications and virtual reality simulations that satisfied his needs, in part. In some ways they were better than sex; he didn't have to deal with a real, living person. Better to be alone, he told himself. Better to avoid entanglements.

Yet there was one slim young woman among the engineering staff who attracted him. She looked almost Asian, but not quite: tall, willowy, soft of speech, her skin smooth and the color of burnt gold, with high sculpted cheekbones and almond eyes that he caught, several times, watching him through lowered lashes.

She reminded him of someone, someone he had taken months of rehabilitation treatments to forget. Someone who haunted the edges of his dreams, a woman that not even his drugs could erase completely from his memory. A woman who had claimed to love him, a woman who had betrayed him. A woman he had murdered, ripping the lying tongue out of her throat with his bare hands.

Harbin woke nights sobbing over her. And now this Eurasian engineer watched him furtively when they were in the same room together, smiled at him seductively when he caught her staring at him.

Harbin tried to ignore her, but he couldn't. Over the weeks and months of building the base, he could not avoid her. And every time he saw her, she smiled and watched him in silence, as if waiting for him to smile back at her, to speak to her, to ask her what her name was or where she was born or why she was here on this godforsaken outpost in the depths of nothingness.

Instead of speaking to her, Harbin brought up her personnel dossier on his office computer. Her name was Leeza Chaptal, born in Selene, her father a French medical doctor, her mother a Japanese-American biologist. She herself was a life-support engineer, and had a year-to-year contract with Humphries Space Systems. She had not volunteered for this job at Vesta; she had been faced with accepting the position or being fired for breach of contract.

She's not happy here, Harbin thought, scanning her dossier. Yet she seems pleasant enough. Her supervisor rates her work highly, he saw.

It wasn't until his phone buzzed that Harbin realized he'd been staring at her dossier photograph for more than fifteen minutes.

HUMPHRIES'S DREAMS

He was a child again, being led by the hand through the majestic marble-walled building where people stood in quiet little groups gazing at the pictures on the walls and speaking in hushed murmurs. The paintings meant nothing to him, nor did the names that his tutor whispered to him: da Vinci, Raphael, Degas, Renoir. Then he saw the picture of the beautiful sailboats gliding across a calm blue sea beneath the summer sun. When he refused to leave it, his tutor sniffed, "Monet. Quite overly popular."

Suddenly it was Christmas, and instead of the painting he wanted, his father presented him with a new computer. When he started to cry with disappointment, his father loomed over him and said sternly, "You can look at all the paintings you want through the web."

And then he was on the boat, the trimaran, and the storm was coming up fast and the boat was heaving wickedly in the monstrous waves and one of the waves broke over the bow and swept him off his feet. He felt the numbing cold water clutching at him, dragging him under, while his father watched from the tossing deck, his arms folded sternly across his chest, his face set in a scowl of disappointment. He doesn't care if I drown! young Martin realized as he thrashed helplessly in the icy water. He doesn't care if I live or die.

"That was foolish of you, Marty," his father growled at him after a crewman had fished him out of the ocean. "Nine years old and you still don't have the brains that god gave to a rabbit."

Martin Humphries, aged nine, dripping wet and shivering with cold, understood from that moment onward that he had no one on Earth to protect him, no one to help him, no one that could ever love him. Not even his mother, drunk most of the time, gave a damn about him. He was alone, except for what and who he could buy.

"This is a dream," he told himself. "This all happened long ago. Mother's been dead for ages and father died years ago. It's all over. He can't humiliate you anymore."

But others could. He saw himself at the board meeting of the Astro Corporation, everyone seated at the long table staring at him.

Sitting at the head of the table in the chairman's seat to which she'd just been elected, Pancho Lane was pointing her accusing finger at him.

"How long are we going to allow the head of our biggest rival to sit on our board of directors?" she demanded. "How long are we going to let Judas sit among us? All he wants is to take control of Astro Corporation, and he'll keep on screwing us every chance he gets, if we don't get rid of him here and now."

The vote was close, but not close enough.

"That's it, then," said Pancho, barely able to conceal the satisfied smirk that played at the corners of her lips. "Martin, you've been kicked off this board. And high time, too."

He saw how white his face was, how his hands trembled no matter how hard he struggled to control them. The others tried to hide their emotions, but he could see they were secretly laughing at him. All of them, even the ones he had thought were on his side.

Feeling cold sweat beading his forehead, his upper lip, he rose shakily to his feet, the blood thundering in his ears, his mind pulsing with ringing, defiant declarations.

But all he could manage to choke out was, "You haven't seen the last of me."

As he stumbled out of the richly carpeted boardroom he could hear muffled laughter behind his back. I'll get them, he swore to himself. Each and every one of them. Especially Pancho, that guttersnipe. I'll get her if it takes every penny, every ounce of sweat, every drop of blood that I've got. I'll get her. I'll see her dead. I'll dance on her grave.

HABITAT *CHRYSALIS*

ig George was at the airlock to greet her when Pancho left her private torch ship *Starpower III* and stepped aboard the rock rats' habitat in orbit about Ceres.

"Welcome to our humble home," George said, with an exaggerated flourish.

Pancho grinned at him. "Good to be here, Georgie. Gonna give me the ten-dollar tour?"

"Sure will."

George led her almost halfway through the rotating complex of connected spacecraft bodies. Pancho enjoyed teasing George about how the habitat looked like a floating junkyard, but once inside the linked vessels she had to admit that the habitat was clean, comfortable, and even attractive. Each interconnected craft was painted in a distinctive color scheme, mostly restful pastels, although there were some bolder, brighter hues here and there, and striking designs decorating some of the bulkheads. The place smelled new, fresh, a far cry from the dust-choked caves and tunnels of Ceres.

As they stepped through the hatches from one spacecraft to another, George proudly showed Pancho the living quarters, common rooms, laboratories, workshops, warehouses and business offices that made up the growing complex.

"Got nearly a thousand people livin' here now," he declared, "with more comin' every week."

"I'm impressed," Pancho said. "I really am. You guys've done a terrific job."

George smiled boyishly behind his thick red beard.

The tour ended at a closed metal door marked NANOTECH LAB. Pancho felt a pang of hopeful surprise.

"Don't tell me Kris is back!"

"Nah," George replied, tapping out the combination on the door's security keypad. "Dr. Cardenas is still off on the Saturn expedition."

As he pushed the door open he added, "But she's not the only nanotech genius in the world, y'know. We've got a few of our own, right here."

The nanotechnology lab was eerily quiet. Pancho saw gleaming cabinets of white and stainless steel lining the walls, and a double row of workbenches that held more metal boxes and instruments. She recognized the gray metal tubing of a scanning field microscope off in one corner, but the rest of the equipment was unfamiliar to her.

"Is anybody working here?" she asked. The lab seemed empty of people, except for the two of them.

"Should be," George said, frowning slightly. "I told 'im we'd be here."

"Excuse me," said a soft voice behind them.

Pancho turned to see an overweight young man with dark hair tied back in a ponytail, a neatly trimmed beard, and a slightly bemused expression on his roundish face. His thick dark brows were raised, as if he were puzzled. His lips were curled slightly into a half smile that seemed apologetic, defensive. He was wearing plain gray coveralls, but had a bright plaid vest over them. No tattoos or jewelry, except for a heavy square gold ring on his right hand.

"I had to take a break," he said in a gentle, almost feminine voice. "I'm sorry I wasn't here when you came in."

George clapped him on the shoulder lightly, but it was enough to make the young man totter. "That's okay, Lev. When you gotta go, you gotta go."

He introduced Pancho to Levi Levinson, then added, "Lev here's from MIT. Brightest lad we've got. Boy genius and all that."

Levinson didn't seem at all embarrassed by George's praise. "I learned a lot from Dr. Cardenas before she left."

"Such as?" Pancho challenged.

Levinson's smile turned slightly superior. "I'll show you. I've got a demonstration all set up." He gestured toward the nearer of the two workbenches.

George dragged over a couple of high stools and offered one to Pancho as he explained, "I was after Kris for years to figure out how we could use nanomachines to separate metals from the ores in the asteroids. Lev here thinks he's solved the problem."

Pancho felt impressed. Turning to Levinson, she asked, "Have you?"
He looked quietly confident, almost smug. All he said was, "Watch."

Pancho watched. Levinson took a dark, lumpy, potato-sized chunk of a metallic asteroid and deposited it into one of the big metal cubicles on the workbench. Half a dozen transparent plastic tubes led from the container to smaller bins farther down the bench. Pancho saw that a digital timer started counting seconds when Levinson clicked the lid closed.

"It's not much of a trick to program nanomachines to separate a specific element from a gross sample," he said. "Nanos are quite capable of taking specific atoms from a sample of material. It's just a matter of programming them properly."

"Uh-huh," said Pancho.

"The problem's always been to separate *all* the different elements in a 'roid simultaneously, without the nanos interfering with one another."

"And in a high-UV environment," George added.

Levinson shrugged his rounded shoulders. "That part was easy. Just harden the nanos so UV won't dissociate them."

Pointing to the sealed container, Pancho asked, "You mean these nanomachines won't be knocked out by ultraviolet light?"

"That's why I keep them sealed inside the container," Levinson answered. "If they got loose they'd start taking the habitat apart, atom by atom."

"Jeeps," Pancho muttered.

"It's perfectly safe," Levinson calmly assured her. "The container is lined with diamond surfaces and none of the nanos are programmed to separate carbon."

"So they can't attack people," George said.

Levinson nodded, but Pancho thought that people also contain iron, phosphorus and a lot of other elements that those nanomachines were programmed to separate. Maybe that's why Kris dragged her feet on this project, she thought.

A bell pinged. An electric motor whirred. Pancho saw little trickles of what looked like dirt or dust sliding down the six transparent tubes toward the bins on the workbench. As she looked closer, though, several of the growing piles seemed to glitter in the light from the overhead lamps.

"The transport tubes are also pure diamond," Levinson said. "Just a precaution, in case a few of the nanomachines are still present in the differentiated samples."

Pancho nodded wordlessly.

Levinson applied a handheld mass spectrometer to each of the piles of dirt, in turn. Pure iron, pure nickel, gold, silver, platinum and lead.

With a wave of one hand, he said, "Voila!"

George clapped his beefy hands together. "Y'see, Pancho? With nanomachines we can mine the metals outta the 'roids easy as pie. All the slugwork gets done by the nanos. All the miners hafta do is sit back and let the little buggers do all the fookin' work!"

"It can be done for minerals, too," Levinson said, in an offhand manner. "Easier, in fact. The nanos work at the molecular level there, rather than atomic."

Pancho looked at each of them in turn. She stood up and planted her hands on her hips. "Fine work," she said. "Only one problem I can see."

"What's that?"

"This'll knock the price of metals and minerals down pretty close to zero."

"Huh?" George grunted.

"You're gonna make it so easy to mine the asteroids that we'll get a glut on the market," Pancho said. "And most of the miners will be thrown out of work, to boot."

George frowned. "I didn't think of that. I was just tryin' t'make their work easier."

"Too easy," said Pancho.

Levinson looked completely unconcerned. "New technology always brings some economic dislocations. But think of the benefits of cheaper raw materials."

"Yeah, sure," said Pancho. Then it hit her with the force of a body blow. "Holy cripes! Once Humphries finds out about this there's gonna be hell to pay!"

"Whattaya mean?" George asked.

"Once this nanotechnology starts being used, there won't be room for two competing companies in the Belt. The only way to make economic sense out of this is for one company to run the whole damned Belt, keep production of raw materials under control and set prices for the buyers. *That's* what he's after!"

"But Humphries doesn't know anything about this," George said.

"Wanna bet?" Pancho snapped.

HUMPHRIES MANSION

I t really works?" Humphries asked. "They've done it?"

"It really works," said Victoria Ferrer, his latest administrative assistant. "Their top nanotech expert, this man Levinson, demonstrated it to Ms. Lane two days ago. She's on her way back here with him now."

Ferrer was a small, light-boned young woman with large, limpid eyes, full sensuous lips and lovely large breasts. When he had first interviewed her for the job, Humphries had wondered if her breasts were siliconed. They seemed oversized for the rest of her. Soon enough he found that they were natural, although enhanced by a genetic modification that Victoria's stagestruck mother had insisted upon when she was pushing her teenaged daughter into a career in show business. Young Vickie went to university instead, and earned honors in economics and finance. Eventually Humphries learned that, as good as Victoria was in bed, she was even better in the office. Ferrer's best asset, he eventually realized, was her brain. But that didn't prevent Humphries from bedding her now and then.

At the moment, though, she was bringing him disturbing news about the nanotechnology work going on at the rock rats' habitat in the Belt.

"That tears it," he said thoughtfully, leaning back in his self-adjusting desk chair. "I should have seen it coming. It's going to knock the bottom out of the market for asteroidal commodities."

"Not necessarily," said Ferrer. She was seated in the plush chair in front of his desk, looking very trim and businesslike in a tailored off-white blouse and charcoal gray slacks.

His brows knitting, Humphries said, "Don't you see? Once they start using nanomachines to get pure metals out of the asteroids, the price for those metals will sink out of sight. Minerals, too. Same thing. The major price factor will be the cost of transportation."

"Only if the rock rats actually use nanos," Ferrer countered.

Humphries sat up a little straighter. "You think they won't?"

With a slight smile, she replied, "I think Ambrose is smart enough to realize that nanomachines could throw most of the miners out of work. I think he'll suppress the idea."

"Buy off the scientist? What's his name, this kid from MIT."

"Levinson," said Ferrer. "I doubt that he can be bought off. He's the kind who'll want the whole world to know how brilliant he is. But Ambrose and the rest of the governing council at Ceres could easily claim that nanomachines are too dangerous to use on the asteroids."

"That sounds farfetched."

She shook her head, just slightly, but enough to let Humphries see that she thought he was wrong. "To operate on the asteroids the nanos would have to be hardened against ultraviolet light. That means the main safety feature that Cardenas built into the nanos years ago would be disabled. Ambrose could argue that the nanos are too dangerous to use."

"And let the rock rats keep on operating the way they have been since the beginning."

"Exactly."

Humphries drummed his fingers on the desktop. "That would avoid a collapse of the market."

"Which is to the rock rats' best interests."

"Sort of like the Luddites smashing the steam-powered looms, back at the beginning of the first industrial revolution."

Ferrer looked puzzled for a moment, and Humphries smiled inwardly. Score one for the boss, he said to himself. I know more than you do.

Aloud, he asked, "You really think Ambrose and the others will suppress this?"

"My information is that he and Ms. Lane have already discussed it. I'm sure he will."

"And use safety precautions as the excuse."

"It's a very good excuse."

Humphries glanced up at the ceiling's smooth cream-colored expanse, then at the holowindow on the far wall that displayed a view of Mount Kilimanjaro when it still had snow on its summit.

"Doesn't matter," he said at last. "In the long run, this development of nanotech mining will be the last straw. I've got to get control of Astro *now*, before that greasemonkey Pancho realizes she can use the nanomachines to undercut my prices and—"

"But if Astro starts using nanomachines for mining the asteroids," Ferrer interrupted, "we could do the same."

"Yeah, and drive the price for asteroidal commodities down to nothing, or close to it," Humphries snapped. "No, I've got to get Astro into my hands now, no more delays or hesitations. Once I've got Astro we can use nanomachines to drive down the cost of mining, but we'll have a monopoly in the damned Belt so we can fix the selling prices!"

Ferrer started to nod, then thought better of it. "What about this new company, Nairobi Industries?"

"They don't have anything going in the Belt."

"They might move that way, eventually."

Humphries made a snorting, dismissive laugh. "By the time they get their base built here on the Moon and start thinking about expanding to the Belt, I'll have the whole thing in my hands. They'll be shut out before they even start."

She looked dubious, but said nothing.

Humphries smacked his hands together. "Okay! The gloves come off. All the preparations are in place. We knock Astro out of the Belt once and for all."

Ferrer still looked less than enthusiastic. She rose from her chair and started for the door.

Before she got halfway across the office, though, Humphries said, "Tell Grigor I want to see him. In half an hour. No, make it a full hour."

And he crooked his finger at her. Dutifully, she turned around and headed back to him.

TORCH SHIP *STARPOWER III*

L ike most torch ships, *Starpower III* was built like a dumbbell, bulbous propellant tanks on one end of a kilometer-long buckyball tether, habitation module on the other, with the fusion rocket engine in the center. The ship spun lazily on the ends of the long tether, producing a feeling of gravity for the crew and passengers.

Pancho's quarters aboard her personal torch ship were comfortable, not sumptuous. The habitation module included the crew's quarters, the bridge, work spaces and storage areas, as well as Pancho's private quarters plus two more compartments for guests.

Pancho was afraid that her lone guest on this trip from Ceres to Selene would become obstreperous. Levi Levinson was flattered almost out of his mind when Pancho told him she wanted to bring him to Selene to meet the top scientists there. "Two of 'em are on the Nobel committee," Pancho had said, with complete truthfulness and a good deal of artful suggestion.

Levinson had immediately packed a travel bag and accompanied her to the torch ship.

Now, though, as they approached Selene, Pancho broke the unpleasant news to him. She invited him to dinner in her private quarters and watched with secret amusement as he goggled at the array of food spread on the table between them by the ship's two galley servers.

"You've made a terrific scientific breakthrough," she told Levinson, once the servers had left. "But I'm not sure the rock rats are gonna take advantage of it."

Levinson's normal expression reminded Pancho of a deer caught in an automobile's headlights. Now his brows shot even higher than usual.

"Not take advantage of it?" he asked, a spoonful of soup trembling halfway between the bowl and his mouth. "What do you mean?"

Pancho had spent most of the day talking with Big George via a tight-beam laser link. George had hammered it out with the rock rats' governing council. They were dead-set against using *anything* that would drop the prices of the ores they mined.

"Fookin' prices are low enough," George had growled. "We'll all go broke if they drop much more."

Now Pancho looked into Levinson's questioning eyes and decided to avoid the truth. The kid's worked his butt off to make this breakthrough, she told herself, and now you've got to tell him it was all for nothing.

"It's the safety problem," she temporized. "The rock rats are worried about using nanos that can't be disabled by ultraviolet light."

Levinson blinked, slurped his soup, then put the spoon back into the bowl. "I suppose some other safety features could be built into the system," he said.

"You think so?"

"Trouble is, the nanos have to work in a high radiation environment. They've got to be hardened."

"And that makes them dangerous," said Pancho.

"Not really."

"The miners think so."

Levinson took a deep, distressed breath. "But if they handle the nanos properly there shouldn't be any problems."

Pancho smiled at him like a mother. "Lev, they're miners. Rock rats. Sure, most of 'em have technical degrees, but they're not scientists like you."

"I could work out protocols for them," he mumbled, half to himself. "Safety procedures for them to follow."

"Maybe you could," Pancho said vaguely.

He stared down into his soup bowl for several moments, then looked back up at her. "Does this mean I can't publish my work?"

"Publish?"

"In *The Journal of Nanotechnology*. It's published in Selene and I thought I'd meet the editors while I'm there."

Pancho thought it over for all of a half-second. A scientific journal. Maybe a hundred people in the whole solar system read it. But one of them will bring the news to Humphries, she was sure. Hell, she said to herself, the Hump prob'ly knows about it already. Not much goes on anywhere that he doesn't know about.

"Sure you can publish it," she said easily. "No problem."

Levinson broke into a boyish smile. "Oh, that's okay then. As long as

I can publish and get credit for my work, I don't care what the stupid rock rats do."

Pancho stared at him, struggling to hide her feelings. Like so many scientists, this kid's an elitist. She felt enormously relieved.

Dorik Harbin knew all about addiction. He'd started taking narcotics when he was a teenager, still in his native Balkan village. The elders fed a rough form of hashish to the kids when they sent the youths out on missions of ethnic cleansing. As he progressed up the ladder of organized murder and rape, his need for drugs became deeper, more demanding. As a mercenary in the employ of Humphries Space Systems he had been detoxed several times, only to fall back into his habit time and again. Ironically, HSS medics supplied the medications as part of the corporation's "incentive program."

Their meds were much better, too: designer drugs, tailored for specific needs. Drugs to help you stay awake and alert through long days and weeks of cruising alone through the Belt, seeking ships to destroy. Drugs to enhance your battle prowess, to make you fiercer, angrier, bloodier than any normal human being could be. Most of all, Harbin needed drugs to help him forget, to blot out the images of helpless men and women screaming for mercy as they floated into space from their broken spacecraft to drift in their survival pods or even alone in their spacesuits, drift like flailing, begging, terrified dust motes until at last death quieted their beseeching voices and they wafted through space in eternal silence.

A lesser man would have been driven to madness by the hopelessness of it all. Humphries's medical specialists took pains to detoxify Harbin's body, to purge his blood stream of the lingering molecules of narcotics. Then other Humphries specialists fed him new medications, to help him do the killings that the corporation paid him to do. Harbin smiled grimly at the irony and remembered Kayyam's words:

> And much as Wine has play'd the Infidel,
> And robb'd me of my Robe of Honor—well,
>   I often wonder what the Vintners buy
> One half so precious as the Goods they sell.

No matter which of the laboratory-designed drugs he took, though, nor how much, they could not erase his dreams, could never blot out the memories that made his sleep an endless torture of punishment. He saw their faces, the faces of all those he had killed over the years, distorted with pain and terror and the sudden realization that their lives were finished, without mercy, without hope of rescue or reprieve or even delay. He heard their screams, every time he slept.

The revenge of the weak against the strong, he told himself. But he dreaded sleep, dreaded the begging, pleading chorus of men and women and babies.

Yes, Harbin knew about addiction. He had allowed himself to become addicted to a woman once, and she had betrayed him. So he had to kill her. He had trusted her, let his guard down and allowed her to reach his innermost soul. He had even dared to dream of a different life, an existence of peace and gentleness, of loving and being loved. And she had betrayed him. When he ripped the lying tongue out of her mouth, she was carrying another man's baby.

He swore never to repeat that mistake. Never to allow a woman to get that close to him. Never. Women were for pleasure, just as some drugs were. Nothing more.

Yet Leeza intrigued him. She went to bed with Harbin easily enough; she even seemed flattered that the commander of the growing base on Vesta took enough notice of her to bring her to his bed. She was compliant, amiable, and energetic in her lovemaking.

Don't get involved with her! Harbin warned himself sternly. Yet, as the weeks slipped by in the dull, cramped underground warrens of Vesta, he found himself spending more and more time with her. She could make him forget the past, at least for the duration of a pleasant dinner together. She could make time disappear entirely when they made love. She could even make Harbin laugh.

Still he refused to allow her into his private thoughts. He refused to hope about the future, refused even to think about any future at all except completing this military base on Vesta and following Martin Humphries's command to hunt down Lars Fuchs and kill him.

But the new orders superseded the old. Grigor told him that Humphries wanted an all-out attack on Astro Corporation ships.

"Forget Fuchs for the moment," Grigor's prerecorded message said. "There are bigger plans in the works."

Harbin knew he was becoming addicted to Leeza when he told her how dissatisfied he was with the new orders.

She lay in bed beside him, her tousled head on his bare shoulder, the only light in the room coming from the glow of starlight from the wallscreen that displayed the camera view of deep space from the surface of Vesta.

"Humphries is preparing to go to war against Astro?" Leeza asked, her voice soft as silk in the starlit darkness.

Knowing he shouldn't be revealing so much to her, Harbin said merely, "It looks that way."

"Won't that be dangerous for you?"

It was difficult to shrug with her head on his shoulder. "I get paid for taking risks."

She was silent for several heartbeats. Then, "You could get paid much more."

"Oh? How?"

"Yamagata Corporation would equal your salary from HSS," she said.

"Yamagata?"

With a slight, mischievous giggle, Leeza added, "And you could still be drawing your pay from Humphries, at the same time."

He turned toward her, brows knitting. "What are you talking about?"

"Yamagata wants to hire you, Dorik."

"How do you know?"

"Because I work for them."

"For Yamagata?"

Her voice became almost impish. "I do the job I was hired to do for Humphries and draw my HSS salary for it. I report on what's happening here to Yamagata, and they pay me the same amount that HSS does. Isn't that neat?"

"It's treason," Harbin snapped.

She raised herself on one elbow. "Treason? To a corporation? Don't be silly."

"It's not right."

"Loyalty to a corporation is a one-way street, Dorik. Humphries can fire you whenever he chooses to. There's nothing wrong with feathering your own nest when you have the opportunity."

"Why is Yamagata so interested in me?"

"They want to know what Humphries is doing. I'm too low in the organization to give them the whole picture. You're the source they need."

Harbin leaned back on his pillow, his thoughts spinning.

"You don't have to do anything against HSS," Leeza urged. "All Yamagata wants is information."

For now, Harbin added silently. Then he smiled in the darkness. She's just like all the others. A traitor. He almost felt relieved that he didn't have to build an emotional attachment to her.

SEVEN MONTHS LATER

HUMPHRIES MANSION

How is she?" Martin Humphries asked, his voice tight with a mixture of anticipation and apprehension.

The holographic image of the obstetrician sitting calmly on a chair in front of Humphries's desk looked relaxed, unruffled.

"It's going to take another hour or so, Mr. Humphries," she said. "Perhaps longer. The baby will arrive when he's good and ready to enter the world."

Humphries drummed his fingers on the desktop. First the brat is three weeks premature and now he's taking his time about being born.

"There's nothing to do but wait," the doctor warned. "Mrs. Humphries is pretty heavily sedated."

"Sedated?" Humphries was instantly alarmed. "Why? By whose order? I wanted a natural childbirth. I told you—"

"Sir, she was sedated when your people wheeled her in here."

"That's impossible!"

The obstetrician shrugged inside her loose-fitting green surgical gown. "I was surprised, too."

"I'm coming over," Humphries snapped.

He clicked off the phone connection before the obstetrician could reply and pushed himself up from his desk chair. He had set up the birthing facility for Amanda down the hall from his office. He had no desire to be present during the mess and blood and pain of childbirth, but the obstetrician's claim that Amanda was heavily sedated alarmed him. She was supposed to be off all the drugs. *She promised me,* Humphries reminded himself, anger rising inside him. *She promised me to stay clean while she was carrying my son.*

Humphries raced down the short corridor between his office and the birthing facility.

She's been doing drugs again, he realized. I've had her detoxed three—no, four times, and she went right back onto them, pregnant or not. She doesn't give a damn about my son, about me. Her and her damned habit. If she's harmed my son I'll kill her.

In his frenzy he forgot that Amanda was the only woman he had ever loved. After two earlier wives and no one knew how many other women, he had fallen truly in love with Amanda. But she never loved him. He knew that. She loved that bastard Fuchs, probably still does, he thought. She's just having this baby to placate me. Fury boiling in him, he swore that if his son wasn't perfect he'd have it terminated before it left the birthing room.

And her with it, Humphries snarled inwardly.

He banged through the door of the birthing facility, startling the green-gowned nurse sitting in the anteroom, her mask pulled down from her face, calmly reading from a palmcomp screen, a cup of coffee in her other hand.

The woman jumped to her feet, sloshing coffee onto the carpeted floor. "Mr. Humphries!"

He strode past her.

"I wouldn't go in there, sir. There's nothing—"

Humphries ignored her and pushed through the door to the birthing room. Amanda lay on the bed, unconscious or asleep, soaked with perspiration, pale as death. Three women in green surgical gowns and masks stood to one side of the bed. Humphries saw that Amanda wore not a trace of makeup. Her china-blue eyes were closed, her lustrous blonde hair matted with sweat. And still she looked so beautiful, so vulnerable, like a golden princess from a fairy tale. His anger melted.

One of the women came up before him, burly, square-shouldered, blocking his view of his wife. "You're not gowned!" she hissed from behind her mask.

Fuming, Humphries went out to the anteroom and demanded that the nurse out there find him a surgical gown and mask. In less than five minutes he was dressed, with plastic booties over his shoes, a mask, gloves, and a ridiculous cap pulled down over his ears.

He went back into the birthing room. It was ominously quiet. Amanda had not moved. The only sound in the room was the slow clicking of one of the monitors clustered around the head of the bed. Humphries stared at the machines. The clicking seemed to be coming from the heart monitor, counting off Amanda's heartbeats. It sounded terribly slow.

THE SILENT WAR

"Well," he whispered to the obstetrician, "how is she doing?"

The woman drew in a breath, then replied, "There are some complications."

"Complications?"

"Her heart. The strain of labor has placed an unusually severe workload on her heart."

"Her heart?" Humphries snapped. Pointing a finger like a pistol at the cardiologist, he demanded, "What about the auxiliary pump?"

"It's doing its job," the cardiologist said firmly. "But there's a limit to how much workload it can carry."

"Will she be all right? Will she get through this all right?"

The obstetrician looked away from him.

He grabbed her shoulder. "My son. Is he all right?"

She looked back at him, but her eyes wavered. "The baby will be fine, Mr. Humphries. Once we get him out of his mother."

Humphries suddenly understood. She's going to die. Amanda's going to die! The only woman I've ever loved in my whole life is going to die giving birth to my son.

His knees gave way. He almost collapsed, but the same burly medic who had pushed him out of the room now grasped his arm in a powerful grip and held him on his feet.

"We're doing everything we can," the obstetrician said as the medic walked Humphries through the door and deposited him on a chair in the anteroom. The nurse out there sprang to her feet again.

Humphries slumped down onto the chair, barely hearing the whispered words between the nurse and medic. The nurse put a cup of steaming coffee in his hand. He ostentatiously poured it onto the carpeting. She looked surprised, then backed away and remained standing by the door to the birthing room. Humphries sat there, his thoughts darker and darker with each passing moment.

Fuchs. He's the cause of all this. This is all his fault. She still loves him. She's only having this baby to keep me happy, to save his putrid ass. Well, if she dies then all my promises are finished. I'll find that son-ofabitch and kill him. I'll get Harbin and every ship I've got out there in the Belt to hunt him down and kill him. I don't care if it takes a thousand ships, I'll see him dead. I'll have him skinned alive. I'll have his balls roasted over a slow fire. I'll—

The squall of a baby's first cry stopped his litany of rage.

Humphries shot to his feet. The nurse was still standing in front of the door.

Which opened slowly. The obstetrician came out, pulling the mask off her face. She looked tired.

"My son?" Humphries demanded.

"The boy's fine," said the woman, unsmiling. "We'll run him through the usual tests in a day or so, but he appears to be normal. A little scrawny, but that's not unusual for a preemie."

Scrawny, Humphries thought. But he'll be all right. He'll grow. He'll be a healthy son.

"Your wife . . ." the obstetrician murmured.

"Is she all right?"

The doctor shook her head slowly.

"Amanda?"

"I'm afraid she didn't make it, sir. Her heart stopped and we couldn't revive her."

Humphries gaped at the woman. "She's dead? Amanda's dead?"

"I'm very sorry, Mr. Humphries," the obstetrician said, her eyes avoiding his. "We did everything that's humanly possible."

"He killed her," Humphries muttered. "The bastard killed her."

"It's not the baby's fault," said the obstetrician, looking alarmed.

"He killed her," Humphries repeated.

HABITAT *CHRYSALIS*

Pancho dropped everything and flew on a full-*g* burn to Ceres, completing the trip from Selene in slightly less than thirty hours.

As her torch ship made rendezvous with the orbiting habitat and docked at one of its airlocks, it felt good to Pancho to get back down to one-sixth gravity. Been living in lunar grav so long it feels normal to me, she thought as she strode through the central passageway of the interlinked spacecraft bodies, heading for Big George's quarters.

When he'd first been elected chief administrator for the rock rats, George had insisted that he would not establish a fancy office nor hire any unnecessary staff personnel. Over the years he had stuck to that promise—in a manner of speaking. His office was still in his quarters, but George's quarters had expanded gradually, steadily, until now they spanned the entire length of one of the spacecraft modules that composed *Chrysalis.*

"Only one side of the passageway," George grumbled defensively when Pancho kidded him about it. "And I haven't hired a single staff member that I didn't absolutely need."

George's "office" was still the sitting room of his quarters. He had no desk, just comfortable furniture scavenged from junked spacecraft. Now he sat in a recliner that had once been a pilot's chair. Pancho was in a similar seat, sitting sideways, her long legs draped over its armrest.

"Looks to me like you're buildin' yourself an empire, George," Pancho teased. "Maybe only a teeny-weeny one, but still an empire."

George glowered at her from behind his brick-red beard. "You di'n't come battin' out here to twit me about my empire, didja?"

"No," said Pancho, immediately growing serious. "I surely didn't."

"Then what?"

"I gotta see Lars."

"See 'im? You mean face to face?"

Pancho nodded somberly.

"What for?"

"Amanda," said Pancho, surprised at how choked up she got. "She's . . . she died."

"Died?" George looked stunned.

"In childbirth."

"Pig's arse," George muttered. "Lars is gonna go fookin' nuts."

"Acute anemia?" Humphries echoed, his eyes narrowing. "How can my son have acute anemia?"

The man sitting in front of Humphries's desk was the chief physician of Selene's hospital. He was a cardiovascular surgeon, a large, imposing man with strangely small and delicate hands, wearing an impeccably tailored business cardigan of ash gray. His expression was serious but fatherly; he was accustomed to dispensing information and wisdom to distressed, bewildered patients and their families. He knew he had to maintain the upper hand with Humphries. Such a powerful man could be troublesome. None of the hospital's lower ranking physicians dared to accept the task of breaking this news to Martin Humphries.

He spread his hands in a placating gesture. "That's not an easy question to answer, Mr. Humphries. The baby has a defective gene, a mutation."

Humphries glanced sharply at Victoria Ferrer, seated to one side of his desk. She kept her face impassive.

"It might have been caused by some stray bit of ionizing radiation," the doctor went on condescendingly, "or even by the low gravity here. We simply don't know enough about the long-term effects of low gravity."

"Could it have been caused by drug use?" Ferrer asked.

Humphries glowered at her. The doctor's self-confidence slipped noticeably for a moment, but he swiftly regained his composure. "We did find an elevated level of barbiturates in Mrs. Humphries's blood, postmortem. But I doubt—"

"Never mind," Humphries snapped. "It doesn't matter. The question now is, how will this affect my son?"

"Chronic anemia is treatable," the doctor answered smoothly. "It can be controlled with medication. He'll be able to lead a completely normal life as long as he takes his medication."

"No problems at all?"

"Not as long as he takes his medication," said the doctor, with his

patented reassuring smile. "Oh, there might be some incidents of asth-
matic attacks, but they should be amenable to antihistamines or adrena-
line therapy. In severe cases we can even—"

"What else? Humphries snapped.

"I beg your pardon?"

"What else is wrong with him?"

The doctor's smile dimmed, then reappeared at full wattage. "His genetic screening looks perfectly normal, otherwise. With proper diet he
should get to the sixth or seventh percentile, size-wise. And if he—"

"You mean he'll be a runt," said Humphries.

Startled, the doctor stammered, "I, eh . . . I wouldn't put it that way,
Mr. Humphries. The boy will be well within normal standards."

"Will he be six feet tall?"

"Six feet . . . that's about one point eight meters, isn't it? No, I doubt
that he'll get that tall."

"Will he be athletic?"

"Well, that all depends. I mean, the anemia will certainly be a factor
in his athletic abilities, of course. But it's much too early . . ."

Humphries let him stumble on, half apologizing, half lecturing on
what it takes to be a good father. Leaning back in his chair, keeping his
hands deliberately in his lap to avoid drumming his fingers impatiently on
the desktop, Humphries saw once again in his mind's eye his newborn
son: a scrawny, red-skinned, squalling little rat-like thing, eyes shut,
mouth open and gasping, miserable little toothpick arms and legs waving
pathetically. A runt. A helpless, useless runt.

He had seen the baby only once, just after Amanda had died. As he
stared down at it, struggling to breathe in its incubator, Humphries had
said silently to it, You killed her. You killed my wife. She died giving life
to you.

He had walked out of the nursery and hadn't seen the baby since that
moment. He knew that if he did, if he went back into the nursery, he'd
want to kill the brat. Smother it in its incubator. Turn off its air. Get rid
of it.

He couldn't do it. There were too many nurses and pediatricians and
servants constantly hovering over the little monster.

Besides, it wasn't really the baby's fault, Humphries told himself. It's
Fuchs. Remember that. It's his fault. He's killed Amanda. He drove her to
use the drugs that killed her and ruined my son. He's hidden behind her
protection all these years. Well, that's over now. Over and done with.

". . . and later on, in a year or two, we can attempt gene replacement
therapy," the doctor was saying. "Or even nanotherapy, since it's legal up
here."

Ferrer was nodding as if she were interested.

"Thank you so much for explaining everything, doctor," Humphries said, getting to his feet.

The physician looked startled, then a flash of anger crossed his face momentarily, but he quickly recovered and got up from his chair.

"Please feel free to call on me at any time, Mr. Humphries. The entire services of the hospital are at your disposal."

"Certainly."

Neither man extended his hand to the other.

Once the physician left the office, Ferrer turned to Humphries. "Should I arrange a christening ceremony?"

"Christening?"

"It's expected for a newborn baby."

"Which comes first," Humphries asked bleakly, "her funeral or the brat's christening?"

Ferrer took a deep breath. Normally it would have roused Humphries but at the moment he ignored it.

"I'll make the arrangements for both," she said softly. "What do you want to name the baby?"

"Name?"

"He's got to have a name."

"Van. It's an old family name. My great-grandfather was named Van. He ran off to South America to avoid being drafted by the U.S. Army. A coward. That's an appropriate name for the little runt, don't you think?"

"I still don't see why you've gotta meet Lars face to face," said Big George.

Pancho swung her legs off the recliner's armrest and got to her feet. "Got something to tell him. Something personal."

"Somethin' more than Amanda's death?"

"Yep."

"Must be fookin' important."

"It is."

"Well," George said, getting up from his chair to stand beside her, "I can try gettin' a message to him. Dunno if he'll respond, though."

"He knows me."

"He *knew* you," George corrected. "Ol' Lars isn't the same man he was back then."

Pancho gave him a long unhappy look, then muttered, "Who the hell is?"

ASTEROID VESTA

Harbin studied the image of Grigor on the wallscreen of his private quarters. A Russian, Harbin said to himself, recalling the way the village elders had spoken of the Russians when he'd been a lad. The Russians are our friends, they intoned, as long as they stay far away from our village.

Grigor's normally dour, downcast features looked almost happy as he gave Harbin the latest orders from Selene. An important executive of the rival Astro Corporation was at Ceres. Probably she would go deeper into the Belt, seeking a meeting with the renegade Fuchs.

"We will receive tracking data from our informant in the IAA facility at Ceres. You will intercept her vessel and eliminate it. Quite possibly you'll be able to eliminate Fuchs at the same time. You are to take as many ships as you deem necessary, but in any event no fewer than five. Humphries wants this job done without fail."

Harbin wanted to answer, "Then let Humphries come out here and do it himself." But he knew that it would take more than half an hour for any reply from him to reach the Moon. Besides, it wouldn't be wise to be so disrespectful to the man who pays all the bills.

So he wiped Grigor's image from his wallscreen and replied merely, "Message received. Will comply."

Five ships. Grigor thinks that more ships will guarantee success. He has no idea of how difficult it is to coordinate a multiship attack out here. And the more ships we use, the sooner the prey will realize it's being tracked.

Harbin shook his head in mild disgust. I could do it alone, one ship with a crew of one. Give me the coordinates of the Astro vessel's course and I'll intercept it and terminate it. And if Fuchs is in the area I'll handle him, too.

Leaning back in his padded chair, Harbin locked his fingers behind his head and thought it over. Fuchs is smart, though. Wily, like a badger. He can sniff out danger a thousand kilometers away. Five ships might make sense. Maybe a few more, to go out ahead of me and take up stations that will cut off his line of retreat. Then I'd have him, finally.

He sat up straight, nodded once at the blank wallscreen, then got to his feet and headed for the command center. He needed the latest tracking data on the Astro vessel.

Big George was staring at a wallscreen, too. Pancho sat beside him in his informal office, her eyes glued to the grainy image of Lars Fuchs.

"I received Pancho's message," Fuchs said, his broad, jowly face downcast, sour-looking. "Unfortunately, I can't risk a meeting. Too many of Humphries's spies might learn of it. Whatever you have to tell me, Pancho, send it in a message."

The image winked off.

Pancho blinked, then turned to George. "That's it? That's his whole message?"

"He doesn't waste words," George replied. " 'Fraid somebody might intercept the beam and get a fix on his location."

"I've got to talk to him," Pancho said, feeling frustrated. "Face to face."

George said, "Lots o' luck."

Getting to her feet, Pancho said, "I can't tell him Mandy's dead over a comm link."

Shaking his unshorn head, George replied, "He's not gonna meet with you, Pancho. I di'n't think he would."

"I'm not going to lead him into a trap, for cripes sake!"

"Not knowingly."

She frowned at him.

"Lars hasn't survived out there for so long by bein' naive," George said. "Humphries has had mercenaries tryin' to bag him. Freelancers, too; the word's gone 'round the Belt that Humphries'll pay a bounty for Lars's head."

Pancho grimaced. "Mandy told me he promised to leave Lars alone."

"Sure he did," George replied, scorn dripping from each syllable.

"I've got to see him."

"It's not gonna happen, Pancho. Face it. Lars is cautious, and I can't say I blame him."

Pancho took a deep breath, telling herself, When you're faced with a stone wall, find a way around it. Or over it. Or tunnel under it, if you have to. What did Dan Randolph always say: When the going gets tough, the tough get going—to where the going's easier.

"George," she asked, sitting down next to him again, "how do you get messages to Lars?"

He hesitated a moment. Then, "He's got a half-dozen or so miniaturized transceivers scattered around on minor asteroids out there. When I squirt a message to one of 'em, I tell him which one I'll be aimin' at on the next message."

"And the transceivers stay on the same 'roids all the time?"

"Naw. Lars moves 'em around. He tells me where they'll be next when he answers me back."

Pancho was silent for a few moments, thinking. At last she said, "So you could send him a message and tell him where you'll be sending the next one."

"And when," George added.

"And then he goes to that rock to pick up your message."

"Right."

"I could be waiting for him at the asteroid where the transceiver is. When Lars shows up, I'll be there to greet him."

George huffed. "And he'll blow you to bits before you can say hello."

"Not if—"

"Count on it," George said.

"I'll take that chance."

Shaking his head, George replied, "Pancho, I can't give you the fookin' coordinates! Lars'll think I betrayed him, for cryin' out loud!"

"I've got to see Lars face to face. I'm willing to take the chance that he'll attack my ship. It's on my head."

George remained adamant for hours. Pancho wheedled, pleaded, begged.

"What's so fookin' important?" George asked. "What is it you've got to tell him to his face?"

Pancho hesitated for a fraction of a second. Then she answered, "George, if I could tell you, I would. But it's for Lars's ears only."

He scratched at his thick beard. "That big, huh?"

Pancho nodded wordlessly.

"All right," he said uneasily. "Tell you what I'll do. I'll go out on the ship with you."

"But you said it'd be dangerous!"

"Yeah. And it will be, believe it. But I think I can work out a scheme that'll keep Lars from blasting us on sight. Besides, I'd rather be there to face him than have him think I ratted him out."

TORCH SHIP *SAMARKAND*

Harbin sat in *Samarkand*'s command chair, his pilot and navigator seated on a level of the bridge slightly below his. The data screens showed a confusing array of ship trajectories heading toward Ceres and away from the asteroid. The ship's computer was sorting out all the information, seeking the one ship that carried Pancho Lane.

She's too clever to use her own vessel, Harbin thought, as one by one the curving lines indicating individual ships' courses winked out. She'll hitch a ride aboard some prospector's ship, or maybe an Astro logistics vessel.

The tracking information came straight from the IAA controllers in the *Chrysalis* habitat orbiting Ceres. Harbin wished that Humphries had enough spies aboard the habitat to watch Pancho Lane and see which vessel she entered, but that kind of information was not available to him.

So he dispatched three armed ships out into the Belt, and kept three more in a very loose formation centered on his own vessel. To an untrained eye it looked like a few more prospectors' ships heading outward. Harbin hoped that's what Fuchs would see.

The welter of curving lines slowly diminished on the screen until only one ship's planned trajectory was displayed. Harbin shook his head, muttering, "Stupid computer." The ship's manifest said it belonged to the government of Ceres and carried none other than their chief administrator, who was going out on an inspection tour of various mining operations in the Belt. The chief rock rat going to visit his little rock rat brethren, Harbin thought.

Then his eyes narrowed. Why is their chief administrator traipsing through the Belt? Has he ever done that before? he asked the computer.

The answer returned almost before he finished uttering the question. Never. This was the first inspection tour on record.

Harbin smiled grimly. Maybe the computer isn't so stupid, after all. He sent a message to Grigor, all the way back at Selene. "Do you have any way of finding out who's on the torch ship *Mathilda II* with the rock rats' chief administrator?"

Grigor replied in little more than an hour. "No passenger list is available. Apparently the vessel carries only its crew of three, and the man Ambrose."

Harbin nodded and remembered that Pancho Lane had once been a professional astronaut. She could probably take the place of a crewman on Ambrose's ship.

To his own navigator he commanded, "Set a course to follow the vessel shown on the computer display. Stay well behind it. I don't want them to know we're following them."

Mathilda II was a great deal more comfortable than the original *Waltzing Matilda*. That old bucket had been a mining ship before it was shot to shreds in the first asteroid war. *Mathilda II* was a comfortably fitted torch ship capable of carrying important passengers while serving as a mobile office for the chief administrator of the Ceres settlement.

Sitting in a swivel chair in the galley, George was explaining, "I left the message for Lars and told him where we'll be waitin' for him. This way we don't surprise him."

Pancho was seated across the galley table from George. They were in the middle of dinner, Pancho picking at a salad while George wholeheartedly attacked a rack of ribs.

"And the spot you picked to rendezvous with him isn't where one of the transceivers is stashed?" she asked.

"Naw," said George, dabbing at his sauce-soaked beard with a napkin. "We'll rendezvous in dead-empty space. I gave him the coordinates. If anybody's followin' us we'll both be able to see 'em long before they can cause any trouble."

Pancho nodded. "And you send all your messages to Lars over a tight laser link?"

"Yup. Just about impossible for anybody to intercept 'em or eavesdrop. If somebody does get into the beam we see it right away as a drop in received power."

"Pretty cute."

"Pretty necessary," George said, picking up another sauce-dripping barbecued rib.

• • •

In the weeks since his encounter with the disguised logistics ship *Roe-buck,* Lars Fuchs had added a new wrinkle to his *Nautilus.*

Ships operating in deep space required radiation shielding. When solar flares erupted and spewed planet-engulfing clouds of deadly ionizing particles through interplanetary space, a ship without shielding was little more than a coffin for its crew. The powerful protons in such clouds were particularly dangerous, capable of killing humans and frying electronics systems within minutes unless they were properly protected.

Most spacecraft shielded themselves by charging their outer skins to a very high positive electrical potential. This diverted the deadly high-energy protons of the radiation cloud. The cloud also contained electrons, however, which were less energetic but capable of discharging the ship's positive electrical field. To keep the electrons at bay, the ships surrounded themselves with a magnetic field, generated by lightweight superconducting wires. Thus spacecraft operating beyond the Earth/Moon system were wrapped in an invisible but powerful magnetic field of their own, and charged their outer skins to high positive potential when a solar storm broke out.

Fuchs, once a planetary geochemist, used *Nautilus*'s electron guns to charge up his craft's skin, then covered the spacecraft with pebbles and dust from a loosely aggregated chondritic asteroid. A radar probe of his spacecraft gave a return that looked like the pebbly surface of a small "beanbag" type of chondritic asteroid. Moreover, the dust and pebbles would scatter a laser beam and absorb its energy even better than the copper shields he had affixed earlier to *Nautilus*'s hull.

If he let his ship drift in a Sun-centered orbit, Fuchs felt confident that *Nautilus* would look to a casual probe just like a small, dumbbell-shaped asteroid. He felt less confident, though, about responding to Big George's latest message.

Pancho wants to meet me face to face, he mused. Why? What's so important that she's coming out here into the Belt to find me?

"I don't like it," he muttered to himself.

Sanja, on duty in the pilot's chair, the son of a former Mongol tribesman, turned his shaved head toward Fuchs and asked, "Sir?"

"Nothing, Sanja," said Fuchs. "Nothing. Once you've reached orbital velocity, cut power and let the ship coast."

MATHILDA II

We have arrived at the designated position," said the pilot. Pancho was sitting in the copilot's chair of *Mathilda II*'s snug, efficiently laid-out bridge. The pilot, seated on her left, was a youngster she had met when she'd come aboard for this flight. He looked like a kid to Pancho, blond and soft-cheeked and scrubbed pink, but he ran the vessel well enough. Good square shoulders, she noticed. Pancho's piloting skills were rusty, she knew, but inwardly she longed for a chance to fly this bucket, just for a little larking around. She couldn't ask, of course. The chairman of the board of Astro Corporation isn't supposed to be a fly-girl. One of the epithets that Humphries often threw at her was "greasemonkey." Pancho had no intention of giving the Humper any ammunition.

Still, she thought as she watched the young man play his fingers over the control panel's keyboard, it'd be fun to goose up the engines and see what this flying machine can do.

"This is the spot, is it?" George asked. Standing behind the pilot's seat, he bent forward slightly to peer out the forward window. Nothing visible except the desert of dark empty space spangled with solemn, unblinking stars.

The pilot's name was Oskar Johannson. Despite his youthful appearance, he was stiffly formal with George and Pancho.

"Yes, sir," he said, pointing to the control panel's main display screen. "These are the coordinates, in yellow, and this is our position, the blinking red cursor. As you can see, sir, they overlap. We are at the proper position."

George nodded. Pancho admired Johannson's strong jaw and gleaming white teeth. Wish he'd smile, she thought. I wonder what it'd take to ruffle his composure a bit.

"No ships in sight?"

"Nothing in view, sir, except a small asteroid about five hundred klicks off, in about the four o'clock position." He tapped the keyboard once. "Five hundred seventeen kilometers, one hundred twenty-two degrees relative to our position, eight degrees elevation."

Pancho grinned at the kid's earnestness. "I thought this position was clear of rocks for at least a thousand klicks all round," she said.

George scratched at his beard, answering, "Rocks get kicked into new orbits all the time, Pancho. Gravity resonances from Jupiter and the other planets are always scrambling the smaller chunks."

Resisting the urge to run the display herself, she said, "An unnumbered rock. Might's well claim it."

"To do that one of us would hafta suit up and go out there and plant a marker on it."

"Why not?" Pancho said, pushing herself up from her seat. "I'll do it. Claim it for Astro."

"Gimme a closer look at it, Oskar," George said.

The radar image showed a dumbbell-shaped chondritic asteroid, slowly tumbling end over end.

"A peanut," George said. "Just like what's-'is-name."

"Ida," said Johannson. "Asteroid number 243."

"Showin' off your college education, Ossie?" asked George.

Johannson actually blushed.

Pushing past George, Pancho said, "I'll go out and claim it. Give me something to do while we're waiting for Lars to show up."

George turned and ducked through the hatch after her. "I'll give you a hand, Pancho."

"I can do it myself," she said, heading up the narrow passageway toward the main airlock, where the space suits were stored.

"You'll need help gettin' into a suit," George called after her. "I'll hafta suit up meself, too, y'know."

"You don't have to—"

"Safety regs," George said firmly. "Somebody's gotta be suited up and ready to go out in case of an emergency."

Pancho hmmphed but didn't object. Safety regulations had saved more than one astronaut's butt, she knew. She allowed George to help her into the suit and check out her seals and systems. Then she helped George and checked him out.

"What's funny?" George asked as he pulled the fishbowl helmet over his wild red mane.

Pancho hadn't realized she was grinning. George seemed about to burst his suit's seams. "Georgie, you look like a red-headed Santa Claus, you know that?"

"Ho, ho, ho," he answered flatly.

Pancho was ready to step into the airlock when Johannson's voice came over the ship's intercom:

"A ship's approaching," he called out. "It's coming up fast."

"Lasers armed and ready, sir," said the weapons technician.

Harbin nodded curtly, his eyes focused on the image of *Mathilda II* on the main screen of *Samarkand*'s bridge. Nothing else in range except a minor asteroid, some five hundred klicks away.

Samarkand carried two powerful continuous-wave lasers, adapted from the cutting tools the rock rats used, plus a high-energy pulsed weapon capable of blowing a centimeter-sized hole in the metal skin of a spacecraft from a distance of a thousand kilometers.

Mathilda's crew module was out of position, Harbin saw; it had rotated away from his fast-approaching ship and was partially shielded by the bulk of the propulsion system, engines and big spherical fuel tanks.

"Stand by," Harbin ordered quietly. The three crew personnel on the bridge with him sat tensely, waiting for the order to fire.

Just a little closer, Harbin said under his breath to the slowly rotating *Mathilda*. Just turn a little bit more.

There. The crew module was clearly visible.

"Fire," Harbin said to the weapons tech. To make certain, he pressed the red button on the keypad set into his command chair's armrest.

"We got her," he whispered triumphantly.

Pancho was inside the airlock, ready to go out and claim the unnamed asteroid, when she heard a gurgling scream in her earphones and warning sirens begin an ear-piercing howl.

"What's that?" she yelled into her helmet microphone.

"Dunno," George's voice replied. "Sounds like the emergency hatches slammed shut."

Pancho banged the airlock control panel, stopping its pumps, then reopened the inner hatch. George was in his space suit, peering down the passageway, his shaggy face frowning with worry.

"Can't get Johannson on the intercom," he muttered.

Pointing to the control panel on the emergency hatch a few meters up the passageway, Pancho said, "We've lost air pressure."

"Better stay in the suits, then," said George as he started toward the closed hatch.

Pancho followed him through three hatches, past the ship's galley and up to the hatch that opened onto the bridge. Red warning lights showed there was no air pressure along the entire way.

"Jesus!" George yelped once he pushed the hatch open.

Looking over the shoulder of George's suit, Pancho saw that the bridge's forward window had been punctured with a fist-sized hole and the control panel was spattered, dripping with bright red blood. Johannson was slumped in his seat, arms hanging, blood-soaked head lolling on his shoulders. George went to him and turned the pilot's chair around slightly. Johannson's eyes had blown out, and blood was still cascading from his open mouth.

For the first time in her long career as an astronaut and executive of a space-based corporation, Pancho vomited inside her fishbowl helmet.

"Hit!" said the weapons tech.

Harbin saw that they had indeed hit the crew module dead-on, probably at the bridge. Good.

"Slow to match the target's velocity," he commanded. "Move in closer."

Now to slice the ship to pieces and make sure no one survives.

Suddenly the lights on the bridge went out. As the dim emergency lights winked on, Harbin saw that his pilot's control board was glaring with red lights.

"What's wrong?" he demanded.

"Malfunction in the weapons pod," said the pilot, his fingers playing over the console keypads. "Electrical failure and—"

The lights blinked. This time Harbin felt the ship shudder slightly.

"We've been hit!" he snapped.

"*Mathilda* isn't firing at us," the navigator said, staring at the main screen. "That vessel isn't armed. It's only a—"

Samarkand lurched noticeably.

"We're spinning!" the pilot shouted. "Number two propulsion tank's been ruptured!"

"They're firing at us," Harbin shouted.

"But they can't!"

"*Somebody*'s firing at us!" he insisted. "Get us out of here! Now!"

"I'm trying to bring the ship under control," the pilot yelled, her voice edgy, nearing panic.

We should get into our suits, Harbin knew. But there's no time for that now.

"Get us out of here!" he repeated, trying to sound calm, measured.

That asteroid, he realized. Somebody's on that asteroid and shooting at us. It must be Fuchs.

Lars Fuchs stood behind his pilot's chair, legs spread slightly, fists on his hips, eyes blazing with anger as he studied the display screen.

They fired on George's ship, he said to himself. Why? Did they think I was aboard? Or were they trying to kill Pancho? Probably both.

"The enemy is escaping," Nodon said. He spoke softly, keeping his tone neutral, making as certain as he could not to anger Fuchs.

"Let them go," Fuchs said. "The dog is whipped, no sense daring him to turn back and snap at us."

None of the crew on the bridge raised any objection.

"Sanja," Fuchs said to the man on the communications console, "see if you can contact the ship they attacked."

Within a few minutes Big George's face appeared on the screen, his brick-red hair and beard still stuffed inside the fishbowl helmet of his space suit.

"We lost one man," George said grimly. "No damage to the ship's systems."

Past George's broad shoulder Fuchs could see space-suited personnel smearing epoxy across the bridge's forward window.

"We'll have air pressure back in half an hour, maybe less," said George.

"Pancho is with you?" Fuchs asked.

"Yep. She's okay."

"You said she wanted to speak with me."

"I'll get her on the line," said George.

Fuchs waited impatiently, fighting the urge to pace the narrow confines of *Nautilus*'s bridge. Within a few minutes Pancho's face replaced George's on his screen. She was apparently in a privacy compartment, still in her space suit.

"He tried to assassinate you," Fuchs said without any preliminaries.

"Humphries?" she replied.

"Who else."

"Maybe he was trying to get you," Pancho said.

"He promised Amanda he wouldn't try to harm me," Fuchs answered, his voice heavy with irony.

An odd expression crossed Pancho's face. He could not determine what was going through her thoughts.

"It might've been a freelancer," she said at last. "Plenty people are after your scalp, Lars."

He shook his head, scowling. "That was no freebooter. He knew where you would be and he knew you were attempting to make a rendezvous with me. Only one of Humphries's agents would have access to such intelligence."

Pancho nodded inside her space-suit helmet. "I guess."

Taking a deep breath, Fuchs said, "Well, Pancho, you wanted to speak with me. Here I am. What is it that's so important?"

That strange expression clouded her face again. "Lars, I need to talk to you face to face about this. Not over a comm link."

"Impossible. You can't come aboard my ship and I won't leave it. Talk now. What is it?"

She hesitated, obviously torn between conflicting emotions.

"Well?" he demanded.

"Lars . . . it's about Amanda. Before she died she—"

"She died?" Fuchs felt his heart constrict beneath his ribs. "Amanda is dead?"

Pancho looked stricken. "I didn't want to tell you like this. I wanted to—"

"She's dead?" Fuchs repeated, his voice gone hollow. He felt as if he needed to sit down, but he couldn't show that weakness here on the bridge, in front of his crew.

"She died in childbirth, Lars."

"Giving birth to his son," Fuchs muttered.

"No, not—"

"He killed her. Humphries killed her just as certainly as if he put a gun to her head and pulled the trigger."

"Lars, you don't understand," said Pancho, almost pleading.

"I understand everything," he growled. "Everything! Now that she's dead even his lying promise to her is gone. Now he'll bend every effort, send every murdering thug he can buy, to kill me. But it won't work, Pancho. He'll never kill me."

"Lars, please. Let me explain—"

"I'll kill him!" Fuchs bellowed, raising his clenched fists above his head. "I'll wipe that smug smile off his face and kill him with these bare hands! I'll repay him for Amanda! I'll kill him!"

He lurched between the two pilots' chairs and punched the communications console so hard that glass broke. Pancho's image disappeared from the display screen.

"I'll kill you, Humphries!" Fuchs screamed to an uncaring universe.

HUMPHRIES MANSION

He got away again?" Humphries squawked.

Standing before his desk, Victoria Ferrer nodded glumly. She wore a plain business suit of dove gray: knee-length skirt and collarless jacket, cut low, with no blouse under it.

Humphries glowered at her. "And Harbin missed Pancho, too?"

"I'm afraid so," Ferrer admitted. "I've had our top military advisor analyze the engagement. Apparently Fuchs has disguised his ship to look like an asteroid—superficially, at least."

"And that psychopath Harbin fell for it."

"As far as the reports show, yes, that's apparently what happened. He damaged *Mathilda II* but not badly enough. The vessel limped back to Ceres. Pancho Lane was not injured."

"And Fuchs got away again," Humphries muttered darkly.

Ferrer said nothing.

"Fire that lunatic Harbin," he snapped. "I don't want him on my payroll for another microsecond."

"But—"

"Fire him!" Humphries shouted. "Get rid of him! Kill him if you have to, just get him out of my way!"

Ferrer sighed patiently. "If you insist."

Noting the way her cleavage moved, Humphries allowed a small grin to creep across his face. "I insist."

"Very well." But instead of turning to leave his office, she remained standing in front of his desk.

"What else?" Humphries asked warily. He knew from long experience that when he had to ask an aide what was on her mind, it wasn't going to be pleasant.

"About your son . . ."

"Alex?"

"No. The baby. Van."

"The runt."

"He's your son, Mr. Humphries, and he needs medical attention."

"See to it, then."

"Don't you want to know—"

"The less I hear about that runt the better I like it. Don't bother me about him. Just do what needs to be done."

She sighed again. This time with disappointment, Humphries could clearly see. "Yes, sir," she said.

Humphries pushed himself up from his desk chair and crooked a finger at her. "Come with me, Victoria. Business hours are finished for this afternoon. Time for fun."

She gave him a look somewhere between surprised and reluctant. "But there's still—"

Coming around the desk, he held out his hand to her. "Vickie, if you wear such enticing clothes you can't blame me for reacting."

She shrugged, which made her even more enticing to him.

Pancho was still steaming by the time she got back to her home in Selene. That's twice the bastard's tried to kill me, she said to herself as she paced through the suite's front corridor to her bedroom. I can't let him have a third shot at me.

She tossed her travel bag onto the bed and told the phone to get her chief of security. Abruptly she canceled the call.

"Find Nobuhiko Yamagata," Pancho said. Silently, she added, Time to fight fire with fire.

It took several minutes for Pancho's computerized communications system to work its way through the Yamagata Corporation's computerized communications system, but at last the wall of Pancho's bedroom seemed to dissolve and she was looking at a three-dimensional image of Nobuhiko. He was on his feet, in a quilted winter parka, its hood pulled down off his head. Pancho could see snow-covered mountains and a crisp blue sky in the background.

"Jeeps," she said, "I hope I haven't busted into your vacation."

Nobuhiko smiled and shook his head. "Only a weekend getaway, Ms. Lane. Your call sounded important."

"It's important to me," Pancho said. "Martin Humphries has tried to murder me again."

"Again?" Nobu's brows rose.

As he listened to Pancho's story, Nobuhiko was thinking that his father's strategy was working perfectly. *She believes Humphries has tried to kill her twice. The first time was our doing, of course. But Humphries is playing his role, too, just as Father predicted.*

". . . so I was thinking that a strategic alliance between our two corporations would make a lot of sense. Together, we could outmaneuver Humphries, and outmuscle him if we have to."

Nobu pretended to be impressed. "The problem is," he said slowly, "that Yamagata Corporation has confined its activities to Earth ever since the greenhouse cliff devastated Japan and so many other nations."

"I know," Pancho said, after the nearly three-second lag that bedeviled communications between the Earth and Moon. "But if our two companies work together, Yamagata can get back into space industries as Astro's partner."

Stroking his chin thoughtfully, Nobu replied, "That is something worth considering, naturally. I will take it up with my board of directors. I'll call a special meeting, as early as I can."

Almost three seconds later Pancho nodded. "Okay. I appreciate that. In the meantime, though, I need some advice. Military advice. Can you recommend someone to me?"

Ahh, thought Nobuhiko, *now we come to the real reason for her call. She is going to war with Humphries and she needs a military force.*

"There are several organizations of mercenaries that might be of service to you."

"I want the best," Pancho said.

"I will send you complete dossiers on the best three organizations," Nobu said, while thinking, *Father will be very impressed. His plan is moving well. Let Astro and Humphries destroy each other. Yamagata Corporation will even help them to do so.*

"Terminated?" Harbin stared at Grigor's message on his screen. "Just like that, they kick me out?"

He was in his quarters in Vesta while the damaged *Samarkand* was undergoing repairs. Leeza Chaptal was in bed with him when Grigor's stinging message came through. Simply one line: *Your services for Humphries Space Systems are hereby terminated. Period.*

Harbin knew it would take at least half an hour for him to get a message back to Grigor. But what could he say? Ask why he'd been cut loose? That was obvious. He'd failed to get Fuchs, and failed to carry out his assignment about Pancho Lane. They were finished with him.

How many have I killed for them? Harbin asked himself. For more than eight years I've done their bidding, and now they kick me out. Terminated. Like some bug they squash under their boots.

Leeza saw the frozen expression on his face, realized that Harbin was raging beneath his mask of icy indifference.

"It's all right," she said, sliding her arms around his neck. "Yamagata will hire you."

"How can you be sure?" he muttered.

"They've wanted to hire you for months. Now there's nothing to prevent you from accepting their offer."

"But if I'm no longer with HSS, why would they hire me? They only wanted me to spy on Humphries for them."

"They'll hire you," she repeated. "I know they will."

"Why?"

Leeza smiled at him. "Because there's going to be a war here in the Belt, and you are a warrior."

ASTRO CORPORATION
HEADQUARTERS

Technically, the principal offices of Astro Corporation were still at La Guaira, off the drowned coast of Venezuela. But Pancho had moved almost all of the corporate headquarters staff to Selene. Most of the board of directors lived in the lunar city, and those who didn't attended board meetings electronically. The three-second communications lag made the meetings tedious to some extent, but Pancho was perfectly willing to accept that. Astro's business was off-Earth; even shipping asteroidal ores Earthside was almost entirely a space operation, and Pancho had always insisted on being where the action was.

Now she sat in the richly paneled boardroom, in her usual place at the head of the long polished conference table. The only other person in the room at this moment was Jacob Wanamaker, known as "Hard-Ass Jake." A retired commander of the International Peacekeeping Force, Wanamaker was a big-shouldered, heavy-bellied, genial-looking older man with a wry, lopsided smile and sad, pouchy brown eyes that had seen much more than their share of death and destruction.

Nobuhiko Yamagata had recommended three military advisors to Pancho: a Japanese mercenary who had fought in miniwars from Indonesia to Chiapas, in Mexico; a Swedish woman who had organized the multinational force that pacified the turmoil in southern Africa; and Hard-Ass Jake. The first two had never been off-Earth; Wanamaker had served several tours aboard a missile-defense space station in Earth orbit. Besides, Jacob Wanamaker had been an admiral in the U.S. Navy before accepting a commission with the IPF, and Pancho figured that fighting in space would be more closely akin to naval warfare than land campaigns.

Once she had personally interviewed the three candidates, Jake won hands down. He was open, easily admitting his lack of experience in space, but the toughness he was famous for showed through his veneer of polite sociability. Pancho had seen men like him when she'd been growing up in west Texas.

"So the trick is," he told her in his rough, sandpaper voice, "to control the lanes of communication. And to do that, you need vessels that are armed and bases for them to be supplied and repaired."

Pancho nodded. "Sounds expensive."

Wanamaker's weather-seamed face was a geological map of hard experience. "War is never cheap, Ms. Lane. The cost is always high: high in blood and high in money. Lots of money."

"It must be exciting, though," she said, probing for his reaction.

Wanamaker cocked a cold eye at her. "Exciting? If you think shitting your pants because you could get killed in the next millisecond is fun, yeah, then I guess you could call it exciting."

It was at that moment that Pancho decided to hire Jacob Wanamaker.

Now they sat in the otherwise empty boardroom, planning strategy.

"HSS has a major base on Vesta," Pancho said. "What do we do about that, attack it?"

Wanamaker pursed his lips for a moment, then replied in his gravelly voice, "Why attack them where they're dug in with solid defenses? That'd cost too many lives."

"But that base is the center of all their operations in the Belt."

"Neutralize it, then. Keep a squadron of ships in the vicinity, close enough to knock off vessels going to or from Vesta, but far away enough to avoid the asteroid's dug-in defenses."

Pancho nodded.

Warming to his subject, Wanamaker gesticulated with his big hands, cupping them together to form an imaginary sphere.

"Matter of fact," he said, "why can't you put three or four of your armed ships together, armor them with asteroidal rock, and keep them on station at a decent distance around Vesta? They'd have more firepower than any individual HSS vessel and more staying power."

"It'd be like a blockade, wouldn't it?" Pancho said.

Wanamaker grinned lopsidedly at her. "You catch on pretty quick."

The rush of pleasure Pancho felt from his praise quickly faded. "But then Humphries'll send out his ships in groups, 'stead of individually, won't he?"

"Yep, convoying would be the countermove."

"It just makes the battles bigger."

"And more expensive."

Suddenly she felt gloomy.

Wanamaker immediately picked up on her mood. "Look, Ms. Lane—"

"Pancho," she corrected absently.

"Okay, Pancho, then. Sherman was right: war is hell, pure and simple. It costs so much in money and blood that if there's any other way to settle your differences with Humphries—any way at all—take it and avoid the bloodshed."

She looked into his earnest brown eyes and said, "I've been trying to avoid this for more'n eight years, Jake. There's no way to get around it, short of giving Humphries total control of the Belt, which means total control of the whole solar system. I won't allow that. I can't."

He puffed his cheeks out in a king-sized sigh. "Then we'll have to fight."

"Guess so," Pancho said morosely.

"You know, battles are won first of all on the morale of the people doing the fighting. Hardly any unit fights to the last man or the last cartridge. Especially mercenaries, such as you'll be using. Somebody decides it's hopeless and gives up before he gets killed."

"Or she," said Pancho.

He acknowledged that with a nod. "Battles are won in the mind and the heart, Pancho. Wars too. The winner is always the guy who won't admit defeat."

She leaned back in her chair, stretched her long legs and stared up at the boardroom's smooth white ceiling.

"Humphries is a stubborn SOB," she said. "And he's not doing the fighting. He sits safe and snug in his house down at the bottom level and gives the orders."

"And pays the bills," Wanamaker added.

Pancho stared at him.

"The way to win this war is to make it too expensive for him to keep on fighting it."

"That means it'll be expensive for Astro, too, and I've got a board of directors to answer to. Humphries can walk all over his board."

With an understanding nod, Wanamaker replied, "Then you're going to have to do some fighting, too, with your board. Just because you're at the top of the chain of command doesn't mean you don't have to put your butt on the line, Pancho."

She tried to smile. "I guess the price of commodities from the Belt is gonna go up."

George was surprised at Pancho's message.

"Go full speed ahead on the nanoprocessing," she said, her lantern-jawed face deadly serious. "It's important that we bring down the costs of mining the rocks."

George studied her image on the wallscreen of his sitting room, thinking, First she says nanoprocessing is gonna knock the bottom outta the market and now she's hot to trot with it. What's goin' on with her?

Pancho's next sentence explained it, at least partially. "Astro's got some big expenses coming up, Georgie. Anything we can do to lower our costs will let us squeeze some extra profits out of the mining operations and help us pay for what's coming up."

"What's coming up?" George asked Pancho's image.

She couldn't answer, of course, not for an hour or so, but George was afraid he already knew. They're gonna fight it out, he figured. No more pokin' here and there, they're gonna fight a fookin' full-scale war. And they're gonna do it right here in the Belt.

"One more thing," Pancho was going on, with hardly a pause for breath. "It's going to be more dangerous out there for Lars than ever before. Tell him it's time for him to come in from the cold. I can give him a new identity, let him live here in Selene if he wants to or even back on Earth. He's got to get out of the Belt, for his own safety."

George nodded at Pancho's image. She looked grave, somber. Like a woman about to go to war, George thought. Then he realized, No. She looks more like a fookin' avenging angel.

Victoria Ferrer watched Humphries's reaction to the latest reports from his far-flung intelligence network.

"Astro's arming ships," he muttered, staring at the display hovering in midair above his desk. "And she's pushing the nanoprocessing scheme."

"She's preparing to go to war," Ferrer said. "Against you."

He looked up at her, his face cold with fury. "With nanoprocessing, Pancho can cut her costs and give Astro an extra layer of profits to finance her war."

"Then we've got to get into nanoprocessing, too."

"Damned quick," Humphries snapped.

"The scientist who perfected the process is here in Selene," Ferrer pointed out. "He came in with Pancho."

"Hire him away from Astro," Humphries said immediately.

"He's not an Astro employee," she said. "Not legally, at least."

"Then hire him. Give him whatever he wants. If he won't come along with us, kidnap him. I want him working for me!"

"I understand," Ferrer said.

Humphries rubbed his hands together. "By god, with nanoprocessing we'll cut the costs of mining down to nothing, almost. Down to the cost of transportation, just about."

"Nanotechnicians don't come cheap."

He sneered at her. "Cheap enough. We'll only need a handful of them. We'll have those little buggers not only mining the ores out of the asteroids, but refining them into pure metals while they do it. What more could you ask for?"

Ferrer looked less enthusiastic. "Lots of miners are going to be thrown out of work."

"So what?" Humphries said offhandedly. "More recruits for the mercenaries."

More cannon fodder, Ferrer thought.

Still in his quarters inside the asteroid Vesta, Dorik Harbin tried to think of the French phrase about the more that things may change, the more they remain the same. Instead, a quatrain from the *Rubaiyat* came to his mind:

> Yesterday, *this* day's madness did prepare:
> Tomorrow's silence, triumph or despair;
>   Drink! for you know not whence you came, nor why;
> Drink! for you know not why you go, nor where.

The irony is almost cosmic, Harbin thought. Humphries fires me because I've failed to kill Fuchs. Yamagata hires me to lead a squadron of mercenaries. Humphries hires Yamagata's mercenaries and bases their ships on Vesta. I didn't have to move, didn't even have to pack a travel bag. Here I am in the same quarters, lower in rank but higher in pay. All I have to do is lead three ships into battle against Astro Corporation. Fuchs has become a sideshow.

His relationship with Leeza Chaptal had changed, though. She had emerged as Yamagata's senior officer among the mercenaries hired by Humphries Space Systems. Now she outranked Harbin, and had little time for him. Which was just as well, Harbin thought. He had no enthusiasm for sleeping with a senior officer. It was one thing to take orders from a woman in battle; in bed, it was a totally different matter.

But Harbin had his consolations. In the travel bag that he didn't have to pack rested a flat gray oblong medical kit that contained a subcutaneous microspray syringe and an array of specially designed medications.

Something for every mood, Harbin thought as he went to the bag and pulled out the kit. Sitting on his bed, he clicked open its lid and examined the vials lined up neatly, each in their clasps. Something to alleviate

depression. Something to enhance sexual performance. This one smoth-
ers fear. That one speeds reaction times. Each one designed specifically
for my metabolism. And Leeza says Yamagata can supply as much as I
need.

Drink! for you know not why you go, nor where. He repeated the line
over and again in his mind as he took a vial from the neat little row and
inserted it into the syringe. Something to make me forget everything, he
thought. Something for oblivion.

He rolled up the sleeve of his uniform and pressed the syringe to the
bare skin of his forearm. Heard its gentle, soothing, reptilian hiss.

He looked up and saw that the wallscreen was displaying a view from
the surface of Vesta. A sliver of bare rock, and then the black emptiness
of infinity. Stars upon stars, all silent and grave, staring back at him. A
barren wilderness of cold and dark.

The drug started to take effect quickly. Harbin lay back on his bed,
thinking, *Oh, wilderness were paradise enow.*

He closed his eyes and begged the silent stars to keep him from
dreaming.

SELENE: EARTHVIEW RESTAURANT

Levi Levinson had never seen such a luxurious restaurant, except in videos. The main eating establishment of Hotel Luna, the Earthview was three levels deep beneath the floor of the crater Alphonsus, big enough to hold a hundred tables covered with heavy damask tablecloths and glittering with silver tableware and sparkling wine glasses and lit by real, actual flickering candles. The spacious room buzzed softly with muted conversations and the barest hint of elegant classical music purring from the overhead speakers. Real, live waiters moved among the tables wearing formal evening clothes. Levinson never gave a thought to the fact that he was wearing his usual coveralls; he had nothing better in his meager wardrobe. Nor did he realize that most of the restaurant's tables were empty. His eyes went to the wide holoscreens mounted on the walls, each showing a real-time view of Earth, glowing blue and white against the endless blackness of space as it hung in the sky above Alphonsus's ring-wall mountains.

He was more than a quarter-hour early for his appointment with Victoria Ferrer, so the table that the maitre d' led him to was empty. He sat ogling the well-dressed tourists and executives at the few other occupied tables, while a waiter poured water for him and left a wine list on the table. Levinson was satisfied with the water. He really wanted a beer, but he felt too self-conscious to ask for one.

After so many weeks in Selene, living in an apartment provided by Astro Corporation, Levinson felt a little guilty about accepting an invitation to dine with an executive from the rival Humphries Space Systems. But what the hell, he thought, I'm not an Astro employee and Pancho Lane has just totally ignored me since she brought me here. It's like she wants me out of the way, hidden like some witness against a crime syndicate back on Earth. I've got nothing better to do until the *Journal of Nanotechnology* publishes my paper. And even there, they've been dragging their feet, like they don't really want to publish it.

Those were the thoughts tumbling through his mind when Victoria Ferrer came up to his table and said:

"You're Dr. Levinson? I'm Vicki Ferrer."

Something in the back of his mind told Levinson he should get to his feet, that's the polite thing. But all he could do was gape at this splendidly beautiful woman standing before him. Ferrer wore a dress of some gold metallic stuff that gleamed in the candlelight and clung to her enticingly.

The waiter held her chair as she sat down, smiling at Levinson. He felt breathless.

Dinner was like some romantic dream. Vicki did the ordering while Levinson simply stared at her, entranced. As they worked their way through the several courses, each accompanied by a special wine, Levinson found himself telling her the story of his life. It sounded plain and dull and boring to him, but she seemed vitally interested in every word.

"And you actually have programmed nanos to process the ores from asteroids?" she asked, her wide brown eyes gleaming with respect, maybe even fascination, he thought.

He went into details about it, but inevitably ended with the disappointing information that the rock rats refused to use his process because they considered it too dangerous.

"It's not really dangerous," Levinson insisted. "I mean, it could be, but I could work out procedures for them that would bring the risk down to a manageable level."

"I'm sure you could," said Vicki, reaching for the sauterne that had been served with dessert.

"But they're not interested in it," Levinson said unhappily.

"Aren't they?"

"No."

She leaned slightly closer to him. "Then why has Pancho Lane ordered her people at Ceres to go ahead with nanoprocessing?"

Levinson blinked at her. "She what?"

"Astro Corporation is preparing to use nanomachines to mine asteroids."

"But that's my work! I published it! I mean, I've got it to the journal and—"

"I'm sure Astro will pay you a royalty of some sort," Ferrer said. "Probably a pittance, just to avoid a lawsuit."

Levinson felt as if someone had stabbed him in the heart.

Ferrer reached across the table and touched his hand. "Lev, how would you like to work for Humphries Space Systems? How would you like to be in charge of a whole operation out in the Belt?"

"Me?"

"You. You're the man we want, Lev. You'll be in charge of nanoprocessing operations at the salary level of a senior executive."

He didn't even bother to ask how much money that meant. He knew it was astronomically more than a laboratory scientist made.

"I'd be very grateful if you said yes, Lev," Victoria Ferrer told him, her voice a whisper, her eyes lowered shyly.

He nodded dumbly. She smiled her warmest at him. Levinson walked on air all the way back to his quarters, with Vicki at his side. She allowed him to give her a fumbling peck on the lips, then left him standing there in the corridor, slightly drunk with wine, more intoxicated with thoughts of being in charge of a major corporate operation and maybe even having this beautiful woman fall in love with him.

He watched her walk down the corridor, then turned to his door and fumbled with the electronic combination lock. Finally stumbling into his apartment, he told himself, This was just our first date. It went pretty damned well. I think she really likes me.

Victoria Ferrer rode the powered stairs down to her own quarters, a quiet smile of accomplishment playing across her lips. We've got him, she said to herself. Martin will be pleased.

SELENE: FACTORY NUMBER ELEVEN

Douglas Stavenger's youthful face was frowning with a mixture of anger and dread as he paced slowly down the length of the factory. Like most lunar manufacturing facilities, Factory Eleven was built out on the surface, open and exposed to the vacuum, protected against the constant rain of micrometeoroids only by a thin dome of honeycomb metal.

"Not much to see, actually," said the factory manager, waving a gloved hand toward the vats where microscopic nanomachines were constructing spacecraft hulls of pure diamond, built atom by atom from carbon soot mined out of asteroids.

Stavenger was wearing one of the new so-called "softsuits" of nanomachined fabric rather than the cumbersome space suit of hard-shell cermet that the factory director wore. The softsuit was almost like a pair of kiddie's pajamas, even down to the attached boots. It was easy to pull on and seal up. The nanomachines held almost-normal air pressure inside the suit without ballooning the way older fabric suits did when exposed to vacuum. Even the gloves felt comfortable, easily flexed. A transparent fishbowl helmet completed the rig, with a small air recycler and even smaller communications unit packed into the belt that went around Stavenger's waist.

"How's the suit feel?" the factory director asked. Her voice sounded a bit uneasy, edgy, in Stavenger's earplug.

"Fine," he said. "I'll bet I could do handsprings in it."

The woman immediately said, "I wouldn't advise that, sir."

Stavenger laughed. "Please call me Doug. Everybody does."

"Yes, sir. I mean, uh, Doug. My name's Ronda."

Stavenger knew her name. And her complete dossier. Although he had not held an official position in Selene's government for decades, Doug Stavenger still kept a steady finger on the lunar nation's pulse. He had the advantage of prestige and the even bigger advantage of freedom. He could go anywhere, see anything, influence anyone. And he did, although usually only in the subtlest manner.

But the time for subtlety was ending quickly. He had asked for this tour of Selene's newest factory because it had been built to supply new torch ships for the corporations competing in the Belt: torch ships armed with powerful lasers, warships built of diamond hulls constructed by nanomachines.

They're killing each other out in the Belt, Stavenger knew. He also knew that sooner or later, one way or the other, the war would come to Selene. What he didn't know was how to prevent it; how to stop the fighting.

"How many orders for ships do you have?" he asked the factory manager.

"Six," she replied. "Three from Astro and three from HSS." She hesitated a beat, then added, "Funny how the orders always come paired up. We never make a ship for one of the corporations without making a ship for the other at the same time."

That had been Stavenger's doing. He had exerted every gram of influence he possessed to keep both Humphries and Pancho from outproducing the other. If they want to fight, Stavenger had reasoned, it's up to us to keep the competition equal. As soon as one of them gets the upper hand they'll be able to dictate the prices for raw materials to us. Selene will have to pay whatever the winner asks for its natural resources. Whoever wins this war in the Belt will win control of Selene as well.

That, Stavenger was determined, would not be allowed to happen.

To the factory manager, he asked as casually as he could manage, "Suppose a third party started ordering spacecraft. Could you supply them on the same schedule you're working now?"

He couldn't see her face through the visor of her hard-shell helmet, but he could sense her nodding. "Sure. We'd have to set up another facility, but that's easy to do: Just pour another concrete pad and roof it over. The nanos do all the real work."

Stavenger nodded. "I see."

Curiosity got the better of the manager. "But who'd be ordering more ships? Who'd this third party be?"

With a soft shrug, he replied, "Oh, I don't know. Maybe Selene."

The manager could not have been more surprised if Stavenger had actually turned a handspring there on the factory floor.

•   •   •

Less than twenty kilometers from the new lunar factory, Lars Fuchs was passing through customs at Selene's Armstrong Spaceport.

He had come to the Moon by a circuitous route, leaving the Belt weeks earlier to return to his native Switzerland, using the passport that Pancho had sent to him through Big George. Although exiled from Ceres and persona non grata at Selene, neither Switzerland nor any other nation of Earth had outlawed Fuchs. Customs officials at the spaceport in Milan had subjected him to a quick but thorough medical examination, including a full-body scan and a blood sample to make certain he did not bear nanomachines.

Thus Lars Fuchs, citizen of Switzerland, returned to his native land. He had spent weeks working out in a centrifuge he'd built aboard *Nautilus,* but still the heavy gravity of Earth made him feel tired, depressed. Even worse was the sight of the sprawling tent city that he glimpsed outside of Milan from the high-speed train as it raced toward the Alps. From the city's newly walled and guarded borders, past Brescia and all the way to the shores of Lake Garda he could see nothing but the shacks and shanties of the homeless, the dispossessed, the haunted, hopeless victims of the greenhouse warming.

After all these years, Fuchs thought, staring through the train window, and still they live like animals.

Then he caught his first glimpse of the Alps. Bare rock, stark and barren as the Moon. Where's the snow? he asked himself, knowing that it was gone, perhaps for centuries, perhaps forever.

His world, the world he had known, was gone also. He didn't realize how much he had loved it, how much he missed it, until he realized that he would never see it again.

As the train plunged into the tunnel at the Brenner Pass, Fuchs stared at his own grim reflection in the window. He looked away, squeezed his eyes shut, and determined to stop thinking about the past. Only the future. Think only of the day when you kill Martin Humphries.

To do that he had to return to Selene, and to accomplish *that* he had to change his identity. Pancho thought she was saving Fuchs's life, protecting the man she had known since he'd first left Earth as an eager graduate student more than a decade earlier. She had provided Fuchs with a new identity and enough money to live comfortably for a few years. At his insistence, she had also done as much for the nine men and women of his crew. *Nautilus* was parked in a Sun-circling orbit deep in the Belt, still disguised to resemble a smallish asteroid. It will be waiting for me when I finish my business with Humphries, Fuchs thought.

He knew what that business was, what it had to be. Pancho hasn't brought me to Earth merely out of friendship. She wants me to get back to Selene. She can't trust any communications link to say it in so many words, but her intention is clear. She wants me to kill Humphries. She knows that's what I want to do, and she's willing to help me do it. It will be a great help to her, of course. But it will be a joy to me. Even if it costs my own life, I will snuff out Humphries.

His thirst for vengeance kindled him for the remainder of his train ride to Bern.

But once in his native Bern he became sad and dispirited, depressed at how the old city had become so shabby, so filled with aimless, homeless men and women, even children, wandering the streets, begging for handouts when the police weren't looking. Fuchs was shocked that the streets were littered with trash; the city that had once sparkled was now grimy, obviously decaying. And at night the streets could even be dangerous, he was warned by the weary-eyed concierge at his hotel.

A week was more than enough for him. Fuchs used the identity Pancho had provided for him to book passage back to Selene. He rented a modest suite for himself at the Hotel Luna, with an expense account to be paid by Astro Corporation. Closer to Humphries, he told himself. Within arm's reach, almost. Close enough to kill. But you must be patient, he thought. You must be careful. Humphries is surrounded by guards and other employees. Pancho can't openly help me to reach him; she can't allow herself to be seen as aiding an assassin. I'll have to act alone. I'll have to get through to Humphries on my own. I don't know how, not yet, but I will do it. Or die in the trying.

He had to disguise his appearance, of course. Lifts in his shoes made him slightly taller. Rigid, spartan dieting had slimmed him somewhat, but no fasting could reduce his barrel chest or thickly muscled limbs. He had grown a thick black beard and wore molecule-thin contact lenses that Astro's people had clandestinely sent him; they altered his retinal pattern enough to fool a computer's simple comparison programming.

Still, Fuchs could not help sweating nervously as he shuffled through the line leading to the customs inspection booth at Selene's Armstrong Spaceport. He had taken a mild tranquilizer but it didn't seem to be helping to calm his growing apprehension.

When he came to the inspection station the computer's synthesized German sounded slightly strange to him, until he realized the machine was not programmed to speak in his own Swiss dialect. He answered its questions as briefly as he could, knowing that the system did not have the voice print of Lars Fuchs in its memory, yet still worried that somehow it might. It didn't. He followed instructions and looked into the retinal scanner for the required five seconds, slowly counting them off in silence.

The automated systems built into the archway directly in front of the inspector's booth scanned his one travel bag and his body without a problem. Fuchs had nothing with him or on him that would trigger an alarm. The human inspector sitting in the booth behind the automated machinery looked bored, his thin smile forced. Fuchs handed him his falsified identity chip and the inspector slipped it into his desktop.

"Karl Manstein?"

"Ja," Fuchs answered.

The inspector asked, "Purpose of your visit?" in standard English; the booth's synthesized computer voice translated his words into German.

"Vacation."

For a heart-stopping moment the inspector studied his screen display, his eyes narrowing. Then he popped Fuchs's thumbnail-sized chip out of his computer and slid it over the countertop to him.

"Welcome to Selene, Herr Manstein. Enjoy your vacation."

"Thank you," Fuchs replied gratefully, scooping up the chip in one meaty hand and hurrying past the inspector, toward the electric-powered cart that would carry him into Selene.

His first task, once he was safely in his suite at the Hotel Luna, would be to send innocuous-seeming messages to his three most trusted crew members, waiting at Ceres. "I have arrived at Selene, and everything is fine." That was the code phrase that would tell them to head for Selene also. Fuchs intended to kill Humphries, and he knew he could not do it alone.

ORE FREIGHTER *SCRANTON*

Chick Egan was mildly surprised to find a ship approaching *Scranton* at high speed. The ore freighter was almost clear of the inner fringe of the Belt, heading toward Selene, carrying a full load of asteroidal metals under contract to Astro Corporation. Astro's people were busily auctioning off the metals on the commodities market at Selene, desperately hoping to get prices high enough to make a minimal profit.

Sitting sideways in the pilot's seat, his legs dangling over the armrest, Egan had been talking with his partner, "Zep" Zepopoulous, about the advisability of getting a laser weapon for the old, slow *Scranton*.

"Makes about as much sense as giving Santa Claus a six-shooter," Zep argued. He was a lean, wiry Greek with thick jet black hair and a moustache to match. "We're in the freight-hauling business, we're not fighters."

Egan's strawberry-blond hair was shorn down to a military buzz cut. "Yeah, but all the other ships are puttin' on lasers. For self-defense."

"This tub isn't worth defending," Zep replied, gesturing around the cramped, shabby cockpit with its scuffed bulkheads and worn-shiny seats. "Somebody wants what we're carrying, we just give it to them and let the insurance carrier worry about it."

"HSS is going after Astro ships," Egan said. "And vice versa."

"We're only under contract to Astro for this one flight. We could sign up with HSS next time out."

"Sam Gunn's arming all his ships," Egan countered. "Astro, HSS, a lot of the independents, too."

"Let 'em," said Zepopoulous. "The day I start carrying weapons is the day I quit this racket and go back to Naxos."

"What's left of it."

"The flooding's stabilized now, they say. I'll be a fisherman, like my father."

"And starve like your father."

That was when the radar pinged. Both men looked at the screen and saw a ship approaching at high speed.

"Who the hell is that?" Zep asked. The display screen showed only blanks where a ship's name and ownership would normally appear.

"Lars Fuchs?" Egan suggested.

"What would he want a load of ores for? We're not an HSS ship, and we don't have any supplies he'd want to take."

Feeling decidedly nervous, Egan turned to the communications unit. "This is *Scranton*. Independent inbound for Selene. Identify yourself, please."

The answer was a laser bolt that punched a hole through the skin of the cockpit. Egan's last thought was that he wished he had armed *Scranton* so he could at least die fighting.

George Ambrose listened to the reports in gloomy silence. The six other members of Ceres's governing council sitting around the oval conference table looked even bleaker.

Eight ships destroyed in the past month. Warships being built at Selene and sent to the Belt by Astro and Humphries Space Systems.

"The HSS base on Vesta has more than two dozen ships orbiting around it," said the council member responsible for relations with the two major corporations. She was a Valkyrie-sized woman with sandy hair and a lovely, almost delicate fine-boned face that looked out of place on her big, muscular body.

"Everybody's carrying weapons," said the councilman sitting beside her.

"It's damned dangerous out there," agreed the woman on the other side of the table.

"What's worrying me," said the accountant, sitting at the table's end, "is that this fighting is preventing ships from delivering their ores to the buyers."

The accountant was a red-faced, pop-eyed overweight man who usually wore a genial smile. Now he looked apprehensive, almost grim.

"Our own economy," he went on, "is based on the business that the miners do. With that business slumping, we're going to be in an economic bind, and damned soon, too."

"Worse than that," said the Valkyrie. "It's only a matter of time before one of the corporations—either Astro or HSS—tries to take over our habitat and make it a base of their own."

"And whichever one takes *Chrysalis*," said the accountant, "the other one will try to take it from them."

"Or destroy us altogether."

Big George huffed out a heavy sigh. "We can't have any fighting here. They'll kill us all."

All their faces turned to him. They didn't have to say a word; George knew the question they wanted answered. *What can we do about it?*

"All right," he said. "I'm gonna send a message to Astro and Humphries. And to Selene, too." Silently he added, With a copy to Doug Stavenger.

"A message?"

"What are you going to say?"

"I'm gonna tell them all that we're strictly neutral in this war they're fightin'," George replied. "We want no part of it. We'll keep on sellin' supplies and providin' R&R facilities for anybody who wants 'em, HSS, Astro, independents, anybody."

The others glanced around the table at one another.

George went on, "But we won't deal with warships. Not from anybody. Only mining ships, prospectors, logistics vessels and the like. We will not supply warships with so much as a toilet tissue."

"A declaration of neutrality," said the accountant.

"Do you think that will be enough?"

"What else can we do?"

"Arm the habitat. Be ready to fight anybody who tries to take us over."

George shook his head ponderously. "This habitat is like an eggshell. We can't fight. It'd just get us all killed."

"We could armor the habitat," the Valkyrie suggested. "Coat the outer hulls with powdered rock, like some of the warships do."

"That'd just postpone the inevitable," George said. "A half-dozen ships could sit out there and pound us into rubble."

"A declaration of neutrality," someone repeated.

"Do you think it would work?"

George spread his big hands. "Anybody got a better idea?"

Silence fell over the conference room.

George drafted his declaration over the next twenty-four hours, with the help of an assistant who had been a history major before coming out to the Belt. The council met again in emergency session, tore the draft to tatters and rewrote it extensively, then—sentence by sentence, almost—wrote a final draft that was quite close to George's original. Only after that did they agree to allow George to send the declaration to Pancho Lane at Astro, Martin Humphries of HSS, and the governing board of Selene. George added a copy for Douglas Stavenger, and then released the statement to the news media of the Earth/Moon region.

For the next several days Big George Ambrose was a minor media attraction. Ceres's neutrality was the first realization for most of the people on battered old Earth that there was a war going on in the Belt: a silent, furtive war taking place far, far away in the dark and cold depths of the Asteroid Belt.

For a few days the Asteroid War was a trendy topic on the news nets, even though no executive of Humphries Space Systems or Astro Corporation deigned to be interviewed or even offer a comment. Sam Gunn, the fast-talking independent entrepreneur, had a lot to say, but the media was accustomed to Gunn's frenetic pronouncements on the evildoings of the big corporations. Nobuhiko Yamagata agreed to a brief interview, mainly to express his regrets that lives were being lost out in the Belt.

Then a major earthquake struck the California coast, with landslides that sent a pair of tsunamis racing across the Pacific to batter Hawaii and drown several Polynesian atolls. Japan braced for the worst, but the hydraulic buffers that Yamagata had built—and been ridiculed for—absorbed enough of the tsunamis' energy to spare the major Japanese cities from extensive destruction. The Asteroid War was pushed to a secondary position in the news nets' daily reporting. Within a week it was a minor story, largely because it was taking place far from Earth and had no direct impact on the Earthbound news net producers.

George Ambrose, however, received a personal message from Douglas Stavenger. It was brief, but it was more than George had dared to hope for.

Seated at the desk in his comfortable home in Selene, Stavenger said simply, "George, I agree that *Chrysalis* could be endangered by the fighting in the Belt. Please let me know what I—or Selene—can do to help."

COMMAND SHIP *ANTARES*

Reid Gormley was a career soldier. He had served with the International Peacekeeping Force in Asia and Africa and had commanded the brilliant strike that had wiped out the paramilitary forces of the Latin American drug cartel. He was widely known in military circles as an able commander: a tough, demanding bantam cock who instilled a sense of pride and invincibility in his troops. He was also vain, cautious, and unwilling to move until he was certain he had an overwhelming superiority of force on his side.

He had come out of retirement to accept a commission with Astro Corporation. Fighting in space was new to him, but then it was new to every commander that the big corporations were hiring. The only experienced space fighters were a handful of mercenaries and renegades like Lars Fuchs. Like most of the other experienced officers who were suddenly finding new careers for themselves, Gormley was certain that a well-motivated, well-trained and well-equipped force could beat mercenaries, who were fighting only for money. As for lone renegades, well, they would be rounded up and dealt with in due time.

It took him nearly six months to bring his force up to the peak of efficiency that he demanded. Like himself, most of the men and women in this Astro Corporation task force were either retired military or younger types who had taken a leave of absence from their regular duties to take a crack at the better pay and more exciting duty offered by the Asteroid War.

Gormley stressed to his troops that while the HSS people were mercenaries, fighting for nothing more than money, they themselves were serving in the best traditions of the military, going into battle to keep the

Asteroid Belt free from the dictatorship of one corporation, fighting to save the miners and prospectors scattered through the Belt from virtual slavery. It never occurred to him that Humphries's mercenaries could say the same thing about him and his troops, with the same degree of truth.

Now he led a force of fourteen ships, armed with high-power lasers and armored with rocky debris crushed from asteroidal stone. His mission was to clear HSS ships from the inner Belt, and then take up a position near Vesta to begin the blockade and eventual strangulation of the major Humphries base.

He had no idea that he was sailing into a trap.

Nobuhiko Yamagata noted that even though it was high summer in Japan, here at the Roof of the World the monastery was still cold, its stone walls icy to the touch of his fingertips. He looked out through the room's only window and consoled himself that at least the Himalayas were still snow-capped. The greenhouse warming had not yet melted them bare.

His father entered the small chamber so silently that when he said, "Hello, son," Nobu nearly hopped off his feet.

Turning, Nobu saw that although his father was smiling, the old man did not look truly pleased. Saito wore his usual kimono. His round face seemed even more youthful than the last time Nobu had visited. Is Father taking youth treatments? Nobuhiko asked himself. He dared not ask aloud.

Kneeling on the mat nearer the window, Saito said, "I just learned that one of our loyal agents was assassinated, together with his wife and children."

Nobu blinked with surprised confusion as he knelt beside his father. "Assassinated?"

"The man who was assigned to make certain that Pancho Lane was not killed in the cable car incident," Saito explained curtly.

"That was months ago."

"His wife and children?" Saito demanded.

Kneading his thighs nervously, Nobu said, "Our security people felt it was necessary. To make certain there would be no possibility of Astro Corporation learning that we caused the accident."

"He was a loyal employee."

"I did not approve the move, Father. I didn't even know about it until after the fact."

Saito gave a low, growling grunt.

"The incident achieved its purpose," Nobu said, trying to get his father's approval. "It started the chain of events that has led to out-and-out war between Astro and Humphries Space Systems."

Saito nodded, although his displeased expression did not change.

"Both Astro and HSS are actually hiring our own people to help them in the fighting," Nobu added. "We're making money from their war."

A slight hint of a smile cracked Saito's stern visage.

Encouraged, Nobu went on, "I believe it's time to consider how and when we step in."

"Not yet."

"If we throw our support to one side or the other, that side will win the war, undoubtedly."

"Yes, I realize that," said the older man. "But it is too early. Let them exhaust themselves further. Already both Astro and HSS are running up huge losses because of this war. Let them bleed more red ink before we make our move."

Nobu dipped his chin in agreement. Then he asked, "Which of them do you think we should support? When the time comes, of course."

"Neither."

"Neither? But I thought—"

Saito raised an imperious hand. "When the proper moment comes, when both Astro and Humphries are tottering on the brink of collapse, we will sweep in and take command of the Belt. Our mercenary units now serving them will show their true colors. The flying crane of Yamagata will stretch its wings across the entire Asteroid Belt, and over Selene as well."

Nobu gasped at his father's grand vision.

He should have been enjoying a restful vacation at Hotel Luna, but Lars Fuchs was not.

In his guise as Karl Manstein, Fuchs was spending the expense-account money Pancho had advanced him as if there was a never-ending supply of it. In truth, it was dwindling like a sand castle awash in the inrushing tide. Hotel Luna may have been threadbare, narrowly avoiding bankruptcy on the trickle of tourists coming to Selene, but its prices were still five-star. Fresh fish from the hotel's own aquaculture ponds; rental wings for soaring like an eagle in the Grand Plaza on one's own muscular strength; guided walks across the cracked and pitted floor of the Alphonsus ringwall, where the wreckage of the primitive *Ranger 9* spacecraft sat beneath a protective dome of clear glassteel; all these things cost money, and then some.

Even though Fuchs/Manstein took in none of the tourist attractions and ate as abstemiously as possible, a suite at Hotel Luna was outrageously expensive. He spent every waking moment studying the layout of Selene, its tunnels and living spaces, its offices and workshops, the machinery systems that supplied the underground city with air to breathe and potable water. In particular, he tried to find out all he could about the lowermost level of Selene, the big natural grotto that Martin Humphries had transformed into a lush garden and luxurious mansion for himself.

About the mansion he could learn nothing. Humphries's security maintained a close guard over its layout and life support systems. Fuchs had to be satisfied with memorizing every detail of the plumbing and electrical power systems that led to the grotto. There was no information available on the piping and conduits once they entered Humphries's private preserve. Perhaps that will be enough, Fuchs thought. Perhaps that will do.

He kept at his task doggedly, filling every moment of each day with his studies, telling himself a hundred times an hour that he would find a way to kill Martin Humphries.

In the night, when he was so exhausted from his work that he could no longer keep his eyes open, the rage returned anew. He and Amanda had roomed at the Hotel Luna once. They had made love in a bedroom like the one he now was in. During the rare moments when he was actually able to sleep he dreamed of Amanda, relived their passion. And awoke to find himself shamed and sticky from his brief dreams.

I'm only a kilometer or so from Humphries, Fuchs told himself over and again. Close enough to kill him. Soon. Soon.

TORCH SHIP *SAMARKAND*

ourteen ships, sir. Confirmed," said Harbin's pilot. The bridge of *Samarkand* was crowded with the pilot, communications technician, weapons tech, the executive officer, and Harbin, seated in the command chair, all of them in bulky, awkward space suits. The navigation officer had been banished to a rearward cabin, connected to the bridge by the ship's intercom.

"A formidable fleet," Harbin murmered.

His own force consisted of only three ships. Although he by far preferred to work alone, Harbin realized that the war had escalated far beyond the point where single ships could engage in one-on-one battles. He was now the leader of a trio of ships, a Yamagata employee, working for Humphries under a contract between HSS and Yamagata.

"They've detected us," the comm tech sang out. "Radar contact."

"Turn to one-fifteen degrees azimuth, maintain constant elevation. Increase acceleration to one-quarter g."

"They're following."

"Good."

Lasers were the weapons that spacecraft used against one another. From a distance of a thousand kilometers their intense beams of energy could slash through the unprotected skin of a spacecraft's hull in a second or less. Defensive armor was the countermove against energy weapons: Warships now spread coatings of asteroidal rubble over their hulls. Newer ships were being built at Selene of pure diamond, manufactured by nanomachines out of carbon soot.

But there was a countermeasure against armored ships, Harbin knew, as he led Astro Corporation's armada of fourteen ships toward the trap.

HSS intelligence had provided Harbin with a very detailed knowledge of the Astro ships, their mission plan, and—most importantly—their commander. Harbin had never met Reid Gormley, but he knew that the pint-sized Astro commander liked to go into battle with a clear preponderance of numbers.

Fourteen ships against three, Harbin thought. Clearly superior. Clearly.

"Don't let them get away!" snapped Gormley as he leaned forward tensely in the command chair of his flagship, *Antares*.

"We're matching their velocity vector, sir," said his navigation officer.

Like their quarry, Gormley's crews had donned their individual space suits. A ship may get punctured in battle and lose air; the suits were a necessary precaution, even though they were cumbersome. Gormley didn't like being in a suit, and he didn't think they were really necessary. But doctrine demanded the precaution and he followed doctrine obediently.

"I want to overtake them. Increase our velocity. Pass the word to the other ships."

"We should send a probe ahead to see if there are other enemy vessels lying outside our radar range," said Gormley's executive officer, a broomstick-lean, coal-black Sudanese who had never been in battle before.

"Our radar can pick up craters on the moons of Jupiter, for god's sake," Gormley snapped back. "Do you see anything out there except the three we're chasing?"

"Nosir," the Sudanese replied uneasily, his eyes on the radar screen. "Only a few small rocks."

Gormley took a quick glance at the radar. "Pebbles," he smirked. "Nothing to worry about."

The Sudanese stayed silent, but he thought, Nothing to worry about unless we go sailing into them. He made a mental note to stay well clear of those pebbles, no matter where the quarry went in its effort to escape.

Wearing a one-piece miniskirted outfit with its front zipper pulled low, Victoria Ferrer had to scamper in her high-heeled softboots to keep pace with Martin Humphries as he strode briskly along the corridor between the baby's nursery and his office.

"Send the brat to Earth," he snapped. "I don't want to see him again."

Ferrer could count the number of his visits to the nursery on the fingers of one hand. She had to admit, though, that the room looked more like a hospital's intensive care ward than an ordinary nursery. Barely more than six months old, little Van Humphries still needed a special high-pressure chamber to get enough air into his tiny lungs. The baby was scrawny, sickly, and Humphries had no patience for a weakling.

"Wouldn't it be better to keep him here?" she asked, hurrying alongside Humphries. "We have the facilities here and we can bring in any specialists the baby needs."

Humphries cast a cold eye on her. "You're not fond of the runt, are you?"

"He's only a helpless baby . . ."

"And you think that getting him attached to you will be a good career move? You think you'll have better job security by mothering the runt?"

She looked genuinely shocked. "That never crossed my mind!"

"Of course not."

Ferrer stopped dead in her tracks and planted her fists on her hips. "Mr. Humphries, *sir:* If you believe that I'm trying to use your son for my own gain, you're completely wrong. I'm not that cold-blooded."

He stopped, too, a few paces farther along the corridor, and looked her over. She seemed sincere enough, almost angry at him. Humphries laughed inwardly at the image of her, eyes flashing with righteous indignation, fists on her hips. Nice hips, he noted. She breathes sexy, too.

"We'll see how warm-blooded you are tonight," he said. Turning, he started along the corridor again. "I want the brat sent Earthside. To my family estate in Connecticut, or what's left of it. That's where his brother is. I've got enough staff and tutors there to start a university. Set up a facility for him there, get the best medical team on Earth to take care of him. Just keep him out of my sight. I don't want to lay eyes on him again. Ever."

Ferrer scurried to catch up with him. "Suppose they can cure him, make him healthy. Maybe nanotherapy or—"

"If and when that happy day arrives, I'll reconsider. Until then, keep him out of my sight. Understand?"

She nodded unhappily. "Understood."

Feeling nettled, fuming, Humphries ducked into his office and slammed the door shut behind him. Send the runt to Connecticut. Alex is down there. My real son. My clone. He's growing up fine and strong. I should've gotten rid of that miserable little brat his first day, the day his mother died. I've got a son; I don't need this other little slug.

Once he got to his desk, Humphries saw that a message from Grigor was waiting for him. He slid into his desk chair and commanded the phone to call his security chief.

Grigor appeared in front of Humphries's desk, seated at his own desk in his own office, a few meters down the hall, dark and dour as usual.

"What is it?" Humphries asked without preamble.

"The Astro flotilla that has been assembled in the Belt is pursuing our Yamagata team, as predicted."

Humphries dipped his chin a bare centimeter. "So the computer wargame is working out, is it?"

"The simulation is being followed. Gormley is rushing into the trap."

"Good. Call me when it's over." Humphries was about to cut the connection when he added. "Send me the video record as soon as it's available."

Grigor nodded. "I think you'll enjoy it," he said, mirthlessly.

"They're veering off," Gormley said, his eyes riveted to the navigation screen. "Follow them! Increase speed. Don't let them get away!"

The Sudanese executive officer noted with some relief that the three fleeing enemy ships had turned away from the sprinkling of small rocks that they had been approaching. They want no more to do with that danger than I do, he said to himself.

"We're well within range," said the weapons officer.

"Locked on?"

Without even glancing at her console, the weapons officer said, "Five lasers are locked onto each of the enemy's vessels, sir."

"Get on their tails," Gormley said. "They may be armored, but they can't armor their thruster nozzles. Hit their thrusters and we've got them crippled."

Of course, thought the Sudanese. But his attention was still on those small rocks off to their starboard. Strange to see such small objects without a larger asteroid that gave birth to them. They're like a reef in the ocean, a danger lurking, waiting to smash unsuspecting ships. Then he thought, For a man who was brought up far from the sea, you've become quite a mariner.

Harbin heard the alarm in the voice of his pilot. "They're firing at us! Firing at all three of us."

"They can't do much damage at this range," he said calmly.

"If they hit our thrusters . . ." The pilot turned in his chair and saw the set of Harbin's jaw. "Sir," he added lamely.

"All ships," Harbin commanded, "increase elevation three degrees, now."

To his exec he said, "Activate the rocks."

"They're maneuvering!" sang out the weapons officer.

Gormley saw it on the nav screen. "Keep locked onto them. Don't let them get away!"

Even the Sudanese had turned his attention away from the small rocks that were now fairly far off to their starboard to concentrate on the battle action. The enemy ships were maneuvering in unison, which was foolish. Far better, when being chased, to maneuver independently and set up a more difficult targeting problem for the attackers.

The collision-avoidance radar began to bong loudly.

"What in blazes is that?" Gormley shouted.

The navigation screen automatically switched to show several dozen meter-sized rocks hurtling toward Gormley's ships. The Sudanese could see glowing plumes of exhaust plasma thrusting the rocks toward them.

How simple! he realized. Set up small rocks with plasma thrusters and guidance chips, lure your enemy toward them, and then fire the rocks into your enemy's ships. How simple. And how deadly.

The rocks were moving at high velocity when they smashed into the Astro Corporation ships. They tore the ships apart, like high-speed bullets fired through tin cans. One of them blasted through the bridge of *Antares,* ripped through the helmeted head of the ship's pilot and plowed out the other side of the bridge while the woman's decapitated body showered blood everywhere. Screams and cries of horror filled the Sudanese's helmet earphones. Cursing wildly, he cut off the suit radio as his chair ripped free of its mounting on the ship's deck and crashed through the gaping hole in the bridge where the rock had gone through. He felt his left arm snap, and a dizzying wave of excruciating pain shot down his spine. Then he felt and heard nothing.

He was spinning slowly, slowly through empty space, still strapped into his broken chair. He could feel nothing below his neck. He could hardly breathe. Through tear-filled eyes he saw the shattered remnants of Gormley's fleet, broken and smashed pieces of spacecraft, bodies floating in their space suits, a proud armada reduced in a few seconds to a slowly spreading patch of debris. Flotsam, he thought idly. We are going to die in this empty wilderness.

"My god," whispered someone on the bridge of *Samarkand.*

Harbin also stared at the destruction. The Astro fleet looked as if it had gone through a shredder. A meatgrinder. Bodies and wreckage were strewn everywhere, spinning, tumbling, coasting through space.

"Should we pick up the survivors?" his pilot asked, in a hushed voice.

Harbin shook his head. "There are no survivors."

"But maybe some—"

"There are no survivors," he repeated harshly. But his eyes lingered on the display screen. A few hundred new asteroids have been added to the Belt, he told himself. Some of them were once human beings.

ASTRO CORPORATION HEADQUARTERS

Wiped out?" Pancho asked, her insides suddenly gone hollow.

"Every ship," said Jake Wanamaker. "No survivors." He looked grim, beaten.

"What happened?"

Wanamaker was standing before her desk like a man facing a firing squad. Pancho pushed herself to her feet and gestured him to one of the comfortably padded chairs arranged around the small oval table in the corner of her office. Feeling shaky, her knees rubbery, she went to the table and sat next to her military commander.

"We're not certain. We got a brief signal that they used small asteroids—some of them no bigger than a man's fist—and rammed them into Gormley's ships."

"How could they do that?" Pancho asked.

"Attach a plasma rocket and a simple guidance system to the rock," said Wanamaker. "It doesn't have to be fancy. Just juice the rocks up to very high velocity and ram them into our ships. Like buckshot hitting paper bags."

"And they're all dead?"

Wanamaker nodded bleakly.

Jesus sufferin' Christ, Pancho thought. Thirteen ships. A hundred and fifty people, just about.

"I think I should tender my resignation," said Wanamaker.

Pancho glared at him. "Giving up?"

He flinched as though she'd slapped him. "No. But a defeat like this . . . you'll probably want a better man to head your war."

Shaking her head slowly, Pancho said, "No, I want you, Jake. One battle doesn't mean we've lost it all."

But inwardly she thought, I want you to keep on heading the military operations. But I'll take charge of this goddamned war. Humphries might have the edge on us militarily, with more mercenaries and more ships and better experience. But there's more than one way to fight a war.

To Wanamaker, she said, "I'm not giving up. Far as I'm concerned, this war's just started."

" 'I have not yet begun to fight,' " he muttered.

"I heard that one," Pancho said. "John Paul Jones, wasn't it?"

Wanamaker nodded.

"Okay. You recruit more mercenaries, I'll buy more ships. For the time being, Humphries has the run of the Belt. He's gonna attack any Astro vessels he can find out there, try to drive us out of the Belt altogether."

"Convoy them."

"Convoy?"

"Don't let them sail alone. Put them in groups. It's harder to attack a formation of armed ships than a single ship."

"Makes sense," Pancho agreed. "I'll send out the word right away."

"I think Yamagata Corporation can provide us with reliable mercenaries."

"Good. Go get 'em."

It took a moment for Wanamaker to realize he'd been dismissed. It only hit him when Pancho pushed her chair back from the conference table and got to her feet. He shot up and started to salute, then caught himself and reddened slightly.

"I've got a lot of work to do," he said, as if excusing himself for leaving the room.

"Me too," said Pancho.

Wanamaker left, and Pancho returned to her desk. She called up reports on where the Astro ships were, and where Humphries's vessels were. A holographic representation of the vast space between Earth and the Belt took form in the air beyond her desk, a huge dark expanse with flickering pinpoints of light showing the positions of the ships, Astro's in blue, HSS's in red. There was a cluster of ships between the Earth and Moon; Pancho blanked them out to simplify the three-dimensional picture.

Cripes, there's a lot of red ones out in the Belt, she said to herself. And those are just the ones we know about. The Humper's prob'ly got a lot more out there, moving around the Belt without any telemetry or identification beacons for the IAA to pick up.

She had the computer identify the ore freighters, logistics carriers, and ships carrying miners to specific asteroids. Then she added the freelancers, the prospectors and miners who worked on their own, independent of the big corporations.

Minutes ticked into hours as she studied the situation. We're outnumbered in the Belt two, three to one, Pancho saw. The Hump's been building up his fleet out there for years now. We've gotta play catch-up.

But why should we play their game? she asked herself. That's what we were doing with Gormley and look what it got us.

She leaned back in her softly yielding desk chair and closed her eyes briefly. What's the point of all those ships out in the Belt? To bring ores to the factories on Earth, or in Earth orbit, or here at Selene, she answered her own question.

She stared at the hologram imagery again. Flickering red dots representing HSS ships were spread through the Belt, with a particular clustering around Vesta. But a thinner trickle of red dots was plying the lanes between the Belt and the Earth/Moon vicinity.

They've gotta bring the goods back here, Pancho saw. That's the whole point of mining the rocks. If we can knock off their ships coming Earthward, we can hit Humphries in the pocketbook, strangle his cash flow, cut his profits down to nothing.

She sat up straight in the desk chair and said aloud, "That's the way to do it! Let him have the Belt for now. Stop him from bringing the ores to market."

We don't need naval tactics, she realized. We don't need battles between fleets of warships. What we need is more like a gang of pirates. Like the old Sea Hawks from Queen Elizabeth I's time. Privateers. Pirates.

And she knew just the man who could lead such a campaign. Lars Fuchs.

"All of them?" Humphries asked, as if the news was too good to be true.

Vicki Ferrer was not smiling, but it was clear from the pleased expression on her face that she was happy to be able to bring her boss a positive report.

"Every Astro ship was destroyed," she repeated.

They were in the big library/bar on the ground floor of Humphries's mansion, alone except for the robot bartender, which stood at its post, gleaming stainless steel reflecting the ceiling lights.

"You're sure?" Humphries asked.

"The report came directly from the Yamagata team. Their idea about using the rocks worked perfectly. The Astro fleet charged right into them. No survivors."

"This calls for champagne!" Humphries strode to the bar. The robot did not move. Nettled slightly at the machine's obtuseness, Humphries called out, "Bartender! Champagne!"

The gleaming dome-topped robot trundled sideways along the bar and stopped precisely at the wine cooler. Two slim arms extruded from its cylindrical body, opened the cooler, and pulled out a bottle of Veuve Cliquot. It trundled back to Humphries and held up the bottle so he could inspect the label.

"Fine," said Humphries. "Open it and let me sample it."

"How does it find the right bottle?" Ferrer asked, coming over to sit on the stool next to him. Even though it was dinner time for most people, she was still in her office attire, a miniskirted baby pink suit that hugged her curves artfully.

"There's a sensor in each hand," said Humphries, watching the dumb machine gripping the cork. If he drops that bottle, Humphries thought, I'll run him through the recycler.

The cork came out with a satisfactorily loud pop and the robot set two champagne flutes on the bar top in front of Humphries, then poured a thimbleful of wine for him to taste.

Humphries tasted, nodded, told the robot to pour. Once it had, he lifted his glass to Ferrer and toasted, "To victory!"

She made a smile and murmured, "To victory."

"We've got them on the run now," Humphries said happily. "I'm going to drive Astro completely out of the Belt!"

Ferrer smiled again and sipped. But she was thinking, Thirteen ships destroyed. How many people did we kill? How many more have to die before this is over?

HOTEL LUNA: RESIDENTIAL SUITE

Pancho could not locate Fuchs. For two days she had her people search for him. They learned that under the false identity she had provided, Fuchs had spent a few days in his native Switzerland, then flown to Selene.

"He's here in Selene?" she asked her security chief.

The man looked uncomfortable. "Apparently."

"Find him," she snapped. "Wherever the hell he is, find him. You got twenty-four hours."

She had just returned to her suite when the phone told her the report on Fuchs came in. She glanced at her wristwatch. Eight minutes before midnight, Pancho saw. They're working overtime.

The suite's décor was set to Camelot, Pancho's fantasy of what King Arthur's fabled castle might have been like. She sat herself on one of the sofas in her bedroom and told the phone to play the report. Through a mullioned window she could see knights jousting on a perfect greensward beneath a cloudless blue sky, watched by a cheering throng standing before tented pavilions complete with colorful pennants that fluttered in the breeze of an eternal springtime.

The young man whose hologram image appeared in the middle of the room might have been one of knights of the Round Table, Pancho thought idly. He was a good-looking blond, strong shoulders, honest open face with sky-blue eyes, his hair stylishly long enough for ringlets to curl around the collar of his jacket. He was sitting at a desk in what appeared to be a smallish office somewhere in the Astro headquarters. The data line hovering to one side of the image identified him as Frederic Karstein, Astro security department.

Pancho listened to the brief report with growing incredulity. And annoyance.

"You mean he was right here in the Hotel Luna?" she asked the image.

The image flickered momentarily. Then the handsome Frederic Karstein said, "Ms. Lane, I'm live now. I can answer your questions in real time, ma'am."

"Are you telling me that Fuchs was living just a couple hundred meters from my own quarters?" she demanded.

"Yes, ma'am, apparently he was."

"And where is he now?"

Karstein shrugged his broad shoulders. "We don't know. He seems to have disappeared."

"Disappeared? How can he disappear?"

"If we knew that, Ms. Lane, we'd probably know where he is."

"You can't just disappear! Selene's not that big, and the whole dog-gone place is under surveillance all the time."

Karstein looked embarrassed. "We're certain he hasn't left Selene. We've checked the passenger lists for all the outgoing flights for the past two weeks, and examined the surveillance camera records."

"So he's someplace here in Selene?"

"It would appear so."

Pancho huffed. "All right. Stay on this. I want him found, and right away, too."

"We'll do our best, Ms. Lane."

She cut the connection and Karstein's image winked out. Dumb blond, Pancho groused to herself.

"Privateers?" Jake Wanamaker asked, his rasping voice croaking out the word. "You mean, like pirates?"

Pancho had invited him to a breakfast meeting in her suite. They sat in the tight little alcove off the kitchen, but the holowalls made it seem as if they were outdoors, beneath a graceful elm tree, with softly rolling grassy hills in the distance and the morning sun brightening a clear sky. She could hear birds chirping happily and almost felt a cool breeze ruffling their table linen.

Pancho took a sip of grapefruit juice, then replied, "Yep. Yo-ho-ho and all that stuff. Cut off Humphries's ships as they're bringing their payloads here to the Moon. Or to Earth."

Wanamaker took a considerable bite out of the sticky bun he was holding in one big hand, chewed thoughtfully for a few moments, then swallowed. "They've beaten the crap out of us in the Belt, sure enough.

It'll be some time before we can build up enough forces to challenge them again."

"But a few ships operating closer to home, outside the Belt . . ." Pancho let the suggestion hang in the air between them.

Wanamaker muttered, "Cut HSS's pipeline to the market. Hit Humphries in the pocketbook."

"That's where it'd hurt him the most."

After washing down his cake with a gulp of black coffee, Wanamaker said, "Set up a blockade."

"Right."

Absently wiping his sticky fingers with his napkin, Wanamaker broke into a wicked grin. "We wouldn't even need crewed ships for that. Just automate some small birds and park them in wide orbits around the Earth/Moon system."

"You can do that?"

He nodded. "They'd be close enough to be remotely operated from here at Selene. It'd be cheaper than using crewed ships."

Pancho had only one further question. "How soon can we get this going?"

Wanamaker pushed his chair back from the table and got to his feet. "Real soon," he said. "Very damned real soon."

Pancho watched him hurry away, thinking, So I won't need Lars after all. Doesn't matter where he's hiding. I won't need him now.

Later that morning, with some reluctance, Pancho slipped on the softsuit and sealed the opening that ran the length of the torso's front. Doug Stavenger was already in his suit. To Pancho he looked as if he'd been packed into a plastic-wrap food container, except for the fishbowl helmet he held cradled in his arms.

"This thing really works?" she asked, picking up her helmet from the shelf in the locker.

Stavenger nodded, smiling at her. "It's been tested for months now, Pancho. I've worn it outside myself several times. You're going to love it."

She felt totally unconvinced. Never fly in a new airplane, she remembered from her first days as a pilot. Never eat in a new restaurant on its opening day.

Plucking at the transparent nanomachined fabric with gloved fingers, she said, "Kinda flimsy."

"But it works like a charm."

"That mean you gotta say prayers over it?"

Stavenger laughed. "Come on, Pancho. Once we're outside you'll wonder how you were ever able to stand those clunky cermet suits."

"Uh-huh." She could see the enthusiasm in his eyes, his smile, his whole demeanor. He's like a kid with a new toy, she thought.

But he was right. It took roughly ten minutes to walk from the airlock at Selene to Factory Number Eleven, out on the floor of the giant crater Alphonsus. Before even five minutes were up, Pancho had fallen in love with the softsuit.

"It's terrific," she said to Stavenger, shuffling along beside her, his boots kicking up gentle clouds of dust. "It's like being without a suit, almost."

"I told you, didn't I?"

Pancho held both hands before her and flexed her fingers. "Hot spit! Even the gloves are easy to work. This is like magic!"

"Not magic. Just nanotechnology."

"And the radiation protection?"

"About the same as a hard-shell suit," Stavenger said. "We could add electromagnetic shielding, but that would probably attract a lot of dust from the ground."

She nodded inside her helmet.

"You're okay for short time periods on the surface," Stavenger went on. "Off the Moon an electromagnetic system can be added to the suits easily enough."

Pancho asked, "Doug, ol' pal, how'd you like to sign a contract with Astro to manufacture and distribute these softsuits?"

He laughed. "No thanks, Pancho. Selene's going to develop this product. We'll sell them at pretty close to cost, too."

Pancho understood the meaning behind his words. If Selene signed up with Astro for selling the suits, Humphries would complain. If Selene gave a contract to HSS, Astro would fight it. She nodded again inside the fishbowl helmet. Better to keep this out of either corporation's hands. Better to let Selene handle this one themselves.

The low curving roof of the factory loomed before them. Stavenger and Pancho climbed the stairs to the edge of the factory's thick concrete slab, then stepped through the "car wash," the special airlock that scrubbed their suits free of dust and other contaminants before they were allowed to enter the ultra-pure domain of the factory itself. Pancho felt the jets and scrubbers pummeling her brutally.

"Hey Doug," she gasped. "You gotta reset these things to go easier."

His voice in her helmet earphones sounded bemused. "We did reset them, Pancho. They would've knocked you flat if we'd left them at the same power level we used for the hard-shell suits."

It took Pancho a few moments to catch her breath once she had stepped out of the "car wash" and onto the factory floor. As Stavenger came up beside her, also breathing heavily, she looked out at the two completed spacecraft. Their diamond hulls looked dark, like ominous shadows lurking beneath the curved roof of the factory.

"There they are," Stavenger said tightly. "One for you and one for Humphries."

She understood the tension in his voice. "Two brand-new warships. So we can go out and kill some more mercenaries."

Stavenger said nothing.

"We've got six more under contract, right?" she asked.

After several heartbeats, Stavenger said, "Yes. And we're building the same number for Humphries."

"So no matter who wins, Selene makes money."

"I don't like it, Pancho. I don't like any of this. If I could convince the governing council to renege on these contracts, I would."

"I don't like it either, Doug. But what else can we do? Let the Humper take over the whole danged solar system?"

He fell silent again.

As they trudged back in silence toward the airlock at Selene, Pancho said to herself: Deadlock. Selene doesn't want either one of us to win. They don't want one side to beat the other and become master of the whole solar system. Even if Astro wins, if *I* win, Selene's scared shitless that they'll be under my thumb. Doug wants to see Humphries and Astro fight ourselves into exhaustion, and then he'll step in and be the peacemaker again.

So they're doing their best to keep us even. They won't make a warship for Humphries without making one for Astro. Keeps them neutral, Doug says. Keeps us in a deadlock, that's what it keeps.

There's gotta be some way out of this, some way to break through and beat the Humper before we're both so broke and dead-flat exhausted that both our corporations go bust.

If I could get Lars to help us, she thought. He might just be able to tip the scales in our favor. But the l'il bugger has disappeared. What's he up to? Why's he gone to ground on me?

Shaking her head inside the fishbowl helmet, Pancho considered: We need an outside force, a partner, an ally. Somebody who can tip the scales in Astro's favor. Outmaneuver Humphries. Overpower him. Some way to outflank HSS.

Then it hit her. Nairobi! That guy from Nairobi Industries wanted a strategic alliance with Astro. I wonder if he's still interested? I'll have to look him up soon's I get back to the office, whatever his name was.

ASTRO CORPORATION
COMMAND CENTER

Jake Wanamaker's command center was a cluster of offices set slightly apart from the rest of Astro Corporation's headquarters. With wry humor, Wanamaker mused that Humphries could do more damage to Astro, at far less cost, by attacking these offices and wiping out the corporation's military command. But even war has its rules, and one of the fundamental rules of this conflict was that no violence would be tolerated anywhere on the Moon. The side that broke that rule would bring Selene and its considerable financial and manufacturing clout into the battle as an enemy.

So despite the purely perfunctory guards stationed at the double doors of the command center, armed with nothing more than sidearms, Wanamaker had little fear of being attacked here in Selene. He went through the doors and down the central corridor, heading for his own office to a chorus of "Good morning, Admiral" accompanied by military salutes. Wanamaker returned each salute scrupulously: good discipline began with mutual respect, he felt.

Wanamaker's office was spartan. The battleship-gray metal furniture was strictly utilitarian. The only decorations on the walls were citations he had garnered over his years of service. The wallscreens were blank as his staff filed in and took their chairs along the scuffed old conference table that butted against his desk. Wanamaker had salvaged them both from his last sea command, an amphibious assault command vessel.

He spent the morning outlining Pancho's idea of setting up a blockade against incoming HSS ore carriers.

"Unmanned craft?" asked one of his junior officers.

"Uncrewed," Wanamaker corrected, "remotely operated from here."

One of the women officers asked, "Here in Selene? Won't that get Stavenger and the governing council riled up?"

"Not if we don't commit any violent acts here in Selene," Wanamaker replied, smiling coldly. Then he added, "And especially if they don't know about it."

"It won't be easy to build and launch the little robots without Stavenger's people finding out about it."

"We can build them easily enough in Astro's factories up on the surface and launch them aboard Astro boosters. No need for Selene to get worked up over this."

The younger officers glanced at each other up and down the conference table, while Wanamaker watched from behind his desk. They get the idea, he saw. I'm not asking for their opinions about the idea, I'm telling them that they've got to make it work.

"Well," his engineering chief said, "we can build the little suckers easily enough. Nothing exotic about putting together a heavy laser with a communications system and some station-keeping gear."

"Good," said Wanamaker.

Gradually the rest of the staff warmed to the idea.

At length he asked, "How long will it take?"

"We could have the first ones ready to launch in a couple of weeks," said the engineer.

Wanamaker silently doubled the estimate.

"Wait," cautioned the intelligence officer, a plump Armenian with long, straight dark hair and darker eyes. "Each of these birds will need sensors to identify potential targets and aim the lasers."

"No worries," said the Australian electronics officer. "We can do that in two shakes of a sheep's tail. Piece of cake."

"Besides," pointed out the engineer, "the birds will be operated from here, with human brains in the loop."

The intelligence officer looked dubious, but voiced no further objections.

"All right, then," said Wanamaker at last. "Let's get to work on this. Pronto. Time is of the essence."

That broke up the meeting. But as the staff officers were shuffling toward the door, Wanamaker called the intelligence officer back to his desk.

"Sit down, Willie," he said, gesturing to the chair on the desk's left side. He knew she disliked to be called by her real name, Wilhelmina. The things parents do to their kids, Wanamaker thought.

She sat, looking curious, almost worried.

Wanamaker took a breath, then said, "We need a diversion."

"Sir?"

"Humphries has beat the hell out of us in the Belt, and it's going to be months before we can start fighting back."

"But Jess said he'd have the first robots on station in two weeks," the intelligence officer countered.

"Two weeks plus Murphy's Law," Wanamaker said.

Her dark eyes lit with understanding. "If anything can go wrong, it will."

"Especially in a wartime situation. I know the staff will push as hard as they can, but I don't expect to be able to hit back to HSS with these robot systems for at least a month, maybe more."

"I see," she said.

"Meanwhile, we need a diversion. Something to knock the HSS people off their feet a little, shake them up, make them realize we're not going to lay down and die."

"Such as?"

He grinned lopsidedly at her. "That's what I want you to figure out, kid."

She did not smile back. "I'll do my best, sir."

ASTEROID 73-241

L evinson felt distinctly uneasy in the space suit. It was bad enough to have to fly out to this remote piece of rock in the middle of nowhere, carrying the heavily armored flask of nanomachines he had produced in the HSS lab at Selene. Now he had to actually go out of the ship like some superjock astronaut and supervise the crew he had brought with him.

"Me?" he had asked, alarmed, when Vickie Ferrer had told him that Martin Humphries himself wanted Lev to personally supervise the experiment.

"You," she had replied, silky smooth. "It's to your advantage to handle the job yourself. Why let someone else take the credit for it?"

As he hung weightlessly between the slowly spinning torch ship and the lumpy dark asteroid, clipped to the tether that was anchored to the ship's airlock, Lev realized that Vickie had played him like a puppet. Her alluring smiles and promising cleavage, her smoky voice and tantalizing hints of what would be possible after he had succeeded with his nanomachines had brought him out here, to this dark and cold emptiness, face to face with a pitted, ugly chunk of rock the size of a football field.

Well, he told himself, when I get back she'll be waiting for me. She said as much. I'll be a big success and she'll be so impressed she'll do whatever I want her to.

Prodded by Ferrer's implicit promises, Levinson had rushed through the laboratory work. Producing nanomachines that were not damaged by ultraviolet light was no great feat; the trick was to keep them contained so they couldn't get loose and start eating up everything in sight. It was after he'd accomplished that that Ferrer had told him he must go out to the Belt and personally supervise the experiment.

So here I am, he said to himself, shuddering inside the space suit. It's so absolutely *empty* out here! Despite his cerebral knowledge that the Asteroid Belt was mostly empty space, he found the dark silence unsettling. It's like being in a football stadium with only one seat occupied, he thought. Like being all alone in an empty city.

There were the stars, of course, but they just made Levinson feel spookier. There were millions of them, countless myriads of them crowding the sky so much that the old friendly constellations he knew from Earth were blotted out, swamped in the multitudes. And they didn't twinkle, they just hung up there as if they were watching, solemn unblinking eyes staring down at him.

"We're ready to unseal the bugs." The voice of one of his technicians grated in his earphones, startling Levinson out of his thoughts.

"They're not bugs," he replied automatically. "They're nanomachines."

"Yeah, right. We're ready to open the jug."

Levinson pulled himself slowly along the tether to its other end, anchored in the solid rock of the little asteroid. His two technicians floated above the rock, able to flit back and forth on the minijet thruster units attached to their backpacks. Levinson, a novice at extravehicular activities, kept himself firmly clipped to the tether. He carried the "jug," a sealed bottle made of pure diamond, on the utility belt around the waist of his space suit.

He planted his feet on the asteroid and, much to his consternation, immediately bounced off. In his earphones he heard one of his techs snicker softly.

"Newton's laws work even out here," he said, to cover his embarrassment.

He approached the rock more slowly and, after two more tries, finally got his boots to stay on the surface. He could see the puffs of dust where he first landed still hanging in the asteroid's minuscule gravity.

The technicians had marked concentric fluorescent circles across the surface of the rock, like a glowing bull's-eye. Cameras back in the ship would record how quickly the nanomachines spread from the release point, chewing up the rock as they went. Levinson went to the center of the circles, tugging on his tether, bobbing up and off the asteroid's surface with each step he took. He heard no giggling from his technicians this time. Probably they've turned their transmitters off, he thought.

It was clumsy working in the space suit's gloves, even with the tiny servomotors on the backs to help him flex the fingers. Finally Levinson unsealed the bottle and placed it, open end down, on the exact center of the bull's-eye. Again, the light gravity worked against him. The bottle bobbed up from the surface as soon as he took his hand off it. Frowning, he pushed it down and held it for a moment, then carefully removed his hand. The bottle stayed put.

Looking up, he saw that both his technicians were hovering well clear of the rock. Scared of the nanomachines, Levinson thought. Well, better to be safe than sorry. He grabbed the tether with both hands and hauled himself off the asteroid, then started his hand-over-hand return to the ship.

The tether suddenly went slack, and for a fearful moment Levinson thought something had gone wrong. Then he saw that it was still fastened to the ship's airlock and remembered that the techs were supposed to set off an explosive charge that released the end of the tether attached to the asteroid. In the vacuum of space he couldn't hear the pop of the explosive bolt. It took a surprisingly tough effort to turn around, but once he did he saw the other end of the tether hanging limply in empty space.

And the asteroid was vanishing! Levinson's eyes goggled at how fast the nanomachines were chewing up the asteroid, leaving a rising cloud of dust that grew so rapidly the solid rock itself was quickly obscured. It's like piranhas eating up a chunk of meat, he thought, recalling videos he had seen of the voracious fish setting a South American stream a-boil as they attacked their prey.

"Start the spectrometer!" Levinson called excitedly as he resumed tugging his way back to the ship.

In less than a minute he could see the sparkling dazzle of a laser beam playing over the expanding dust cloud.

Puffing with exertion, he saw as he approached the airlock that its hatch was closed. His two assistants had jetted to the ship ahead of him, he realized.

"What're you getting?" he asked into his helmet microphone.

The technician running the spectrometer aboard the ship answered, "Iron, lead, platinum, silver—"

"Pure elements or compounds?" Levinson demanded, watching the asteroid dissolve like a log being chewed up by a wood chipper.

"Atomic species mostly. Some compounds that look pretty weird, but most of it is pure atomic species."

The weird stuff must be the nanos, Levinson thought. He had programmed them to shut down after forty-eight hours. At this rate there wouldn't be anything left of the asteroid in forty-eight hours except a cloud of individual atoms.

Wow! he thought. It works even better than I expected. Vickie's going to be impressed, all right.

ADMIRAL WANAMAKER'S OFFICE

The spare, austere office was empty except for Wanamaker himself and Wilhelmina Tashkajian, his intelligence officer. She was short, round, dark, and, according to the scuttlebutt that floated around the office, a pretty good amateur belly dancer. All Wanamaker knew for certain was that she had a fine, sharp mind, the kind that can analyze information and draw valid conclusions more quickly than anyone else on his staff. That was all he wanted to know about her.

They sat on opposite sides of the conference table that extended from the admiral's desk. Like all of Wanamaker's officers, Tashkajian wore plain gray coveralls with her name and rank spelled out on a smart-chip badge clipped to the flap of her breast pocket. Wanamaker himself wore the same uniform.

He looked up from the report on the display screen built into the table's top. "They're testing nanomachines?"

She nodded, her dark eyes somber. "Humphries recruited the scientist that Pancho brought back here from Ceres. Snatched him right out from under our noses."

Wanamaker grimaced. "She should have kept him on Astro's payroll."

"Too late for that, sir."

"And they're already in test phase?"

Another nod. "From the information we've gathered, they went through the laboratory phase very quickly, and then sent this Dr. Levinson and a crew of technicians out to the Belt. Conclusion: They're testing nanomachines on an asteroid."

"Does Pancho know this yet?"

"She gets a copy of my reports automatically."

4

"Any response from her?"

"Not yet, sir. I just put out the report this morning. Not everyone reacts as fast as you." She smiled slightly, then added, "Sir."

He allowed himself to smile back at her a little.

"The real question," she said, "is whether HSS is developing nanomachines for processing ores out of the asteroids or as weapons."

"Weapons?" Wanamaker's gray brows rose.

"If they can chew up rocks, they can chew up spacecraft, buildings, even people."

He sank back in the stiff metal chair. "Weapons," he muttered. "My god."

"It's a possibility, isn't it?" she asked.

"I suppose it is."

Tashkajian waited a heartbeat, then said, "I've been thinking about your request for a diversion, sir."

"Is this a change of subject?"

"Not entirely, sir."

Looking slightly puzzled, Wanamaker said, "Go ahead."

"Suppose we attacked HSS's base at Vesta," she began.

"Most of it's underground," said Wanamaker. "They're well dug in. And well defended."

"Yes, sir, I understand. But they have certain facilities on the surface of the asteroid. Communications antennas. Launchpads. Airlocks to the interior. Even their defensive laser weapons. They're all up on the surface."

"So?"

"So we strew the surface with nanomachines that eat metals."

Wanamaker's eyes flickered. She couldn't tell from his stony expression whether he was impressed or disgusted.

She plunged on, "The nanomachines would destroy metal structures, even eat into the asteroid itself. It might not wipe out the base but it would certainly disrupt their operations. It would be the diversion you've asked for."

He was silent for several moments. Then he asked, "And how do you get a ship close enough to Vesta to accomplish this raid? They'd blast the ship into molecules before it got close enough to be dangerous to them."

"I think I've got that figured out, too, sir."

He saw that she was deadly serious. She wouldn't bring this up unless she thought she had the entire scheme in hand, he realized.

"Go ahead," he said.

"We send the ship in when there's a solar flare."

Wanamaker blinked. "Do you think . . ." His voice trailed off.

"I've checked out the numbers, sir." With growing confidence she went on, "A category four solar flare emits a huge cloud of ionized particles. Scrambles communications on all frequencies, including radar! A ship could ride inside the cloud and get close enough to Vesta to release the nanomachines."

Immediately, he countered, "Solar flare clouds don't block laser beams."

"Yessir, I know. But laser sweeps aren't generally used for spotting spacecraft unless the radar scans have found a bogie. They use laser scans to identify an unknown radar blip."

"Riding inside a radiation cloud is pretty damned hazardous."

"Not if the ship is properly shielded, sir."

He fell silent once again, thinking.

"The radiation storm would drive all HSS personnel off the surface of Vesta. They'd all be deep underground, so our nanomachines would destroy their surface facilities without killing any of their personnel."

Wanamaker tried to scowl and wound up almost smiling, instead. "A humane attack on the enemy."

"A diversion that could cripple the HSS base on Vesta, at least temporarily, and check their domination of the Belt, sir."

"If there's a big enough flare to give you the cloud you need," he cautioned.

"That's what got me thinking about this idea in the first place," she said, clearly excited. "We're in the middle of a solar maximum period. Plenty of sunspots and lots of flares."

He nodded curtly. "Let me see the numbers."

"Yes, sir!"

HABITAT *CHRYSALIS*

Victoria Ferrer felt distinctly uneasy in the rock rats' habitat, in orbit around the asteroid Ceres. Although she dressed as modestly as she could, she still felt that every move she made was being watched by men—and women—who focused on her the way a stalking leopard stares at its prey.

The habitat itself was comfortable enough. The gravity was the same as the Moon's, or so close that she couldn't notice any difference. As a visitor Ferrer had a small but well-appointed compartment to herself, and the adjoining cabin to use as an office. There was a galley in the next segment of the structure, and even a passably decent restaurant on the other side of the wheel-shaped assemblage. With her expense account, she could afford to take most of her meals in the restaurant.

Ferrer had expected the rock rats to be scruffy, feisty, hard-rock types. Prospectors and miners, existing at the edge of human civilization, independent individualists eking out their living in the vast dark emptiness of the Belt, surviving in a world of danger and loneliness. To her surprise, she found that most of the residents of *Chrysalis* were shopkeepers, accountants, technicians employed in the service industries. Even the actual miners and prospectors had technical educations. They operated complex equipment out in the Belt; they had to know how to keep a spacecraft functioning when the nearest supply or maintenance depot was millions of kilometers away.

But they stared at her. Even in plain coveralls buttoned up to her chin, she felt their eyes on her. Fresh meat, she thought. A new face. A new body.

Her mission at Ceres was twofold. She was recruiting more hands for the army of mercenaries that the war demanded out of the growing numbers of unemployed miners and prospectors. And she was waiting for the return of Levinson and his nanotech team, to see firsthand the results of their experiment on an actual asteroid.

It had been pathetically easy to keep Levinson on a string. Every time they met he stared at her with hungry puppy eyes. If he comes back with a success he'll expect me to reward him, Ferrer thought. It won't be so easy to put him off then. But if he's successful I can let him down gently and maneuver him off to some other woman. God knows there are plenty here at Ceres who would be happy to get connected with a scientist who can take her back to Earth.

She tried to clear her mind of worries about Levinson and concentrate on the unemployed miner sitting on the other side of her desk. The clean-cut young man was trying his best not to ogle, but his eyes kept returning to the front of her shapeless turtleneck sweater. Momma and her damned genetic engineering, Ferrer thought. I should have brought sloppy old sweatshirts, or, better yet, a space suit.

She kept their discussion strictly on business, without a hint of anything else. Humphries had sent her here to recruit crews for HSS ships and she had no interest in anything else.

"I don't understand your reluctance," she said to the miner. "We're offering top salary and benefits."

He looked a decent-enough fellow, Ferrer thought: freshly shaved and wearing well-pressed slacks and an open-necked shirt. His dossier, on her desktop screen, showed he had an engineering degree and had spent the past four years working as a miner under contract to Astro Corporation. He'd quit a month ago and hadn't found a new job yet.

Fidgeting nervously in his chair, he answered, "Look, Ms. Ferrer, what good will all that salary and benefits do me when I'm dead?"

She knew what he meant, but still she probed, "Why do you say that?"

Making a sour face, the miner said, "You want to hire me as a crewman on one of your HSS ships, right? Everybody knows HSS and Astro are fighting it out in the Belt. People are being killed every day, just about. I'd rather bum around here on *Chrysalis* and wait for a real job to open up."

"There are a lot of unemployed miners here," Ferrer said.

"Yeah, I know. Some got laid off, like me. Some just quit, 'cause it's getting too blamed dangerous out in the Belt. I figure I'll just wait until you guys have settled your war. Once the shooting stops, I'll go back to work, I guess."

"That could be a long wait," she pointed out.

With a frowning nod, he replied, "I'd rather starve slowly than get killed suddenly."

Ferrer admitted defeat. "Very well. If you change your mind, please contact us."

Getting up from the chair in a rush, as if happy to be leaving, the miner said, "Don't hold your breath."

Ferrer conducted two more interviews that afternoon with exactly the same results. Miners and prospectors were abandoning their jobs to get away from the fighting. *Chrysalis* was filling up with unemployed rock rats. Most of them had run through what little savings they had accumulated and were now depending for their living on the scanty largesse of *Chrysalis*'s governing board. Hardly any of them accepted employment aboard HSS ships. Or Astro's, Ferrer found with some satisfaction. Of the fourteen men and women she had personally interviewed, only two had signed up, both of them women with babies to support. All the others had flatly refused her offers.

I'd rather starve slowly than get killed suddenly. That was their attitude.

Sitting alone in her office as the day waned, Ferrer sighed heavily. I'm going to have to report to Humphries, she told herself. He's not going to like what I have to tell him.

Levinson was glad to be out of the space suit. In fact, he was whistling cheerily as he made his way from the airlock of the torch ship toward the compartment they had given him. In two days we'll be back at Ceres, and then Vickie and I ride a torch ship back to Selene. I'll bet we spend the whole journey shacked up together.

"Shouldn't whistle aboard ship," said one of the technicians, coming up the passageway behind him. "It's considered bad luck."

Levinson grinned at her. "That's an old superstition," he said.

"No it's not. It dates back to sailing days, when orders were given by playing a whistle. So they didn't want anybody whistling and messing up the signaling system."

"Doesn't apply here," Levinson said loftily.

"Still, it's considered—"

"EMERGENCY," the overhead speaker blared. "PRESSURE LOSS IN MAIN AIRLOCK COMPARTMENT."

The blood froze in Levinson's veins. The airtight hatch up the passageway slammed shut. His knees went rubbery.

"Don't piss yourself," the technician said, smirking at him. "It's probably something minor."

"But the hatch. We're trapped here."

"Naw. You can open the hatch manually and get to your quarters. Don't sweat it."

At that instant the hatch swung open and two of the ship's crew pushed past them, heading for the airlock. They looked more irritated than frightened.

Feeling marginally better, Levinson followed the tech through the hatch and toward his own compartment. Still, when the hatch automatically slammed shut again, he jumped like a startled rabbit.

He was opening the accordion-pleated door to his compartment when the overhead speaker demanded, "DR. LEVINSON REPORT TO THE BRIDGE IMMEDIATELY."

Levinson wasn't exactly certain where the bridge was, but he thought it was farther up the passageway that ran the length of the habitation module. With his pulse thumping nervously in his ears, he made his way past two more closed hatches and finally stepped into what was obviously the bridge. The ship's captain was standing with his back to the hatch, half bent over between the backs of two side-by-side chairs, both occupied by crew members. All three men were peering at readouts on the instrument panel.

The hatch slammed behind him, making him flinch again. The captain, grim-faced, whirled on him.

"It's those goddamned bugs of yours! They're eating up my ship!"

Levinson knew it couldn't be true. Pea-brained rocket jocks! Anything goes wrong, they blame the nearest scientist.

"The nanomachines are on the asteroid," he said, with great calm and dignity. "Or what's left of it. They couldn't possibly be aboard your ship."

"The hell they're not!" roared the captain, jabbing an accusing finger at the displays on the instrument board. Levinson could see they were swathed in red.

"They couldn't—"

"They were in that dust cloud, weren't they?"

"Well, yes, perhaps a few," he admitted.

"And the loose end of your fucking tether was flapping around in the cloud, wasn't it?"

Levinson started to reply, but his mouth went so dry he couldn't form any words.

"You brought the mother-humping bugs aboard my ship, damn you!"

"But . . . but . . ."

"They're eating out the airlock compartment! Chewing up the metal of the hull, for chrissakes!" The captain advanced toward Levinson, hands clenched into fists, face splotched with red fury. "You've got to stop them!"

"They'll stop themselves," said Levinson, backing away a step and bumping into the closed hatch. "I built a time limit into them. Once the time limit is reached they run out of power and shut themselves down."

The captain sucked in a deep breath. His face returned almost to its normal color. "They'll stop?"

"Yessir," Levinson said. "Automatically."

"How soon?"

Levinson swallowed and choked out, "Forty-eight hours."

"Forty-eight *hours*?" the captain bellowed.

Levinson nodded, cringing.

The captain turned back toward the two crewmen seated at the instrument panel. "Contact *Chrysalis*. Report our situation to them."

The crewman in the left-hand seat asked, "Anything else to tell them, sir?"

The captain fumed in silence for a moment, then muttered, "Yeah. Read them your last will and testament. We're going to die here. All of us."

Levinson wet his pants.

LAST RITES

L evinson had never been so terrified. He stumbled back to his compartment, slid the door shut after three trembling tries, then yanked his palmcomp out of his coveralls, tearing the pocket slightly, and called up the numbers he needed to calculate how long the torch ship would last.

The tiny corner of his mind that still remained rational told him the calculation was meaningless. He had no firm idea of how fast the nanomachines were disassembling the ship, and only the haziest notion of how massive the ship was. You're just rearranging the deck chairs on the *Titanic*, he told himself. But he knew he had to do something, anything, to try to stave off the terror that was staring him in the face.

We could make it to Ceres in less than forty-eight hours, he thought, if the captain pushes the engines to their max. If the nanomachines don't destroy the engines first. Okay, we get to Ceres, to the habitat *Chrysalis*. They won't let us in, though, because they'd be afraid of the nanos damaging them.

But the machines will shut themselves down in forty-eight hours, Levinson reminded himself. Less than that, now; it was about two hours ago that we dispersed them on the asteroid.

How fast are they eating up the ship? he asked himself. Maybe I can make some measurements, get at least a rough idea of their rate of progress. Then I could—

He never finished the sentence. The curving bulkhead of his compartment, formed by the ship's hull, suddenly cracked open. Levinson watched in silent horror as a chunk of metal dissolved before his goggling eyes. The air rushed out of the compartment with such force that he fell to his knees. His lungs collapsed as he sank to the metal deck of the compartment, blood gushing from every pore. He was quite dead by the time his nanomachines began taking him apart, molecule by molecule.

Martin Humphries was talking with his six-year-old son, Alex, in the family's estate in Connecticut.

"Van cries all the time," Alex said, looking sad. "The doctor says he's real sick."

"Yes, that's true," said Humphries, feeling nettled. He wanted to talk about other things than his stunted younger son.

"Can I come to see you?" Alex asked, after the three-second lag between Earth and Moon.

"Of course," Humphries replied. "As soon as your school year ends you can come up here for a week or so. You can take walks on the Moon's surface and learn how to play low-games."

He watched his son's face, so like the pictures of himself at that age. The boy blossomed into a huge smile when he heard his father's words.

"With you, Daddy?"

"Sure, with me, or one of my staff. They can—"

The amber light signaling an incoming call began blinking. Humphries had given orders that he was not to be disturbed except for cataclysms. He glared at the light, as if that would make it stop claiming his attention.

"I've got to go now, Alex. I'll call you again in a day or so."

He clicked off the connection, and never saw the hurt disappointment on his son's face.

Whoever was calling had his private code. And the message was scrambled as well, he saw. Scowling with impatience, Humphries instructed the computer to open the message. Victoria Ferrer's features appeared in three dimensions in the hologram above his desk. She looked tired, depressed.

"I'm on a torch ship on my way back to Selene," she said. "Still too far out for a two-way conversation, but I know you'll want to hear the bad news right away."

He started to ask what she was talking about, then realized that she wouldn't hear his question for a good twenty minutes or more.

"The nanomachine experiment backfired. The bugs got loose on the ship and totally destroyed it. Nothing left but a cloud of atoms. Everybody killed, including Levinson."

She gave a few more details, then added, "Oh, by the way, the recruiting was pretty much a flop, too. Those rock rats are too smart to volunteer for cannon fodder."

Her message ended.

Humphries leaned back in his desk chair and stared at the wall screen that displayed a hologram of Jupiter's colorful swirling clouds.

Completely destroyed the ship and killed everybody aboard, he repeated to himself. What a weapon those little bugs could make!

ORE CARRIER *STARLIGHT*

S
tarlight was an independent freighter. For years it had plied between Ceres and Selene, taking on cargoes of ore in the Belt and carrying them on a slow, curving ellipse to the waiting factories on the Moon and in Earth orbit. Its owners, a married couple from Murmansk, had kept strictly aloof from the big corporations, preferring to make a modest living out of carrying ores and avoiding entanglements. Their crew consisted of their two sons and daughters-in-law. On their last trip to Selene they had tarried a week longer than usual so that their first grandchild—a girl—could be born in the lunar city's hospital. Now, after a trip with the squalling new baby to the Belt, they were returning to Selene, happy to be away from the fighting that had claimed so many Astro and HSS ships.

The Astro drone had no proper name, only a number designation: D-6. The *D* stood for "destroyer." It was an automated vessel, remotely controlled from Astro's offices in Selene. The controllers' assignment was to attack any HSS vessels approaching the Moon. The particular controller on duty that morning had a list of HSS ships in her computer, complete with their names, performance ratings, and construction specifications. She suspected that *Starlight* was a disguised version of a Humphries freighter and spent most of the morning scanning the vessel with radar and laser probes.

Astro's command center was kept secret from Humphries's people, of course; it was also kept secret from the government of Selene, which insisted that no hostilities should take place in its jurisdiction. So the controller watched *Starlight* passively, without trying to open up a communications link with the freighter or even asking the International Astronautical Authority offices about the ship's registration and identity.

To her credit, the Astro controller instructed D-6 to obtain close-up imagery of the approaching freighter. Unfortunately, the destroyer's programming was new and untried; the drone had been rushed into use too soon. The onboard computer misinterpreted the controller's order. Instead of a low-power laser scan, the destroyer hit *Starlight* with a full-intensity laser beam that sawed the vessel's habitation module neatly in half, killing everyone aboard.

Pancho was heading for the Moon's south pole when the news of the *Starlight* fiasco reached her.

She was flying in a rocket on a ballistic trajectory to the Astro power station set on the summit of the highest peak in the Malapert Mountains. Taller than Everest, Mt. Dickson's broad, saddle-shaped summit was always in sunlight, as were its neighboring peaks. Astro workers had covered its crest with power towers topped by photovoltaic cells. The electricity they generated was carried back to Selene by cryogenically cooled cables of lunar aluminum that ran across the rugged, crater-pocked highlands for nearly five thousand kilometers.

For the few brief minutes of the rocket's arcing flight southward, the handful of passengers hung weightlessly against their seat restraint straps. To her surprise, Pancho actually felt a little queasy. You've been flying a desk too long, girl. She thought about how the future growth of the Moon would almost certainly be in the polar regions. Water deposits were there, she knew, and you could build power towers that were always in sunlight, so you got uninterrupted electricity, except for Earth eclipses, but that was only a few minutes out of the year. It was a mistake to build Selene near the equator, she thought.

Back in those days, though, it started as a government operation. Moonbase. Some bean-counting sumbitch of a bureaucrat figured it'd be a couple of pennies cheaper in propellant costs to build near the equator than at either polar region. They picked Alphonsus because there were vents in the crater floor that outgassed methane now and then. Big lollapalooza deal! *Water*'s what you need, and the ice deposits at the poles are where the water is. Even so, it isn't enough. We have to import water from the rock rats.

As the rocket vehicle fired its retros in preparation for landing at the Astro base, Pancho caught a glimpse through her passenger window of the construction already underway at Shackleton Crater, slightly more than a hundred kilometers distant. Nairobi's found the money they needed, she told herself. She had followed their progress in the weekly reports her staff made, but seeing the actual construction sprawling across the floor of Shackleton impressed her more than written reports or imagery. Where's their money coming from? she asked herself. Her best investigators had not been able to find a satisfactory answer.

She had brought one of the new nanomachine space suits with her, folded and packed in her travel bag. Stavenger had even supplied her with a nanofabric helmet that could be blown up like a toy balloon. Pancho packed it but firmly decided that if she had to use the softsuit she'd find a regular bubble helmet to go with it.

There was no need for a space suit. Once the ballistic rocket touched down, a flexible tunnel wormed from the base's main airlock to the ship's hatch. Pancho walked along its spongy floor to the airlock, where the director of the base was waiting for her, looking slightly nervous because he wasn't entirely sure why the company's CEO had suddenly decided to visit his domain.

Pancho allowed him to tour her through the base, which looked to her a lot like most of the other lunar facilities she had seen. It was almost entirely underground; the work on the surface of maintaining the solar cells and building new ones was done by robotic machines teleoperated from the safety of the underground offices.

"Of course, we're not as luxurious down here as Selene," the base director explained in a self-deprecating tone, "but we do have the basic necessities."

With that, he ushered Pancho into a tight, low-ceilinged conference room that was crowded with his senior staff people, all of them anxious to meet the CEO and even more anxious to learn why she had come to see them. The conference table was set with sandwiches and drinks, with a scale model of the base sitting in the middle of the table.

There weren't enough chairs for everyone, so Pancho remained standing, munched on a sandwich, sipped at a plastic container of fruit juice, and chatted amiably with the staff—none of whom dared to sit down while the CEO remained standing.

At last she put her emptied juice container back on the table. As if on signal, all conversations stopped and everyone turned toward her.

She grinned at them. "I guess you're wondering why I dropped in on y'all like this," Pancho said, reverting to her west Texas drawl to put them at their ease.

"It's not every day that the chief of the corporation comes to see us," the base director replied. A few people tittered nervously.

"Well," said Pancho, "to tell the truth, I'm curious 'bout what your new neighbors are up to. Any of you know how to get me invited over to the Nairobi complex?"

SELENE NEWS
MEDIA CENTER

Despite its rather glitzy title, the news media center was little more than a set of standard-sized offices—most of them crammed with broadcasting equipment—and one cavernous studio large enough to shoot several videos at the same time.

Edith Stavenger stood impatiently just inside the studio's big double doors, waiting while the camera crew finished its final take on a training vid for the new softsuits. A young woman who actually worked a tractor on the surface was serving as a model, showing how easy it was to pull the suit on and seal its front.

Many years earlier Edith Stavenger had been Edie Elgin, a television news reporter in Texas, back in the days when the first human expedition to Mars was in training. She had come to the Moon as a reporter during the brief, almost bloodless lunar war of independence. She had married Douglas Stavenger and never returned to Earth. She still had the dynamic, youthful good looks of a cheerleader, golden blonde hair and a big smile full of strong bright teeth. She was still bright-eyed and vigorous, thanks to rejuvenation therapies that ranged from skin-cell regeneration to hormone enhancement. Some thought that she had taken nanomachines into her body, like her husband, but Edith found no need for that; cellular biochemistry was her fountain of youth.

She had served as news director for Selene for a while but, at her husband's prodding, semi-retired to a consultant's position. Doug Stavenger wanted no dynasties in Selene's political or social structure and Edith agreed with him, almost completely. She clung to her consultant's position, even though she barely ever tried to interfere with the operation of the news media in Selene.

But now she had a reason to get involved, and she waited with growing impatience for the head of the news department to finish the scene he was personally directing.

The young model took off her fishbowl helmet and collapsed the transparent inflatable fabric in her hands. Then she unsealed her softsuit, peeled it off her arms and wriggled it past her hips. She'd be kind of sexy, Elgin thought, if she weren't wearing those coveralls.

At last the scene was finished, the crew clicked off their handheld cameras, and the news director turned and headed for the door.

"Edie!" he exclaimed. "I didn't know you'd come up here."

"We've got to talk, Andy."

The news director's name was Achmed Mohammed Wajir, and although he traced his family roots back to the Congo, he had been born in Syria and raised all over the Middle East. His childhood had been the gypsy existence of a diplomat's son: never in one city for more than two years at a time. His father sent him to Princeton for an education in the classics, but young Achmed had fallen in love with journalism instead. He went to New York and climbed through the rough-and-tumble world of the news media until a terrorist bomb shattered his legs. He came to Selene where he could accept nanotherapies that rebuilt his legs, but he could never return to Earth while he carried nanomachines inside him. Wajir soon decided he didn't care. The Moon's one-sixth g made his recovery easier, and at Selene the competition in the news business was even gentler than the gravity.

As they pushed through the studio's double doors and out into the corridor, Wajir began, "If it's about this *Starlight* accident—"

"Accident?" Elgin snapped. "It's a tragedy. Seven innocent people killed, one of them a baby."

"We played the story, Edie. Gave it full coverage."

"For a day."

Wajir had once been slim as a long-distance runner, but years behind a desk—or a restaurant table—had thickened his middle. Still, he was several centimeters taller than Elgin and now he drew himself up to his full height.

"Edie," he said, "we're in the news business, and *Starlight* is old news. Unless you want to do some sob-sister mush. But even there, there's no relatives left to cry on camera for you. No funeral. The bodies have drifted to god knows where by now."

Edith's normal cheerful smile was long gone. She was dead serious as they walked along the corridor past glass-walled editing and recording studios.

"It's not just this one terrible tragedy, Andy," she said. "There's a war going on and we're not covering it. There's hardly a word about it any-where in the media."

"What do you expect? Nobody's interested in a war between two corporations."

"Nobody's interested because we're not giving them the news they need to get interested!"

They had reached Wajir's office. He opened the door and gestured her inside. "No sense us fighting out in the hallway where everybody can hear us," he said.

Edith walked in and took one of the big upholstered chairs in front of his wide, expansive desk of bioengineered teak. Instead of going to his swivel chair, Wajir perched on the edge of his desk, close enough to Edith to loom over her.

"We've been over this before, Edie. The news nets Earthside aren't interested in the war. It's all the way to hell out in the Asteroid Belt and it's being fought by mercenaries and you know who the hell cares? Nobody. Nobody on Earth gives a damn about it."

"But we should make them care about it," she insisted.

"How?" he cried. "What do we have to do to get them interested? Tell me and I'll do it."

Edith started to snap out a reply, but bit it back. She looked up at Wajir, who was leaning over her, his ebony face twisted into a frown. He's been a friend for a long time, she told herself. Don't turn him into an enemy.

"Andy," she said softly, "this disaster of the *Starlight* is only the tip of the iceberg. The war is spreading out of the Belt. It's coming here, whether we like it or not."

"Good. Then we can cover it."

She felt her jaw drop with surprise, her brows hike up.

"I'm not being cynical," he quickly explained. "We can't get news coverage from the Belt."

"If it's the expense, maybe I could—"

Shaking his head vigorously, Wajir said, "It's not the money. The Belt's controlled by the corporations. Astro and HSS have it sewn up between them."

"There are independents."

"Yeah, but the war's between Astro and HSS and neither one of them wants news reporters snooping around. They won't talk to us here and they won't ferry us out to the Belt."

"Then I'll go," Edith heard herself say.

Wajir looked genuinely shocked. "You?"

"I used to be a reporter, back in the Stone Age," she said, smiling for the first time.

"They won't take you, Edie."

"I'll fly out on an independent ship," she said lightly. "I'll go to *Chrysalis* and interview the rock rats there."

He pursed his lips, rubbed at his nose, looked up at the ceiling. "The big boys won't like it."

"You mean the big corporations?"

Wajir nodded.

"I don't really care whether they like it or not. I'll go out on an independent ship. Maybe Sam Gunn will give me a ride on one of his vessels."

"If he's got any left," Wajir muttered. "This war is bankrupting him."

"Again? He's always going bankrupt."

"Seriously, Edie," he said, "this could be dangerous."

"Nobody's going to hurt Douglas Stavenger's wife. There are *some* advantages to being married to a powerful man."

"Maybe," Wajir admitted. "Maybe. But I don't like this. I think you're making a mistake."

Damned if it isn't the same guy who came to see me in my office, Pancho thought as she looked at the holographic image of the handsome Nairobi executive. She was in the office of the Astro base's director, which he had lent her for the duration of her visit to the south polar facility. Leaning back in the creaking, stiffly unfamiliar chair, Pancho saw the man's name spelled out beneath his smiling, pleased image: Daniel Jomo Tsavo.

"Ms. Lane," he said, looking pleasantly surprised, "what an unexpected pleasure."

He was just as good-looking as she remembered him, but now instead of wearing a conservative business suit he was in well-worn coveralls, with the edge of a palmcomp peeping out from his breast pocket. He gets his hands dirty, Pancho thought, liking him all the more for it.

"You're the head of the Nairobi base?" Pancho asked him.

His smile turned brighter. "After my visit with you, my superiors assigned me to managing the construction of our facilities here."

"I didn't know," said Pancho.

"I suppose they thought it was cheaper to keep me here than fly me back home," he said, self-deprecatingly.

"So you've been down here at the south pole all this time."

"Yes, that's true. I had no idea you had come to the Mountains of Eternal Light," Tsavo said.

"Came down to check out how my people are doing here," she lied easily, "and thought maybe I could take a peek at how you're getting along."

"By all means! It would be an honor to have you visit our humble facility, Ms. Lane."

She arched a brow at him. "Don't you think you can call me Pancho by now?"

He chuckled and looked away from her, seemingly embarrassed. "Yes, I suppose so . . . Pancho."

"Good! When can I come over, Daniel?"

For a moment he looked almost alarmed, but he quickly recovered. "Um, our facilities are not very luxurious, Pancho. We weren't expecting illustrious visitors for some time, you see, and—"

"Can it, Danny boy! I can sleep on nails, if I have to. When can I come over?"

"Give me a day to tidy up a bit. Twenty-four hours. I'll send a hopper for you."

"Great," said Pancho, recognizing that twenty-four hours would give him time to check with whoever his bosses were and decide how to handle this unexpected visit.

"By the way," she added, "are you folks still interested in a strategic partnership with Astro Corporation?"

Now his face went almost totally blank. Poker-playing time, Pancho realized.

"Yes," he said at last. "Of course. Although, you realize, with this war going on, the financial situation has changed a good deal."

"Tell me about it!"

He smiled again.

"Okay, then, we can talk about it when I get to your base."

"Fine," said Daniel Jomo Tsavo.

DATA BANK: SOLAR FLARE

The minor star that humans call the Sun is a seething, restless million-kilometer-wide thermonuclear reactor. Deep in its core, where the temperature exceeds thirty million degrees, intact atoms cannot exist. They are totally ionized, their electrons stripped from their nuclei. Under those immense temperatures and pressures hydrogen nuclei—bare protons—are forced together to create nuclei of helium. This process of fusion releases particles of electromagnetic energy called photons, which make their tortuous way through half a million kilometers of incredibly dense ionized gas, called plasma, toward the Sun's shining surface.

Furiously boiling, gigantic bubbles of plasma rise and sink again, cooling and reheating, in an endless cycle of convection. Immense magnetic fields play through the plasma, warping it, shredding it into slender glowing filaments longer than the distance between the Earth and its Moon. Vast arches of million-degree plasma form above the solar surface, expanding, hurling themselves into space or pouring back down into the Sun in titanic cascades.

Over cycles of roughly eleven years the Sun's violence waxes and wanes. During periods of maximum solar activity the Sun's shining face is blotched with sunspots, slightly cooler regions that look dark compared to the surrounding chromosphere. Solar flares erupt, sudden bursts of energy that can release in a few seconds the equivalent of a hundred million *billion* tons of exploding TNT: more energy than the entire human race consumes in fifty thousand years.

The electromagnetic radiation from such a flare—visible light, radio waves, ultraviolet and X-rays—reaches the Earth's vicinity in about eight minutes. This is the warning of danger to come. Close behind, a few minutes or a few hours, comes the first wave of extremely energetic protons and electrons, traveling at velocities close to the speed of light.

The energy in these particles is measured in *electron volts*. One electron volt is a minuscule bit of energy: It would take five million electron volts to light a fifty-watt lamp. But protons with energies of forty to fifty million electron volts can easily penetrate a quarter-inch of lead, and particles from solar flares with energies of more than fifteen thousand *billion* electron volts have reached the Earth.

Yet the most violent effects of the solar flare are still to come.

The flare has ejected a gigantic puff of very energetic plasma into interplanetary space. The cloud expands as it moves outward from the Sun, soon growing to dimensions larger than the Earth. When such a cloud hits the Earth's magnetosphere it rattles the entire geomagnetic field, causing a magnetic storm.

The auroras at Earth's north and south poles flare dramatically, and the "northern lights" (and southern) are seen far south (and north) of their usual haunts. The ionosphere—the belt of ionized particles some eighty kilometers above Earth's surface—runs amok, making a shambles of long-range radio transmissions that are normally reflected off its ionized layers.

On the Moon and even out in the Asteroid Belt all surface activity is halted when a solar flare bathes the region in lethal radiation. All spacecraft that operate beyond the Moon carry protective electromagnetic shielding to divert the energetic particles of the flare's cloud. Otherwise the people in those spacecraft would swiftly die, killed by the invisible bullets of ionizing radiation.

Within a few days the deadly cloud wafts away, dissipates in interplanetary space. Earth's ionosphere settles down. The auroras stop flaring. Space-suited workers can return to the surface of the Moon and the asteroids. The solar system returns to normal. Until the next solar flare.

WEATHER FORECAST

Jersey Zorach was a dour, dark, stolid astrophysicist who studied the weather in space. Despite his being a third-generation American, born and raised just outside Chicago, he had never outgrown his Latvian heritage of being burdened with a sense of impending doom.

He sat in his messy little cubbyhole of an office, a squat, untidy man built rather like a fireplug, with a thick thatch of unruly prematurely gray hair flopping down over his forehead, surrounded by beeping display screens, stacks of books, reports, video chips and the scattered remains of many meals he had eaten at his desk.

Since interplanetary space is a nearly perfect vacuum, most people smiled or even laughed when Zorach told them his profession, waiting for a punch line that never came. There was no rain or snow in space, true enough. But Zorach knew there was a wind of ghostly microscopic particles blowing fitfully from the Sun, a solar wind that sometimes reached hurricane velocities and more. There was a constant drizzle of cosmic particles sleeting in from the distant stars as well.

And there were clouds, sometimes. Invisible but quite deadly clouds.

For years he had worked to make precise predictions of solar flares. He studied the Sun until his eyes burned from staring at its seething, roiling image. He made mountains of statistical analyses, trying to learn how to forecast solar flares by matching existing data on earlier flares and making "backcasts" of them. He spun out holographic maps of the interplanetary magnetic field, knowing that those invisible threads of energy steered the radiation clouds that were thrown out by solar flares.

Nothing worked. His predictions were estimates at best. Everyone praised him and the results he was obtaining, but Zorach knew he had yet to predict a single flare. Not one, in all the years he had been working on them.

So he wasn't surprised when one of the display screens in his cluttered office suddenly pinged. Turning to it, he saw nothing unusual to the unaided eye. But the alphanumerics strung along the bottom of the screen told him clearly that a new solar flare had just erupted.

A big one, he saw. Big and nasty. He knew the automated system was already sending warnings to every human habitat and outpost from Selene to the colony in orbit around distant Saturn. But he pecked at his own phone and called Selene's safety office to make certain they started bringing everybody in from the surface. It was a point of honor with him. If I can't predict the bloody storms, he said to himself, at least I can make certain no one is killed by them.

Deep below the Moon's surface in his private grotto, Martin Humphries had no worries about solar flares or the radiation clouds that accompanied them.

He was ambling slowly through the colorful garden in the patio outside the elaborately carved front door of his mansion, with Victoria Ferrer at his side. The heady aroma of solid beds of roses and peonies filled the air, and he felt victory was close enough almost to touch.

"We're winning," Humphries said happily. "We've got Astro on the run."

Ferrer, walking slowly alongside him, nodded her agreement. But she warned, "This latest move of Astro's could cut off the ore shipments coming in from the Belt."

Humphries disagreed with a wave of his hand in the air. "Drones attacking our automated freighters? I'm not worried about that."

"You should be. This could be serious."

"Don't be stupid," Humphries sneered. "This fiasco with that *Starlight* vessel has brought Pancho's little scheme out into the open."

"But they could strangle your profits if—"

"I'm going to get rid of Astro's drones at one stroke," Humphries said confidently.

Ferrer looked at him questioningly.

"Set up a meeting for me with Doug Stavenger."

"Stavenger?"

"Uh-huh. Once Stavenger has his nose rubbed into the fact that Astro's controlling those birds from inside Selene, he'll close down their operation."

"He will?"

"Yes indeed he will," said Humphries, smiling broadly. "He's made it clear to me and that little guttersnipe that he doesn't want any fighting in Selene. No fighting anywhere on the Moon."

"But does that mean he'll demand that Astro close down its control center for the drones?"

"Damned right he will. And he'll make it stick, too."

Ferrer was silent for a moment, thinking. Then, "Pancho will just move the control center off the Moon. Put up a space station."

"And we'll blast it to smithereens." Humphries clapped his hands together. "I only hope the damned greasemonkey is aboard when we wipe it out."

Ferrer thought it over and had to admit that her boss was correct. HSS mercenaries had scored major victories over Astro forces in the Belt. Astro had sprung a surprise with their drones attacking HSS freighters as they approached the Moon, but Humphries was probably right in thinking that Stavenger would force them to move that operation out of the safety of Selene. Of course, zapping that independent freighter and wiping out that family didn't help Astro's cause. Not at all.

Yet she heard herself ask, "What about Fuchs? He's still lurking out there somewhere."

"Fuchs?" Humphries snorted disdainfully. "He's a spent force. Once we've cleaned out Astro we can hunt him down at our leisure. He's as good as dead; he just doesn't know it yet."

For weeks, Lars Fuchs had been living in the machinery and storage spaces in Selene's "basement."

On the Moon, where the deeper below the surface you are, the safer you are from the radiation and temperature swings and the thin but constant infall of micrometeors that pepper the surface, Selene's "basement" was its topmost level.

Just below the Grand Plaza and its extensions, Selene's highest underground level was entirely devoted to the pumps and power converters and other life-support equipment that provided the city's air, water, light and heat. Living quarters were on the lower levels, the lower the more prestigious—and expensive.

The "basement" also held the warehouses that stocked spare parts, clothing, preserved foods, and the tanks of water that Selene's residents drank and washed in. In short, the "basement" had all the supplies that a renegade, a fugitive, a homeless exile would need to survive.

During the years he had lived at Ceres, Fuchs had listened for hours to Big George Ambrose talking about the "bad old days" when he had lived as a fugitive in Selene's shadowy underground economy, surviving on his wits and the petty pilfering that provided food and shelter for him and his fellow nonpersons. Even Dan Randolph had once spent a few months hiding from the authorities in Selene.

So Fuchs had politely checked out of the Hotel Luna, afraid that sooner or later he would be identified and forced to return to Earth, and toted his meager travel bag up toward the kilometer-long tunnel that led to Armstrong Spaceport. Instead of going to the spaceport, though, he found one of the access hatches marked MAINTENANCE AND SUPPLY SECTION: AUTHORIZED PERSONNEL ONLY, quickly decoded its simple security lock, and disappeared into the shadowy "basement," where machinery throbbed incessantly and the air was heavy with the odors of lubricating oil and ozone from the electrical machinery.

Color-coded pipes and electrical conduits ran overhead. Maintenance robots trundled back and forth along the walkways between the pulsating machinery and the warehouse stacks. Simpleminded machines programmed to alert human controllers of malfunctioning equipment or water leaks, the robots were fairly easy to avoid. Fuchs could see the red lights set into their tops flashing through the dimly lit passageways while they were still far enough distant to get out of range of their optical sensors.

There was a scattering of other people hiding there, too, a ragged handful of men and women who preferred to scratch out an underground living rather than submit to Selene's laws. Some of them were wild-eyed from drugs, or raving alcoholics; others were simply unable or unwilling to live by other people's rules. Fuchs met a few of them, barely avoided a fight when one of them pulled a knife and ordered him to swear loyalty. Fuchs bent his knee and agreed, then quickly moved as far away from the megalomaniac as he could and never saw him again.

Fuchs settled down in the "basement," content to sleep in a bedroll and eat canned foods pilfered from the warehouse stocks. He spent his waking hours peering at his palmcomp, studying the schematics of Selene's air ducts and water pipes, searching for a way to penetrate the lunar city's lowest level, where Humphries lived in his magnificent mansion.

As the weeks passed, Nodon, Sanja, and Amarjagal arrived at Selene one by one, each of them bearing identification as Astro Corporation employees, lowly technicians. Their one-room corporate apartments were sufficient for them, luxurious compared to Fuchs's hideout in the storeroom shelves in the "basement."

Fuchs visited his crew members, furtively making his way through Selene's corridors to spend long hours with them, planning how he might kill Martin Humphries.

SHINING MOUNTAIN BASE

Daniel Jomo Tsavo hated the three-second lag in communications between the Earth and Moon. It upset him to ask a question and then wait and wait and wait until the answer came back. Yet there was no way around the lag. And now the safety people have warned us that a solar storm is on its way; normal communications will be disrupted and all work on the surface will have to stop until the storm passes. Ah well, he said to himself, this call to Yamagata is on a tight laser-beam link. The storm should not affect it, unless it's powerful enough to fry the laser transmitter on the surface.

"Pancho Lane wants to visit your base?" Nobuhiko Yamagata replied at last.

Tsavo nodded vigorously. "She just called. She's at the Astro facility in the Malapert Mountains, no more than a hundred kilometers from where I sit."

Again the interminable lag. Tsavo used the time to study Yamagata. His round, flat face looked frozen, his eyes hooded, his expression unreadable. Yet he must be thinking furiously, Tsavo thought. Come on, come on. Tell me what I should do.

"This is a striking opportunity," Yamagata said at last.

Tsavo agreed heartily. "I took it on my own authority to invite her to come over tomorrow."

Yamagata again seemed lost in thought. At last he said, "Don't delay. Bring her to your base as quickly as you can. I will send an interrogation team immediately on a high-g burn. There is much we can learn from her."

• • •

Pancho felt slightly nervous being out on the surface with a solar flare cloud on its way. The scientists had estimated that it would take more than six hours for the radiation to even begin building up, but still she felt edgy about it. She was wearing a standard hard-shell space suit as she followed the Astro base director along the crest of Mount Randolph. Approaching storm or not, the director wanted to show off what his people were doing and Pancho had no intention of showing any fear in front of her own people.

I should be testing the softsuit I brought with me, she said to herself. Yet she answered silently, You know what they say about test engineers: more guts than brains. I'll wear a softsuit when they've been in use for a year or two. Momma Lane didn't raise any of her daughters to get themselves killed trying out new equipment.

She was being conducted on a quick walk through the small forest of gleaming white towers that reached up into the bright sunlight. Their wide, circular tops were dark with solar cells that drank in the Sun's radiant energy and converted it silently to electricity. They look like great big mushrooms, Pancho thought. Then she corrected herself. Nope, they look more like giant penises. She giggled inwardly. A forest of phalluses. A collection of cocks. Monumental pricks, all standing at attention.

"As you can see," the base director's voice rasped in her earphones, "another advantage of the power towers is that the solar cells are placed high enough above the surface so they're not bothered by dust."

It took an effort for Pancho to control her merriment. "You don't need to clean 'em off," she said, trying to sound serious.

"That's correct. It saves quite a bit of money over the long run."

She nodded inside her helmet. "What about damage from micrometeoroids?"

"The cells are hardened, of course. Deterioration rate is about the same for the ground arrays around Selene."

"Uh-hmm." Pancho seemed to recall a report that said otherwise. "Didn't the analysis that—"

A new voice broke into their conversation. "Ms. Lane, ma'am, we have an incoming call for you from the Nairobi base at Shackleton."

"Put it through on freak two," she said.

It was voice only, but she recognized Tsavo's caramel-rich baritone. "Ms. Lane, Pancho, this is Daniel. I'm sending a hopper over to your facility within the next half-hour. Please feel free to visit us whenever you're ready to."

Grinning, delighted, Pancho answered, "I'll get over there soon's I can, Danny."

"You know that a solar storm is approaching," he said.

Pancho nodded inside her helmet. "Yup. I'll get to you before it hits."

"Fine. That's wonderful."

Pancho cut her inspection tour short, apologizing to the base director, who frowned with undisguised disappointment.

Sure enough, there was a Nairobi Industries hopper standing on its spindly little legs, waiting for her at the launchpad. It was painted a vivid green with the corporate logo—an oval Masai shield and two crossed spears—stenciled just below the glassteel bubble of the cockpit.

She dashed to the room that the base director had given her for her quarters, picked up her still-unopened travel bag, and headed out toward the pad. She called Jake Wanamaker on her handheld to tell him where she was going and why. Then she buzzed her security chief and asked him why in the name of hell-and-gone he hadn't been able to locate Lars Fuchs yet.

"I want him found," she insisted. "And pronto."

At that moment, Lars Fuchs was huddled with his three crew members in a narrow, shadowy niche between one of the big electrical power converters and the open-shelved storehouse that he used as his sleeping quarters.

"This is where you live, Captain?" Amarjagal asked, in a whisper that was halfway between respect and disbelief.

"This is my headquarters," Fuchs replied evenly. "For the time being."

Nodon said, "You could move in with me, sir. There is no need for you—"

"I'll stay here. Less chance of being discovered."

The three Mongols glanced at one another, but remained silent.

Over the weeks since Fuchs had gone underground he had learned the pattern of the maintenance robots that trundled along the walkways set between the machinery and storehouses in Selene's uppermost level. It was easy enough to avoid them, and he swung up into the higher tiers of the warehouse each night to spread his bedroll for sleep. It was a rugged sort of existence, but not all that uncomfortable, Fuchs told himself. As long as he kept his pilfering of food and other supplies down to the bare necessities, Selene's authorities didn't bother to track him down. From what Big George had told him, it was easier for the authorities to accept a slight amount of wastage than to organize a manhunt through the dimly lit machinery spaces and storehouses.

The one thing that bothered Fuchs was the constant humming, throbbing that pervaded this uppermost level of Selene. He knew that Selene's nuclear power generators were buried more than a hundred kilometers away, on the far side of Alphonsus's ringwall mountains. Yet there was a constant electrical crackle in the air, the faint scent of ozone that triggered uneasy Earthly memories of approaching thunderstorms. Fuchs felt that it shouldn't bother him, that he should ignore the annoyance. Still, his head ached much of the time, throbbing in rhythm to the constant electrical pulse.

He had chosen this site for his headquarters because he could commandeer the big display screen that had been erected on one side of the storehouse shelving. It had been placed there to help the occasional human operator to locate items stacked in inventory. Fuchs used its link to Selene's main computer to study schematics of the city's water and air circulation systems. He was searching for a way into Humphries's mansion. So far his search had proved fruitless.

"The man must be the biggest paranoid in the solar system," Fuchs muttered.

"Or the greatest coward," said Amarjagal, sitting on the walkway's metal grating beside him, her sturdy legs crossed, her back hunched like a small mountain.

Nodon and Sanja sat slightly farther away, their shaved skulls sheened with perspiration in the overly warm air. This close together, Fuchs could smell their rancid body odors. They have showers in their quarters, he knew. Perhaps they're worried about their water allotments. Fuchs himself washed infrequently in water tapped from one of the main pipes that ran overhead. No matter how careful he was he always left puddles that drew teams of swiftly efficient maintenance robots, buzzing officiously. Fuchs feared that sooner or later human maintenance workers would come up to determine what was causing the leaks.

"Every possible access to his grotto is guarded by triply redundant security systems," Fuchs saw as he studied the schematics. "Motion detectors, cameras, heat sensors."

Nodon pointed with a skinny finger, "Even the electrical conduits are guarded."

"A mouse couldn't squirm through those conduits," said Sanja.

"The man is a great coward," Amarjagal repeated. "He has much fear in him."

He's got a lot to be afraid of, Fuchs thought. Then he added, But not unless we find a way into his mansion.

No matter how they studied the schematics, they could find no entry into Humphries's domain, short of a brute force attack. But there are only four of us, Fuchs reminded himself, and we have no weapons. Humphries must have a security force patrolling his home that's armed to the teeth.

Nodon shook his head unhappily. "There is no way that I can see."

"Nor I," Amarjagal agreed.

Fuchs took in a deep, heavy breath, then exhaled slowly, wearily. "I can," he said.

The three of them turned questioning eyes to him.

"One of you will have to change your job, get a position with Selene's maintenance department."

"Is that possible?" asked Amarjagal.

"It should be," Fuchs replied. "You're all qualified technicians. You have identity dossiers from Astro Corporation."

"I'll do it," said Nodon.

"Good."

"And after Nodon begins working for the maintenance department?" Amarjagal asked.

Fuchs eyed her dispassionately. Of the three, she was the feistiest, the most likely to ask questions. Is it because she's a woman? Fuchs wondered.

"I'll have to acquire an identification chip for myself, so I can get down to Selene's lowest level."

"How can you get one?"

"I'll need help," he admitted.

The three Asians looked at him questioningly.

"I'll call Pancho. I'm sure she can get an identification tag for me that will give me access to Humphries's grotto."

He was grasping at a straw and he knew it. Even worse, when he called Pancho from one of the phones set along the walkways of the machinery spaces, he was told that Ms. Lane was away from her office and unavailable.

"Where is she?" Fuchs asked.

"Ms. Lane is unavailable at present," the phone's synthesized voice answered. "Please leave your name and someone will get back to you as soon as possible."

Fuchs had no intention of leaving his name. "Can I reach her, wherever she is?"

"Ms. Lane is unavailable at present," the computer replied cheerfully.

"How long will she be gone?"

"That information is unknown, sir."

Fuchs thought swiftly. No sense trying to pry information out of a stupid machine, he thought. Besides, he didn't want to stay on the phone long enough to draw the attention of Selene's security monitors.

"Tell her that Karl Manstein called and will call again."

Feeling desperate, trapped, he punched the phone's OFF key.

• • •

It wasn't easy to surprise Douglas Stavenger. No matter that he had been officially retired from any formal office for decades, he still kept himself informed on everything that happened in Selene. And beyond, to a considerable extent.

He knew that his wife was pressing the news media chief for more coverage of the war raging out in the Belt. He knew that the corporations were pushing in the opposite direction, to keep the story as hushed up as possible. The *Starlight* tragedy had forced some light into the situation, but both Astro and Humphries Space Systems exerted every gram of their enormous power to move the media off the story as quickly as possible.

But now, as he sat at the breakfast table with his wife, Stavenger was truly shocked by her revelation.

"You're going to Ceres?"

Edith smiled prettily over her teacup. "Nobody else wants to open up this story, Doug, so I'm going to do it."

He fought down an impulse to shake his head. For several moments he said nothing, staring at his bowl of yogurt and honey, his thoughts spinning feverishly.

Yet when he looked up at her again all he could think to say was, "I don't like it, Edie."

"I'm not sure that I like it myself, darling, but somebody's got to do it and I don't see anyone else stepping up to the task."

"It's dangerous out there."

Her smile widened. "Now who's going to harm the wife of Doug Stavenger? That would bring Selene into the war, wouldn't it?"

"Not automatically, no."

"No?" She arched a brow at him.

He conceded, "I imagine the corporations would fear Selene's response."

"If anyone harmed me," she went on, quite seriously, "you'd see to it that Selene came into the war on the other side. Right? And that would throw the balance of power against the corporation that harmed me. Wouldn't it?"

He nodded reluctantly.

"And that would decide the war. Wouldn't it?"

"It could."

"It would, and you know it. Everybody knows it, including Pancho Lane and Martin Humphries." She took another sip of tea, then put the cup down with a tiny clink of china. "So I'll be perfectly safe out there."

"I still don't like it," he murmured.

She reached across the little table and grasped his hand. "But I've got to, Doug. You can see that, can't you? It's important: not just to me but to everybody involved, the whole solar system, for god's sake."

Stavenger looked into his wife's earnest eyes and knew he couldn't stop her.

"I'll go with you, then," he said.

"Oh no! You've got to stay here!"

"I don't think—"

"You're my protection, Doug. What happens if we both get killed out there? Who's going to lead Selene?"

"The duly elected governing council."

"Oh, sure," she sneered. "Without you pulling their strings they'll dither and shuffle and do nothing, and you know it."

"No, I don't know that."

She smiled again. "I need your protection, Doug, and I can only get it if you're here at Selene, keeping things under control."

"You give me more credit than I deserve."

"And you're the youngest éminence grise in the solar system."

He laughed. It was an old standing joke between them.

"Besides," Edith went on, "if you come out to Ceres all the attention will be on you. They'll fall all over themselves trying to show you that everything's all right. I'll never get a straight story out of anybody."

He kept the argument going for nearly another half-hour, but Stavenger knew that his wife would do what she wanted. And so would he. Edith will go to Ceres, he realized, and I'll stay here.

Nobuhiko was brimming with excitement when he called his father to tell him that Pancho Lane was walking into the Nairobi base on the Moon.

The elder Yamagata was in his cell in the monastery, a fairly sizable room whose stone walls were covered now with bookshelves and smart screens. The room was furnished sparsely, but Nobu noticed that his father had managed to get a big, square mahogany desk for himself.

Saito was sitting on his haunches on a tatami mat, however, directly under the big wallscreen that displayed an intricate chart that Nobu guessed was the most recent performance of the Tokyo stock exchange.

"She's going into the Nairobi base voluntarily?" Saito asked.

"Yes!" gushed Nobu. "I've ordered an interrogation team to get there immediately! The Africans can drug her and the team wring her dry and she'll never even know it!"

Saito grunted. "Except for her headache the next day."

Nobu wanted to laugh, but held back.

His father said nothing for long, nerve-racking moments. Finally, "You go to Shackleton. You, yourself."

"Me? But why—"

"No interrogation team knows as much about our work as you do, my son. You can glean much more from her than they could without you."

Nobu thought it over swiftly. "But if somehow she recognizes me, remembers afterward . . ."

"Then she must be eliminated," Saito answered. "It would be a pity, but it would be quite necessary."

COMMAND SHIP
SAMARKAND

Since the battle that shattered Gormley's fleet, the HSS base at Vesta had been busy. Ships were sent out in groups of two or three to hound down Astro freighters and logistics vessels. Although Astro's crewed ships were armed, they were no match for the warships with their mercenary crews that Humphries was pouring into the Belt.

Sitting in the command chair of *Samarkand,* in charge of three attack ships, Dorik Harbin wondered how long the war could possibly go on. Astro's vessels were being methodically eliminated. It was clear that Humphries's mercenaries were on the verge of sweeping Astro entirely out of the Belt. Astro's pitiful effort to stop HSS freighters from delivering ores to the Earth/Moon region had backfired hideously with the *Starlight* fiasco.

Yet the rumor was that more Astro ships were heading for the Belt. Better-armed ships, vessels crewed by mercenaries who were smart enough to avoid massed battles. The war was settling down to a struggle of attrition. Which corporation could better sustain the constant losses of ships and crews? Which corporation would decide the war was costing too much and call it quits?

Not Humphries, Harbin thought. He had met the man and seen the tenacity in his eyes, the dogged drive to succeed no matter what the cost. It's only money to him, Harbin realized. He isn't risking his neck, he's in no danger of shedding his own blood. What does he care how many are killed out here in the empty silence of the Belt?

His communications technician flashed a red-bordered message onto the bridge's main screen. A solar flare warning. Scanning the data, Harbin saw that it would be several days before the cloud reached the Belt's inner fringes.

"Run a diagnostic on the radiation shield system," he commanded, thinking, Make sure now that the shield is working properly, and if it's not you've got three or four days to repair it.

"We have a target, sir!"

His weapons tech's announcement stirred Harbin out of his thoughts. The flare warning disappeared from the main screen, replaced by three small blips, nearly nine thousand kilometers away, too distant for their telescopic cameras to resolve into a clear optical image.

With the touch of a fingertip on his armrest keypad, Harbin called up the computer's analysis. Their trajectory was definitely not the Sun-centered ellipse of asteroids; they were moving in formation toward Ceres. Not HSS ships, either; the computer had all their flight plans in its memory.

"Three on three," he muttered.

As *Samarkand* and its two accompanying warships sped toward the Astro vessels, the display screen began to show details. One of them was a typical dumbbell-shaped freighter, toting a large, irregularly shaped mass of ores. The other two were smaller, sleeker, obviously escorts designed to protect the freighter. Both the escorts were studded with asteroidal rock, armor to absorb and deflect laser beams.

Harbin's ships, including *Samarkand,* were also covered with asteroidal rubble, for the same reason. He saw that the Astro freighter was not so armored. They probably hope to use their cargo as a shield, he thought.

"Parallel course," he commanded. "Remain at a distance of fifteen hundred klicks. No closer, for the present."

"It's a long shot for the lasers," his weapons tech said, her heavy, dark face looking decidedly unhappy. "And they're armored, too."

Harbin nodded. "It's the freighter we want. I don't care about the escorts."

The weapons technician gave him a puzzled frown, then returned her attention to her screens.

Harbin studied the image on the main screen. The Astro escort vessels look more like rock piles than warships, he thought. I suppose we do too. He smiled grimly. Between the two corporations, we must be using more ores as ship's armor than we're selling to the markets on Earth. Well, that will end sooner or later. No war lasts forever.

Unbidden, a couplet from the *Rubaiyat* came to his mind:

> One Moment in Annihilation's waste,
> One moment, of the well of life to taste—

"We've been pulsed by search radar," his pilot reported.

Harbin nodded. "They know we're here."

"They're making no move toward us."

"No," Harbin replied. "Two escorts are not going to come after the three of us. They'll stick close to their freighter and wait for us to make a move on them."

"What move shall we make, sir?"

"Just continue the parallel course at this distance." Turning to the communication tech, seated beside the pilot, Harbin added, "Make certain that our two other ships follow me closely."

As the comm tech relayed his orders, Harbin thought, How to separate those two escorts from the freighter? If we go in to attack we'll be moving into their massed fire. I've got to find a way to split them apart.

For long, nerve-stretching minutes the two little formations flew in parallel, too distant for either to waste power on laser shots that would be absorbed by the ships' protective shields of asteroidal rubble. The Astro ships were hurrying out of the Belt, heading Earthward, to bring the freighter's massive load of ores to the waiting markets.

"We'll be reaching fuel bingo in forty-five minutes, sir," the pilot announced.

Harbin acknowledged the warning with a nod. Fuel bingo: the turnback point. The farthest distance from their refueling base at Vesta that *Samarkand* and its two accompanying ships could safely go.

How to separate those escorts from the freighter? Harbin asked himself, over and over. He played one scheme after another in his mind. He riffled through the tactical computer's preset plans. Nothing that he could use. He was pleased to see that the computer's data bank included his own tactics against Gormley.

And that gave him the idea he needed.

"You two," he said, jabbing a finger at the communications and weapons technicians. "Get to the main airlock and suit up. Now!"

They unbuckled their seat harnesses and scampered to the bridge's hatch. Once they announced that they were in their space suits, Harbin went back to the airlock to brief them on what they had to do. Neither of them relished the idea of going outside, he could see that on their faces even through the thick visors of their helmets. That didn't matter to Harbin. There was no other way for his scheme to work.

He made his way back to the bridge and resumed his position in the command chair. The executive officer monitored the two technicians as they left the airlock and followed Harbin's orders. Within half an hour they reported that they had successfully discharged the electrostatic field that held the rocks of their armor shield tightly around the hull of the ship.

"Some of the rocks are floating loose now," the weapons tech reported, her voice tense. "Most of 'em are holding in place against the hull, though."

"Good," Harbin said tightly. "Come back aboard."

"Yes, *sir.*" He could hear the relief in their voices. They were technicians, not trained astronauts. Working outside was not a chore they enjoyed.

While they were wriggling out of their space suits back at the airlock, Harbin commanded his pilot to turn and commence a high-speed run at the Astro ships. The other two HSS vessels were to remain on their courses.

The two technicians struggled back into their seats as *Samarkand*'s fusion engines accelerated the ship to a full g and then even beyond. Harbin heard metal groaning and creaking as the trio of Astro ships grew visibly bigger in the main screen.

The loosened rocks of the rubble shield were being pushed mechanically by the bulk of the accelerating ship. They were no longer held to the hull by the electrostatic field. Harbin heard thumps and bangs as some of the rocks separated entirely from the ship, but most of them obediently followed Newton's laws and hung on the ship's hull.

Harbin could see the Astro warships deploying to meet his solo attack. He felt sweat trickling down his ribs, cold and annoying. Once we let loose the rocks we'll have no protection against their lasers, he knew. But they'll be too busy to fire on us. He hoped.

"Decelerate," he ordered. "Reduce to one-half g."

The pilot tried to slow the ship smoothly, but still Harbin felt as if his insides were being yanked out of him. The comm tech moaned like a wounded creature and the entire ship seemed to creak and complain, metal screeching against metal.

As the ship slowed, though, the thousands of rocks of her rubble shield—fist-sized and smaller—kept on moving in a straight line, blindly following their own inertia as they hurtled toward the Astro vessels.

"Turn one hundred eighty degrees," Harbin snapped.

The sudden lurching turn was too much for the comm tech; she retched and slumped over the armrest of her chair. *Samarkand* was no racing yacht. The ship turned slowly, slowly toward the right. Some of the remaining rocks ground against the hull, a dull grating sound that made even the pilot look up with wide, frightened eyes.

Harbin paid no attention to anything but the main screen. The Astro vessels were in the path of a speeding avalanche of stones as most of *Samarkand*'s erstwhile shielding came plunging toward them.

"Keep the stones between us and them," Harbin told the pilot. "We can still use them to shield us."

The display screen was filled with the rubble now. Harbin saw a brief splash of laser light as one of the Astro warships fired into the approaching avalanche. With his armrest keyboard he widened the scope of the display.

The Astro captains knew what had happened to Gormley, too. For a heartstopping few seconds they maintained their formation, but then their nerve broke and the two escorting warships scattered, leaving the bigger, more ponderous freighter squarely in the path of the approaching stones.

The freighter tried to maneuver away from the avalanche but it was too slow, too cumbersome to escape. Its captain did manage to turn it enough so that its bulky cargo of asteroidal ores took the brunt of the cascade.

Harbin watched, fascinated, as the blizzard of rocks struck the freighter. Most of them hit the massive cargo of ores that the ship carried in its external grippers. Harbin saw sparks, puffs of dust, as the stones struck in the complete silence of airless space.

"I wouldn't want to be in that shooting gallery," the executive officer muttered.

Harbin glanced away from the screen momentarily, saw that the weapons tech was tending to the comm technician, who was sitting up woozily in her chair.

The rocks continued to pound the freighter. Harbin saw a flash of glittering vapor that quickly winked out. Must have hit part of the crew module, he thought. That was air escaping.

"Where are those two escort ships?" he asked aloud.

The pilot chuckled. "On their way back to Selene, from the looks of it."

Why not? Harbin thought. They don't have a ship to escort anymore. Why risk their butts in a three-against-two engagement?

He called his two other ships and told them to stand by in case the two Astro warships returned. Then he commanded his pilot to move *Samarkand* closer to the crippled freighter.

"We've got to finish her off," he said.

The pilot asked, "Do you want me to open a frequency to her? I can take over the comm console, sir."

Harbin shook his head. He had no desire to talk with the survivors, if there were any still alive aboard the freighter. His job now was to complete the destruction of the ship, which meant that anyone still breathing aboard her was going to die.

"No need to talk to them," he said to the pilot. Then, to the weapons tech, "Get back to your post and arm the lasers. Time to finish this job."

SELENE: ASTRO COMMAND CENTER

Admiral Wanamaker had expected his intelligence officer to be excited, or perhaps worried. Instead, she looked deadly calm. And determined.

"Willie," he said, "I can't let you go on this mission. I'm sure you understand why."

Tashkajian remained standing in front of his desk, her dark eyes unwavering. "This mission is my idea, sir. I don't think I should expect others to take risks that I'm not prepared to take myself."

Gently, trying not to injure her pride, Wanamaker said, "But I need you here, Willie. You're my intelligence officer, and a damned good one. I can't afford to risk you."

Her steadfast pose faltered just a little. "But, sir, it's not right for me to stay here while the crew dashes out to the Belt inside that radiation cloud."

He smiled slightly. "You assured me it was perfectly safe, Willie."

"It is!" she blurted. "But . . . well, you know, there's always a chance . . ." Her voice trailed off for a moment, then she snapped, "Dammit, sir, you know what I mean!"

"Yes I do," he admitted. "But you're not going. You've picked a crew and the ship is ready to go out inside the radiation cloud to attack the HSS base at Vesta. You are staying here, where you belong. Where I need you to be."

"That's not fair, sir!"

"I have no intention of being fair. This is a war we're fighting, not some playground game."

"But—"

"The ship goes without you," Wanamaker said, as firmly as he could manage. "That is final."

•   •   •

"Welcome to Shining Mountain Base," said Daniel Tsavo, beaming so widely Pancho thought she could see his molars.

He was standing at the end of the flexible tube that had been snaked out to the hopper from the airlock of the base structure.

Shifting the travel bag on her shoulder, Pancho took his extended hand, smiling back at him, and looked around. The interior of the Nairobi facility looked bare-bones, no-nonsense efficiency. Undecorated metal walls. Ribbed dome overhead. Tractors scuffed and grimy with lunar dust.

"Nice of you to invite me," Pancho said, knowing that she had actually invited herself.

"I'm glad you got here before the solar storm strikes. We'll be safely underground before the radiation begins to mount."

"Sounds good to me," said Pancho.

Tsavo led her to a pair of gleaming metal doors. They slid open to reveal an elevator.

"Most of our base is underground, of course," he said as he gestured her into the cab.

"Just like Selene."

"Just like Selene," he agreed as the doors slid shut and the cab began dropping so fast Pancho's stomach lurched.

Wanamaker had been dead-set against this visit. When Pancho had told him she was going to look over the Nairobi base, his holographic image had turned stony.

"Pancho, the head of the corporation shouldn't walk into a potential enemy base all by herself."

"Enemy?" Pancho's brows had shot up. "Nairobi's not an enemy of ours."

"How do you know?" Wanamaker had demanded. "You're at war, Pancho, and anybody who isn't an ally is potentially an enemy."

Pancho didn't believe it.

"At least take a security team with you," Wanamaker insisted.

"I can take care of myself."

As Tsavo guided her along the tunnels of the Nairobi base, though, Pancho began to wonder about her bravado. The place was larger than she had expected, much larger. Construction crews in dark blue coveralls seemed to be everywhere, drilling, digging, hauling equipment on electrically powered minitractors, yelling to each other, lifting, banging. The noise was incredible and incessant. Tsavo had to shout to make himself heard. And everything smelled brand new: fresh paint, concrete dust, sprays of lubricants and sealants in the air.

Pancho smiled and nodded as Tsavo shouted himself hoarse explaining what they were walking through. Living quarters would be there, offices on the other side of that corridor, laboratories, storerooms, a big conference room that could be converted into a theater, the base control center: all still unfinished, raw concrete and lunar rock and plans for the future.

Many of the workers were Asians, Pancho saw.

"Contract labor," Tsavo explained, his voice getting rougher with each word. "They have the experience and skills, and they are cheaper than training our own people."

Deeper and deeper into the base they walked, down inclined ramps marked TEMPORARY ACCESS and through tunnels whose walls were still bare rock.

Jeeps, Pancho thought, this place is *huge*. They're really building a city here, sure enough.

She hoped that the minibeacon her communications people had planted under the skin of her left hip would be able to send its coded signal through the rock. Jake's put up a set of six of polar orbiting satellites to keep track of me, she reminded herself; there'd be one close enough to pick up my signal all the time. I'll be okay. They'll know exactly where I am.

Yet for the first time in years she found herself thinking about Elly. Pancho had always felt safe with Elly tucked around her ankle. The gengineered krait had been her faithful bodyguard. Nobody messed with her once they realized she had a lethally poisonous snake to protect her. No matter that Elly's venom had been replaced with a strong sedative. Very few people had enough nerve to push things to the point where the snake would strike. Little Elly had been dead for more than ten years now, and Pancho had never worked up the resolve to get another such companion. Blubbery fool, she chided herself. Sentimental over a slithering snake, for cripes sake.

She tugged at the asteroidal sapphire clipped to her left earlobe. Like the rest of her jewelry, Pancho's earrings held surprises, weapons to defend her, if need be. But damn, she thought, there's a miniature army down here. I'd never be able to fight my way through all these bozos.

Sitting in the little wheeled chair in her office, just off the master bedroom of her home in Selene, Edith Elgin Stavenger used the three-second lag between Earth and Moon to catch up on the dossier of the woman she spoke with. For more than a week she had been chasing down executives in the news media on Earth, trying to stir their interest and support for her upcoming flight to Ceres.

THE ASTEROID WARS

Edith's cozy office seemed to be split in two, and the head of the North American News Syndicate appeared to be sitting behind her massive, gleaming cherrywood desk, talking with Edith as if they were actually in the same room—except for that three-second lag. Edith had the woman's dossier up on the wallscreen to one side of her own petite, curved desk.

"It's not a story, Edie," the media executive was saying. "There's no news interest in it."

The executive's name was Hollie Underwood, known in the industry as Holy Underhand or, more often, Queen Hollie. Thanks to rejuvenation therapies, she looked no more than thirty: smooth skin, clear green eyes, perfectly coiffed auburn hair. Edith thought of *The Picture of Dorian Gray* and wondered how withered and scarred with evil her portrait might be. Her reaction to Edith's idea was typical of the news media's attitude.

"There's no interest in it," Edith replied smoothly, "because no one's telling the story to the public."

Then she waited three seconds, watching Underwood's three-dimensional image, wondering how much the woman's ruffled off-white blouse must have cost. Pure silk, she was certain.

"Edie, dear, no one's telling the story because there's no story there. Who cares about a gaggle of mercenaries fighting each other all the way out there in the Asteroid Belt?"

Edith held her temper. Very sweetly, she asked, "Does anyone care about the cost of electrical power?"

Underwood's face went from mild exasperation to puzzled curiosity. At last she asked, "What's the price of electricity got to do with this?"

Feeling nettled that an executive of Underwood's level didn't understand much of anything important, Edith replied patiently, "The greenhouse flooding knocked out more than half of the coastal power plants around the world, didn't it?"

Without waiting for a reply, she went on, "Most of the loss in generating capacity is being taken up by solar power satellites, right? And where do you think the metals and minerals to build those satellites come from?"

Before Underwood could reply, Edith added, "And the fuels for the fusion generators that the power companies are building come from Jupiter, you know. This war is driving up their prices, too."

By the time she answered, Underwood was looking thoughtful. "You're saying that the fighting out in the Asteroid Belt is affecting the price of metals and minerals that those rock rats ship back to Earth. And the price of fusion fuels, as well."

"And the price of those resources affects the ultimate price you flatlanders pay for electricity, yes." Edith grimaced inwardly at her use of the derogatory *flatlanders,* but Underwood seemed to pay it no attention.

"So it costs us a few cents more per kilowatt hour," she said at last. "That's still not much of a story, is it."

Edith sat back in her little desk chair. There's something going on here, she realized. Something circling around below the surface, like a shark on the hunt.

She studied Underwood's face for a few silent moments. Then she asked, "How much advertising is Astro Corporation buying from you? Or is it Humphries?"

Once she heard the question Underwood reddened. "What do you mean? What are you implying?"

"The big corporations don't want you to go public about their war, do they? They're paying for this cover-up."

"Cover-up?" Underwood snapped, once she heard Edith's accusation. "There isn't any cover-up!"

"Isn't there?"

Underwood looked furious. "This conversation is *over!*" Her image winked out, leaving Edith alone in her snug little office.

She nodded to herself and smiled. That hit a nerve, all right. The big boys are paying off the news media to keep the war hushed up. That's what's going on.

Then Edith's smile faded. Knowing the truth would be of little help in getting the story to the public.

How to break through their wall of silence? Edith wished she knew.

ASTRO CORPORATION HEADQUARTERS

Jake Wanamaker actually banged his fist against the wall. He stomped past the row of consoles in the communications center and punched the wall hard enough to dent the thin metal paneling.

"She just waltzed in there all by herself and now you can't even make contact with her?"

The communications technicians looked scared. Old as he was, Wanamaker was still a formidable figure, especially when he was radiating anger. For several heartbeats no one in the comm center said a word. Console screens blinked and beeped softly, but everyone's attention was focused on the big admiral.

"Sir, we got good tracking data on her until she got to the Nairobi base."

"Those minibeacons are supposed to be able to broadcast through solid rock," Wanamaker snarled. "We hung a half-dozen satellites in polar orbits, didn't we? Why aren't they picking up her signal?"

"It must be the solar flare, sir," said another of the technicians. "It's screwing up communications."

Glowering, Wanamaker said, "You people assured me that the frequency the system uses wouldn't be bothered by a flare."

The chief comm tech, a cadaverous, sunken-eyed old computer geek, called across the room, "Their base must be shielded. Faraday cage, maybe. Wouldn't be too tough to do."

"Great!" Wanamaker snapped. "She's in a potential enemy's camp and we can't even track her movements."

"If she gets outside again the satellites'll pick up her signal," said the chief tech, hopefully.

"*If* she gets outside again," Wanamaker muttered.

"Not while the solar storm's in progress," said one of the younger techs, wide-eyed with worry. "Radiation level's too high. It'd be suicide."

Rumors spread through a tightly knit community such as Selene like ripples widening across a pond. One comm tech complained to a fellow Astro employee about the tongue-lashing Wanamaker gave to everyone in the communications center. The Astro employee mentioned to her husband that Pancho Lane had disappeared down at the Astro base near the south pole. Her husband told his favorite bartender that Pancho Lane had gone missing. "Probably shacked up with some guy, if I know Pancho," he added, grinning.

At that point the rumor bifurcated. One branch claimed that Pancho had run off with some guy from Nairobi Industries. The other solemnly insisted that she had been kidnapped, probably by Martin Humphries or some of his people.

Within hours, before Wanamaker or anyone in the Astro security office could even begin to clamp down a lid on the story, Selene was buzzing with the rumor that Pancho was either off on a love tryst or kidnapped and probably dead.

Nodon heard the story during his first hours of work as a maintenance technician in the big, echoing garage that housed the tractors and tour busses that went out onto the surface of Alphonsus's crater floor. He went through the motions of his new job and, as soon as his shift ended, hurried up into the "basement" to find Fuchs.

Fuchs was not at the stacks of shelving where Nodon and the others had met him before. Nodon fidgeted nervously, not knowing whether he should start searching through the dimly lit walkways or wait where he was for Fuchs to return. A maintenance robot came trundling along the walkway, its red dome light blinking. Nodon froze, plastering his back against the storeroom shelves. The robot rolled past, squeaking slightly. The maintenance robot needs maintenance, Nodon thought.

Half a minute behind the robot came Lars Fuchs, in his usual black pullover and slacks, and the usual dark scowl on his face.

"Kidnapped?" Fuchs gasped when Nodon told him the tale.

"Perhaps dead," the Mongol added.

"Humphries did this?"

To his credit, Nodon admitted, "I don't know. No one seems to know."

"It couldn't be anybody else," Fuchs growled.

Nodon agreed with a nod.

"Down at the south pole, you say? They captured her down there?"

"That is the story. Some say she has run off with a lover."

"Pancho wouldn't do that. She wouldn't have to. If she wanted a lover she'd do it right here in Selene, where she's safe."

Nodon said nothing.

"It's got to be Humphries," Fuchs muttered, as much to himself as his companion. "He's probably having her taken to his mansion, down below."

"Do you think so?"

"Even if he hasn't, that's where *he* is. We've got to get in there. And quickly."

Daniel Tsavo tried to hide his nervousness as he toured Pancho through the construction areas and finally down into the finished section of the Nairobi base, where he and the other corporate executives resided. It was blessedly quiet down at this lowest level; the constant battering noise of the twenty-four-hour-a-day construction was muffled by thick airtight hatches and acoustical insulation. As they walked along the carpeted corridor toward the executive dining room, Tsavo kept Pancho on his right, as he had done all through the brief tour, so that he could hear the microreceiver embedded in his left ear without being obvious about it.

It troubled him that Nobuhiko Yamagata himself was speeding to the base on a high-g rocket from Japan. The interrogation team had already arrived, but their work was suspended until Yamagata arrived.

Pancho, meanwhile, was trying to sort out in her mind everything she had seen in this brief tour of the unfinished base. It's enormous! she thought. They're not just building a phase-one facility here, they're putting up a whole city, all in one shot. This place'll be just as big as Selene.

Tsavo tried hard not to hold his left hand up to his ear. He was waiting for news that Yamagata had arrived, waiting for his instructions on what to do with Pancho.

"Pretty fancy setup you guys have for yourselves," Pancho teased as they walked along the corridor. Its walls were painted in soothing pastels. The noise of construction was far behind them. "Nice thick carpets on the floor and acoustic paneling on the walls."

"Rank has its privileges," Tsavo replied, making himself smile back at her.

"Guess so." Where are they getting the capital for all this, Pancho wondered. Nairobi Industries doesn't have this kind of financial muscle. Somebody's pouring a helluva lot of money into this. Humphries? Why would the Humper spend money on Nairobi? Why invest in a competitor? 'Specially when he's sinking so much into this goddamn war. I wouldn't be able to divert this much of Astro's funding; we'd go broke.

"Actually," Tsavo said, scratching at his left ear, "all this was not as expensive as you might think. Most of it was manufactured at Selene."

"Really?"

"Truly."

Pancho seemed impressed. "Y'know, back in the early days of Moon-base they thought seriously about putting grass down in all the corridors."

"Grass?"

"Yep. Life-support people said it'd help make oxygen, and the psychologists thought it'd make people happier 'bout having to live underground."

"Did they ever do it?"

"Naw. The accountants ran the numbers for how much electricity they'd need to provide light for the grass. And the maintenance people complained about the groundskeeping they'd have to do. That killed it."

"No grass."

"Except up in the Main Plaza, of course."

Tsavo said, "We plan to sod our central plaza, too. And plant trees."

"Uh-huh," said Pancho. But she was thinking, If Humphries isn't bankrolling Nairobi, who is? And why?

The receiver in Tsavo's ear buzzed. "Mr. Yamagata is expected in two hours. There is to be no interrogation of Ms. Lane until after he has arrived. Proceed with dinner as originally planned."

At that precise moment, Pancho asked, "Say, when's dinner? I haven't had anything to eat since breakfast."

"Perfect timing," Tsavo murmured, stopping at a set of double doors. Using both hands, he pushed them open. Pancho saw a conference room that had been transformed into a dining room. The central table was set for eight, and there were six people standing around the sideboard at the far end of the oblong room, where drinks had been set up. Two of them were women, all of them dark-skinned Africans.

Tsavo introduced Pancho to his Nairobi Industries colleagues, then excused himself to go to the next room for a moment, where the servers waited with a group of six Japanese men and women.

"No drugs," Tsavo told their chief. "We'll have a normal dinner. We can sedate her later."

TORCH SHIP *ELSINORE*

Doug Stavenger rode with Edith all the way up to the torch ship, waiting in a tight orbit around the Moon. He went with her through *Elsinore*'s airlock as the ship's captain personally escorted his passenger to her quarters, a comfortable little cabin halfway down the passageway that led to the bridge.

Once the captain had left them alone and had slid the passageway door shut, Stavenger took his wife in his arms.

"You don't have to do this, Edie," he said.

"Yes I do," she replied. She was smiling, but her eyes were steady with firm resolve.

"You could send someone else and have him report what he finds to you. You could stay here at Selene and produce the news show or documentary or whatever—"

"Doug," she said, sliding her arms around his neck, "I love you, darling, but you have no idea of how the news business works."

"I don't want you risking your neck out there."

"But that's the only way to get the story!"

"And there's a solar storm approaching, too," he said.

"The ship's shielded, darling." She nuzzled his nose lightly, then said, "You'd better be getting back to Selene before the radiation starts building up."

He frowned unhappily. "If something should happen to you . . ."

"What a story it would make!" She smiled as she said it.

"Be serious."

Her smile faded, but only a little. "I'm being serious, Doug. The only way to break this conspiracy of silence is for a major news figure to go to

Ceres and report on the situation firsthand. If Selene broadcasts my story it'll be picked up by independents on Earth. Then the Earthside nets will *have* to cover it. They'll have no choice."

"And if you get killed in the process?"

"I won't," she insisted. "I'm not going to go out into the Belt. I'll stay at Ceres, on the habitat the rock rats have built for themselves, where it's perfectly safe. That's one of the tricks of this business: Give the appearance of being on the front line, but stay at headquarters, where it's safe."

Stavenger tightened his grip around her waist. "I really don't want you to go, Edie."

"I know, dearest. But I have to."

Eventually he gave up and released her. But all the way back to Selene on the little shuttle rocket, all the way back to his home in the underground city's third level, Doug Stavenger could not shake the feeling that he would never see his wife again. He told himself he was being a foolish idiot, overly protective, overly possessive, too. Yet the feeling would not leave him.

Two ships left Selene, heading toward the Belt. *Elsinore,* carrying Edith Elgin, was going to the habitat *Chrysalis,* in orbit around the asteroid Ceres. *Cromwell,* an Astro Corporation freighter, was ostensibly going to pick up a load of ores that she would tote back to Selene.

Both ships turned on their electromagnetic radiation shielding as soon as they broke orbit around the Moon. The vast and growing cloud of energetic ionizing radiation that had been spewed out by the solar flare soon engulfed them both. Aboard *Elsinore,* the ship's crew and her sole passenger watched the radiation count climb with some unavoidable trepidation. Aboard *Cromwell,* the crew counted on the radiation cloud to shield their approach to Vesta. *Cromwell* carried no human passengers, of course. Its cargo was a pair of missiles that carried heavily insulated warheads of nanomachines, the type commonly called gobblers.

Unable to communicate with *Cromwell,* and equally unable to contact Pancho, Jake Wanamaker had nothing better to do but pace the communications center and glower at the technicians working the consoles. At last he thumped himself down at an empty console and pulled up Pancho's messages. Maybe there's something in here that can tell me what she thinks she's up to, he told himself, knowing it was just an excuse to engage in some busywork before he started smashing the furniture.

A long string of routine calls, mostly from Astro offices or board members. But one of the messages was highlighted, blinking in red letters. A Karl Manstein. No identification; just a call with no message attached. Yet it was highlighted. Wanamaker routed the call through Astro's security system, and the Mainstein name dissolved before his eyes, replaced by the name *Lars Fuchs.*

Lars Fuchs had called Pancho, Wanamaker realized. He remembered that she had wanted to contact Fuchs and was chewing out her security people because they couldn't find him.

The man's right under their noses, Wanamaker said to himself. Right here in Selene. But he left no callback number.

Wanamaker had the computer trace the origin of Fuchs's call. It had come from a wall phone up in the equipment storage area. Is he hiding up there? Wanamaker wondered.

He picked up the console microphone and instructed the communications computer to put through any call from Fuchs or Karl Manstein directly to him.

Nothing to do but wait, Wanamaker thought, leaning back in the console's little wheeled chair. Wait to see what's happening with Pancho. Wait to find out how *Cromwell*'s mission to Vesta turns out. Wait for Fuchs to call again.

He hated waiting.

Then he realized that someone was standing behind him. Swiveling the chair he saw it was Tashkajian, looking just as somber and apprehensive as he felt.

Martin Humphries was strolling through his expansive underground garden when Victoria Ferrer hurried along the curving brick path, breathless with news of the rumors about Pancho.

"Who the hell would kidnap Pancho?" Humphries snickered.

Walking alongside him through the wide beds of colorful flowers, Ferrer said, "The betting upstairs is that you did."

"Me? That's ridiculous."

"Is it?" she asked.

"I wouldn't mind having her assassinated. But why kidnap her?"

Ferrer shrugged slightly. "She might have run off with some guy. They say this man running the Nairobi operation is quite a slab of beefcake."

"Pancho wouldn't do that," Humphries said, shaking his head.

"Well, the Astro security people are floundering around, wondering where she is."

Humphries stopped in the middle of the path and took in a deep breath of flower-fragrant air. "Well, let's hope that she's dead. But I doubt it. Pancho's a tough little guttersnipe."

SELENE: STORAGE CENTER FOURTEEN

Fuchs paced along the dimly lit walkway between storage shelves and humming, vibrating equipment, trying to avoid the scattering of renegades and outcasts that lived among the shadows, turning aside whenever he saw the flashing red light of an approaching maintenance robot. He rubbed at the back of his neck, which was tight with tension. Absently, his hand moved to massage the bridge of his nose. His head ached and he felt frustrated, angry, aching, and—worst of all—uncertain.

What to do? What to do? Humphries must have had Pancho kidnapped. Who else would do it? Right at this moment they're probably flying Pancho back here to his mansion. If they haven't killed her already. What can I do? How can I help her?

He knew the answer. Get to Humphries and kill him. Kill the murdering bastard before he kills Pancho. Kill him for Amanda. For all the rock rats he's killed out in the Belt. Execute him, in the name of justice.

He snorted at his own pretensions. Justice. No, what you want is vengeance. Don't talk of justice; you want revenge, nothing less.

Alone as he paced the walkway, he nodded his aching head fiercely. Vengeance. Yes. I will have vengeance against the man who destroyed my life. Who destroyed everything and everyone I hold dear.

And what risks are you willing to take for your vengeance? he asked himself. You have three people with you; Humphries has a small army of security guards down there in his mansion. How can you even think of getting to him? There is no one in Selene who will help you. No one in the entire solar system would lift a finger for you, except Pancho and she's a prisoner or perhaps already dead.

Fuchs abruptly stopped his pacing. He found himself in front of a large wall screen, set up against the side of a massive, chugging water pump that was painted bright blue. The screen was mounted on rubberized shock absorbers, to separate it from the pump's constant vibration. In the faint light from a distant overhead lamp Fuchs saw his reflection in the blank screen: a short, stocky man with a barrel chest, stubby arms and legs, a bristling black beard and deep-set eyes that glowed like twin lasers. He was dressed in shapeless black slacks and a pullover shirt, also black as death.

No more thinking, he told himself. No more planning. Get Sanja and the others and *strike*. Tonight. Humphries dies tonight or I do. He almost smiled. Possibly both of us.

His headache disappeared along with his uncertainty.

"It was a really great dinner," Pancho said as Tsavo walked her along the corridor. "You got some sharp people working for you. I enjoyed talking with them."

Tsavo beamed at her compliments. "I'm glad you enjoyed it."

During dinner he had learned that Nobuhiko Yamagata had landed, scant minutes ahead of the leading edge of the solar storm, and had gone immediately to his interrogation team. Now the voice whispering electronically in his left ear told him to take Pancho to her quarters and let her fall asleep. To help make her sleep, Yamagata's people had injected a strong sedative in the bottle of wine that waited on Pancho's bedside table.

"It's been a really good visit," Pancho was saying. "I'm glad I came."

Still smiling for her, Tsavo said, "You'll stay the night, of course."

Pancho grinned back at him. He was a centimeter or so taller than her own lanky height, and she liked tall men.

"I'd love to, Dan, but I've got to get back to my own people. They're expecting me."

"But the storm," he said earnestly. "All surface activities are suspended until the radiation goes down to normal."

Pancho teased, "Is that what your dinner was for? To keep me here long enough for the storm to hit?"

He looked shocked. "No! Not at all. But now that it's hit, you'll have to stay the night."

She said nothing as he led her a few more paces down the carpeted corridor and stopped at an unmarked door. Sliding it open, he ushered her into a spare but comfortable-looking bedroom, with a small desk set in one corner and a wallscreen that showed the view outside the base. Pancho saw several hoppers standing out there, including the green one she had flown in on. And a transfer vehicle, the kind that brought people in from ships in orbit; that hadn't been there when she'd landed. In the bright sunlight outside she could see that it was anodized sky blue.

Then she noticed that her travel bag had been placed on the bed, unopened. And there was a bottle of wine sitting tilted in a chiller bucket on the low table in front of the cushioned sofa.

"Champagne," she noted. "And two glasses."

Tsavo put on a slightly sheepish look. "Even before the storm came up I had hoped you'd stay the night."

"Looks like I'll have to. I ought to call my people at Malapert, though, and let them know I'm okay."

He hesitated, as if debating inwardly with himself. Pancho couldn't hear the whispered instructions he was getting.

"All right," he said, flashing that killer smile again. "Let me call my communications center."

"Great!"

He went to the phone on the desk and the wallscreen abruptly switched to an image of a man sitting at a console with a headset clipped over his thick dark hair.

"I'm afraid, sir, that the solar storm is interfering with communications at this time."

Tsavo seemed upset. "Can't you establish a laser link?"

Unperturbed, the communications tech said, "Our laser equipment is not functional at this time, sir."

"Well get it functioning," Tsavo said hotly. "And let me know the instant it's working."

"Yes, sir." The wallscreen went dark.

Pancho pursed her lips, then shrugged. "Guess my people at Malapert will have to get along without me till the storm lets up."

Tsavo looked pleased. Smiling, he asked, "Would you like some wine?"

COMMAND SHIP
SAMARKAND

Harbin was heading back to the HSS base at Vesta. *Samarkand* had not escaped its one-sided battle against the Astro freighter unscathed. The loosed rocks and pebbles of his ship's armor shield had dented and buckled parts of the hull, and now *Samarkand* was totally unarmored, easy prey for any warship it should happen to meet.

He was worried about the ship's radiation shielding. Even though the diagnostics showed the system to be functioning properly, with a solar storm approaching he preferred to be safely underground at Vesta.

Still, he left his two other vessels to continue their hunt through this region of the Belt while he made his way back to Vesta for refurbishment.

It will be good to have a few days of R&R, he thought as he sat in the command chair. Besides, my medicinals are running low. I'll have to get the pharmacy to restock them.

He turned the con over to his executive officer and left the bridge, ducking through the hatch and down the short passageway to his private quarters. Making his way straight to his lavatory, he opened the medicine chest and surveyed the vials and syringes stored there. Running low, he confirmed. But there's enough here to get me through the next few nights. Enough to let me sleep when I need to.

He reached for one of the vials, but before he could take it in his fingers the intercom buzzed.

"Sir, we have a target," the exec's voice said. Then she added, "I think."

Harbin slammed the cabinet door shut. "You think?" he shouted to the intercom microphone set into the metal overhead of the lav.

"It's an odd signature, sir."

Incompetent jackass, Harbin said to himself. Aloud, "I'm on my way."

He strode to the bridge, simmering anger. I can't trust this crew to do anything for themselves. I can't even leave them alone long enough to take a piss.

But as he slid into the command chair he saw that the display on the main screen was indeed fuzzy, indistinct.

"Max magnification," he commanded.

"It is at maximum," the comm tech replied. She too was staring at the screen, a puzzled frown furrowing her pale Nordic countenance.

Harbin glanced at the data bar running across the bottom of the display. Just over twelve hundred kilometers away. The object was spinning slowly, turning along its long axis every few seconds.

"Size estimate," he snapped.

Two pulsating cursors appeared at each end of the rotating object. Blinking alphanumerics said 1.9 METERS.

"It's too small to be a ship," said the pilot.

"A robot vehicle?" the weapons technician asked. "Maybe a mine of some sort?"

Harbin shook his head. He knew what it was. "Turn off the display."

"But what is it?" the communications tech wondered aloud.

"Turn it off!"

The screen went dark. All four of his officers turned to stare at him questioningly.

"It's a man," Harbin said. "Or a woman. Someone in a space suit. Someone dead. Killed in a battle out there, probably months ago."

"Should we—"

"Ignore it," he snapped. "It can't hurt us and there's nothing more we can do to it. Just leave it alone."

The officers glanced at each other.

"A casualty of war," Harbin said grimly as he got out of the command chair. "Just forget about it. I'm going back to my quarters. Don't disturb me with any more ghosts."

He went back to his cabin, stripped off his sweaty uniform and stretched out on his bunk. It will be good to get back to Vesta, he thought. This ship needs refurbishment. So do I.

This war can't last much longer, he told himself. We've driven most of the Astro ships out of the Belt. They'll come back with more, I suppose, and we'll destroy them. We'll keep on destroying them until they finally give up. And what then? Do I retire back to Earth? Or keep on working? There's always money to be made for a mercenary soldier. There's always someone willing to pay for killing someone else.

He closed his eyes to sleep, but instead he saw a space-suited figure tumbling slowly through the star-flecked emptiness, silently turning over and over, for all eternity alone in the cold, dark emptiness, forever alone.

His eyes snapped open. Harbin thought about taking a shot that would let him sleep, but he didn't want to dream. So he lay on the bunk for hours, wide awake, staring at the hard metal of the overhead.

"Wish I could call my people and tell 'em I'll be spending the night here," Pancho said. "When's that laser link going to start working?"

Wine bottle in one hand, pneumatic corkscrew in the other, Daniel Tsavo suddenly looked uneasy.

"They'll know you're safe down here," he said, with a slightly labored smile. "Let's have some wine and stop worrying."

Pancho made herself smile back at him. "Sure, why not? You open the bottle while I freshen up a little."

She went to the lavatory and closed its door firmly. Pecking at her wristwatch, she saw that its link with the satellites that were supposed to be tracking her was dead. She tried the phone function. That was down, too.

Pancho leaned against the sink, thinking furiously. I'm cut off from the outside. He wants me to stay here overnight. Fun and games? Maybe, but there's more to it than just a romp in the sheets. This place is *huge*. They're spending more money on construction than Nairobi's got on its books. A lot more. Somebody big is bankrolling them.

And then it hit her. Tsavo said to me, "Welcome to Shining Mountain Base." That's what the Japanese call this mountain range: the Shining Mountains. And that transfer ship outside is painted in Yamagata Corporation's blue.

Yamagata's behind all this, Pancho finally realized. They're bankrolling Nairobi. And now they've got me here; I waltzed right in and they're not going to let go of me that easy.

She heard the pop of a champagne cork through the flimsy lavatory door. Ol' Danny boy's working for Yamagata, Pancho said to herself. And I'll bet there's enough happy juice in that wine to get me to babble my brains out to him.

I've got to get out of here, she told herself. And quick.

Nobuhiko Yamagata paid scant attention to the bows and self-effacing hisses of his underlings. He went straight from the transfer rocket that had landed him at Shining Mountain Base to the room where Pancho Lane would be interrogated. It was in the base's infirmary, a small room where his interrogation team surrounded an empty gurney.

Father is right, Nobu said to himself. I can learn much more from Pancho than these hirelings could.

The team was gowned and masked, like medics. Two young women were helping Nobu into a pale green surgical gown. Within minutes he was masked, gloved, and capped with one of the ridiculous-looking shapeless hats that came down over his ears.

Then he stood by the gurney, waiting. The members of the interrogation team flanked him in silence.

Well, Nobuhiko thought, everything is prepared. Everyone is here except Pancho.

SHINING MOUNTAIN BASE

Won't you have some champagne?" Tsavo asked smoothly, offering Pancho one of the crystal flutes that he had filled with the bubbly wine.

"Love to," said Pancho, smiling her best smile for him.

As he handed her the glass Pancho let it slip from her fingers. She watched with inner amusement as the glass tumbled slowly in the gentle lunar gravity, wine spilling from its lip in languid slow motion. Pancho could have grabbed the glass before it started spilling, but she watched it splash champagne over her coveralls while Tsavo stood there looking shocked.

"Aw gosh," she said as the glass bounced on the thick carpeting. "Sorry to be so clumsy."

Tsavo recovered enough to say, "My fault."

Looking down at the wine-spattered front of her coveralls, Pancho said, "I better dry this off." She headed for the lavatory, stopping momentarily to unclip one of her earrings and place it on the night table beside the bed.

There are many ways to incapacitate an opponent who's bigger and stronger than you are, Pancho reminded herself as she firmly closed the lavatory door. One of them is to blind the sumbitch.

She leaned her back against the door and squeezed her eyes shut, but still she saw the flash behind her closed eyelids. Tsavo screamed. By the time Pancho had the lav door open again he was staggering across the bedroom.

"I can't see!" he shrieked. "I'm blind!"

He crashed into the coffee table, knocking the bottle and chiller bucket to the floor and tumbled into the sofa with a painful thump, groaning, pawing at his eyes.

"I'm blind! I'm blind!"

"Sorry, Danny boy," Pancho said as she scooped her travel bag off the bed. "You'll get your sight back in a few hours, more'n likely."

She left him moaning in a tumbled sobbing heap on the floor by the sofa and dashed out into the corridor.

Now we find out how much security they got here, Pancho said to herself, actually grinning as she raced on her long legs up the carpeted corridor.

Fuchs had thought about calling Astro Corporate headquarters to try to speak with one of Pancho's aides, but decided against it. None of them would have the authority to give him the help he needed, nor the wit to see the necessity of it. With Pancho out of the picture, Fuchs realized he was on his own.

Just as well, he told himself as he rode the powered stairs down to Selene's bottommost level. It's better not to involve Pancho or anyone else. What I have to do I'll do for myself.

Nodon, Sanja and Amarjagal were waiting for him at the bottom of the last flight of stairs. The corridor down at this level was empty, as Fuchs had expected it to be. Only the very wealthiest lived down here, in the converse of penthouses on Earth. No crowds here, he said to himself as the four of them strode down the broad, empty, quiet corridor. Fuchs saw that the walls here were decorated with bas reliefs, the floor softly carpeted. Security cameras watched them, he knew, but they looked like a quartet of maintenance workers, nothing to set off an alarm.

So far.

"Have you set the maintenance computer?" Fuchs asked Nodon.

The younger man nodded, his big liquid eyes looking slightly frightened. "Yes, sir. The water will be shut off to this level in . . ." he glanced at his wristwatch, ". . . three minutes."

"Good," said Fuchs. He had no idea how long it would take the maintenance people to discover that the water to level seven had been shut off. Long enough to get the four of us inside Humphries's grotto, he hoped.

The corridor ended in a blank stone wall with a heavy metal hatch set in it. Beside the hatch was a keypad.

"Do you have the access number?" Fuchs asked Nodon.

"I haven't had enough time on my job with the maintenance department to be assigned down here," Nodon said, his voice little more than an apologetic whisper. "But I know the emergency numbers that work on the upper levels."

"Try them."

Nodon hunched slightly before the keypad and began tapping numbers. Fuchs watched with gathering impatience. One of those numbers should override the security code, he told himself. Humphries has to allow Selene emergency crews inside his private preserve, he's got to. Not even he can refuse to allow emergency workers to enter his area. That's written into Selene's basic safety regulations.

The hatch suddenly gave off a metallic click. In the stillness of the empty corridor it sounded like a gunshot.

"That's it!" Fuchs hissed. He set a meaty hand against the cold steel of the hatch and pushed. It opened slowly, silently. A gust of soft, warm air brushed past him as the hatch swung all the way open.

Fuchs gaped at what he saw. A huge expanse filled with brilliant flowers, warm artificial sunlight glowing from the lamps high overhead, the very air heavy with scents he hadn't smelled since he'd left Earth. And trees! Tall, stately, spreading their leafy branches like arms open to embrace him.

"It's a paradise," Amarjagal whispered, her eyes wide with awe. Nodon and Sanja stood beside her, mouths agape. Fuchs felt tears welling up.

With an angry shake of his head he growled, "Come on. Their security alarms must be going off. Their cameras are watching us."

He started up the brick path that wound through beds of bright colorful flowers, heading for the mansion they could see through the trees.

Paradise, Fuchs thought. But this paradise has armed men guarding it, and they'll be coming out to stop us in a few minutes.

Nobuhiko pushed up the sleeve of his green surgical gown and looked at his watch. Turning to the chief of the interrogation team, he demanded, "Well, where is she? I've been waiting for more than half an hour."

The man's mask was slightly askew. He pushed back his shower-cap hat, revealing a line pressed into his high forehead by the cap's elastic band.

"Tsavo was to bring her here," he said.

"They should be here by now," said Nobuhiko.

The man hesitated. "Perhaps they are . . ."

"They are what?"

With a shrug, the man said, "They spent a night together back at Selene, when they first met. Perhaps they are in bed together now."

One of the gowned and masked women tittered softly.

Nobuhiko was not amused. "Send someone to find them. At once."

Her travel bag clutched under one arm, Pancho walked briskly along the corridor, trying to remember the route she had followed when Tsavo brought her down to this level. Cripes, she thought, it was only an hour or two ago but I'm not sure of which way we came. My memory's shot to hell.

She thought about the stealth suit she had used so many years ago to sneak into Humphries's mansion unseen. I could use a cloak of invisibility right about now, she told herself as she glanced up at the corridor's ceiling, searching for surveillance cameras. She couldn't see any, but she knew that didn't mean there weren't any watching.

She spotted a pair of metal doors at the end of the corridor. The elevator! Pancho sprinted to it and leaned on the button set into the wall.

Now we'll find out if they're watching me. If the elevator's working, it means they don't know I'm on the loose.

The elevator doors slid smoothly open and Pancho stepped into the cab. It wasn't until the doors shut again and the elevator started accelerating upwards that she thought it might be a trap. Jeeps! They could have an army of guards waiting for me up at the top level.

TORCH SHIP *ELSINORE*

An ordinary passenger riding out to the rock rats' habitat at Ceres would have been quickly bored in the cramped confines of the torch ship. *Elsinore* was accelerating at one-sixth g, so that its sole passenger would feel comfortable at the familiar lunar level of gravity. But like all the ships that plied between the Moon and the Belt, *Elsinore* was built for fast, efficient travel, not for tourist luxuries. There was no entertainment aboard except the videos broadcast from Selene or Earth. Meals were served in the neatly appointed but decidedly small galley.

Edith had dinner with the ship's captain and one of his officers, a young Asian woman who said little but listened attentively to the ship's passenger and her skipper.

"We'll be vectoring out of the radiation cloud tomorrow," the captain announced cheerfully, over his plate of soymeat and mushrooms. "Ceres is well clear of the cloud's predicted path."

"You don't seem worried about it," Edith said.

He made a small shrug. "Not worried, no. Respectful, though. Our radiation shielding is working, so we're in no danger. And by this time tomorrow we should be out of it altogether."

"Will the cloud reach the Belt at all?" she asked.

"Oh yes, it's too big and intense to dissipate until it's well past the orbit of Jupiter. Ceres is well clear of it, but a good half of the Belt is going to be bathed in lethal radiation."

Edith smiled for him and turned her attention to her own dinner of bioengineered carp fillet.

After dinner, Edith went to her cabin, sent a laser-beamed message to her husband back at Selene, then started working on the first segment of the documentary she had planned.

Sitting on the tiny couch of her cabin with the video camera perched on its mobile tripod by the bed, she decided to forgo the usual Edie Elgin cheerleader smile. Covering a war was a serious matter.

"This is Edie Elgin, aboard the torch ship *Elsinore*," she began, "riding out to the Asteroid Belt, where a deadly, vicious war is taking place between mercenary armies of giant corporations. A war that could determine how much you pay for electrical energy and all the natural resources that are mined in the Belt."

She got to her feet and walked slowly around the little cabin, the camera automatically pivoting to keep her in focus.

"I'll be living in this cabin for the next six days, until we arrive at Ceres. Most of the men and women who go out to the Belt to work as miners or prospectors or whatever travel in much less comfortable quarters."

Edith went to the door and out into the passageway. The camera trundled after her automatically on its tripod as she began to show her viewers the interior of the torch ship. As she spoke, she hoped that this segment wouldn't be too boring. If it is I can cut it down or eliminate it altogether, she thought. I don't want to bore the viewers. That is, assuming anybody wants to watch the show once it's finished.

Cromwell was cruising toward the Belt at a more leisurely pace, allowing the radiation cloud to engulf it. The ship's five-person crew could not feel the radiation that surrounded the ship nor see it, except in graphs the computer drew from the ship's sensors.

"The shielding is working fine," the skipper kept repeating every few minutes. "Working just fine."

His four crew members wished he'd change the subject.

Eventually, he did. "Set course thirty-eight degrees azimuth, maintain elevation."

Embedded in the radiation cloud, *Cromwell* headed toward Vesta.

Suddenly panicked, Pancho stabbed at the panel of buttons in the elevator. The cab lurched to a stop and the doors slid open. The pounding, growling, roaring sounds of construction immediately blasted her ears but she paid them no attention as she walked briskly out into the unfinished expanse.

She saw that she wasn't at the topmost level, the dome where there was an airlock that led to the rocket hoppers sitting outside. Must be a rampway that leads up, she thought hopefully. Better stay away from the elevators.

A construction worker driving an orange tractor yelled at her in Japanese. Pancho couldn't understand his words, but she recognized the tone: *What the hell are you doing here? Get back where you belong!*

With a grin she hollered back to him, "That's just what I'm trying to do, buddy. Which way is up?"

The head of base security was perspiring visibly. Nobuhiko glared at the black man and demanded, "Well, where is she? She has to be *someplace!*"

Yamagata had left his interrogation team in their silly green gowns and bustled off to the security chief's office, tearing off the surgical gown they had given him and throwing it angrily to the floor as his own quartet of bodyguards hastened along behind him.

The security chief was standing behind his desk, flanked by a wall of display screens, most of them blank.

"She *was* here," he said, punching a keypad on his desktop, "with Mr. Tsavo."

One of the screens lit up to show Pancho and Tsavo in the bedroom. Nobu watched Pancho spill her champagne, go to the lavatory—and then the screen flared with painful brilliance.

Blinking, a red afterimage burning in his eyes, Yamagata said through gritted teeth, "I don't want to know where she *was*. I want to know where she is now."

The security chief wiped at his tearing eyes. "She must have gone up into the construction area. The surveillance cameras on those levels haven't been activated yet."

Before the exasperated Yamagata could say anything, the security chief added, "I've ordered all the airlocks sealed and placed guards at all the space suit storage areas. She can't get outside."

Nobu thought, That's something, at least. She's trapped inside the base. We'll find her, then. It's only a matter of time.

We make an unlikely invasion force, Fuchs thought as he and his three crew members walked purposively through the flowering garden toward Humphries's mansion.

But that might be a good thing, he realized. The more unlikely we appear, the less seriously the guards will take us. We might still have surprise on our side.

Not for long, he saw. A pair of men were striding down the winding path toward them, both of them tall, broadshouldered, with the hard-eyed look of professional security guards. They were clad in identical slate-gray tunics and slacks: not quite uniforms, but close enough. Fuchs wondered what kinds of weapons they carried.

"What are you doing here?" the one on the left called, raising a hand to stop Fuchs and his people.

"Emergency maintenance," said Fuchs, slowing but not stopping. "Water stoppage."

"We didn't get any emergency call," said the other one. He was slightly shorter, Fuchs saw, and looked somewhat younger.

"It registered on our board," Fuchs lied. Stretching out an arm to point, he said, "You can see the problem from here, up on your roof."

The shorter one turned almost completely around. The other glanced over his shoulder. Fuchs launched himself at the older one, ramming his head into the man's midsection. He heard a satisfying "Oof!" and the two of them went down, Fuchs on top. Nodon kicked the man in the head and he went limp. Getting to his feet, Fuchs saw that Amarjagal and Sanja had knocked the other one unconscious as well.

Swiftly, they tied the two men with their own belts and dragged them into the bushes, but not before taking their guns and communicators.

Fuchs looked over one of the pistols as they ran toward the mansion. Laser pistols. Fuchs remembered how the rock rats had turned their hand-held tools into makeshift weapons, years ago. These were specifically designed as sidearms. Nodon held the other gun.

"STOP WHERE YOU ARE!" boomed an amplified voice.

Fuchs yelled back, "This is an emergency! Quick! We haven't a moment to lose!"

The front door of the mansion opened as they raced up to it, and another pair of guards in identical slate-gray outfits—one of them a woman—stepped out, looking puzzled.

"What's going—"

Fuchs shot the man and before she could react Nodon shot the woman. The infrared laser beams were invisible but Fuchs saw the smoking little circular wound in his man's forehead as he slumped to the ground.

"Come on," Fuchs said, waving his crew forward. Amarjagal and Sanja stopped long enough to take the guns from the unconscious guards, then they stepped over their inert bodies and into the mansion's entryway.

I'm in his house! Fuchs marveled. I'm actually in Humphries's home! He realized he hadn't expected to get this far.

A woman in a black servant's dress came out of a door down the hall, carrying a silver tray laden with covered dishes. Fuchs rushed toward her. When she saw the gun in his hand she gave out a frightened squeak, dropped the tray with a loud crash, and fled back into the kitchen.

"Never mind her," Fuchs snarled. "Find Humphries."

•   •   •

Finally ending her video tour of the ship, Edith returned to her cabin. She felt tired, but decided to review what she had shot and mark the scenes for future editing.

Once her face appeared on the cabin's wallscreen, though, she studied it minutely for signs of aging. To her relief, she could find none. The rejuvenation therapies were still working.

Then she wondered if that might not be counted against her, back on Earth. They might think I'm filled with nanomachines, like Doug. That would prejudice them against me, maybe.

She shrugged to herself and shut down the display. Faced with a choice between flatlander prejudices and physical youth, she opted for youth. With a yawn she looked toward her bed. Time for some beauty sleep, Edith said to herself, wishing that Doug were here with her.

HUMPHRIES MANSION

The house was huge, Fuchs realized, and divided into two sections. On one side of the hallway that extended from the entrance there seemed to be a warren of offices and laboratories. Fuchs and his crew glanced into a few of them; they were unoccupied, quiet, dark. Offices for his staff, Fuchs guessed, empty at this time of night.

Impatiently he waved his three aides back to the hallway.

"Sanja," he directed, pointing down the hall, "you find that woman. She must know where Humphries is. "We'll look through the other side of the house."

Humphries was upstairs, in the master bedroom suite, sitting at his computer desk. The war is going well, he said to himself as he studied the latest figures on battle casualties. In another couple of months we'll have booted Astro out of the Belt altogether.

Yet when he turned to his intelligence department's latest assessment, his face contorted into a frown. Astro's building more ships, gearing up for a counterattack. That damned greasemonkey doesn't know when she's beaten.

He heard a muffled clatter from downstairs. One of the servants must have dropped something. Leaning back in his yielding desk chair he realized that he had ordered a snack more than half an hour ago. Where the hell was it?

With a shake of his head he returned to his musings about the war. They claim Pancho's disappeared. More likely she's down at that Nairobi base trying to get their support. And I've got a board of directors meeting coming up. They'll yell bloody murder about the p-and-l figures. This war's bleeding us. But once we win it, they'll all shut up. They'll have to.

His thoughts returned to Pancho. The little guttersnipe. If she's building a new fleet of warships here at Selene it makes sense to attack the factories where they're being built. But that would bring Stavenger into the war on her side. I don't want Selene coming in against—

"The water turned off."

Annoyed, Humphries turned to see Victoria Ferrer standing in the doorway to his office, wrapped in a white full-length robe, its sash cinched around her waist. Her hair was glistening wet.

"What?" he snapped.

"The water turned off," she repeated, "right in the middle of my shower."

At that moment the report hovering above his desk abruptly disappeared, replaced by the intense face of his chief security guard.

"Sir, we have intruders on the premises."

"Inside the house?"

"Yessir. Downstairs. I suggest you go to top security mode immediately."

"Damned right! And you get them! Call everyone you've got. Get them!"

Down in his basement office, the security chief clicked off his phone, thinking furiously. Only twelve guards on night duty, he knew. Still, he glanced at the screen showing the duty roster. They've already knocked out four of them. He told the phone to call up every guard on the payroll— another two dozen of them—and get them to the mansion immediately.

Humphries has his suite sealed off, so they can't get to him unless they can cut through three centimeters of reinforced cermet, he thought. Even with laser pistols that will take some time. The boss is safe enough. He called for a view of the master suite and saw that Ferrer was in there with Humphries. He grinned to himself. Hell, he might even enjoy this, as long as she's sealed into the bedroom with him.

Then he turned his attention to the screen showing three of the four intruders making their way up the main staircase to the upper floor.

Fuchs was leading Nodon and Amarjagal cautiously up the main stairway, peering intently at the upper landing to see if any more security guards were up there. Suddenly he heard the heavy slamming of doors. A voice blared from speakers hidden in the ceiling:

"WE HAVE YOU ON CAMERA AND ARE AUTHORIZED TO USE LETHAL FORCE IF NECESSARY. THE HOUSE IS SEALED

AND THERE IS NO WAY FOR YOU TO ESCAPE. DROP YOUR WEAPONS AND PUT YOUR HANDS ON TOP OF YOUR HEADS."

Fuchs hesitated for barely a fraction of a second, then rushed up the stairs, the two others behind him. As they reached the landing, Sanja started up the steps behind them.

"The front doorway has been sealed with a metal slab!" he called.

The windows, too, were covered with heavy metal grillwork, Fuchs saw as he glanced around the upstairs hallway. The hall was lined with real wooden furniture: tables and chests and sideboards. Actual paintings hung along the walls.

They think we're burglars or thieves, Fuchs thought. They're trying to make certain we can't get away. But I don't want to get away, I want to find Humphries.

"Where are you, Humphries?" he shouted at the ceiling. "Show yourself, coward!"

Nodon, his eyes so wide that Fuchs could see white all around the pupils, said in a tight whisper, "They must be sending more guards. We're trapped!"

All the lights went off, plunging them into almost total darkness. Within an instant, though, Nodon pulled a hand torch from his coverall pocket. Its feeble beam made the hallway look eerie, mysterious.

Fuchs rushed to a heavy walnut table against the wall. With one sweep of his arm he sent the flower vase and smaller porcelain pieces atop it crashing to the carpeted floor.

"Help me turn this thing over and drag it over to the top of the stairs. We can stop them from getting up here."

Sanja and Amarjagal tipped the table over with a heavy thud, and the four of them pushed it to the head of the stairs and wedged it there between the wall and the staircase railing. Down below they heard the pounding of running feet and saw the shadowy figures of security guards coming along the downstairs hall. They must have been stationed in the basement, Fuchs thought, straining to make out how many of them there were. No more than six, he estimated.

He whispered to the two men, "Get the statues, the chairs, anything you can lift and bring them here. Amarjagal, go down the hallway a few meters so you can fire on them as they come up the stairs."

If they think we're going to surrender, they have a big surprise coming, Fuchs thought grimly. I'm not leaving this house until I see Humphries dead at my feet.

SHINING MOUNTAIN BASE

Pancho jogged up the rampway, long legs pumping easily as she made her way to the top level of the base. Trotting along the final section of ramp she could see the ribbed vaulting of the surface dome overhead. Almost there, she said to herself.

But she skidded to a halt when she spotted a quartet of men standing by the row of space suits that hung next to the airlock. They were all Japanese, their coveralls sky blue and bearing the white flying crane emblem of Yamagata Corporation. Each of them had an ugly-looking sidearm strapped to his waist.

They saw her, too. Two of them started to sprint toward her as Pancho reversed her course and started back down the ramp, back toward the noisy, bustling construction crews and the minitractors that were hauling loads of steel beams and drywall sheeting. She swung her legs over the ramp's railing and jumped lightly to the dusty floor several meters below.

The noise was an advantage to her, she thought. Nobody's going to hear those guards yelling, and these construction guys don't have comm units in their ears. She loped alongside one of the electric-powered minitractors and hopped into the cart it was towing, landing with a plop amidst coils of wire and bouncing, flexing lengths of plastic piping.

She lay flat, hoping that the guards didn't see her hitchhike maneuver. The minitractor trundled on for several minutes; all Pancho could see was the bare beams supporting the ceiling overhead.

She was thinking as hard and fast as she could. Airlocks are up on the next level, but they're all guarded. So are the suits. Even if I could grab a space suit the guards would grab me before I had time to put one on. And there's the damn-dratted solar storm outside, too. Not the best time for a walk on the surface.

I could use the softsuit, she reminded herself. It's right here, tucked into my travel bag. Never used the blow-up helmet before but Doug said it works okay. Yeah, maybe. Maybe not. What choice do I have?

The big problem was to get to an airlock without being seen. Suddenly Pancho broke into a fierce grin. No, the problem is how do I get some explosives so I can *make* a new airlock for myself!

Doug Stavenger tried to busy himself with catching up on the minutes of Selene's governing council meetings. But as he read the reports of the water board and the maintenance department and the safety office, the words blurred into meaningless symbols before his eyes. Irritated, nervous, he told his computer to show him the latest report on the solar storm.

One wall of the office in his home seemingly dissolved into a three-dimensional image of the Earth/Moon system. It was bathed in a hot pink glow that represented the radiation cloud. Stavenger muted the sound, preferring to read for himself the figures on radiation intensity and predicted time duration of the storm displayed across the bottom of the holographic image.

"Add traffic," he said quietly.

Several yellow dots appeared in the image. One of them was identified as *Elsinore*, the ship Edith was aboard.

"Project trajectories."

Slim green curving lines appeared, the one attached to *Elsinore* arcing out to the right and out of the cloud.

"Add destinations."

Elsinore's projected path ended at a dot labeled "Ceres." Stavenger noted almost subliminally that of all the ships in the region, there was one named *Cromwell* but that had no projected destination visible. No course vector for it showed at all. It was deep inside the radiation cloud, too.

As he watched, *Cromwell*'s dot winked out. Stavenger stared at the display. Either the ship's suddenly been destroyed or they've turned off all their tracking and telemetry beacons. There were no other ships near it, as far as the imagery showed. So it can't have been attacked by somebody.

Why would they turn off all their beacons? Stavenger asked himself. It took only a moment's thought for him to understand.

Pancho jumped off the cart as the minitractor rolled past a jumbled pile of equipment and crates of supplies lying in what seemed a haphazard disorder on the dusty concrete floor. The driver saw her and yelled at her over his shoulder in Japanese as the tractor trundled away from her.

"Same to you, buddy," Pancho hollered back, bowing politely to the driver.

Slinging her travel bag over one shoulder, she ducked behind the nearest pile of crates and started searching through the trove. No explosives, but in the midst of the scattered pieces of equipment she saw something that might be almost as good: a welding laser. Kneeling beside the laser's finned barrel, she clicked its ON switch and felt her heart sink. The power supply's battery indicator was way down in the red. I need a power source, she told herself.

Suddenly the loudspeakers hanging on poles every fifty meters or so blared into harsh, rapid Japanese. Pancho didn't understand the words but she knew the tone: There's an intruder sneaking around here. Find her!

All the construction noise stopped. It was eerie, Pancho thought. The banging, buzzing, yelling construction site went absolutely still. It was as if everybody froze.

But only for a moment. Hunkered behind a crate, Pancho saw the blue-clad construction workers looking around uncertainly. Foremen and women strode out among them, snapping orders. The workers gathered themselves into parties of four, five and six and began methodically searching the entire floor. Pancho figured they were doing the same on the other levels, too.

Feeling like a mouse in a convention hall filled with cats, Pancho knelt behind the crate. The laser was within reach, but without a power supply it was useless. And even if I get outside, she told herself, I'll have to sprint through the storm to get into one of the hoppers sitting out on the launchpad. The outlook ain't brilliant.

Then she saw the same minitractor she had ridden on heading across the cement-dusty floor toward her. Two men were squeezed into its cab alongside the driver.

He remembers me hitching the ride, Pancho realized, and he's bringing the goons to search the area. She smiled. The tractor could serve as a power supply for the laser, she thought. All I have to do is get rid of those three guys. She unclipped her other earring and held it tightly in her palm.

Sitting on the bare concrete floor, her back pressed against the plastic crate, Pancho listened to the tractor coming up and stopping. Voices muttering in Japanese. They're getting out, she knew. Poking around.

She clambered to her feet. The three saw her immediately. Pancho noticed with some surprise that the hard-hatted driver was a young woman. The other two, bareheaded, were stony-faced men. And armed with guns.

"You!" one of the men shouted in English, pointing a pistol at her. "Don't move!"

Pancho slowly raised both hands above her head, the earring still clutched in her right palm. Wait, she said to herself, flicking the catch of the earring with her thumb. Let them get just a little closer.

Now! She tossed the earring at them and flung both arms over her eyes. The flash of light still seared through her closed lids and burned a red afterimage on her retinas. But once she opened her eyes she found that she could see well enough. The two goons were writhing on the ground, screeching in Japanese. The woman driver was staggering around blindly. Blinking painful tears, Pancho grabbed the laser in both hands, pushed past the dazed and groping driver, and dumped it into the back of the tractor. Even in one-sixth g, it was heavy.

Quickly she detached the cart and slipped into the tractor's cab. She put it in gear and headed for the nearest ramp, up to the top level.

HABITAT *CHRYSALIS*

Big George scowled at the display splashed across his wall screen as he sat in his favorite recliner, feet up, a frosty mug of beer at his side. Solar storm, he said to himself. Big one.

The IAA forecasters were predicting that the storm would not reach Ceres. The cloud of ionized particles followed the interplanetary magnetic field, and the field's loops and knots were guiding it across the other side of the solar system, far from Ceres's position. George felt grateful. *Chrysalis* was protected by electromagnetic shielding, just as most spacecraft were, but George had no great ambition to ride out a storm.

Poor bastards on Vesta are gonna get it, he noted. Hope they've got the sense to get their arses underground in time. George shrugged and reached for his beer. At least they've got plenty of warning.

The display showed spacecraft traffic. *Elsinore* was the only vessel George was interested in. Edith Elgin was aboard, coming to Ceres to do a video report on the war out here. About fookin' time somebody in the news media paid attention, George thought.

Elsinore was swinging clear of the radiation cloud, he saw. She'll be here in four days and some, George said to himself. Good. We'll be waitin' for her.

He took a long swallow of beer. There was nothing else for him to do, except wait.

HUMPHRIES MANSION

Fuchs crouched behind the makeshift barricade jammed at the top of the stairs, peering into the shadows. Some light from the garden outside was leaking through the grills covering the upstairs windows. He could hear movement downstairs, but it was almost impossible to see anything with all the indoor lights off. Nodon has a hand torch, he knew, but to turn it on would simply give the guards a target to shoot at.

"Nodon," he whispered, "pull down some of the drapes on the windows."

The crewman scuttled away, and Fuchs heard ripping noises, then a muffled thud.

A strong voice called from the first floor, "Whoever you are, you can't get out of here. You're trapped. Better give yourselves up and let us turn you over to the authorities."

Fuchs bit back the snarling reply he wanted to make. Nodon slithered up and pushed some bunched-up fabric into his hands. "Will this do, Captain?" he asked.

"We'll see," Fuchs whispered back.

A light flashed momentarily in the darkness and a man yowled with pain. Amarjagal, halfway across the landing, had fired her gun at someone creeping silently up the steps. But not silently enough. The Mongol woman had heard him and shot him with her laser pistol. Its beam was invisible, but the fabric of the guard's clothing flashed when it was hit. Fuchs heard the man tumbling down the carpeted stairs.

We need some light, Fuchs said to himself. If I can set this drapery afire we can use it as a torch.

Another spark of light splashed against the table, just past Fuchs's ear. He smelled burning wood.

"Behind us!" Sanja screamed in his native Mongol dialect.

Fuchs turned as both Sanja and Nodon fired blindly down the hallway. There's another staircase! he realized. Fool! Fool! You should have thought of that, should have—

Nodon screamed with pain as a bolt struck him and grabbed his shoulder. Fuchs snatched the gun from Nodon's fingers and fired blindly down the hall. In the corner of his eye he saw Amarjagal shooting at a pair of figures crawling up the steps.

Dropping Nodon's gun, Fuchs bunched the drapery fabric in one hand and fired his gun into it. The stuff smoldered. He fired again, and it burst into flame. So much for fire-retardant materials, he thought. Put a hot enough source on it and it will burn.

"Shoot at them," he ordered Sanja. "Keep their heads down."

Sanja obediently fired down the hallway, even picking up Nodon's gun and shooting with both hands.

Fuchs scrambled to his feet and plunged down the hall, bellowing like a charging bull, firing his own gun with one hand and waving the blazing drapery over his head with the other. Whoever was down there was still ducking, not firing back. Fuchs saw the back stairwell, skidded to a stop and threw the fiery fabric down the steps. For good measure he sprayed the stairwell with his gun.

He saw several men backing down the stairs as the drapery tumbled down. The carpeting on the steps began to smoke and an alarm started screeching in the flickering shadows.

Humphries had gone from his office into his adjoining bedroom, eyes wide with fright. He could feel his heart pounding beneath his ribs, hear the pulse thundering in his ears so loudly he barely heard Ferrer shouting at him.

Somebody's broken into my house, screeched a voice in his head. Somebody's gotten into my home!

The emergency lights were on and the cermet shutters had sealed off the bedroom from the office and the hallway beyond it. Nobody can get to me, Humphries told himself. There's two fireproof doors between me and them. I'm safe. They can't reach me. The guards will round them up. I'm safe in here.

Still in her white terrycloth robe, Ferrer grabbed him by both shoulders. "It's Fuchs!" she shouted at him. "Look at the display!"

The wall screen showed a stubby miniature bear of a man charging down the hallway outside, swinging a blazing length of drapery.

"Fuchs?" Humphries gasped. It was difficult to make out the man's face in the false-color image of the infrared camera. "It can't be!"

Ferrer looked angry and disgusted. "It is! The computer's matched his image and his voice. It's Fuchs and three of his henchmen."

"Here?"

"He's come to kill you!" she snapped.

"No! He can't! They'll—"

"FIRE!" the computer's emergency warning sounded. "FIRE IN THE REAR STAIRWELL."

Humphries froze, staring at the wall screen, which now showed the rear stairs blazing.

"Why don't the sprinklers come on?" he demanded.

"The water's off," she reminded him.

"No water?" Humphries bleated.

"The building's concrete," Ferrer said. "Seal off the burning area and let the fire consume all the oxygen and kill itself. And anybody in the burning section."

Humphries felt the panic in him subside a little. She's right, he thought. Let the fire burn itself out. He stood up straighter, watching the wallscreen's display.

"Anybody caught in there," he said, pointing shakily, "is going to get burned to death. Fuchs is going to roast, just as if he were in hell."

Hurrying back to the makeshift barricade at the top of the main staircase, Fuchs could smell smoke wafting up from the rear stairs.

"FIRE!" said a synthesized voice, calm and flat but heavily amplified. "FIRE IN THE REAR STAIRWELL."

"We've got to get out of here," Sanja hissed in his ear.

"No!" Fuchs snapped. "Not till we get Humphries."

Amarjagal crawled to them. "More guards down there," she said. "They will charge up the stairs."

From the corner of his eye Fuchs could see the flickering light of the flames in the rear stairwell. They can't attack us from that direction, he thought. Then he realized, And we can't retreat that way, either.

Laser bolts sizzled against the upturned table and scorched the wall behind them.

"Here they come!"

Even in the shadowy light Fuchs could see a team of guards charging up the stairs, firing their handguns as others down in the entryway also fired up at them.

Fuchs rolled to one side of the table, where his crew had laid a heavy marble bust from one of the tables down the hall. He noticed that one of the laser blasts had ignited a painting on the wall behind them. Grunting with the effort, he lifted the bust with both hands, raised it above the edge of the upturned table, and hurled it down the stairs. It bounced down the steps, scattering the approaching guards like a bowling ball. Sanja and Amarjagal fired at them. Fuchs heard screams of pain.

"We must get out of here," Amarjagal said flatly. There was no panic in her voice, not even fear. It was simply a statement of fact.

And Fuchs knew she was right. But they were surrounded, trapped. And Humphries was untouched.

SHINING MOUNTAIN BASE

Been a long time since I drove a tractor, Pancho said to herself as she puttered up the ramp toward the base's topmost level. They haven't changed much since my astronaut days, she thought. Haven't improved them.

The fact that the Nairobi base was so big was an advantage to her. They're scurrying all over the place looking for me; got a lot of territory to search. I'll be in good shape until those three blind mice down there start talking.

The tractor reached the top of the ramp and Pancho steered past a knot of blue-coveralled construction workers, heading for a quiet, empty spot along the base of the dome. She figured it would take the better part of half an hour to get the laser going and cut a reasonably sized hole in the dome's metal wall. Better get into the softsuit before then, she told herself. Unless you want to breathe vacuum.

Nobuhiko felt sorry for Daniel Tsavo. The man sat in a little folding chair in the base's infirmary, hunched almost into a fetal position, his fists balled up on his lap, his unseeing eyes aimed at the floor. It must be terrible to be blind, Nobu thought, even if it's only temporary.

A pair of doctors and three nurses were finishing their ministrations, taping a bandage across Tsavo's eyes while the man kept up a low angry mumble about what Pancho had done to him.

Keeping his face impassive as he listened to Tsavo's muttered story, Nobu couldn't help feeling some admiration for Pancho. She walked into the lion's den knowingly, he realized. She came here to learn what Nairobi is doing. I wonder if she understands now that Nairobi is a tool of Yamagata Corporation? And if she does, what should I do about it?

I should call my father, Nobuhiko thought. But not here. Not now. Not in front of these aliens. Wait. Have patience. You've come all the way to the Moon, be patient enough to wait until they capture Pancho. Then we'll find out how much she knows. Once we determine that, it will be time to decide what to do with her.

Pancho was thinking of Yamagata as she toted the laser from the back of the minitractor to the base of the dome's curving metal wall. This topmost level of the base was quieter than the lower levels. Construction here was nearly complete, except for small groups scattered across the dome's floor, painting and setting up partitions. There were guards at all the airlocks, though, and more guards stationed along the lockers where space suits were stored.

She kept low and stayed behind the tractor, hoping that anyone searching for her up at this level would see nothing more than a tractor parked near an empty section of the wall. Until the laser starts flashing sparks of molten metal, and by then it'll be too late to stop me. I hope.

Why is Yamagata backing Nairobi? she asked herself as she plugged the power cable into the tractor's thermionic generator. Nobuhiko told me Yamagata's not involved in space operations, they're concentrating all their efforts on Earth. Yeah, sure. What was it Dan Randolph used to say: "And rain makes applesauce." Nobu was lying through his teeth at me. Sumbitch is using Nairobi to get established on the Moon. But why?

It wasn't until she had the laser ready to go and was pulling the soft-suit out of her travel bag that the answer hit Pancho. Yamagata's getting ready to take over the Belt! They're letting Astro and Humphries slaughter each other and they'll step over the bloody corpses and take control of everything! They're even *helping* us to fight this damned stupid war!

Suddenly Pancho felt angry. At herself. I should've seen this, she fumed silently. If I had half the smarts god gave a warty toad I would have figured this out months ago. Damn! Double damn it all to hell and back! I've been just as blind as I made those people downstairs.

Okay, she told herself. So you've been outsmarted. Just don't go and kill yourself. Check out this suit carefully.

The softsuit was easy to put on. You just stepped into it the same way you stepped into a pair of coveralls, put your arms through the sleeves, and sealed up the front like it was Velcro. The nanomachines are activated by the body's heat, she knew. Wriggling her fingers inside the skin-thin gloves, she wondered all over again how the virus-sized nanobugs could keep her safe from the vacuum of space without stiffening up the way normal gloves and fabric suits did.

She had never worn a nanotech helmet before. It hung limply in her gloved hands, like an empty plastic sack. Reading the illustrated instructions off her palmcomp, Pancho blew it up like a kid's balloon. It puffed out to a rigid fishbowl shape. It felt a little spongy to her, but Pancho pulled the helmet over her head and sealed it to the suit's collar by running two fingers along the seam. Same as sealing a freezer bag, she thought.

No life-support pack; only a slim green cylinder of oxygen, good for an hour. Or so the instructions said.

Okay, she told herself. You got one hour.

It was difficult for the Nairobi security woman to understand what the nearly hysterical Japanese woman was saying. She kept pawing at her eyes and sobbing uncontrollably. The two African guards, both men, were still sprawled on the concrete floor, unconscious.

She called her boss on her handheld and reported her finding: one tractor driver and two guards, all three of them incapacitated, blinded.

"Where's the tractor?" Her boss's face, even in the handheld's minute screen, scowled implacably at her.

"Not here," she replied.

The boss almost smiled. "Good. All tractors have radio beacons. Get the number of the tractor out of the driver, then we can track its beacon and find out where the fugitive is."

"Assuming the fugitive is with the tractor," she said, before thinking.

His scowl deepened. "Yes, assuming that," he growled.

It wasn't wise to second-guess the boss, she remembered too late.

Pancho hesitated as she held the laser's cutting head next to the curving metal wall. I cut a hole and the air whooshes out. None of the people up here are in suits. They could get killed.

Then she shook her head. This dome's too big for that. The air starts leaking out, they'll pop some emergency sheets that'll get carried to the hole and plug it up long enough for them to get a repair crew to fix it. Nobody's going to get hurt except you, she said to herself, if you don't get your butt in gear.

She thumbed the laser's control switch. Its infrared beam was invisible, but a thin spot of cherry-red instantly began glowing on the metal wall. Holding the laser head in both her gloved hands like an old-fashioned power drill, Pancho slowly lifted it in an arc-like shape. She felt nothing inside the softsuit, but noticed that dust was swirling along the floor and disappearing into the thin, red-hot cut. Punched through, she thought. Nothing but vacuum outside.

The wall was thick, and the work went slowly, but finally Pancho cut a hole big enough for her to crawl through. Dust and scraps of litter were rushing through it now. But as she turned off the laser and ducked the hole, she saw there was another wall beyond it. Drat-damn it! Meteor shield.

It was a flimsy wall of honeycomb metal set up outside the actual dome structure to absorb the constant hail of micrometers that rained down on the Moon's surface. Grumbling to herself, Pancho took up the laser again and started cutting once more. This one'll go a lot faster, she told herself.

She heard a voice bellowing in Japanese, very close, but ignored it, sawing frantically with the laser to cut through the meteor shield and get outside.

"You there!" a man's voice yelled in English. "Stop that or I'll shoot!"

ORE CARRIER *CROMWELL*

Despite his outward show of confidence as he sat in the command chair on the bridge, *Cromwell*'s skipper felt decidedly nervous as the creaking old ore ship cruised toward Vesta inside the radiation cloud. As surreptitiously as he could, he kept an eye on the console that monitored the radiation levels inside and outside his ship. A glaring red light showed that the sensors outside were reporting lethally high radiation, enough to kill a man in minutes. Next to that baleful red glow on the control panel a string of peaceful pale green lights reported that radiation levels inside the ship were close to normal.

Good enough, the captain said to himself. So far. We still have a long way to go.

He had worked out with the special weapons tech how close they would have to be to Vesta before releasing the twin missiles that contained the nanomachines. They had developed three possible scenarios. The first one was the basic plan of attack, the flight path they would follow if everything went as planned and they were not detected by Humphries's people. That was the trajectory they were following now, sneaking along inside the radiation cloud until they reached the predetermined release point.

If they were detected on their way in to Vesta, or if the ship developed some critical malfunction such as a breakdown of its radiation shielding (a possibility that made the skipper shudder) then they would release the missiles early and hope that they would not be seen or intercepted by Vesta's defense systems. The skipper and the weapons tech had worked out a release point for that contingency. It was only six hours from where they now were.

Their third option was to call off the attack altogether. That decision would be entirely—and solely—up to the captain. Only a major disaster would justify abandoning the attack, such as a serious malfunction of the ship's systems or an interception by HSS vessels.

Cruising blind and deaf inside the radiation cloud, watching the sensor readings on the control panel, the skipper thought that of the three options before him he much preferred number two. *Let's get to the early release point, fire the damned missiles at Vesta, and get the hell out of here before something goes wrong.*

He got up from the command chair. All four of his crew turned from their consoles toward him.

"I'm going to catch some zees," he said gruffly. "You take your normal relief, one at a time. Ms. Yamaguchi, you have the con. Wake me in five hours."

"Yes, sir. Five hours."

The captain ducked through the hatch. His quarters were immediately aft of the bridge. *Five hours,* he thought. *I'll make my decision after a good nap, when my mind is fresh.*

He knew what he wanted that decision to be.

HUMPHRIES MANSION

In his basement office, Humphries's security chief watched the screens on the wall to one side of his desk with growing dismay. Four guys are holding off two dozen of my people. The dumb bozos are just sitting there like a bunch of petrified chipmunks. And now the back staircase is on fire. Humphries is gonna fry my ass for this.

Angrily he punched the keyboard on his desk. "What the hell are you punks doing, waiting for hot dogs so you can have a fuckin' barbecue?"

He had only a voice link with his team upstairs, no video. "I got six people wounded here."

"You got a dozen and a half untouched! Go get the intruders!"

"Why should we rush 'em and take more casualties? They're not goin' anywhere. We can wait 'em out."

"While the fuckin' house burns down?" the chief yelled.

"Then we'll burn 'em out!"

The chief thought it over swiftly. Humphries is sealed into his master suite. They can't get to him. The fire's triggered the automatic alarms. That upstairs hallway is closed off by airtight doors. Windows are already sealed. Okay. We'll let the fire do the job.

It was getting smoky in the upstairs hall. Leaning his back against the overturned table Fuchs peered down the hallway and saw flames licking at the carpet, spreading toward them.

"We must get out," Amarjagal repeated.

The flames reached the drapes on the farthest window. They began smoldering.

Coughing, Sanja added, "It is useless to die here, Captain."

Fuchs wanted to pound his fists on the floor. Humphries was a few meters away, cowering behind his protective cermet barrier. The coward! Fuchs raged. The sniveling coward. But he's smarter than I am. He's prepared for this attack, while I've led my people into a stupid assault that will gain us nothing even if we live through it. He pictured Humphries's smirking face and felt the rage rising inside him even hotter than the flames creeping toward them.

"THE ENTIRE HALLWAY AREA IS SEALED OFF," the loud-speaker voice declared. "THE FIRE'S GOING TO SUCK ALL THE OXYGEN OUT OF YOUR AIR. YOU HAVE THREE CHOICES: SUFFOCATE, ROAST, OR SURRENDER."

Sitting cross-legged on his oversized bed, Humphries yelled at the wallscreen image of his security chief, "You're letting them burn up the second-floor hallway? Do you have any idea of the value of the artwork on those walls? The furniture alone is worth more than your salary!"

The security chief looked distinctly uncomfortable. "Sir, it's the only way to get them. They've wounded six of my people already. No sense getting more of them hurt."

"That's what I pay them for!" Humphries raged. "To protect me! To kill that sonofabitch Fuchs! Not to burn my house down!"

Ferrer was sitting on an upholstered chair on the far side of the spacious room, her robe demurely pulled down below her knees.

The security chief was saying, "You're perfectly safe inside your suite, Mr. Humphries. The walls are concrete and your door is fireproof reinforced cermet."

"And my hallway's going up in flames!"

"They started the fire, sir, my people didn't. And now they either surrender or the fire kills them."

"While your people sit on their asses."

Stiffly, the security chief replied, "Yessir, while my people keep the rest of the house secure and wait for the intruders to give themselves up."

Humphries stared at the chief's image for a long moment, panting with frustrated rage. Then he snarled, "Don't look for a bonus at Christmas."

"We're trapped here," Amarjagal said, still as unemotional as a wood carving.

Fuchs saw the flames licking up the window draperies, heard them hissing, edging along the carpeting toward them. But the smoke was no worse than it had been before: annoying, but not suffocating.

"Where's the smoke going?" he muttered.

"Captain, we must do something," said Sanja, his voice tense. "We can't stay here much longer."

Fuchs scrambled to his feet and took a few steps along the hall. He saw the smoke curling up from the blazing drapes and streaming across the ceiling in a thin, roiling layer. It grew noticeably thinner halfway along the hall.

"Help me," he called to Sanja as he grabbed a heavy chest of inlaid ebony. The two men wrestled it into the middle of the hall and Fuchs clambered up onto it.

A ventilator, he saw, its grillwork cleverly disguised to look like an ornamental design on the ceiling. It was closed, he realized, but not completely. Some of the smoke was being sucked up through it. He pushed against it with both hands. It gave, but only slightly.

Sanja immediately understood. He took a copper statuette from the nearest table and handed it up to Fuchs, base first. Fuchs pounded at the ventilator grill with the fury of desperation. It dented, buckled. With an animal roar he smashed at it again and the ventilator gave way with a screech of metal against metal. Immediately, the smoke slithering along the ceiling began pouring into the opening.

"It's big enough to crawl through!" he shouted.

"Nodon," said Amarjagal, on her feet now. "He's unconscious."

"Carry him. Come on."

Fuchs hauled himself up into the ventilator shaft. It was filled with smoke and utterly dark inside. Coughing, he reached down for Nodon's still-unconscious body. This shaft can't be too long, he thought. We're up near the roof. There must be an outlet nearby.

Crawling, coughing, eyes streaming with burning tears, he dragged Nodon's limp body through the shaft. Its metal walls felt hot to his fingers, but he slithered along, knowing that either he found his way out of the building or he would soon die.

The security chief was peering at his display screens, straining to see what was going on in the dim shadows of the upstairs hall. The only light came from the flickering flames. The intruders were moving around, he felt sure, but it was almost impossible to make out anything definite in the smoke. Even the infrared cameras were virtually useless now. Several of the window draperies were blazing; the flames overloaded the surveillance cameras' light sensitive photocells. All he could see was overexposed flickers of flame and inky black shadows shambling around.

The fire's contained to the upstairs hall, he saw, checking the other screens. Thank god for small miracles. I'll probably have to resign after this. If Humphries doesn't fire me outright.

• • •

Pacing the length of the big bedroom, Humphries muttered, "I don't like this. I don't like being cooped up in here."

Victoria Ferrer suppressed an incipient smile. He's really frightened, she thought. Normally, if we were locked in his bedroom together he'd peel this robe off me and pop me between the sheets.

"I don't like waiting," he said, louder.

"Think of it this way," she suggested, not moving from the chair where she sat, "Fuchs is dying out there. When those fireproof doors open again you can go out and stand over his dead body."

He nodded, but it was perfunctory. The thought of victory over Fuchs obviously didn't outweigh his innate fear for his own life.

Fuchs's lungs were burning. The metal walls of the ventilator shaft were scorching hot now as he crawled along blindly, dragging Nodon's inert body with one pain-cramped hand. He couldn't see Amarjagal or Sanja behind him. He didn't even know if they were still there. His entire world had narrowed down to this smoke-filled, blistering hot purgatory.

Through tear-filled eyes he saw a light up ahead. It can't be, he told himself. I'm starting to hallucinate. The garden outside is still in its night-time lighting mode. There can't be bright lighting out there—

His heart clenched in his chest. Unless the guards have turned up all the outdoor lights! Like a badger, Fuchs scuttled along the upward-slanting shaft, leaving Nodon and the others behind. Light! Air! He bumped his head against a metal grill, feeling blessedly cool air caressing his hot, sooty face. The smoke was streaming out. Fresh air was seeping in.

With his bare hands Fuchs battered the grill, punched it until his knuckles were raw and bleeding, butted it with his head, finally forced it open by wedging his feet against the sides of the shaft and leaning one powerful shoulder against the thin metal and pushing with all his strength. It gave way at last.

He took one huge gulp of fresh air, wiped at his eyes with grimy hands, then ducked back down the shaft to grab Nodon by the collar of his coveralls and haul him up onto the roof. Amarjagal's head popped up behind Nodon's booted feet. She too was grimy, soot-streaked. But she smiled and pulled herself out of the shaft.

"Stay low," Fuchs hissed. "The guards must be patrolling the grounds."

Sanja came up, and crawled on his belly to lay beside Fuchs. They looked out onto the splendid garden just beyond the mansion's wall and, farther, to the trees and green flowering shrubbery of this artificial Eden planted deep below the surface of the Moon.

And there were guards standing out there, armed with assault rifles, ready to shoot to kill.

SHINING MOUNTAIN BASE

You there!" the guard yelled. "Stop that or I'll shoot!"

Pancho realized that her necklace was tucked inside the dratted softsuit. She couldn't reach it. Couldn't whip it off her neck and toss it at the goon. Prob'ly wouldn't have time to do it before he drilled me, anyway, she thought as she slowly climbed to her feet and raised both gloved hands over her helmeted head. She nudged the laser slightly with her boot. It was still on, still cutting away at the honeycomb shield outside the dome's wall.

"Who the devil are you?" the guard demanded, walking slowly around the minitractor, a pistol leveled at Pancho's navel. He looked African but spoke like an Englishman. "And what the devil do you think you're doing?"

Pancho shrugged inside the softsuit. "Nothin'," she said, trying to look innocent.

"My god!" the guard yelped, seeing that hole cut into the dome wall and the bright red hot spot the laser was making on the honeycomb shield. "Turn that thing off! Now! Don't you realize you could—"

At that instant the honeycomb cracked open and a rush of air knocked Pancho flat against the curving dome wall. The guard was staggered but kept his senses enough to realize what was happening. He turned and ran as fast as he could, which wasn't very fast because he was leaning against a gale-force wind trying to rush out of the hole Pancho had cut.

The loudspeakers started yammering in Japanese, then in another language Pancho didn't understand. She slid down to the floor and slithered out of the break, hoping the softsuit wouldn't catch or tear on the broken edges of the holes the laser had made.

Outside, she looked around the barren lunar landscape. The dome was on the crest of the ringwall mountains that surrounded Shakleton. The ground sloped away, down toward the floor of the crater. Nothing to see but rocks and minicraters, some of them no bigger than a finger-poke into the stony ground. Damn! Pancho thought. I'm on the wrong side of the dome.

Without hesitation she began sprinting, looking for the launchpads, happy to be able to run inside a space suit. Inside the old hard-shell suits it was impossible to do anything more than lumber along like Frankenstein's monster.

That guard'll be okay, she told herself. There's plenty of air inside the dome. They'll get the leak plugged before anybody's in any real danger. Jogging steadily, she grinned to herself. Meantime, while they're chasing around trying to fix the damage I've done, I'll get to one of the hoppers and head on home.

A sickly pale green splotch of color appeared on the left side of her helmet. The earphones said, "Radiation warning. Radiation level exceeding maximum allowable. Get to shelter immediately."

"I'm trying!" Pancho said, surprised at the suit's sophistication.

Before she took another dozen strides the color went from pastel green to bright canary yellow.

"Radiation warning," the suit said again. "Radiation level exceeding maximum allowable. Get to shelter immediately."

Pancho gritted her teeth and wondered how she could shut off the suit's automated voice synthesizer. The launchpads were still nowhere in sight.

Nobuhiko was back at the base's infirmary, this time in a screened-off cubicle barely large enough to hold a bed, looking down on a heavily sedated Daniel Tsavo. A spotless white bandage covered the upper half of the Kenyan's black face. He was conscious, but barely so, as the tranquilizing drug took effect.

". . . she blinded me," he was mumbling. "Blind . . . can't see . . ."

Yamagata glanced impatiently at the African doctor standing on the other side of Tsavo's bed. "It's only temporary," the doctor said, trying to sound reassuring. He seemed to be speaking to Yamagata, rather than his patient. "The retinal burns will heal in a few days."

"Failed," Tsavo muttered. "Failure . . . blind . . . nowhere to go . . . career ruined . . ."

Bending slightly over the bed, Nobuhiko said, "You haven't failed. You'll be all right. Rest now. Everything will be fine in a day or two."

Tsavo's right hand groped toward the sound of Yamagata's voice. Nobuhiko instinctively backed away from it.

"Did you find her?" the Kenyan asked, his voice suddenly stronger. "Did you get what you wanted from her?"

"Yes, of course," Nobuhiko lied. "You rest now. Everything has turned out very well."

Tsavo's hand fell back to the sheets and he breathed a heavy sigh. The doctor nodded as if satisfied that the drugs had finally done their job. Then he made a small shooing gesture.

Nobuhiko understood. He turned away from the bed and stepped out of the tiny cubicle. He wrinkled his nose at the smell of antiseptics that pervaded this part of the infirmary. He had spent many hours in hospitals, when his father was dying. The odor brought back the memory of those unhappy days.

The pair of aides waiting for him out in the corridor snapped to attention almost like elite-corps soldiers, even though they wore ordinary business suits.

"Have they found her?" Nobuhiko asked in Japanese.

"Not yet, sir."

Nobu frowned as he started walking toward the exit, allowing his aides to see how displeased he was. To come all this way to the Moon, he thought, and have her slip away from us. Hot anger simmered through him.

The senior of the two assistants, noting the obvious displeasure on his master's face, tried to change the subject:

"Will the black man recover his sight?"

"Apparently," Nobuhiko snapped. "But he is not to be trusted with any important tasks. Never again."

Both aides nodded.

As they reached the double doors of the infirmary the handheld of the senior aide beeped. He flicked it open and saw a Yamagata engineer in a sky-blue hard hat staring wide-eyed in the miniaturized screen.

"The dome has been penetrated!" the engineer blurted. "We have sent for repair crews."

The aide looked stricken. He turned to Yamagata, wordlessly asking him for instructions.

"*She* did this," Nobu said. "Despite all our guards and precautions, Pancho has gotten away from us. She's outside."

"But the radiation storm!" the junior aide said, aghast. "She'll be killed out there."

Suddenly Nobu felt all his anger dissolve; all the tension that had held him like a vise for the past several hours faded away. He laughed. He threw his head back and laughed aloud, while his two aides gaped at him.

"Killed out there?" he said to them. "Not likely. Not Pancho. We couldn't hold her in here with a thousand guards. Don't think that a little thing like a solar storm is going to stop her."

His two aides said nothing even though they both thought that their master had gone slightly insane.

"Radiation warning," the suit repeated for the umpteenth time. "Radiation level exceeding maximum allowable. Get to shelter immediately."

Pancho made a silent promise to herself that when she got back to Selene she would rip the voice synthesizer out of this goddamned suit and stomp on it for an hour and a half.

The color splashed across the left side of her bubble helmet was bright pink now. I'm absorbing enough radiation to light a concert hall, she thought. Unbidden, the memory of Dan Randolph's death from radiation poisoning rose in her mind like a ghostly premonition of things to come. She saw Dan lying on his bunk, too weak even to lift his head, soaked in sweat, gums bleeding, hair coming out in bunches, dying while Pancho looked on, helpless, unable to save him.

You got a lot to look forward to, she growled to herself.

Her loping stride had slowed to a walk, but she was still doggedly pressing forward across the outer perimeter of the dome. You don't really appreciate how big something is until you have to walk around it, she told herself. Everything always looks bigger on foot.

And there it was! Around the curve of the dome she saw one, then two and finally three spacecraft sitting on concrete launchpads. She recognized the little green one that had brought her here from the Astro base, about a hundred klicks away.

Would they have guards placed around those birds? Pancho asked herself, without slowing her pace toward the launchpads.

Naw, she answered. Not in this storm. That'd be suicide duty. Not even Yamagata would ask his people to do that. Then she added, I hope.

Aside from the splotch of color in her helmet and the automated voice's irritating, repetitive warning, there was no visible, palpable sign of the radiation storm. Pancho was striding along the rocky, barren lunar crest, kicking up slight plumes of dust with each step. Outside the nanomachined fabric of her softsuit was nothing but vacuum, a vacuum thousands of times rarer than the vacuum just above Earth's atmosphere, nearly four hundred thousand kilometers away. Instinctively she glanced up for a sight of Earth, but the black sky was empty. Only a few of the brightest stars shone through the heavy tinting of her helmet. You can always see Earth from Selene, she said to herself. Maybe that's an advantage over this polar location that we hadn't realized before.

She started to hurry her pace toward the rocket hopper but found it was too tiring. Uh-oh, she thought. Fatigue's one of the first signs of radiation sickness.

She knew the vacuum out here wasn't empty. A torrent of subatomic particles was sleeting down upon her, mostly high-energy protons. The suit absorbed some of them, but plenty of others were getting through to smash into the atoms of her body and break them up. When she glanced at the color swatch in her helmet, though, it had gone down from bright pink to a sultry auburn.

Jeeps, Pancho exclaimed silently, the radiation level's going down.

"Radiation warning," the suit repeated yet again. "Radiation level exceeding maximum allowable. Get to shelter immediately."

"I'm goin'," Pancho groused. "I'm goin'."

Radiation's decreasing. The storm's ending. Maybe I'll make it through this after all. But then she thought that Yamagata might send some goons out to the launchpads if the radiation level's gone down enough. Despite the aches in her legs and back, she pushed herself to walk faster.

HUMPHRIES MANSION:
ON THE ROOF

Smoke was billowing up through the ventilator that Fuchs had smashed open. The guards down in the garden below pointed to it. One of them pulled a handheld from his tunic pocket and started talking into it.

We've got to get off this roof and out to the exit hatch, Fuchs thought. And quickly, before they get all their guards out here and we're hopelessly surrounded.

Turning, he saw that Nodon was sitting by himself, his eyes open. He looked groggy, but at least he was conscious.

"Nodon," Fuchs whispered, hunkering down beside the wounded man, "can you walk?"

"I think so, Captain." Nodon's right shoulder had stopped bleeding, but the charred spot on his coveralls showed where the laser beam had hit him. The arm hung limply by his side.

Turning to Amarjagal, Fuchs gestured toward the two guards below. "Get those two when I give the word. Sanja, help me carry Nodon."

Sanja nodded wordlessly while Amarjagal checked the charge on the pistol in her hand. As Fuchs slid one beefy arm around Nodon's slim waist he saw the two guards looking up in their direction. One of them was still speaking into his handheld.

"Now!" he shouted, hauling Nodon to his feet.

Amarjagal shot the one with the handheld squarely in the forehead, then swung her aim to hit his companion in the chest. They both tumbled into the bushes that lined the garden walkway.

With Sanja helping to support Nodon, Fuchs yelled, "Jump!" and all four of them leaped off the roof to land with a thump amid the shrubbery that lined the mansion's wall. Lunar gravity, Fuchs thought gratefully. On Earth we would have broken our bones.

Half-dragging Nodon, they started up the bricked path, hobbling toward the heavy airtight hatch that was the only exit from the grotto. Fuchs heard shouts from behind them. Turning his head, he saw a trio of guards boiling out of the mansion's front door, pistols in their hands. A tendril of pale gray smoke drifted out of the open door.

"Stop while you're still alive," one of the guards shouted. "There's no way you can get out of here."

"Amarjagal, help Sanja," Fuchs commanded, slipping the wounded man out of his grasp and dropping to one knee. He snapped a quick shot at the three guards, who scattered to find shelter in the shrubbery. Fuchs fired at them until his pistol ran out of power. One of the flowering shrubs burst into flame and a guard leaped out from behind it.

Running back to the others Fuchs yelled, "Give me your guns! Quick!"

They obediently dropped their pistols onto the path, hardly breaking stride as they carried the wounded Nodon toward the hatch. Nodon's the only one who knows the emergency codes to open the hatch, Fuchs thought. He'd better be conscious when we get there or we're all dead.

He ducked behind the sturdy bole of a tree and peered up the pathway. No one in sight. They could be crawling through the shrubbery, Fuchs realized. He checked the three guns at his feet. Picking the one with the fullest charge, he began spraying the greenery, hoping to ignite it. Some of the plants smoldered but did not flame. Fuchs growled a curse as his pistol died; he picked up the next one.

In his bedroom, Humphries was screaming at his security chief.

"What do you mean, the whole house is burning? It *can't* burn, you stupid shit! The firewall partitions—"

"Mr. Humphries," the chief snapped stiffly, "the partitions have failed. The intruders opened a ventilator shaft and the fire is spreading through the eaves beneath the roof. You'll have to abandon your suite, sir, and pretty damned quick, too."

Humphries glared at the screen.

"I'm leaving," said the chief. "If you want to roast, go right ahead."

The phone screen went blank. Humphries look up at Ferrer. "This can't be happening," he said. "I don't believe it."

She was at the door, ready to make a break for it. "At least Fuchs and his crew have left the house," she said, trying to stay calm.

"They have?"

"That's what the guards outside reported. Remember? They're having a firefight out there right now."

"Firefight?" Humphries couldn't seem to get his mind working properly. Everything was happening too fast, too wildly.

"We've got to get out, Martin," she insisted, almost shouting.

Humphries thought it was getting warm in the bedroom. That's my imagination, he told himself. This whole suite is insulated, protected. They can't get to me in here.

Something creaked ominously overhead. Humphries shot a glance at the ceiling, but it all looked normal. He looked around wildly. *The whole building's on fire,* he heard the security chief's voice in his mind. I pay that stupid slug to protect me, Humphries said to himself. He's finished. I'll get rid of him. Permanently.

"How do you open this hatch?" Ferrer asked. She was standing at the bedroom doorway, the door itself flung open but the protective cermet partition firmly in place.

Humphries eyes were on the window, though. "My garden!" he howled, staring at the flames licking across the branches of several of the trees.

"We've got to get out—" Ferrer put a hand on the cermet hatch and flinched back. "It's hot!"

The phone was dead, Humphries realized. The controls for the fireproof partitions were automated. As long as the sensors detected a fire, the hatches would remain closed unless opened manually. But the controls are down in the security office, in the basement, Humphries realized. And that yellow little bastard has run away.

I could override the controls from my computer, he thought. But that's in the sitting room, and we're shut off from it!

He could feel the panic bubbling inside him, like the frothing waves of the sea rising over his head to drown him.

Ferrer was standing in front of him, shouting something, her eyes wide with fear. Humphries couldn't hear what she was saying. His mind was repeating, The whole house is on fire! over and over again. Glancing past her terrified face through the bedroom window he saw that the garden was blazing as well.

Ferrer slapped him. Hard. A stinging smack across his face. Instinctively Humphries slapped her back as hard as he could. She staggered back, the imprint of his fingers red against her skin.

"You little bitch! Who do you think you are?"

"Martin, we've got to get out of here! We've got to get through the window and outside!"

Perhaps it was the slap, or perhaps the sight of the always cool and logical Ferrer looking panicked, terrified. Whatever the reason,

Humphries felt his own panic subside. The fear was still there, but he could control it now.

"It's burning out there," he said, pointing toward the window.

Her face went absolutely white. "The fire will consume all the oxygen in the air! We'll suffocate!"

"*They'll* suffocate," Humphries said flatly. "Fuchs and whatever riffraff he's brought with him."

"And the guards!"

"What of it? They're a useless bunch of brain-dead shits."

"But we'll suffocate too!" Ferrer shouted, almost screaming.

"Not we," he said. "You."

The six-hundred-meter-long concrete vault of Selene's Grand Plaza is supported, in part, by two towers that serve as office buildings. Selene's safety office is located in one of those towers, not far from Douglas Stavenger's small suite of offices.

This late at night, the safety office was crewed by only a pair of men, both relaxed to the point of boredom as they sat amid row after row of old-fashioned flat display screens that showed every corridor and public space in the underground city. On the consoles that lined one wall of their sizeable office were displayed the readouts from sensors that monitored air and water quality, temperature, and other environmental factors throughout the city.

They were playing chess on an actual board with carved onyx pieces, to alleviate their boredom. The sensors and displays were automated; there was no real need for human operators to be present. There was hardly ever any problem so bad that a plumber or low-rate electrician couldn't fix it in an hour or less.

The senior safety officer looked up from the chess board with a malicious grin. "Mate in three."

"The hell you will," said the other, reaching for a rook.

Alarms began shrilling and lurid red lights started to flash across several of the consoles. The rook fell to the floor, forgotten, as the men stared goggle-eyed, unbelieving, at the screens. Everything looked normal, but the alarms still rang shrilly.

Running his fingers deftly across the master console's keyboard, the senior of the two shouted over the uproar, "It's down at the bottom level. Temp sensors into overload."

"That's Humphries's area," said his junior partner. "We got no cameras down there."

Shaking his head, the other replied, "Either the sensors are whacked out or there's a helluva fire going on down there."

"A fire? That's im—"

"Look at the readings! Even the oxygen level's starting to go down!"

"Holy mother of god!"

The senior man punched at the emergency phone key. "Emergency! Fire on level seven. I'm sealing off all the hatches and air vents."

"There's people down there!" his assistant pointed out. "Martin Humphries himself! If we seal them in, they'll all die!"

"And if we don't seal them in," the senior man snapped, his fingers pecking furiously across the keyboard, "that fire'll start sucking the oxygen out of the rest of the city. You want to kill everybody?"

LUNAR HOPPER

Hoppers are meant for short-range transportation on the Moon. They are ungainly looking vehicles, little more than a rocket motor powered by powdered aluminum and liquid oxygen, both scraped up from the lunar regolith. Atop the bulbous propellant tanks and rocket nozzle is a square metal mesh platform no more than three meters on a side, surmounted by a waist-high podium that houses the hopper's controls. The entire craft sits on the ground on a trio of spindly legs that wouldn't be strong enough to hold its weight in normal Earth gravity.

Pancho felt bone-weary as she slowly climbed the flimsy ladder up to the hopper's platform. She felt grateful that this particular little bird had a glassteel bubble enclosing the platform. It'll gimme some protection against the radiation, she told herself. She got to the top, pulled herself up onto the aluminum mesh and let the trapdoor hatch slam shut. All in the total silence of the airless Moon.

There were no seats on the hopper, of course. You rode the little birds standing up, with your boots snugged into the fabric loops fastened to the platform.

The radiation sensor display on the side of her helmet had gone down to a sickly bilious green and the automated voice had stopped yakking at her. Pancho felt grateful for that. Either the radiation's down enough so the warning system's cut out or I've got such a dose the warning doesn't matter anymore, she thought.

She felt bilious green herself: queasy with nausea, so tired that if there had been a reclining seat on the hopper she would've cranked it back and gone to sleep.

Not yet, she warned herself. You go to sleep now, girl, and you prob'ly won't wake up, ever.

Hoping the radiation hadn't damaged the hopper's electronic systems, Pancho clicked on the master switch and was pleased to see the podium's console lights come on. A little on the weak side, she thought. Fuel cells are down. Or maybe my vision's going bad.

Propellant levels were low. Nairobi hadn't refueled the bird after it had carried her here to their base. Enough to make it back to the Astro base? Despite her aches and nausea, Pancho grinned to herself. We'll just hafta see how far we can go.

Nobuhiko had followed one of the engineers to the base flight control center, a tight little chamber filled with consoles and display screens, most of them dark, most of the desks unoccupied. Still the room felt overly warm, stifling, even with Yamagata's retinue of bodyguards stationed outside in the corridor.

One console was alight, one screen glowing in the shadows of the control center. Nobu bent over the Nairobi flight controller seated at that console. He saw Pancho's lanky figure slowly climbing the ladder of the green-anodized hopper.

The Yamagata engineer standing at his side gasped. "She's not wearing a space suit!"

"Yes she is," Nobu replied. "A new type, made of nanomachines."

To the flight controller he asked, "Can you prevent her from taking off?"

Looking up briefly, the controller shook his head. "No, sir. She can control the vehicle autonomously. Of course, without a flight plan or navigational data, she won't be able to find her destination. And the vehicle's propellant levels are too low for anything but a very short flight."

"We could send a team out to stop her," suggested the Yamagata engineer.

Nobuhiko took a breath, then replied, "No. Why send good men out into that radiation storm?"

"The storm is abating, sir."

"No," he repeated. "Let her take off. If she is to die, let it be a flight accident. I'll have the Nairobi public relations people make up a plausible story that keeps Yamagata Corporation out of it."

Nobuhiko straightened up and watched the little lunar hopper take off in a sudden spurt of stark white gas and gritty dust, all in total silence.

He almost wished Pancho good fortune. An extraordinary woman, he thought. A worthy opponent. Too bad she's going to die.

•   •   •

As soon as the hopper jerked off the ground Pancho turned on its radio, sliding her finger along the frequency control to search for Malapert's beacon. She knew roughly which direction the Astro base lay in. The hopper had only limited maneuverability, however; it flew mainly on a ballistic trajectory, like an odd-looking cannon shell.

"Pancho Lane calling," she spoke into her helmet microphone. She wanted to yell, to bellow, but she didn't have the strength. "I'm in a hopper, coming up from the Nairobi Industries base at Shackleton crater. I need a navigation fix, pronto."

No reply.

She looked down at the bleak lunar landscape sliding by, trying to remember landmarks from her flight in to Shackleton. Nothing stood out. It all looked the same: bare rock pitted by innumerable craters ranging from little dimples to holes big enough to swallow a city. Rugged hills, all barren and rounded by eons of meteors sandpapering them to worn, tired smoothness. And rocks and boulders strewn everywhere like toys left behind by a careless child.

Pancho felt worn and tired, too. Her mind was going fuzzy. It would be *so* good to just fold up and go to sleep. Even the hard metal deck of the hopper looked inviting to her.

Stop it! she commanded herself. Stay awake. Find the base's radio beacon. Use it to guide you in.

She played the hopper's radio receiver up and down the frequency scale, seeking the automated homing beacon from the Malapert base. Nothing. Feeling something like panic simmering in her guts, Pancho thought, Maybe I'm heading in a completely wrong direction. Maybe I'm so way off that—

A steady warm tone suddenly issued from her helmet earphones. Pancho couldn't have been more thrilled if the world's finest singer had begun to serenade her.

"This is Pancho Lane," she said, her voice rough, her throat dry. "I need a navigational fix, pronto."

A heartbeat's hesitation. Then a calm tenor voice said to her, "Malapert base here, Ms. Lane. We have you on our radar. You're heading seventeen degrees west of us. I'm feeding correction data to your nav computer."

Pancho felt the hopper's tiny maneuvering thruster push the ungainly bird sideways a bit. Her legs felt weak, rubbery. Bird's on automatic now, she thought. I can relax. I can lay down and—

A red light on the control console glared at her like an evil eye and the hopper's computer announced, "Propellant cutoff. Main engine shutdown."

Pancho's reply was a heartfelt, "Shit!"

BRUSHFIRE

Fuchs backed slowly along the brick path, a nearly spent laser pistol in each hand, his eyes reflecting the lurid flames spreading across the wide garden that filled the grotto. Burn! he exulted. Let everything burn. His garden. His house. And Humphries himself. Let the fire burn him to death, let him roast in his own hell.

Coughing, he finally turned and sprinted heavily up the path toward the airlock hatch that they had come in through. The others were already there; Nodon was even standing on his own feet, although he looked pale, shaky.

Fuchs was panting as he came up to them. "Hard . . . to breathe," he gasped.

Amarjagal wasted no time on the obvious. "The airlock is sealed. The emergency code doesn't work."

Fuchs stared at her flat, normally emotionless face. Now she was staring back at him, cold accusation in her eyes.

Sanja said, "The fire . . . it's eating up the oxygen."

"Get the airlock open!" Fuchs commanded. "Nodon, try all the emergency codes."

"I have," Nodon said, almost wailing. "No use . . . no use . . ."

Fuchs leaned his back against the heavy steel hatch and slid down onto his rump, suddenly exhausted. Most of the garden was ablaze now, roaring with flames that crawled up the trees and spread across the flowering bushes, burning, destroying everything as they advanced. Gray smoke billowed up and slithered along the rough rock ceiling as if trying to find an opening, the slightest pore, a way to escape the inferno of this death trap.

•   •   •

Humphries was coldly logical now. The closet in his bedroom was built to serve as an emergency airlock. There was even a space suit stashed in there, although Humphries had never put it on. The Earthbound architect who had designed the mansion had been rather amused that Humphries insisted on such precautions, but the knowing smirk on his face disappeared when Humphries bought out his firm, fired him, and sent him packing back to Earth.

The mansion had been completed by others, and the emergency airlock built to the tightest possible specifications.

Knowing that there were two extra tanks of breathable air in there, Humphries headed for his closet.

"What are you doing?" Ferrer screamed at him. "We've got to get out!"

"You get yourself out," he said icily, remembering the slap she had given him. "I'll stay here until this all blows over."

He slid open the door to his closet. All that Ferrer could see was a row of clothing neatly arrayed on hangers.

"What've you got in there?" she demanded from the other side of the bedroom. She no longer looked smoothly sultry, enticing. Her dark hair was a disheveled tumble, her white robe rumpled, hanging half open. She seemed frightened, confused, far from alluring.

"Enough air to last for a day or more," he said, smiling at her.

"Oh thank god!" she said, rushing toward the closet.

Humphries touched the stud set in the closet's interior door frame and an airtight panel slid quickly shut. He saw the shocked surprise on her face just before the panel shot home and closed her off from his view.

He heard her banging on the steel panel. "Martin! Open the door! Let me in!"

He walked back deeper into his closet, trying to shut out her yammering. Pushing a row of slacks aside he saw the space suit standing against the closet's back wall like a medieval suit of armor.

"Martin! Please! Let me in!"

"So you can slap me again?" he muttered. "Go fry."

The chief of the emergency crew nearly dropped his handheld when he recognized who was coming up the corridor toward them.

"Mr. Stavenger!"

"Hello . . . Pete," Stavenger said, after a quick glance at the crew chief's nametag. "What's the situation here?"

Stavenger could see that a team of three men and four women were assembling a portable airlock and sealing it over the hatch that opened onto the grotto. The crew chief said as much.

"How long will this take?" Stavenger asked.

"Another ten minutes. Maybe twelve."

"Once it's ready, how many people can you take through it at one time?"

The crew chief shook his head. "It's only big enough for two."

"There are at least thirty people in there," Stavenger said. "They're running out of oxygen pretty quickly."

"We got another crew working on the water lines. If we can get the sprinklers working we oughtta be able to put the fire out pretty quick."

"But those people need air to breathe."

"I know," said the crew chief. "I know."

Fuchs saw dark-clad figures stumbling up the path, coughing, staggering. He scrambled to his feet and picked up one of the nearly spent pistols.

"Stop where you are!" he shouted, coughing himself.

The closest man tossed his pistol into the bushes. "Let us out!" he yelled. "The fire . . ."

The others behind him also threw their guns away. They all lurched toward Fuchs, coughing, rubbing at their eyes. Behind them the flames inched across the flowers and grass, climbed nimbly up the trunk of a tree. Its crown of leaves burst into flame.

"The hatch is locked," Fuchs told them. "We're all trapped in here."

The security guards didn't believe him. Their leader rushed to the hatch, tapped frantically at the keyboard panel.

"Jesus, Mary and Joseph," he growled. "Of all the sonofabitch fuckups . . ."

"It's automatic, I imagine," said Fuchs, resignedly. "Nothing we can do about it."

The security guard stared at him. "But they should have emergency teams. Something—"

At that moment a voice rumbled through the heavy hatch, "This is Selene emergency services. Is anybody there? Rap on the hatch."

Fuchs almost leaped with sudden joy and hope. He banged the butt of his pistol against the steel hatch.

"Okay. We're setting up an airlock. Once it's ready we'll be able to start taking you out. How many of you are there?"

Fuchs counted swiftly and then rapped on the hatch eleven times, thinking, We might live through this after all. We might get out of this alive.

FLIGHT PLANS

Pancho knew she had to think swiftly, but the fog of fatigue and radiation sickness made her feel as if she were wrapped in heavy wet blankets.

Propellant bingo, she said to herself. There's still enough juice for an automated landing. But not enough to reach the base. Override the automatics and push this bird as far as she'll go? Do that and you won't land, you'll crash on the landing pad—if you get that far. Let the bird coast and come down wherever it reaches? Do that and you'll land in the middle of nowhere. No, you won't land, you'll crash on the rocks.

"We have a good track on you, Ms. Lane, and we're getting some satellite imagery, as well," said the Malapert controller's voice. "You're not going to reach the base, I'm afraid. We're gearing up a search and rescue team. If you can find a reasonably flat place to set down, we'll come out and get you."

"Copy search and rescue operation," Pancho said, her throat painfully dry. "I'll set her down as close to the base as I can."

If I can stay on my feet long enough, she added silently.

"Malapert?" she called, her voice little more than a croak now.

"Malapert here, Ms. Lane."

"Better include some medics in the S&R team. I got me a healthy dose of radiation."

The barest fraction of a second's hesitation. Then, "Understood, Ms. Lane."

Okay, Pancho said to herself. Now all you gotta do is stay awake long enough to put this bird on the ground without breaking your neck.

She wanted to smile. *If I wasn't so pooped-out tired, this would be kinda fun.*

Some half a billion kilometers away, Dorik Harbin decided to leave *Samarkand*'s bridge and inspect the ship personally. They were fully enveloped by the radiation storm now, and although all the ship's systems were performing adequately, Harbin knew that the crew felt edgy about flying blind and deaf inside a vast cloud of high-energy particles that could kill an unshielded man in moments.

The monitors on the control panels were all in the green, he saw, except for a few minor pieces of machinery that needed maintenance. *I'll get the crew working on them,* Harbin thought as he got up from his command chair. *It will be good for their morale to have something to do instead of just waiting for the radiation level to back down to normal.*

He gave the con to his pilot and stepped to the hatch. Turning back for a moment, he glanced once more at the radiation shielding monitors. All green. Good.

Aboard *Cromwell* the skipper awoke minutes before his number one called on the intercom. He hauled himself out of his bunk, washed his face and pulled on a fresh set of coveralls. No need to brush his hair: It was shaved down to within a centimeter of his scalp.

He entered the bridge and saw that all the ship's systems were operating within nominal limits. And they were still sailing inside the cloud of ionized particles. Its radiation intensity had diminished, though, he noted. The cloud was thinning out as it drifted outward from the Sun.

"Are we still shielded against radar?" he asked his communication technician.

"Theoretically, sir," the man answered with a nod.

"I'm not interested in theory, mister," snapped the skipper. "Can the radars on Vesta spot us or not?"

The technician blinked once, then replied, "No, sir. Not unless they pump up their output power to two or three times their normal operational mode, sir."

Not unless, the captain grumbled to himself.

"You holler out loud and clear if we get pinged," he told the comm tech.

"Yes, sir. Loud and clear."

Pointing at the weapons technician, the skipper said, "Time for a skull session. In my quarters."

The weapons tech was actually a physicist from Astro Corporation's nanotechnology department, so tall he was continually banging his head on the hatches as he stepped through them, so young he looked like a teenager, but without the usual teenaged pose of sullen indifference. Instead, he was bright, cheerful, enthusiastic.

Yet he looked somber now as he ducked low enough to get through the hatch without thumping his straw-thatched head against the coaming.

"We'll be at the decision point in a few minutes," the captain said as he sat on his bunk and gestured the younger man to the only chair in the compartment.

"Eighteen minutes," said the physicist, "and counting."

"Is there any reason why we shouldn't release the missiles then?"

The physicist's pale blond brows rose questioningly. "The plan calls—"

"I know what the plan calls for," the captain interrupted impatiently. "What I'm asking is, are the missiles ready to be released?"

"Yessir, they are. I checked them less than an hour ago."

The captain looked into the youngster's cool blue eyes. I can fire off the missiles and get us the hell out of here, he told himself.

"But if we wait until the final release point their chances of getting to Vesta without being detected or intercepted are a whole lot better," said the younger man.

"I understand that."

"There's no reason I can see for releasing them early."

The captain said nothing, thinking that this kid was a typical scientist. As long as all the displays on the consoles were in the green he thought everything was fine. On the other hand, if I fire the missiles early and something goes wrong, he'll tell his superiors that it was my fault.

"Very well," he said at last. "I want you to calculate interim release points—"

"Interim?"

"Give me three more points along our approach path to Vesta where I can release those birds."

"Three points short of the predetermined release point?"

"That's right."

The kid broke into a grin. "Oh, that's easy. I can do that right here." And he pulled his handheld from the breast pocket of his coveralls.

SELENE: LEVEL SEVEN

I t's getting warmer in here, Humphries thought. Then he told himself, No, it's just your imagination. This space is insulated, fireproof. He pushed through a row of suits hanging neatly in the closet and touched one hand to the nearest of the three green tanks of oxygen standing in a row against the back wall. I've got everything I need. They can't burn me out.

Slowly he edged past the suits and slacks and jackets and shirts, all precisely arranged, all facing the same direction on their hangers, silent and waiting for him to decide on using them. He brushed their fabrics with his shoulder, was tempted to finger their sleeves, even rub them soothingly on his cheek. Like a baby with its blanket, he thought. Comforting.

Instead he went to the door, still sealed with the cermet partition. Tentatively, he touched it with his fingertips. It wasn't hot. Not even very warm. Maybe the fire's out, he supposed. Ferrer wasn't pounding on the door anymore. She gave up on that. I wonder if she made it out of the house? She's tough and smart; could she survive this fire? He suddenly felt alarmed. If she lives through it, she'll tell everybody I panicked! She'll tell them I crawled into my emergency shelter and left her outside to die!

Humphries felt his fists clenching so hard his fingernails were cutting painfully into his palms. No, the little bitch will *threaten* to tell everything and hang that threat over my head for the rest of her life. I'll have to get rid of her. Permanently. Pretend to give her whatever she wants and then get Harbin or some other animal to put her away.

His mind decided, Humphries paced the length of his clothes closet once more, wondering how he would know when it was safe to leave his airtight shelter.

•   •   •

At least the flames aren't advancing as fast as they were, Fuchs thought as he lay sprawled on the brick pathway in front of the airlock. The grotto was a mass of flames and smoke that seemed to get thicker every second. Their heat burned against his face. Nodon had lapsed into unconsciousness again; Amarjagal and Sanja lay on the grass beside him, unmoving, their dark almond-shaped eyes staring at the fire that was inching closer. The black-clad security guards sprawled everywhere, coughing, their guns thrown away, their responsibilities to Humphries forgotten.

One of the women guards asked, "How long . . ." She broke into a racking cough.

As if in answer to her unfinished question, the voice from the other side of the hatch boomed, "We've got the airlock set up. In thirty seconds we'll open the hatch. We can take two people at a time. Get your first two ready."

Fuchs pawed at his burning eyes and said, "Amarjagal and Nodon."

The woman slung Nodon's good arm around her bulky shoulders and struggled up to her feet, with Sanja helping her. Some of the security guards stirred, and Fuchs reached for the laser pistol on the ground next to him.

"We'll all get through," he said sternly. "Two at a time."

The guards stared sullenly back at him.

"Which of you is in charge?" Fuchs asked.

A big-shouldered man with his gray hair cut flat and short rolled over to a sitting position. Fuchs noted that his belly hung over the waistband of his trousers.

"I am," he said, then coughed.

"You will decide the order in which your people go through the hatch," said Fuchs, in a tone that brooked no argument. "You and I will be the last two."

The man nodded once, as the heavy steel hatch clicked and slowly swung open.

Stavenger stood out in the corridor beyond the emergency airlock and watched the survivors of the fire come out, two by two.

Like Noah's Ark, he thought.

Most of them were Humphries security people, their faces smudged with soot as black as their uniforms. There were three Asians, one of them in the gray coveralls of Selene's maintenance department.

"The last two coming through," said one of the emergency team.

An odd couple, Stavenger thought. One tall and broad-shouldered, the other short and thickset. Both in black outfits. Then he recognized the dour face of the shorter man. Lars Fuchs! Stavenger realized. That's Lars Fuchs!

"Anybody else in there?" the emergency team's chief asked.

"Nobody alive," said the Humphries' security chief.

"Okay," the chief called to his team. "Seal the hatch and let the fire burn itself out."

Stavenger was already speaking into his handheld, calling for a security team to arrest Lars Fuchs. There's only one reason for him to be here in Humphries's private preserve, Stavenger knew. He's killed Martin Humphries.

If it weren't so infuriating it would almost be funny, Humphries thought as he sat huddled in his closet.

The idiotic architect who designed this for me never bothered to install a phone inside the shelter because everybody carries handhelds or even implants. I don't have an implant and I hate those damned handhelds beeping at me. So now I'm sitting here with no goddamned way to let anybody know I'm alive. And I don't dare go outside because the fire might still be burning. Even if it isn't, it's probably used up all the oxygen out there and I'd suffocate.

Damn! Nothing to do but wait.

Humphries detested waiting. For anything, even his own rescue.

CRASH LANDING

round's coming up awful fast, Pancho said to herself. She had allowed the little hopper to follow its ballistic trajectory, knowing it was going to come down way short of the Astro base in the Malapert Mountains. How short she didn't really care anymore. Her main concern—her *only* concern now—was to get this bird down without killing herself.

Any landing you can walk away from is a good landing, she told herself as the bare, rock-strewn ground rushed up at her. Find a flat, open spot. Just like Armstrong in the old Apollo 11 Eagle. Find a flat, open spot.

Easier said than done. The rolling, hilly ground sliding past her was pitted with craters of all sizes and covered so thickly with rocks and boulders that Pancho thought of a teenaged boy she had dated whose face was covered with acne.

Funny what the mind dredges up, she thought.

"Pay attention to the real world," she muttered.

She fought down a wave of nausea as the ground rushed up at her. It would be *sooo* good to just lay down and go to sleep. Her legs felt like rubber, her whole body ached. Without thinking of it consciously she ran her tongue across her teeth, testing for a taste of blood. Bad sign if your gums start bleeding, she knew. Symptom of radiation sickness, big time.

"Pay attention!" she screamed at herself.

"Say again?" came the voice of the flight controller at Malapert.

"Nothin'," Pancho replied, apologetically. They've still got me on their radar, she thought. Good. They'll know where the body's buried.

There! Coming up on the right. A fairly flat area with only a few dinky little rocks. It's sloping, though. On a hillside. Not so bad. If I can reach it.

Pancho nudged the tee-shaped control yoke and the hopper's maneuvering thrusters squirted out a few puffs of cold gas, enough to jink the ungainly little craft toward the open area she had spotted.

Shit! More rocks than I thought. Well, beggars can't be choosers. Only enough juice for one landing.

She tapped the keyboard for the automatic landing sequence, not trusting herself to do the job manually. The hopper shuddered as its main engine fired, killed its velocity, and the little craft dropped like a child's toy onto the stony, sloping ground. All in total silence.

Pancho remembered enough from her old astronaut training to flex her knees and brace her arms against the control podium. The hopper thumped into the ground, one flat landing foot banging into a rock big enough to tip the whole craft dangerously. For a wild moment Pancho thought the hopper was going to tumble over onto its side. It didn't, but the crash landing was violent enough to tear away the loop that held her right foot to the platform grillwork. Her leg flew up, knocking her so badly off balance that her left leg, still firmly anchored in its foot loop, snapped at the ankle.

Pancho gritted her teeth in the sudden pain of the broken bone as she thudded in lunar slow motion to the grillwork platform.

Feeling cold sweat breaking out of every pore of her body, she thought, Well, I ain't dead yet.

Then she added, Won't be long before I am, though.

ASTRO CORPORATION COMMAND CENTER

I might as well move a cot in here, thought Jake Wanamaker as he paced along the row of consoles. A technician sat at each of them, monitoring display screens that linked the command center with Astro ships and bases from the Moon to the Belt. Lit only by the ghostly glow of the screens, the room felt hot and stuffy, taut with the hum of electrical equipment and the nervous tension of apprehensive men and women.

There were only two displays that Wanamaker was interested in: Malapert base, near the lunar south pole, and *Cromwell,* about to start its runup to the asteroid Vesta.

Wanamaker hunched over the technician monitoring the link with *Cromwell.* Deep inside the cloud of high-energy particles, radio contact was impossible. But the ship's captain had sent a tight-beam laser message more than half an hour earlier. It was just arriving at the Astro receiving telescope up on the surface of the Moon.

The screen showed nothing but a jumbled hash of colors.

"Decoding, sir," the seated technician murmured, feeling the admiral's breath on the back of her neck.

The streaks dissolved to reveal the apprehensive-looking face of *Cromwell*'s skipper. The man's eyes looked wary, evasive.

"We have started the final run to target," he stated tersely. "The radiation cloud is dissipating faster than predicted, so we will release our payload at the point halfway between the start of the run and the planned release point."

The screen went blank.

Turning her face toward Wanamaker, the technician said, "That's the entire message, sir."

His immediate reaction was to fire a message back to *Cromwell* ordering the captain to stick to the plan and carry the nanomachines all the way to the predecided release point. But he realized that it would take the better part of an hour for a message to reach the ship. *Nothing I can do,* he told himself, straightening up. He stretched his arms over his head, thinking, *The captain's on the scene. If he feels he needs to let the package go early it's for a good reason.* But Wanamaker couldn't convince himself. *The captain's taking the easiest course for himself,* he realized. *He's not pressing his attack home.*

Turning slowly, he scanned the shadowy room for Tashkajian. She was at her desk on the other side of the quietly intense command center. *This is her plan,* Wanamaker thought. *She worked it out with the captain. If there's anything wrong with his releasing the package early, she'll be the one to tell me.*

But what good will it do? I can't get the word to him in time to straighten him out.

Tashkajian got up from her little wheeled chair as he approached her desk.

"You saw the report from *Cromwell?*" Wanamaker asked.

"Yes, sir."

"And?"

She hesitated a moment. "It's probably all right. The missiles are small and Vesta's radars will still be jammed by the radiation."

"But he said the cloud was breaking up."

"Our reports from the IAA monitors—"

A whoop from one of the consoles interrupted them. "They found her!" a male technician hollered, his face beaming. "They found Pancho! She's alive!"

The first that Pancho realized she'd passed out was when the excruciating pain woke her up. She blinked her gummy eyes and saw that somebody in a bulbous hard-shell space suit was lifting her off her back, broken ankle and all.

"Jesus Christ on a Harley!" she moaned. "Take it easy, for chrissakes."

"Sorry," the space-suited figure said. Pancho heard his words in her helmet earphones.

"That leg's broken," she said. Nearly sobbed, actually, it hurt so badly.

"Easy does it," the guy in the space suit said. Through a haze of agony Pancho realized there were three of them. One holding her shoulders, another her legs, and the third hovering at her side as they carried her away from the wreck of the hopper.

"I'll immobilize the ankle as soon as we get you to our hopper," the guy said. "I'm a medic, Ms. Lane."

"I can tell," she groused. "Total indifference to pain. Other people's pain."

"We didn't know your ankle was broken, ma'am. You were unconscious when we reached you. Almost out of air, too."

Screw you, Pancho thought. But she kept silent. I oughtta be pretty damn grateful to these turkeys for coming out and finding me. Each step they took, though, shot a fresh lance of pain through her leg.

"We had to land more than a kilometer from your crash site," the medic said. "Not many places around here to put down a hopper safely."

"Tell me about it."

"We'll be there in ten-fifteen minutes. Then I can set your ankle properly."

"Just don't drop me," Pancho growled.

"The ground is very stony, very uneven. We're doing the best we can."

"Just don't drop me," she repeated.

They only dropped her once.

When the Selene emergency team brought Fuchs, his three crew, and the Humphries security people to the hospital, Fuchs had the presence of mind to give his name as Karl Manstein. Medical personnel put each survivor of the fire onto a gurney and wheeled them to beds separated by plastic curtains.

Fuchs knew he had to get out of the hospital as quickly as possible, with his crew. He lay on the crisp white sheets staring at the cream-colored ceiling, wondering how far away from him the others were. Nodon's wounded, he remembered. That's going to make an escape more difficult.

It's only a matter of time before they realize Manstein is an alias, a fiction. Then what?

But a new thought struck him and suddenly he smiled up at the ceiling, alone in his curtained cubicle.

When he and the Humphries security chief finally staggered through the hatch and the temporary airlock that the Selene emergency crew had erected, the head of the emergency team had asked them, "Anybody else in there?"

The security chief had shaken his head gravely. "Nobody alive," he had said.

Humphries is dead! Fuchs exulted. Lying on his hospital bed, his eyes still stinging and his lungs raw from the smoke, he wanted to laugh with glee. I did it! I killed the murdering swine! Martin Humphries is dead.

• • •

Martin Humphries was quite alive, but gnawingly hungry. He had never in his life known hunger before, but as he paced, or sat, or stretched out on the thick carpeting of his closet hideaway, his empty stomach growled at him. It *hurt,* this hollow feeling in his belly. It stretched the minutes and hours and drove his mind into an endless need for food. Even when he tried to sleep his dreams were filled with steaming banquets that he somehow could not reach.

Thirst was even worse. His throat grew dry, his tongue seemed to get thicker in his mouth, his eyes felt gritty.

I could die in here! he realized. A hundred times he went to the airtight panel, touched it gingerly with his fingertips. It felt cool. He pressed both hands on it. Flattened his cheek against it. The fire *must* be out by now, he thought. His wristwatch told him that more than twenty hours had gone by. The fire's got to be out by now. But what about the air? Is there any air to breathe on the other side of the panel?

Somebody will come, he assured himself. My security chief knows about this shelter. If he wasn't killed in the fire. If he didn't suffocate from lack of oxygen. Ferrer. Victoria might have gotten out. She'll tell them I'm here. But then he wondered, Will she? I wouldn't let her in here with me; she could be sore enough to let me rot in here, even if she got out okay. But even so, *somebody* will send people to go through the house, assess the damage. The Selene safety inspectors. The goddamned insurance people will be here sooner or later.

Later, a sardonic voice in his mind told him. Don't expect the insurance adjusters to break their butts getting here.

It's all that motherless architect's fault, Humphries fumed. Idiot! Builds this emergency shelter without a phone to make contact with the outside. Without sensors to tell me if there's air on the other side of the door. I'll see to it that he never gets another commission. Never! He'll be panhandling on street corners by the time I get finished with him.

There's not even a water fountain in here. I could die of thirst before anybody finds me.

He slumped to the floor and wanted to cry, but his body was too dehydrated to produce tears.

BALLISTIC ROCKET

From her seat by the narrow window Pancho could see out of the corner of her eye the rugged lunar highlands gliding swiftly past, far below. She was the only passenger on the ballistic rocket as it arced high above the Moon's barren surface, carrying her from Astro's Malapert base back to Selene. Her ankle was set in a spraycast; she was heading for Selene's hospital, and injections of nanomachines that would mend her broken bones and repair the damage that radiation had done to her body.

Pancho had precious little time to study the scenery. She was deep in conversation with Jake Wanamaker, whose craggy unsmiling face reminded her of the rocky land below.

". . . should be releasing the nanomachines right about now," Wanamaker was saying.

"And everybody on Vesta is belowground?" Pancho asked.

"Ought to be, with that radiation cloud sweeping over them. Anybody up on the surface is going to be dead no matter what we do."

Pancho nodded. "All right. Now what's this about Humphries's mansion burning down?"

Wanamaker grimaced with distaste. "A group of four fanatics infiltrated into the grotto down there on the bottom level. Why, we don't know yet. They're being held by Selene security in the hospital."

"And they burned the house down?"

"Set the whole garden on fire. The place is a blackened wasteland."

"Humphries?"

"No sign of him. Selene inspectors are going through the place now. Apparently the house is still standing, but it's been gutted by the fire."

Strangely, Pancho felt no elation at the possibility that Humphries was dead. "Have they found his body?"

"Not yet."

"And the people who attacked the place are in the hospital?"

"Under guard."

Pancho knew only one person in the entire solar system who would be crazy enough to attack Humphries in his own home. Lars Fuchs.

"Was Lars Fuchs one of the attackers?"

Wanamaker's acid expression deepened into a dark scowl. "He gave his name as Karl Manstein. I don't think Selene security has tumbled to who he really is."

For an instant Pancho wondered how Wanamaker knew that Manstein was an alias for Fuchs. But she put that aside as unimportant. "Get him out of there," she said.

"What?"

"Get him out of the hospital. Out of Selene. Send him back to the Belt, to Ceres, anywhere. Just get him loose from Selene security."

"But he's a murderer, a terrorist."

"I brought him to Selene to help in our fight against Humphries," Pancho half-lied. "I don't want Stavenger or anybody else to know that."

"How am I supposed to get him past Selene's security guards?" Wanamaker asked, clearly distressed.

Pancho closed her eyes for a moment. Then, "Jake, that's your problem. Figure it out. I want him off the Moon and headed back to the Belt. Yesterday."

He took a deep breath, then replied reluctantly, "Yes, ma'am." For an instant she thought he was going to give her a military salute.

"Anything else?" Pancho asked.

Wanamaker made a face that was halfway between a smile and a grimace. "Isn't that enough?"

Ulysses S. Quinlan felt awed, his emerald-green eyes wide with admiration, as he stood in the middle of the huge downstairs living room of the Humphries mansion. Or what was left of it. The wide, spacious room was a charred and blackened desolation, walls and ceiling scorched, floor littered with burned stumps of debris and powdery gray ash.

Born in Belfast of an Irish father and Irish-American mother, Quinlan had grown up to tales of civil wars. To please his father he played football from childhood, which eventually brought him an athletic scholarship to Princeton University, back in the States—which pleased his mother, even though she cried to be separated from her only child. Quinlan studied engineering, and worked long years on the frustrating and ultimately pointless seawalls and hydromechanical barriers that failed to prevent the rising ocean from flooding out most of Florida and the Gulf Coast regions as far south as Mexico's Yucatan peninsula.

He suffered a nervous breakdown when Houston was inundated, and was retired at full pension precisely on his fortieth birthday. To get away from oceans and seas and floods he retired to the Moon. Within a year he was working in Selene's safety department, as happy and cheerful as he'd been before the disastrous greenhouse floods on Earth.

Now he whistled through his breathing mask as he goggled at the size of the mansion's living room.

"The grandeur of it all," he said as he shuffled through the gray ash and debris.

"Like the old Tsars in Russia," said his partner, a stocky redheaded Finnish woman. He could hear the contempt in her tone, even through her breathing mask.

"Aye," agreed Quinlan, thudding the blackened wall with a gloved fist. "But he built solid. Reinforced concrete. The basic structure stood up to the flames, it did."

His partner reluctantly agreed. "They could have contained the fire to one area if somebody hadn't allowed it to spread to the roof."

Quinlan nodded. "A pity," he murmured. "A true pity."

They wore the breathing masks to protect their lungs from the fine ash that they kicked up with each step they took. The grotto had been refilled with breathable air hours earlier. Quinlan and his Finnish partner were inspecting the ruins, checking to make certain that no hint of fire reignited itself now that there was oxygen to support combustion again.

They spent a careful hour sifting through the debris of the lower floor. Then they headed cautiously up the stairs to the upper level. The wooden facings and lush carpeting of the stairway had burned away, but the solid concrete understructure was undisturbed by the fire.

Upstairs was just as bad a mess as below. Quinlan could see the broken and charred remains of what had once been fine furniture, now lying in shattered heaps along the walls of the hallway. The windows were all intact, he noticed, and covered with metal mesh screens. He must have built with tempered glass, Quinlan thought. Bulletproof? I wonder.

Following the floor plan displayed on their handhelds, they pushed through the debris at the wide doorway of the master bedroom suite. Quinlan whistled softly at the size of it all.

"That must have been the bed," his partner said, pointing to a square block of debris on the floor.

"Or his airport," muttered Quinlan.

"Hey, look at this." The Finn was standing in front of an intact door panel. "The fire didn't damage this."

"How could that be?" Quinlan wondered aloud, stepping over toward her.

"It's plastic of some sort," she said, running her gloved had along the panel.

"Ceramic, looks like."

The redhead checked her handheld. "Should be a closet, according to the floorplan."

"How in the world do you get into it, though?" Quinlan looked for a door latch or a button but could see nothing along the soot-blackened door frame.

He tried to slide the door open. It wouldn't budge. He tapped it, then rapped. "It's locked from the inside, seems like."

At that instant the door slid open so fast they both jumped back a startled step or two.

Martin Humphries stood tottering on uncertain legs, glaring at them with red-rimmed blazing in his eyes.

"About time," he croaked, his voice bricky-dry.

"Mr. Humphries!"

Humphries staggered past them, looked at the ruins of his palatial bedroom, then turned back on them fiercely.

"Water! Give me water."

Quinlan yanked the canteen from his belt and wordlessly handed it to the angry man. Humphries gurgled it down greedily, water spilling down his chin and dripping onto the front of his wrinkled shirt. Even through the breathing mask, Quinlan could smell the man's foul body odor.

Humphries put the canteen down from his lips, but still held onto it possessively. Wiping his chin with the back of his free hand, he coughed once, then jabbed a finger at Quinlan.

"Phone," he snapped, his voice a little stronger than before. "Give me a phone. I'm going to hang that murdering bastard Fuchs by his balls!"

ASTEROID VESTA

Although the military base on Vesta belonged to Humphries Space Systems, its key personnel were mercenaries hired by HSS from several sources. Leeza Chaptal, for example, was a Yamagata Corporation employee. She was now effectively the base commander, since the HSS man nominally in charge of the base was a business executive, by training and education an accountant, by disposition a bean-counter.

Leeza left him to shuffle paperwork (electronically, of course) and he left her to run the two-hundred-odd men and women who made up the military strength of the base: engineers, technicians, astronauts, soldiers. It was a wise arrangement. The HSS man dealt with numbers, while Leeza handled the real work.

With the solar storm raging, though, there was very little real work being done. Leeza had called in everyone from the surface. Huddled safely in the caverns and tunnels deep underground, there was little for the military to do other than routine maintenance of equipment and that oldest of all soldierly pursuits: griping.

In truth, Leeza herself felt uncomfortable burrowed down like a mole in its den. Even though she seldom went to the surface of Vesta, it unnerved her to realize that she *could not* go up to the surface now, could not get out of these cramped little compartments carved out of the asteroid's rocky body, could not stand up on the bare pebbled ground—even in a space suit—and see the stars.

She paced slowly along the consoles in the base command center, looking over the shoulders of the bored technicians sitting at each desk. The storm was weakening, she saw. Radiation levels were beginning to decline. Good, she thought. The sooner this is over, the better. Four HSS vessels were hanging in docking orbits up there, waiting for the radiation to recede enough so they could begin shuttling their crews down to the base. And Dorik Harbin was approaching in his ship, *Samarkand*.

Dorik had been distant for weeks now; perhaps it was time to bring him closer. Leeza smiled inwardly at the thought. *He doesn't like the fact that I outrank him*, she knew. *But a few of the right pills and he'll forget all about rank. Or maybe I should try something that will make him obedient, submissive. No*, she decided. *I like his passion, his ferocity. Take that away from him and there's nothing special left.*

"Unidentified vehicle approaching," said the tech monitoring the radar.

Leeza felt her scalp tingle. *Anything that the radar could spot through this radiation cloud must be close, very close.*

"Two bogies," the technician called out as Leeza hurried to his chair.

They were speeding toward Vesta, and so close that the computer could calculate their size and velocity. *Too small to be attack ships*, Leeza saw, swiftly digesting the numbers racing across the bottom of the display. *Nukes? Nuclear bombs couldn't do much damage to us while we're buttoned up down here.* For the first time she felt grateful for the solar storm.

"They're going to impact," said the technician.

"Yes, I can see," Leeza replied calmly.

The two approaching missiles fired retrorockets at the last instant and hit the hard, stony ground almost softly. *A crash landing*, she thought. *No explosion. Timed fuzing?*

She walked a few paces to the communications console. "Do you have a camera in the vicinity where those two bogies landed?"

The comm tech already had the scene on her main display screen. It was grainy and dim, but Leeza saw the crumpled wreckage of two small missiles lying on the bare ground.

"Is that the best magnification you can get?" she asked, bending over the technician's shoulder to peer at the screen.

The technician muttered something about the radiation up there as she pecked at her keyboard.

The display went blank.

"Nice work," Leeza sneered.

"It shouldn't have done that," said the technician, defensively.

"Radar's out!" called the radar tech.

Leeza straightened up and turned in his direction.

"Radiation monitors have gone dead."

"No response from the surface camera at the crash site," the comm tech said. "Hey, two more cameras have gone out!"

Leeza turned slowly in a full circle. Every console was conking out, screens going dark while red failure-mode lights flared.

"What's going on up there?" Leeza asked.

No one answered.

No less than fourteen Humphries Space Systems employees attended Martin Humphries between his burned-out mansion and the finest suite in the decaying Hotel Luna, four flights above the fire-blackened grotto. Flunkies and lackeys ranging from his personal physician to a perky blonde administrative assistant with a brilliant smile from HSS's personnel department were already waiting for their CEO as Quinlan and his surprised partner helped Humphries through the temporary airlock and into Selene's bottommost corridor.

The head of his security department, the never-smiling Grigor, fell into step alongside Humphries as they started toward the powered stairs.

"Your assistant, the woman Ferrer . . ."

"What about her?" Humphries asked, suddenly worried that Victoria had survived the fire and was ready to tell the world how he had abandoned her.

"They found her body in the upstairs hallway," said Grigor morosely. "Dead of smoke inhalation."

Humphries felt a surge of relief flow through him. But he growled, "Fuchs. He's responsible for this. I want Fuchs's balls on a platter."

"Yessir," said Grigor. "I'll see to it right away."

"And fire that dumb sonofabitch who was in charge of security for my house!"

"Immediately, sir."

"You've got to rest, Mr. Humphries," the doctor said, placing a placating hand on Humphries's arm. "You've been through an ordeal that would—"

"Fuchs!" Humphries raged, shaking loose of the doctor. "Find him! Kill the bastard!"

"Right away, sir."

Humphries fumed and ranted all the way up the power stairs and into the sumptuous hotel suite that the woman from the personnel department had reserved for him. A full dinner was waiting on a wheeled table set up in the sitting room. Humphries blurted orders and demands as he stormed into the suite and went straight to the lavatory. Even while he stripped off his sweaty clothes and stepped into the steaming shower he still yelled at the aides—including the blonde—swirling around him.

"And another thing," he called from the shower. "Get my insurance adjusters down to the mansion and see to it that they have a complete list of its contents. Goddamned fire ruined everything in there. Everything!"

Aides scurried and took notes on their handhelds. The doctor wanted to give Humphries an injection of tranquilizers, but he would have none of it.

"But you've got to rest," the doctor said, backing away from his employer's raging shouts.

"I'll rest when Fuchs's body is roasting over a slow fire," Humphries answered hotly while he struggled into a robe being held for him by the head of his public relations department.

He stormed into the sitting room, glared at the dinner waiting for him, then looked up at the small crowd of aides, assistants and executives.

"Out! All of you! Get the hell out of here and leave me alone."

They hurried toward the door.

"You!" He pointed at Grigor. "I want Fuchs. Understand me?"

"I understand, sir. It's as good as done. He can't get out of Selene. We'll find him."

"It's his head or yours," Humphries growled.

Grigor nodded, looking more morose than usual, and practically bowed as he backed away toward the door.

The doctor stood uncertainly in the center of the sitting room, a remote sensing unit in his hand. "I should take your blood pressure, Mr. Humphries."

"Get OUT!"

The doctor scampered to the door.

Humphries plopped himself down on the wide, deep sofa and glowered at the covered plates arranged on the wheeled table. A bottle of wine stood in a chiller, already uncorked.

He looked up and saw that everybody had left. Everybody except the blonde, who stood at the door watching him.

"Do you want me to leave, too?" she asked, with a warm smile.

Humphries laughed. "No." He patted the sofa cushion beside him. "You come and sit here."

She was slim, elfin, wearing a one-piece tunic that ended halfway down her thighs. Humphries saw a tattoo on her left ankle: a twining thorned stem that bore a red rose.

"The doctor said you should rest," she said, with an impish smile.

"He also said I need a tranquilizer."

"And a good night's sleep."

"Maybe you can help me with that," he said.

"I'll do my best."

He discovered that her name was Tatiana Oparin, that she worked in his personnel department, that she was ambitious, and that she would be delighted to replace the late Victoria Ferrer as his personal aide. He also discovered that the rose around her ankle was not her only tattoo.

•   •   •

Grigor Malenkovich noted, in his silent but keen-eyed way, that Tatiana stayed behind in Humphries's suite. Good, he thought. She is serving her purpose. While she keeps Humphries occupied I can start the search for Fuchs without his hounding me.

The place to start is the hospital, he told himself. All four of the intruders have been brought there. They are under guard. One of them is undoubtedly Fuchs himself. Or, if not, then he knows where Fuchs is.

He went directly to the hospital, only to be told by Selene's security officers that all the people taken from the fire scene were under protective custody.

"I want to ask them a few questions," said Grigor.

The woman in the coral red Selene coveralls smiled patiently at him. "Tomorrow, Mr. Malenkovich. You can be present when we interrogate them."

Grigor hesitated a moment, then asked, "Why not now? Why wait?"

"The medics say they need a night's rest. One of them was wounded, you know, and all of them have had a pretty rugged time of it."

"All the better. Question them while they are tired, worn down."

The woman smiled again, but it seemed forced. "Tomorrow, Mr. Malenkovich. Once the medics okay it. We'll talk to them tomorrow."

Grigor thought it over. No sense getting into a quarrel with Selene security, he decided. Besides, Humphries is busy enjoying a good night's rest—or something of the kind.

"You can't take patients out of the hospital without authorization," said the doctor. He was young, with a boyish thatch of dark brown hair flopping over his forehead. Wanamaker thought he probably made out pretty well with the female hospital staffers.

He kept his thoughts to himself, though, and put on his sternest, darkest scowl.

"This is an Astro Corporation security matter," he insisted, his voice low but iron-hard.

They were standing at the hospital's admittance center, little more than a waist-high counter with a computer terminal atop it. The doctor had been summoned by the computer, which normally ran the center without human intervention. Wanamaker had waited until midnight to fetch Fuchs and his people out of the hospital. Minimal staff on duty. He had brought six of the biggest, toughest-looking Astro employees he could find. Two of them actually worked in the security department. The other four consisted of two mechanics, one physical fitness instructor from Astro's private spa, and a woman cook from the executive dining room.

The doctor looked uncertainly at the identification chip Wanamaker held out rigidly at arm's length. He had already run it through the admittance center's computer terminal and it had verified that Jacob Wanamaker was an executive of Astro Corporation's security department.

"I should call Selene's security department," the doctor said.

"Aren't they guarding the four?" Wanamaker demanded, knowing that they had been called off by one of his own people who had hacked into their computer system.

"Not on this shift," said the doctor. "They'll be back in the morning, at oh-eight-hundred."

"All right then," Wanamaker said. "I'll deal with them in the morning. Right now, I've been instructed to take the four to Astro headquarters."

Wanamaker was thinking, If this young pup doesn't cave in I'll have to slug him. He didn't want to do that. He wanted this extraction to be painless.

The young man's face was too bland to frown effectively, but he screwed up his features and said, "This hospital is run by the governing board of Selene, not Astro or any other corporation."

Wanamaker nodded knowingly. "Very well. You contact your governing board and get their okay."

The doctor glanced at the wall clock. "It's almost one A.M.!"

"Yes, that's right."

"They'll all be asleep."

"Then you'll have to wake them." Wanamaker hoped fervently that the kid didn't think of calling Selene's security department. That could create a problem.

Before the doctor could make up his mind, Wanamaker suggested, "Why don't you call Douglas Stavenger?"

"Mr. Stavenger?" The doctor's eyed widened. "He knows about this?"

"And he's given his approval," Wanamaker lied.

"Well . . ."

"Is there any medical reason to keep them hospitalized?" Wanamaker demanded.

The doctor shook his head. "No, they're supposed to be released in the morning."

"Very well then. Give me the release forms and I'll sign them."

"I don't know . . ."

Wanamaker didn't wait any further. He walked past the puzzled, uncertain young doctor. His six subordinates marched in step behind him, trying to look fierce, as Wanamaker had instructed them to do.

ARMSTRONG SPACEPORT

As the cart trundled to a stop at the end of the tunnel that led back to Selene, Wanamaker noticed that the lower half of Pancho's right leg was wrapped in a cast. She looked grim, almost angry, as she sat behind the cart's wheel with her leg sticking out onto the fender.

Fuchs was standing beside Wanamaker, also far from happy. His three aides were already on their way to the little rocket shuttlecraft that would take them up to the vessel waiting in orbit above the Moon's rugged, airless surface.

"Humphries is alive and well," said Pancho, without getting down from the electric cart. "No thanks to you, Lars."

His mouth a downcast slash, Fuchs answered, "Too bad. The world would be better off with him dead."

"Maybe so, but all you did was kill a dozen or so of his people. Now he's got a perfectly good excuse to go after your ass, ol' buddy."

Fuchs started to reply, thought better of it, and said nothing.

Turning to Wanamaker, Pancho asked, "What've you got for him?"

"The only available armed vessel is a new attack ship, *Halsey*.

Pancho nodded brusquely. "Okay, Lars. That's your new ship. Officially, you've hijacked it while it was sitting in lunar orbit waiting for a crew to be assigned to it."

"You're giving it to me?" Fuchs asked, flabbergasted.

"You're stealing it. We'll add it to your long list of crimes."

His broad, normally downcast face broke into a bitter smile. "Pancho . . . I . . . I don't know what to say."

She did not smile back at him. "Just get your butt up to the ship and get the hell out of here as fast as you can. Go back to the Belt and hide out with the rock rats. Humphries is going to come after you with everything he's got."

Fuchs nodded, understanding. "I'm only sorry that I didn't kill him. He deserves to die."

"So do we all, ol' buddy," said Pancho. "Now, *git*! Before a platoon of HSS security goons comes boiling down the tunnel."

Fuchs grasped her hand and, bending slightly, kissed it. Pancho's face turned red.

"Go on, git. There's gonna be plenty hell to pay; I've got to get busy."

Almost laughing, Fuchs turned and started trotting down the corridor that led to the waiting shuttlecraft, a thickset, sturdy little badger of a man clad in black, his short arms pumping as he ran.

Wanamaker shook his head. "When Humphries finds out you've helped him escape . . ."

Pancho grinned at him. "Hell, Jake, he got away from you. You're the one who sprang him out of the hospital. He got away from you and stole a brand-new Astro spacecraft. I might have to dock your pay or something."

Wanamaker broke into a craggy smile. "You are some piece of work, Ms. Lane. Really some piece of work."

"Come on," Pancho said, patting the plastic of the seat beside her. "I'll give you a ride back to town. We got a lot of work to do."

"What do you mean, he's disappeared?" Humphries demanded.

Grigor stood before him like a dark wraith, his eyes downcast. With a shrug, he repeated, "Fuchs is gone."

They were in the sitting room of Humphries's suite in the Hotel Luna. Tatiana Oparin had discreetly remained in the bedroom when Grigor had arrived, before Humphries's breakfast order had come from room service.

"He *can't* be gone!" Humphries shouted, pounding the pillows of the sofa on which he sat. Clad only in a silk hotel robe, his thin, almost hairless legs reminded Grigor of a chicken's.

Standing before the sofa, to one side of the coffeetable, Grigor reported, "He was under Selene's custody last night, in the hospital. This morning, when we went to interrogate him, he and his crew were gone."

"Gone? How could he be gone? Where did he go? How could he get out?"

"An Astro Corporation security detail removed him from the hospital shortly after one A.M.," Grigor replied, his voice as flat and even as a computer's. "There is no trace of him after that."

Leaping to his feet so hard that his robe flapped open, Humphries screamed, "Find him! Search every centimeter of the city and *find him!* Now! Use every man you've got."

"Yes, sir."

"Don't stand there! Find him!"

As Grigor turned toward the door, the phone chimed. Scowling, Humphries saw that the wallscreen displayed the name of the caller: Pancho Lane.

"Phone answer," he snapped.

Pancho's angular, light tan features took shape on the wallscreen, slightly bigger than life.

"Martin, I have some unpleasant news for you."

He glared at her image as he pulled the maroon robe tightly around himself.

"Lars Fuchs somehow stole our newest ship and lit out of lunar orbit a few hours ago. He's prob'ly heading back to the Belt."

"He stole one of your ships?" Humphries asked, his voice dripping sarcasm.

"Yup," said Pancho. "Slipped away from a phony security detail that sprang him out of the hospital last night."

Humphries's innards felt like a lake of molten lava. "He had lots of help, then, didn't he?"

Keeping her face immobile, Pancho admitted, "Well, he's got some friends among my Astro people, yeah. We're looking into it."

"I'm sure you are."

She almost smiled. "I just thought you'd want to know."

"Thank you, Pancho."

"Any time, Martin." The screen went dark.

Humphries stepped to the small table at the end of the sofa, yanked up the lamp sitting atop it, and heaved it at the wallscreen. It bounced off and thudded to the carpeted floor.

"Guttersnipe bitch! She helped him get away. Now he's running back to the Belt to hide out with his rock rat friends."

Grigor said, "We could intercept him."

Humphries glared at his security chief. "He'll be running silent. You'd have to search the whole region between here and the Belt. There aren't enough ships—"

"He'll have to put in somewhere for supplies," said Grigor. "The *Chrysalis* habitat at Ceres is the only place for that."

Still glowering, Humphries said, "They won't take him in. They exiled him, years ago."

Nodding slightly, Grigor countered, "Perhaps. But he will contact a ship in the region for supplies."

"Or capture one, the damned pirate."

"Either way, *Chrysalis* is the key to his survival. If we control the habitat at Ceres, we will get him into our grasp, sooner or later."

Humphries stared at his security chief for a long, silent moment. Then he said, "All right. Tell our people at Vesta to send a force to Ceres and take control of *Chrysalis*."

An unhappy expression twisted Grigor's normally dour face. "We seem to have lost contact with Vesta," he said, the words coming out swiftly, all in a rush.

"What?"

"I'm sure it's only temporary."

"Lost contact?" Humphries's voice rose a notch.

"It might be the solar storm," said Grigor, almost to himself, "although the cloud is well past the Belt now."

"Lost contact with the whole base?" Humphries shouted. "The entire base?"

"For more than twelve hours," Grigor admitted, almost in a whisper.

Humphries wanted to scream. And he did, so loudly and with such fevered anger that Tatiana Oparin rushed into the sitting room. When she failed to calm him down she called the HSS medical department for Humphries's personal physician.

COMMAND SHIP *SAMARKAND*

Harbin hated these one-way messages. I have to sit here like an obedient dog while my master speaks to me, he grumbled silently. Yet there was no other way. Grigor was at Selene, Harbin in his private compartment aboard *Samakand,* so deep in the Belt that it took light the better part of an hour to span the distance between them.

Grigor's face, in the display screen, looked even dourer than usual. He's worried, Harbin thought. Frightened.

". . . completely wiped out Humphries's home here in Selene and killed four security guards," the security chief was saying, speaking rapidly, nervously. "They also killed Humphries's personal assistant, the woman Ferrer. The attack was led by Lars Fuchs."

Fuchs attacked Humphries in his own home! Harbin marveled. He felt some admiration for such daring. Strike your enemy as hard as you can. Strike at his heart.

Grigor was droning on, "Astro has apparently spirited Fuchs away. Most likely he's on his way back to the Belt. He must have friends at Ceres, allies who will give him supplies and more crewmen. Your orders are to find Fuchs and kill him. Nothing else matters now. Bring Fuchs's head to Mr. Humphries. He will accept nothing less."

Harbin nodded. This isn't the first time that Humphries has demanded Fuchs's life, he recalled. But this will be the last time. The final time. Fuchs has frightened Humphries. Up until now Humphries has fought this war in comfort and safety. But now Fuchs has threatened him, terrified him. Now he'll move heaven and Earth to eliminate the threat that Fuchs represents. Now it's time for Fuchs to die.

"Something else," Grigor added, his eyes shifting nervously. "The base on Vesta has gone silent. We don't know why. I've diverted one of our attack ships to the asteroid to see what's happened. You stay clear of Vesta. Head directly for Ceres and the habitat *Chrysalis*. Get Fuchs. Let me worry about Vesta."

The security chief's morose face disappeared from Harbin's screen, leaving him alone in his compartment.

Let him worry about Vesta, Harbin thought sourly. And what do I do about supplies? Where do I get fuel and food for my crew? How do I get all the way over to Ceres on what's left in my propellant tanks? I've stripped this ship's armor, too. What if I run into an Astro attack vessel? Grigor can give orders, but carrying them out is up to me.

Doug Stavenger was also feeling frustrated about the long time lag between Selene and the Belt. Edith, aboard *Elsinore,* was approaching Ceres. She would be arriving at the *Chrysalis* habitat in less than twenty-four hours.

". . . so it turns out that if you'd stayed here," he was saying to her, "you'd have had a big story at your doorstep. Humphries isn't letting any news media into his home, not even inside his garden, or what's left of it. But from what the safety inspectors tell me the house is a burned-out shell and that big, beautiful garden of his is almost completely destroyed."

He hesitated, leaned back in his recliner and tried to group his thoughts coherently. It was difficult speaking to a blank screen. It was like talking to yourself.

"Edie, this war's gone far enough. I've got to do something to stop it. They're fighting here in Selene now and I can't permit that. If that fire had spread beyond Humphries's garden it could have killed a lot of people here. Everyone, maybe, if we couldn't get it under control. I can't let them pose that kind of a threat to us. I've got to stop them."

Yes, Stavenger told himself. You've got to stop them. But how? How can you stop two of the most powerful corporations in the solar system from turning Selene into a battleground?

When his message arrived at *Elsinore,* Edith Elgin saw the concern, the deep lines of apprehension creasing her husband's handsome face.

But in her mind a voice was exulting, Fuchs is heading here! He has to be. He has friends among the rock rats. One way or another he's going to sneak back to Ceres, at least long enough to refuel and restock his ship. And I'll be there to interview him!

She was so excited that she hopped up from the chair she'd been sitting in to view her husband's message and left her cabin, heading up the narrow passageway toward the bridge. I've got to find out exactly when we dock at *Chrysalis,* she told herself. And see if the captain can spot any other ships heading toward the habitat. Fuchs may be running silent, but his ship will show up on radar, now that we're clear of the radiation cloud.

Lars Fuchs was indeed heading for Ceres, running silently, all beacons and telemetry turned off. Hands clasped behind his back, mouth turned down in a sullen scowl, he paced back and forth across the bridge of the *Halsey,* his mind churning.

The ship was running smoothly enough, for its first flight in deep space. Its systems were automated enough so that the four of them could run it as a skeleton crew. Nodon's shoulder was healing, and Sanja had assured Fuchs that there were more crewmen waiting for them at *Chrysalis.*

Fuchs was officially exiled from the rock rats' habitat, and had been for nearly ten years. But they'll let me take up a parking orbit, he thought. Just for a day or so. Just long enough to take on more crew and supplies.

Then what? he asked himself. I have *Nautilus* waiting for me in the Belt, and now this new ship. Can I find enough people to crew them both? Humphries will be coming after me with everything he's got. Fuchs nodded to himself. Let him. Let him chase me all through the Belt. I'll bleed him dry. I failed to kill him, but I can hurt him where the pain is greatest: in his ledger sheets. Every ship he sends after me is an expense that drains his profits. Every HSS ship that I destroy will pour more red ink on him. I'll bleed him dry.

Until he kills me, Fuchs realized. This war between us can end in only one way. I'm a dead man. He told me that years ago.

He caught a glimpse of himself reflected in one of the blank screens on the bridge. A bitter, angry face with a thin slash of sneering lips and deepset eyes that burned like hot coals.

All right, he said to his image. He'll kill me. But it will cost him plenty. I won't go easily. Or cheaply.

Big George Ambrose was fidgeting uncomfortably at the conference table. His chair was just a tad too small for his bulk, its arms just high enough to force him to hunch his shoulders slightly. After a couple of hours it got painful.

And this meeting had been going on for more than a couple of hours. The governing board of *Chrysalis* was having one of its rare disagreements. Usually the board was little more than a rubber stamp for George's decisions. None of the board members really wanted any responsibility.

They were all picked at random by the habitat's personnel computer, and required to serve a year on the governing body. Each of the eight men and women wanted to be back at their jobs or at home or taking in a video or at the pub. Anywhere but stuck in this conference room, wrangling.

George thought the pub was a good idea. Maybe we should have our fookin' meetings there, he said to himself. Get them all half blind and then take a vote.

But this was a serious issue, he knew. It had to be faced squarely. And soberly.

Pancho had warned George that Lars Fuchs was in a spacecraft heading for the Belt. It didn't take a genius to realize that he'd have to get supplies from somewhere, and Ceres was the only somewhere there was.

"He might not come here at all," said one of the board members, an edgy-looking woman in a high-mode pullover that sported more cutouts than material. "He might just hijack a ship or two and steal the supplies he needs. He *is* a pirate, after all."

"That's why we exiled him in the first place," said the bland-looking warehouse operator sitting next to her.

"That's not entirely true," George pointed out.

"But we did exile him," the warehouseman retorted. "So we don't have to allow him to dock here."

"That all happened ten years ago," said one of the older board members, a former miner who had started a new career as an armaments repairman.

"But he was exiled for life, wasn't he?"

"Right," George admitted.

"So there."

The woman sitting directly across from George, a plumpish redhead with startling violet eyes, said, "Listen. Half the HSS ships in the Belt are going to be looking for Fuchs. If he puts in here they'll grab him."

"This is neutral territory," George said. "Everybody knows that. We've established it with HSS and Astro. We service any ship that comes to us, and they don't do any fighting within a thousand klicks of our habitat."

"That doesn't mean we have to service Fuchs. He's an exile, remember."

"There's something else involved," George added. "We have a news media star heading here. She'll arrive tomorrow. Edith Elgin."

"I've watched her shows from Selene!"

"Isn't she married to Douglas Stavenger?"

"What's she coming here for?"

"To do a documentary about the war," George explained.

"Do we want to have a documentary about the war? I mean, won't that be bad publicity for us?"

"She'll want to interview Fuchs, I bet."

"That'd be a great way to get everybody's attention: an interview with the notorious pirate."

"It'll make us look like a den of thieves."

"Can we stop her?"

All eight of them looked to George.

Surprised at this turn, George said, "We'd have a helluva time shooing her away. She's got a right to report the news."

"That doesn't mean we have to help her. Let her interview Fuchs somewhere else."

But George was thinking, Humphries's people are smart enough to watch her and wait for Fuchs to show up. Wherever she interviews Fuchs, it's going to be fookin' dangerous for both of them.

ASTEROID VESTA

An individual nanomachine is like an individual ant: mindless but unceasingly active. Its blindly endless activity is of little consequence by itself; even the most tireless exertions of a device no bigger than a virus can be nothing but invisibly minuscule in the human scale of things.

But while an individual ant can achieve little and has not enough brain to accomplish more than instinctual actions, an ant *colony* of many millions of blindly scurrying units can strip a forest, build a city, act with a purposefulness that seems little short of human intelligence.

So it is with nanomachines. An individual unit can accomplish little. But strew millions of those virus-sized units over a restricted area and they can build or destroy on a scale that rivals human capacities.

The asteroid Vesta is a spheroid rich in nickel-iron, some 500 kilometers in diameter. The Humphries Space Systems base on Vesta was burrowed, for the most part, more than twenty meters below the asteroid's pitted, airless, bare surface.

The nanomachines that were strewn across a small area of the asteroid's surface operated in a far different regime of scale and environment. Their world was a universe of endlessly vibrating, quivering molecules where electromagnetic forces held atoms in tight clusters, and Brownian motion buffeted atoms, molecules and nanomachines alike. On that scale of size, the nanomachines were giant mechanical devices, like huge bulldozers or derricks, bulling their way through the constantly jostling, jiggling molecules.

Each nanomachine was built with a set of grippers that fit the shape of the molecule that made up high-grade steel. Each nanomachine had the strength to seize such molecules and pull them apart into their constituent atoms of iron, carbon, chromium, and nickel.

Drawing their energy from the unceasing Brownian vibrations of the molecules themselves, the nanomachines patiently, mindlessly, tirelessly chewed through every molecule of steel they could find, tearing them apart. On the molecular scale of the nanomachines this was a simple operation. It would end only when the quantum-dot timing devices built into each individual nanomachine told it to stop and disassemble itself.

Or when the nanos ran out of steel to chew on. Whichever came first.

Leeza Chaptal was the first to understand what was happening. As she stood in the control center deep underground and watched the monitor screens go blank, one by one, she realized that only the sensors and other equipment up on the surface were failing.

The technicians seated at their consoles around her had gone from surprise to irritation to outright fear.

"Something's wiping out everything up on the surface," one of them said, needlessly. They could all see that.

"Those missiles," said Leeza. "They must be responsible for this."

"But what . . . how?"

"There wasn't any explosion," said one of the puzzled technicians. "Nothing seismic registered except their crashing on the surface."

"And then everything started blanking out."

"Nanomachines," Leeza guessed. "They must have brought in nanomachines that are eating up our surface installations."

All the techs turned to her in wide-eyed fear. Nanomachines. They had all heard stories about how they could chew up everything, including people, and turn everything in their path into a dead, formless gray goo.

"Somebody's got to go up the surface and see what's going on up there."

Nobody budged.

Leeza hadn't expected volunteers. "I'll go myself," she said.

Leeza's heart was already thumping loudly as she clumped to the hatch in the awkward, bulbous hard-shell space suit. Then she saw that the display on the hatch opening onto the vertical shaft that led up to the surface showed that there was nothing but vacuum on its other side.

Omygod, she gasped silently. They've eaten through the hatch at the top of the shaft.

Should I go through? What if they infect my suit? What if they start chewing on me?

Yet she had to know what was going on, had to learn the nature and depth of the attack they were undergoing.

Turning to the two maintenance engineers who had helped her into the suit, she said through its fishbowl helmet, "Get back on the other side of the hatch down the corridor."

They didn't need to be told twice. Both of them scampered down the corridor and squeezed through the hatch together, neither one of them willing to wait for the other. Leeza heard the metallic thud when they slammed the hatch and sealed it.

Okay, she told herself. Just a quick peek. A fast reconnaissance. Nothing heroic.

With gloved fingers she tapped the code on the hatch's control panel. It popped open slightly, and she noticed a puff of gritty dust from the floor swirl through the crack.

Breathing heavily inside her helmet, she pushed the hatch all the way open and stepped tentatively through. The lamps fixed to the shoulders of her space suit reflected light off the steel wall of the shaft.

"Looks all right so far," she said into her helmet microphone to the techs in the control center watching her progress in the corridor's surveillance camera.

"Some dust or dirt accumulated on the floor of the shaft," she reported, kicking up little lingering clouds of dust as she turned a full circle.

She had to crane her neck painfully to look up the length of the shaft. Sure enough, the hatch up at the top was gone. She could see a swatch of stars in the circular opening up there. Feeling jumpier with every heartbeat, Leeza unclipped the hand torch from her waist and shone it up the shaft. The gleaming reflection from the smooth steel lining ended about halfway up.

"The metal lining of the shaft seems to have been eroded or something," she said. A pebble pinged on her helmet. She would have jumped halfway out of her skin if she hadn't been inside the cumbersome suit.

"It's eating the metal!" she yelped.

"Get back inside," said one of the techs from the control center. "Get back before they start chewing on you!"

Leeza didn't wait to be told twice.

There was no nanotech expert among the HSS crew at the Vesta base. And no way to call for advice or information, with all the surface antennas gone. Leeza ordered the entire team into the galley, the only room large enough to hold the nearly two hundred men and women in the base at the same time.

"It's nanomachines," she concluded, after reporting to them what was happening. "They seem to be attacking metal. Maybe they're specifically programmed to destroy steel, maybe it's any metal at all. We don't know. But either way, we're in deep trouble."

"They could eat out all the hatches and open the whole complex to vacuum!" said one of the mercenary soldiers.

"That's what they're in the process of doing," Leeza admitted.

The head of the logistics storeroom, a soft-looking sandy-haired man with a bold blue stylized wolf tattooed across his forehead, spoke up:

"They're coming down the shaft and eating at the airtight hatch, right?"

"Right," said Leeza.

"And when they've gone through that first hatch they'll come along the corridor toward the next hatch, right?"

"We all know that!" snapped a dark-haired woman in pale green coveralls. "They'll eat up anything metal."

"Well," said the logistics man, "why don't we spray the corridors and hatches with something nonmetallic?"

"Spray?"

"We've got sprayguns, ceramics torches, butterknives, for chrissakes. Cover every square millimeter of exposed metal with something nonmetallic. Slather it on good and thick. Maybe that'll stop the nanos."

"That's ridiculous!"

"Maybe not."

"It's worth a try."

Leeza agreed that it was worth a try. If nothing else, it would keep everybody busy, instead of waiting in dread for the nanomachines to kill them.

COMMAND SHIP
SAMARKAND

Agreat way to go into battle, thought Dorik Harbin: out of fuel, stripped of armor, and low on rations.

Sitting in the command chair on *Samarkand*'s bridge, Harbin turned his gaze from the main display screen to the thick quartz port set into the bulkhead on his left. They were close enough to the *Chrysalis* for him to see it without magnification; the habitat's linked circle of metal-skinned modules glinted faintly in the light from the distant Sun, a tiny spark of human warmth set against the cold, silent darkness of infinite space.

"I have contact with *Chrysalis,* sir," his communications technician said, turning halfway in her chair to look at Harbin.

"Main screen," he ordered.

A woman's face appeared on the screen, ascetically thin, high cheekbones, hair cropped down to a bare fuzz, almond-shaped dark eyes full of suspicion.

"Please identify yourself," she said, her voice polite but hard-edged. "We're not getting any telemetry data from you."

"You don't need it," Harbin said, reflexively rubbing one hand over his fiercely dark beard. "We're looking for Lars Fuchs. Surrender him to us and we'll leave you in peace."

"Fuchs?" The woman looked genuinely puzzled. "He's not here. He's an exile. We wouldn't—"

"No lies," Harbin snapped. "We know Fuchs is heading for your habitat. I want him."

Her expression turned from surprise to irritation. "How can we produce him when he's not here?"

"Who's in charge there?" Harbin demanded. "I want to speak to your top person."

"That'd be Big George. George Ambrose. He's our chief administrator."

"Get him."

"He's not here."

Harbin's jaw clenched. "Are you joking, or do you want me to start shooting?"

Her eyes widened. "George is aboard the *Elsinore*. Greeting some VIP from Selene."

"Patch me through to him."

Sullenly, the woman said, "I'll try."

The screen went blank. Harbin turned to his comm tech. "Did she cut me off?"

The technician shrugged. "Maybe it wasn't deliberate."

Harbin thought otherwise. They're playing a delaying game. Why? Do they know we're almost out of propellant? Why are they being stubborn?

Aloud, he commanded, "Show me the ships parked at the habitat."

The technician murmured into the pin microphone at her lips and the main screen lit up. *Chrysalis* showed up as a circle in the middle of the display. Harbin counted eleven ships co-orbiting nearby. One of them was identified as *Elsinore,* a passenger-carrying torch ship. The others appeared to be freighters, ore carriers, logistics supply vessels.

We'll have to take the propellants and supplies we need from them, Harbin said to himself. After we've found Fuchs.

He called up *Elsinore*'s manifest. Registered to Astro Corporation. Just in from Selene. No cargo. Carrying only one passenger, someone identified as Edith Elgin, from Selene.

From Selene, he thought. Who would pay the expense of sending a torch ship from Selene to Ceres for just one passenger? Lars Fuchs must be aboard that ship. He has to be. The passenger they've identified on their manifest, this Edith Elgin, must be a front for Fuchs.

It must be.

Harbin rose from his command chair. "Take the con," he said to his pilot. "I'll be back in a few moments. If *Chrysalis*'s chief administrator calls, let me know immediately."

He ducked through the hatch and walked the few steps to the door of his private quarters. They're not going to give up Fuchs willingly, Harbin thought. They might know that we're low on supplies, or guess it. Maybe they think they can wait us out. They could be calling for more Astro attack ships to come to their aid.

He looked at his bed. How long has it been since I've slept? he asked himself. With a shake of his head he answered, No matter. This is no time for sleep. He went past the bed and into his lavatory. There he opened the slim case that housed his medications. I'll need to be alert, razor-sharp, he told himself. He picked one of the vials and fitted it to the hypospray. Rolling up the sleeve of his tunic, he pressed the spraygun against his bare skin and pushed the plunger.

He felt nothing. For good measure he fitted another vial to the hypospray and shot the additional dose into his bloodstream.

Big George was walking Edith Elgin down the passageway to *Elsinore*'s main airlock, where his shuttlecraft had docked.

"You won't need a space suit," George was saying. "We'll go straight into the shuttle and then we'll dock with *Chrysalis*. Shirtsleeve environment all the way."

Edith smiled, delighted with this big, shaggy mountain of a man with the wild brick-red hair and beard. He would look terrific on video.

"I'm looking forward to seeing how the rock rats live," she said, secretly berating herself for not having a microcam attached to her and slaved to wherever her eyes focused. Always be ready to shoot, she reminded herself. You're letting an opportunity slip away.

"Aw, there aren't many ratties in the habitat. Mostly clerks and shop-keepers. The real rock rats are out in the Belt, workin' their bums off."

"Even with this war going on?" she asked.

George nodded. "No work, no eat."

"But isn't it dangerous, with ships being attacked?"

"Sure it is. But—"

"URGENT MESSAGE FOR MR. AMBROSE," the overhead intercom speakers blared.

George swiveled his head around, spotted a wall phone, and hurried to it. Edith followed him.

A bone-thin woman's face showed in the wall phone's little screen. "An unidentified ship has taken up a parking orbit. They're demanding we surrender Lars Fuchs to them."

"Lars isn't here," George said.

"I told him that but he said we either give him Fuchs or he starts shooting!"

"Bloody fookin' maniac," George growled.

"He wants to talk to you."

"Right. I want to talk to him. Put me through."

• • •

Harbin felt perfectly normal. Bright, alert, ready to deal with these miserable rock rats or whatever other enemies came at him.

For the moment, though, he was sitting in his command chair and staring into the sky-blue eyes of a man sporting a thick mane of blazing red hair and an equally wild-looking beard.

Stroking his own neatly cropped beard, Harbin said, "It's very simple. You surrender Fuchs to me or I'll destroy you."

"We don't have Fuchs," George Ambrose said, obviously working hard to hold back his temper.

"How do I know that's true?"

"Come aboard and look for yourself! He's not here."

"He is aboard *Elsinore,* don't deny it."

"He isn't. He's not here. You're welcome to come aboard and search the ship from top to bottom."

"I'm not such a fool. You've already spirited him away to your habitat."

"Search the habitat then!"

"With a dozen men? You could hide him from us easily."

Ambrose started to say something, thought better of it, and sucked in a deep breath. At last he said, "Look, whoever the fook you are. *Chrysalis* is neutral territory. We're not armed. We have no weapons. You're welcome to search the habitat to your heart's content. We'll resupply your ship and fill your propellant tanks for you. What more can I offer you?"

"Lars Fuchs," said Harbin, implacably. This stubborn fool is beginning to anger me, he realized. He could feel the rage building, deep within him, like a seething pit of hot lava burning its way toward the surface.

"Lars isn't here!" Ambrose insisted. "He's not anywhere near here! We exiled the poor bloody bastard years ago. He's persona non grata."

Harbin leaned forward in his chair, his eyes narrowing, his hands clenching into fists. "You have one half-hour to produce Fuchs. If you haven't given him to me by then, I will destroy your precious habitat and everyone in it."

SELENE: DOUGLAS STAVENGER'S QUARTERS

Doug Stavenger sat tensely in the armchair at one end of his living room's sofa. At the matching chair on the other end sat Pancho Lane. Between them, Martin Humphries was on the sofa, beneath a genuine Bonestell painting of a sleek rocket sitting on the Moon's rugged surface.

Pancho looks wary, Stavenger thought, like a gazelle that's been caught in a trap. The trousers of her trim sea-green business suit hid the cast on her left ankle.

Humphries looks worried, too, he realized. I've never seen him so uptight. Maybe being nearly killed has finally knocked some sense into his head.

"This war has gone far enough," Doug Stavenger said, leaning forward earnestly. "Too far, in fact. It's got to stop. Now."

Neither Pancho nor Humphries said a word. They look like two schoolkids who've been sent to the principal's office for discipline, Stavenger thought.

He focused on Pancho. "Despite Selene's demands, and my personal request to you, Astro has used its facilities here to direct military operations."

She nodded, lips tight. "Yep, that's true."

"And you produced a disaster."

Pancho nodded again.

Turning to Humphries, he said, "And that fire in your personal preserve could have wiped out all of Selene."

"I didn't start the fire," Humphries snapped. "It was that murdering sonofabitch Fuchs."

"And why was he trying to get to you?" Pancho interjected.

"He's a killer! You know that. Everybody knows it. He even killed one of my assistants, Victoria Ferrer!"

"And how many have you killed?" Pancho retorted. "You've tried to kill Lars more'n once."

For the first time in long, long years Stavenger felt angry. Truly angry. These two stubborn idiots were threatening Selene and everyone living in it.

"I don't care who started the fire," he said coldly, "the fact is that you're running your war from here. It was inevitable that the fighting would spread to Selene."

"I'm sorry for that," Pancho said. "Really sorry. But I had nothing to do with Fuchs's attack on the mansion."

Humphries glared at her. "Didn't you? You brought Fuchs here to Selene, didn't you? You protected him while he plotted to kill me!"

"I brought him to Earth to save his hide from your hired killers," Pancho countered, with some heat.

"Enough!" Stavenger snapped. "You want to fight your war, then fight it elsewhere. You're both leaving Selene."

"What do you mean?" Humphries demanded.

"Both Humphries Space Systems and Astro Corporation will move out of Selene. That includes the two of you, all your employees, and all your equipment. I want you both out, lock, stock and barrel. Within the week."

"You can't do that!"

"Can't I?" Stavenger said, meeting Humphries's angry gaze. "The governing council of Selene will formally declare both your corporations to be outlaw operations. If you don't move out by the deadline they will seize all your assets and forcibly exile any of your people still remaining here."

"That's illegal," Pancho blurted.

"It won't be by this time tomorrow," said Stavenger. "I guarantee it."

Humphries jabbed an accusing finger at him. "You can't expect me to—"

"I do expect you to clear out of Selene. Now. Immediately. I don't care where you go. I don't care if you slaughter each other out in the Belt or in the pits of hell. But you will *not* drag Selene into this war. And you will not endanger this community. Is that clear?"

Humphries glowered at him for a silent moment, then seemed to relax and lean back into the sofa's ample cushions.

"So I'll go to Hell Crater," he said, with a smirk.

Stavenger turned to Pancho. "And you?"

She shrugged. "Maybe Malapert. Maybe we'll set up shop in one of the habitats at L-4 or L-5."

Humphries sneered at her. "Good idea. I can wipe you out with a single nuke, then."

Stavenger suddenly shot out of his chair, grabbed Humphries by the collar of his tunic and hauled him to his feet.

"Why don't I just break your damned neck here and now and get this war over with?" he snarled.

Humphries went white. He hung limply in Stavenger's grasp, not even able to raise his hands to defend himself.

Stavenger pushed him back onto the sofa. "Martin, I can see that you're not going to stop this war of your own volition. It won't stop until you're stopped."

Some color returned to Humphries's face. With a trembling hand he pointed to Pancho. "What about her? She started it!"

"*I* started it?" Pancho yelped. "That's the biggest motherhumping lie I ever heard."

"You started arming your ships!"

"You tried to assassinate me!"

"I did not!"

"The cable car from Hell Crater, remember? You're saying you didn't do that?"

"I didn't!"

"Liar."

"I didn't do it!"

"Then who the hell did?"

"Not me!"

Stavenger's phone chimed, interrupting their finger-pointing.

"Phone answer," Stavenger called.

Edith Elgin's face appeared on the screen. She looked tense, worried, almost frightened. "Doug, I know you're going to hear about this one way or the other. The rock rats' habitat at Ceres is being threatened by somebody who wants Lars Fuchs. It must be a Humphries operation. I'm safe on the *Elsinore* so far, but we don't know what's going to happen. This could get ugly."

The screen went blank.

"Edith!" Stavenger called.

The screen remained gray, but a synthesized voice said, "Transmission was interrupted at the source. The system will attempt to reconnect."

Stavenger whirled on Humphries. "If anything happens to my wife I'll kill you. Understand me? I'll kill you!"

TORCH SHIP *ELSINORE*

Well at least lemme get back to *Chrysalis,*" Big George was saying to the image on the screen, "and show you that Fuchs isn't there."

The fierce, dark-bearded man shook his head grimly. "No one will transfer from your ship to the habitat. How do I know that you won't smuggle Fuchs in with you?"

With obvious exasperation, George replied, "Because Fuchs isn't here! Come and see for your fookin' self!"

"I am not leaving my ship," said the intruder. "You will produce Lars Fuchs or face the consequences."

Big George and Edith were in her quarters aboard *Elsinor,* trying to reason with the scowling image on the screen. As George fumed and attempted to explain the situation to the intruder, Edith surreptitiously went to the travel kit resting on the shelf above her bed. Hoping she was out of the comm screen camera's view, she slipped one of the microcams she had brought with her out of the kit and attached it to the belt of her dress. It looked like an additional buckle, or perhaps a piece of stylish jewelry.

"I know Fuchs is with you," the dark-bearded man was saying, his voice flat and hard. "Don't try to tell me otherwise."

"But he's not," George replied for the umpteenth time. "Send a crew over here and inspect the ship."

"So that you can overpower them and cut my forces in half?" The man shook his head.

He's paranoid, Edith thought as she stepped to George's side, hoping the microcam was focused on the wall screen.

"Look," George said, straining to remain patient, "this ship isn't armed. The habitat isn't armed—"

"You provide weapons to the rock rats," said the intruder.

"No," George answered. "We provide mining equipment. If the rats get any weapons it's from logistics ships that the corporations send to the Belt."

"That's a lie. Where is Fuchs? My patience is running thin."

"He's not fookin' here!" George thundered.

In truth, Lars Fuchs was aboard *Halsey,* cruising past the orbit of Mars, nearly 200 million kilometers from Ceres. At his ship's present rate of acceleration, he would reach the *Chrysalis* habitat in a little more than three days.

He knew nothing of the circumstances unfolding at Ceres. As his ship traveled through the dark emptiness toward the Belt, Fuchs had plenty of time to think, and remember, and regret.

A failure. A total failure, he accused himself. Humphries killed my wife, destroyed my life, turned me into a homeless wandering exile, a Flying Dutchman doomed to spend my life drifting through this eternal night, living off whatever scraps I can beg or steal from others. I talk of vengeance, I fill my dreams with visions of hurting Humphries again and again. But it's all futile. All in vain. I'm a beaten man.

Amanda, he thought. My beautiful wife. I still love you, Amanda. I wish it had all turned out differently. I wish . . .

He squeezed his eyes shut and strove with all his might to drive the vision of her out of his thoughts. You're alive, he told himself sternly. You still exist, despite all he's done to you. Humphries had driven you into a life of piracy. He's made me into an outcast.

But I still live. That's my only true revenge on him. Despite everything he's done, despite everything he can do, I still live!

Aboard *Samarkand,* Harbin stared with dilated eyes at the floundering, fuming image of the red-bearded George Ambrose.

"You will produce the man Fuchs," Harbin said tightly, "or suffer the consequences. You have less than fifteen minutes remaining."

He cut the connection to *Elsinore.* Turning to his weapons technician, sitting at his console to Harbin's right, he asked, "Status of the lasers?"

"Sir, we have full power to all three of them."

"Ready to fire on my command?"

"Yessir."

"Good," said Harbin.

The executive officer, a blade-slim Japanese woman, suggested, "Perhaps we should send a boarding party to the ships parked around the habitat."

"To search for Fuchs?" Harbin asked lazily. He was starting to feel calm, almost tranquil. The injection must be wearing off, he thought. Too much stress burns the drug out of the bloodstream. I need another shot.

"If he's aboard any of those ships we can find him," the exec said.

"How many troops could we send, do you think? Six? Ten? A dozen?"

"Ten, certainly. Armed with sidearms and minigrenades. Those civilians in the ships wouldn't dare stand in their way."

Harbin felt just the slightest tendril of drowsiness creeping along his veins. It would be good to get a full night's sleep, he thought. Without dreams.

Aloud, he asked, "And what makes you think that there are nothing but civilians in those ships?"

The exec blinked rapidly, thinking, then replied, "Their manifests show—"

"Do you believe that if *Elsinore,* for example, were carrying a company of armed mercenaries they would show it on their manifest?"

She gave Harbin a strange look, but said nothing.

He went on, "Why do you think that red-bearded one is so anxious to have us search his ship? It's an obvious trap. He must have troops there waiting to pounce on us."

"That's—" The exec hesitated, then finished, "That's not likely, sir."

"No, not likely at all," Harbin said, grinning lopsidedly at her. "You would have done well against Hannibal."

"Sir?"

Harbin pushed himself out of the command chair. "I'm going to my quarters for a few minutes. Call me five minutes before their time is up."

"Yes, sir," said the exec.

Harbin knew something was wrong. If the drug is burning out of my system I ought to be feeling withdrawal symptoms, he thought. But I'm tired. Drowsy. Did I take the right stuff? I can't direct a battle in this condition.

Once he popped open the case that held his medications he focused blurrily on the vials still remaining, lined up in a neat row along the inside of the lid. Maybe I'm taking too much, he considered. Overdosing. But I can't stop now. Not until I've got Fuchs. I've got to get him.

He ran his fingertips over the smooth plastic cylinders of the medications. Something stronger. Just for the next half hour or so. Then I can relax and get a good long sleep. But right now I need something stronger. Much stronger.

HABITAT *CHRYSALIS*

Yannis Ritsos was the last of a long line of rebels and poets. Named after a famed Greek forebear, he had been born in Cyprus, lived through the deadly biowar that racked that tortured island, survived the fallout from the nuclear devastation of Israel, and worked his way across the Mediterranean to Spain where, like another Greek artist, he made a living for himself. Unlike El Greco, however, Yanni supported himself by running computer systems that translated languages. He even slipped some of his own poetry into the computers and had them translate his Greek into Spanish, German and English. He was not happy with the results.

He came to Ceres not as a poet, but as a rock rat. Determined to make a fortune in the Asteroid Belt, Yanni talked a fellow Greek businessman into allowing him to ride out to the Belt and try his hand at mining. He never got farther than the *Chrysalis* habitat, in orbit around Ceres. There he met and married the beautiful Ilona Mikvicius and, instead of going out on a mining ship, remained at Ceres and took a job in the habitat's communications center.

Sterile since his exposure to the nuclear fallout, totally bald for the same reason, Yanni longed to have a son and keep the family line going. He and Ilona were saving every penny they could scratch together to eventually pay for a cloning procedure. Ilona knew that bearing a cloned fetus was dangerous, but she loved Yanni so much that she was willing to risk it.

So Yannis Ritsos had everything to live for when Dorik Harbin's ship came to the *Chrysalis* habitat. He had suffered much, survived much, and endured. He felt that the future looked, if not exactly bright, at least promising. But he was wrong. And it was his own rebellious soul that put an end to his dreams.

"Sir," the comm tech called out, "someone aboard *Elsinore* is sending a message to Selene."

Harbin, fresh from a new injection of stimulant, turned to his weapons technician. "Slag her antennas," he commanded. "All of them."

The technician nodded and bent over his console.

In her compartment aboard *Elsinore*, Edith Elgin stopped in mid-sentence as the wall screen suddenly broke into jagged, hissing lines of hash.

"Something's wrong," she said to Big George. "The link's gone dead."

George frowned. "He doesn't want us talkin' to anybody. Prob'ly knocked out the antennas."

"You mean he attacked this ship?" Edith was shocked.

Nodding, George said, "And he'll do worse in another fifteen minutes if we don't produce Lars."

"But Fuchs isn't here!"

"Tell it to him."

Yannis Ritsos was alone on duty in *Chrysalis*'s communications center when Harbin's ultimatum came through.

It was a dull night shift; nothing but boringly routine chatter from the far-scattered ships of the miners and prospectors, and the coded telemetry sent routinely from their ships. With everything in the center humming along on automatic, and no one else in the comm center at this late hour, Yanni opened the computer subroutine he used to write poetry.

He had hardly written a line when the central screen suddenly lit up to show a dark-bearded man whose eyes glittered like polished obsidian.

"Attention, *Chrysalis*," the stranger said, in guttural English. "This is the attack vessel *Samarkand*. You are harboring the fugitive Lars Fuchs. You will turn him over to me in ten minutes or suffer the consequences of defiance."

Annoyed at being interrupted in his writing, Yanni thought it was some jokester in the habitat pulling a prank.

"Who is this?" he demanded. "Get off this frequency. It's reserved for incoming calls."

The dark-bearded face grew visibly angry. "This is your own death speaking to you if you don't turn Fuchs over to me."

"Lars Fuchs?" Yanni replied, only half believing his ears. "God knows where he is."

"I know where he is," the intruder snapped. "And if you don't surrender him to me I will destroy you."

Irritated, Yanni shot back, "Fuchs hasn't been here for years and he isn't here now. Go away and stop bothering me."

Harbin stared at the comm screen in *Samarkand*'s bridge. They're stalling for time, he thought. They're trying to think of a way to hide Fuchs from me.

He took a deep breath, then said with deadly calm, "Apparently you don't believe me. Very well. Let me demonstrate my sincerity."

Turning to the weapons tech, Harbin ordered, "Chop one of the habitat's modules."

The man swallowed hard, his Adam's apple bobbing up and down. "Sir, there are civilians in those modules. Innocent men and women—"

"I gave you an order," Harbin snapped.

"But—"

"Get off the bridge! I'll take care of this myself."

The weapons tech glanced at the others on the bridge, looking for support.

"*Chrysalis* is unarmed, sir," said the pilot softly, almost in a whisper.

Cold fury gripped Harbin. "Get out. All of you," he said, his voice hard as ice. "I'll tend to this myself."

The entire bridge crew got up and swiftly went to the hatch, leaving Harbin alone in the command chair. He pecked furiously at the keyboards on his armrests, taking control of all the ship's systems.

Fools and weaklings, he raged to himself. They call themselves mercenaries but they're no good for anything except drawing their pay and pissing their pants in fear. *Chrysalis* is unarmed? I'll believe that when pigs fly. They're harboring Fuchs and they're stalling for time, trying to hide him, trying to lure me into sending my crew over there so they can ambush and slaughter them. I've seen ambushes, I've seen slaughters. They're not going to do that to me or my crew.

He called up the weapons display for the main screen, focused on the module of the *Chrysalis* closest to his ship and jabbed a thumb against the key that fired the lasers. Three jagged lines slashed across the thin skin of the module. Puffs of air glittered briefly like the puffs of a person's breath on a winter's day.

"Give me Fuchs," he said to the comm screen.

Yanni heard screams.

"What's going on?" he asked the empty communications center.

The face on the screen smiled coldly. "Give me Fuchs," he said.

Before Yanni could reply, the comm center's door burst open and a woman in bright coral coveralls rushed in. "Module eighteen's been ripped apart! They're all dead in there!"

Yanni gaped at her. She was from the life support crew, he could see by the color of her coveralls. And she was babbling so loud and fast that he could barely understand what she was saying.

"We're under attack!" she screamed. "Call for help!"

"Call who?" Yanni asked.

The executive officer stepped through the hatch into the bridge.

"Sir," she said crisply, her face a frozen expressionless mask, "I have a squad of twenty ready to board *Chrysalis* and search for Fuchs. They are armed with pistols and minigrenades, perfectly capable of dealing with whatever resistance the rock rats may try to offer."

Harbin stared at her. Why are these fools trying to undermine me? I know what to do. You kill your enemies. Kill them all. Men, women, children, dogs, cattle, all and every one of them. Burn down their village. Burn their crops. Blast the trees of their orchards with grenades. Leave nothing alive.

"Sir, did you hear me?" the exec asked, stepping closer to him.

Harbin swiveled the chair slightly toward her. "My hearing is perfect," he said calmly. "Tell your troops to stand down. I won't need them."

"They can search the habitat—"

"No," Harbin said softly, almost gently. "That won't be necessary. Why risk them when we can destroy the habitat from here?"

"But Fuchs—"

"Fuchs will die with the rest of the rock rats," Harbin said. He wanted to laugh. It was all so simple. You killed your enemies and then they will never be able to hurt you again. Why can't she see that? It's so logical, so beautifully clear.

He dismissed the executive officer and began to calmly, methodically, thoroughly destroy *Chrysalis* and everyone in it.

TORCH SHIP *ELSINORE*

T he wall screen in Edith's compartment lit up to show the ship's captain. He looked shaken.

"You'd better come up to the bridge and see this," he said, his voice trembling. "They're destroying the habitat."

Big George boiled out into the passageway and charged up toward the bridge, Edith running hard behind him.

The captain and the two crew members on the bridge looked ashen, dazed.

Through the observation port Edith could see *Chrysalis*; three of its modules were ripped apart, chunks of metal and structure floating aimlessly. As she watched, invisible laser beams began slicing through another module. Air burst into the vacuum of space in glittering wisps of ice and dissipated in an eyeblink. All in silence: total, deadly, complete silence. Shapes came tumbling through one of the gouges torn in the module's skin. Bodies, Edith realized. Those are human bodies.

"The bloody fookin' bastard," George growled. He pounded both fists against the thick quartz of the observation port. "Bloody fookin' BAS-TARD!" he bellowed.

"Can't we do something?" Edith asked the captain.

He shook his head. "Not a thing."

"But there must be *something*! Call for help!"

"Our antennas are out. Even if we had Fuchs aboard or knew where he is, we wouldn't be able to tell him now."

Edith felt the strength ebbing out of her. I'm watching a thousand people dying. Being killed. George looked on the verge of tears. The captain was a white-faced statue.

"There's nothing we can do?" she asked.

"Nothing except wait," said the captain. "We're probably next."

Once he realized what was happening, Yanni bolted from the useless comm center and down the habitat's central passageway. Ilona! I've got to find Ilona! Their quarters were three modules down the passageway; at this time of night she should be in their bedroom, asleep.

He had to fight his way past a screaming mob at the module's airlock, fighting to grab the pitifully few space suits stored there.

Why is this happening? Yanni asked himself as he ran toward the hatch that led to his wife. Why are they killing us?

Then the bulkhead ahead of him split apart and a blast of air like a whirlwind lifted him off his feet and out into the dark cold emptiness beyond. He had just time enough to understand that it didn't matter why or who or anything else. He was dead and Ilona was too.

The exec simply stood by Harbin's side as he carefully, precisely cut up the modules of the *Chrysalis* habitat. When the last unit was reduced to a broken shambles he looked up at her and saw fear in her eyes: fear and shock and disgust.

"There," Harbin said, lifting both hands from the armrest keyboards. "It's done. Fuchs is dead. I've accomplished my mission."

The exec seemed to stir, as if coming out of a trance. "Are . . ." Her voice caught, and she coughed slightly. "Are you certain he was in the habitat?" Then she added, "Sir?"

Harbin ignored her question. "They're all dead. Now we can go home and be safe."

He got up from the command chair slowly, almost leisurely, and stretched his arms up to the metal overhead.

"I'm rather tired. I'm going in for a nap. You have the con."

"Yes, sir," she said. As she watched him go to the hatch and duck through it, she thought about the ships in parking orbits around *Chrysalis*. Witnesses to the slaughter. And Fuchs might in reality be aboard any one of them.

She shook her head. I can testify that he did it on his own. He even dismissed the rest of us from the bridge. I returned to try to dissuade him, but he wouldn't listen to me. I couldn't disobey a superior officer, and I certainly couldn't overpower the man. He acted alone, she rehearsed her testimony. It was entirely his doing.

She slipped into the command chair and summoned the rest of the bridge crew. One of the ships parked nearby was an HSS logistics vessel.

We'll refuel and reprovision from her, the exec thought, and then double back to Vesta.

Harbin saw several of his troopers idling in the galley, down at the end of the passageway from the bridge. Still in full armor, bristling with guns and grenades.

"Stand down," he called to them. "We won't be boarding the habitat." And he giggled. There's no habitat to board, he added silently.

As he entered his privacy compartment he seemed to recall that there was an incoming ship that might be harboring Fuchs. He shook his head foggily. No, that can't be. I killed Fuchs. I killed them all. All of them.

He tottered to the lav and splashed cold water on his face. Drug's wearing off, he realized. They wear off quicker and quicker. I must be building a tolerance to them. Have to tell the medics when we get back to Vesta. Need something stronger, better lasting.

He flopped onto his bed and closed his eyes. Sleep, he told himself. I need sleep. Without dreams. No dreaming. Please don't let me dream.

Doug Stavenger would not allow either Pancho or Humphries to leave his living room. They sat there and watched him desperately trying to reestablish contact with his wife, at Ceres.

Pancho offered him the full resources of Astro Corporation. After checking with her handheld she told Stavenger, "We've got three ships docked at Ceres. I've sent an order for them to report to me here."

"That will take an hour or more," Stavenger said.

Pancho shrugged. "No way I can make it happen faster."

Humphries remained on the sofa, silent, his eyes following Stavenger's every move, every gesture. Pancho felt contempt for the man. And a certain tiny speck of pity. Doug'll kill him, she knew, if anything's happened to his wife. All of Humphries's money can't help him one little iota now. Doug'll tear him apart.

They waited, Stavenger sending urgent, desperate messages to every ship in the Belt, Humphries sitting frozen with fear, Pancho churning the entire situation over and over in her mind, time and again, going over every detail she could think of, reliving the chain of events that had led to this place, this moment, this fearful point in spacetime.

"There's somebody else who oughtta be here," she said at last.

Stavenger froze the image on the wall screen and turned to look at her, obviously annoyed at her interruption.

"Yamagata," Pancho went on, despite his irritation. "Nobuhiko Yamagata should be here, if you want to stop this war."

Humphries stirred himself. "Just because his corporation provides mercenary troops—"

"He's behind this whole thing," Pancho said.

Stavenger gave her his full attention. "What do you mean?"

"Yamagata's the money behind the Nairobi base at the south pole," said Pancho. "He's been renting mercenaries to Astro and HSS, both."

"So?"

She jabbed a finger at Humphries. "You say you didn't set up that accident with the cable car?"

"I didn't," Humphries said.

"Then who else would've done it? Who's sittin' fat and happy while you and me bleed ourselves to death? Who stands to take over if Astro and HSS go broke?"

"Yamagata," Humphries breathed.

"Yamagata?" Stavenger echoed, still not believing it.

"Yamagata," Pancho insisted.

Stavenger turned back to his wall screen. "Phone, get Nobuhiko Yamagata. Top priority."

Leeza Chaptal was back in her space suit, but this time it was covered in slick, shining oil. Still, she was trembling inside it as the airlock hatch swung open.

The metal cladding of the circular shaft was obviously eaten away down almost to the level of her eyes. But no further, she saw. In the twelve hours since she'd last been in the shaft, the nanomachines had progressed only a meter or so down the shaft.

"I think they've stopped," she said into her helmet microphone.

"How can you be sure?" came the reply in her earphones.

Leeza unhooked the hand laser from her equipment belt. "I'm going to mark a line," she said, thumbing the laser's switch. A thin uneven line burned into the steel coating. She realized that her hands were shaking badly.

"Okay," she said, backing through the hatch and pushing it shut. "I'll come back in an hour and see if they've chewed past my mark."

She clumped in the ungainly suit back to the next hatch and rapped on it. "Fill the tunnel with air and open up," she ordered. "I've got to pee."

"They're leaving," Edith saw.

Still standing in the bridge of *Elsinore* with the captain and Big George, she saw the ship that had destroyed the habitat accelerate away from the area, dwindling into the eternal darkness, its rocket thrusters glowing hotly.

"Running away from the scene of the crime," said the captain.

George said nothing, but Edith could see the fury burning in his eyes. Suddenly he shook himself like a man coming out of a trance. Or a nightmare.

He started for the hatch.

"Where are you going?" the captain asked.

"Airlock," George replied, over his shoulder. Squeezing his bulk through the hatch, he said, "Space suits. Gotta see if anybody's left alive in *Chrysalis*."

Edith knew there couldn't be any survivors. But George is right, she thought. We've got to check.

And she stirred herself, realizing that she had to record this disaster, this atrocity. I've got to get this all on camera so the whole human race can see what's happened here.

SELENE: PEACE CONFERENCE

Three days after the *Chrysalis* atrocity, the conference took place in Doug Stavenger's personal office, up in the tower suite that housed Selene's governing administrators and bureaucrats. It was very small, very private, and extremely well-guarded.

Only four people sat at the circular table in the center of the office: Pancho, Humphries, Nobuhiko Yamagata and Douglas Stavenger himself. No aides, no assistants, no news reporters or anyone else. Selene security officers were stationed outside the door and patrolled the corridors. The entire area had been swept for electronic bugs.

Once the four of them were seated, Stavenger began, "This meeting will be held in strict privacy. Only the four of us will know what we say."

The others nodded.

"None of us will leave this room until we have come to an agreement to stop this war," Stavenger added, his face totally grim. "There will be no exceptions and no excuses. There's a lavatory through that door," he pointed, "but the only way out of here is through the door to the corridor and no one is leaving until I'm satisfied that we've reached a workable understanding."

Humphries bristled. "What gives you the right to—"

"Several thousand dead bodies scattered across the Asteroid Belt," Stavenger snapped. "I'm representing *them*. You are going to stop this damned war or you are going to starve to death right here at this table. There is no third option."

Yamagata smiled uneasily. "I came here voluntarily, at your request, Mr. Stavenger. This is no way to treat a guest."

Gesturing in Pancho's direction, Stavenger replied, "Ms. Lane was your guest at the Nairobi base at Shackleton crater, wasn't she? And you damned near killed her."

Nobuhiko's brows knit momentarily. Then he said, "I could call for help, you know."

Without any change in his expression, Stavenger said, "There's no way to get a message out of this room. I've had it shielded. Your hand-helds won't get a signal past these walls."

Pancho leaned back in her chair and stretched her legs beneath the table. "Okay, then. Let's start talking."

Harbin had spent the three days since the attack on *Chrysalis* drifting in and out of a drug-induced stupor. His executive officer ran the ship while he slept and dreamed eerily distorted fantasies that always ended in blood and death.

By the time they reached Vesta, he had run out of medications and was beginning to sober up.

He was washing his bearded, pouchy-eyed face when someone tapped at his door.

"Enter," he called, mopping his face with a towel.

The exec slid the door back and stepped into his compartment. Harbin realized the bed was a sweaty, tangled mess, and the cramped compartment smelled like the hot insides of an overused gym shoe.

"We're about to enter a parking orbit around Vesta, sir," she said stiffly.

"The base is back in operation?" he asked. As he spoke the words he realized that he didn't care if the base was operating again. It meant nothing to him, one way or the other.

"Yes, sir. The nanomachine attack was limited to the surface installa-tions, for the most part. No one was killed or even injured."

Harbin knew from the look on her face that there was more to come. "What else?"

"I have received orders to relieve you of command. Mr. Humphries personally called and demanded to know who was responsible for the destruction of the *Chrysalis* habitat. When he found out it was you he went into a rage. Apparently he knows you from an earlier experience."

Harbin felt as if he were watching this scene from someplace far away. As if he was no longer in his body, but floating free, drifting through nothingness, alone, untouched, untouchable.

"Go on," he heard himself say.

"He wants you brought to Selene to stand trial for war crimes," the exec said, her words stiff, brittle.

"War crimes."

"The *Chrysalis* massacre. He also said that you murdered an employee of his, several years ago."

"I see."

"I've been ordered to relieve you of command and confine you to your quarters. Sir."

Harbin almost smiled at her. "Then you should follow your orders."

She turned and grasped the door handle. Before she stepped through the doorway, though, she said, "It's on all the news nets. They've been playing it for the past two days."

She left him, sliding the door shut. There was no lock on the door. It didn't matter, Harbin thought. Even if it were locked the accordion-fold was so flimsy he could push through it easily. If he wanted to.

Harbin stood in his musty, messy compartment for a moment, then shrugged. *The moving finger writes*, he thought. *Nor all thy tears wash out a word of it.*

Why can't I feel anything? He asked himself. I'm like a block of wood. A statue of ice. The *Chrysalis* massacre, she called it. Massacre?

Shrugging his shoulders, he told the wall screen to display a news broadcast.

A woman's shocked, hollow-eyed face appeared on the screen, her name—Edie Elgin—spelled out beneath her image. She wore no makeup, her hair was disheveled, her voice little more than a shaky whisper.

". . . been working for several hours now," she was saying, "trying to determine if there are any survivors. So far, none have been found."

The scene suddenly changed to show the shattered remains of the *Chrysalis* habitat: broken, crumpled cylinders of metal glinting against the blackness of space, jagged pieces floating nearby, bodies drifting.

And Edie Elgin's voice, choked with sorrow and horror, nearly sobbing, was saying, "Nearly eleven hundred people were living in the habitat when it was attacked. They had no weapons, no defenses. They were methodically slaughtered by their unidentified attacker."

Harbin sank down onto his bed, staring at the screen. The icy armor that had surrounded him began to melt away. For the first time in many days he felt an emotion. He felt pain.

"Yamagata Corporation is not responsible for the *Chrysalis* tragedy," Nobuhiko said sternly. "Our employees were working under a contract with Humphries Space Systems."

"I never ordered them to attack the habitat," Humphries replied, with some heat. "I just wanted them to find Fuchs."

Pancho said, "Lars is somewhere in the Belt by now. You'll never find him."

"Yes I will. He tried to kill me!"

"That wasn't my doing," Pancho said.

Stavenger slapped a palm on the table, silencing them. "I don't care who did what to whom. The past is over and done with. We're here to prevent this kind of thing from happening again. I want an end to this fighting."

"Sure," Humphries said easily. "I'm willing to stop it. But I want Fuchs's head on a platter."

"What you want," said Pancho, "is total control of the Belt and all its resources."

"Isn't that what you want, too?" Humphries countered. Turning to Yamagata, he added, "And you, as well?"

Keeping his face expressionless, Nobuhiko replied, "Now that you have introduced nanomachine processing to mining the asteroids, there is good economic sense in having one corporation establish a monopoly in the Belt."

"But which corporation?" Humphries asked.

The three of them stared at each other.

"Wait a minute," Stavenger interrupted. "You're all forgetting something that's important."

They turned toward him.

"There's more to mining the asteroids than making profits," he said. "More involved in this than acquiring power."

Humphries smirked. "I can't imagine what it could be."

But Pancho's face lit up. "It's what Dan Randolph wanted in the first place! Back when we made the flight out to the Belt in the old *Starpower*!"

"And what was that?" Nobuhiko asked.

"To help the people on Earth," said Pancho. "Help 'em recover from the greenhouse cliff. Bring 'em the raw materials for rebuilding. Bring 'em the fuels for fusion power generators. *That's* what Dan started out to do!"

"And that's what you've all lost sight of," said Stavenger.

"Well, that's our principal market, I agree," Humphries said. "But that doesn't mean—"

Pancho cut him off. "We oughtta be selling the ores from the asteroids at the lowest possible price. And the fusion fuels, too."

"And building more solar power satellites," Stavenger added.

"To help rebuild Japan," Yamagata murmured.

"To help rebuild the world," said Pancho.

Stavenger smiled gently. "And to help expand human habitats on the Moon and elsewhere, in deep space."

"We can do that!" Pancho agreed eagerly.

"But not with the three of you cutting each other's throats," Stavenger said.

"Only one corporation should manage the resources of the Belt," Yamagata said firmly. "Competition is pointless, once nanoprocessing reduces the prices of asteroidal ores."

"Not ores," Humphries reminded him. "The nanomachines will produce pure metals."

"And minerals," Pancho added.

Humphries gave her an exaggerated bow of his head.

"But which corporation will gain the monopoly?" Yamagata asked.

"None of us," said Pancho.

"What?" Humphries snapped. "It's got to be one of us. Nobody else has the capability."

"Selene does," Pancho said, staring straight at Stavenger.

Looking back at her, he admitted, "I've been thinking that way, too."

Humphries exploded, "If you think you're going to muscle me out of what's rightfully mine—"

Pancho waved him down. "Don't pop your cork, Martin. I know how we can do this and keep our shareholders happy."

"I don't see how that can be done," Humphries groused.

"Nor do I," Nobuhiko added.

Grinning, Pancho clasped her hands together and leaned them on the conference table. "It's simple. We each sign a contract with Selene for them to operate our asteroid business. We get the profits, minus a small percentage to Selene."

"A manager's fee," said Stavenger.

"Right," Pancho agreed. "Selene manages our operations and sets the market prices for the asteroidal products. The three of us just sit back and collect the profits."

Yamagata took in a deep breath. Then, "I presume that Selene will set the prices as low as possible."

"Very likely," Stavenger said. "Those people on Earth need the resources. We won't put power trips ahead of the people's needs."

"Power trips?" Humphries snarled. "You'll have all the power."

"That's right," Stavenger replied amiably. "Selene will be the arbiter for the rest of the solar system. No more competition. No more killing. No more war."

"I don't like it," said Humphries.

Yamagata asked, "Can Selene be trusted with such power?"

"Can anyone else in this room?" Stavenger retorted.

A heavy silence fell across the conference table.

Finally Pancho said, "I'm willing to try it—on a five-year time limit. That way, if we're not happy with Selene's performance when the time's up, we don't have to renew the contract."

"But only if two of the three corporations refuse to renew," said Stavenger. "No single corporation can back out of the contract, it will take a majority vote."

"Agreed," said Pancho.

"I would like to consult my people back on Earth before agreeing," Yamagata said.

"I still don't like it," Humphries grumbled.

"C'mon, Martin," Pancho reached over and shook him slightly by the shoulder. "It'll make life a lot easier for you. You'll still be the richest sumbitch in the solar system. All you'll have to do is sit back and pull in the profits. No more worries."

"No more slaughters," Stavenger said, his face still deadly serious. "Regardless of your intentions, Martin, it was your orders that led to the *Chrysalis* massacre."

"That would never hold up in a court of law."

"Don't be too certain of that. War crimes courts can be very harsh."

Humphries leaned back in his chair, his mouth a tight line, his eyes closed. At last he sat up straight and asked Stavenger, "Will you still exile me?"

Stavenger smiled. "No, I don't think that would be necessary, Martin. You can rebuild your home down below. Besides, I rather think I'd like to have you close by, where I can keep an eye on you."

FINAL ADJUSTMENTS

The three-second lag in communications between Earth and the Moon did not irritate Nobuhiko Yamagata. He found it useful; it gave him a few moments to think before responding to his father.

Saito's face grew solemn when Nobu told him of the tentative agreement they had hammered out.

"But this will keep Yamagata from moving back into space operations," the older man complained.

"Not entirely," Nobuhiko replied. "We will gain only a small share in the profits from asteroidal mining, true enough. But the price for asteroidal resources will become so low that we will be able to continue our rebuilding programs and invest in new space ventures, as well."

"Lower our costs," Saito muttered. "H'mm. I see."

In the end, the elder Yamagata agreed that his son's best course was to accept the agreement. By the time Nobuhiko ended his conversation with his father, Saito was already talking about building solar power satellites in orbit about the planet Mercury.

"The sunlight is much more intense that close to the Sun," he said. "Perhaps I will leave this dreary monastery and lead the Mercury project myself."

Soaked with well-earned perspiration, Martin Humphries held Tatiana Oparin's naked body close to his own and contemplated his future.

"Maybe I won't rebuild the house," he said, gazing up at the darkened ceiling of the hotel bedroom. It sparkled with a thousand fluorescent flecks of light, like stars on a summery evening back on Earth.

"Not rebuild it?" Tatiana murmured drowsily.

"I could go back to Connecticut. That's where my boys are living. The runt's nothing much, but Alex is turning into a real son. Just like his father." He laughed at his private joke.

"You'd leave the Moon?"

"Just for a visit. To see the kids. And there's other family still down there. Can't take too much of them."

"But you'll still live here at Selene, won't you?"

"Maybe. Maybe not. Hell Crater's an interesting place. Maybe I'll buy into one of the casinos there. Be a playboy instead of a captain of industry. Might make a nice change for me."

"You would make an excellent playboy," said Tatiana, snuggling closer to him.

Humphries laughed in the darkness. This is a lot easier than running a corporation, he thought. Let the others do the work. I'll spend the profits.

Stavenger spent much of his evening sending a long, detailed report to his wife about the peace conference.

"I think it could work," he concluded. "I think we can make it work."

Edith was on her way back to him, he knew. She had survived the atrocity at Ceres unscathed, physically. Her news coverage, complete with computer-graphic simulations of the actual attack based on her eye-witness description, had been the biggest news event since the green-house floods had first struck. There was already talk of a Pulitzer for her.

None of that mattered to Stavenger. Edith's all right, he thought. She's on her way back. She wasn't hurt. It was an emotional trauma for her, but she wasn't physically harmed. She'll be all right. I'll help her recover.

Edith's news reporting had been the key to making the peace agreement, Stavenger realized. With the *Chrysalis* massacre in full view of every person in the solar system, Humphries and the others had no choice except to come to some sort of an agreement to end the fighting.

Now comes the hard part, Stavenger told himself. Now we have to make the agreement work.

Pancho was packing her travel bag when the call from Jake Wanamaker came through. She invited him to come to her residence.

By the time he buzzed at the front door, Pancho was packed and ready to go. She carried her travel bag to the door and let it drop to the floor, then opened the door to let Wanamaker in. In the languid lunar gravity, the bag thumped on the carpeting as Wanamaker stepped into the entryway.

"Going somewhere?" he asked.

"Yep," said Pancho, ushering him into the sitting room. "But I got lots of time. Want a drink?"

The room's décor was set to the Mediterranean isle of Capri: steep, green-clad cliffs studded with little white-walled villages clinging here and there, and the placid sea glittering beneath a warm Sun.

Wanamaker asked for a bourbon and water. Pancho had the autobar pour her an ice-cold *lemoncello*, to go with the scenery.

She gestured him to a comfortably wide armchair, and perched herself on the smaller upholstered chair next to it. They clinked glasses. Pancho noticed that Jake took a healthy swig of his bourbon, rather than a polite little sip.

"What's on your mind?" Pancho asked.

He gave her a sheepish grin. "Looks like I'm out of a job."

"Guess so," she said. "Your contract runs to the end of the year, though."

"I don't feel right taking money for doing nothing."

Pancho considered this for a moment, then heard herself say, "So why don't you come with me? Be my bodyguard."

His brows shot up. "Bodyguard? Where are you going?"

With a shrug, she admitted, "Dunno. Just want to get away from all this. I'm going to resign from Astro Corporation."

"Resign?"

"Yep. I sorta fell into this job by accident. Took me a lotta years to realize I don't really want to be a corporate executive."

"So you're going to travel?"

"For a bit. My sister's out at the Saturn habitat. Thought maybe I'd have a look-see out there."

"You don't need a bodyguard for that," Wanamaker said.

Pancho grinned at him. "Okay then, I'll be your bodyguard. How's that?"

Realization dawned on Wanamaker's face. He broke into a wide grin.

Shanidar was in orbit around Vesta. There was a delay getting the crew transferred down to the base because most of the surface facilities had been eaten away by the nanomachine attack. Just as well, Harbin thought. He was in no hurry to leave the ship.

He had remained in his quarters, as ordered by the executive officer. He had not slept for several days. Without his medications, sleep brought dreams, and Harbin did not like what his dreams showed him.

He replayed the news broadcasts of his attack on *Chrysalis* over and over. Each time it seemed worse to him, more horrifying, more damning.

What does life hold for me now? he asked himself. They'll send out some troops to arrest me. Then a trial, probably back on Earth. And then what? A firing squad? More likely a lethal injection. Or perhaps life in prison.

I can save them the trouble, he thought.

His mind resolved, Harbin slid open the pleated door to the passageway and headed toward the rear of the ship, away from the bridge. I've got to do this quickly, he knew, before they realize I've left my quarters.

He went straight to the weapons locker, unattended now that the ship was in orbit and the crew waiting to transfer to their base. The grenade storage bins were locked, but Harbin knew all the combinations. He tapped out the proper sequence and the lock clicked open.

A small one, he told himself. You don't want to damage the ship too much.

A minigrenade, hardly larger than his thumbnail. Enough explosive in it, however, to blast open an airlock hatch. Or something else.

"Hey, what're you doing?"

Harbin whirled to see one of his crewmen coming down the passageway.

"Oh, it's you, Captain." The man looked suddenly embarrassed. "Sir, eh—you're supposed to be confined to your quarters."

"It's all right, trooper," Harbin said reassuringly. "Nothing to worry about. *For all the Sin wherewith the Face of Man is blackened . . .*"

"Sir?" the crewman asked, puzzled. Then he saw the minigrenade in Harbin's hand. His eyes went wide.

"Nothing," Harbin muttered. He flicked the grenade's fuse with his thumbnail as he spun around to place his body between the crewman and the blast. The explosion nearly tore him in half.

ASTEROID 67-046

What do you mean, Dorn's not available?" Humphries shouted at the blank phone screen. "Get me the officer on watch aboard the Humphries Eagle."

"All exterior communications are inoperable at the present time," replied the phone.

"That's impossible!"

"All exterior communications are inoperable at the present time," the phone repeated, unperturbed.

Humphries stared at the empty screen, then turned slowly toward Elverda Apacheta. "He's cut us off. We're trapped in here."

Elverda felt the chill of cold metal clutching at her. Perhaps Dorn is a madman, she thought. Perhaps he is my death, personified.

"We've got to do something!" Humphries nearly shouted.

Elverda rose shakily to her feet. "There is nothing that we can do, for the moment. I am going to my quarters and take a nap. I believe that Dorn, or Harbin or whatever his identity is, will call on us when he is ready to."

"And do what?"

"Show us the artifact," she replied, silently adding, I hope.

Legally, the artifact and the entire asteroid belonged to Humphries Space Systems. It had been discovered by a family—husband, wife, and two sons, ages five and three—that made a living from searching out iron-nickel asteroids and selling the mining rights to the big corporations. They filed their claim to this unnamed asteroid, together with a preliminary description of its ten-kilometer-wide shape, its orbit within the asteroid belt, and a sample analysis of its surface composition.

Six hours after their original transmission reached the commodities market computer network on Earth—while a fairly spirited bidding was going on among four major corporations for the asteroid's mineral rights—a new message arrived at the headquarters of the International Astronautical Authority, in London. The message was garbled, fragmentary, obviously made in great haste and at fever excitement. There was an artifact of some sort in a cavern deep inside the asteroid.

One of the faceless bureaucrats buried deep within the IAA's multi-layered organization sent an immediate message to an employee of Humphries Space Systems. The bureaucrat retired hours later, richer than he had any right to expect, while Martin Humphries personally contacted the prospectors and bought the asteroid outright for enough money to end their prospecting days forever. By the time the decision-makers in the IAA realized that an alien artifact had been discovered they were faced with a fait accompli: the artifact, and the asteroid in which it resided, were the personal property of the richest man in the solar system.

Martin Humphries was something of an egomaniac. But he was no fool. Graciously he allowed the IAA to organize a team of scientists who would inspect this first specimen of alien intelligence. Even more graciously, Humphries offered to ferry the scientific investigators all the long way to the asteroid at his own expense. He made only one demand, and the IAA could hardly refuse him. He insisted that he see this artifact himself before the scientists were allowed to view it.

And he brought along the solar system's most honored and famous artist. To appraise the artifact's worth as an art object, he claimed. To determine how much he could deduct from his corporate taxes by donating the thing to the IAA, said his enemies. But over the days of their voyage to the asteroid, Elverda came to the conclusion that buried deep beneath his ruthless business persona was an eager little boy who was tremendously excited at having found a new toy. A toy he intended to possess for himself. An art object, created by alien hands.

For an art object was what the artifact seemed to be. The family of prospectors continued to send back vague, almost irrational reports of what the artifact looked like. The reports were worthless. No two descriptions matched. If the man and woman were to be believed, the artifact did nothing but sit in the middle of a rough-hewn cavern. But they described it differently with every report they sent. It glowed with light. It was darker than deep space. It was a statue of some sort. It was formless. It overwhelmed the senses. It was small enough almost to pick up in one hand. It made the children laugh happily. It frightened their parents. When they tried to photograph it, their transmissions showed nothing but blank screens. Totally blank.

As Humphries listened to their maddening reports and waited impatiently for the IAA to organize its handpicked team of scientists, he ordered his security manager to get a squad of hired personnel to the asteroid as quickly as possible. From corporate facilities at the Jupiter station and the moons of Mars, from three separate outposts among the Asteroid Belt itself, Humphries Space Systems efficiently brought together a brigade of experienced mercenary security troops. They reached the asteroid long before anyone else could, and were under orders to make certain that no one was allowed onto the asteroid before Martin Humphries himself reached it.

"The time has come."

Elverda woke slowly, painfully, like a swimmer struggling for the air and light of the surface. She had been dreaming of her childhood, of the village where she had grown up, the distant snowcapped Andes, the warm night breezes that spoke of love.

"The time has come."

It was Dorn's deep voice, whisper-soft. Startled, she flashed her eyes open. She was alone in the room, but Dorn's image filled the phone screen by her bed. The numbers glowing beneath the screen showed that it was indeed time.

"I am awake now," she said to the screen.

"I will be at your door in fifteen minutes," Dorn said. "Will that be enough time for you to prepare yourself?"

"Yes, plenty." The days when she needed time for selecting her clothing and arranging her appearance were long gone.

"In fifteen minutes, then."

"Wait," she blurted. "Can you see me?"

"No. Visual transmission must be keyed manually."

"I see."

"I do not."

A joke? Elverda sat up on the bed as Dorn's image winked out. *Is he capable of humor?*

She shrugged out of the shapeless coveralls she had worn to bed, took a quick shower, and pulled her best caftan from the travel bag. It was a deep midnight blue, scattered with glittering silver stars. Elverda had made the floor-length gown herself, from fabric woven by her mother long ago. She had painted the stars from her memory of what they had looked like from her native village.

As she slid back her front door she saw Dorn marching down the corridor with Humphries beside him. Despite his slightly longer legs, Humphries seemed to be scampering like a child to keep up with Dorn's steady, stolid steps.

"I demand that you reinstate communications with my ship," Humphries was saying, his voice echoing off the corridor walls. *"I'll dock your pay for every minute this insubordination continues!"*

"It is a security measure," Dorn said calmly, without turning to look at the man. *"It is for your own good."*

"My own good? Who in hell are you to determine what my own good might be?"

Dorn stopped three paces short of Elverda, made a stiff little bow to her, and only then turned to face his employer.

"Sir: I have seen the artifact. You have not."

"And that makes you better than me?" Humphries almost snarled the words. *"Holier, maybe?"*

"No," said Dorn. *"Not holier. Wiser."*

Humphries started to reply, then thought better of it.

"Which way do we go?" Elverda asked in the sudden silence.

Dorn pointed with his prosthetic hand. *"Down,"* he replied. *"This way."*

The corridor abruptly became a rugged tunnel again, with lights fastened at precisely spaced intervals along the low ceiling. Elverda watched Dorn's half-human face as the pools of shadow chased the highlights glinting off the etched metal, like the Moon racing through its phases every half-minute, over and again.

Humphries had fallen silent as they followed the slanting tunnel downward into the heart of the rock. Elverda heard only the clicking of his shoes at first, but by concentrating she was able to make out the softer footfalls of Dorn's padded boots and even the whisper of her own slippers.

The air seemed to grow warmer, closer. *Or is it my own anticipation?* She glanced at Humphries; perspiration beaded his upper lip. The man radiated tense expectation. Dorn glided a few steps ahead of them. He did not seem to be hurrying, yet he was now leading them down the tunnel, like an ancient priest leading two new acolytes—or sacrificial victims.

The tunnel ended in a smooth wall of dull metal.

"We are here."

"Open it up," Humphries demanded.

"It will open itself," replied Dorn. He waited a heartbeat, then added, *"Now."*

And the metal slid up into the rock above them as silently as if it were a curtain made of silk.

None of them moved. Then Dorn slowly turned toward the two of them and gestured with his human hand.

"The artifact lies twenty-two point nine meters beyond this point. The tunnel narrows and turns to the right. The chamber is large enough to accommodate only one person at a time, comfortably."

"Me first!" Humphries took a step forward.

Dorn stopped him with an upraised hand. The prosthetic hand. *"I feel it my duty to caution you—"*

Humphries tried to push the hand away; he could not budge it.

"When I first crossed this line, I was a soldier. After I saw the artifact I gave up my life."

"And became a self-styled priest. So what?"

"The artifact can change you. I thought it best that there be no witnesses to your first viewing of it, except for this gifted woman whom you have brought with you. When you first see it, it can be—traumatic."

Humphries's face twisted with a mixture of anger and disgust. *"I'm not a mercenary killer. I don't have anything to be afraid of."*

Dorn let his hand drop to his side with a faint whine of miniaturized servomotors.

"Perhaps not," he murmured, so low that Elverda barely heard it.

Humphries shouldered his way past the cyborg. *"Stay here,"* he told Elverda. *"You can see it when I come back."*

He hurried down the tunnel, footsteps staccato.

Then silence.

Elverda looked at Dorn. The human side of his face seemed utterly weary.

"You have seen the artifact more than once, haven't you?"

"Fourteen times," he answered.

"It has not harmed you in any way, has it?"

He hesitated, then replied, *"It has changed me. Each time I see it, it changes me more."*

"You . . . you really are Dorik Harbin?"

"I was."

"Those people of the Chrysalis . . . *?"*

"DORIK HARBIN KILLED THEM ALL. YES. THERE IS NO EXCUSE FOR IT, NO PARDON. IT WAS THE ACT OF A MONSTER."

"But why?"

"Monsters do monstrous things. Dorik Harbin ingested psychotropic drugs to increase his battle prowess. Afterward, when the battle drugs cleared from his bloodstream and he understood what he had done, Dorik Harbin held a grenade against his chest and set it off."

"Oh my god," Elverda whimpered.

"He was not allowed to die, however. Yamagata Corporation's med-

ical specialists rebuilt his body and he was given a false identity. For many years he lived a sham of life, hiding from the authorities, hiding from his own guilt. He no longer had the courage to kill himself; the pain of his first attempt was far stronger than his own self-loathing. Then he was hired to come to this place. Dorik Harbin looked upon the artifact for the first time, and his true identity emerged at last."

Elverda heard a scuffling sound, like feet dragging, staggering. Martin Humphries came into view, tottering, leaning heavily against the wall of the tunnel, slumping as if his legs could no longer hold him.

"No man . . . no one . . ." He pushed himself forward and collapsed into Dorn's arms.

"Destroy it!" he whispered harshly, spittle dribbling down his chin. "Destroy this whole damned piece of rock! Wipe it out of existence!"

"What is it?" Elverda asked. "What did you see?"

Dorn lowered him to the ground gently. Humphries's feet scrabbled against the rock as if he were trying to run away. Sweat covered his face, soaked his shirt.

"It's . . . beyond . . ." he babbled. "More . . . than anyone can . . . nobody could stand it . . ."

Elverda sank to her knees beside him. "What has happened to him?" She looked up at Dorn, who knelt on Humphries's other side.

"The artifact."

Humphries suddenly ranted, "They'll find out about me! Everyone will know! It's got to be destroyed! Nuke it! Blast this whole asteroid to bits!" His fists windmilled in the air, his eyes were wild.

"I tried to warn him," Dorn said as he held Humphries's shoulders down, the man's head in his lap. "I tried to prepare him for it."

"What did he see?" Elverda's heart was pounding; she could hear it thundering in her ears. "What is it? What did you see?"

Dorn shook his head slowly. "I cannot describe it. I doubt that anyone could describe it—except, perhaps, an artist: a person who has trained herself to see the truth."

"The prospectors—they saw it. Even their children saw it."

"Yes. When I arrived here they had spent eighteen days in the chamber. They left it only when the chamber closed itself. They ate and slept and returned here, as if hypnotized."

"It did not hurt them, did it?"

"They were emaciated, dehydrated. It took a dozen of my strongest men to remove them to my ship. Even the children fought us."

"But—how could . . ." Elverda's voice faded into silence. She looked at the brightly lit tunnel. Her breath caught in her throat.

"Destroy it," Humphries mumbled. "Destroy it before it destroys us!

Don't let them find out. They'll know, they'll know, they'll all know." He began to sob uncontrollably.

"You do not have to see it," Dorn said to Elverda. "You can return to your ship and leave this place."

Leave, urged a voice inside her head. *Run away. Live out what's left of your life and let it go.*

Then she heard her own voice say, as if from a far distance, "I've come such a long way."

"It will change you," he warned.

"Will it release me from life?"

Dorn glanced down at Humphries, still muttering darkly, then returned his gaze to Elverda.

"It will change you," he repeated.

Elverda forced herself to her feet. Leaning one hand against the warm rock wall to steady herself, she said, "I will see it. I must."

"Yes," said Dorn. "I understand."

She looked down at him, still kneeling with Humphries's head resting in his lap. Dorn's electronic eye glowed red in the shadows. His human eye was hidden in darkness.

He said, "I believe your people say, Vaya con Dios."

Elverda smiled at him. She had not heard that phrase in forty years. "Yes. You too. Vaya con Dios." She turned and stepped across the faint groove where the metal door had met the floor.

The tunnel sloped downward only slightly. It turned sharply to the right, Elverda saw, just as Dorn had told them. The light seemed brighter beyond the turn, pulsating almost, like a living heart.

She hesitated a moment before making that final turn. What lay beyond? What difference, she answered herself. *You have lived so long that you have emptied life of all its purpose.* But she knew she was lying to herself. Her life was devoid of purpose because she herself had made it that way. She had spurned love; she had even rejected friendship when it had been offered. Still, she realized that she wanted to live. Desperately, she wanted to continue living no matter what.

Yet she could not resist the lure. Straightening her spine, she stepped boldly around the bend in the tunnel.

The light was so bright it hurt her eyes. She raised a hand to her brow to shield them and the intensity seemed to decrease slightly, enough to make out the faint outline of a form, a shape, a person . . .

Elverda gasped with recognition. A few meters before her, close enough to reach and touch, her mother sat on the sweet grass beneath the warm summer sun, gently rocking her baby and crooning softly to it.

Mamma! she cried silently. Mamma. The baby—Elverda herself—looked up into her mother's face and smiled.

And the mother was Elverda, a young and radiant Elverda, smiling down at the baby she had never had, tender and loving as she had never been.

Something gave way inside her. There was no pain; rather, it was as if a pain that had throbbed sullenly within her for too many years to count suddenly faded away. As if a wall of implacable ice finally melted and let the warm waters of life flow through her.

Elverda sank to the floor, crying, gushing tears of understanding and relief and gratitude. Her mother smiled at her.

"I love you, Mamma," she whispered. "I love you."

Her mother nodded and became Elverda herself once more. Her baby made a gurgling laugh of pure happiness, fat little feet waving in the air.

The image wavered, dimmed, and slowly faded into emptiness. Elverda sat on the bare rock floor in utter darkness, feeling a strange serenity and understanding warming her soul.

"Are you all right?"

Dorn's voice did not startle her. She had been expecting him to come to her.

"The chamber will close itself in another few minutes," he said. "We will have to leave."

Elverda took his offered hand and rose to her feet. She felt strong, fully in control of herself.

The tunnel outside the chamber was empty.

"Where is Humphries?"

"I sedated him and then called in a medical team to take him back to his ship."

"He wants to destroy the artifact," Elverda said.

"That will not be possible," said Dorn. "I will bring the IAA scientists here from the ship before Humphries awakes and recovers. Once they see the artifact they will not allow it to be destroyed. Humphries may own the asteroid, but the IAA will exert control over the artifact."

"The artifact will affect them—strangely."

"No two of them will be affected in the same manner," said Dorn. "And none of them will permit it to be damaged in any way."

"Humphries will not be pleased with you, once he recovers."

He gestured up the tunnel, and they began to walk back toward their quarters.

"Nor with you," Dorn said. "We both saw him babbling and blubbering like a baby."

"What could he have seen?"

"What he most feared. His whole life has been driven by fear, poor man."

"What secrets he must be hiding!"

"He hid them from himself. The artifact showed him his own true nature."

"No wonder he wants it destroyed."

"He cannot destroy the artifact, but he will certainly want to destroy us. Once he recovers his composure he will want to wipe out the witnesses who saw his reaction to it."

Elverda knew that Dorn was right. She watched his face as they passed beneath the lights, watched the glint of the etched metal, the warmth of the human flesh.

"You knew that he would react this way, didn't you?" she asked.

"No one could be as rich as he is without having demons driving him. He looked into his own soul and recognized himself for the first time in his life."

"You planned it this way!"

"Perhaps I did," he said. "Perhaps the artifact did it for me."

"How could—"

"It is a powerful experience. After I had seen it a few times I felt it was offering me . . ." he hesitated, then spoke the word, "salvation."

Elverda saw something in his face that Dorn had not let show before. She stopped in the shadows between overhead lights. Dorn turned to face her, half machine, standing in the rough tunnel of bare rock.

"You have had your own encounter with it," he said. "You understand now how it can transform you."

"Yes," said Elverda. "I understand."

"After a few times, I came to the realization that there are thousands of my fellow mercenaries, killed in engagements all through the asteroid belt, still drifting where they were killed. Miners and prospectors, as well. Floating forever in space, alone, unattended, ungrieved for."

"Thousands of mercenaries?"

"The Chrysalis massacre was not the only bloodletting in the Belt," said Dorn. "There have been many battles out here. Wars that we paid for with our blood."

"Thousands?" Elverda repeated. "Thousands of dead. Could it have been so brutal?"

"Men like Humphries know. They start the wars, and people like me fight them. Exiles, never allowed to return to Earth again once we take the mercenary's pay."

"All those men—killed."

Dorn nodded. "And women. The artifact made me see that it was my duty to find each of those forgotten bodies and give each one a decent final rite. The artifact seemed to be telling me that this was the path of my atonement."

"Your salvation," she murmured.

"I see now, however, that I underestimated the situation."

"How?"

"Humphries. While I am out there searching for the bodies of the slain, he will have me killed."

"No! That's wrong!"

Dorn's deep voice was empty of regret. "It will be simple for him to send a team after me. In the depths of dark space, they will murder me. What I failed to do for myself, Humphries will do for me. He will be my final atonement."

"Never!" Elverda blazed with anger. "I will not permit it to happen."

"Your own life is in danger from him," Dorn said.

"What of it? I am an old woman, ready for death."

"Are you?"

"I was . . . until I saw the artifact."

"Now life is more precious to you, isn't it?"

"I don't want you to die," Elverda said. "You have atoned for your sins. You have borne enough pain."

He looked away, then started up the tunnel again.

"You are forgetting one important factor," Elverda called after him.

Dorn stopped, his back to her. She realized now that the clothes he wore had been his military uniform. He had torn all the insignias and pockets from it.

"The artifact. Who created it? And why?"

Turning back toward her, Dorn answered, "Alien visitors to our solar system created it, unknown ages ago. As to why—you tell me: Why does someone create a work of art?"

"Why would aliens create a work of art that affects human minds?"

Dorn's human eye blinked. He rocked a step backward.

"How could they create an artifact that is a mirror to our souls?" Elverda asked, stepping toward him. "They must have known something about us. They must have been here when there were human beings existing on Earth."

Dorn regarded her silently.

"They may have been here much more recently than you think," Elverda went on, coming closer to him. "They may have placed this artifact here to communicate with us."

"Communicate?"

"Perhaps it is a very subtle, very powerful communications device."

"Not an artwork at all."

"Oh yes, of course it's an artwork. All works of art are communications devices, for those who possess the soul to understand."

Dorn seemed to ponder this for long moments. Elverda watched his solemn face, searching for some human expression.

Finally he said, "That does not change my mission, even if it is true."

"Yes it does," Elverda said, eager to save him. "Your mission is to preserve and protect this artifact against Humphries and anyone else who would try to destroy it—or pervert it to his own use."

"The dead call to me," Dorn said solemnly. "I hear them in my dreams now."

"But why be alone in your mission? Let others help you. There must be other mercenaries who feel as you do."

"Perhaps," he said softly.

"Your true mission is much greater than you think," Elverda said, trembling with new understanding. "You have the power to atone for the wars that have destroyed your comrades, that have almost destroyed your soul."

"Atone for the corporate wars?"

"You will be the priest of this shrine, this sepulcher. I will return to Earth and tell everyone about these wars."

"Humphries and others will have you killed."

"I am a famous artist, they dare not touch me." Then she laughed. "And I am too old to care if they do."

"The scientists—do you think they may actually learn how to communicate with the aliens?"

"Someday," Elverda said. "When our souls are pure enough to stand the shock of their presence."

The human side of Dorn's face smiled at her. He extended his arm and she took it in her own, realizing that she had found her own salvation. Like two kindred souls, like comrades who had shared the sight of death, like mother and son they walked up the tunnel toward the waiting race of humanity.

My son, if sinners entice you,
Do not consent. . . .
Keep your feet from their path;
For their feet run to evil,
And they hasten to shed blood. . . .
But they lie in wait for their own blood;
They ambush their own lives.
So are the ways of everyone who gains by violence.
It takes away the life of its possessors.

—The Book of Proverbs
Chapter 1, verses 10–19